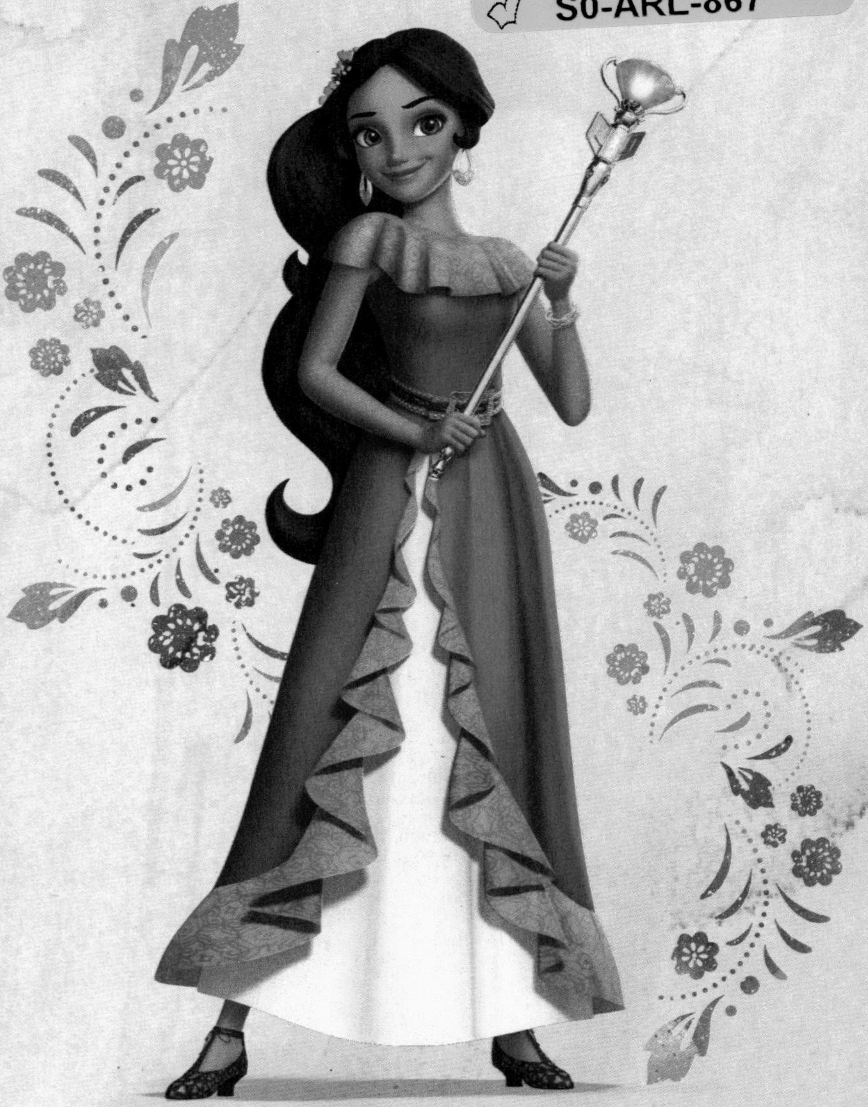

Published simultaneously in the United States and Canada by Joe Books Ltd,
489 College Street, Suite 203, Toronto, ON M6G 1A5

www.joebooks.com

First Joe Books edition: September 2017

Print ISBN: 978-1-77275-488-9
ebook ISBN: 978-1-77275-653-1

Names, characters, places, and incidents featured in this publication are
either the product of the author's imagination or are used fictitiously.

Any resemblance to actual persons (living or dead), events, institutions,
or locales, without satiric intent, is coincidental.

Adaptation, design, lettering, layout, and editing by First Image.

Library and Archives Canada Cataloguing in Publication
information is available upon request

Printed and bound in Canada
1 3 5 7 9 10 8 6 4 2

Adventure Takes Flight

CINESTORY COMIC

JOE BOOKS LTD

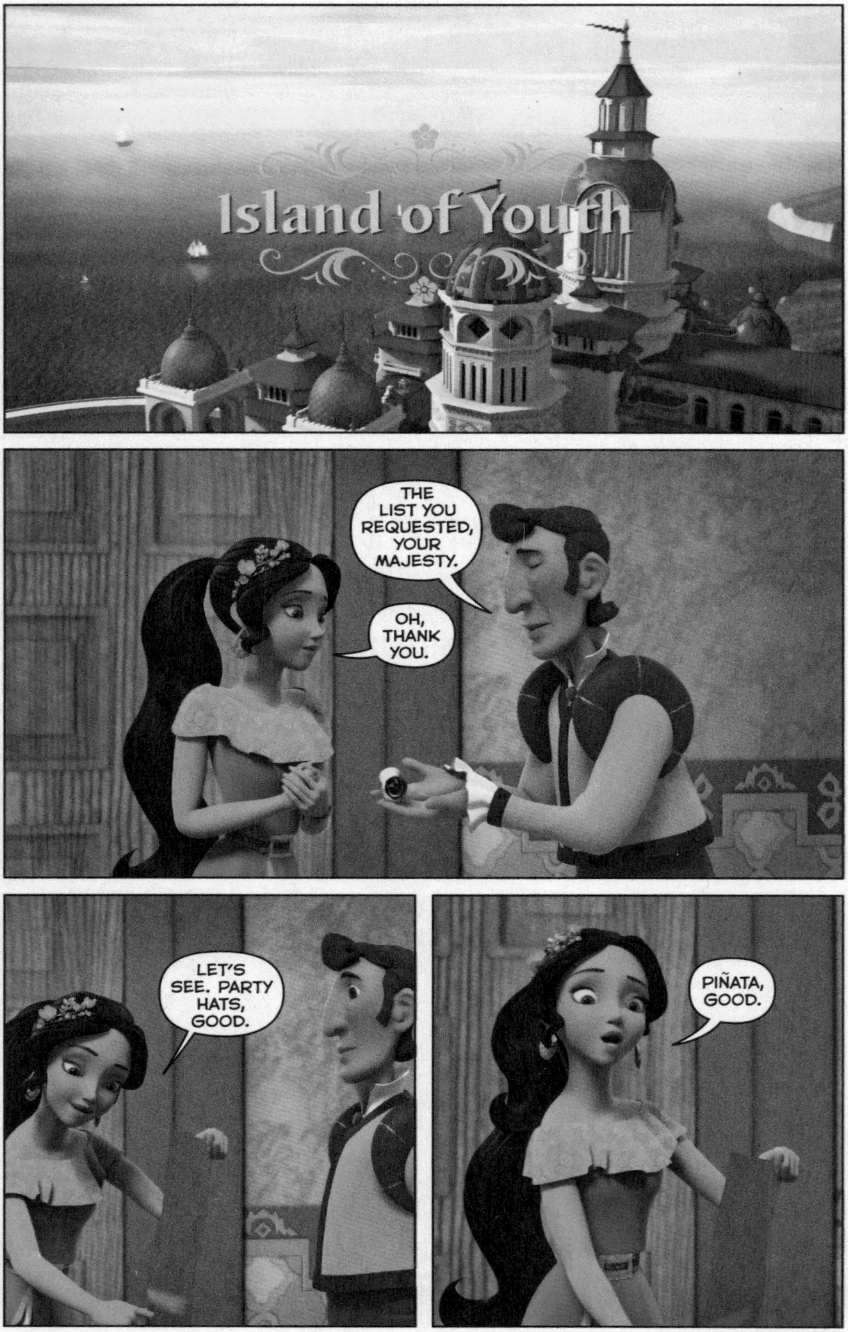
Island of Youth
THE LIST YOU REQUESTED, YOUR MAJESTY.
OH, THANK YOU.
LET'S SEE. PARTY HATS, GOOD.
PIÑATA, GOOD.

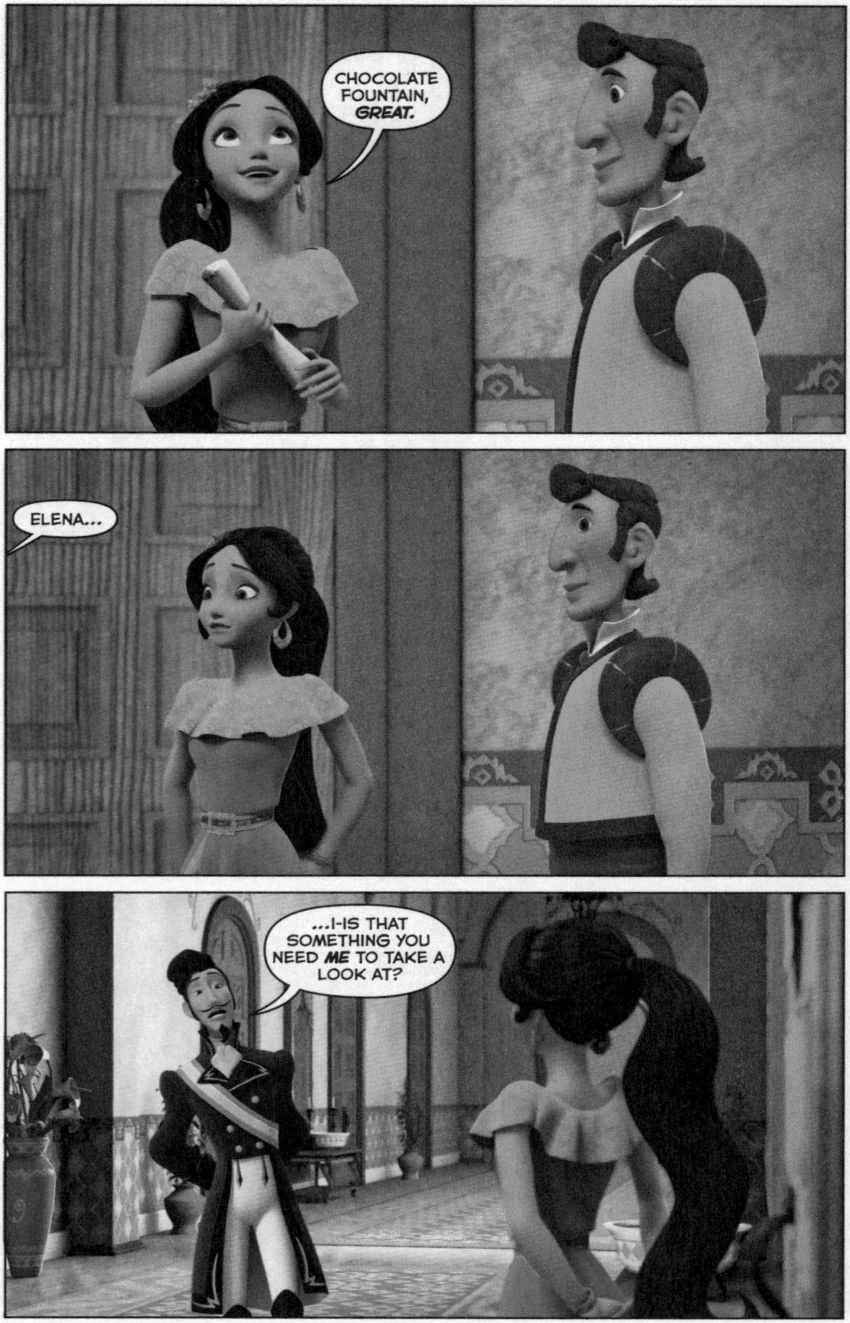
CHOCOLATE FOUNTAIN, *GREAT.*
ELENA...
...I-IS THAT SOMETHING YOU NEED *ME* TO TAKE A LOOK AT?

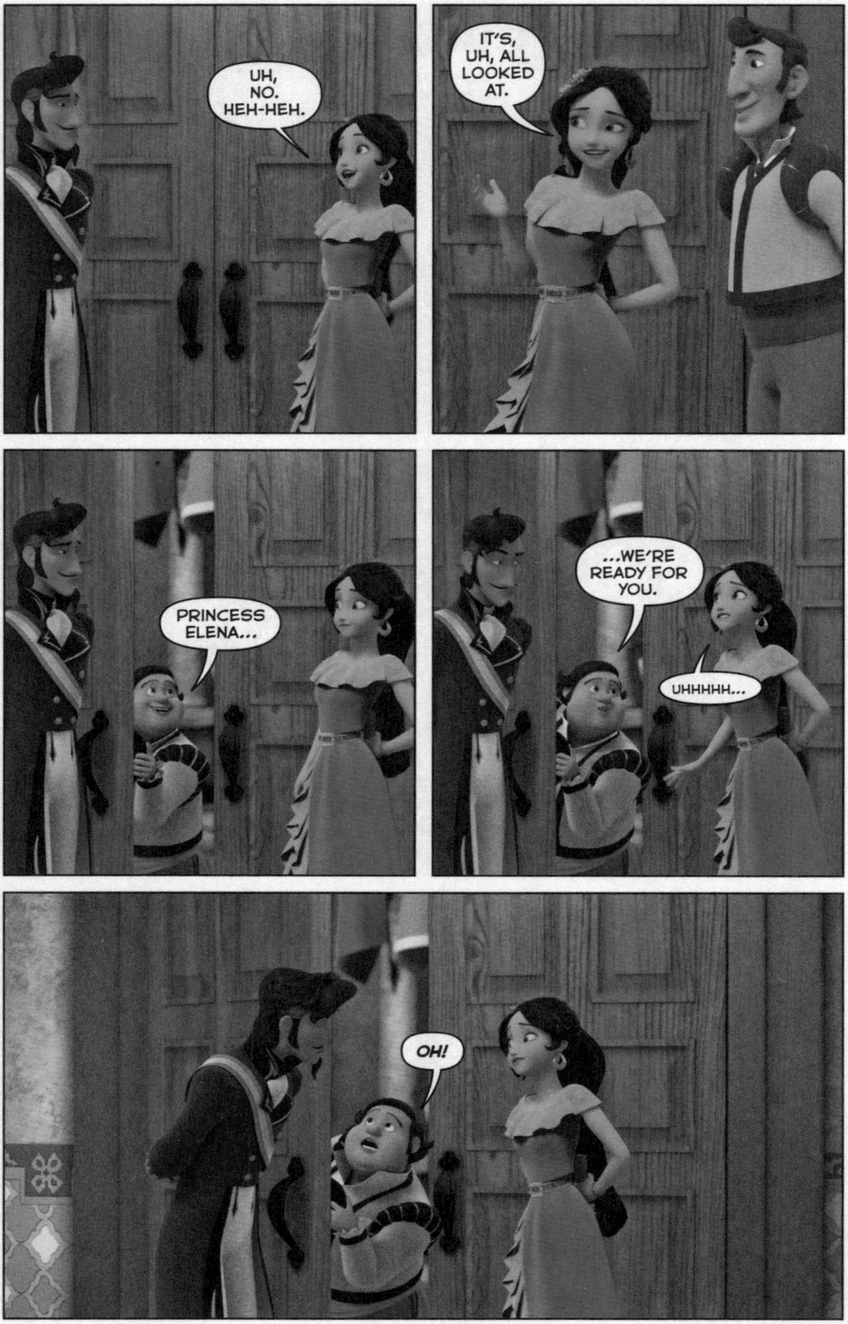
UH, NO. HEH-HEH.
IT'S, UH, ALL LOOKED AT.
PRINCESS ELENA...
...WE'RE READY FOR YOU.
UHHHHH...
OH!

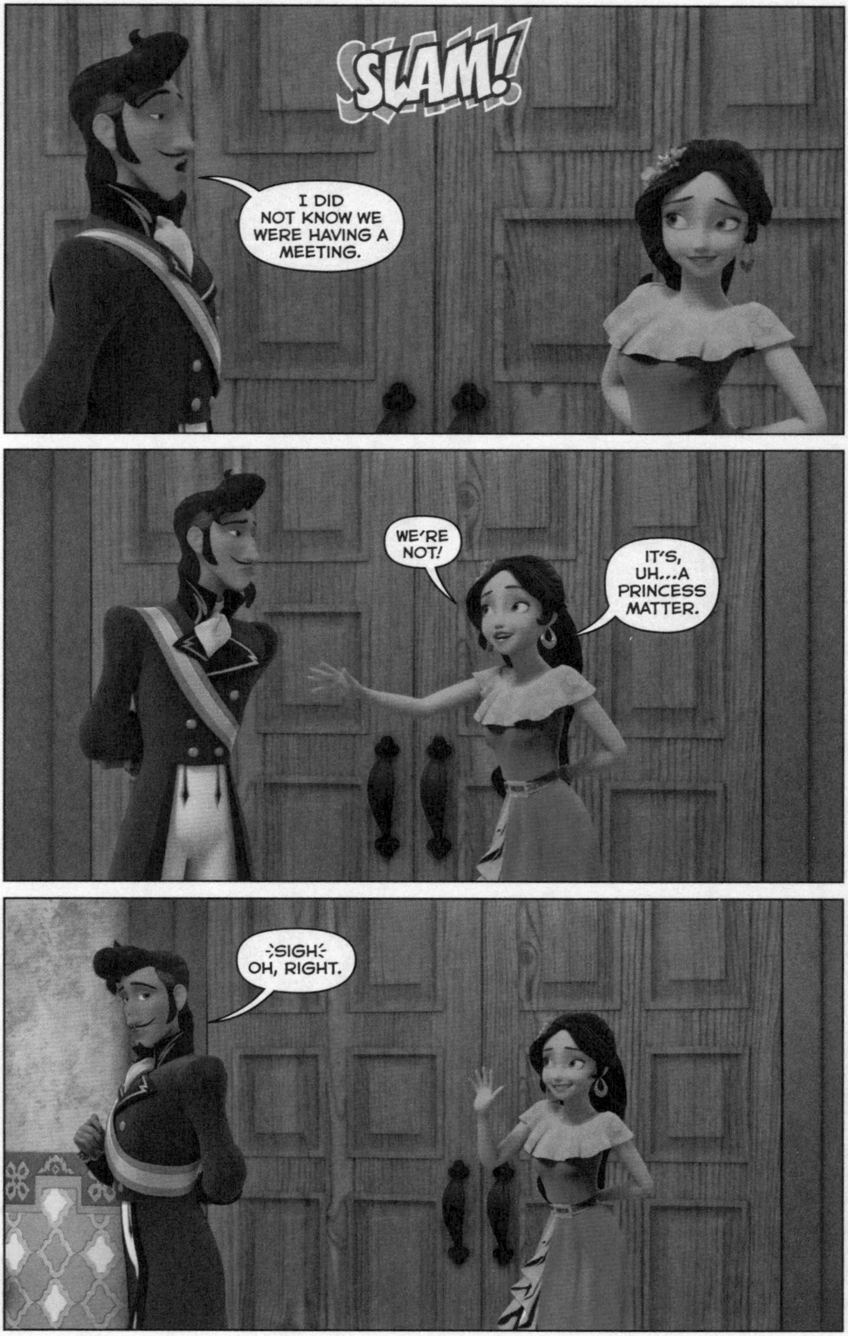
SLAM!
I DID NOT KNOW WE WERE HAVING A MEETING.
WE'RE NOT!
IT'S, UH...A PRINCESS MATTER.
SIGH
OH, RIGHT.

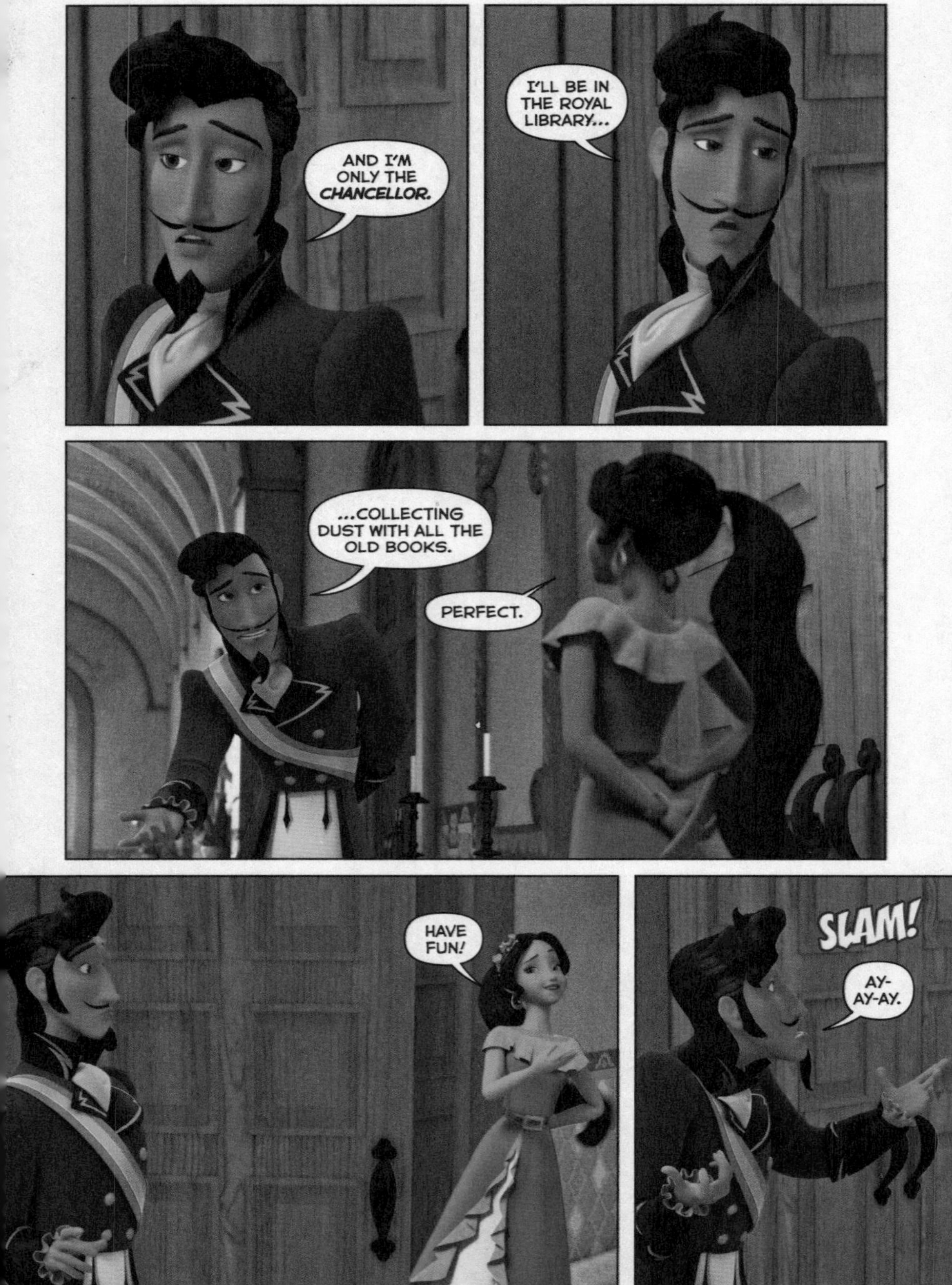
AND I'M ONLY THE *CHANCELLOR.*
I'LL BE IN THE ROYAL LIBRARY...
...COLLECTING DUST WITH ALL THE OLD BOOKS.
PERFECT.
HAVE FUN!
SLAM!
AY-AY-AY.

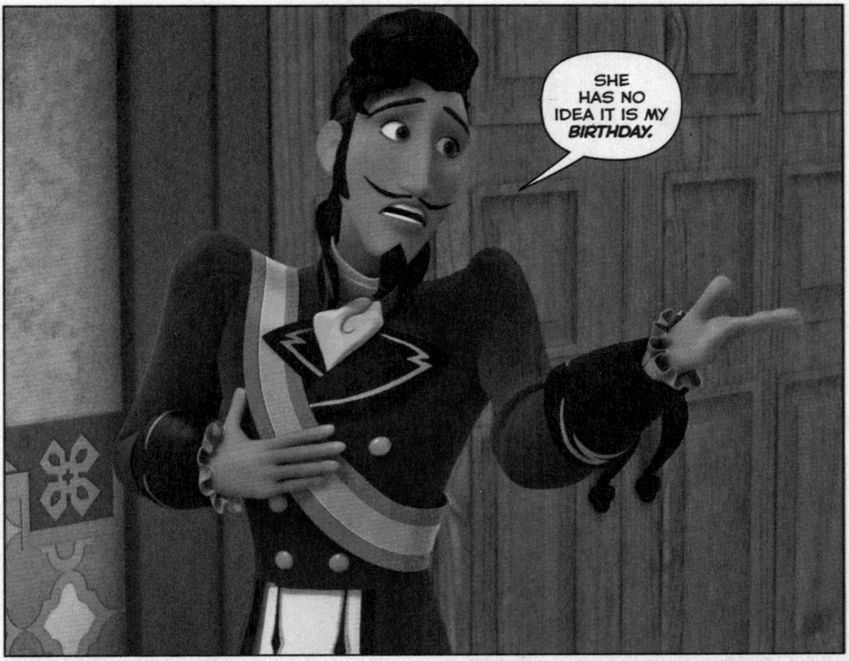
SHE HAS NO IDEA IT IS MY *BIRTHDAY.*

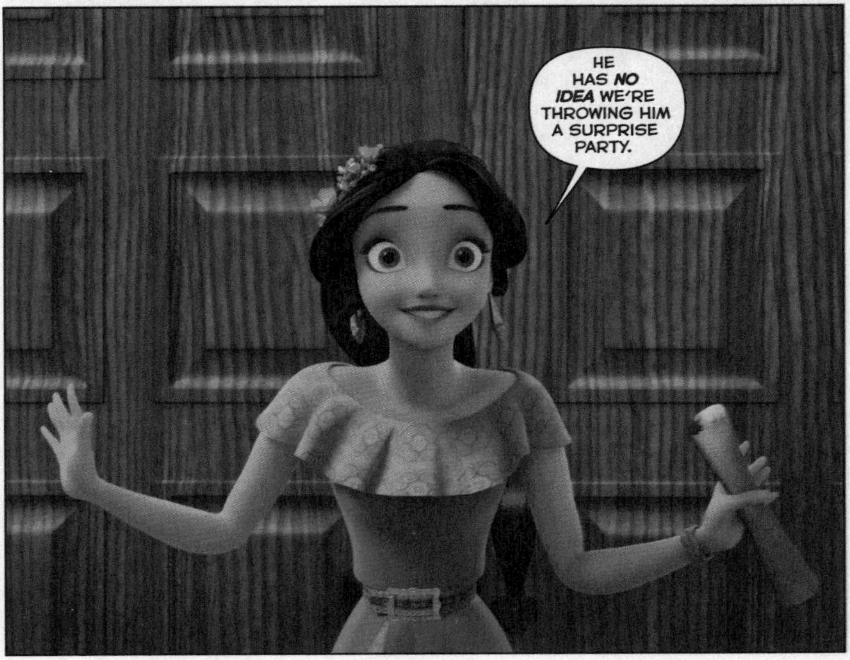
HE HAS *NO IDEA* WE'RE THROWING HIM A SURPRISE PARTY.

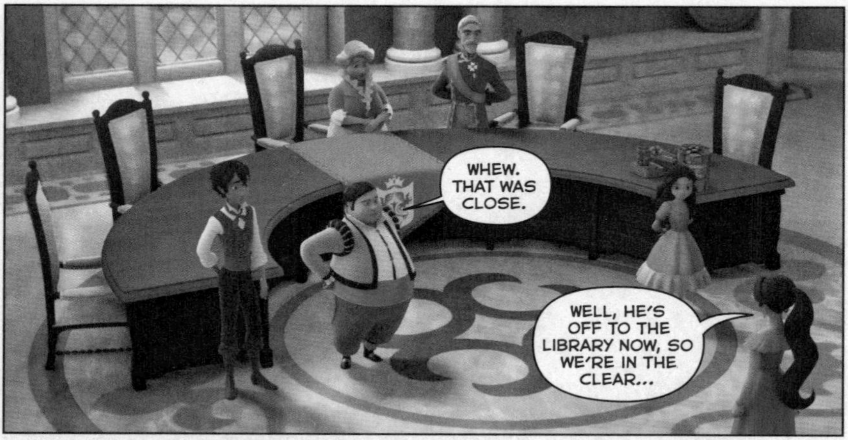
WHEW. THAT WAS CLOSE.
WELL, HE'S OFF TO THE LIBRARY NOW, SO WE'RE IN THE CLEAR...

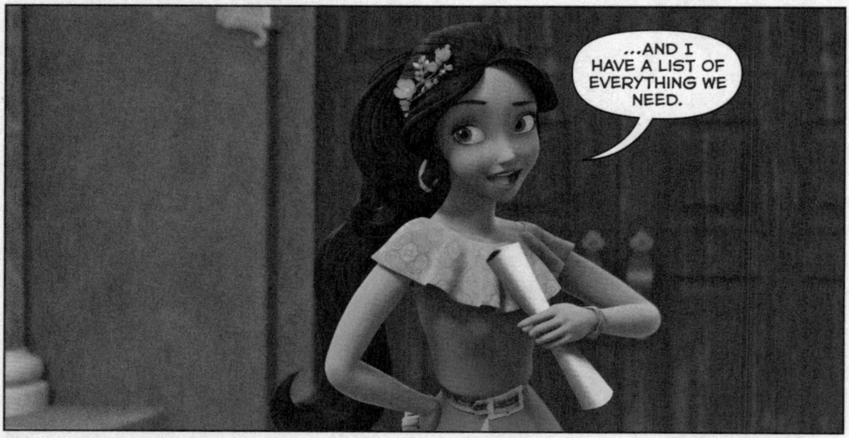
...AND I HAVE A LIST OF EVERYTHING WE NEED.

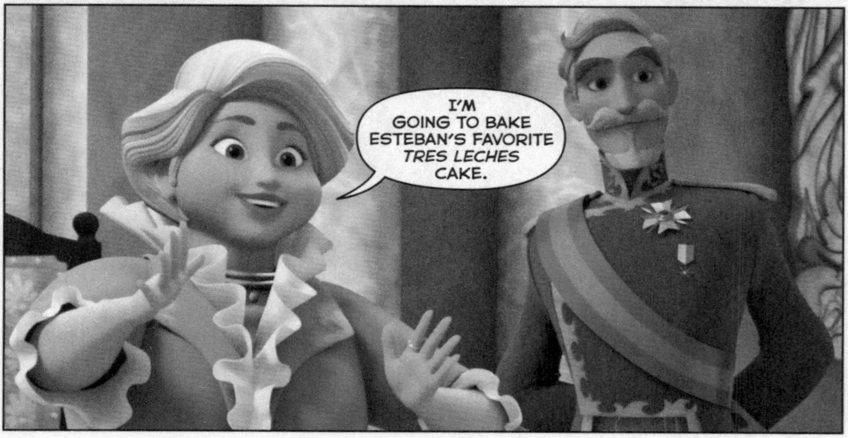
I'M GOING TO BAKE ESTEBAN'S FAVORITE *TRES LECHES* CAKE.

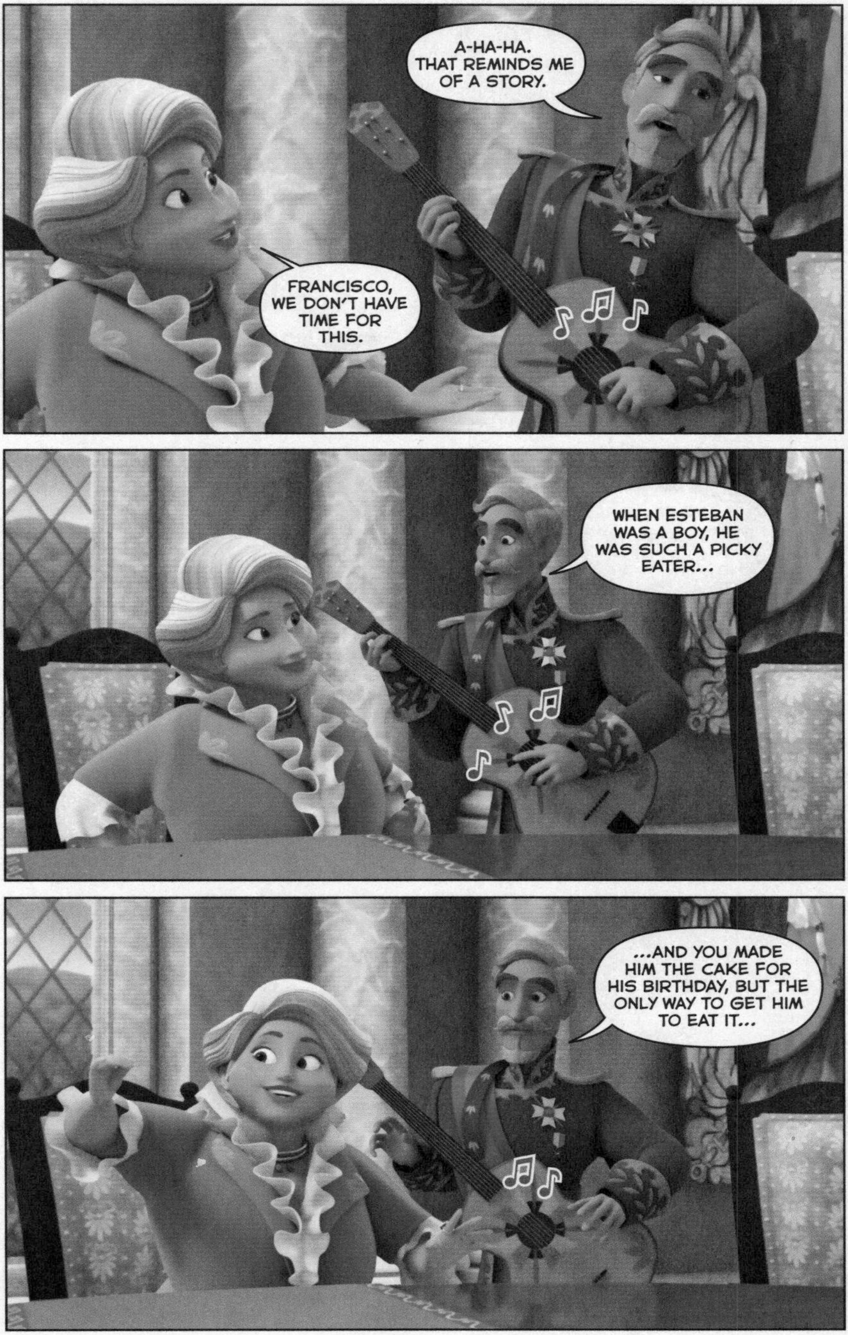
A-HA-HA. THAT REMINDS ME OF A STORY.
FRANCISCO, WE DON'T HAVE TIME FOR THIS.
WHEN ESTEBAN WAS A BOY, HE WAS SUCH A PICKY EATER...
...AND YOU MADE HIM THE CAKE FOR HIS BIRTHDAY, BUT THE ONLY WAY TO GET HIM TO EAT IT...

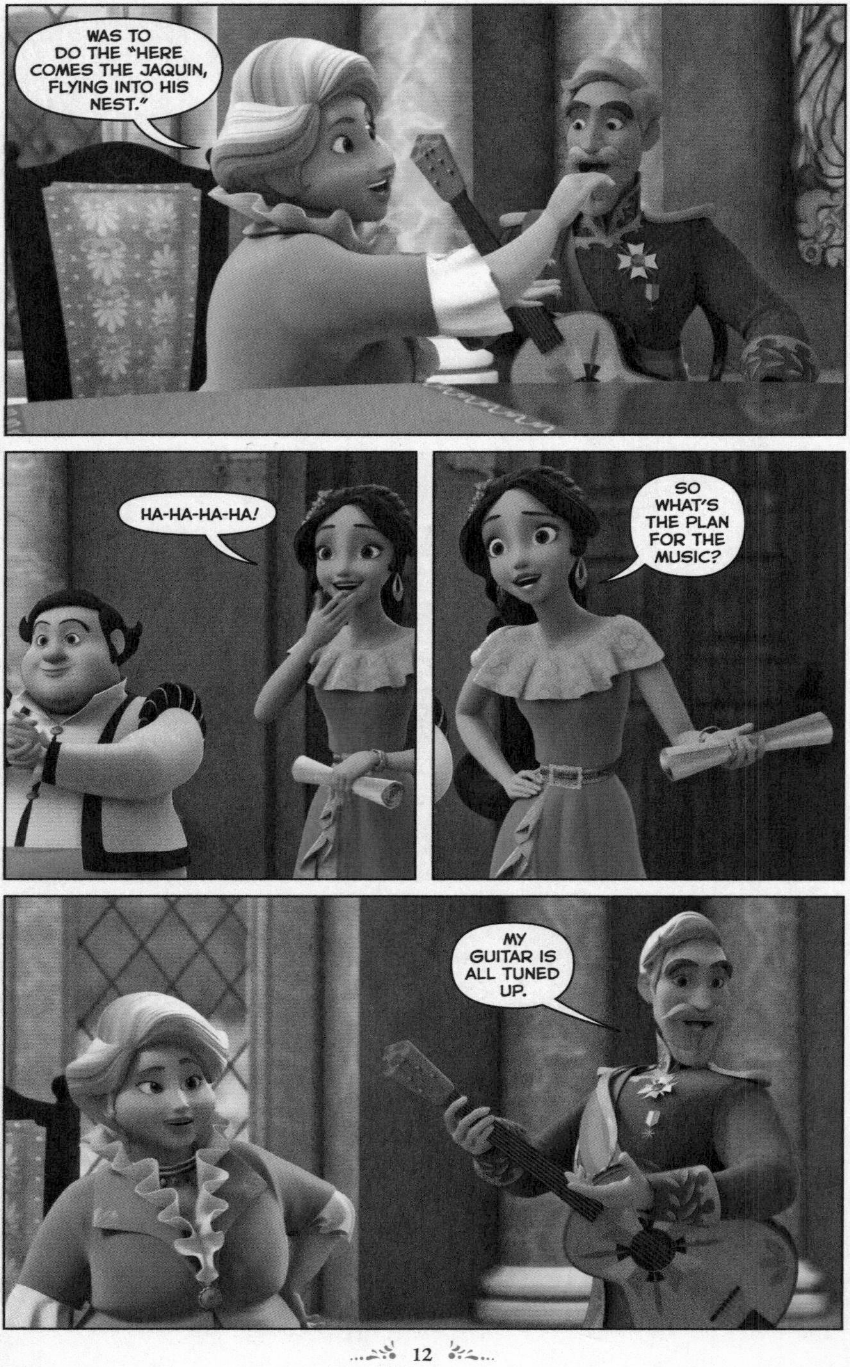
WAS TO DO THE "HERE COMES THE JAQUIN, FLYING INTO HIS NEST."
HA-HA-HA-HA!
SO WHAT'S THE PLAN FOR THE MUSIC?
MY GUITAR IS ALL TUNED UP.

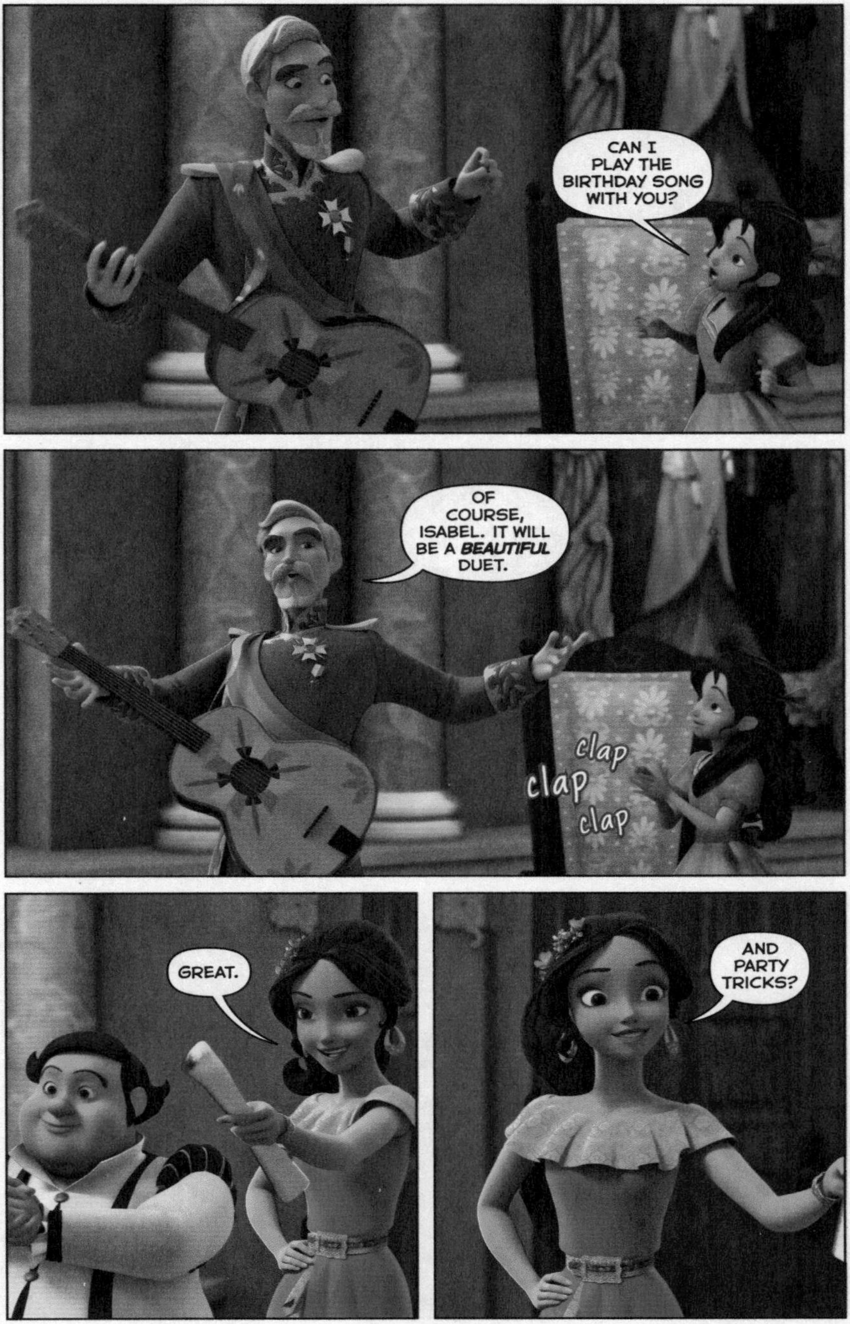
CAN I PLAY THE BIRTHDAY SONG WITH YOU?
OF COURSE, ISABEL. IT WILL BE A *BEAUTIFUL* DUET.
clap clap clap
GREAT.
AND PARTY TRICKS?

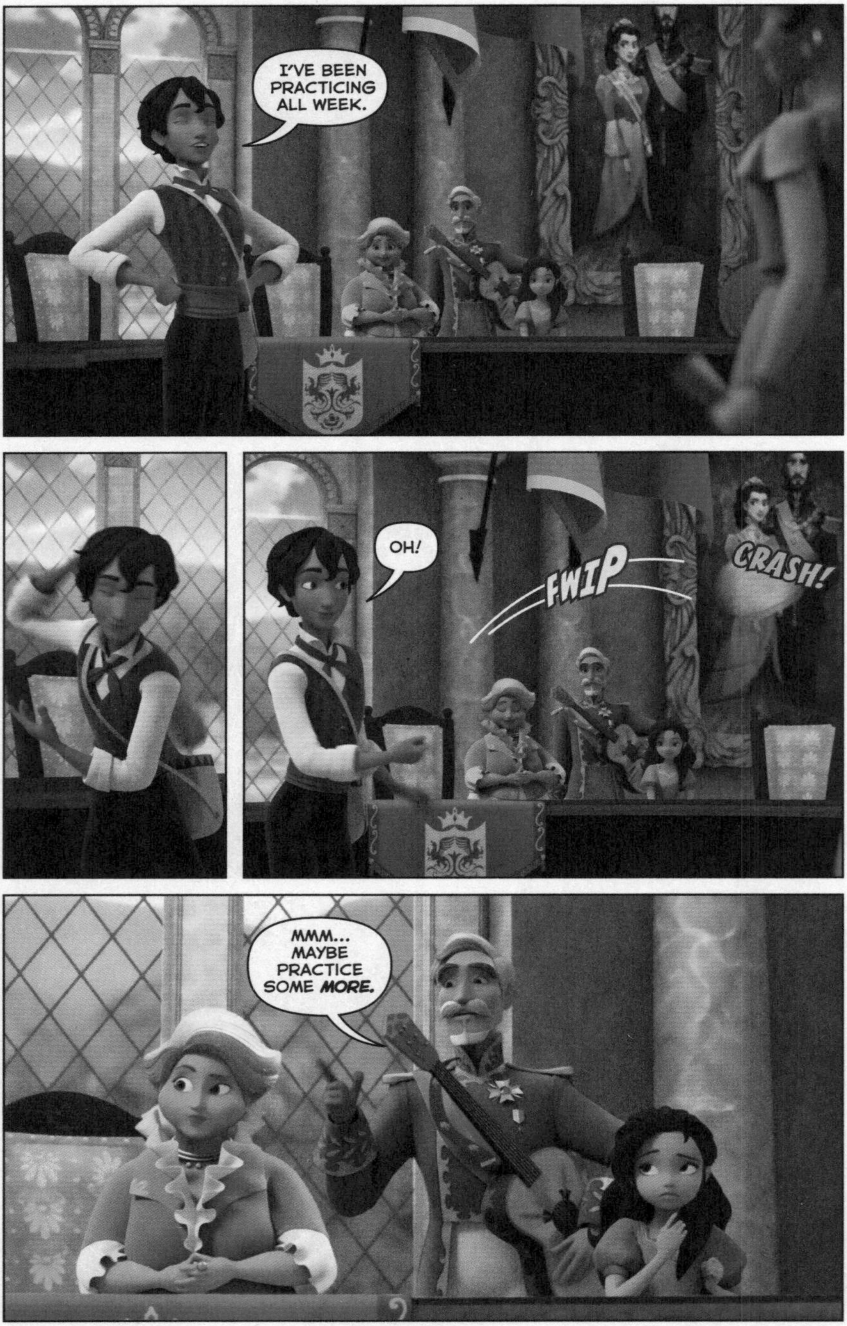
I'VE BEEN PRACTICING ALL WEEK.
OH!
FWIP
CRASH!
MMM... MAYBE PRACTICE SOME *MORE.*

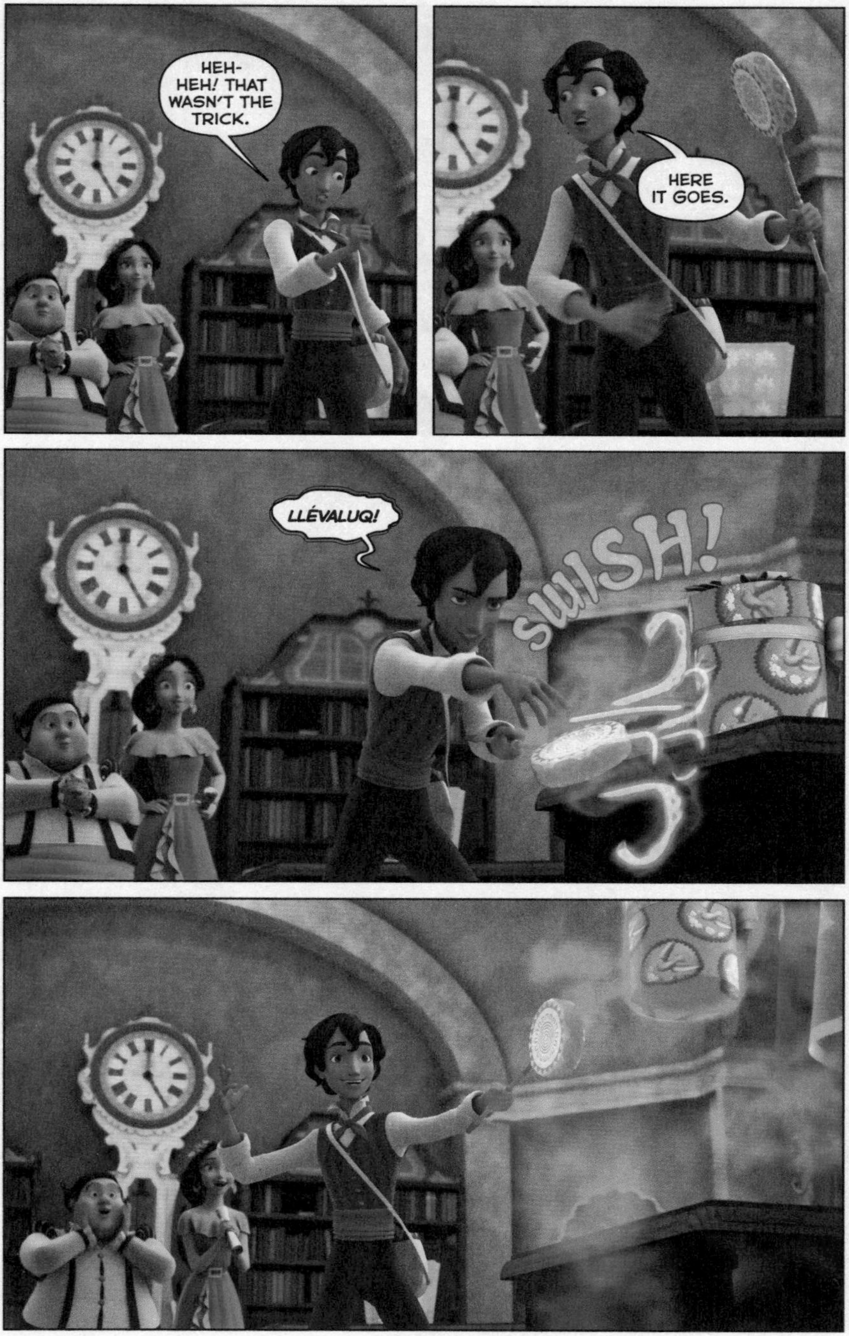
HEH-HEH! THAT WASN'T THE TRICK.
HERE IT GOES.
LLÉVALUQ!
SWISH!

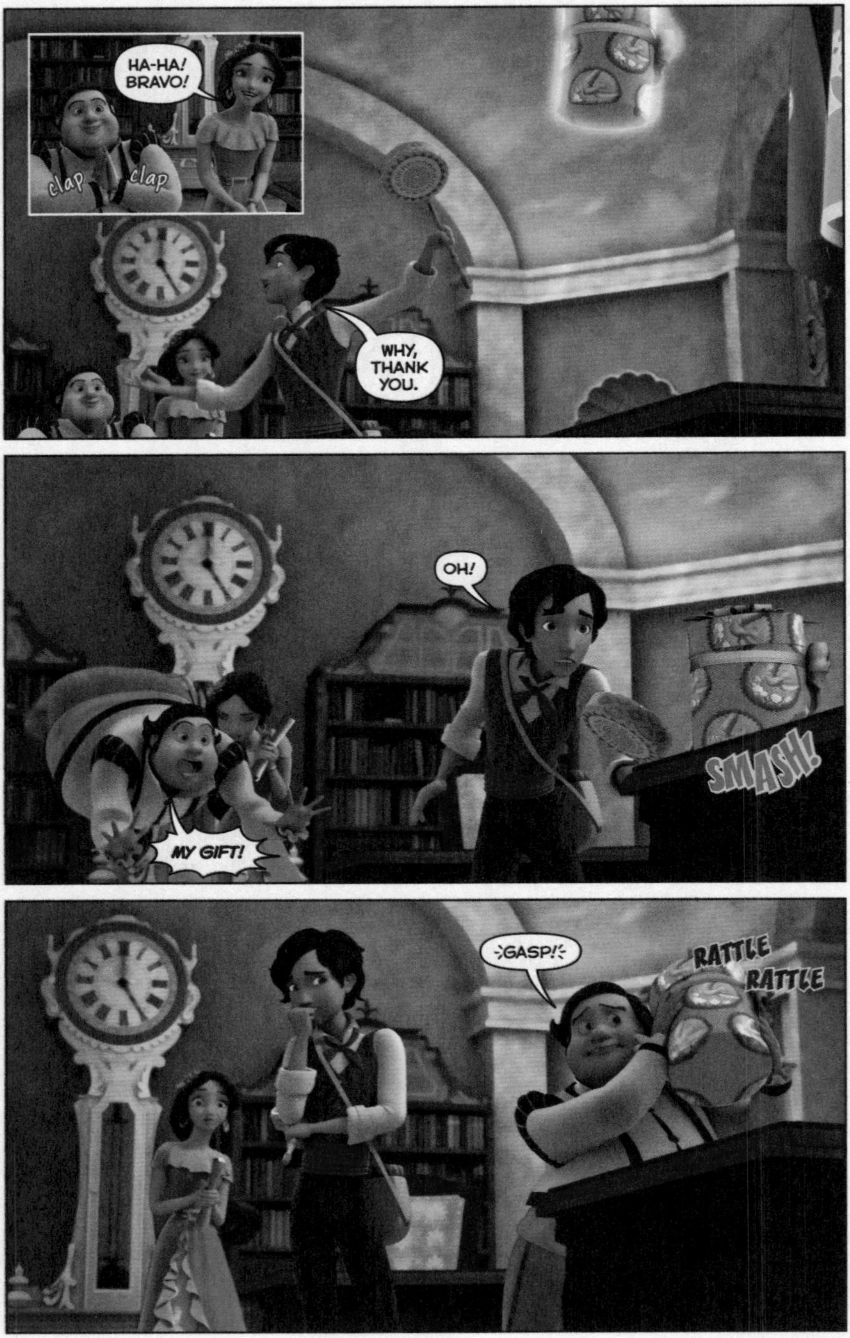

HA-HA! BRAVO!
clap clap
WHY, THANK YOU.
OH!
SMASH!
MY GIFT!
GASP!
RATTLE RATTLE

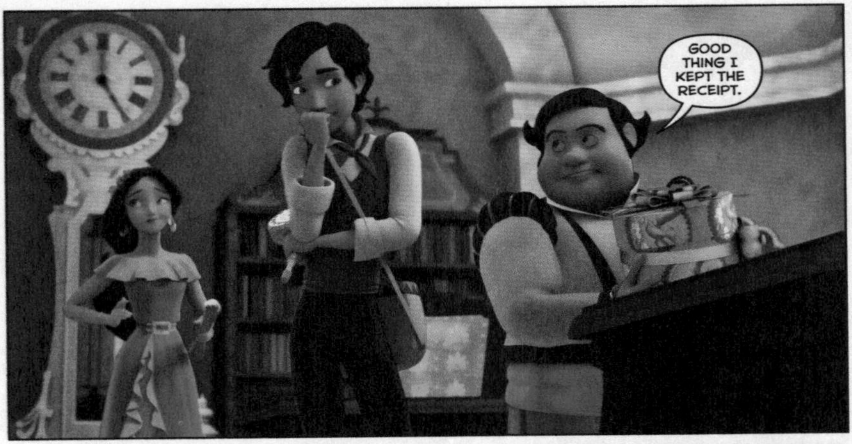
GOOD THING I KEPT THE RECEIPT.

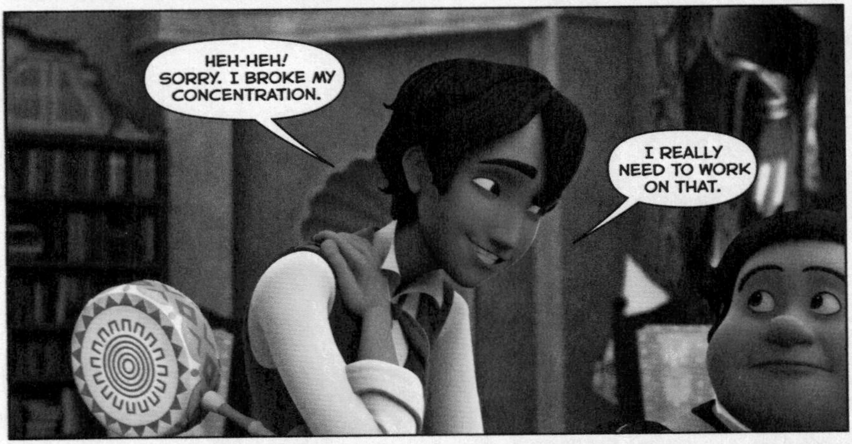
HEH-HEH! SORRY. I BROKE MY CONCENTRATION.
I REALLY NEED TO WORK ON THAT.

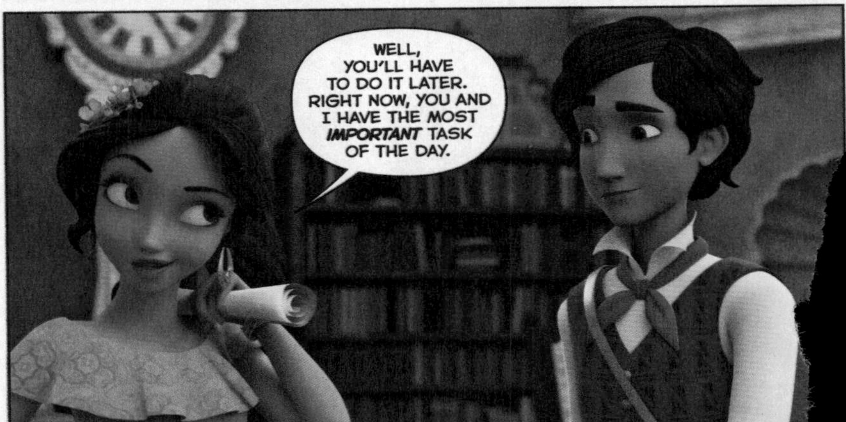
WELL, YOU'LL HAVE TO DO IT LATER. RIGHT NOW, YOU AND I HAVE THE MOST *IMPORTANT* TASK OF THE DAY.

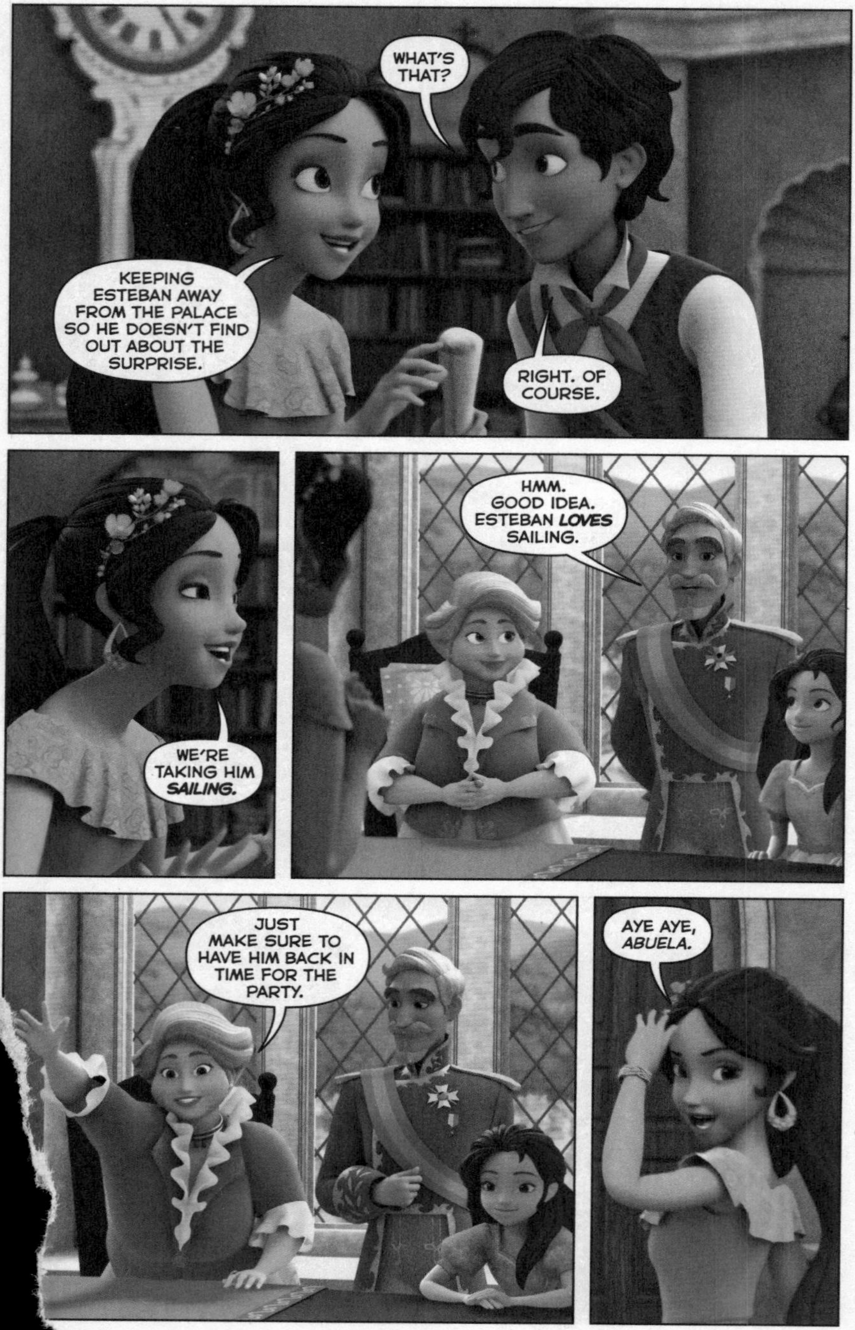
KEEPING ESTEBAN AWAY FROM THE PALACE SO HE DOESN'T FIND OUT ABOUT THE SURPRISE.
WHAT'S THAT?
RIGHT. OF COURSE.
WE'RE TAKING HIM *SAILING.*
HMM. GOOD IDEA. ESTEBAN *LOVES* SAILING.
JUST MAKE SURE TO HAVE HIM BACK IN TIME FOR THE PARTY.
AYE AYE, *ABUELA.*

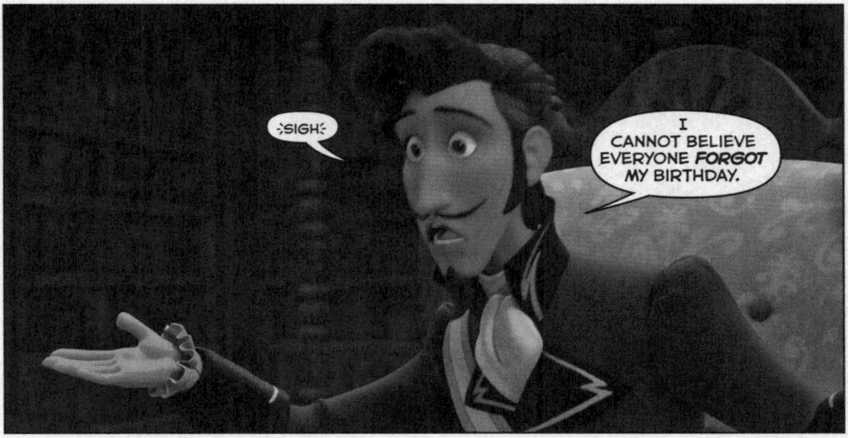
SIGH
I CANNOT BELIEVE EVERYONE ***FORGOT*** MY BIRTHDAY.

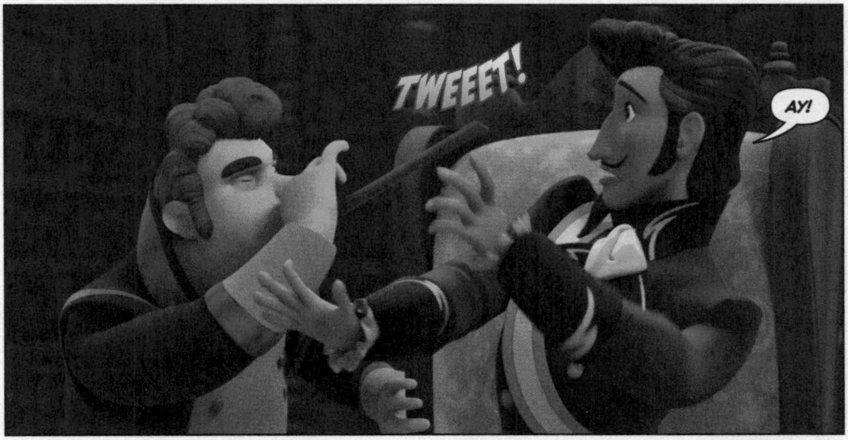
TWEEET!
AY!

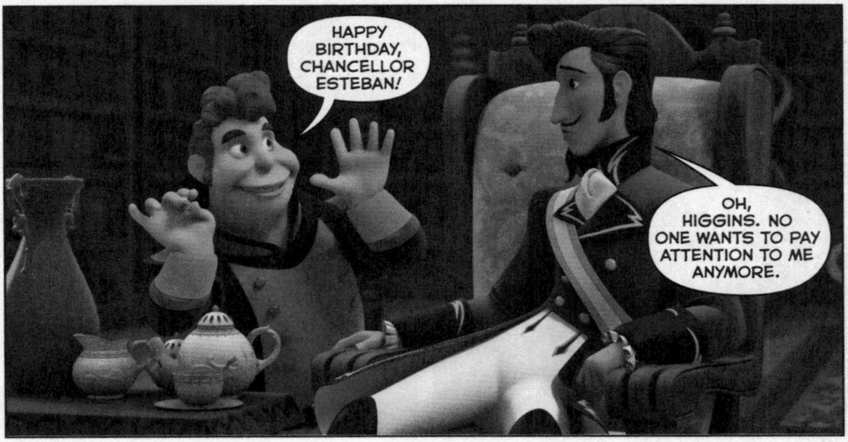
HAPPY BIRTHDAY, CHANCELLOR ESTEBAN!
OH, HIGGINS. NO ONE WANTS TO PAY ATTENTION TO ME ANYMORE.

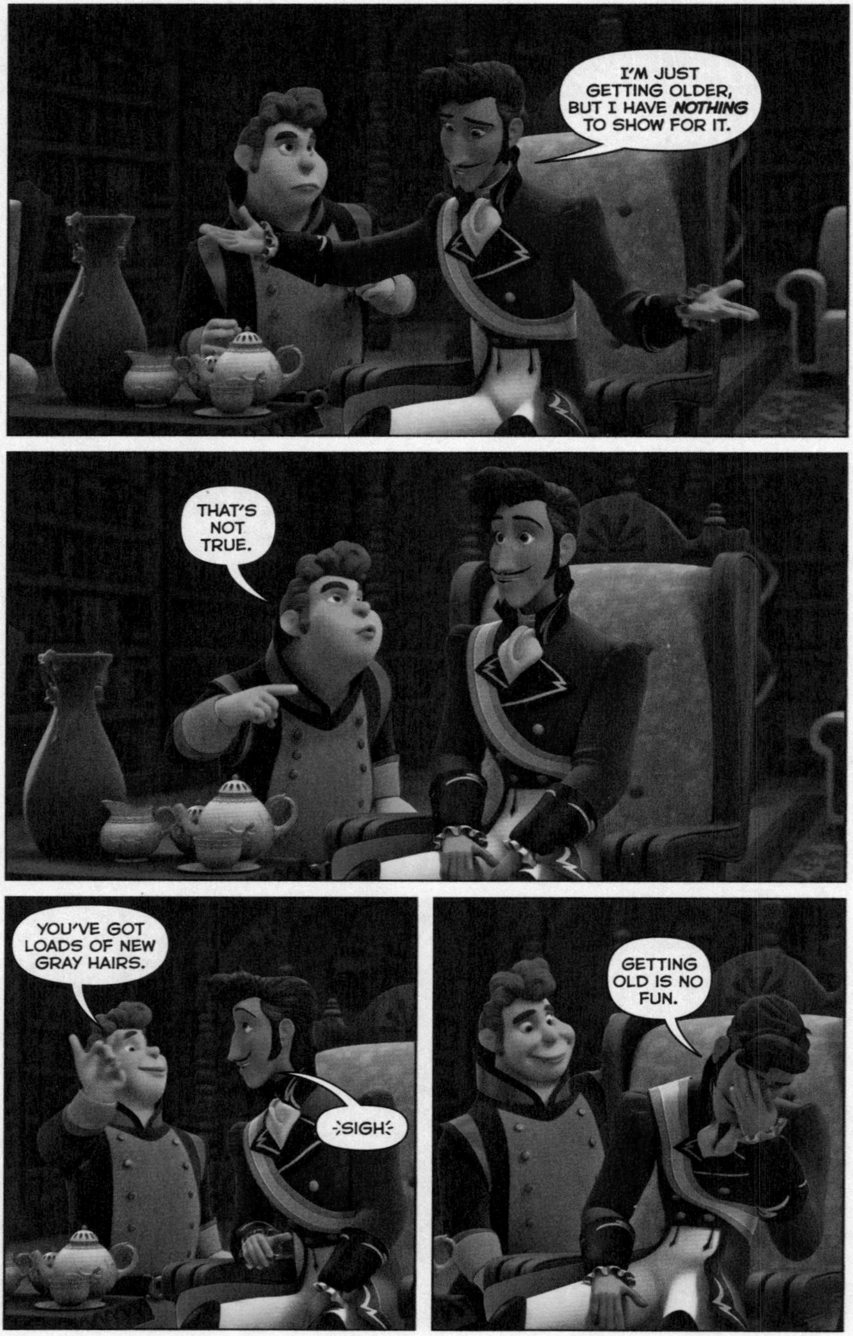
I'M JUST GETTING OLDER, BUT I HAVE *NOTHING* TO SHOW FOR IT.
THAT'S NOT TRUE.
YOU'VE GOT LOADS OF NEW GRAY HAIRS.
SIGH
GETTING OLD IS NO FUN.

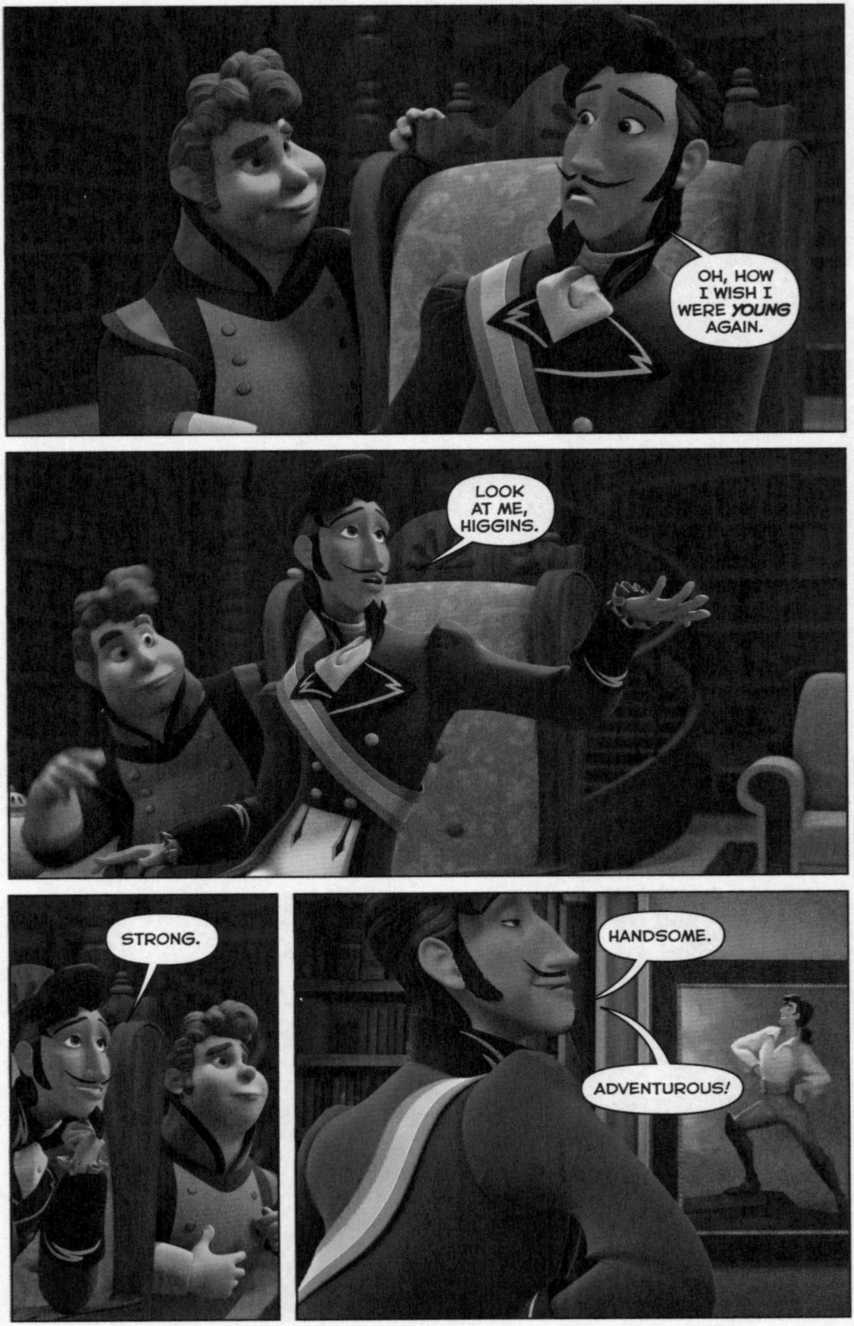
OH, HOW I WISH I WERE *YOUNG* AGAIN.
LOOK AT ME, HIGGINS.
STRONG.
HANDSOME.
ADVENTUROUS!

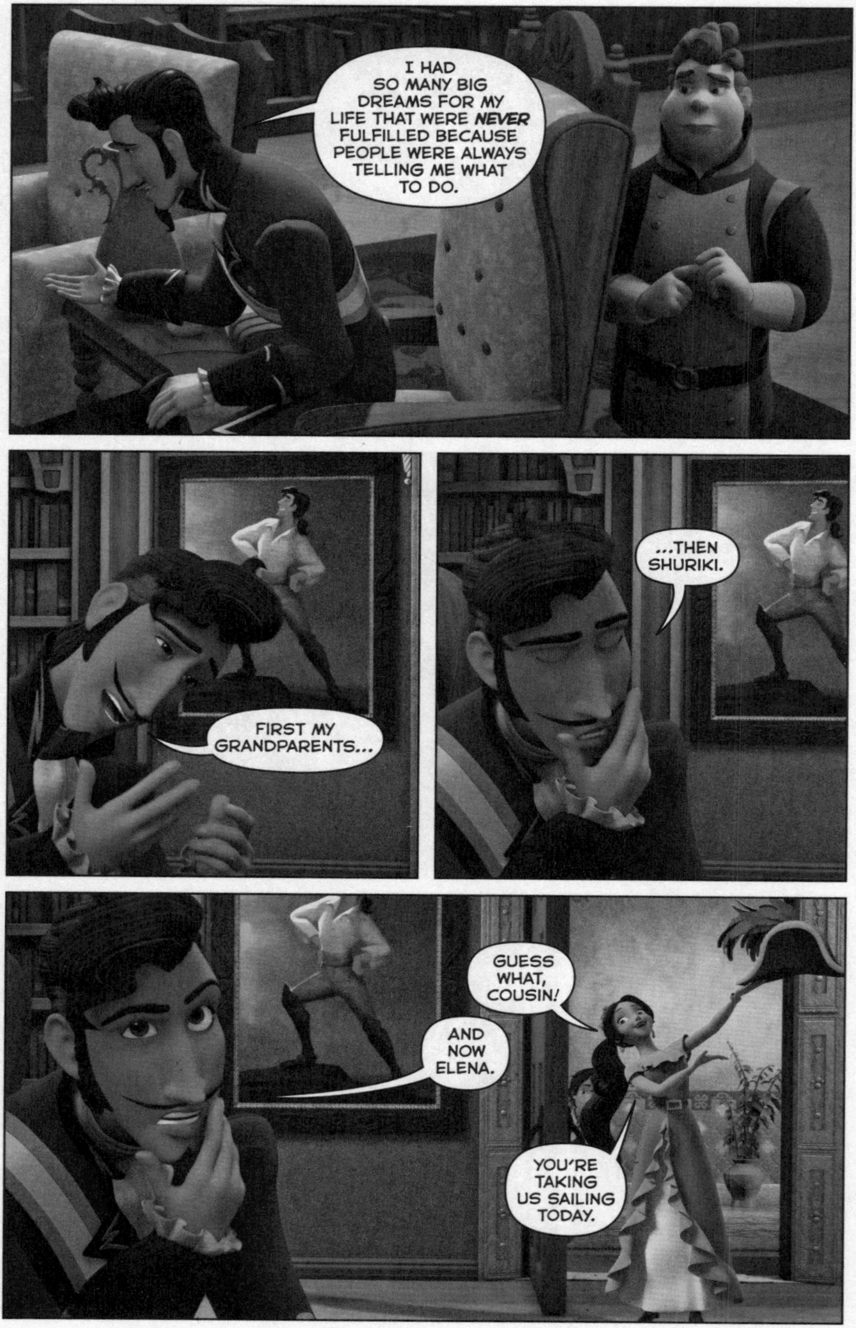
I HAD SO MANY BIG DREAMS FOR MY LIFE THAT WERE *NEVER* FULFILLED BECAUSE PEOPLE WERE ALWAYS TELLING ME WHAT TO DO.
FIRST MY GRANDPARENTS...
...THEN SHURIKI.
AND NOW ELENA.
GUESS WHAT, COUSIN!
YOU'RE TAKING US SAILING TODAY.

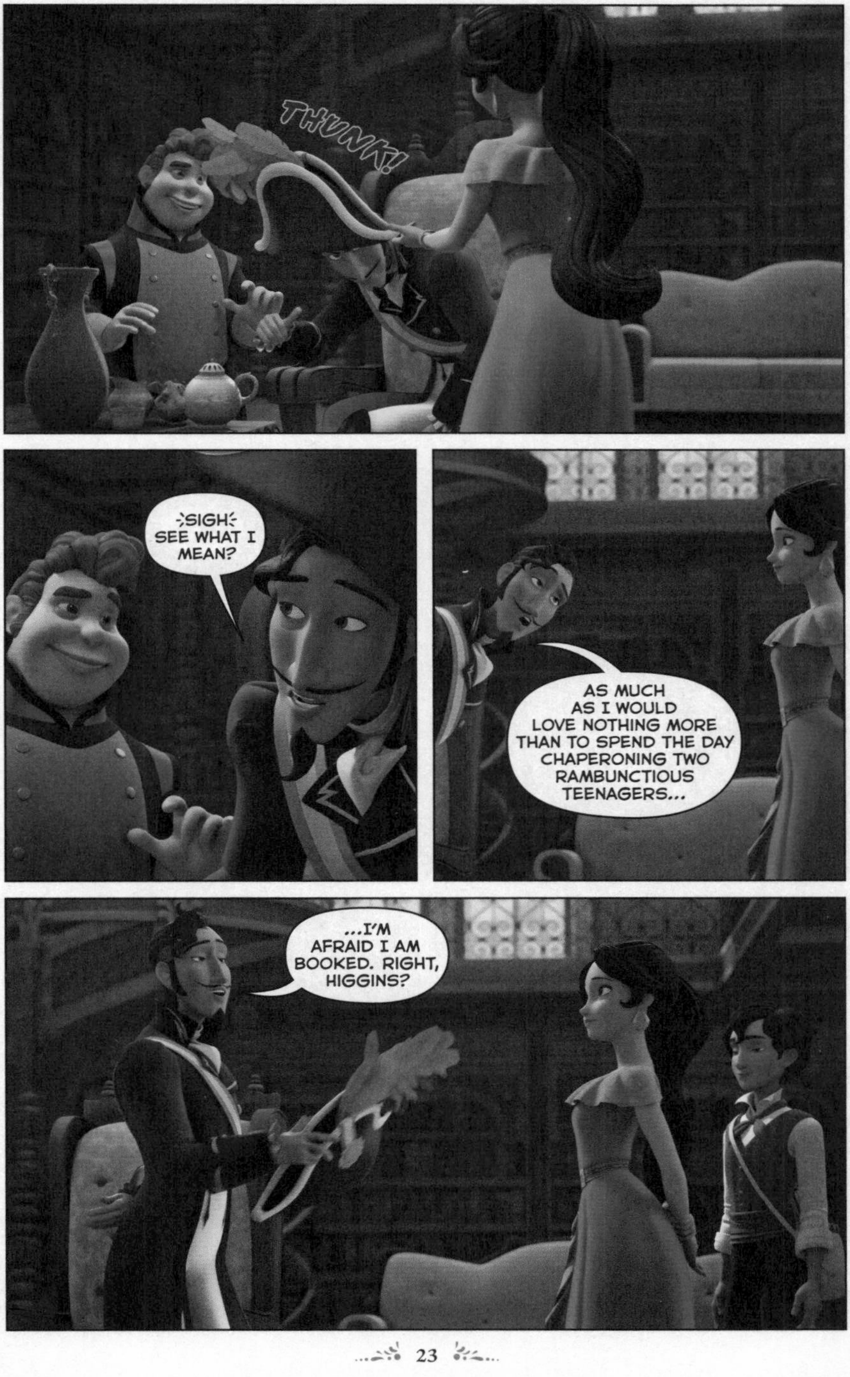
THUNK!
-SIGH-
SEE WHAT I
MEAN?
AS MUCH
AS I WOULD
LOVE NOTHING MORE
THAN TO SPEND THE DAY
CHAPERONING TWO
RAMBUNCTIOUS
TEENAGERS...
...I'M
AFRAID I AM
BOOKED. RIGHT,
HIGGINS?

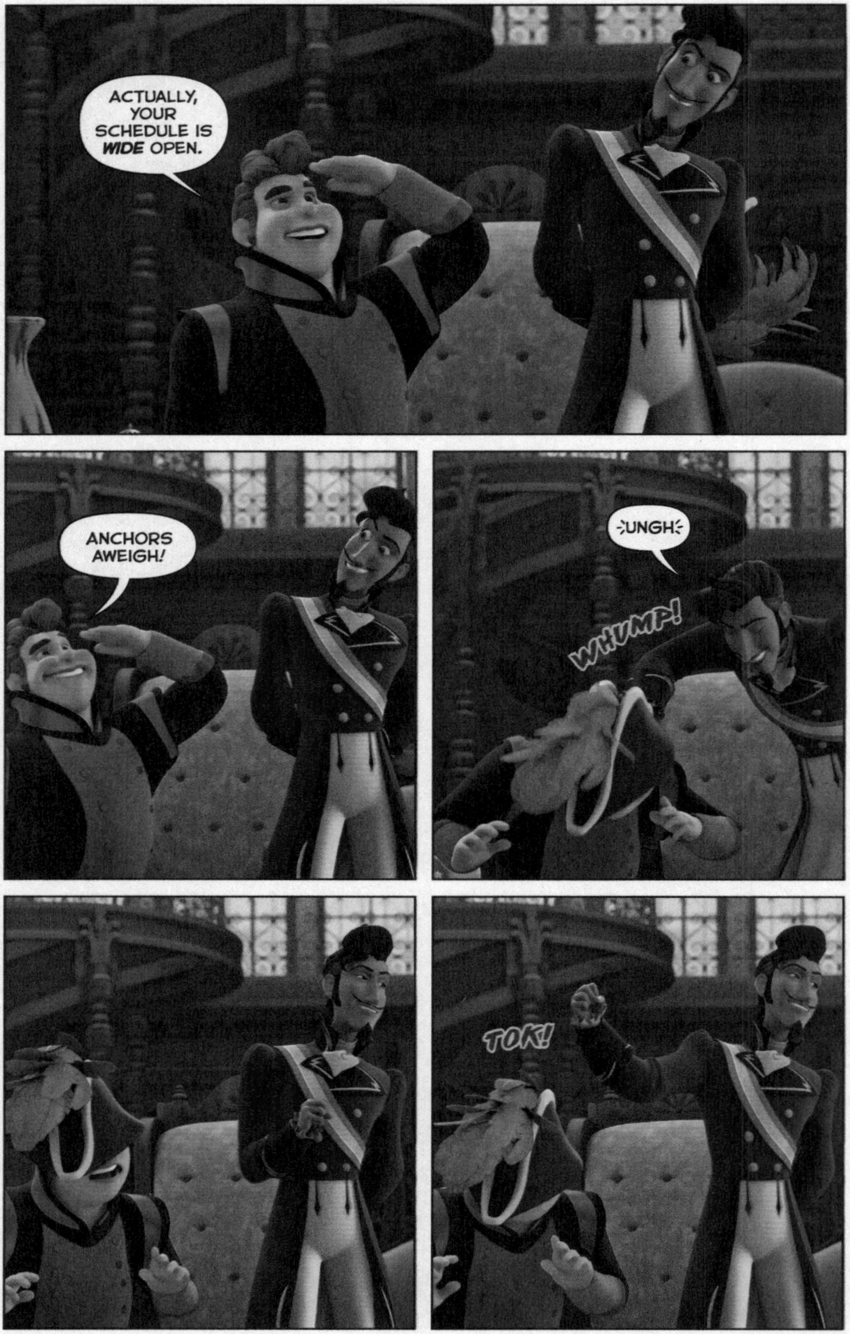
ACTUALLY, YOUR SCHEDULE IS *WIDE* OPEN.
ANCHORS AWEIGH!
UNGH
WHUMP!
TOK!

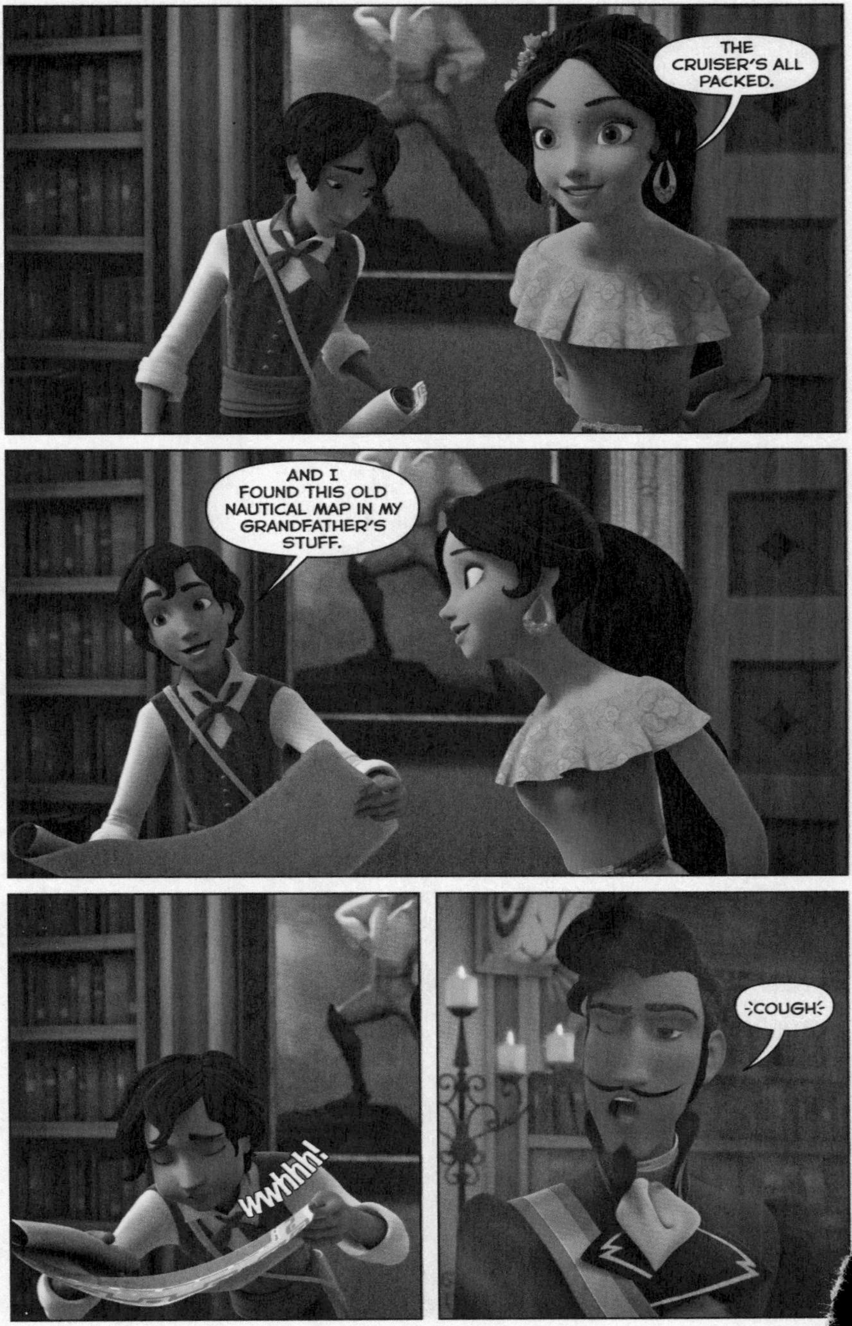
THE CRUISER'S ALL PACKED.
AND I FOUND THIS OLD NAUTICAL MAP IN MY GRANDFATHER'S STUFF.
WHHH!
COUGH

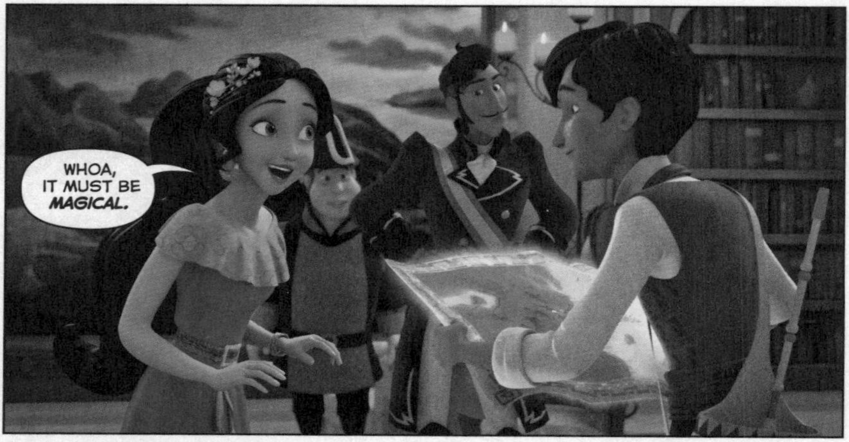
WHOA, IT MUST BE MAGICAL.

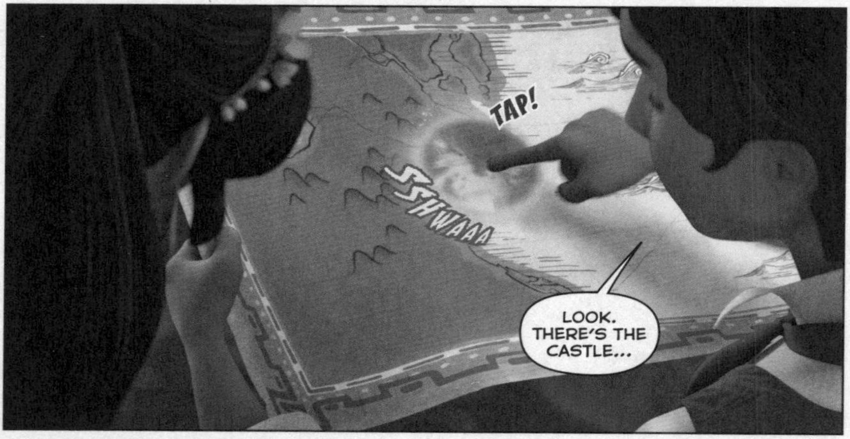
TAP!
SSHWAAA
LOOK. THERE'S THE CASTLE...

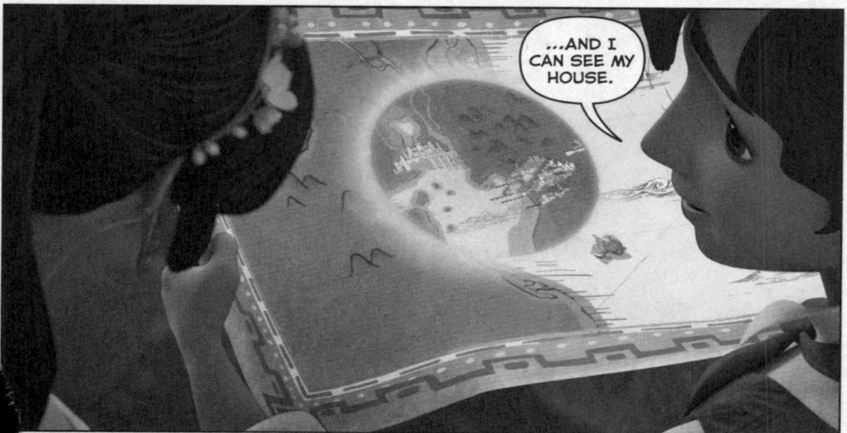
...AND I CAN SEE MY HOUSE.

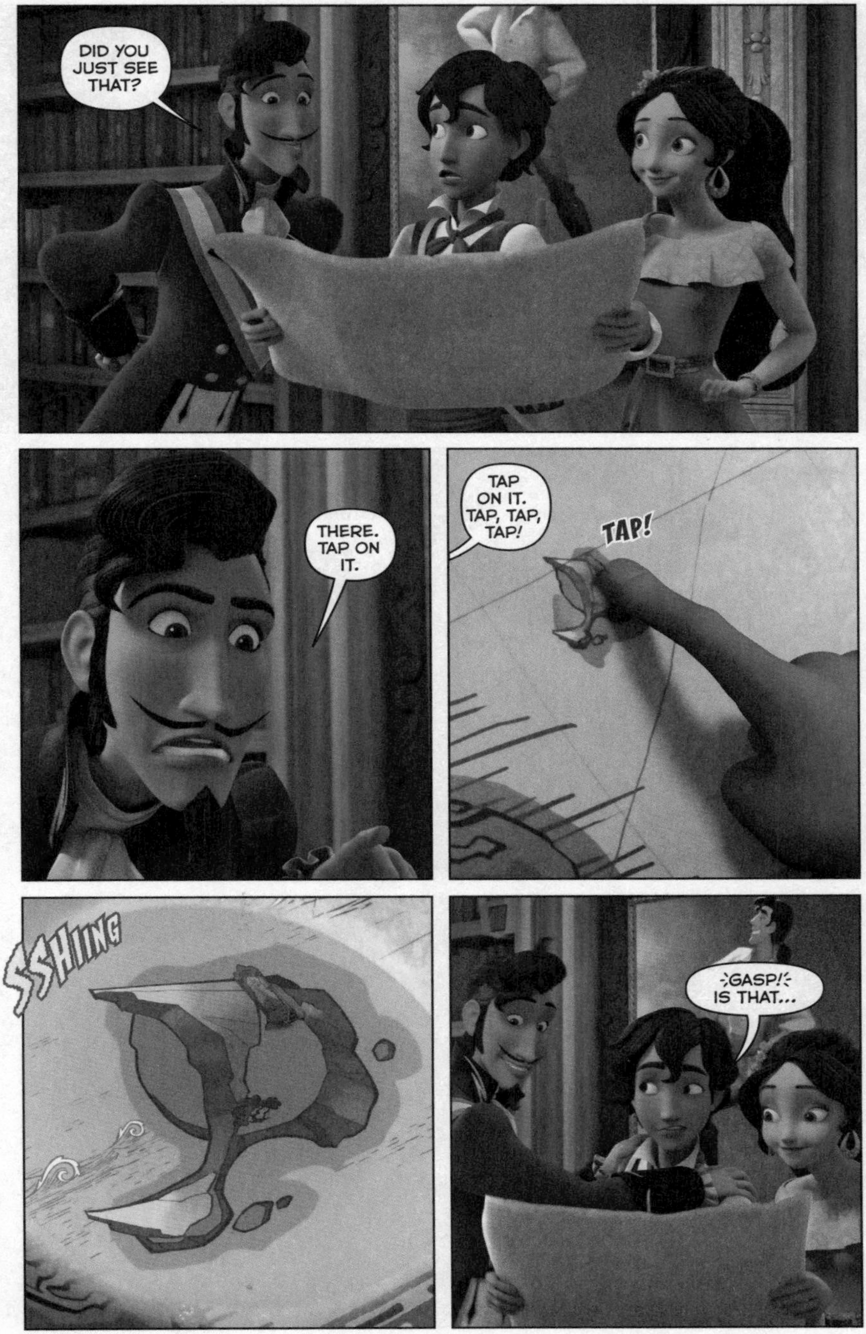
DID YOU JUST SEE THAT?
THERE. TAP ON IT.
TAP ON IT. TAP, TAP, TAP!
TAP!
SSHIING
GASP! IS THAT...

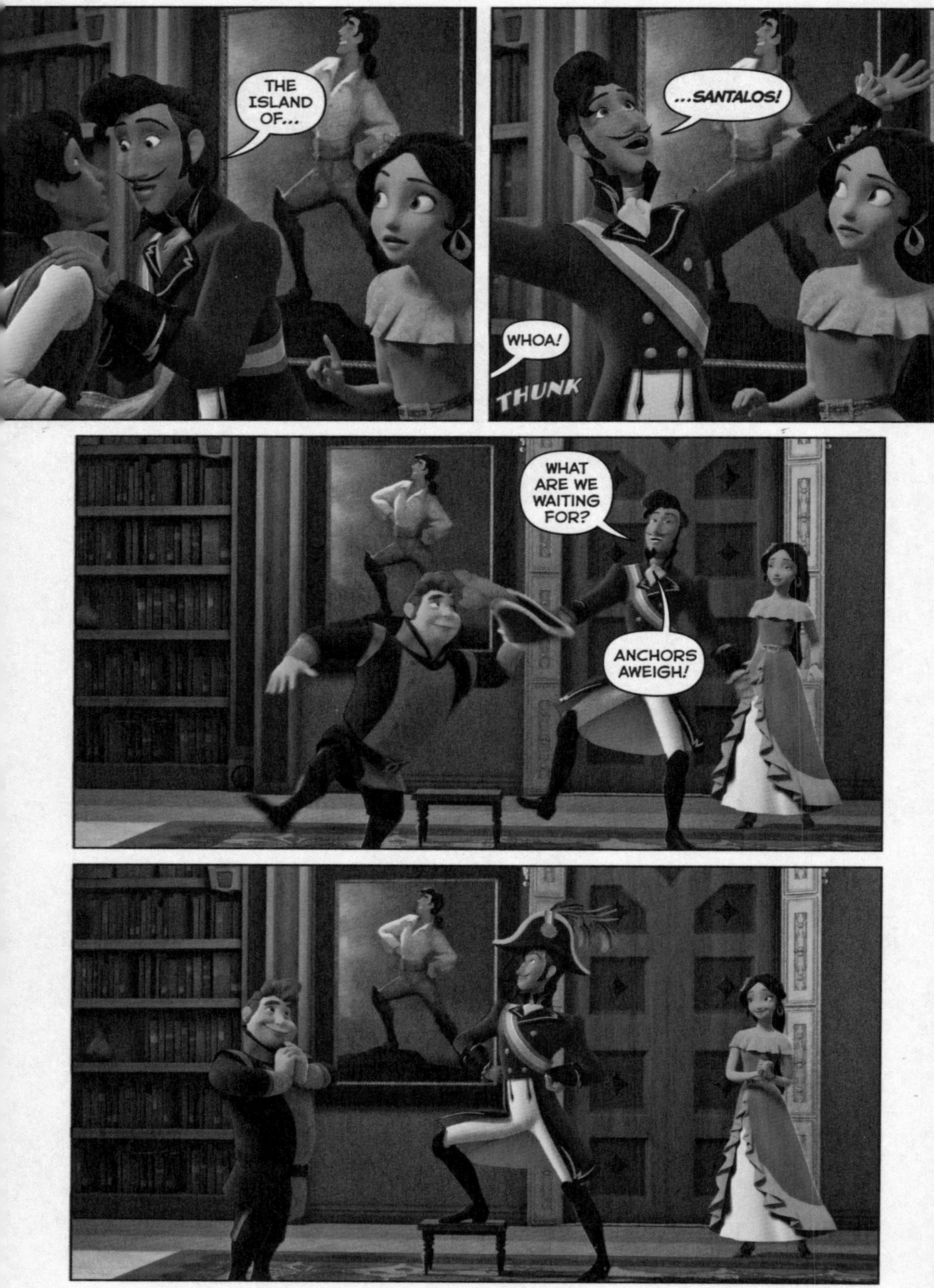
THE ISLAND OF...
...SANTALOS!
WHOA!
THUNK
WHAT ARE WE WAITING FOR?
ANCHORS AWEIGH!

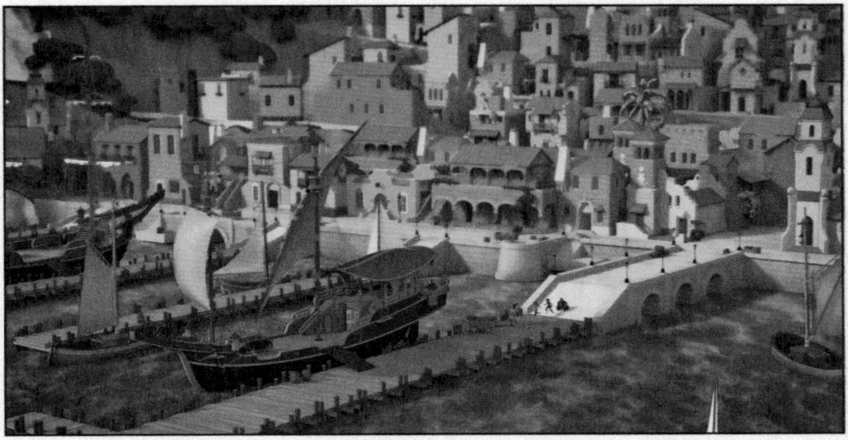

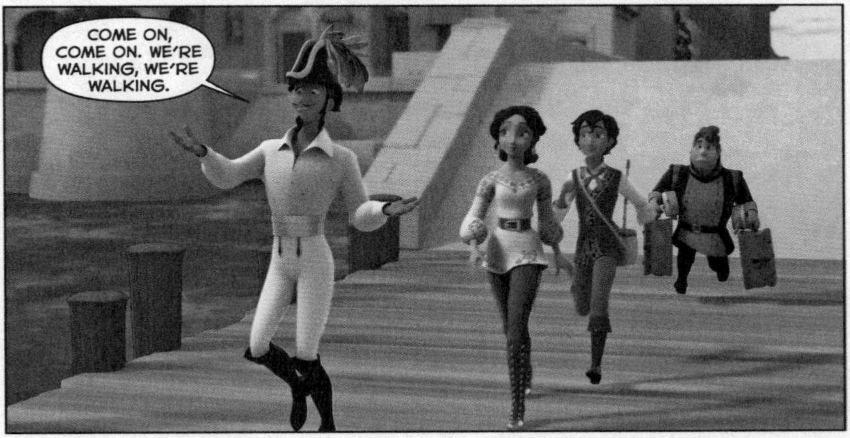
COME ON, COME ON. WE'RE WALKING, WE'RE WALKING.

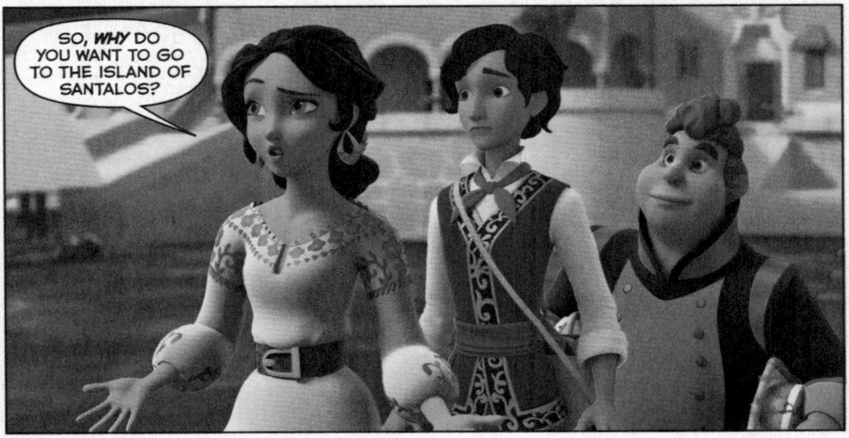
SO, *WHY* DO YOU WANT TO GO TO THE ISLAND OF SANTALOS?

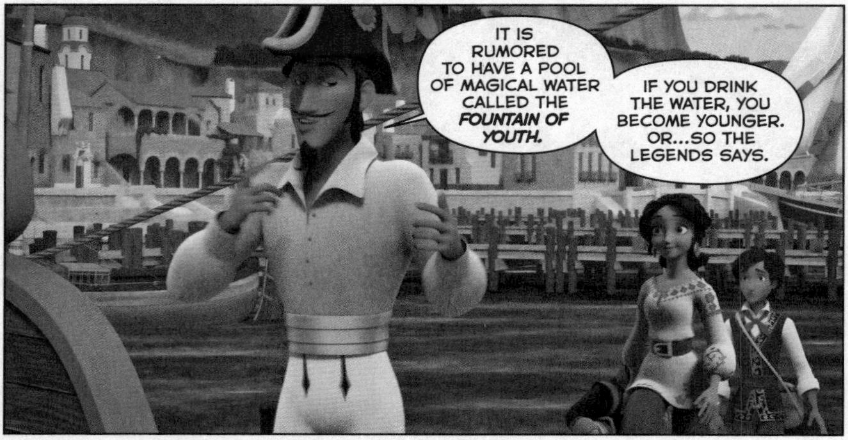
IT IS RUMORED TO HAVE A POOL OF MAGICAL WATER CALLED THE *FOUNTAIN OF YOUTH.*
IF YOU DRINK THE WATER, YOU BECOME YOUNGER. OR...SO THE LEGENDS SAYS.

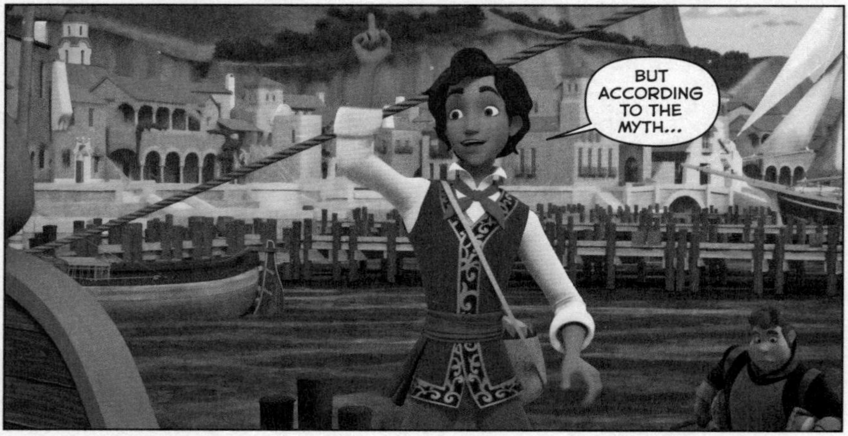
BUT ACCORDING TO THE MYTH...

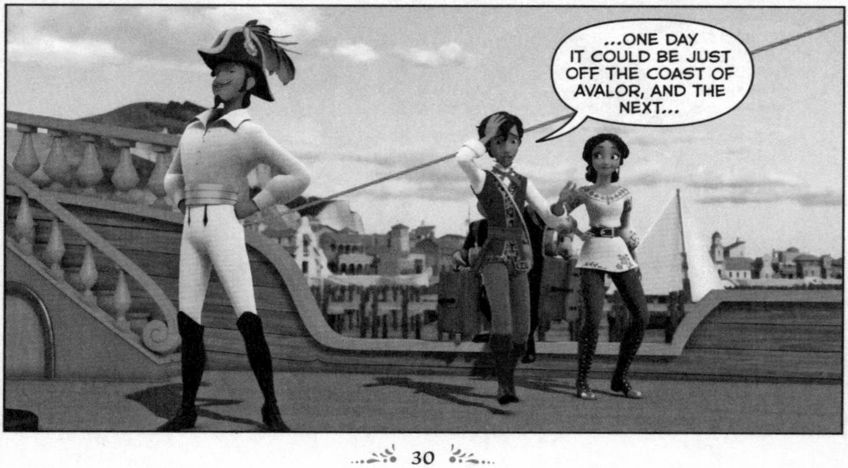
...ONE DAY IT COULD BE JUST OFF THE COAST OF AVALOR, AND THE NEXT...

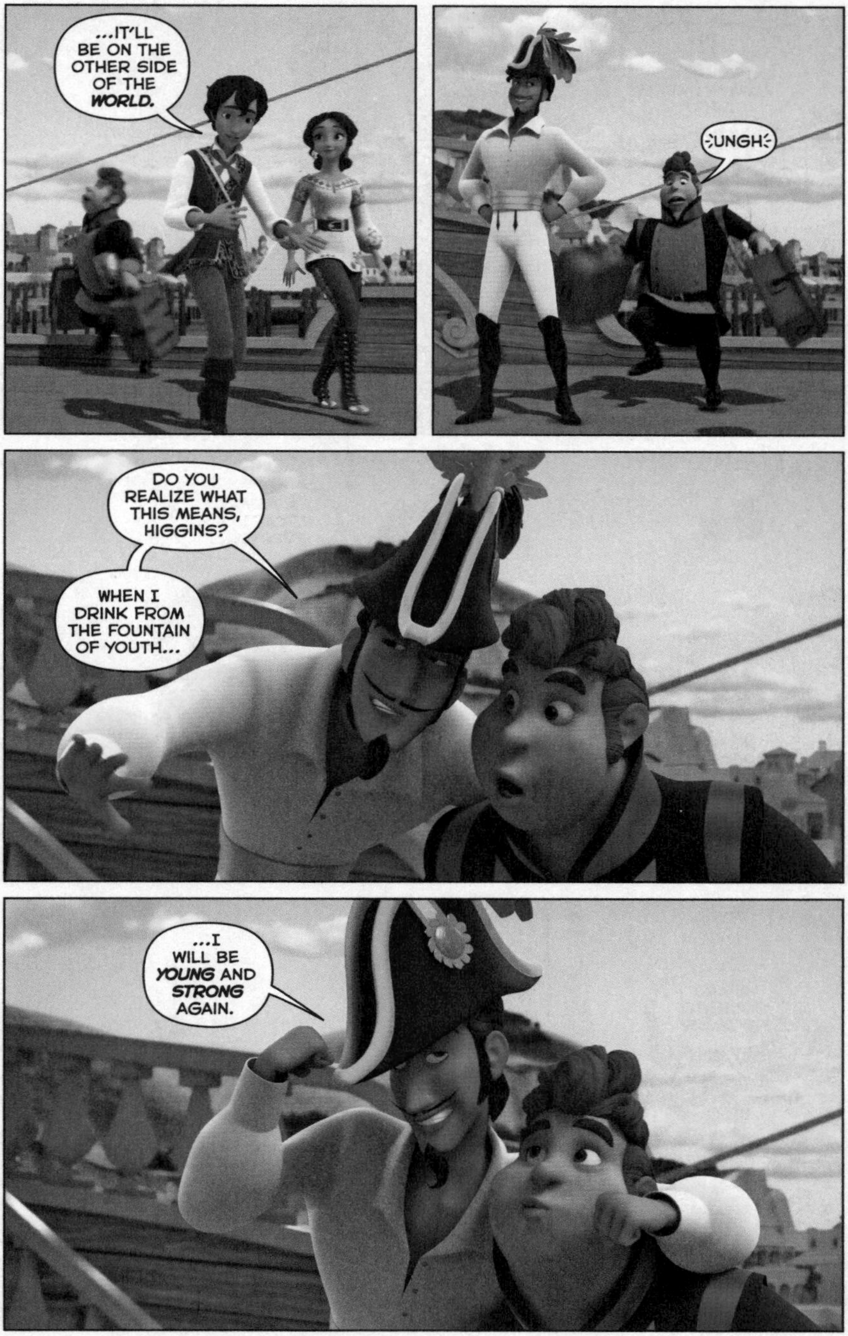
...IT'LL BE ON THE OTHER SIDE OF THE *WORLD.*
UNGH
DO YOU REALIZE WHAT THIS MEANS, HIGGINS?
WHEN I DRINK FROM THE FOUNTAIN OF YOUTH...
...I WILL BE *YOUNG* AND *STRONG* AGAIN.

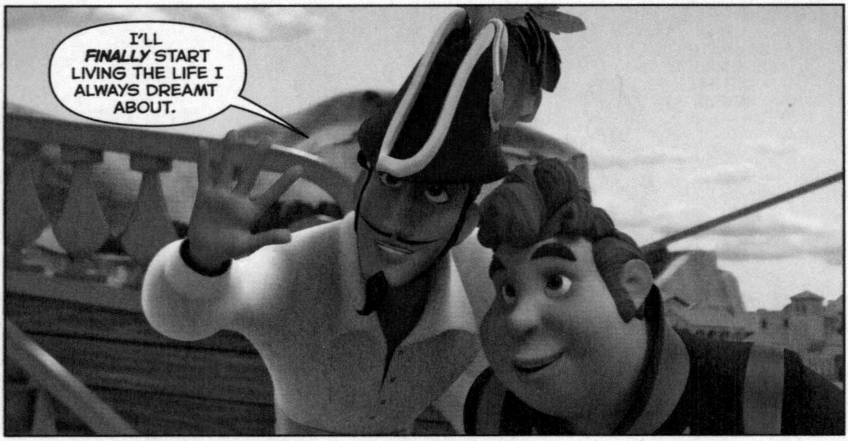
I'LL FINALLY START LIVING THE LIFE I ALWAYS DREAMT ABOUT.

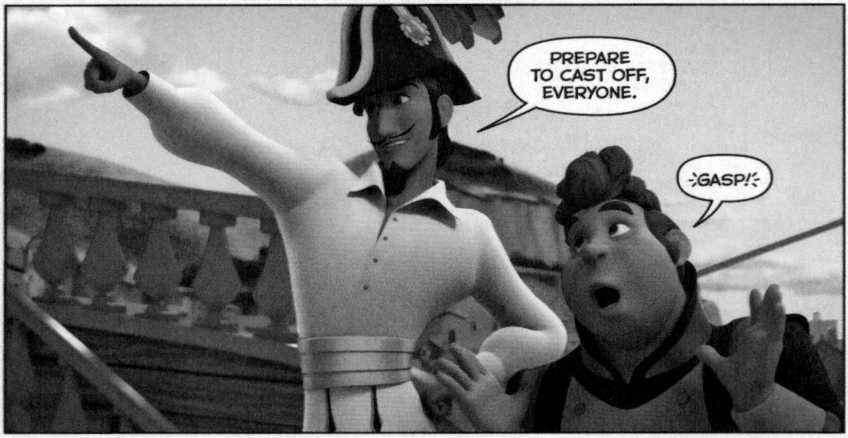
PREPARE TO CAST OFF, EVERYONE.
GASP!

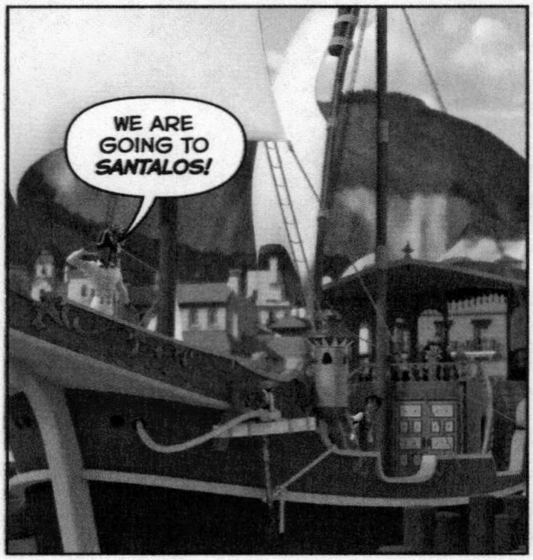
WE ARE GOING TO SANTALOS!

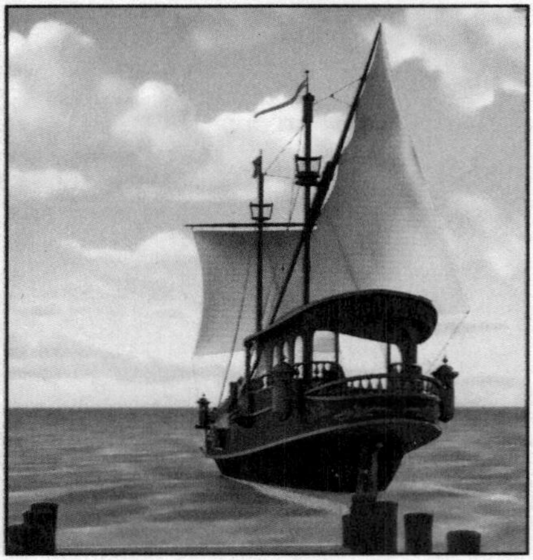

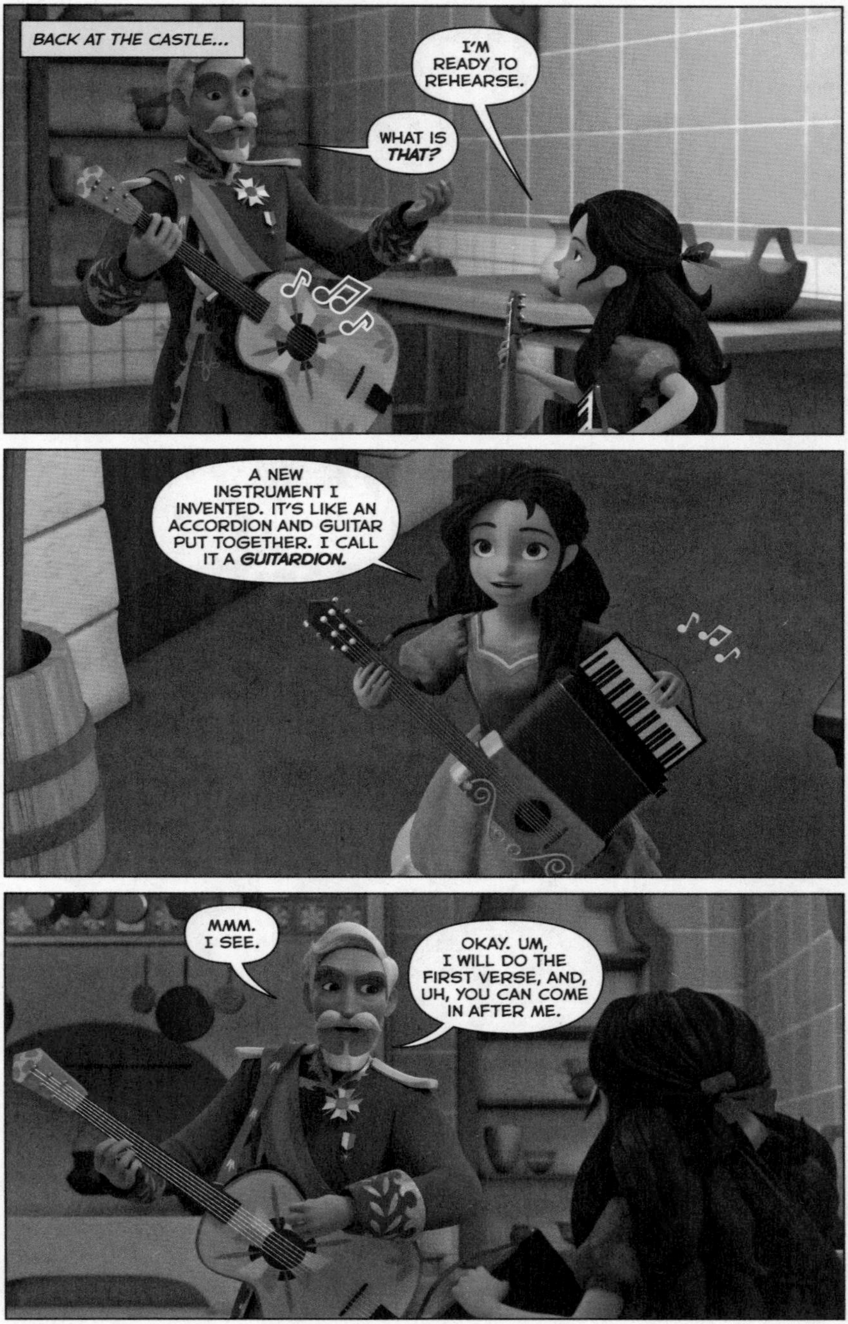
BACK AT THE CASTLE...
I'M READY TO REHEARSE.
WHAT IS *THAT?*
A NEW INSTRUMENT I INVENTED. IT'S LIKE AN ACCORDION AND GUITAR PUT TOGETHER. I CALL IT A ***GUITARDION.***
MMM. I SEE.
OKAY. UM, I WILL DO THE FIRST VERSE, AND, UH, YOU CAN COME IN AFTER ME.

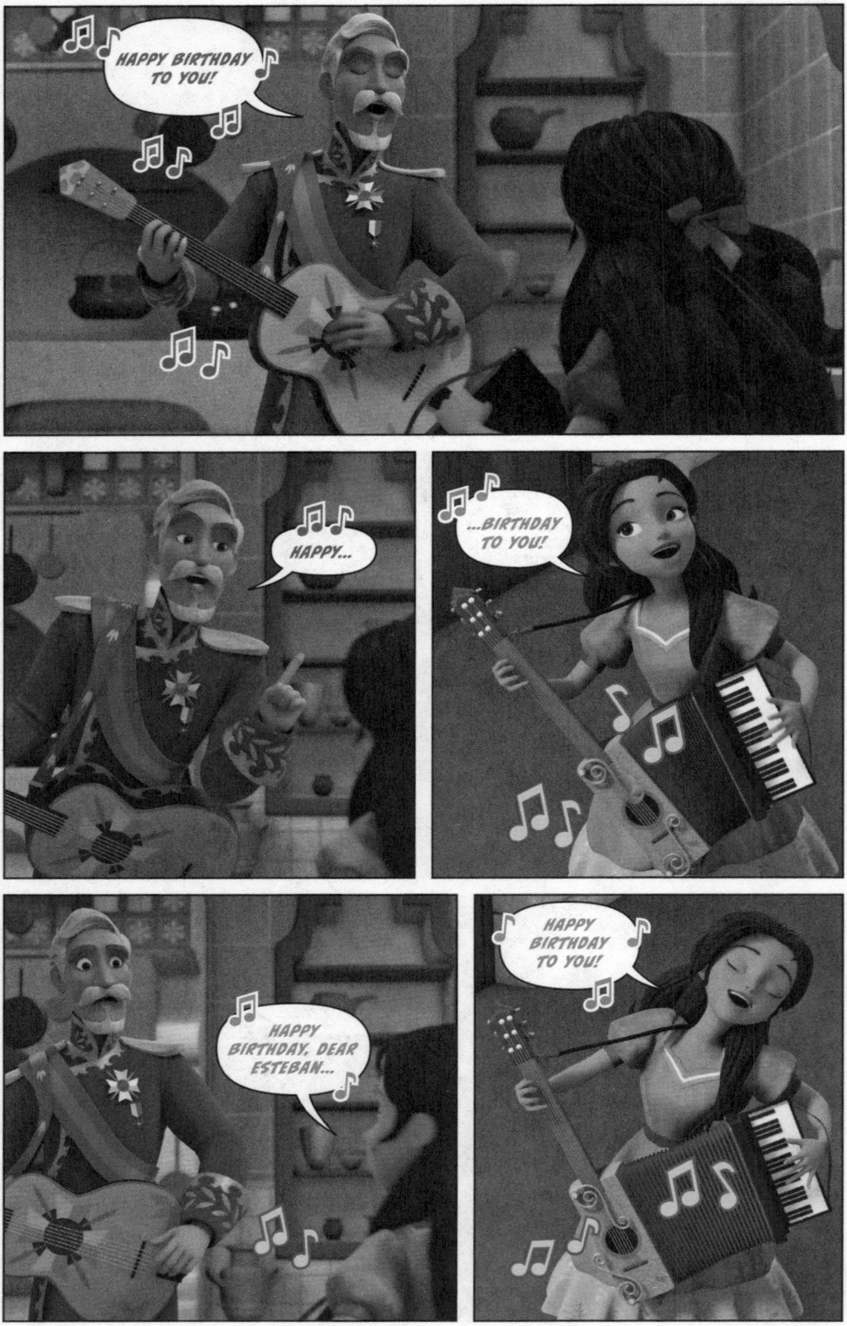

HAPPY BIRTHDAY TO YOU!
HAPPY...
...BIRTHDAY TO YOU!
HAPPY BIRTHDAY, DEAR ESTEBAN...
HAPPY BIRTHDAY TO YOU!

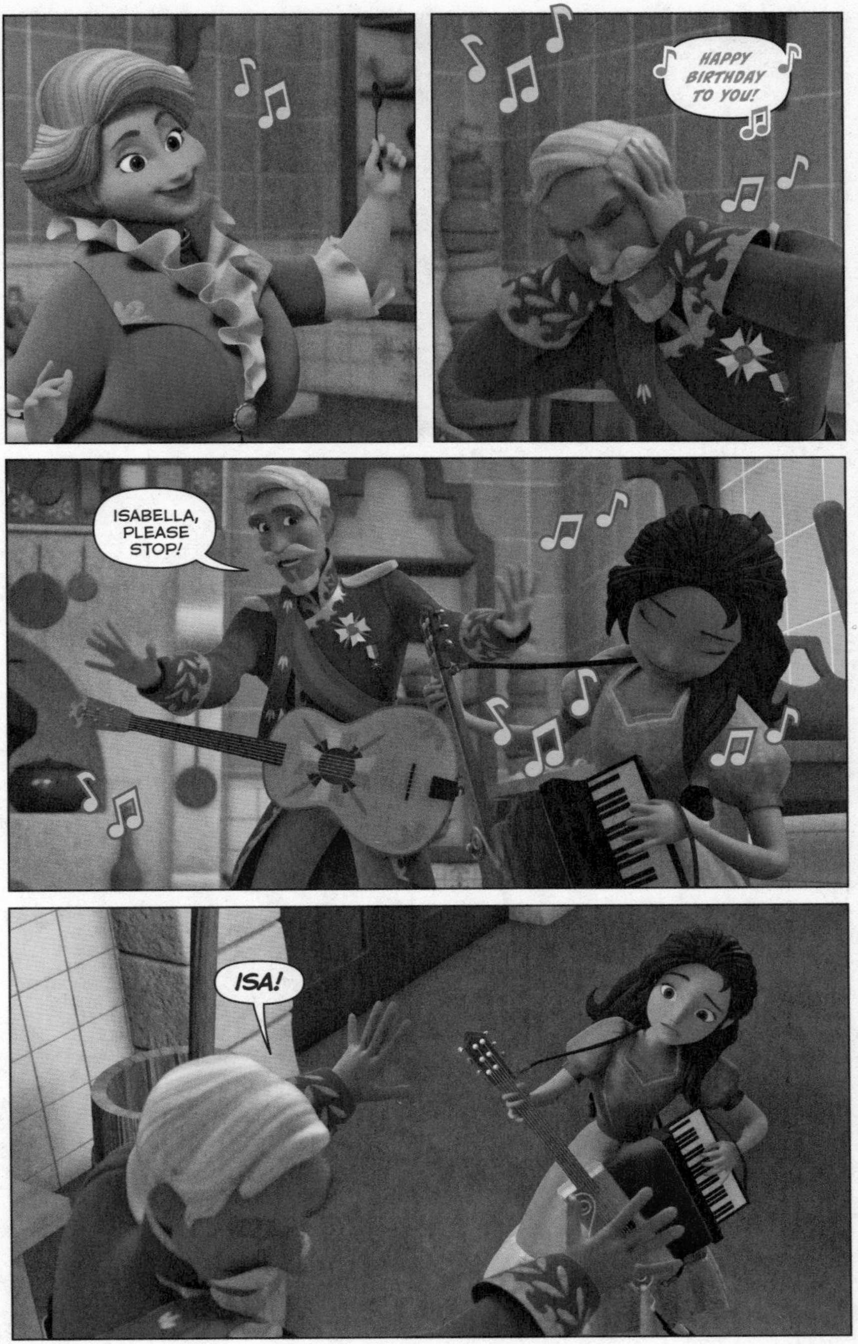
HAPPY BIRTHDAY TO YOU!
ISABELLA, PLEASE STOP!
ISA!

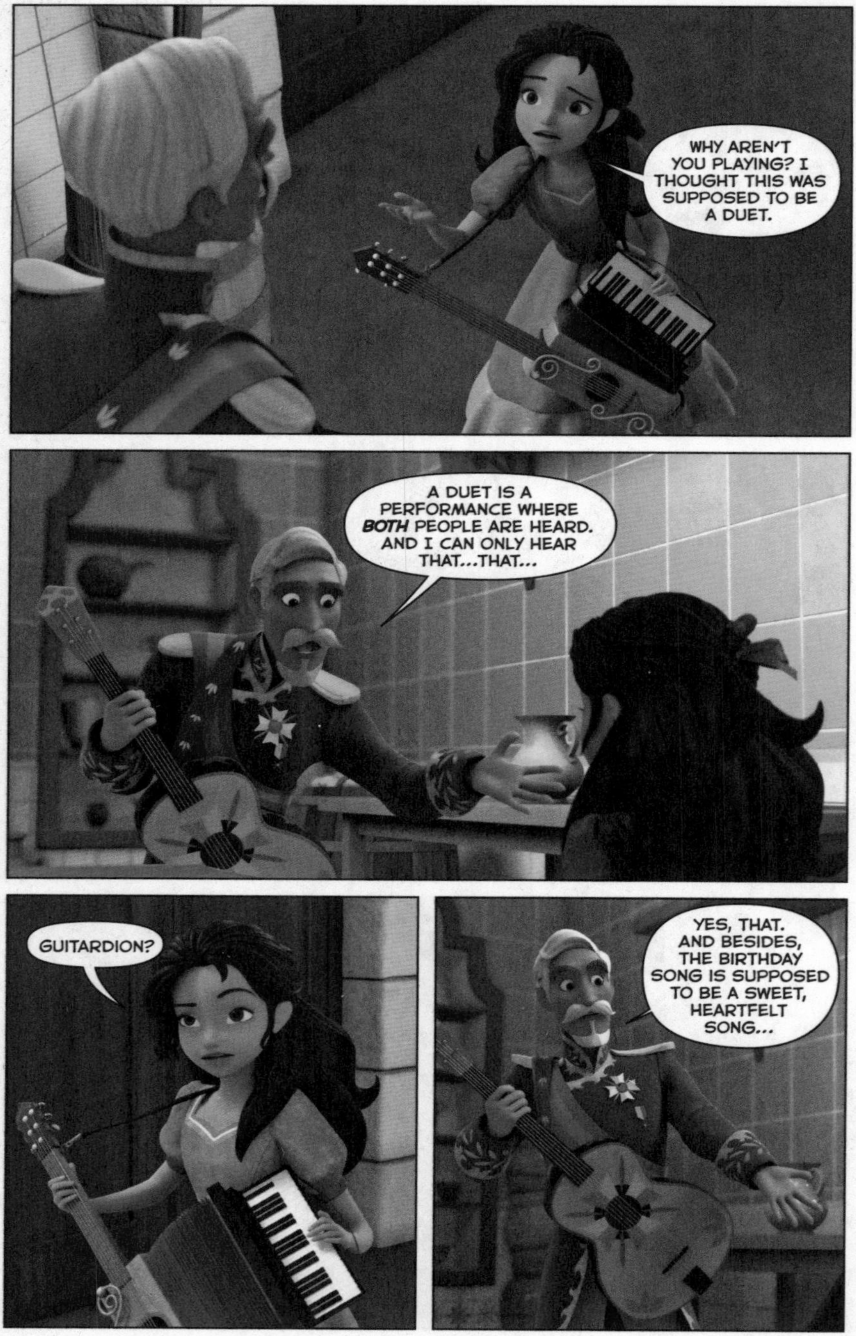
WHY AREN'T YOU PLAYING? I THOUGHT THIS WAS SUPPOSED TO BE A DUET.
A DUET IS A PERFORMANCE WHERE *BOTH* PEOPLE ARE HEARD. AND I CAN ONLY HEAR THAT...THAT...
GUITARDION?
YES, THAT. AND BESIDES, THE BIRTHDAY SONG IS SUPPOSED TO BE A SWEET, HEARTFELT SONG...

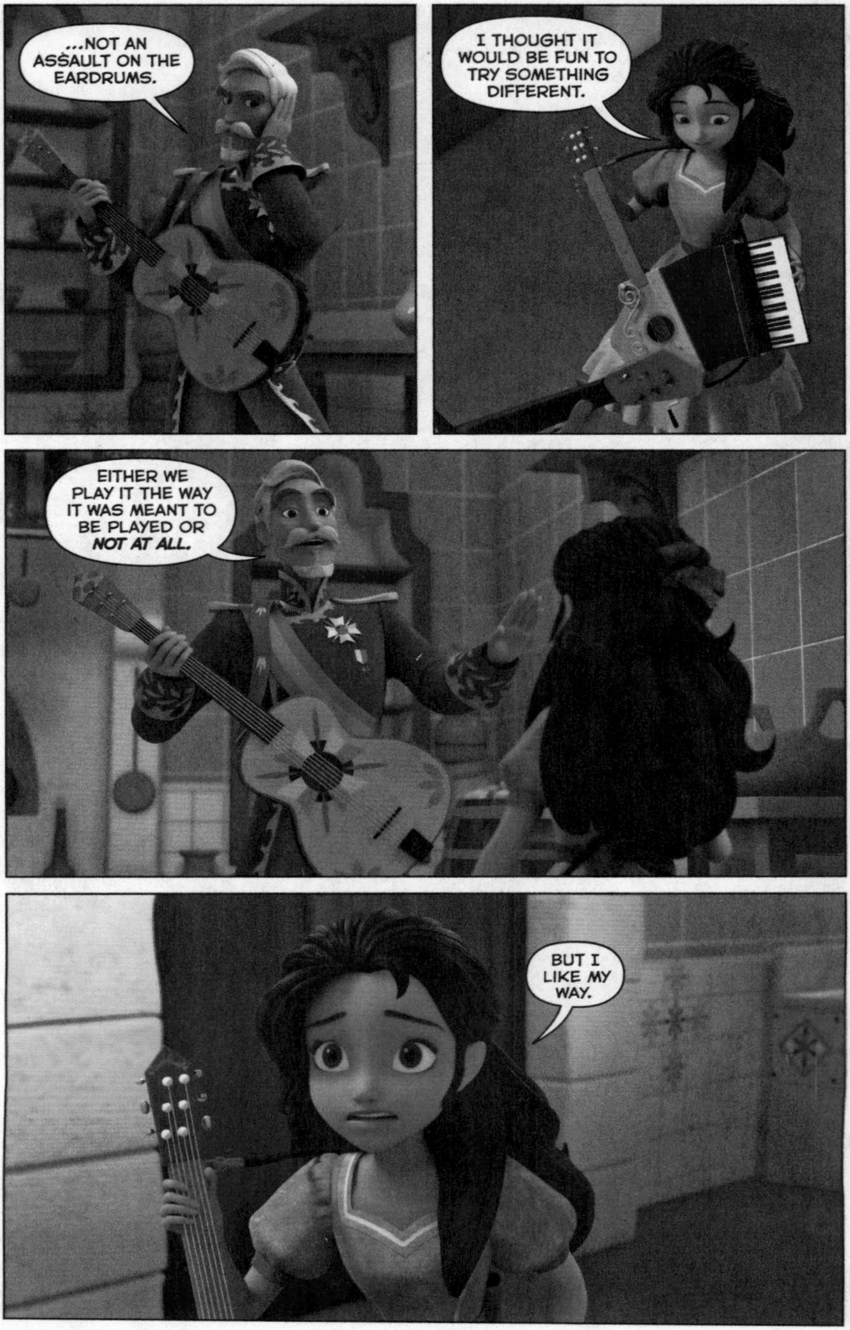
...NOT AN ASSAULT ON THE EARDRUMS.
I THOUGHT IT WOULD BE FUN TO TRY SOMETHING DIFFERENT.
EITHER WE PLAY IT THE WAY IT WAS MEANT TO BE PLAYED OR *NOT AT ALL.*
BUT I LIKE MY WAY.

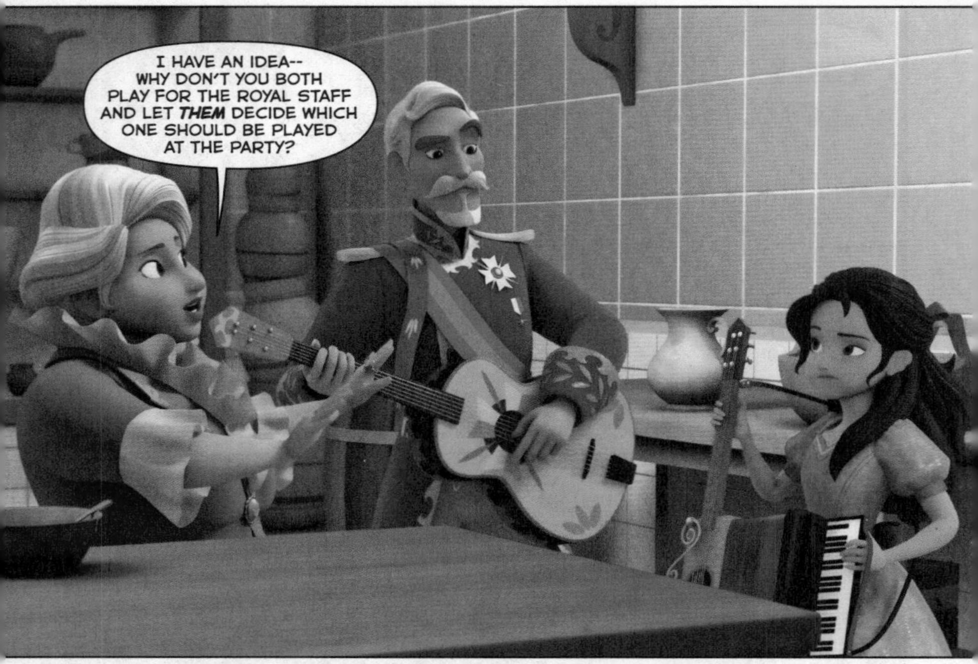
I HAVE AN IDEA-- WHY DON'T YOU BOTH PLAY FOR THE ROYAL STAFF AND LET *THEM* DECIDE WHICH ONE SHOULD BE PLAYED AT THE PARTY?

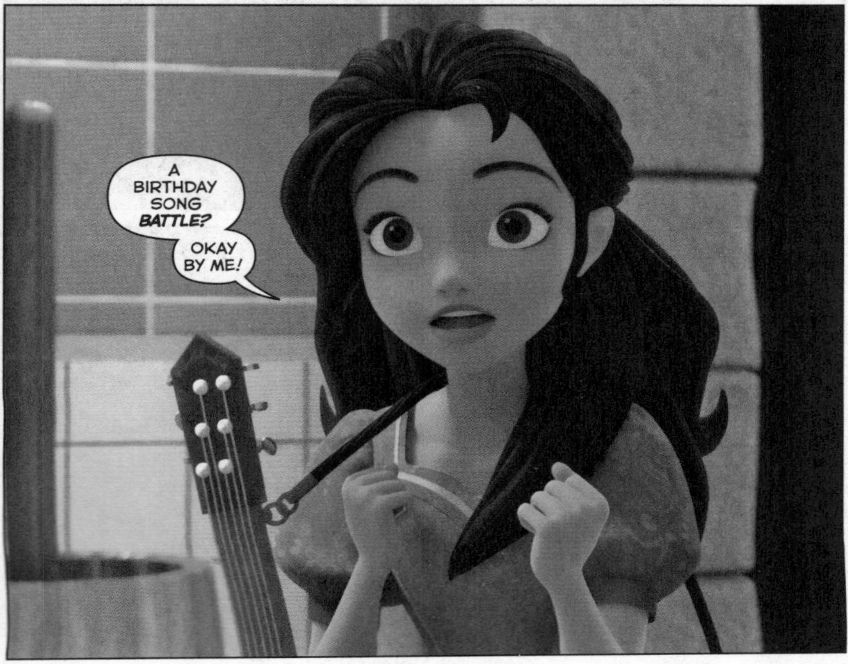
A BIRTHDAY SONG *BATTLE?*
OKAY BY ME!

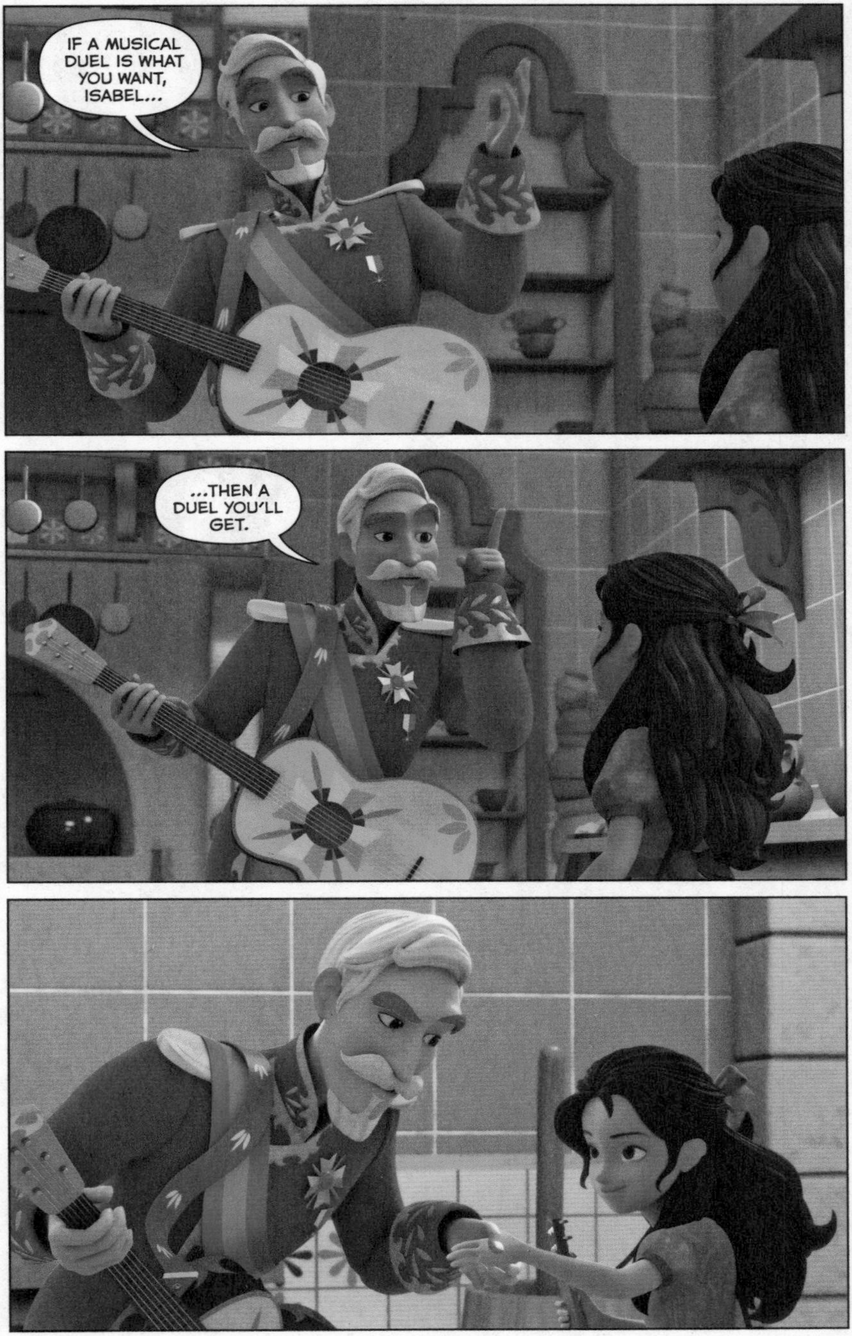
IF A MUSICAL DUEL IS WHAT YOU WANT, ISABEL...
...THEN A DUEL YOU'LL GET.

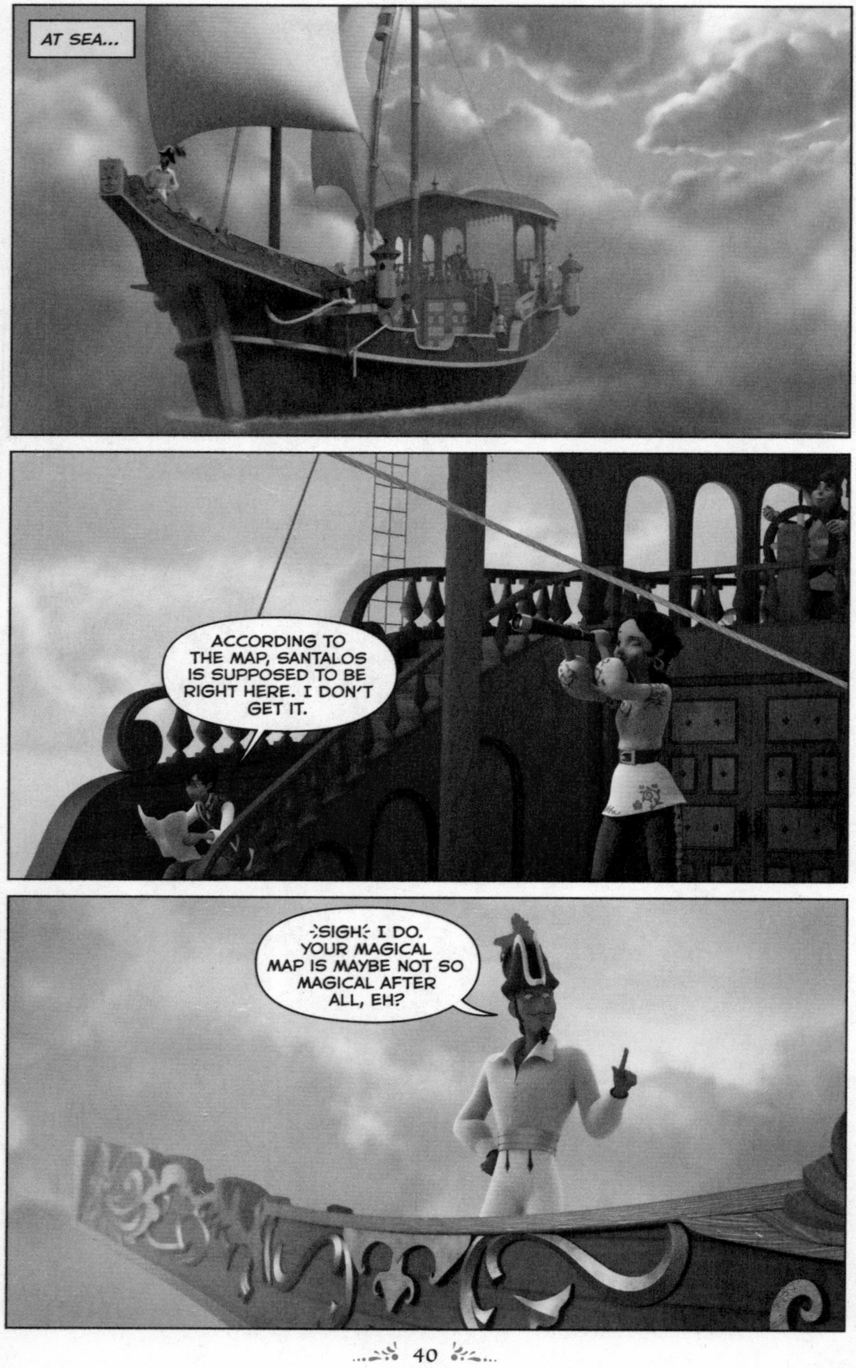
AT SEA...
ACCORDING TO THE MAP, SANTALOS IS SUPPOSED TO BE RIGHT HERE. I DON'T GET IT.
SIGH I DO. YOUR MAGICAL MAP IS MAYBE NOT SO MAGICAL AFTER ALL, EH?

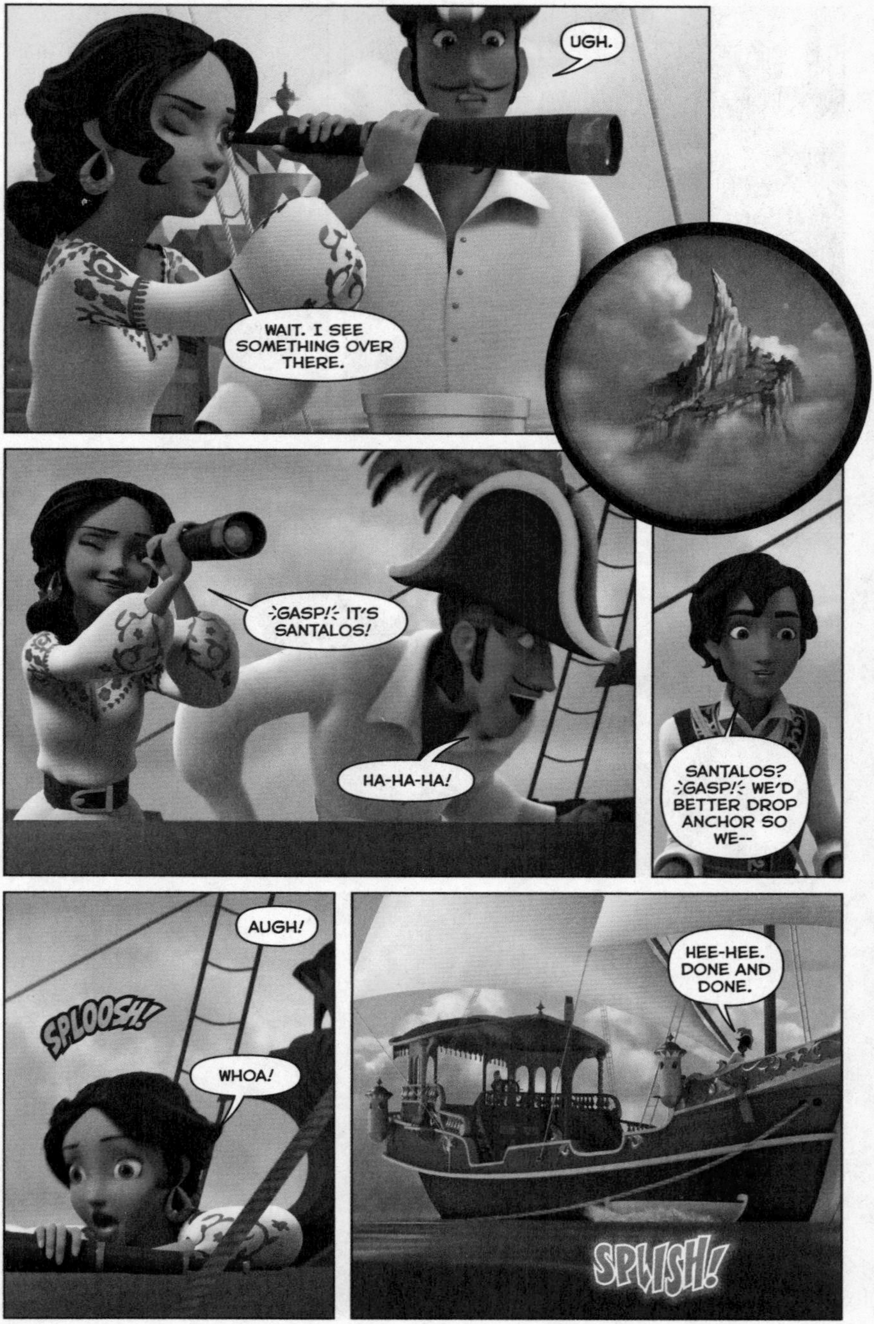
UGH.
WAIT. I SEE SOMETHING OVER THERE.
·GASP!· IT'S SANTALOS!
HA-HA-HA!
SANTALOS? ·GASP!· WE'D BETTER DROP ANCHOR SO WE--
AUGH!
SPLOOSH!
WHOA!
HEE-HEE. DONE AND DONE.
SPLISH!

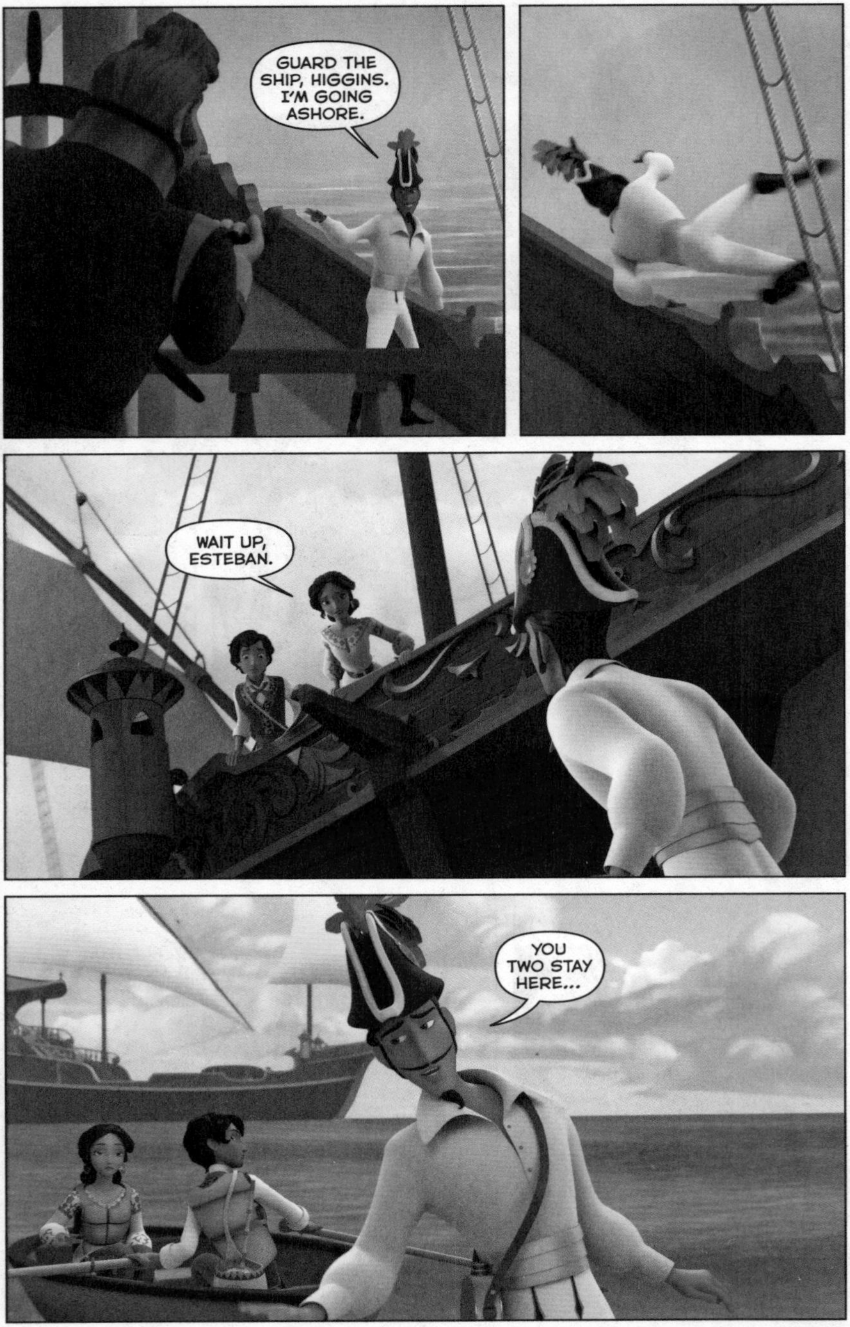
GUARD THE SHIP, HIGGINS. I'M GOING ASHORE.
WAIT UP, ESTEBAN.
YOU TWO STAY HERE...

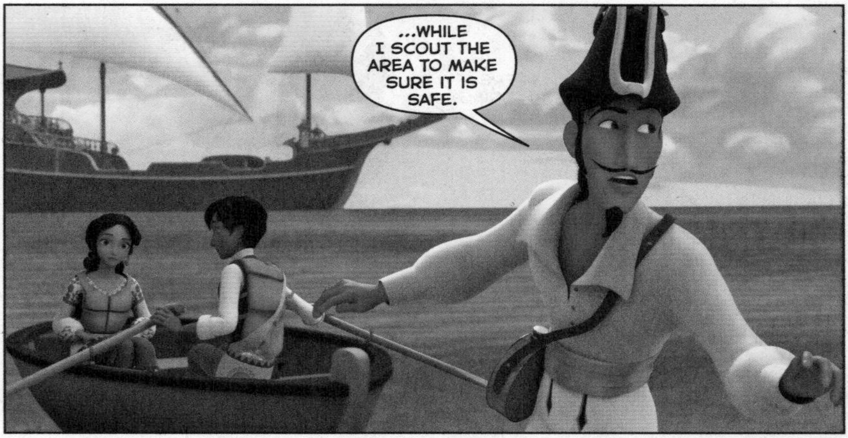
...WHILE I SCOUT THE AREA TO MAKE SURE IT IS SAFE.

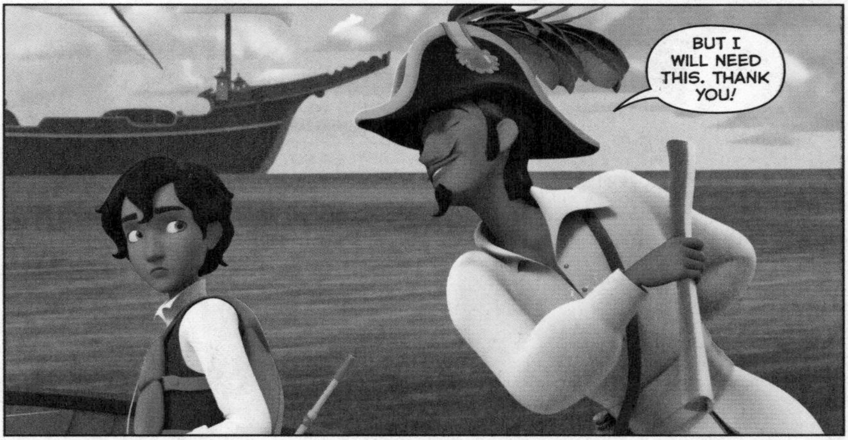
BUT I WILL NEED THIS. THANK YOU!

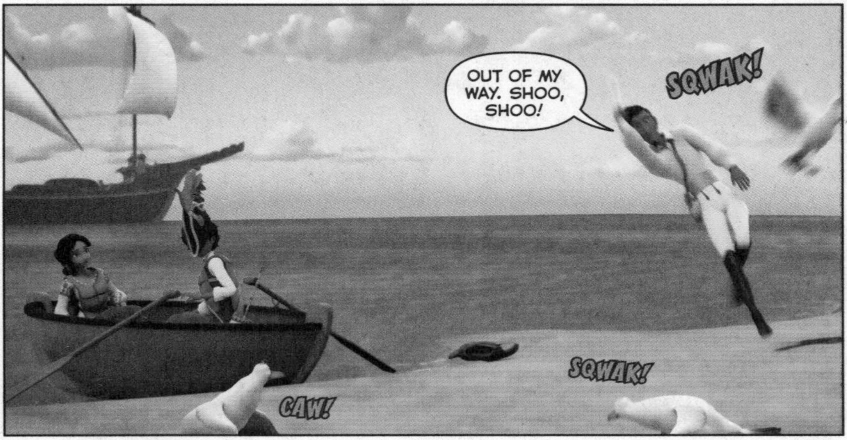
OUT OF MY WAY. SHOO, SHOO!
SQWAK!
SQWAK!
CAW!

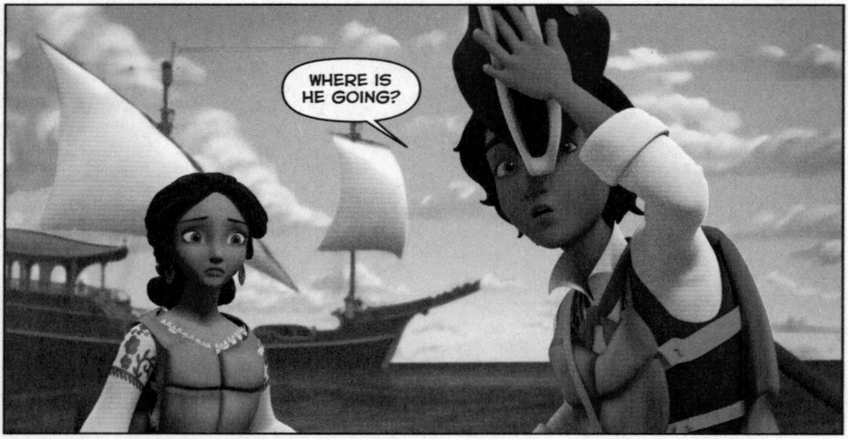
WHERE IS HE GOING?

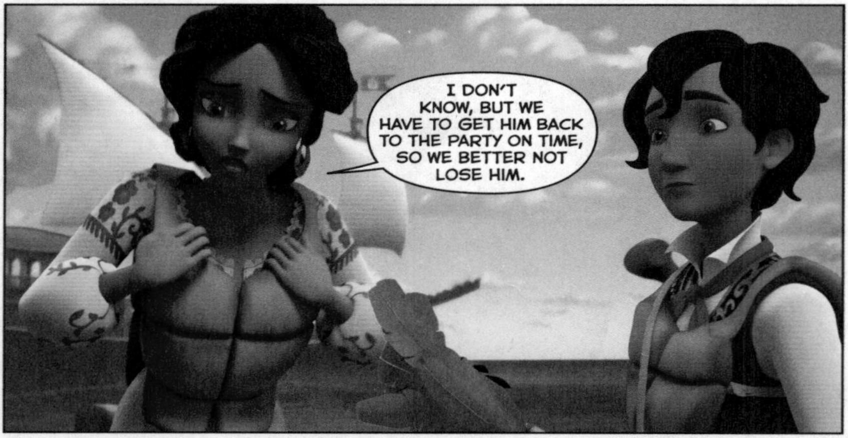
I DON'T KNOW, BUT WE HAVE TO GET HIM BACK TO THE PARTY ON TIME, SO WE BETTER NOT LOSE HIM.

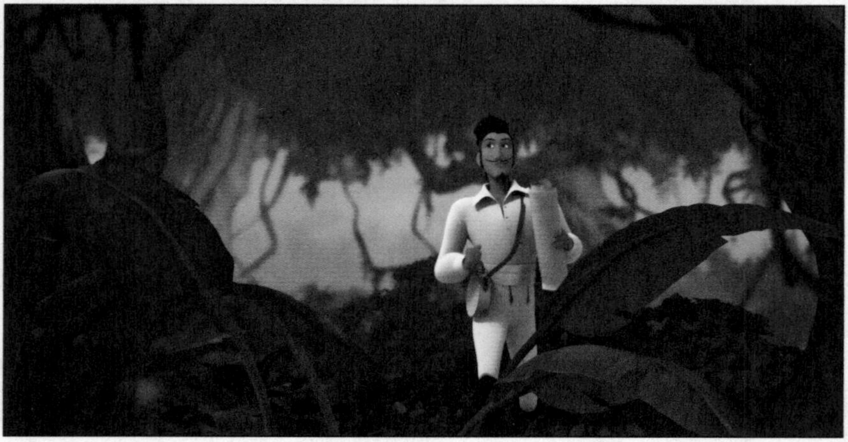

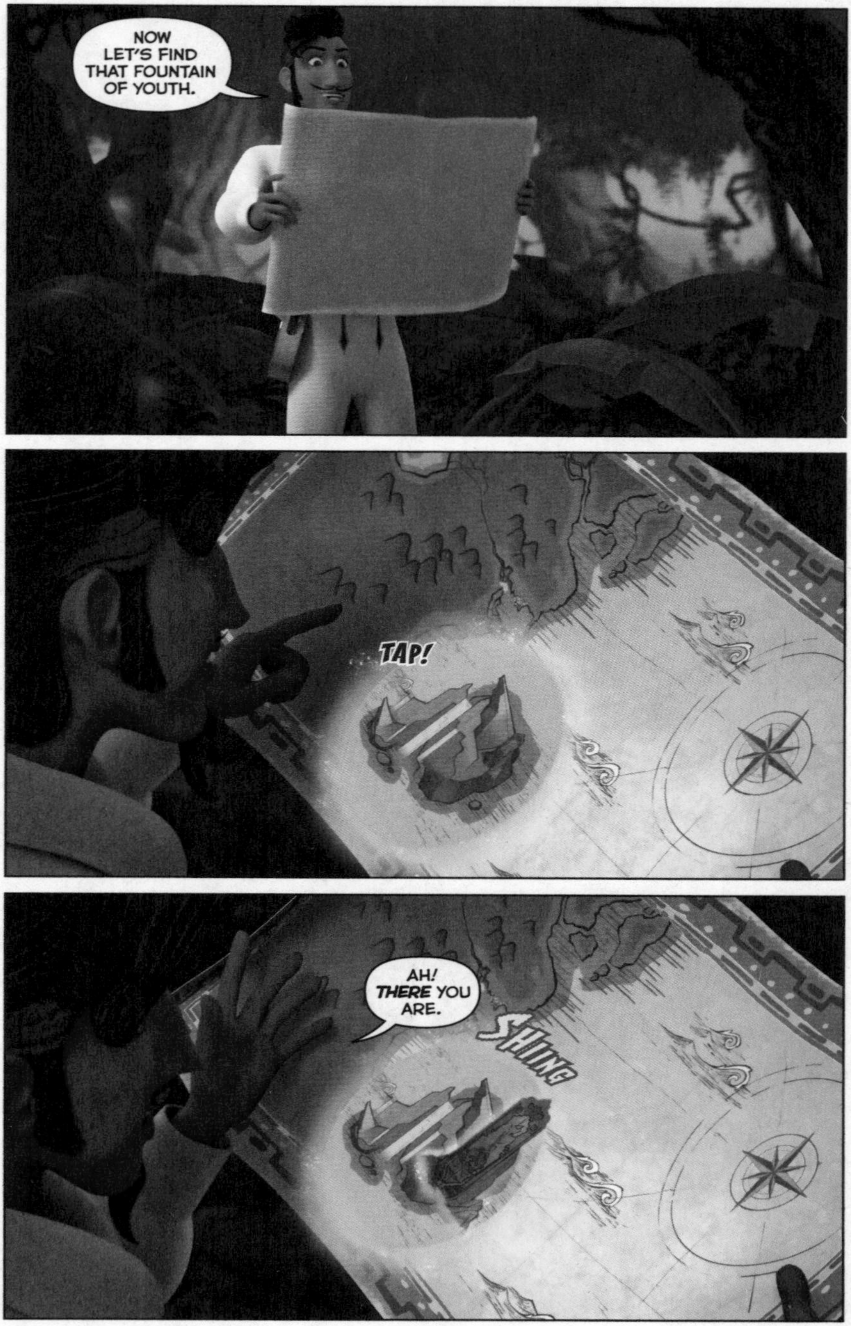
NOW LET'S FIND THAT FOUNTAIN OF YOUTH.
TAP!
AH! *THERE* YOU ARE.
SHIING

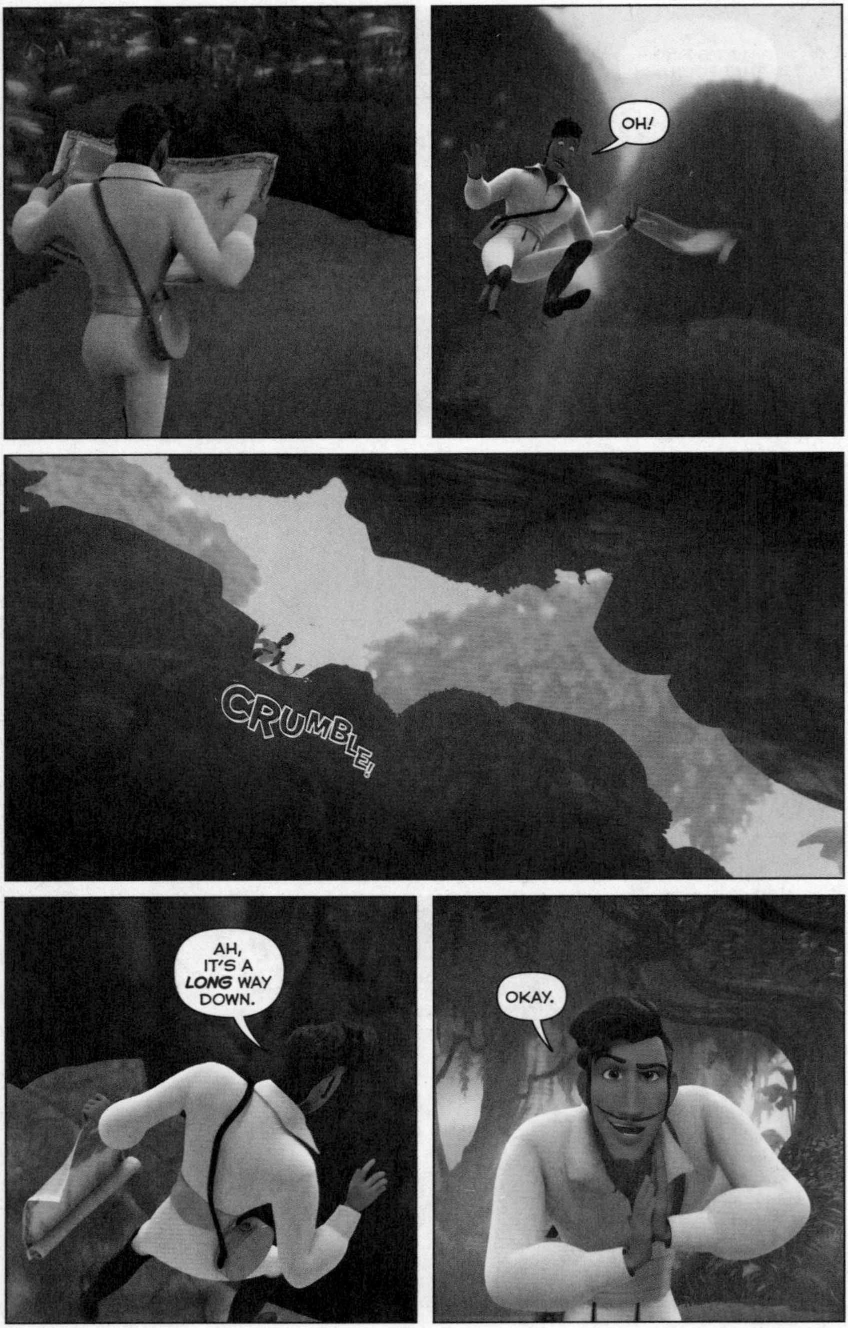
OH!
CRUMBLE!
AH, IT'S A LONG WAY DOWN.
OKAY.

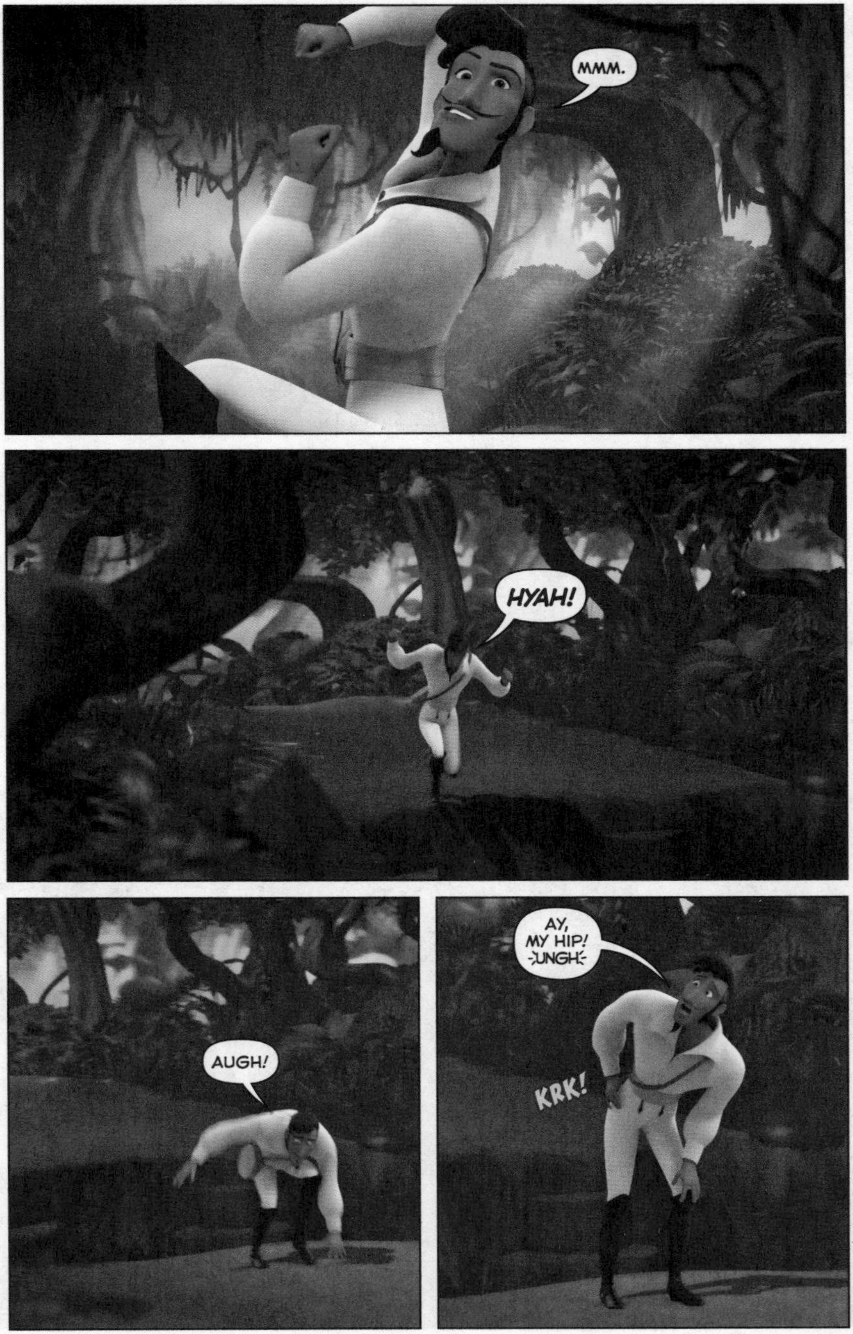
MMM.
HYAH!
AUGH!
AY, MY HIP! UNGH
KRK!

OH, THERE IT IS.

THE *FOUNTAIN OF YOUTH.*

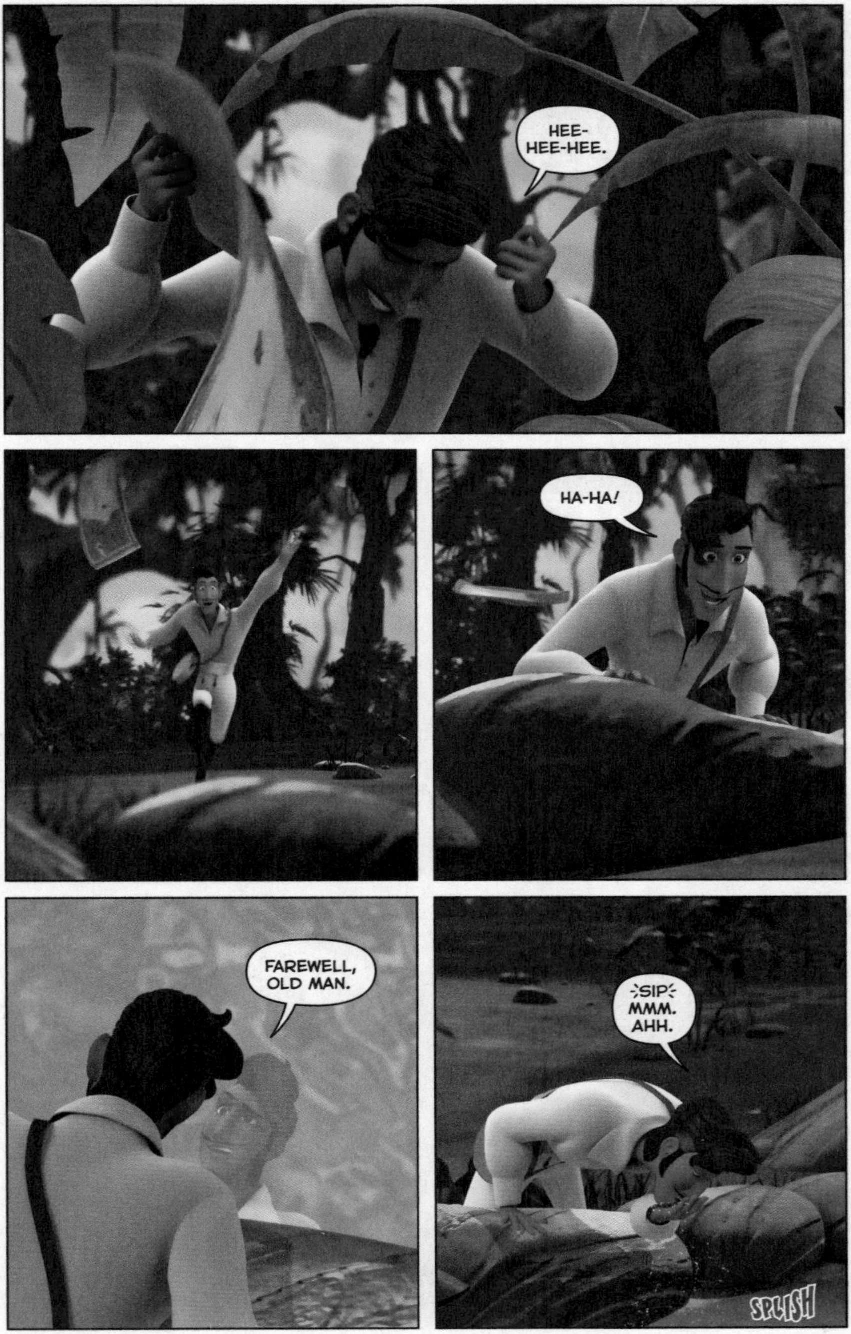
HEE-
HEE-HEE.
HA-HA!
FAREWELL,
OLD MAN.
SIP
MMM.
AHH.
SPLISH

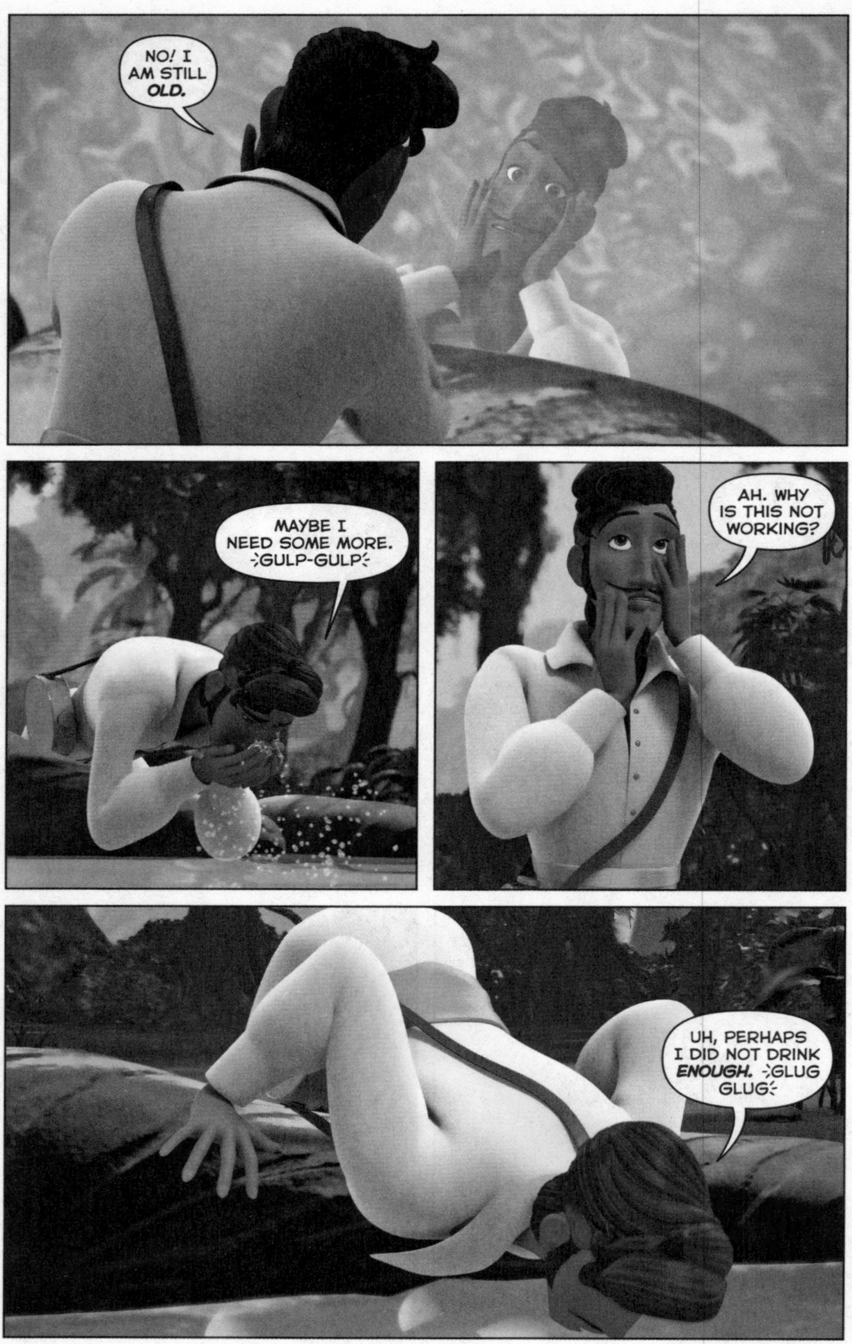
NO! I AM STILL *OLD.*
MAYBE I NEED SOME MORE. -GULP-GULP-
AH. WHY IS THIS NOT WORKING?
UH, PERHAPS I DID NOT DRINK *ENOUGH.* -GLUG GLUG-

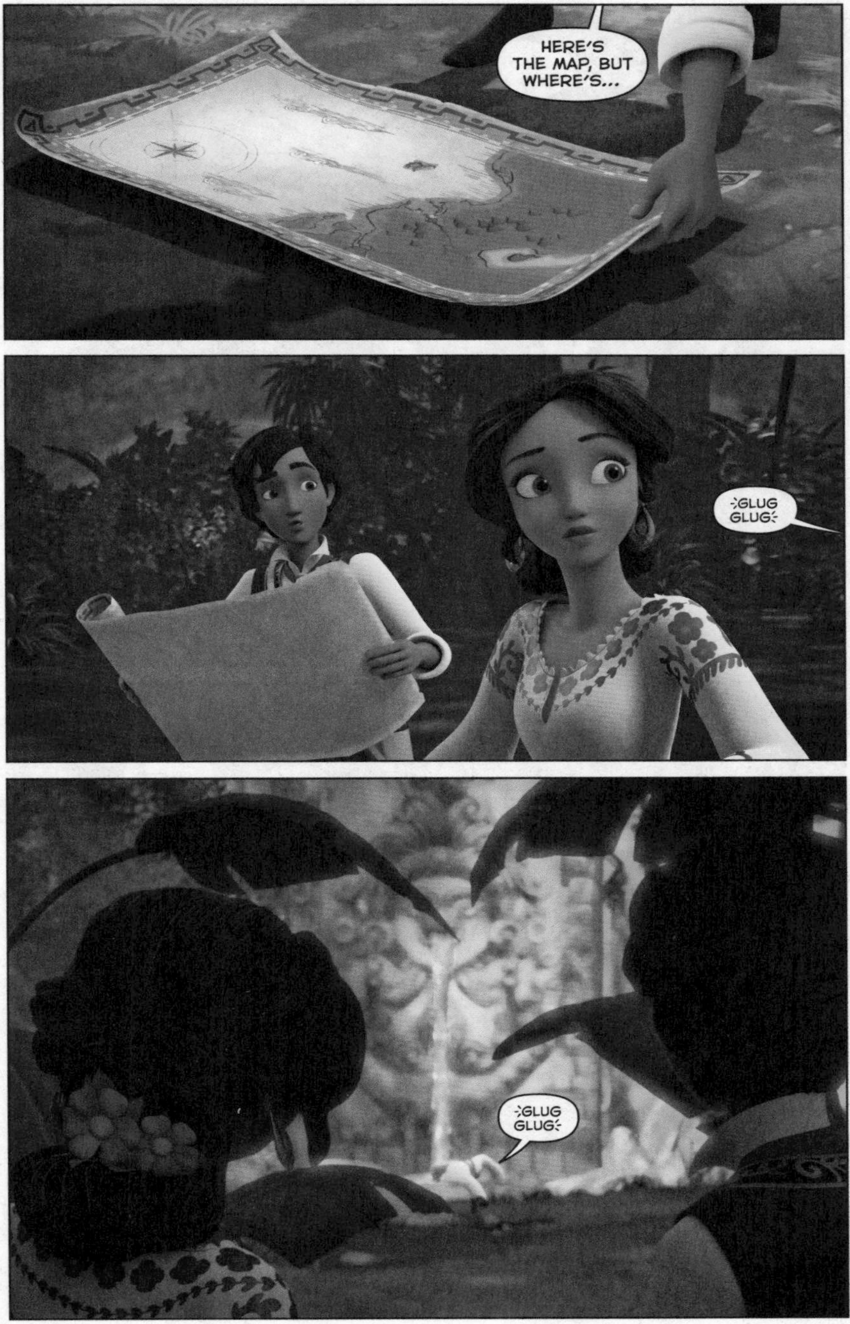
HERE'S THE MAP, BUT WHERE'S...
GLUG GLUG
GLUG GLUG

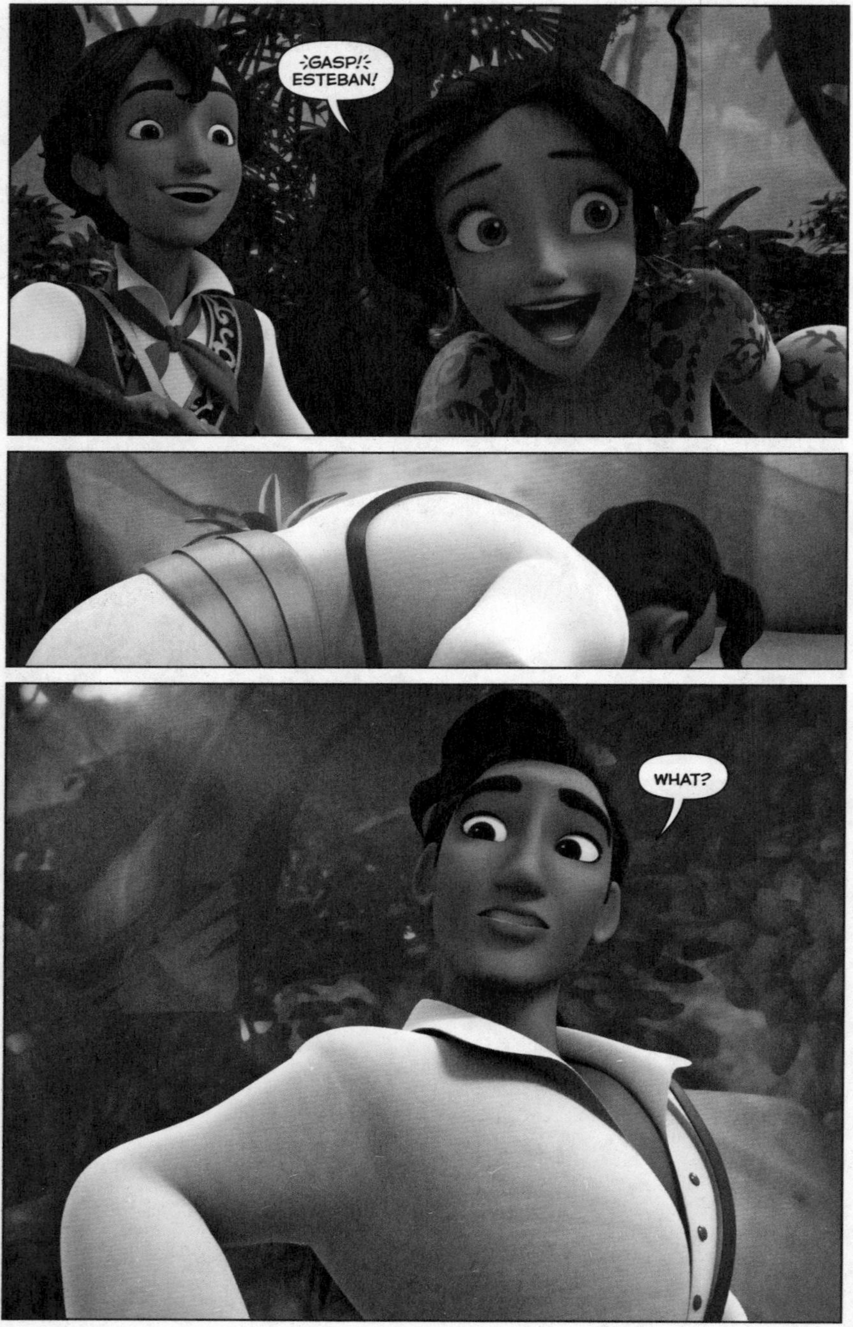
GASP!
ESTEBAN!
WHAT?

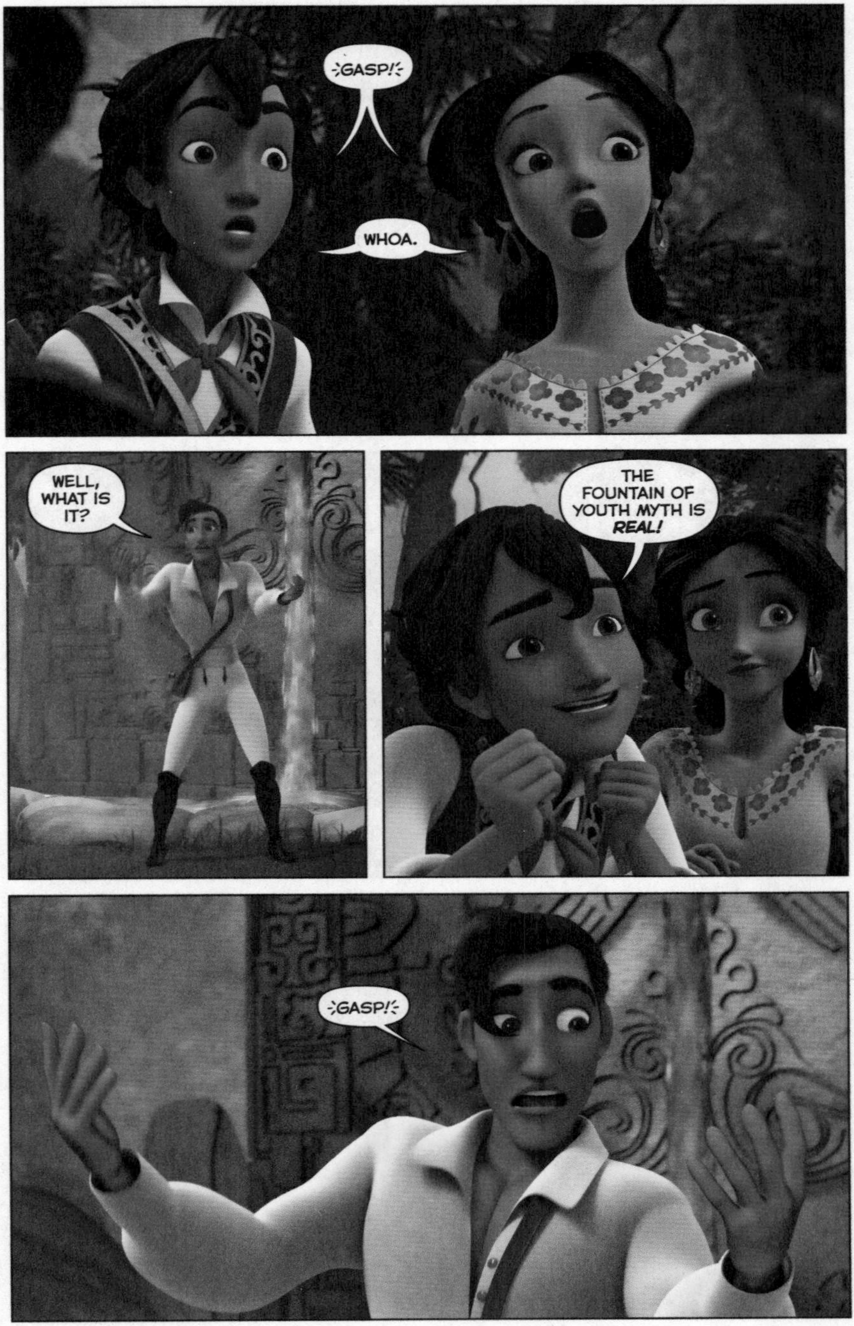
GASP!
WHOA.
WELL, WHAT IS IT?
THE FOUNTAIN OF YOUTH MYTH IS *REAL!*
GASP!

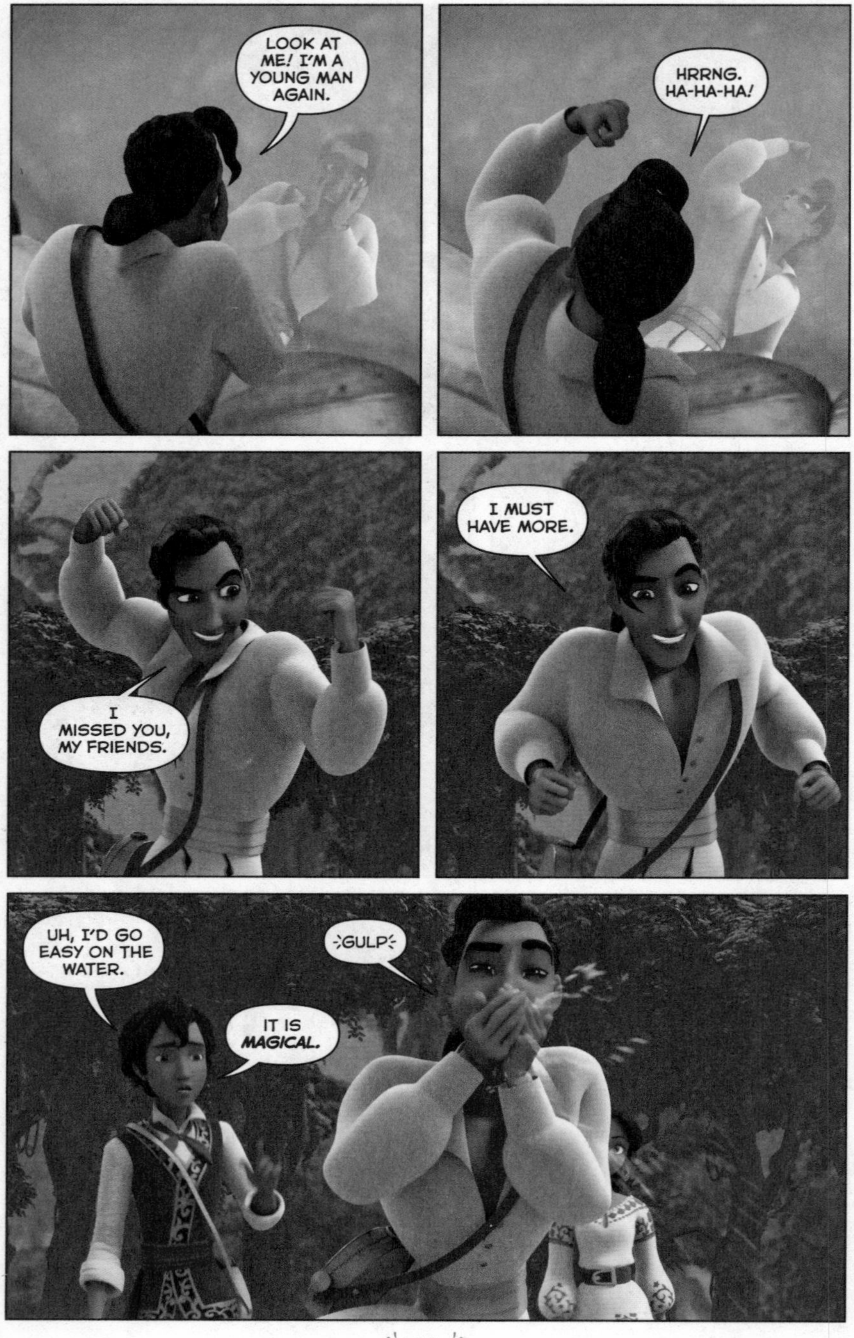
LOOK AT ME! I'M A YOUNG MAN AGAIN.
HRRNG. HA-HA-HA!
I MISSED YOU, MY FRIENDS.
I MUST HAVE MORE.
UH, I'D GO EASY ON THE WATER.
IT IS *MAGICAL.*
GULP

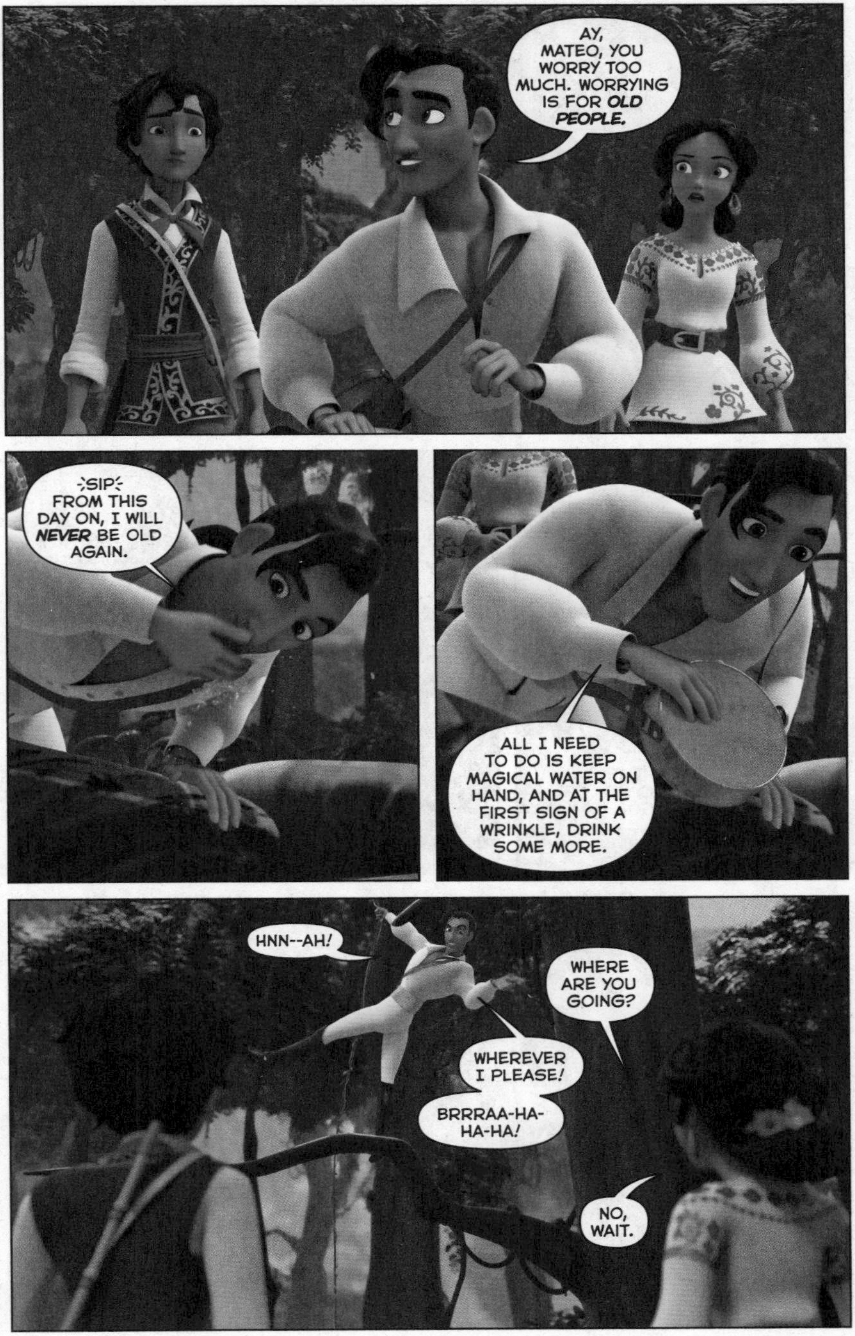
AY, MATEO, YOU WORRY TOO MUCH. WORRYING IS FOR **OLD PEOPLE.**
SIP
FROM THIS DAY ON, I WILL ***NEVER*** BE OLD AGAIN.
ALL I NEED TO DO IS KEEP MAGICAL WATER ON HAND, AND AT THE FIRST SIGN OF A WRINKLE, DRINK SOME MORE.
HNN--AH!
WHERE ARE YOU GOING?
WHEREVER I PLEASE!
BRRRAA-HA-HA-HA!
NO, WAIT.

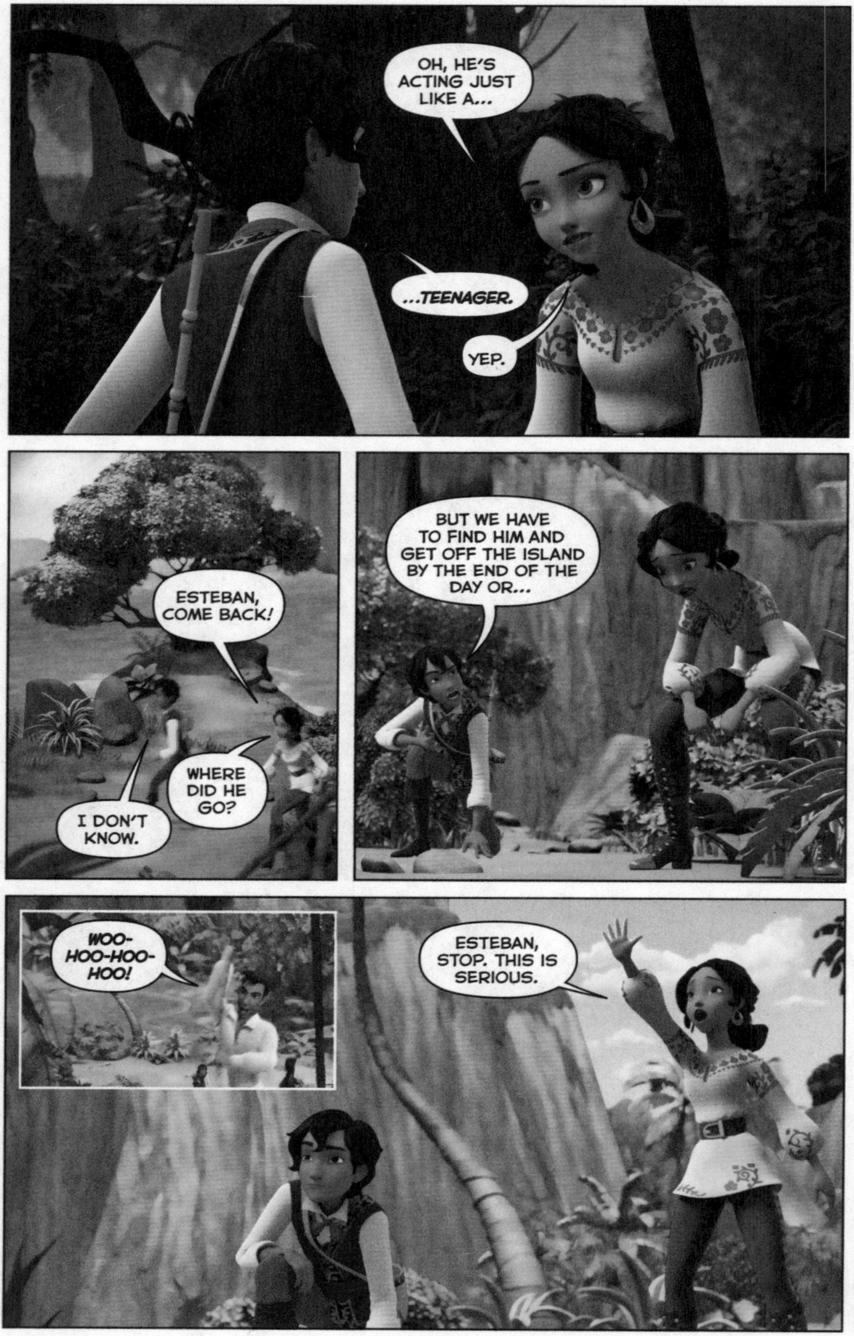
OH, HE'S ACTING JUST LIKE A...
...TEENAGER.
YEP.
ESTEBAN, COME BACK!
WHERE DID HE GO?
I DON'T KNOW.
BUT WE HAVE TO FIND HIM AND GET OFF THE ISLAND BY THE END OF THE DAY OR...
WOO-HOO-HOO-HOO!
ESTEBAN, STOP. THIS IS SERIOUS.

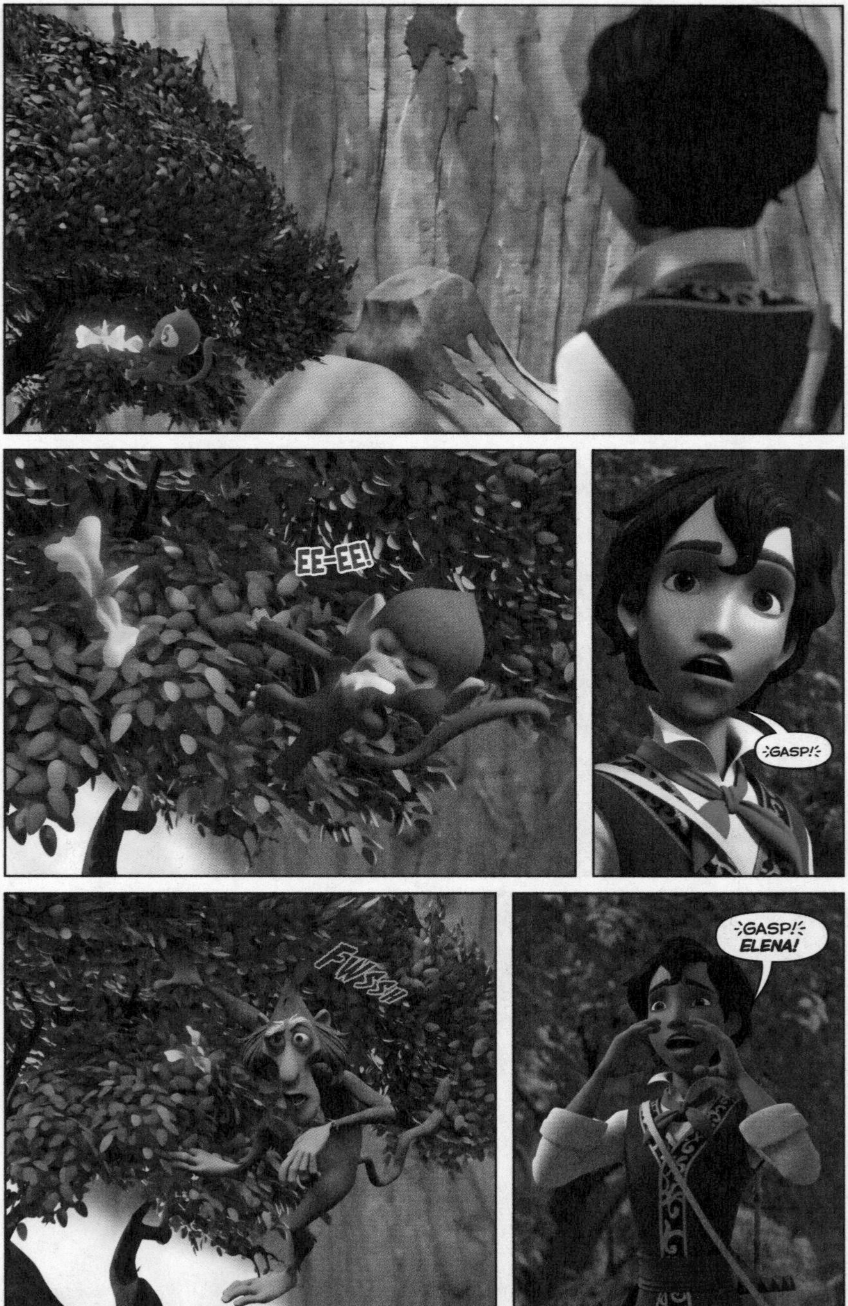
EE-EE!
¡GASP!¡
FWSSH
¡GASP!¡ ELENA!

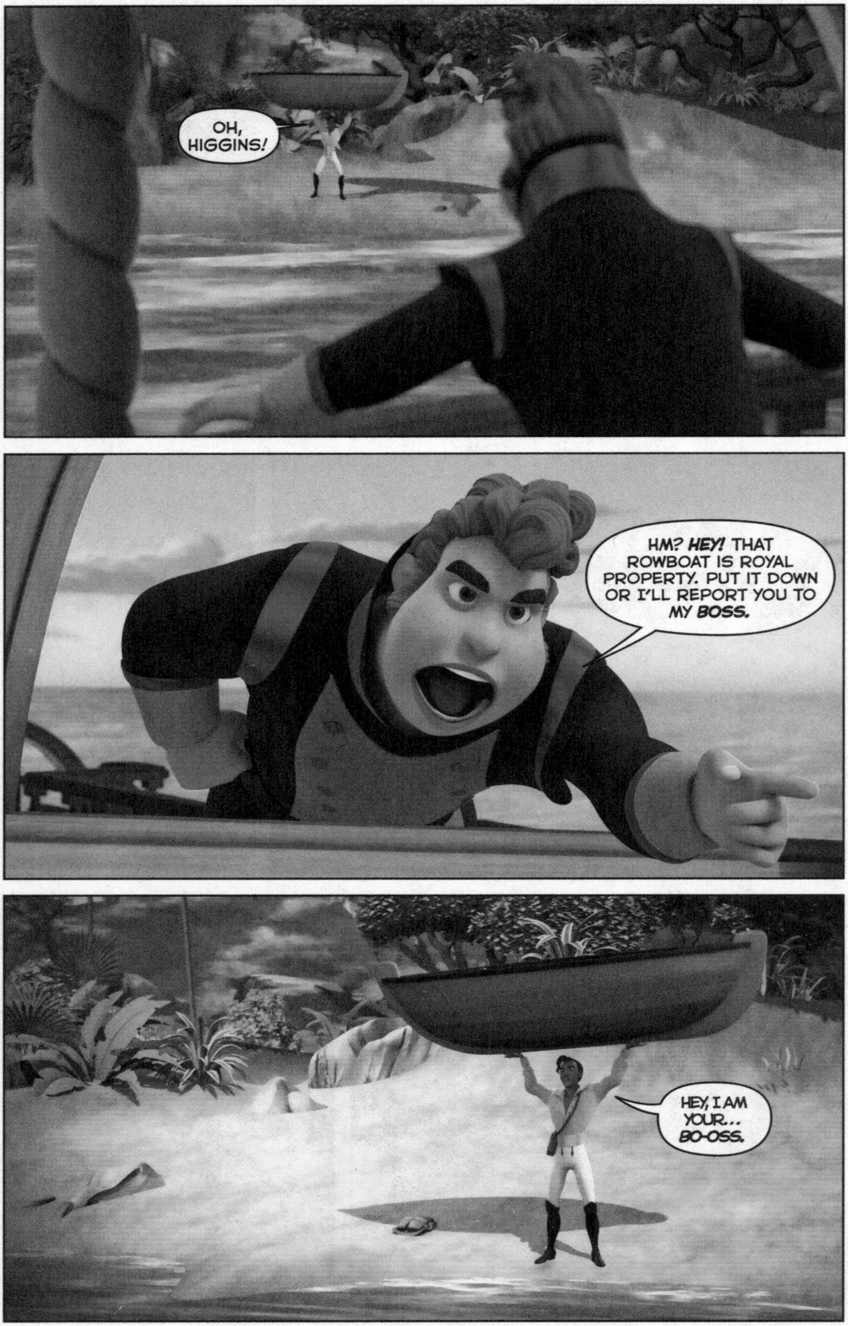
OH, HIGGINS!
HM? HEY! THAT ROWBOAT IS ROYAL PROPERTY. PUT IT DOWN OR I'LL REPORT YOU TO MY BOSS.
HEY, I AM YOUR... BO-OSS.

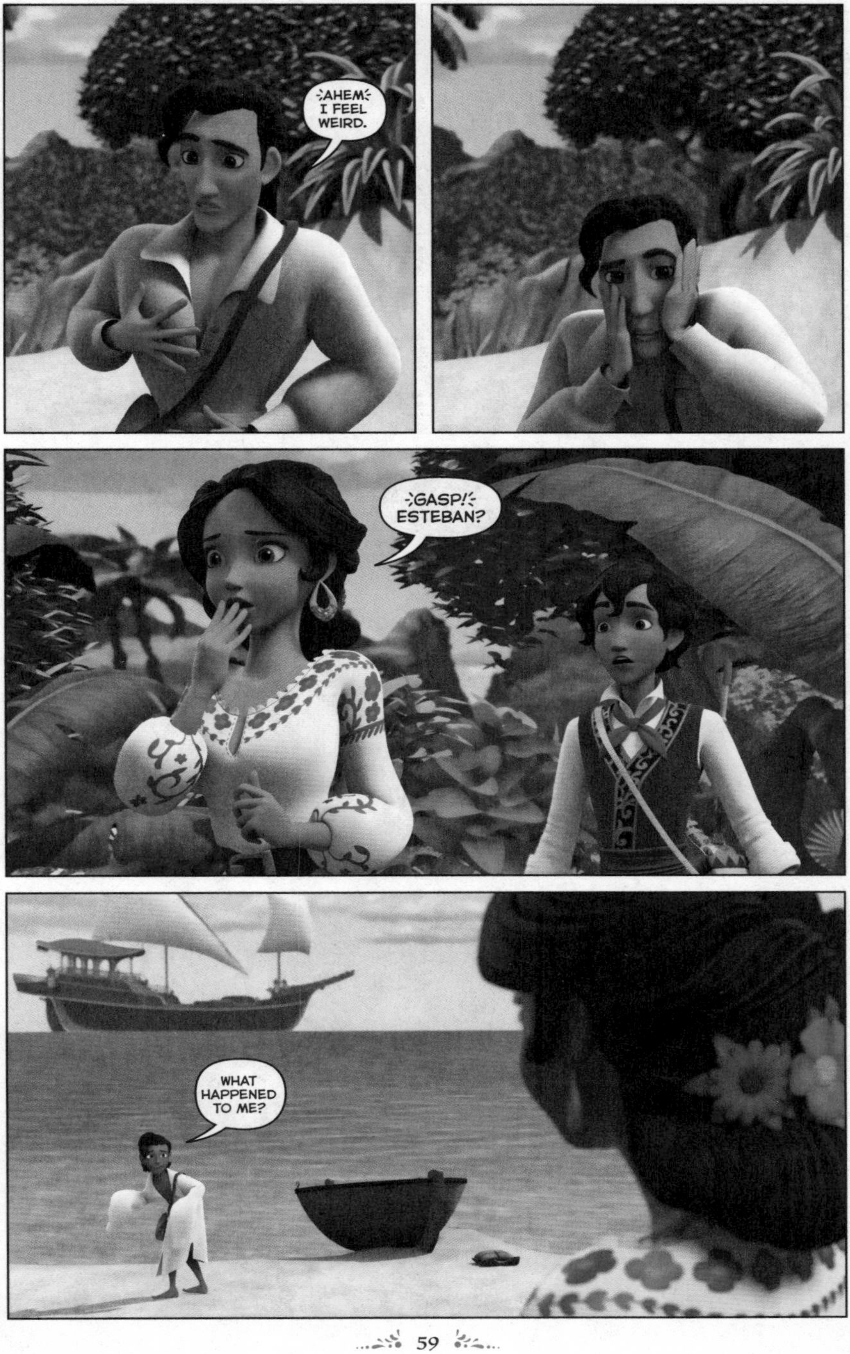

-AHEM- I FEEL WEIRD.
-GASP!- ESTEBAN?
WHAT HAPPENED TO ME?

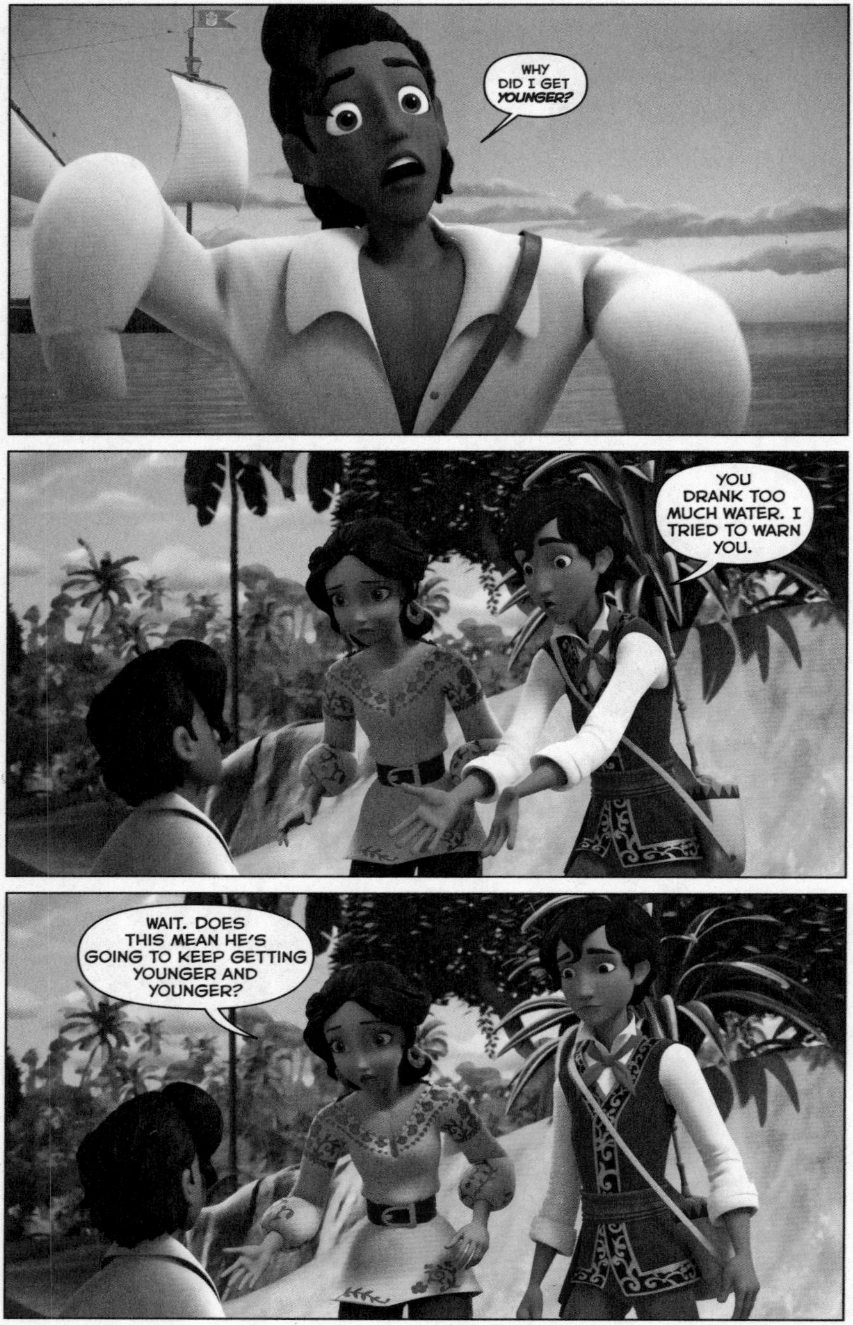
WHY DID I GET *YOUNGER?*
YOU DRANK TOO MUCH WATER. I TRIED TO WARN YOU.
WAIT. DOES THIS MEAN HE'S GOING TO KEEP GETTING YOUNGER AND YOUNGER?

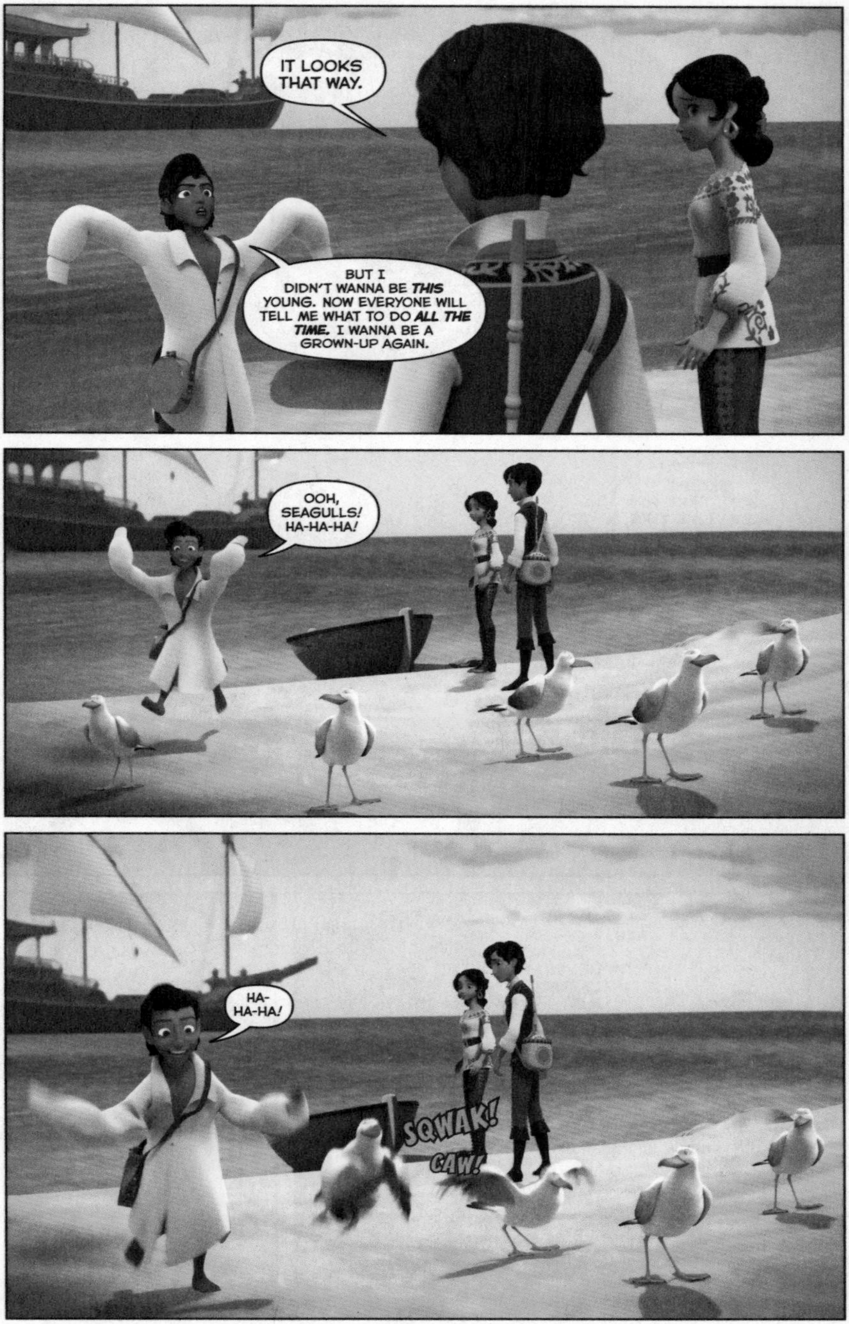
IT LOOKS THAT WAY.
BUT I DIDN'T WANNA BE ***THIS*** YOUNG. NOW EVERYONE WILL TELL ME WHAT TO DO ***ALL THE TIME.*** I WANNA BE A GROWN-UP AGAIN.
OOH, SEAGULLS! HA-HA-HA!
HA-HA-HA!
SQWAK!
CAW!

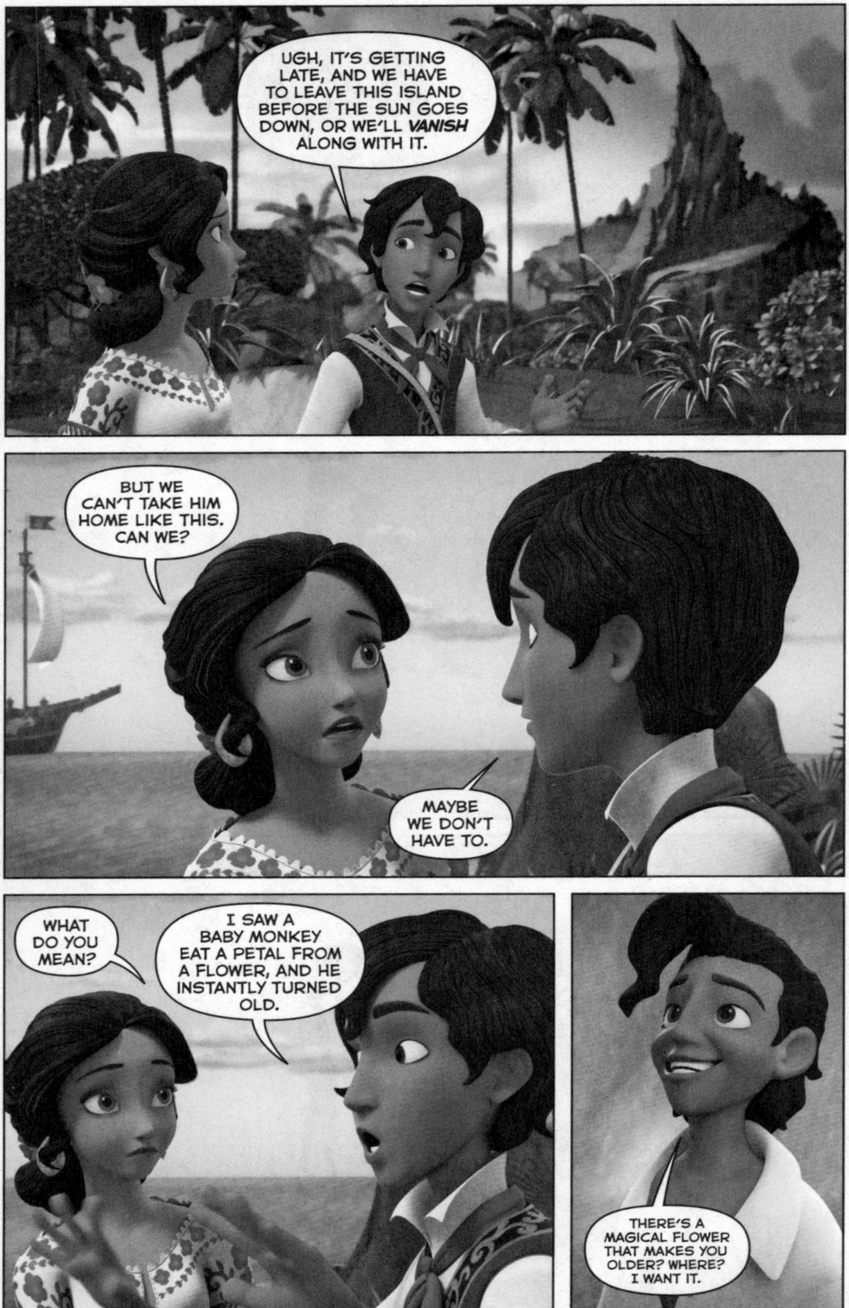
UGH, IT'S GETTING LATE, AND WE HAVE TO LEAVE THIS ISLAND BEFORE THE SUN GOES DOWN, OR WE'LL *VANISH* ALONG WITH IT.
BUT WE CAN'T TAKE HIM HOME LIKE THIS. CAN WE?
MAYBE WE DON'T HAVE TO.
WHAT DO YOU MEAN?
I SAW A BABY MONKEY EAT A PETAL FROM A FLOWER, AND HE INSTANTLY TURNED OLD.
THERE'S A MAGICAL FLOWER THAT MAKES YOU OLDER? WHERE? I WANT IT.

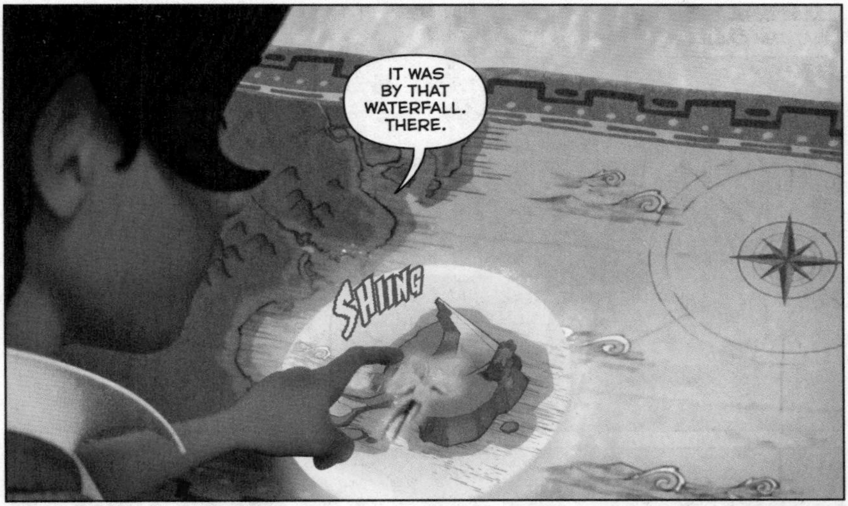
IT WAS BY THAT WATERFALL. THERE.
SHIING

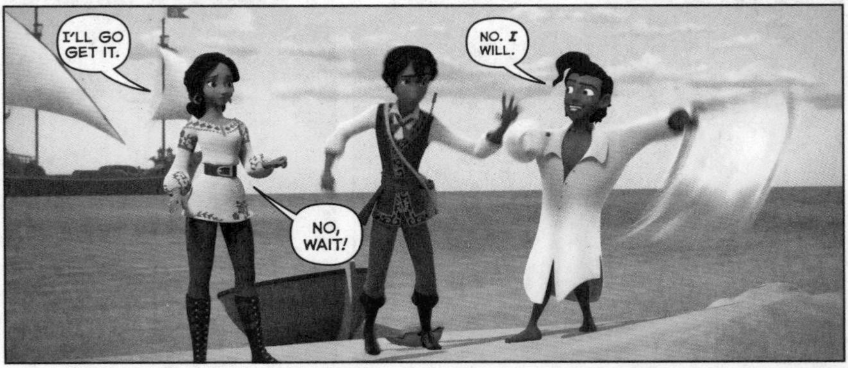
I'LL GO GET IT.
NO. *I* WILL.
NO, WAIT!

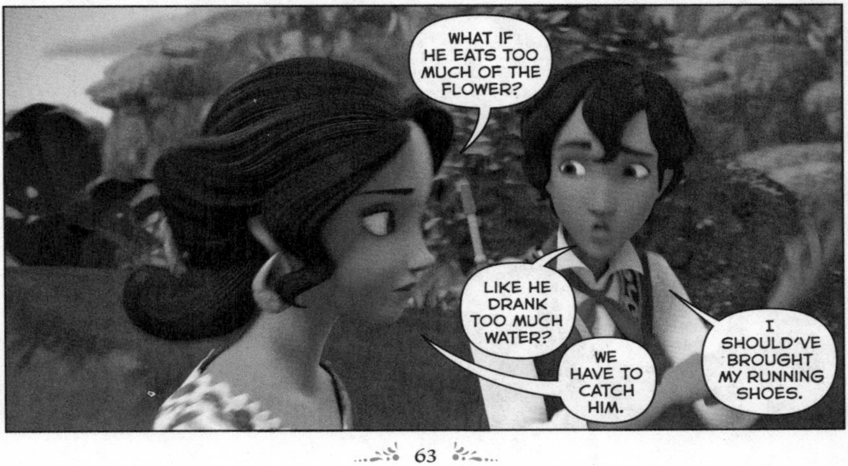
WHAT IF HE EATS TOO MUCH OF THE FLOWER?
LIKE HE DRANK TOO MUCH WATER?
WE HAVE TO CATCH HIM.
I SHOULD'VE BROUGHT MY RUNNING SHOES.

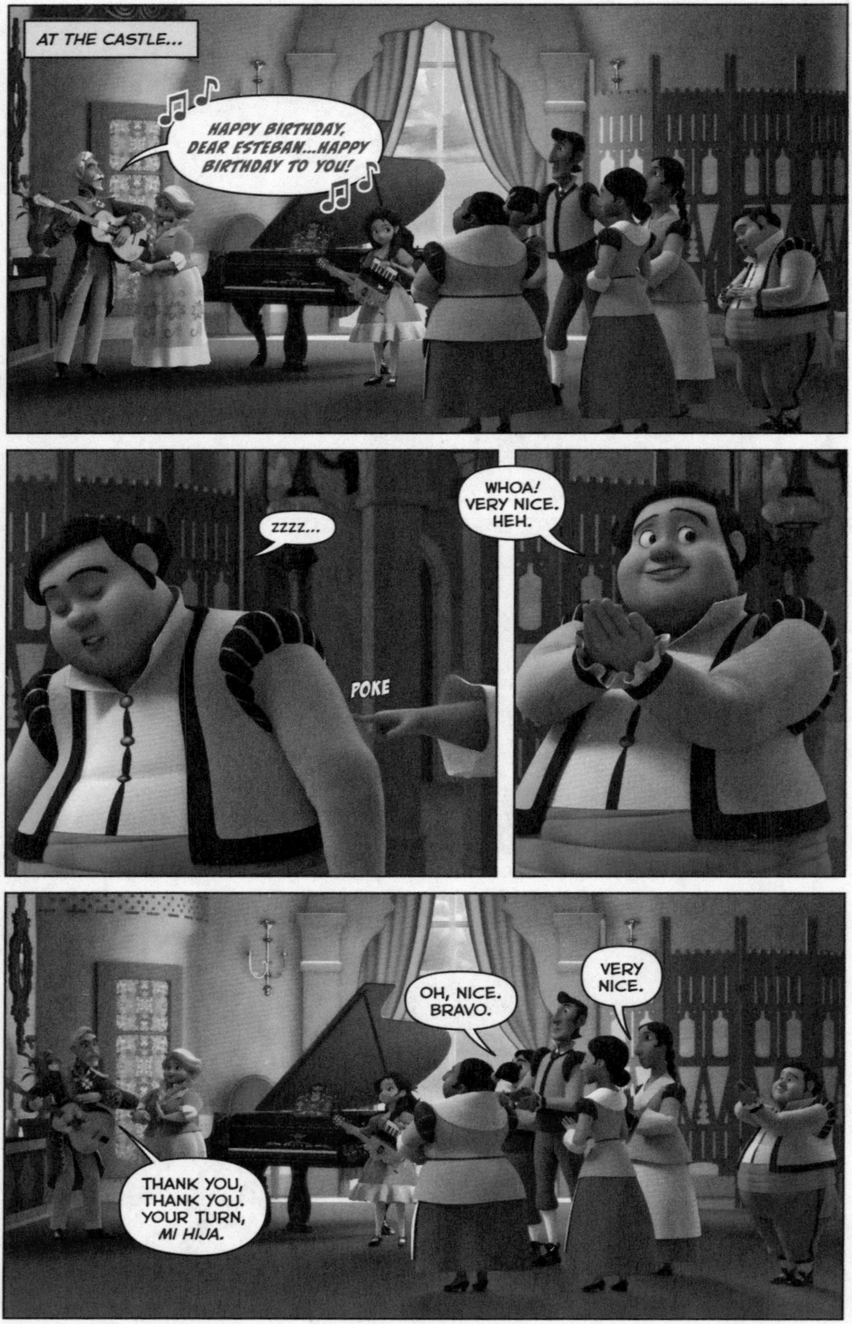
AT THE CASTLE...
HAPPY BIRTHDAY, DEAR ESTEBAN...HAPPY BIRTHDAY TO YOU!
ZZZZ...
POKE
WHOA! VERY NICE. HEH.
OH, NICE. BRAVO.
VERY NICE.
THANK YOU, THANK YOU. YOUR TURN, MI HIJA.

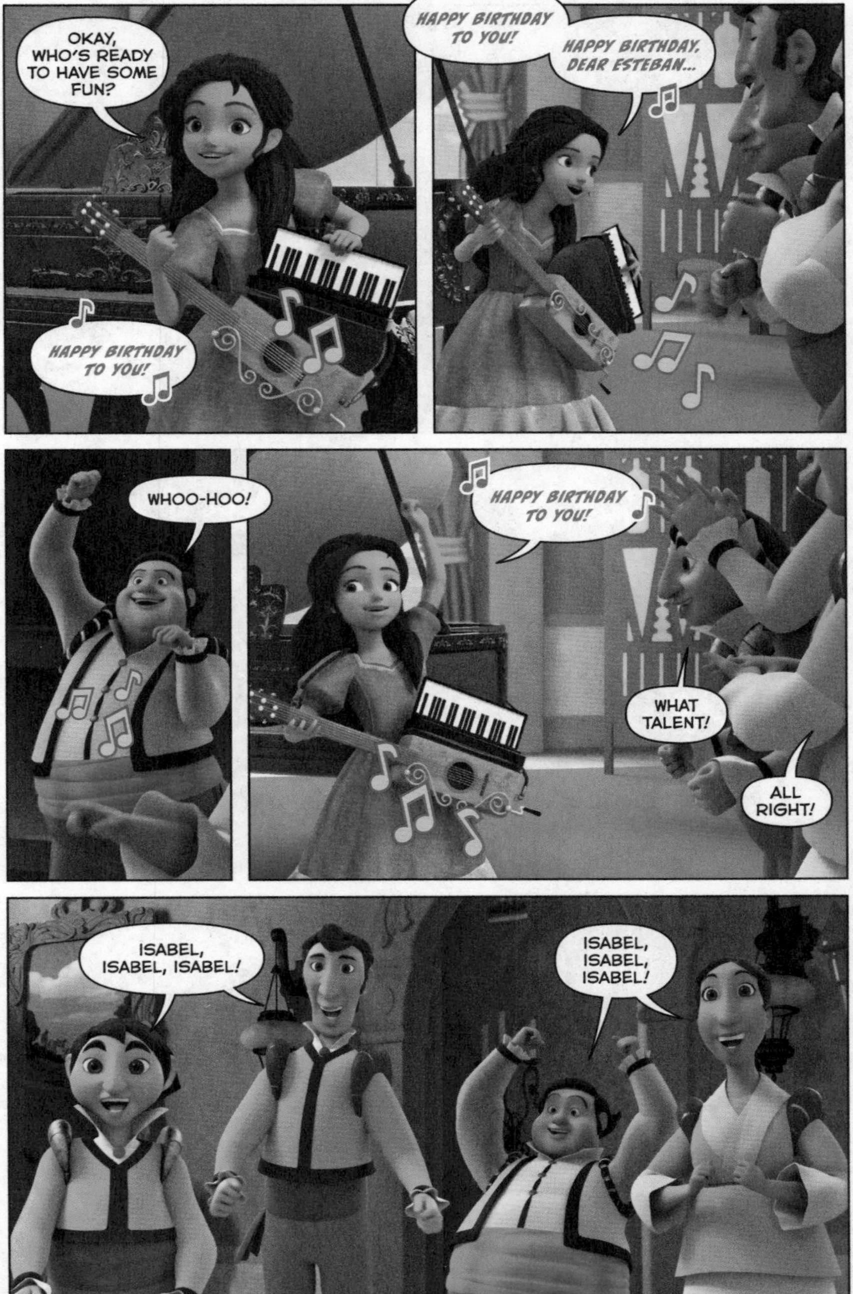
OKAY, WHO'S READY TO HAVE SOME FUN?
HAPPY BIRTHDAY TO YOU!
HAPPY BIRTHDAY TO YOU!
HAPPY BIRTHDAY, DEAR ESTEBAN...
WHOO-HOO!
HAPPY BIRTHDAY TO YOU!
WHAT TALENT!
ALL RIGHT!
ISABEL, ISABEL, ISABEL!
ISABEL, ISABEL, ISABEL!

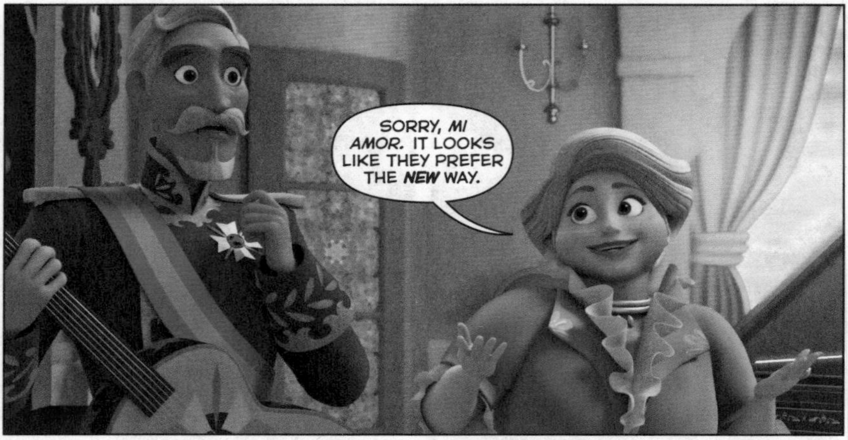
SORRY, *MI AMOR.* IT LOOKS LIKE THEY PREFER THE ***NEW*** WAY.

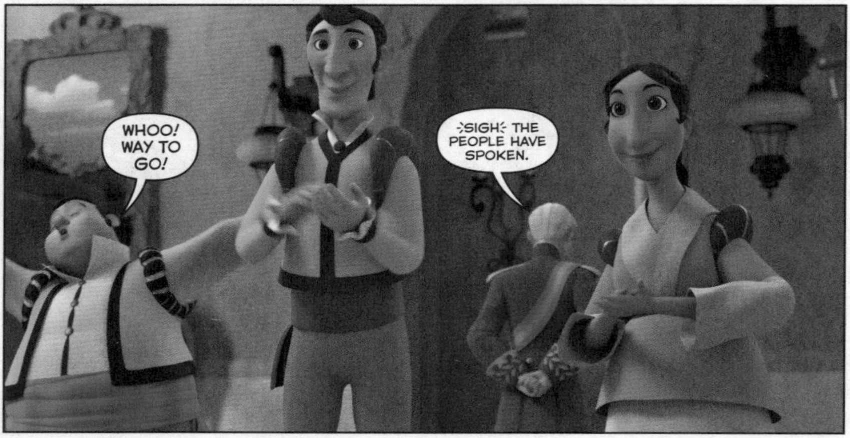
WHOO! WAY TO GO!
SIGH THE PEOPLE HAVE SPOKEN.

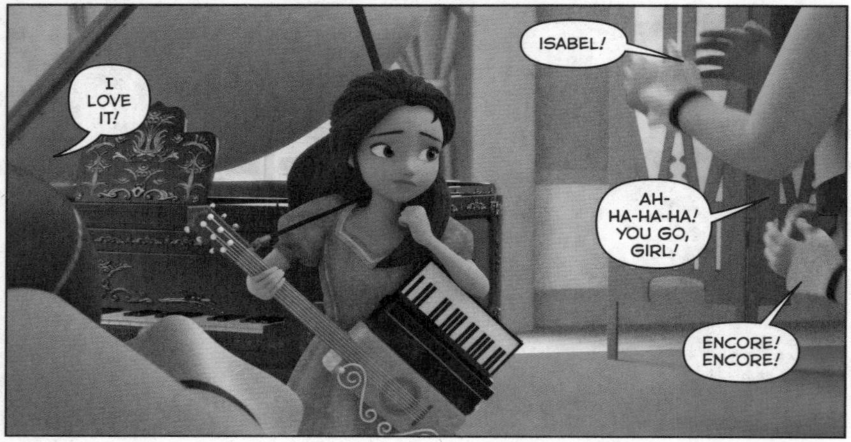
I LOVE IT!
ISABEL!
AH-HA-HA-HA! YOU GO, GIRL!
ENCORE! ENCORE!

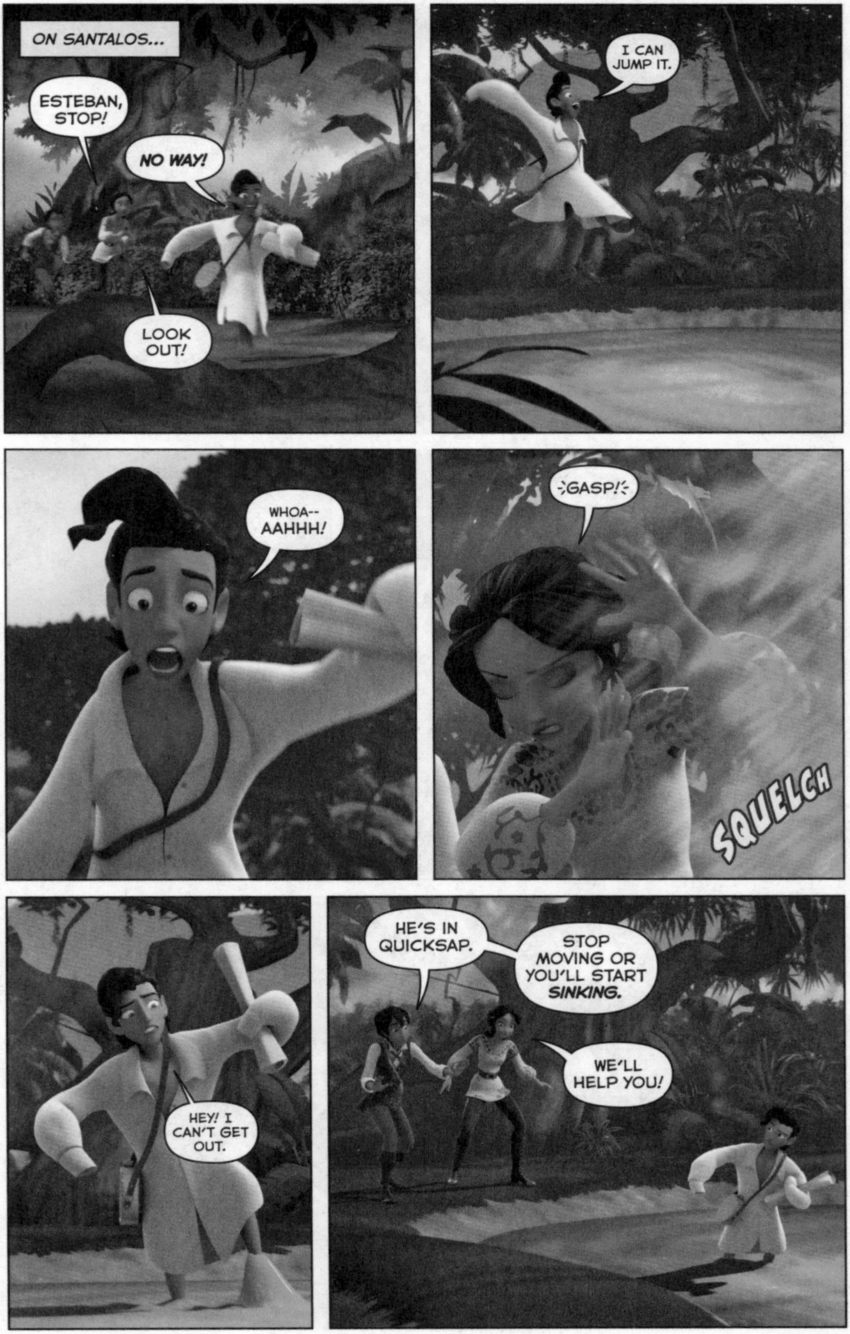
ON SANTALOS...
ESTEBAN, STOP!
NO WAY!
LOOK OUT!
I CAN JUMP IT.
WHOA--AAHHH!
GASP!
SQUELCH
HEY! I CAN'T GET OUT.
HE'S IN QUICKSAP.
STOP MOVING OR YOU'LL START SINKING.
WE'LL HELP YOU!

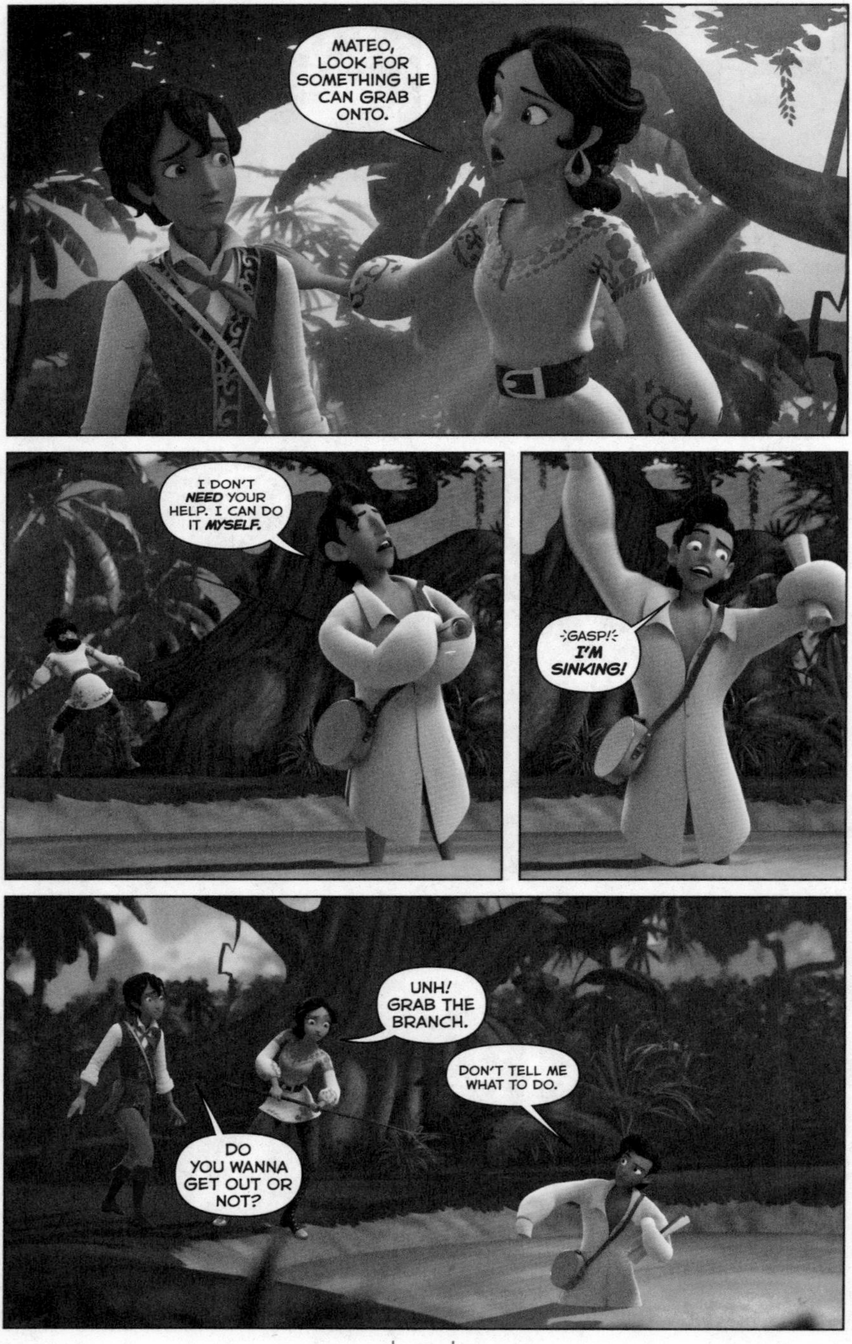
MATEO, LOOK FOR SOMETHING HE CAN GRAB ONTO.
I DON'T *NEED* YOUR HELP. I CAN DO IT *MYSELF.*
GASP! *I'M SINKING!*
UNH! GRAB THE BRANCH.
DON'T TELL ME WHAT TO DO.
DO YOU WANNA GET OUT OR NOT?

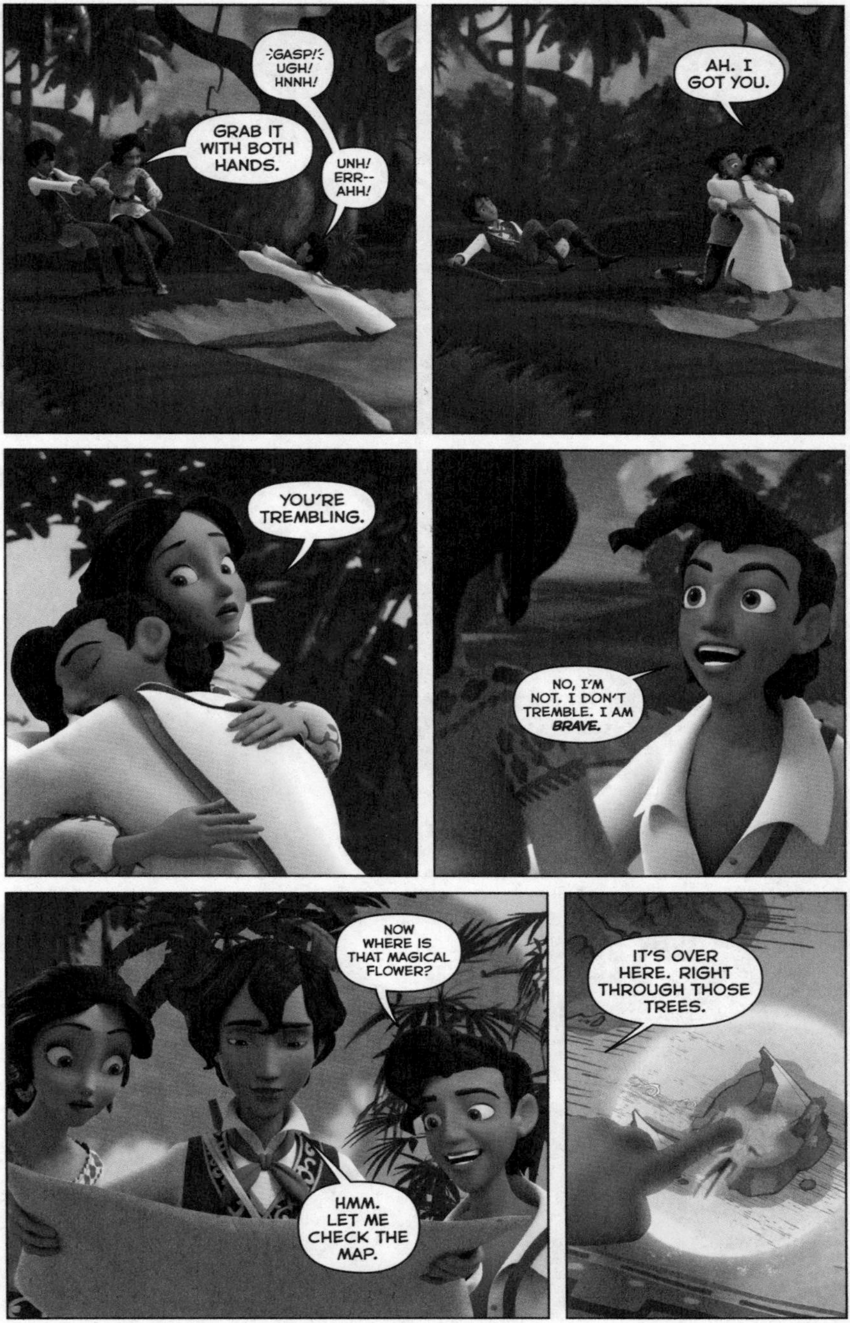
GASP! UGH! HNNH!
GRAB IT WITH BOTH HANDS.
UNH! ERR-- AHH!
AH. I GOT YOU.
YOU'RE TREMBLING.
NO, I'M NOT. I DON'T TREMBLE. I AM *BRAVE.*
NOW WHERE IS THAT MAGICAL FLOWER?
HMM. LET ME CHECK THE MAP.
IT'S OVER HERE. RIGHT THROUGH THOSE TREES.

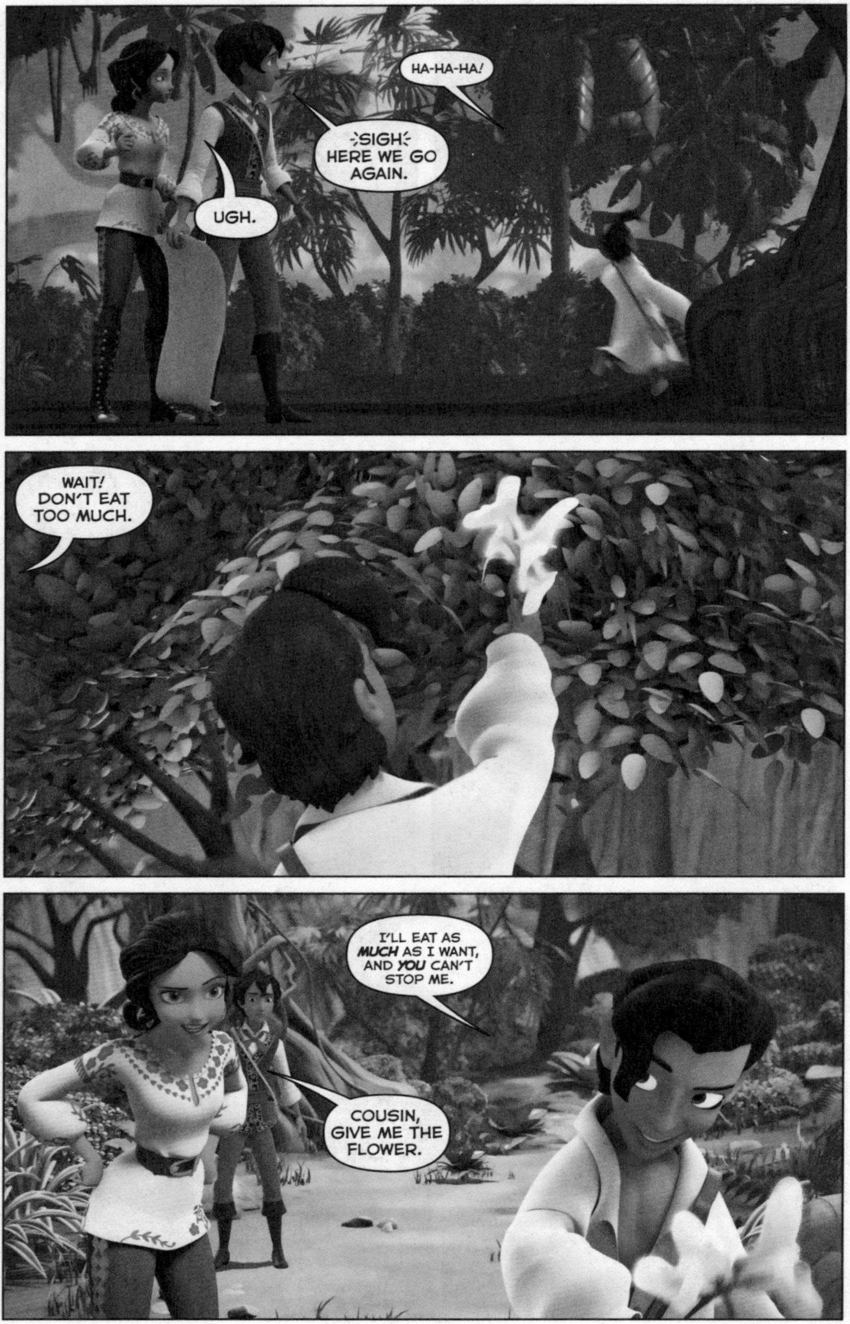
HA-HA-HA!
SIGH
HERE WE GO AGAIN.
UGH.
WAIT! DON'T EAT TOO MUCH.
I'LL EAT AS *MUCH* AS I WANT, AND *YOU* CAN'T STOP ME.
COUSIN, GIVE ME THE FLOWER.

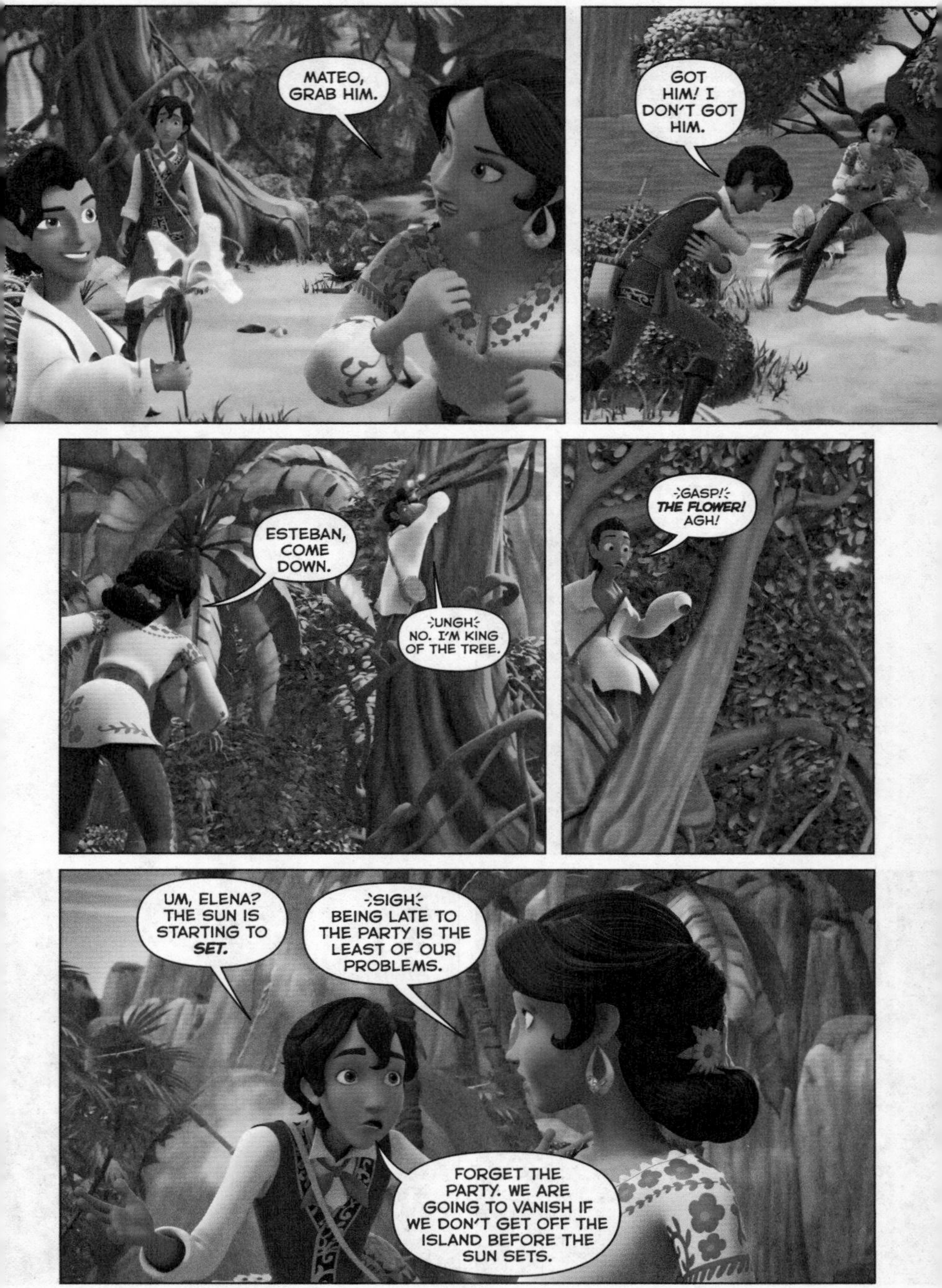
MATEO, GRAB HIM.
GOT HIM! I DON'T GOT HIM.
ESTEBAN, COME DOWN.
UNGH NO. I'M KING OF THE TREE.
GASP! THE FLOWER! AGH!
UM, ELENA? THE SUN IS STARTING TO SET.
SIGH BEING LATE TO THE PARTY IS THE LEAST OF OUR PROBLEMS.
FORGET THE PARTY. WE ARE GOING TO VANISH IF WE DON'T GET OFF THE ISLAND BEFORE THE SUN SETS.

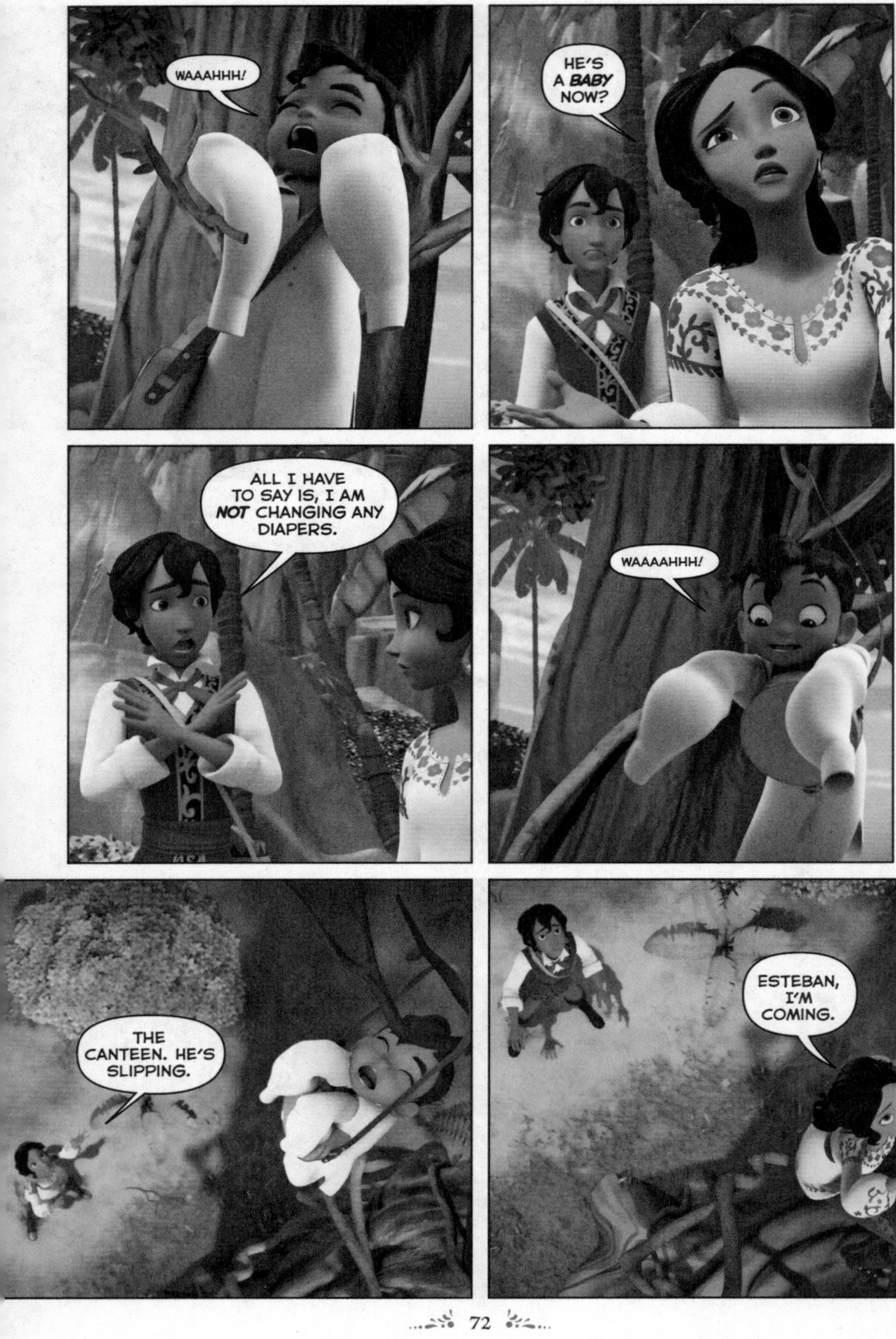
WAAAHHH!
HE'S A *BABY* NOW?
ALL I HAVE TO SAY IS, I AM *NOT* CHANGING ANY DIAPERS.
WAAAAHHH!
THE CANTEEN. HE'S SLIPPING.
ESTEBAN, I'M COMING.

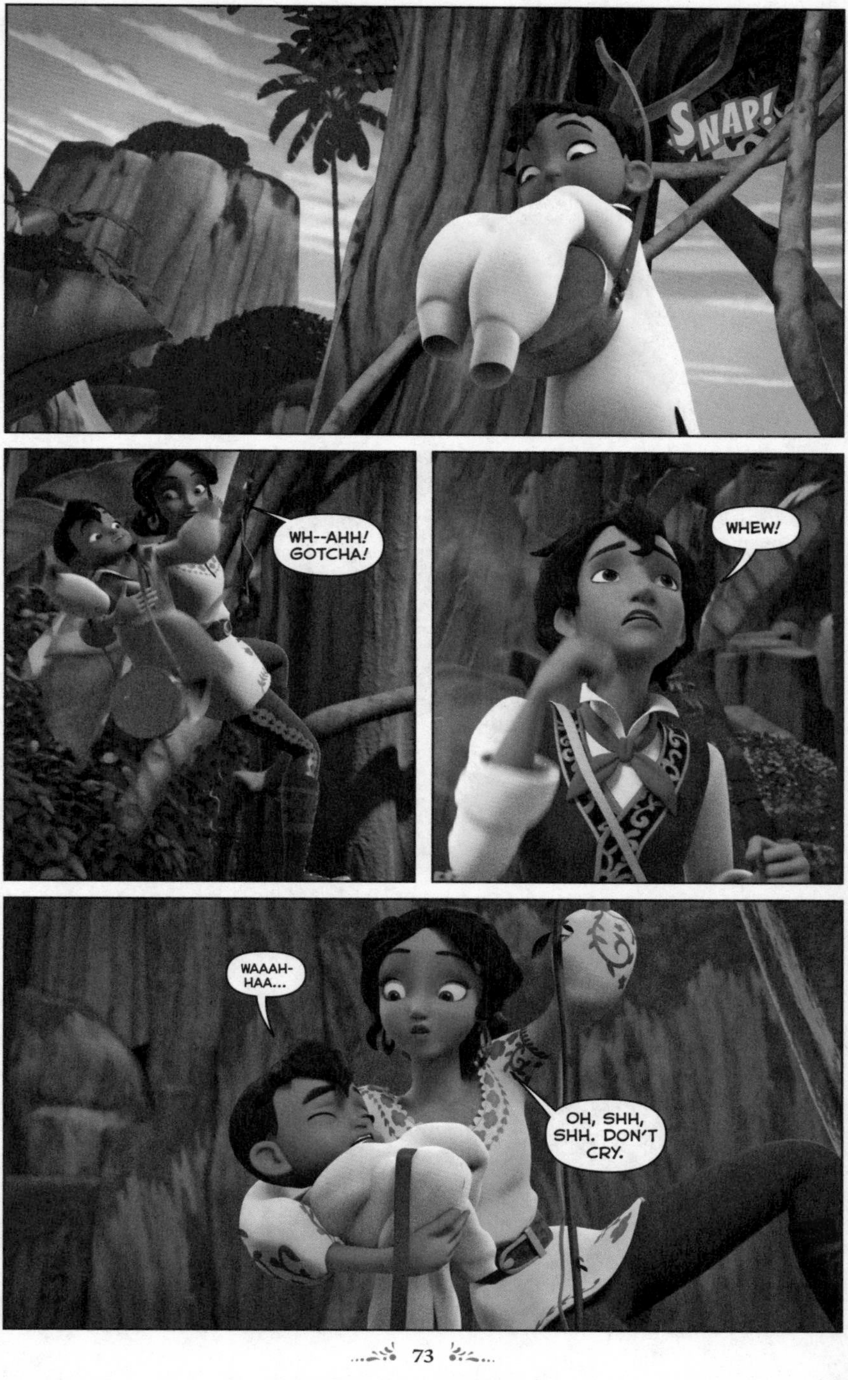
SNAP!
WH--AHH! GOTCHA!
WHEW!
WAAAH-HAA...
OH, SHH, SHH. DON'T CRY.

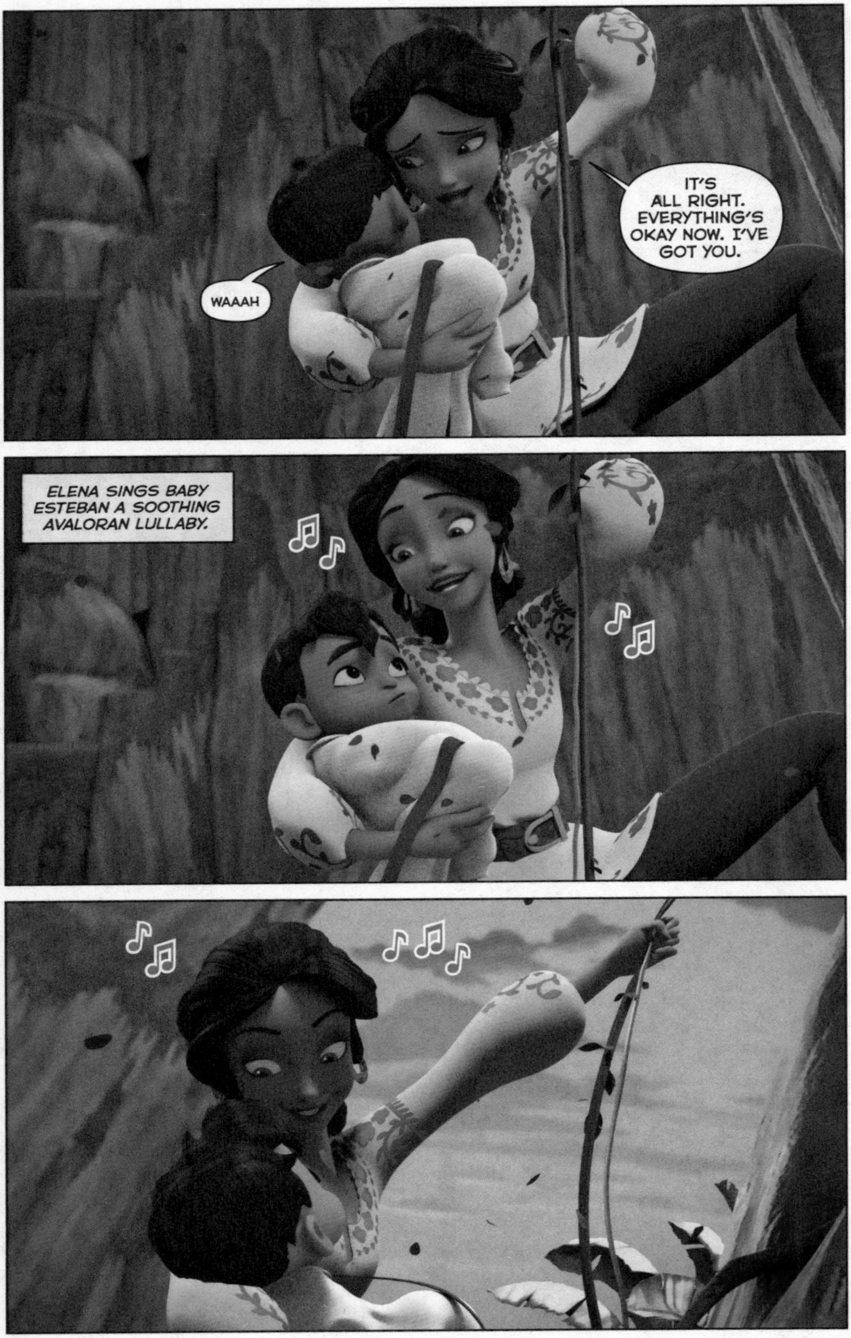
WAAAH
IT'S ALL RIGHT. EVERYTHING'S OKAY NOW. I'VE GOT YOU.
ELENA SINGS BABY ESTEBAN A SOOTHING AVALORAN LULLABY.

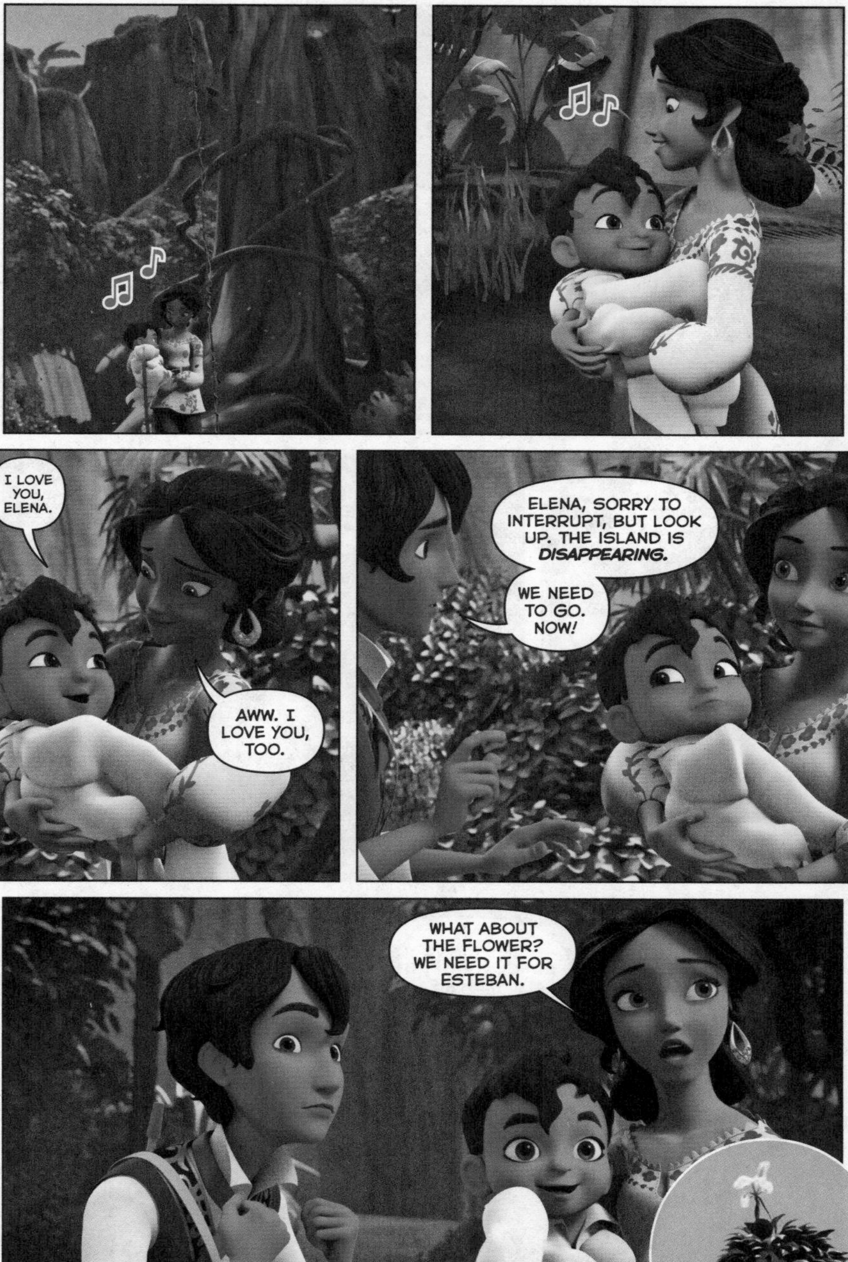
I LOVE YOU, ELENA.
AWW. I LOVE YOU, TOO.
ELENA, SORRY TO INTERRUPT, BUT LOOK UP. THE ISLAND IS *DISAPPEARING.*
WE NEED TO GO. NOW!
WHAT ABOUT THE FLOWER? WE NEED IT FOR ESTEBAN.

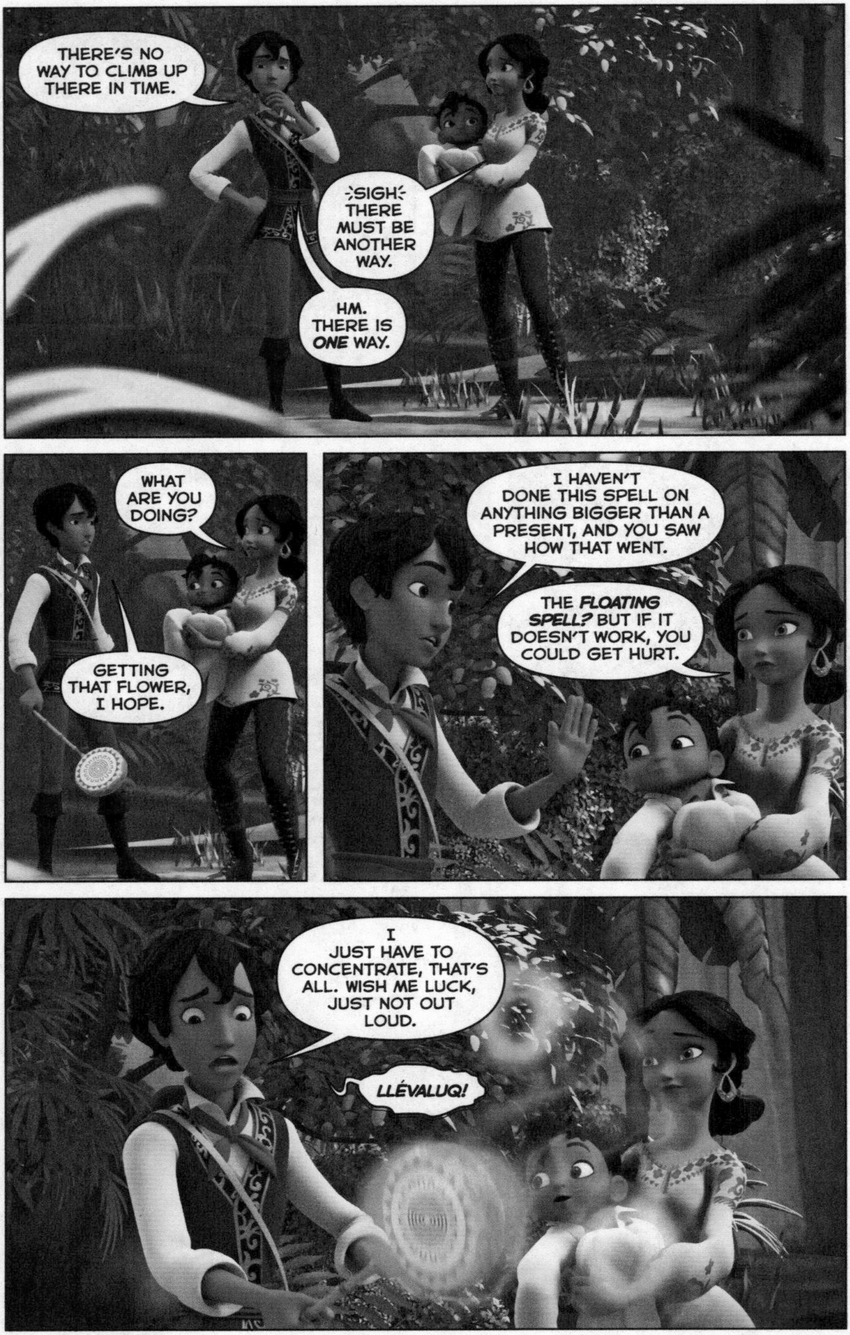
THERE'S NO WAY TO CLIMB UP THERE IN TIME.
SIGH THERE MUST BE ANOTHER WAY.
HM. THERE IS *ONE* WAY.
WHAT ARE YOU DOING?
GETTING THAT FLOWER, I HOPE.
I HAVEN'T DONE THIS SPELL ON ANYTHING BIGGER THAN A PRESENT, AND YOU SAW HOW THAT WENT.
THE ***FLOATING SPELL?*** BUT IF IT DOESN'T WORK, YOU COULD GET HURT.
I JUST HAVE TO CONCENTRATE, THAT'S ALL. WISH ME LUCK, JUST NOT OUT LOUD.
LLÉVALUQ!

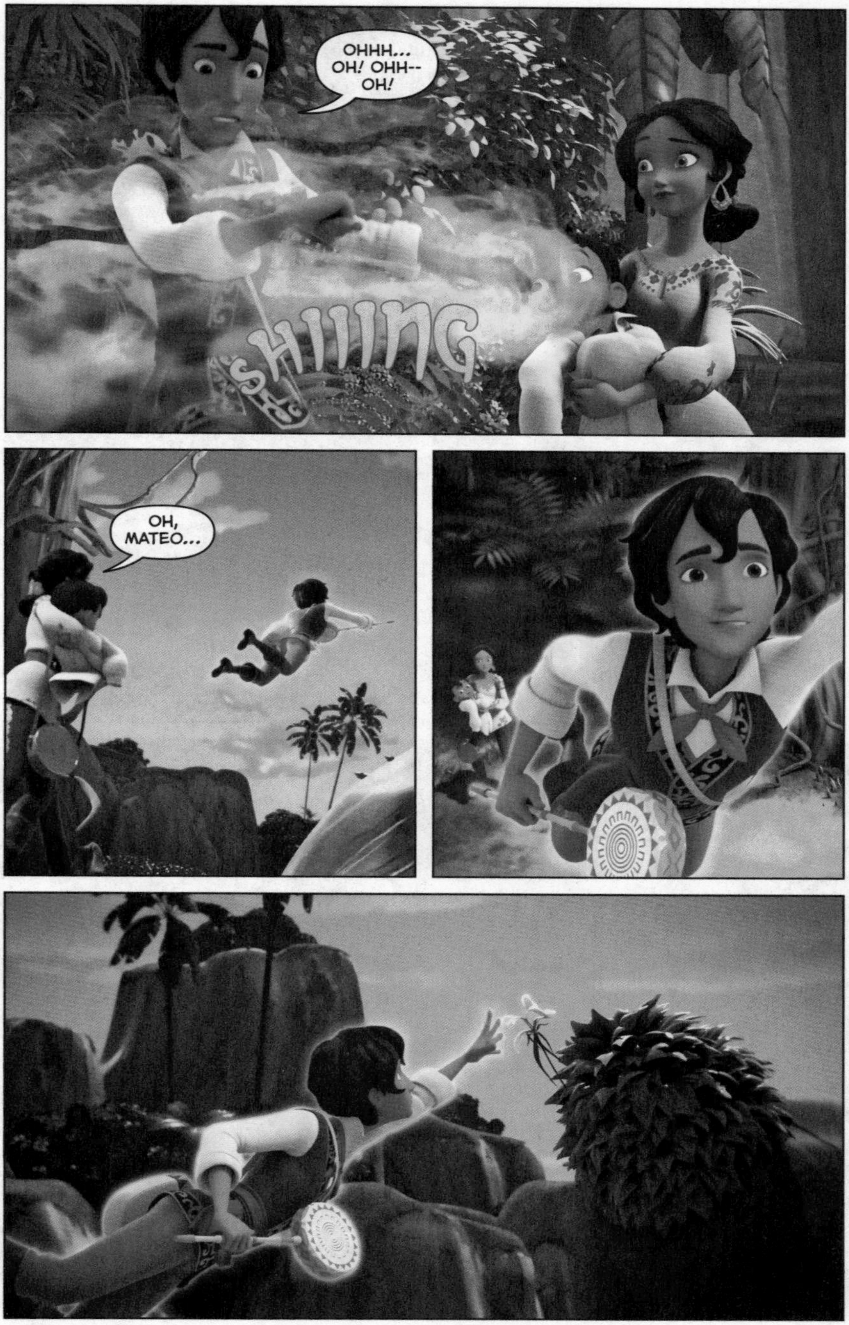
OHHH... OH! OHH-- OH!
SHIIING
OH, MATEO...

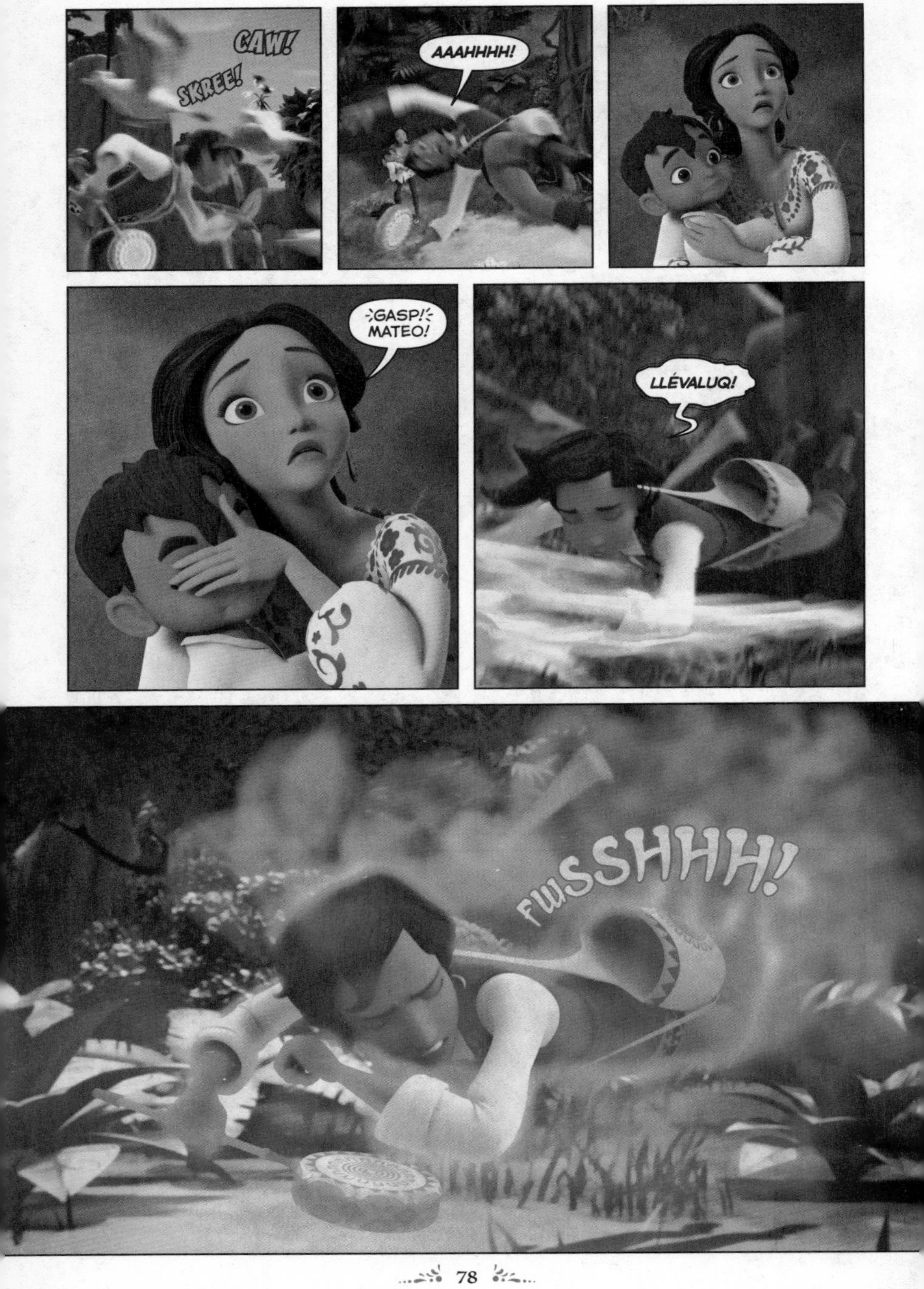
CAW!
SKREE!
AAAHHHH!
¡GASP!
MATEO!
LLÉVALUQ!
FWSSHHH!

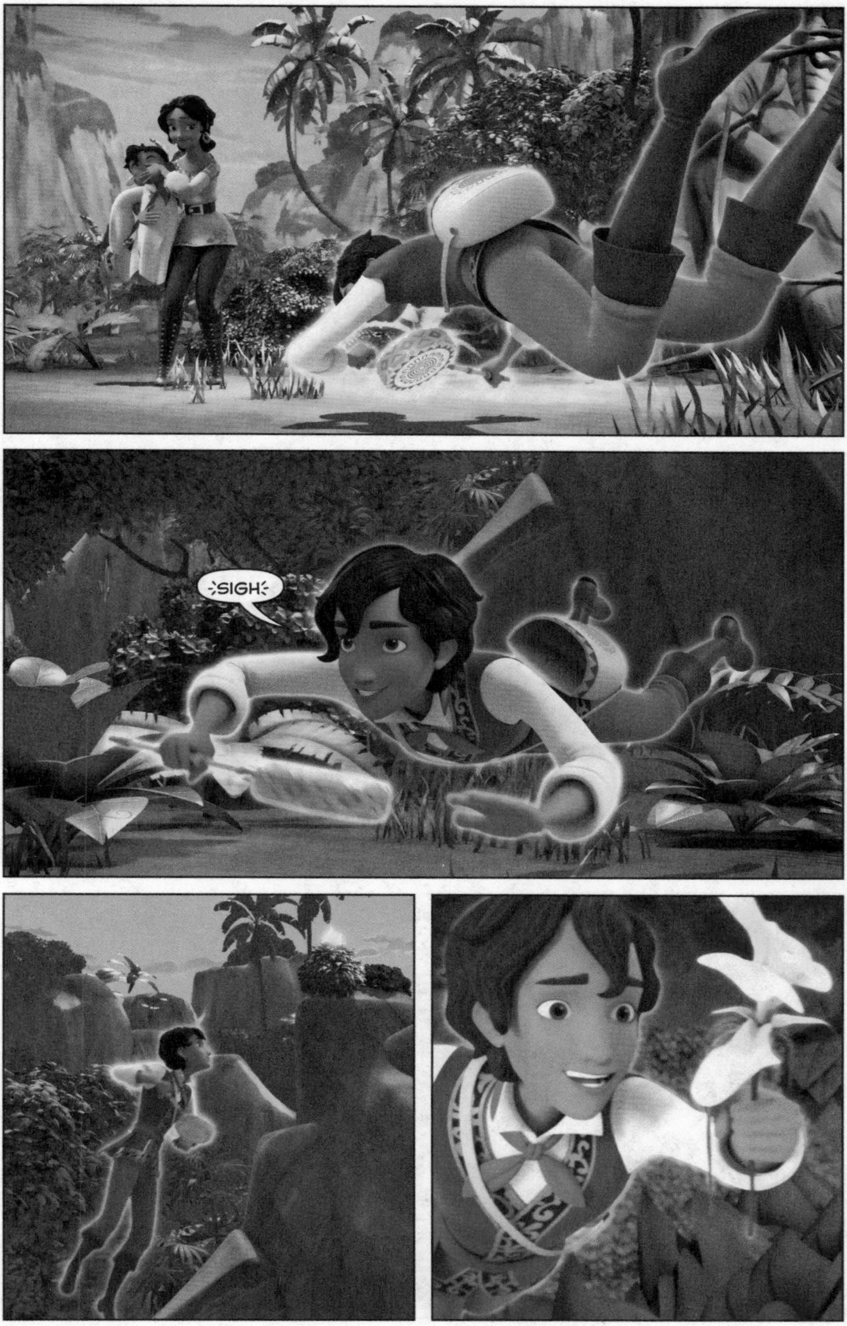
SIGH

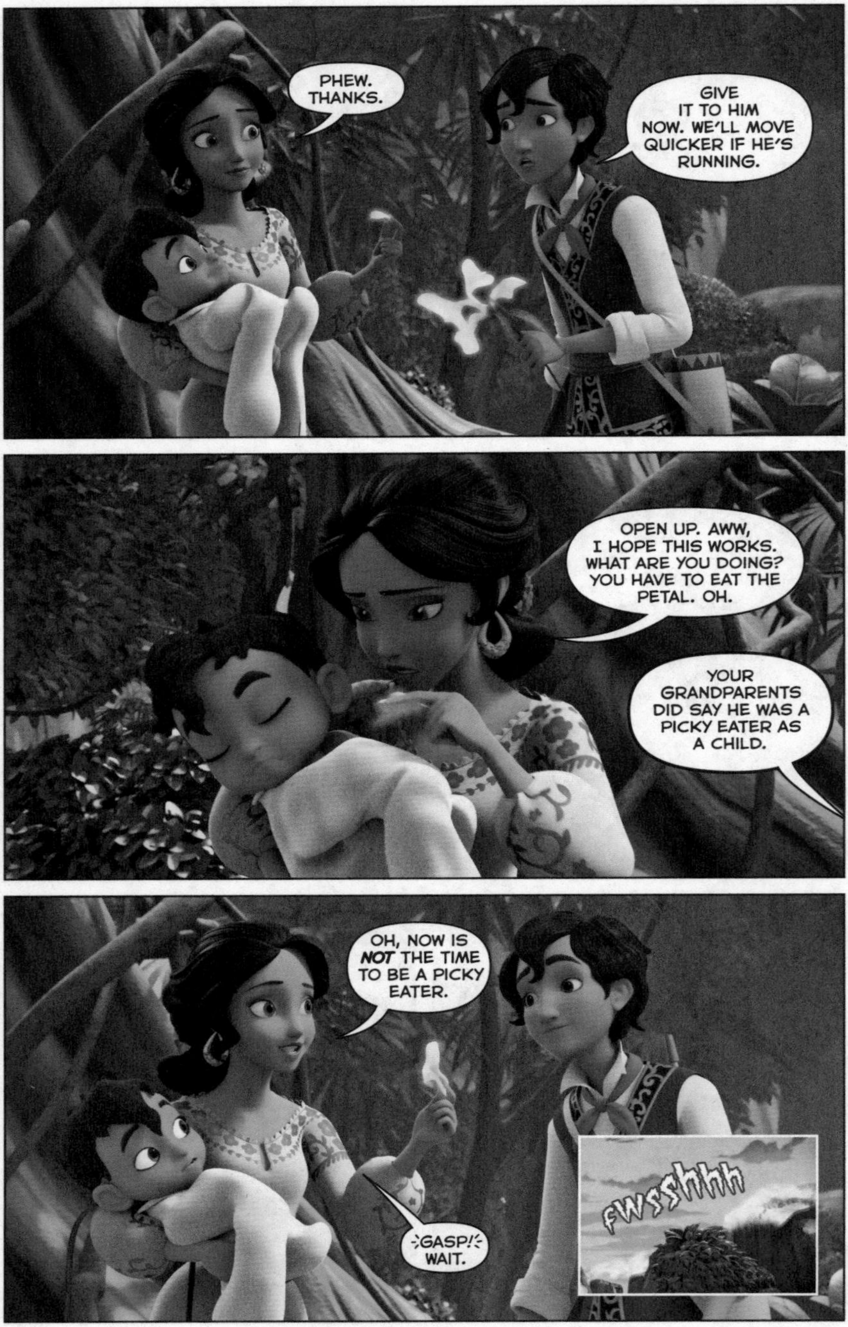
PHEW. THANKS.
GIVE IT TO HIM NOW. WE'LL MOVE QUICKER IF HE'S RUNNING.
OPEN UP. AWW, I HOPE THIS WORKS. WHAT ARE YOU DOING? YOU HAVE TO EAT THE PETAL. OH.
YOUR GRANDPARENTS DID SAY HE WAS A PICKY EATER AS A CHILD.
OH, NOW IS ***NOT*** THE TIME TO BE A PICKY EATER.
GASP! WAIT.
FWSSHHH

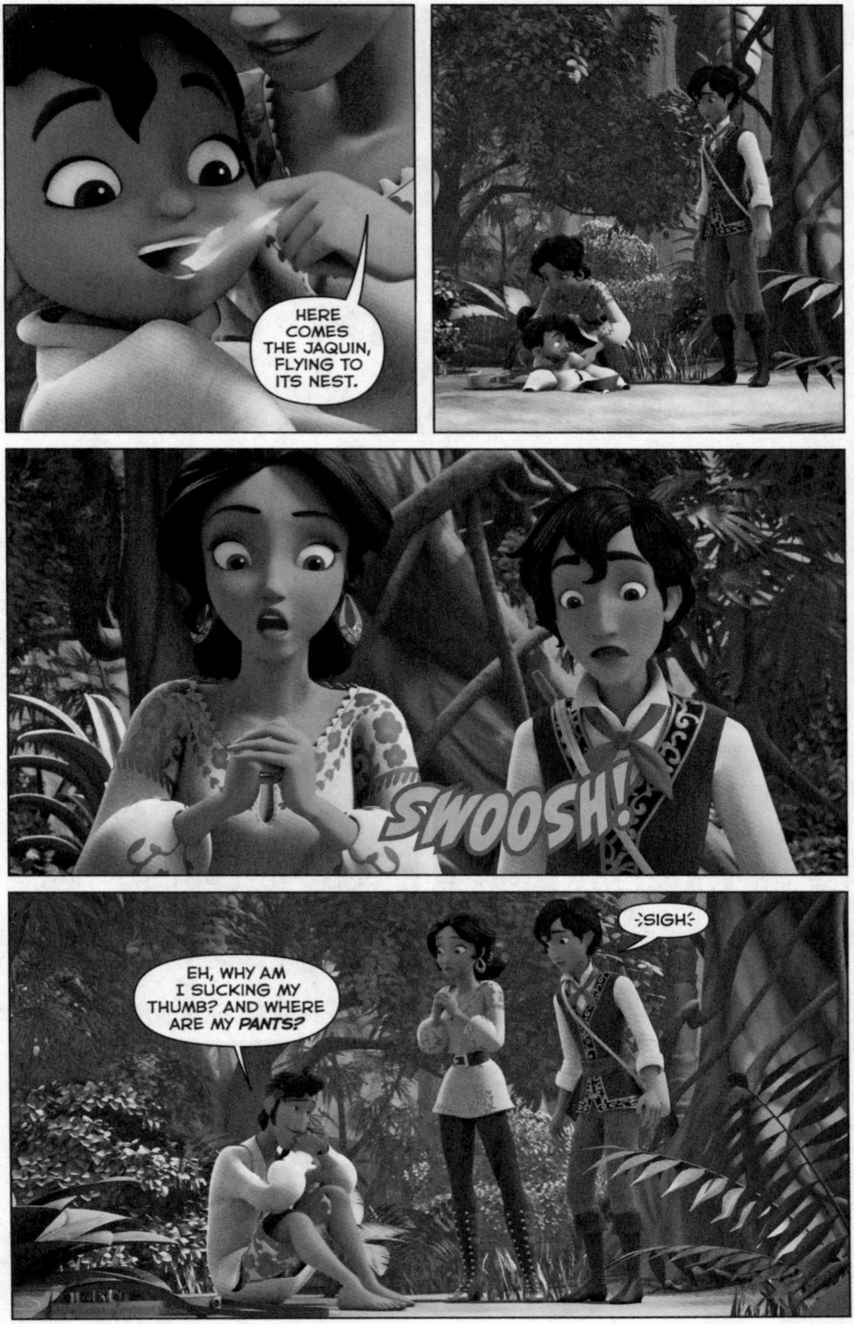
HERE COMES THE JAQUIN, FLYING TO ITS NEST.
SWOOSH!
EH, WHY AM I SUCKING MY THUMB? AND WHERE ARE MY *PANTS?*
SIGH

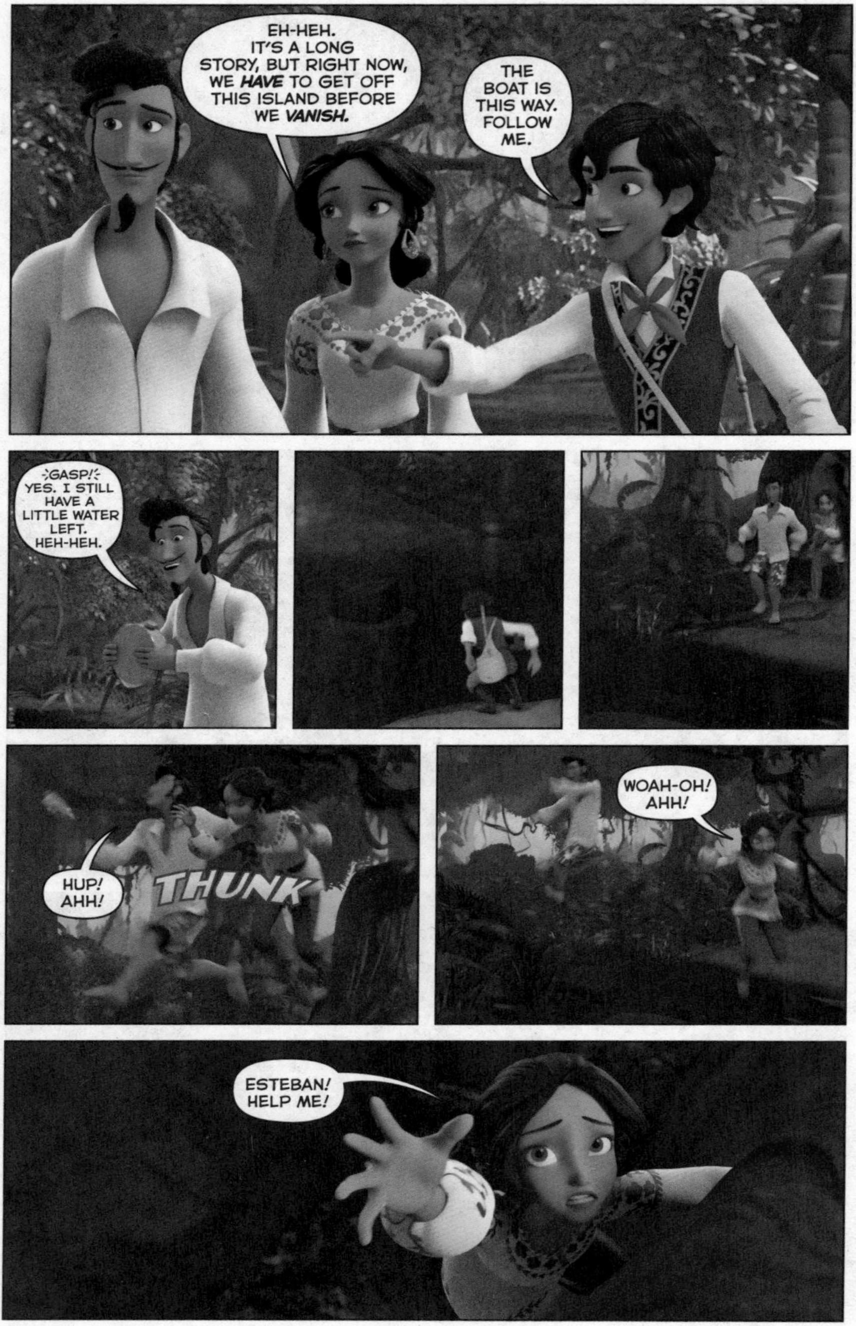
EH-HEH. IT'S A LONG STORY, BUT RIGHT NOW, WE *HAVE* TO GET OFF THIS ISLAND BEFORE WE *VANISH.*
THE BOAT IS THIS WAY. FOLLOW ME.
GASP! YES. I STILL HAVE A LITTLE WATER LEFT. HEH-HEH.
HUP! AHH!
THUNK
WOAH-OH! AHH!
ESTEBAN! HELP ME!

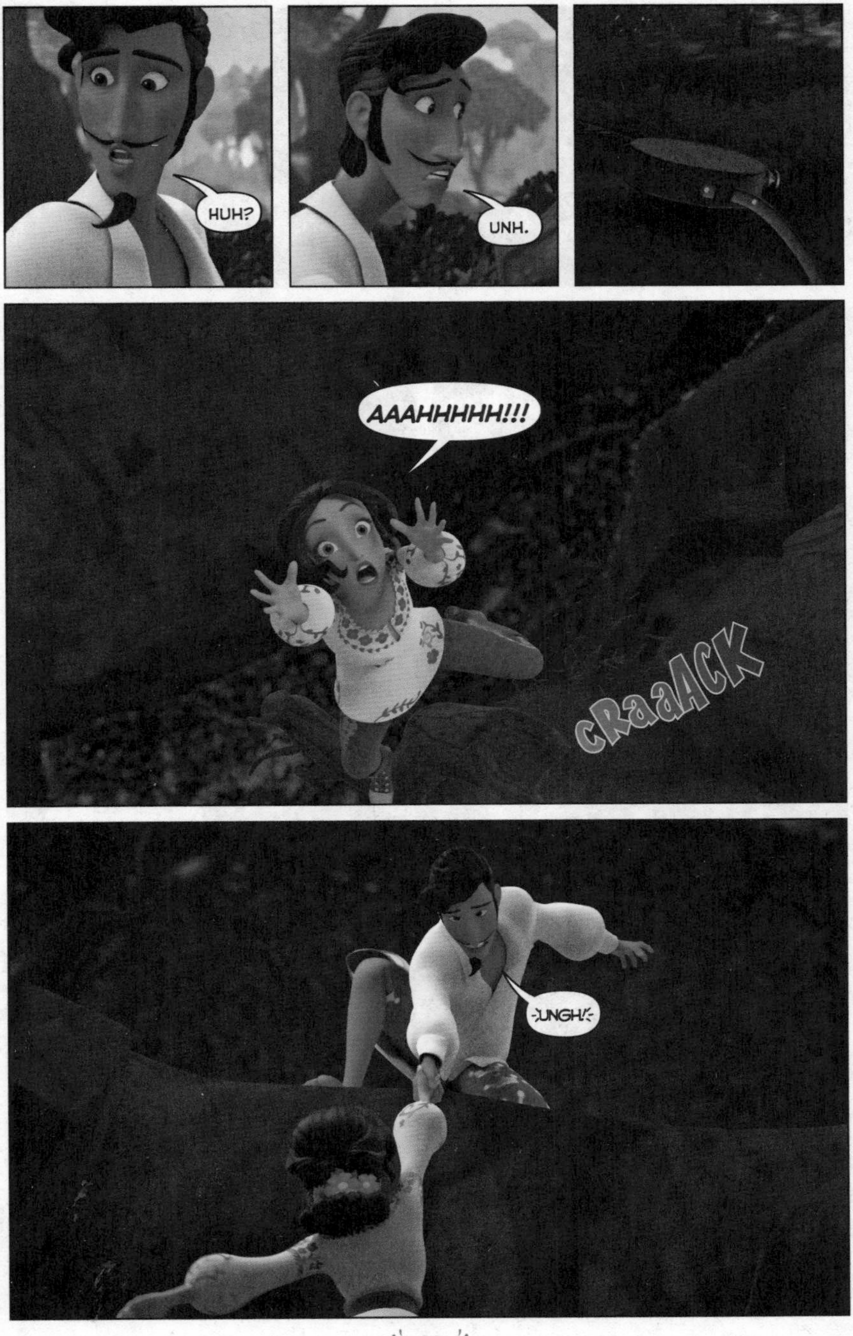
HUH?
UNH.
AAAHHHHH!!!
cRaaACK
UNGH!

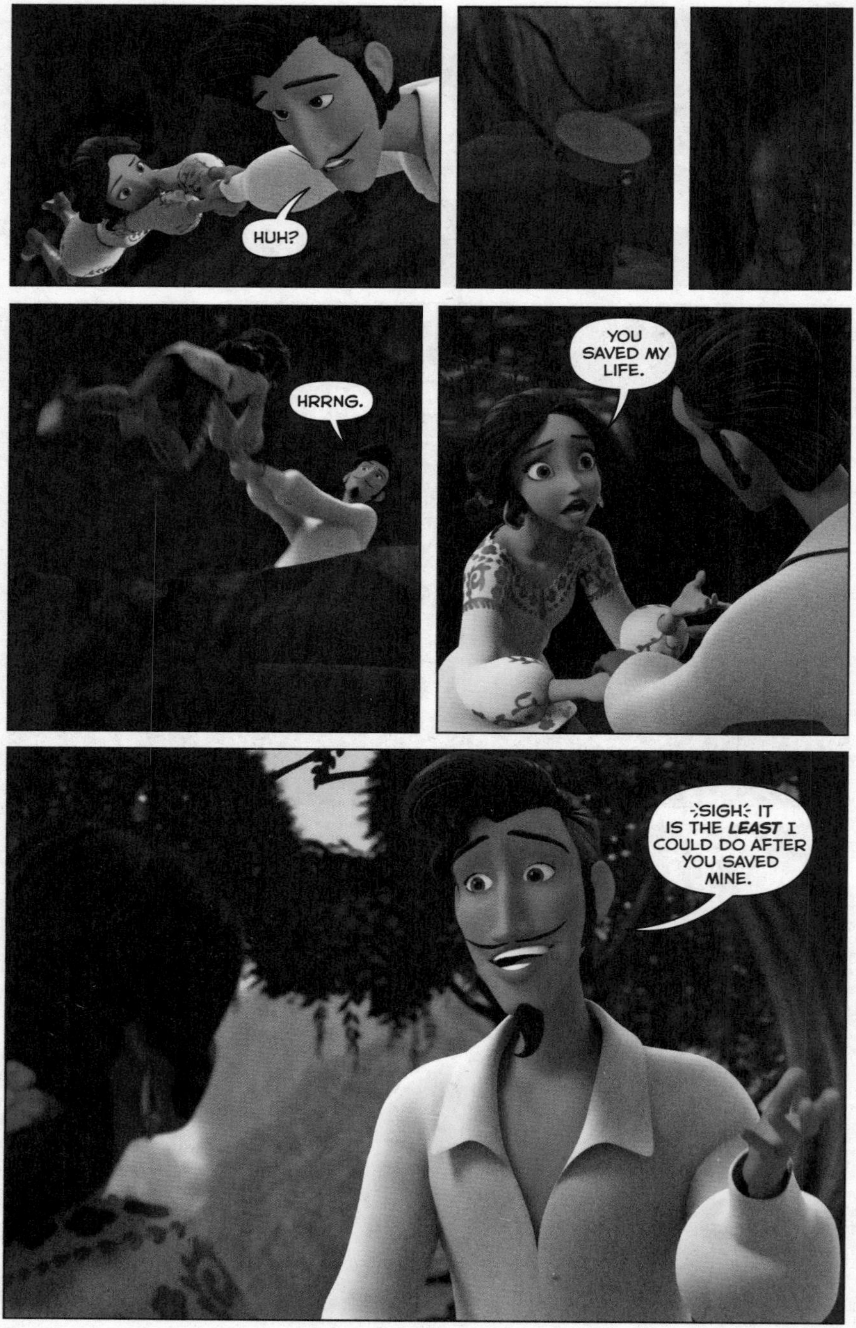
HUH?
HRRNG.
YOU SAVED MY LIFE.
⁘SIGH⁘ IT IS THE *LEAST* I COULD DO AFTER YOU SAVED MINE.

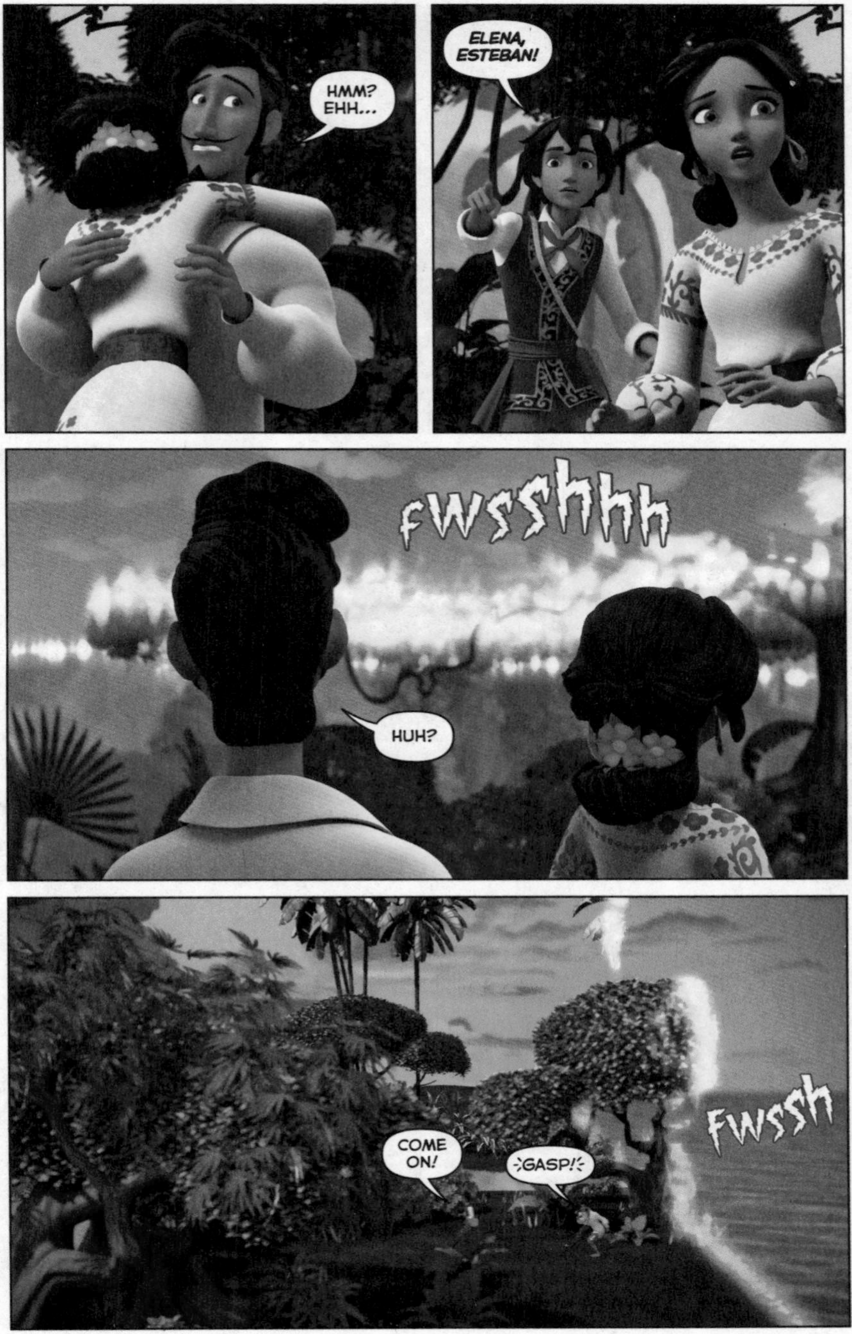
HMM? EHH...
ELENA, ESTEBAN!
FWSSHHH
HUH?
COME ON!
GASP!
FWSSH

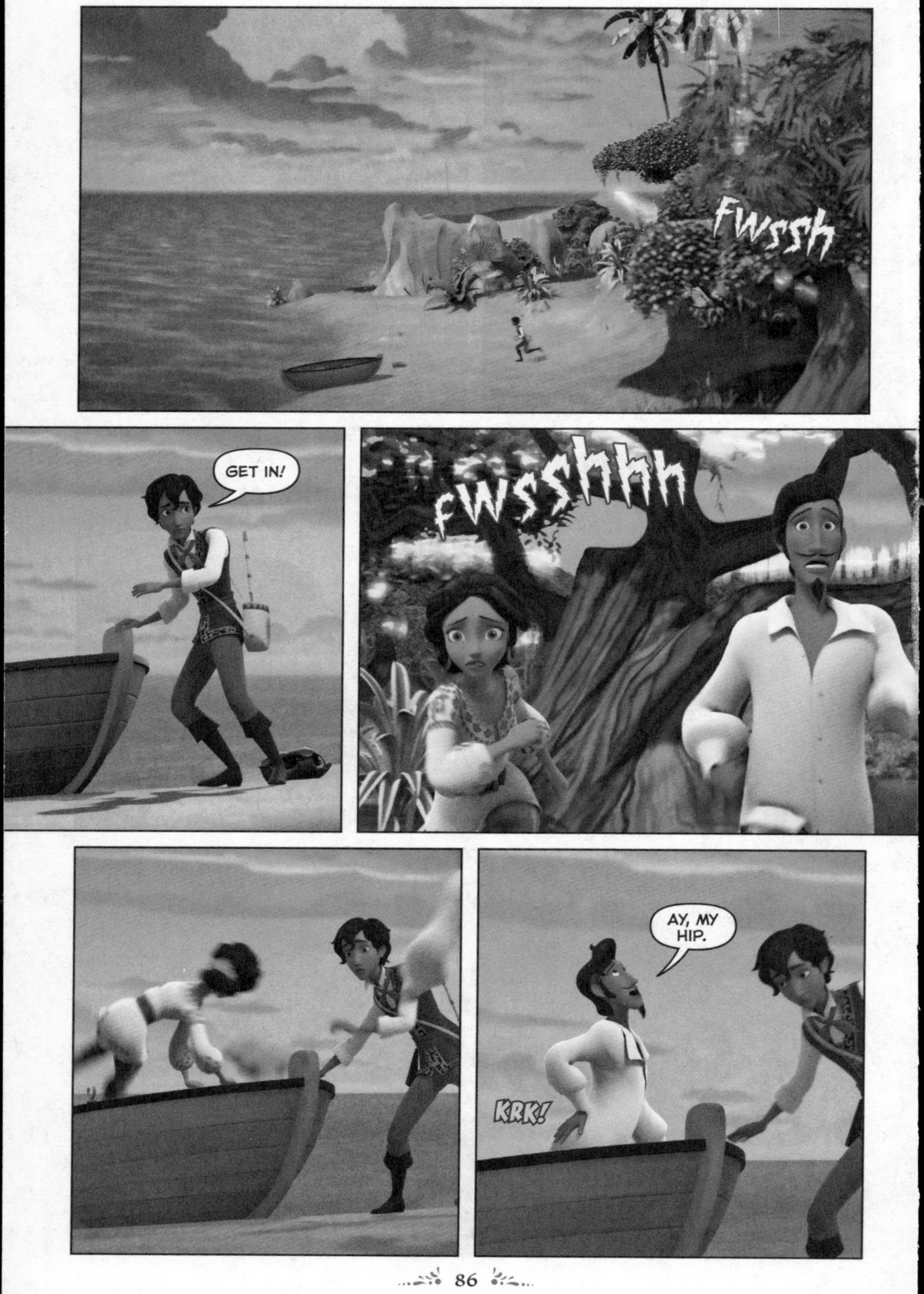
fwssh
GET IN!
fwsshhh
AY, MY HIP.
KRK!

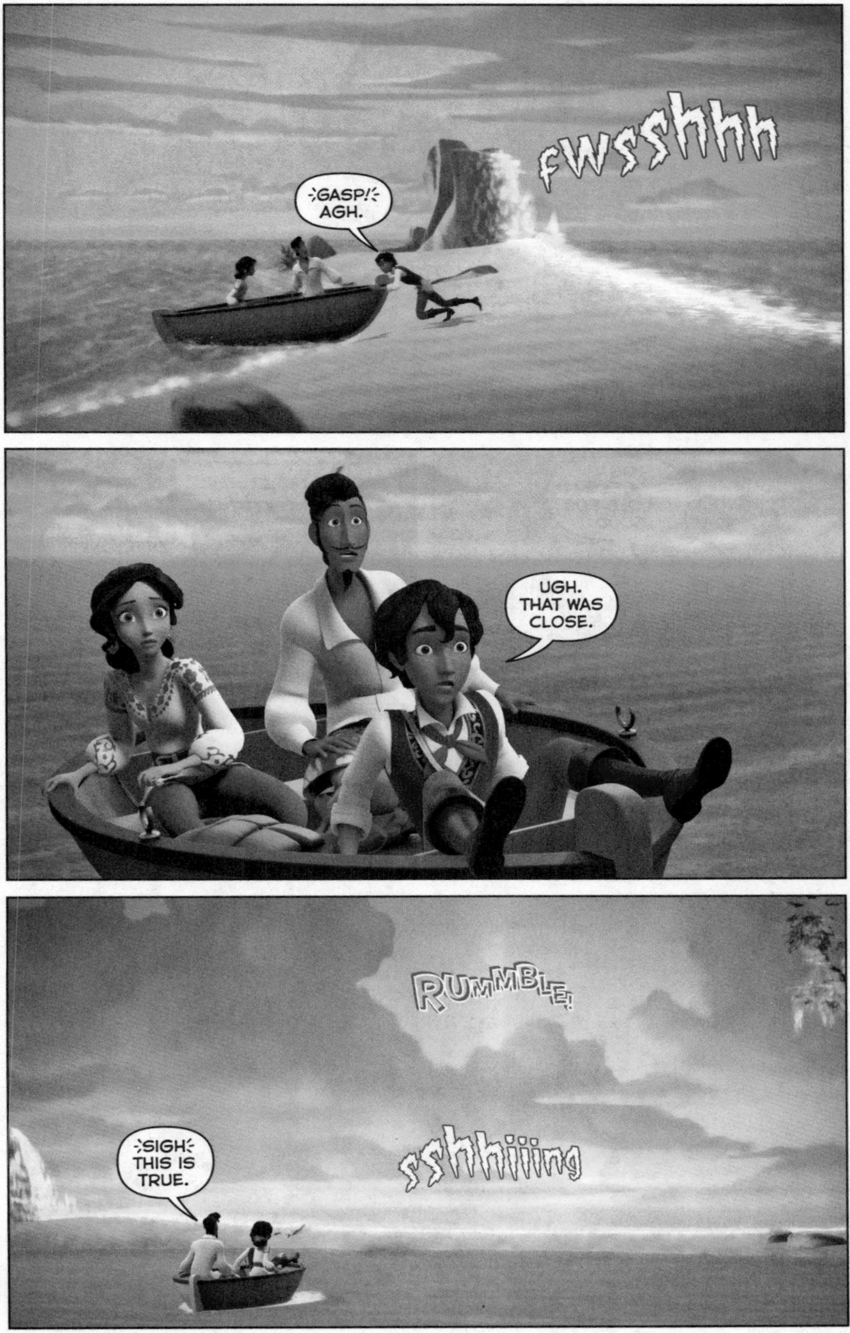
FWSSHHH
GASP! AGH.
UGH. THAT WAS CLOSE.
RUMMBLE!
SIGH THIS IS TRUE.
RSHHIIING

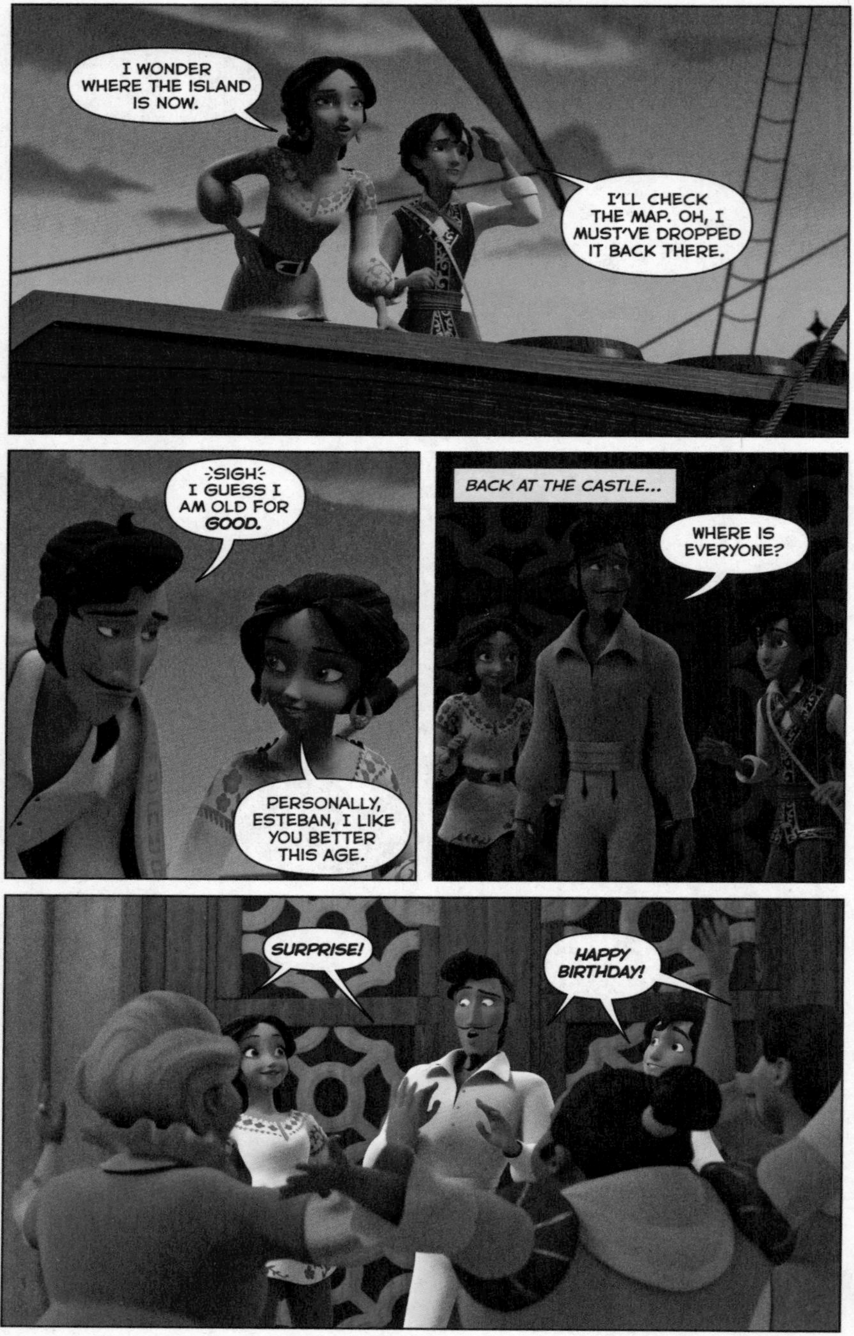
I WONDER WHERE THE ISLAND IS NOW.
I'LL CHECK THE MAP. OH, I MUST'VE DROPPED IT BACK THERE.
SIGH I GUESS I AM OLD FOR *GOOD.*
PERSONALLY, ESTEBAN, I LIKE YOU BETTER THIS AGE.
BACK AT THE CASTLE...
WHERE IS EVERYONE?
SURPRISE!
HAPPY BIRTHDAY!

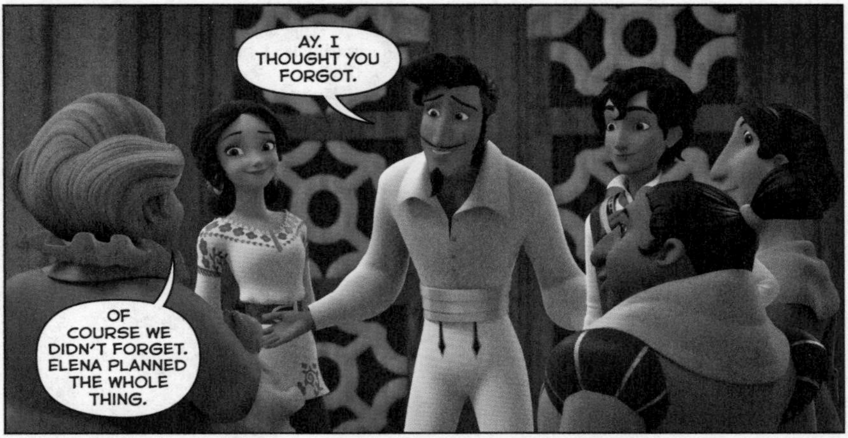
AY. I THOUGHT YOU FORGOT.
OF COURSE WE DIDN'T FORGET. ELENA PLANNED THE WHOLE THING.

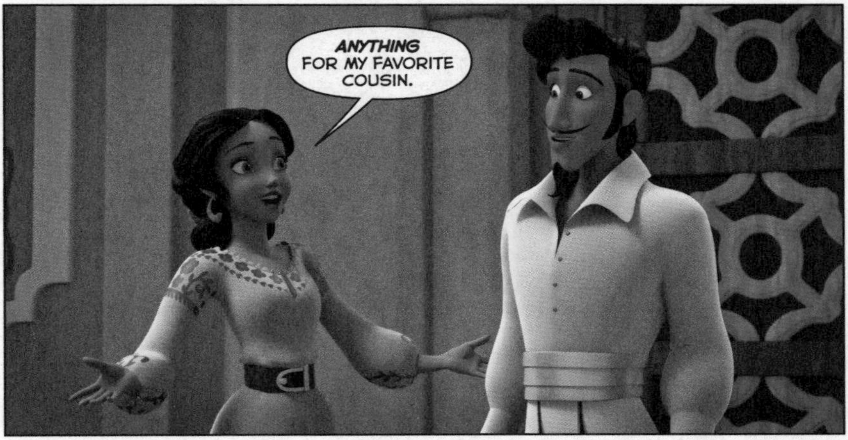
ANYTHING FOR MY FAVORITE COUSIN.

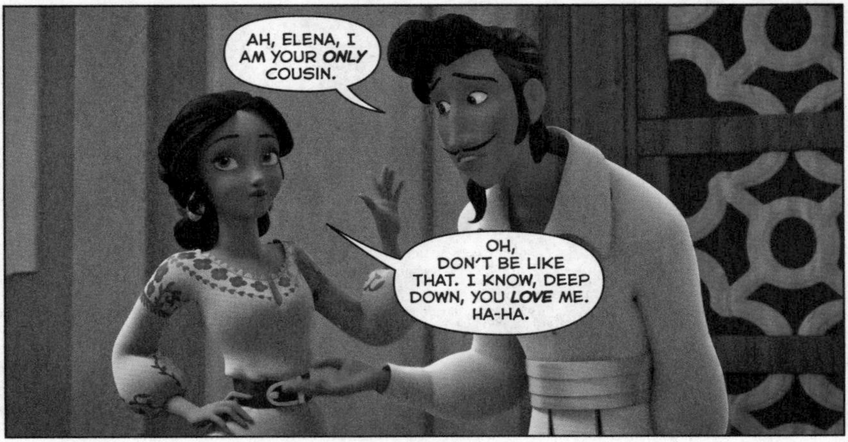
AH, ELENA, I AM YOUR *ONLY* COUSIN.
OH, DON'T BE LIKE THAT. I KNOW, DEEP DOWN, YOU *LOVE* ME. HA-HA.

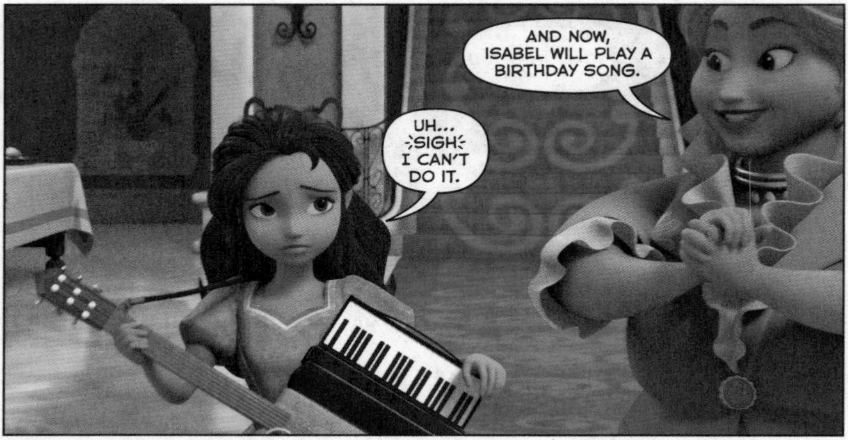
AND NOW, ISABEL WILL PLAY A BIRTHDAY SONG.
UH... ⁘SIGH⁘ I CAN'T DO IT.

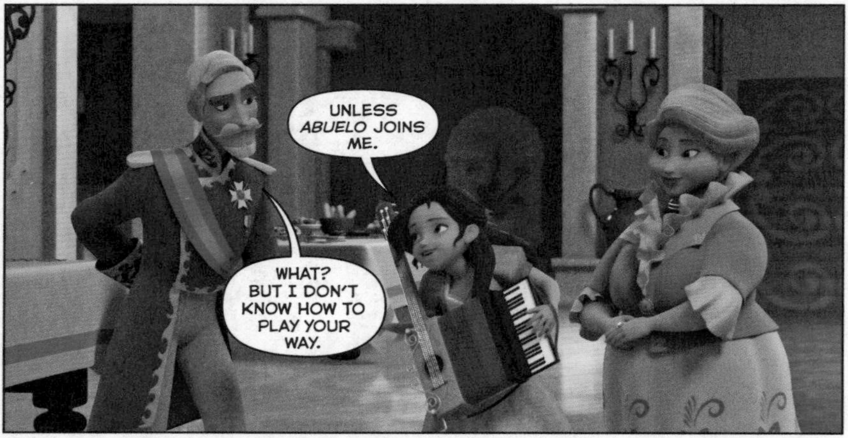
UNLESS *ABUELO* JOINS ME.
WHAT? BUT I DON'T KNOW HOW TO PLAY YOUR WAY.

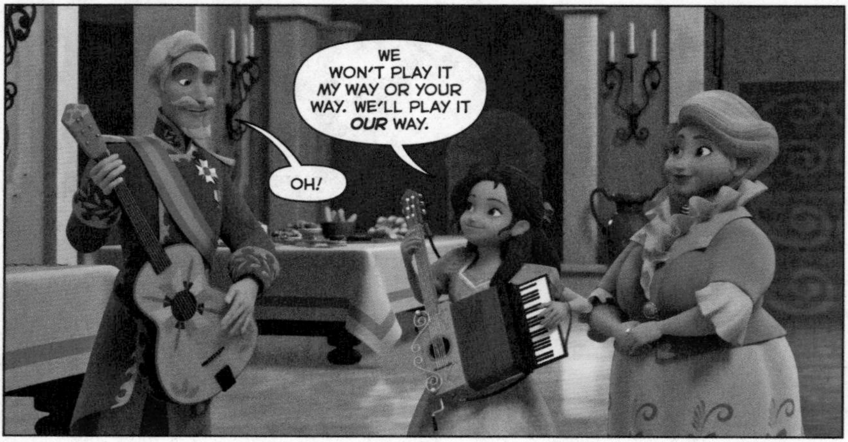
WE WON'T PLAY IT *MY* WAY OR *YOUR* WAY. WE'LL PLAY IT ***OUR*** WAY.
OH!

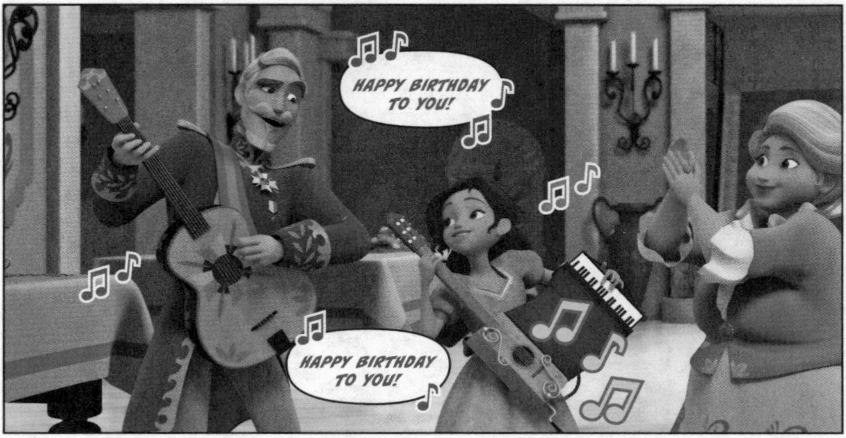
HAPPY BIRTHDAY TO YOU!
HAPPY BIRTHDAY TO YOU!

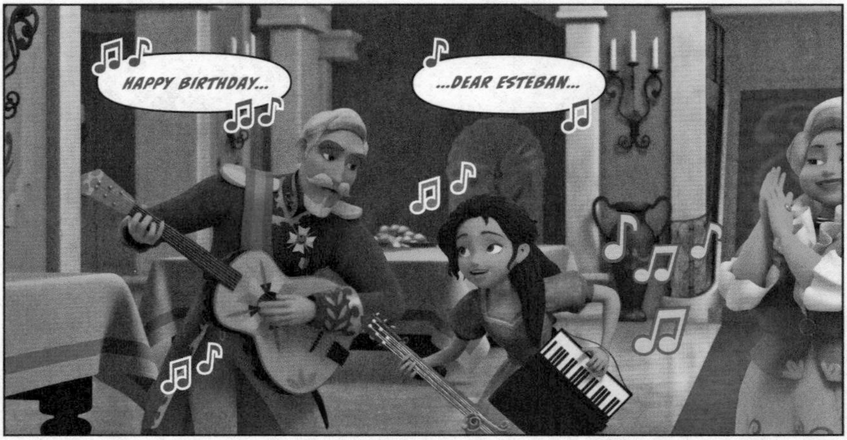
HAPPY BIRTHDAY...
...DEAR ESTEBAN...

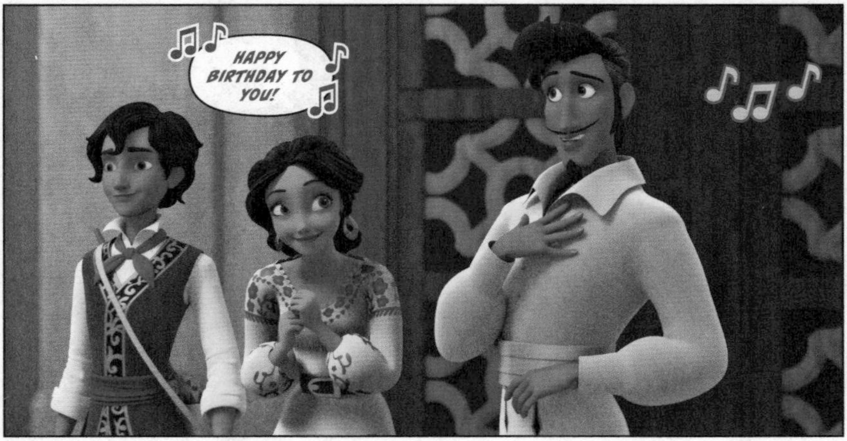
HAPPY BIRTHDAY TO YOU!

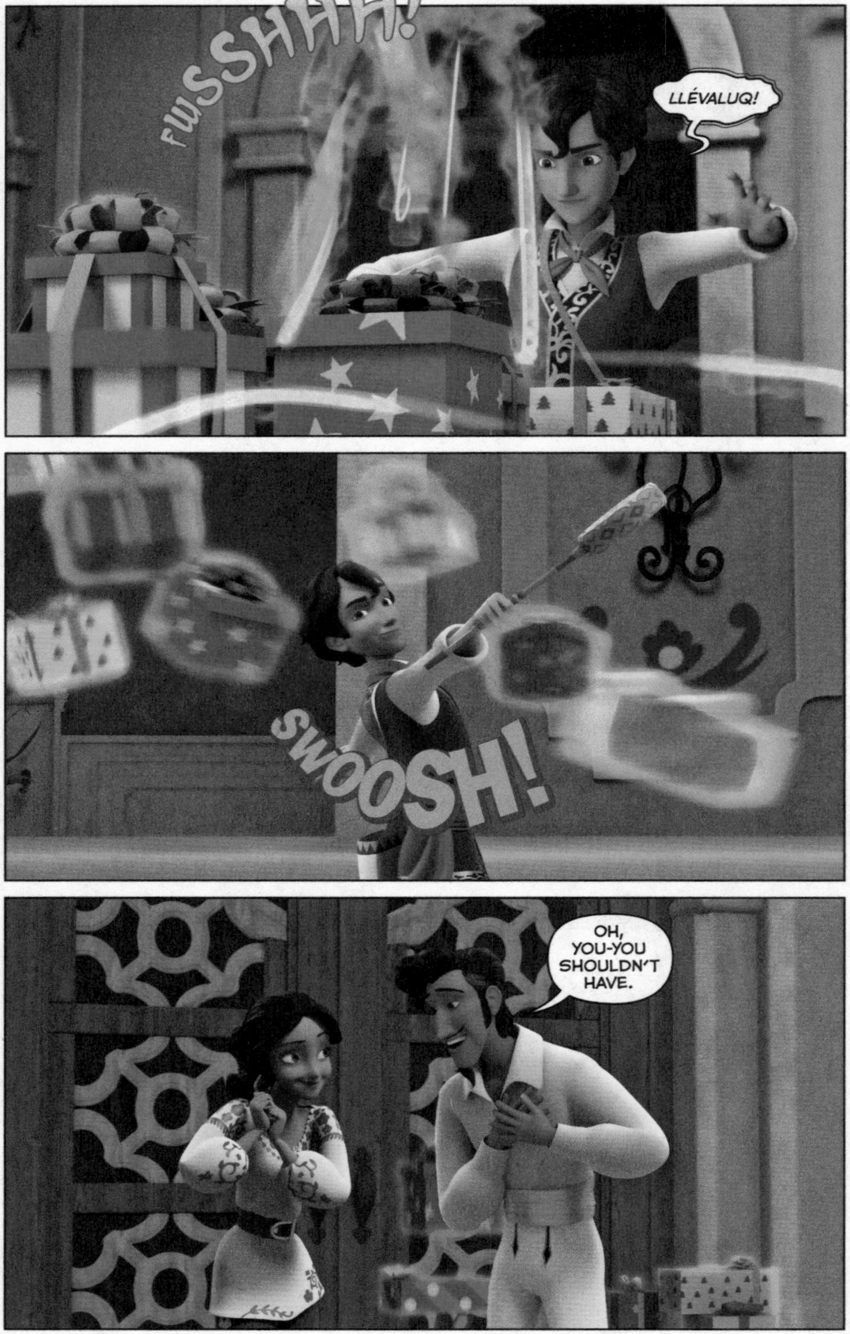
FWSSHHH!
LLÉVALUQ!
SWOOSH!
OH, YOU-YOU SHOULDN'T HAVE.

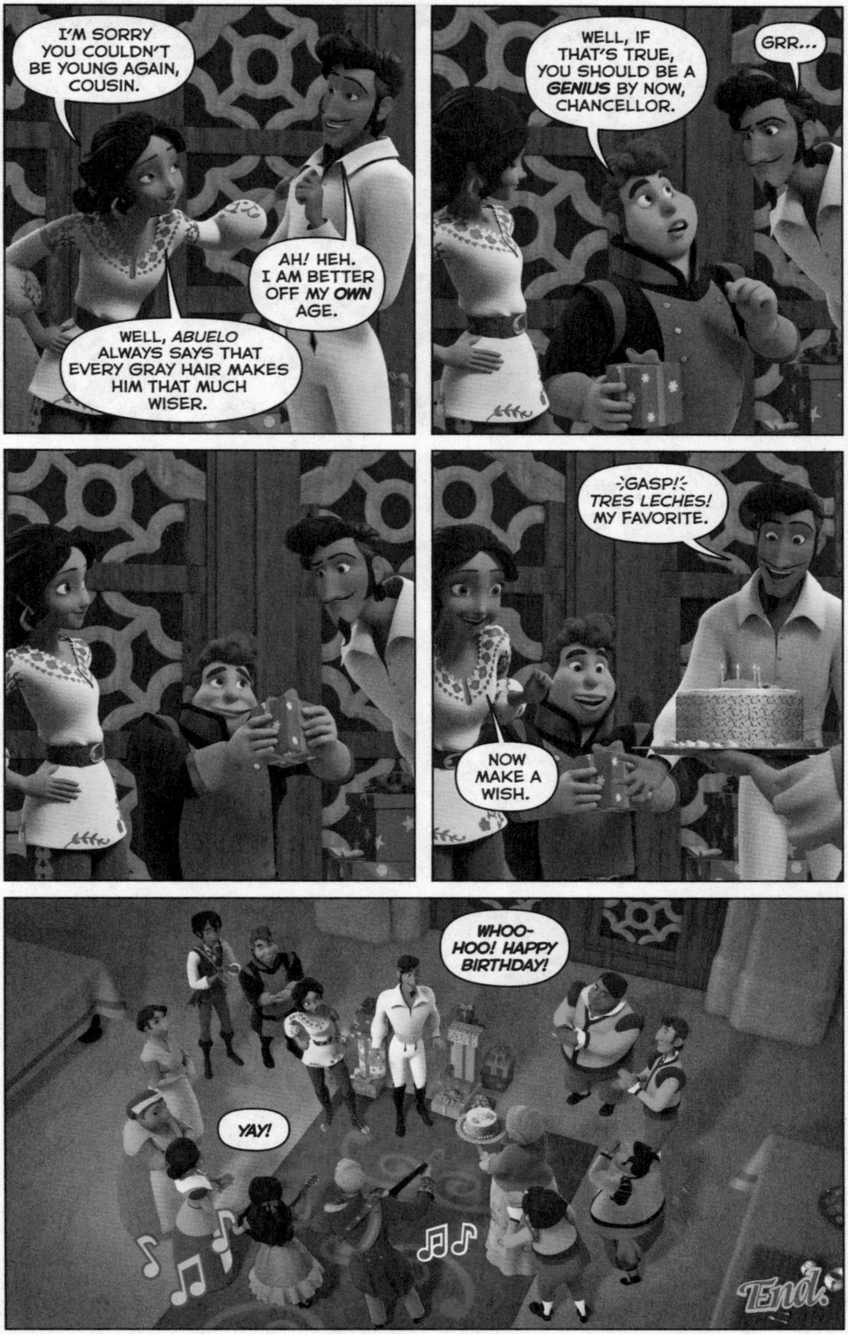
I'M SORRY YOU COULDN'T BE YOUNG AGAIN, COUSIN.
AH! HEH. I AM BETTER OFF MY *OWN* AGE.
WELL, *ABUELO* ALWAYS SAYS THAT EVERY GRAY HAIR MAKES HIM THAT MUCH WISER.
WELL, IF THAT'S TRUE, YOU SHOULD BE A ***GENIUS*** BY NOW, CHANCELLOR.
GRR...
GASP! *TRES LECHES!* MY FAVORITE.
NOW MAKE A WISH.
WHOO-HOO! HAPPY BIRTHDAY!
YAY!
End.

Spellbound

MOZE-- MORT--O--LOZ. UGH, COME ON, MATEO, GET IT RIGHT.

HEY, MR. ALMOST-THE-ROYAL WIZARD.

YAHHH!

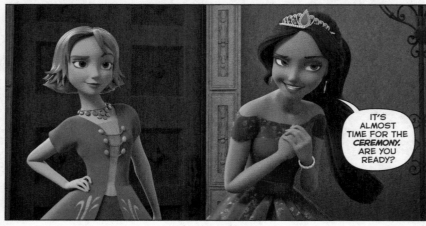

IT'S ALMOST TIME FOR THE *CEREMONY.* ARE YOU READY?

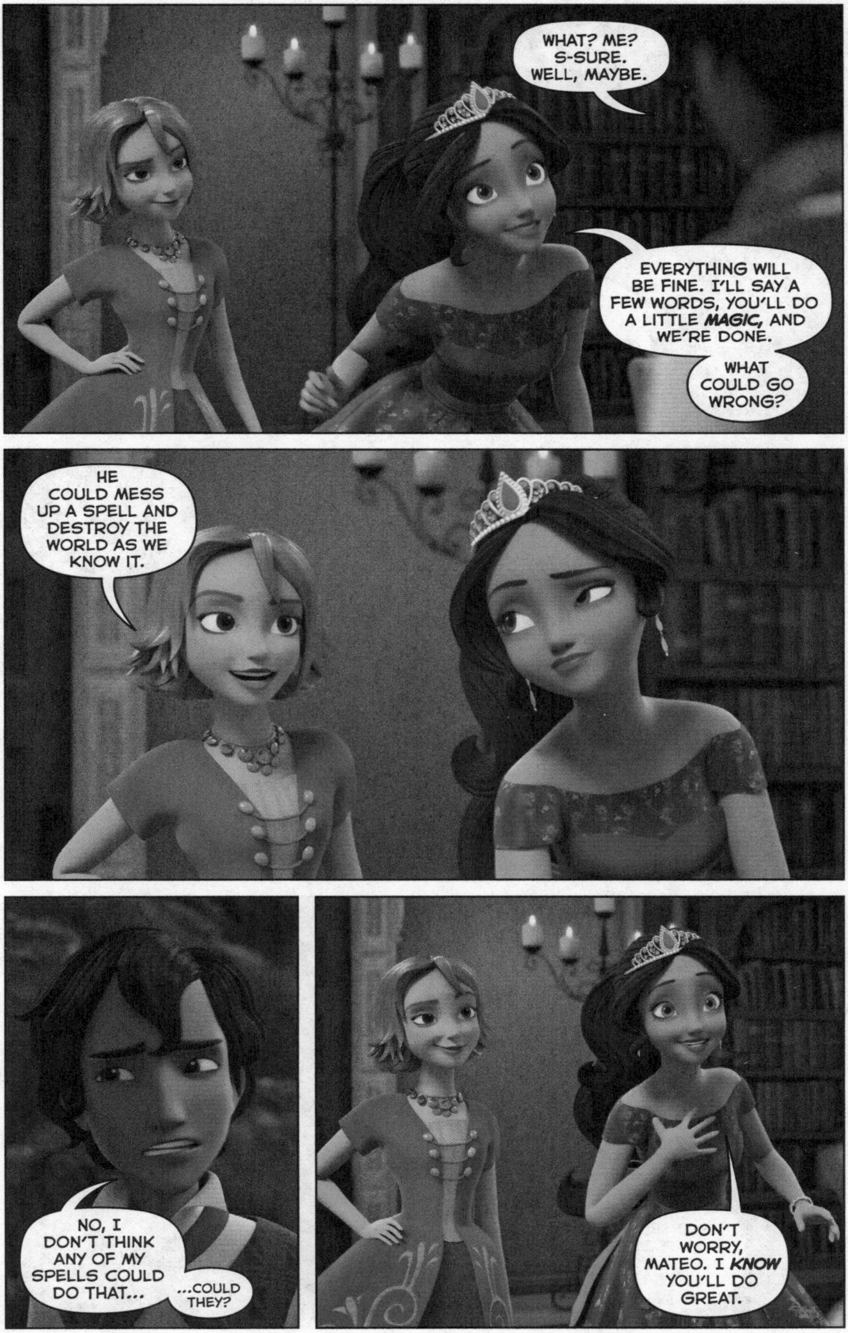
WHAT? ME? S-SURE. WELL, MAYBE.
EVERYTHING WILL BE FINE. I'LL SAY A FEW WORDS, YOU'LL DO A LITTLE *MAGIC,* AND WE'RE DONE.
WHAT COULD GO WRONG?
HE COULD MESS UP A SPELL AND DESTROY THE WORLD AS WE KNOW IT.
NO, I DON'T THINK ANY OF MY SPELLS COULD DO THAT...
...COULD THEY?
DON'T WORRY, MATEO. I *KNOW* YOU'LL DO GREAT.

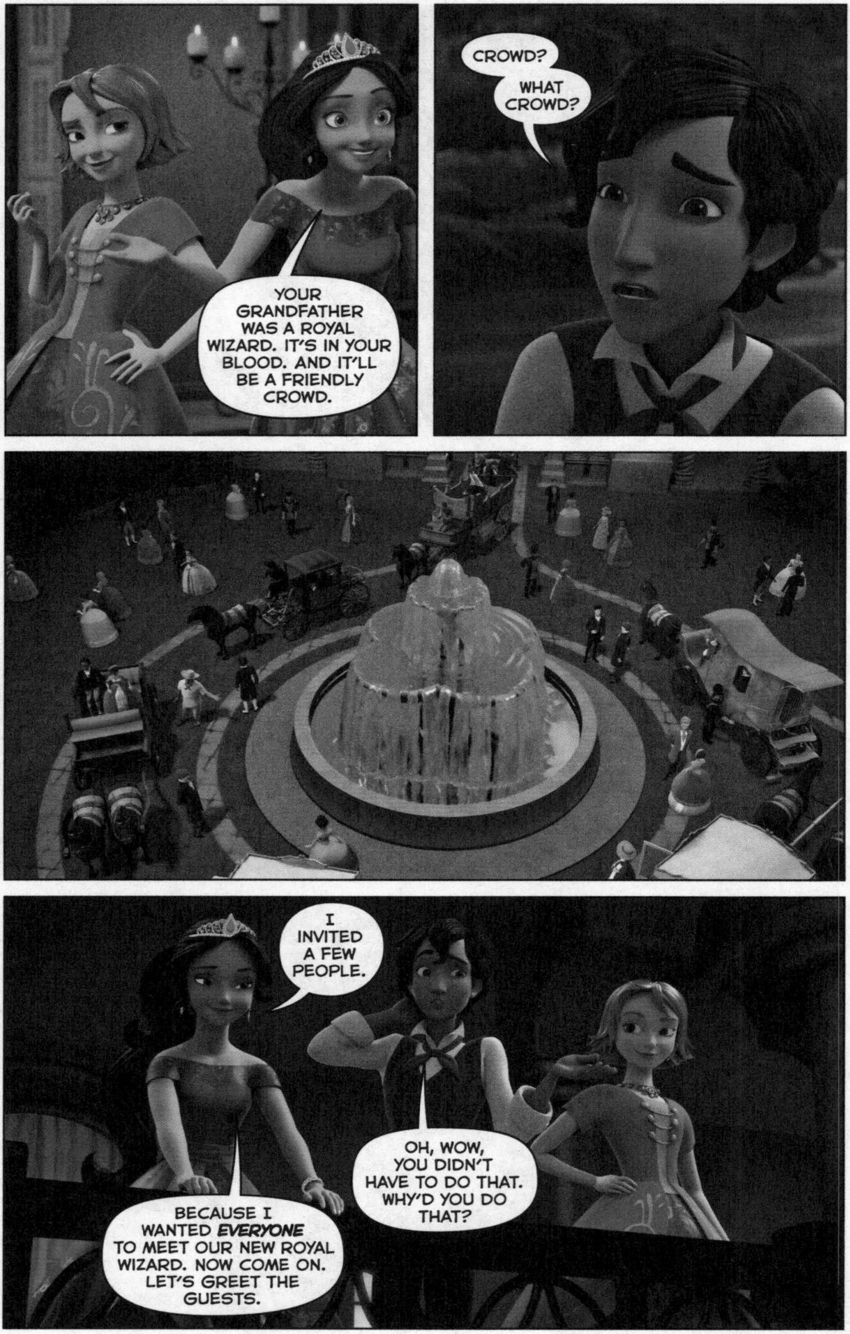
YOUR GRANDFATHER WAS A ROYAL WIZARD. IT'S IN YOUR BLOOD. AND IT'LL BE A FRIENDLY CROWD.
CROWD?
WHAT CROWD?
I INVITED A FEW PEOPLE.
OH, WOW, YOU DIDN'T HAVE TO DO THAT. WHY'D YOU DO THAT?
BECAUSE I WANTED *EVERYONE* TO MEET OUR NEW ROYAL WIZARD. NOW COME ON. LET'S GREET THE GUESTS.

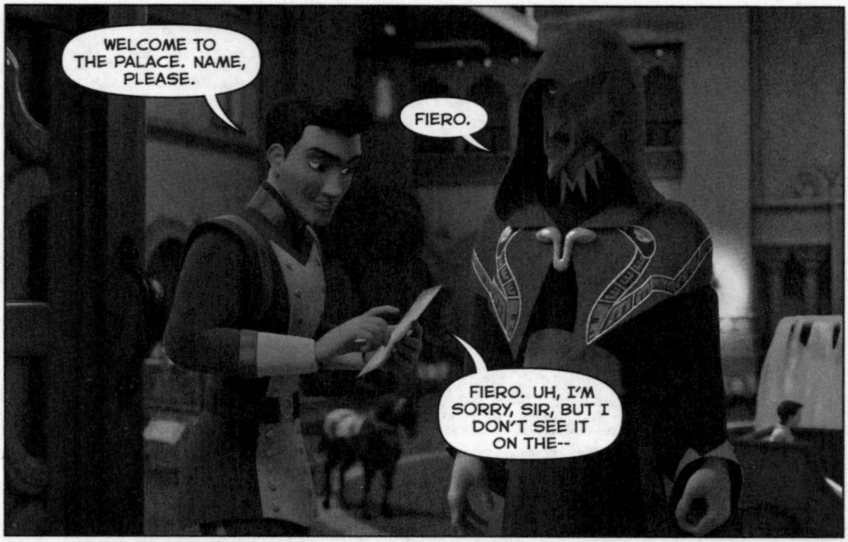
WELCOME TO THE PALACE. NAME, PLEASE.
FIERO.
FIERO. UH, I'M SORRY, SIR, BUT I DON'T SEE IT ON THE--

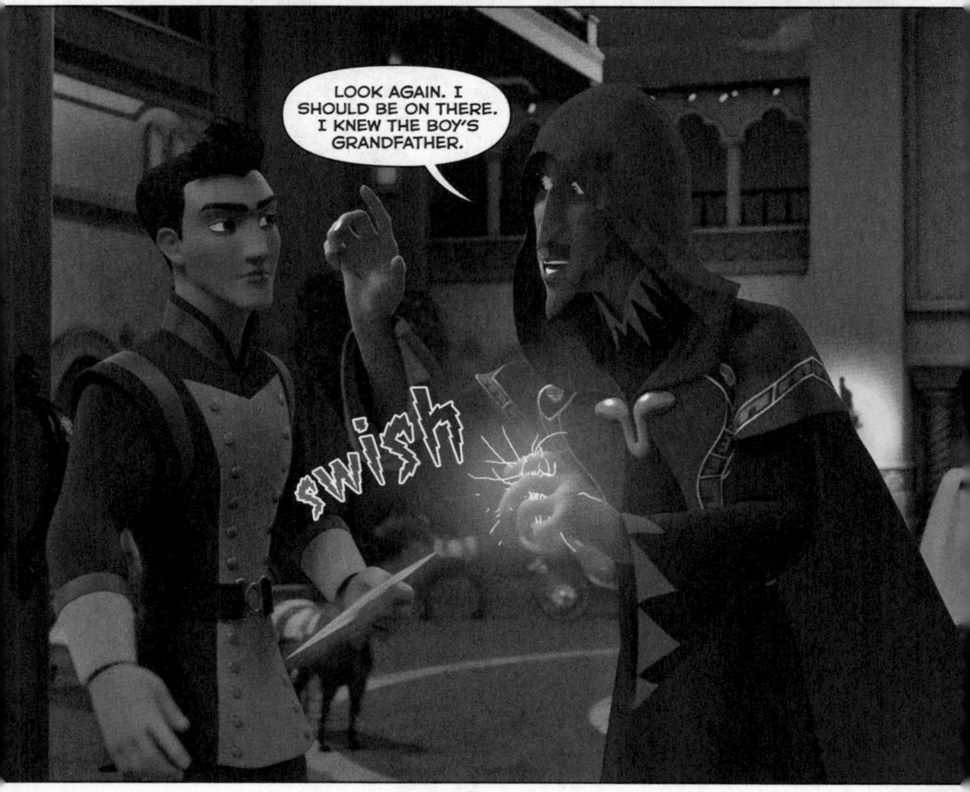
LOOK AGAIN. I SHOULD BE ON THERE. I KNEW THE BOY'S GRANDFATHER.
swish

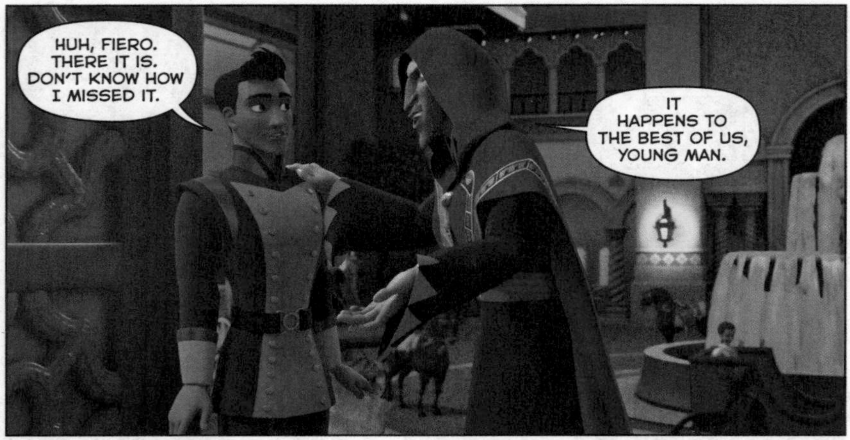
HUH, FIERO. THERE IT IS. DON'T KNOW HOW I MISSED IT.
IT HAPPENS TO THE BEST OF US, YOUNG MAN.

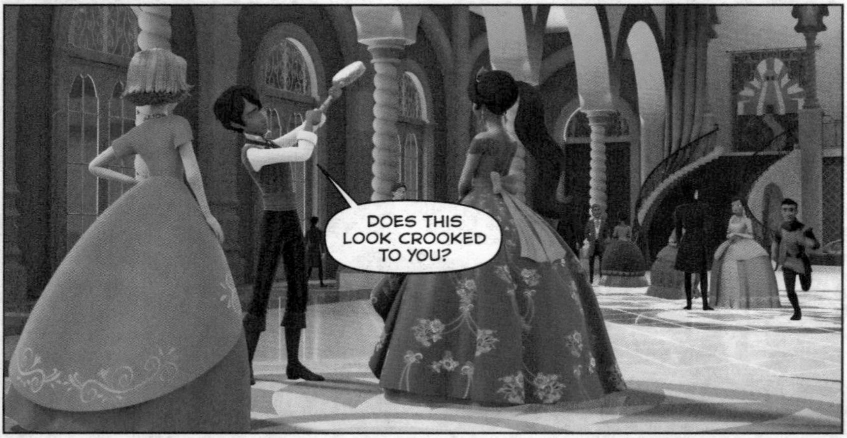
DOES THIS LOOK CROOKED TO YOU?

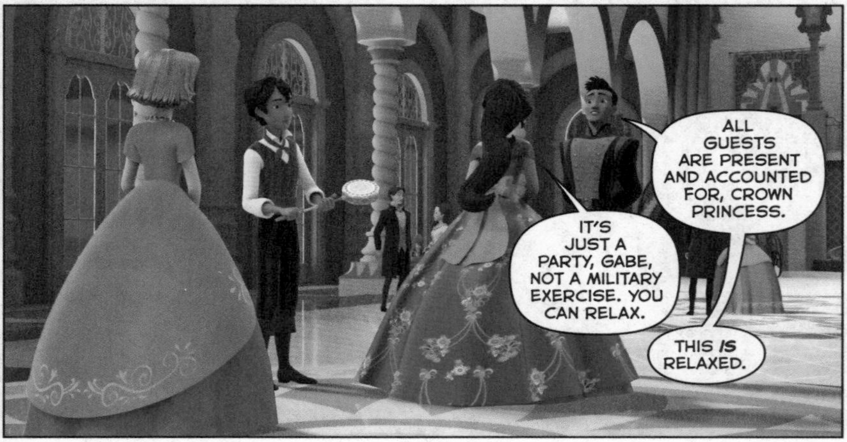
ALL GUESTS ARE PRESENT AND ACCOUNTED FOR, CROWN PRINCESS.
IT'S JUST A PARTY, GABE, NOT A MILITARY EXERCISE. YOU CAN RELAX.
THIS *IS* RELAXED.

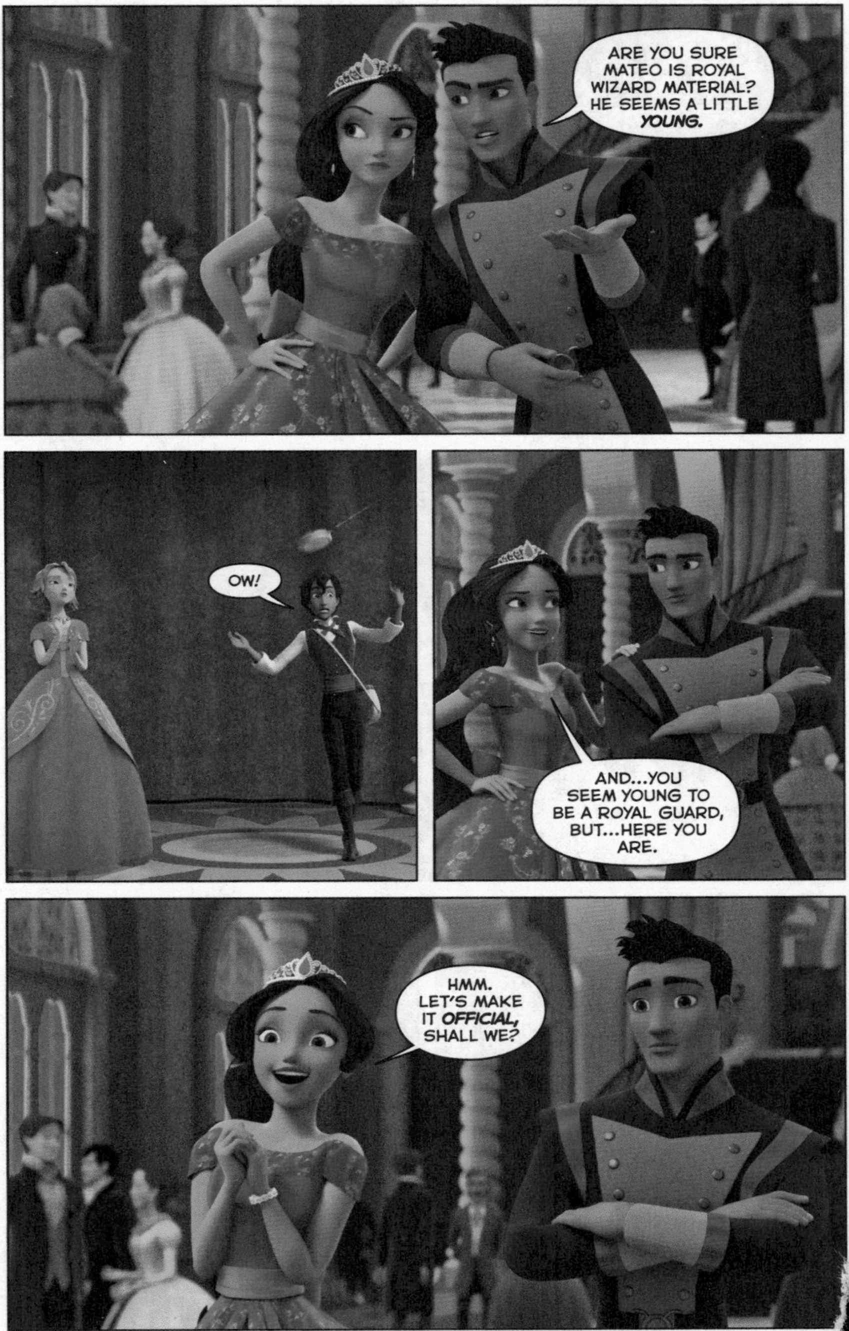
ARE YOU SURE MATEO IS ROYAL WIZARD MATERIAL? HE SEEMS A LITTLE *YOUNG.*
OW!
AND...YOU SEEM YOUNG TO BE A ROYAL GUARD, BUT...HERE YOU ARE.
HMM. LET'S MAKE IT *OFFICIAL,* SHALL WE?

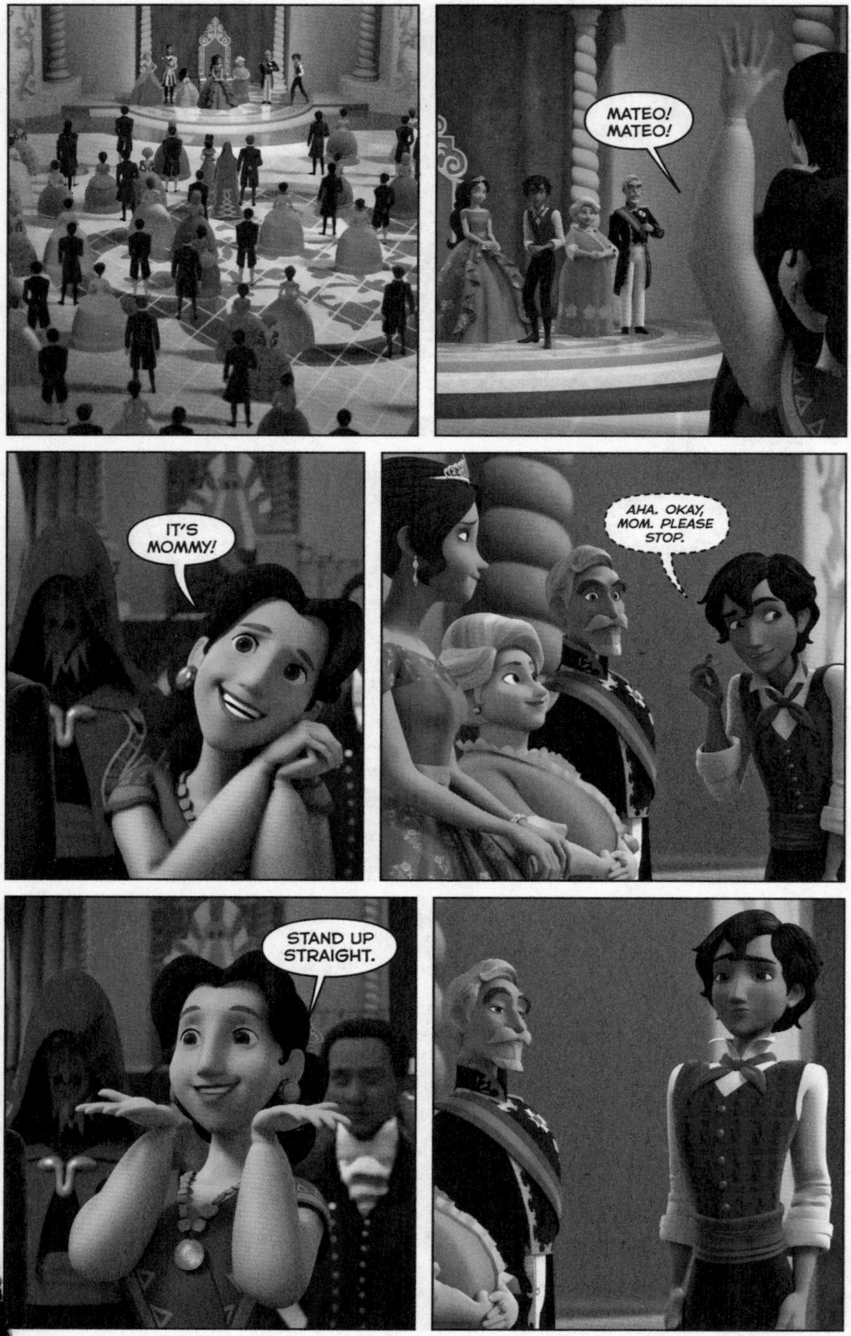
MATEO! MATEO!
IT'S MOMMY!
AHA. OKAY, MOM. PLEASE STOP.
STAND UP STRAIGHT.

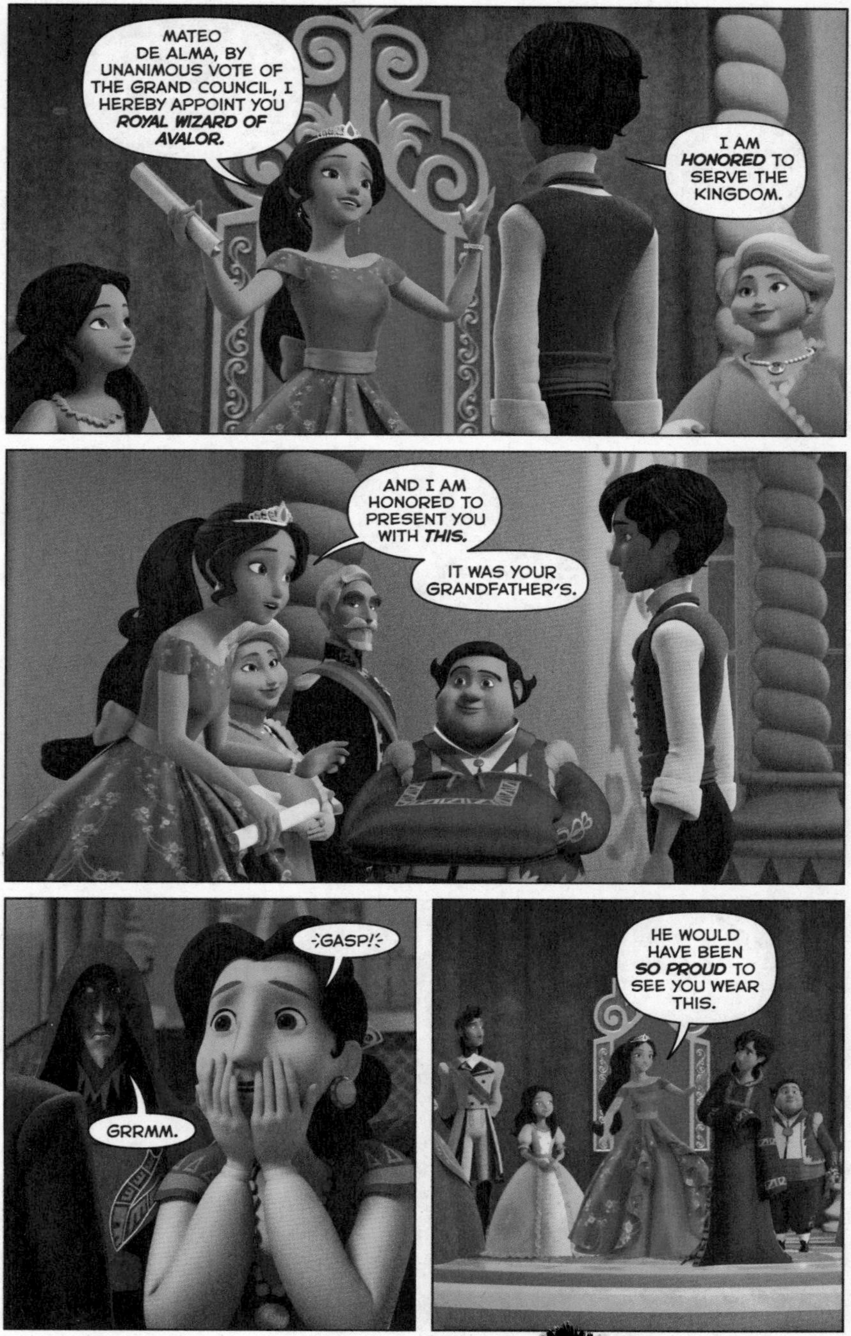
MATEO DE ALMA, BY UNANIMOUS VOTE OF THE GRAND COUNCIL, I HEREBY APPOINT YOU ***ROYAL WIZARD OF AVALOR.***
I AM ***HONORED*** TO SERVE THE KINGDOM.
AND I AM HONORED TO PRESENT YOU WITH ***THIS.***
IT WAS YOUR GRANDFATHER'S.
GASP!
GRRMM.
HE WOULD HAVE BEEN ***SO PROUD*** TO SEE YOU WEAR THIS.

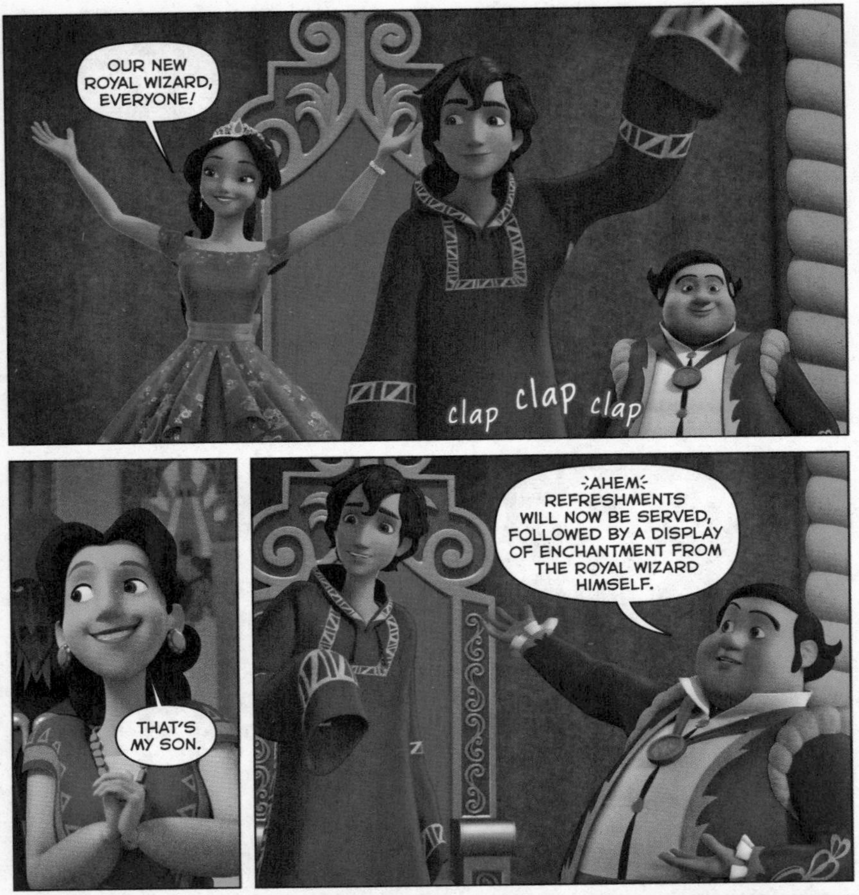
OUR NEW ROYAL WIZARD, EVERYONE!
clap clap clap
THAT'S MY SON.
AHEM REFRESHMENTS WILL NOW BE SERVED, FOLLOWED BY A DISPLAY OF ENCHANTMENT FROM THE ROYAL WIZARD HIMSELF.
EH-HEH-HEH. FOLLOWED BY AN EVEN *BIGGER* SURPRISE.

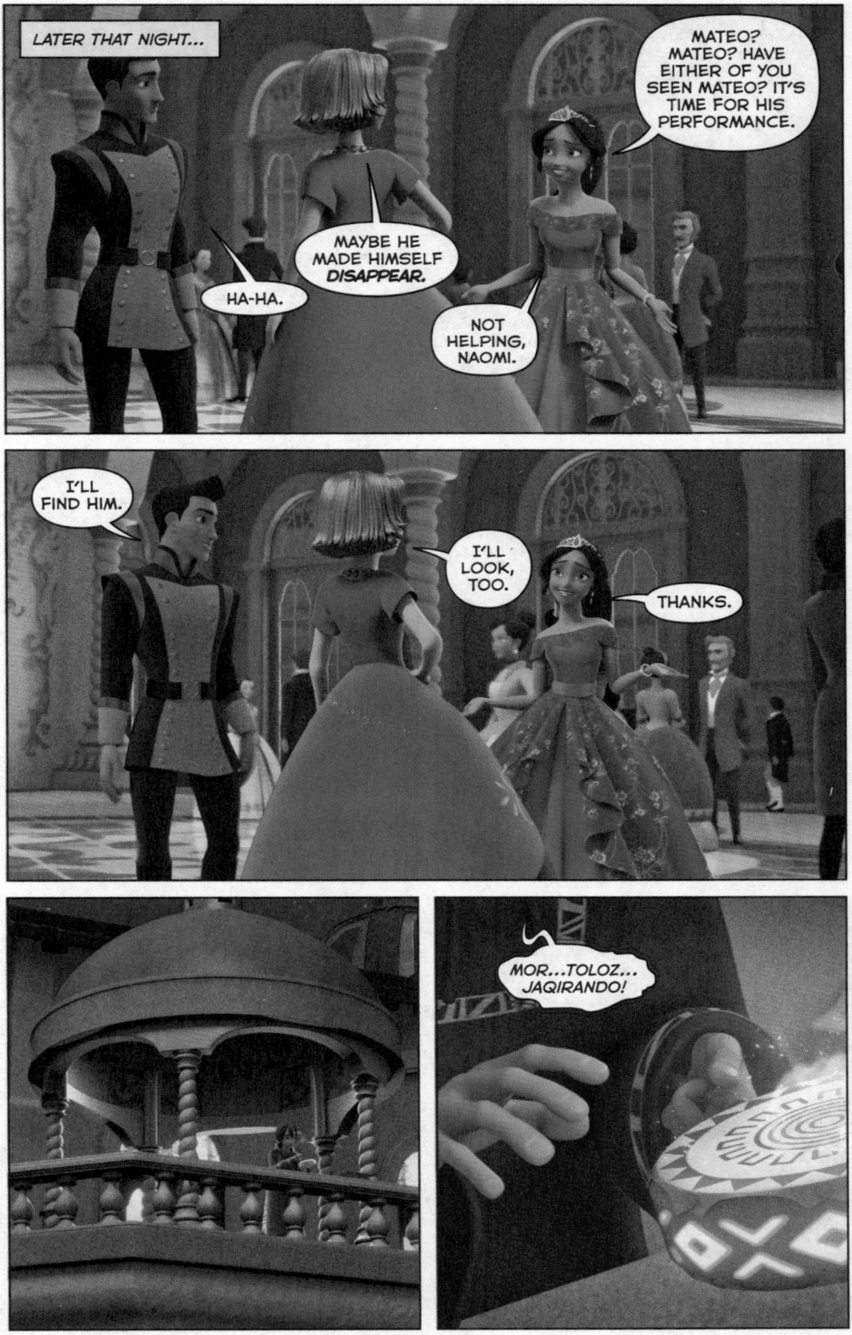
LATER THAT NIGHT...
MATEO? MATEO? HAVE EITHER OF YOU SEEN MATEO? IT'S TIME FOR HIS PERFORMANCE.
MAYBE HE MADE HIMSELF ***DISAPPEAR.***
HA-HA.
NOT HELPING, NAOMI.
I'LL FIND HIM.
I'LL LOOK, TOO.
THANKS.
MOR...TOLOZ... JAQIRANDO!

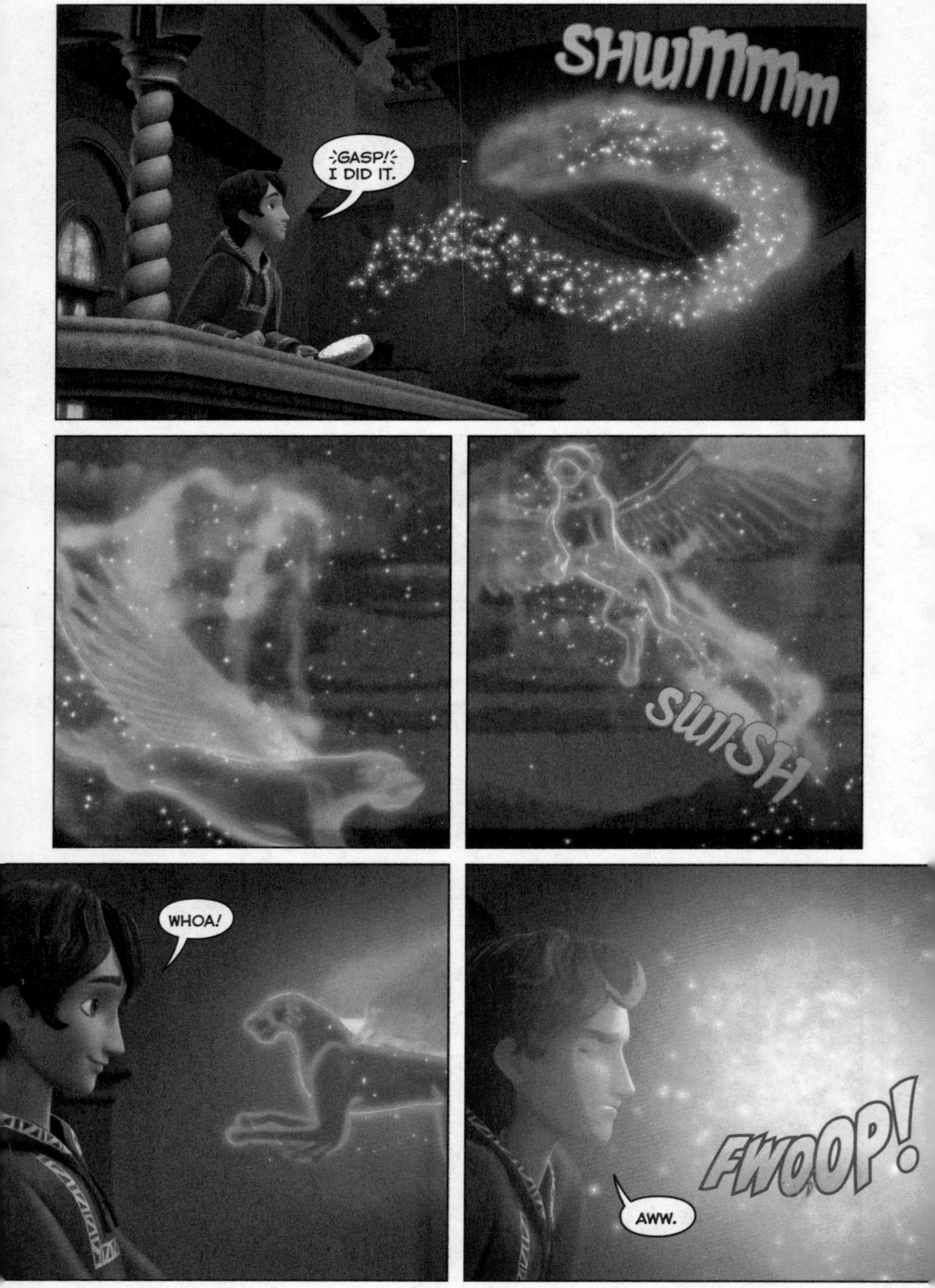

SHWMMM
GASP! I DID IT.
SWISH
WHOA!
FWOOP!
AWW.

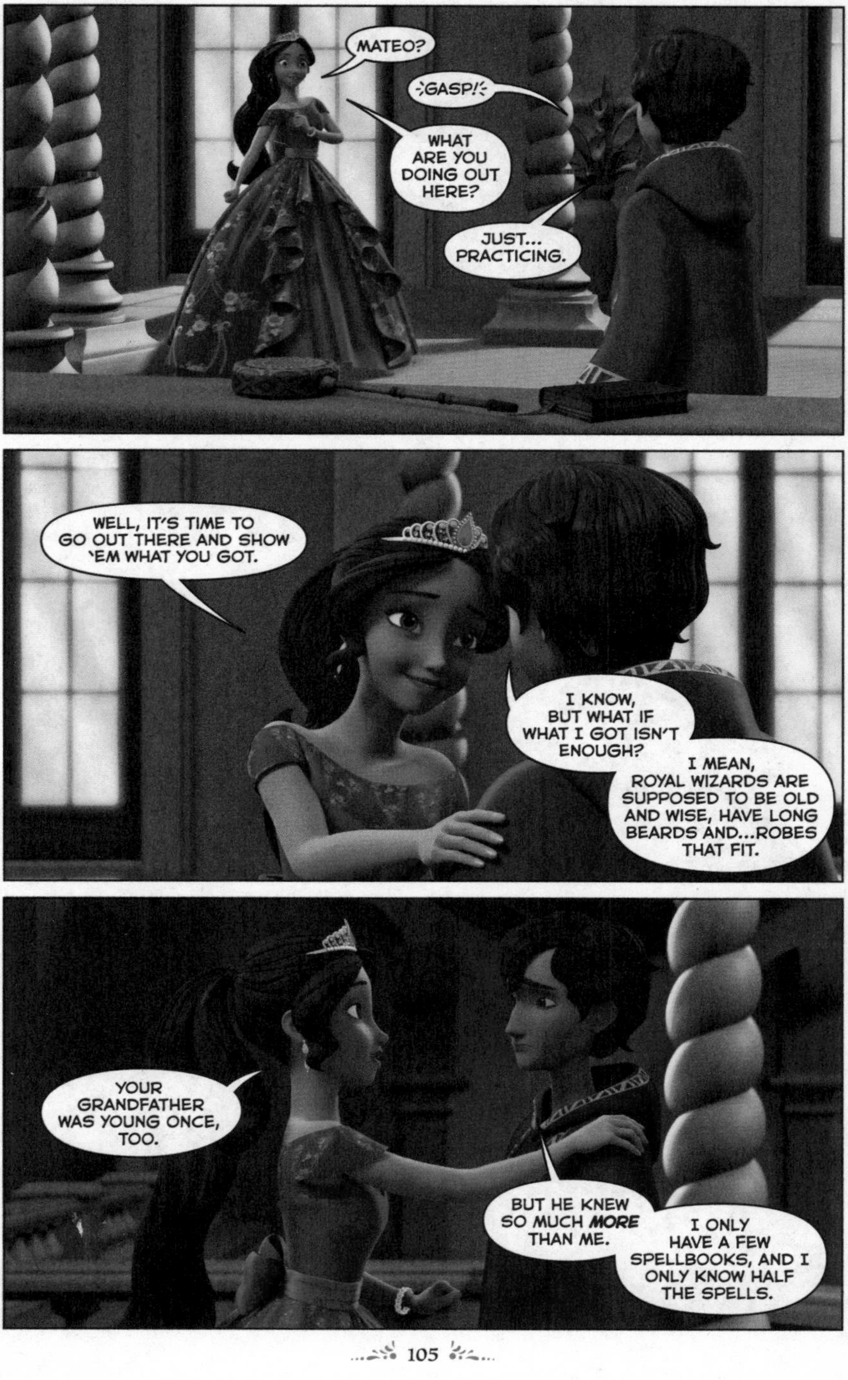
MATEO?
GASP!
WHAT ARE YOU DOING OUT HERE?
JUST... PRACTICING.
WELL, IT'S TIME TO GO OUT THERE AND SHOW 'EM WHAT YOU GOT.
I KNOW, BUT WHAT IF WHAT I GOT ISN'T ENOUGH?
I MEAN, ROYAL WIZARDS ARE SUPPOSED TO BE OLD AND WISE, HAVE LONG BEARDS AND...ROBES THAT FIT.
YOUR GRANDFATHER WAS YOUNG ONCE, TOO.
BUT HE KNEW SO MUCH *MORE* THAN ME.
I ONLY HAVE A FEW SPELLBOOKS, AND I ONLY KNOW HALF THE SPELLS.

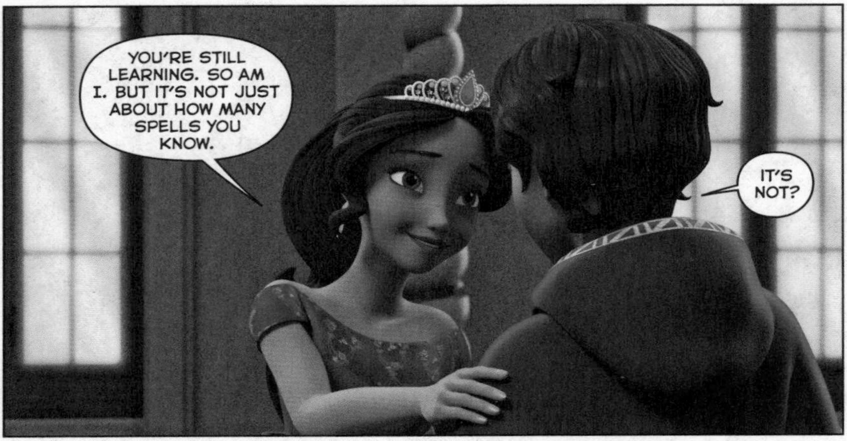
YOU'RE STILL LEARNING. SO AM I. BUT IT'S NOT JUST ABOUT HOW MANY SPELLS YOU KNOW.
IT'S NOT?

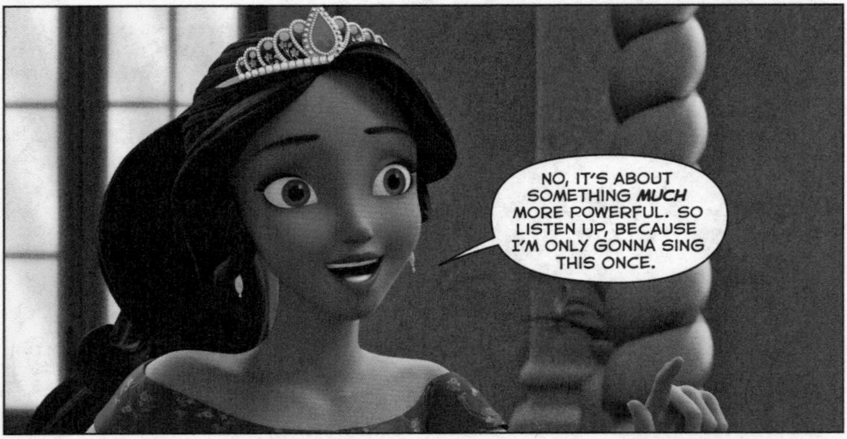
NO, IT'S ABOUT SOMETHING *MUCH* MORE POWERFUL. SO LISTEN UP, BECAUSE I'M ONLY GONNA SING THIS ONCE.

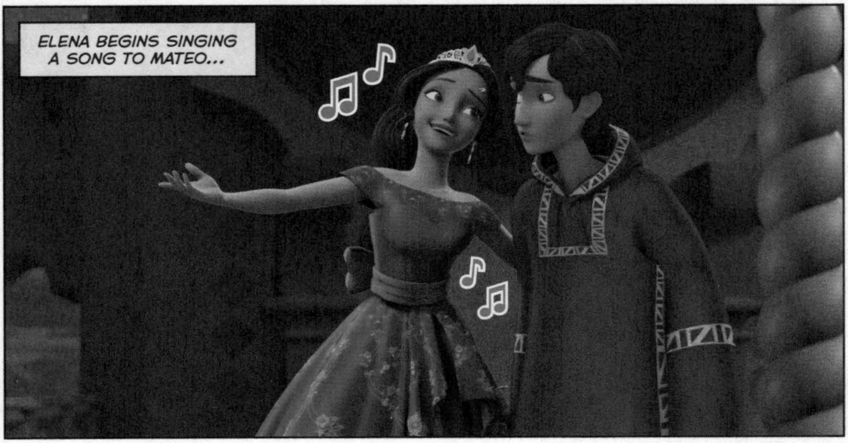
ELENA BEGINS SINGING A SONG TO MATEO...

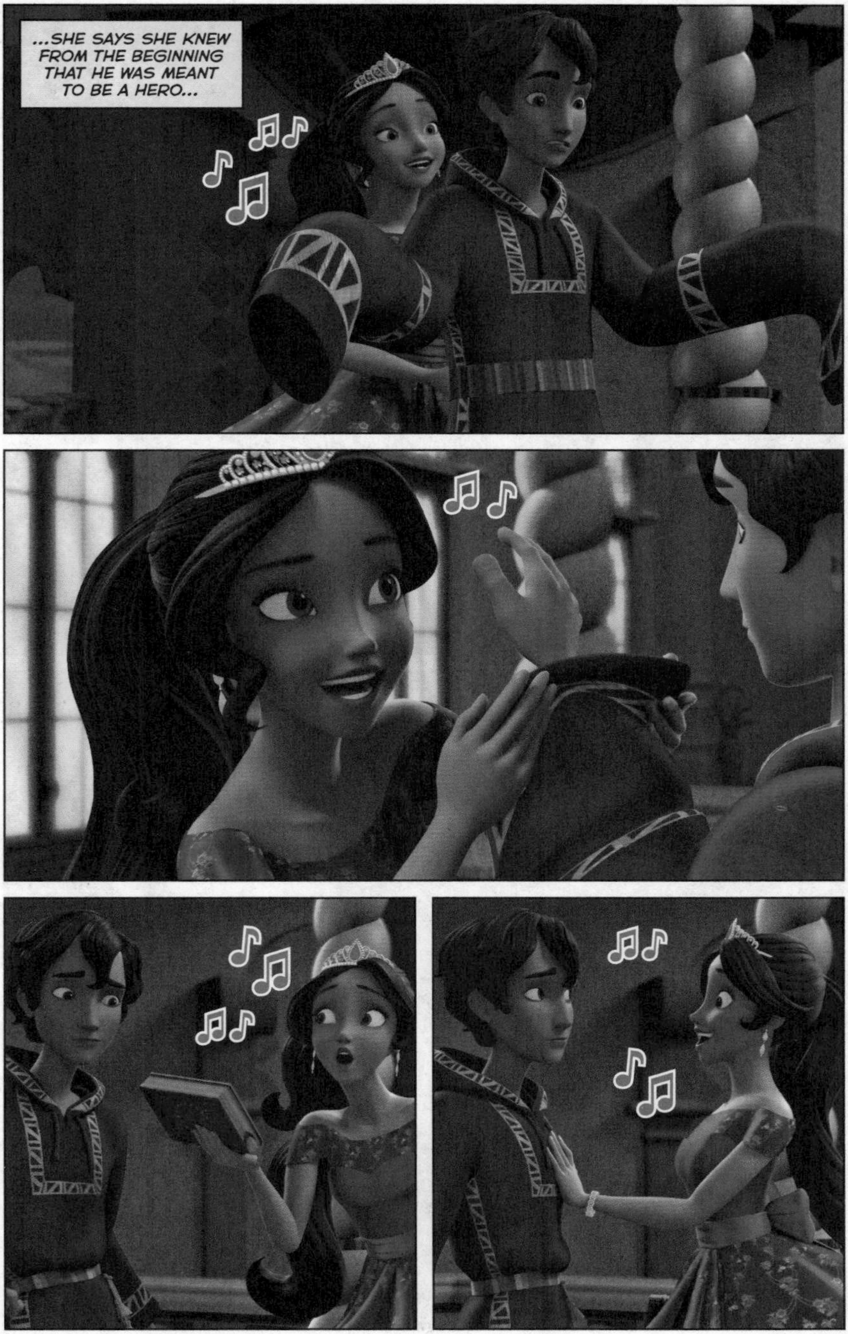
...SHE SAYS SHE KNEW FROM THE BEGINNING THAT HE WAS MEANT TO BE A HERO...

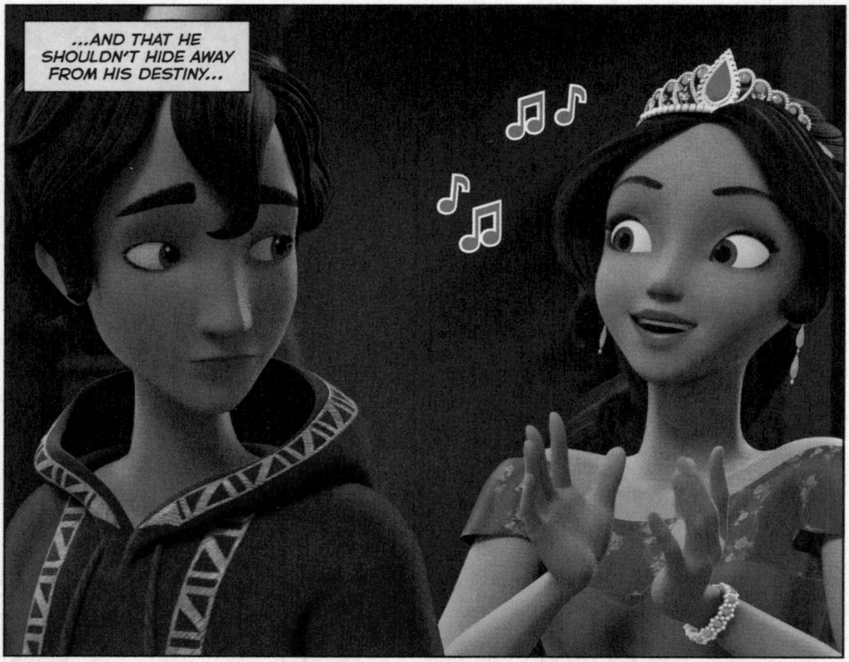
...AND THAT HE SHOULDN'T HIDE AWAY FROM HIS DESTINY...

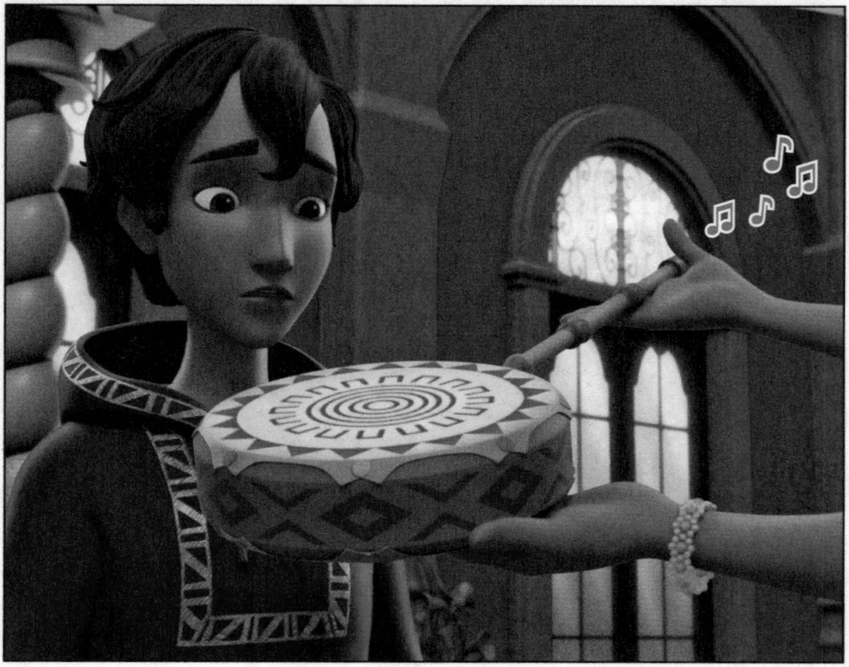

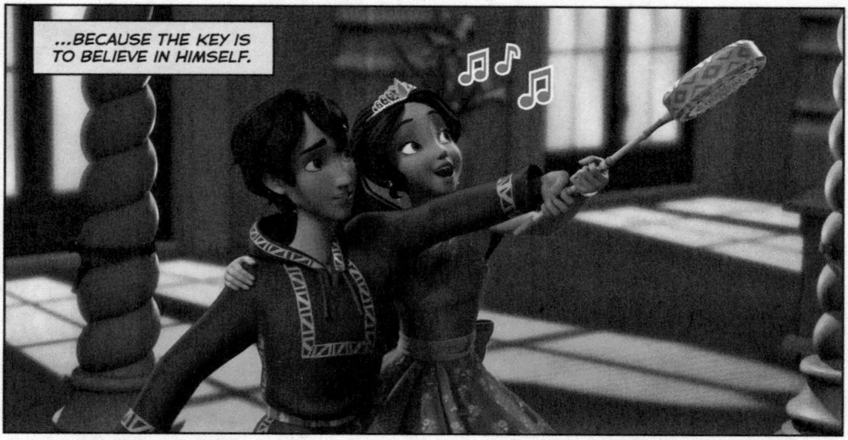
...BECAUSE THE KEY IS TO BELIEVE IN HIMSELF.

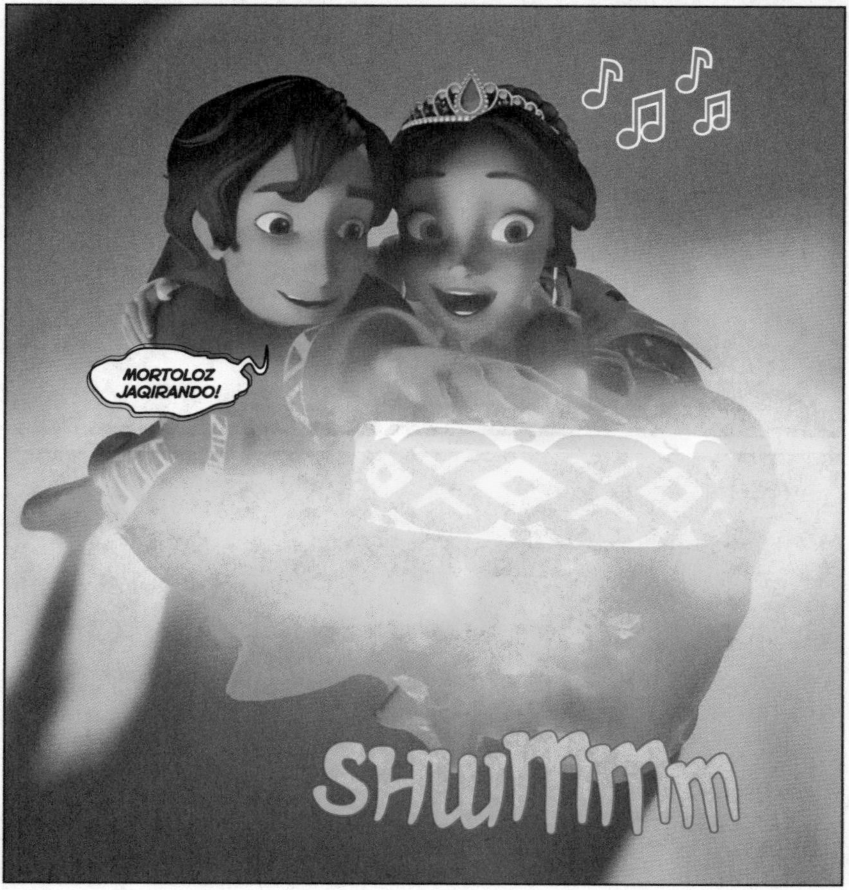
MORTOLOZ JAQIRANDO!
SHUMMM

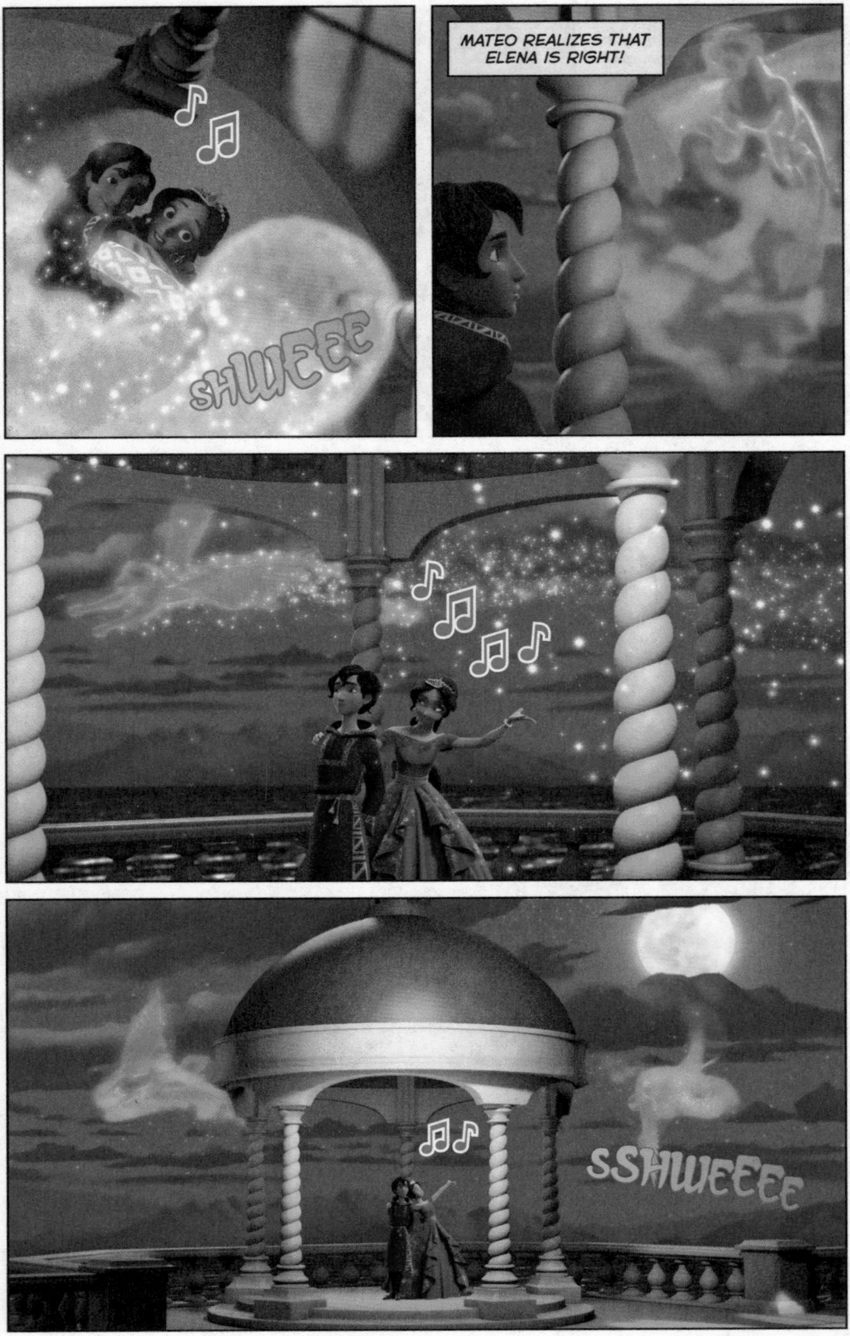
SHWEEE
MATEO REALIZES THAT
ELENA IS RIGHT!
SSHWEEEE

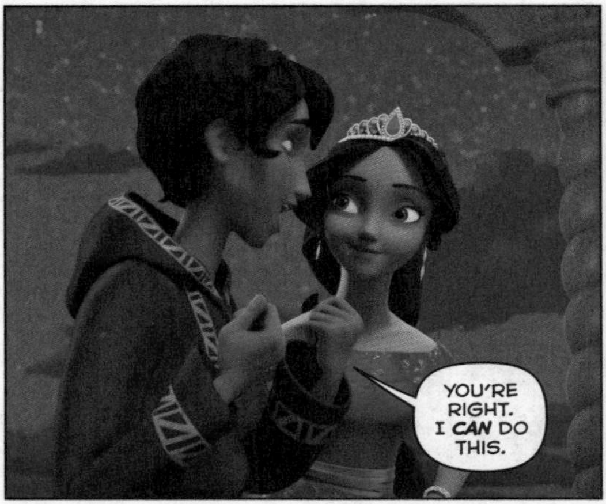
YOU'RE RIGHT. I **CAN** DO THIS.

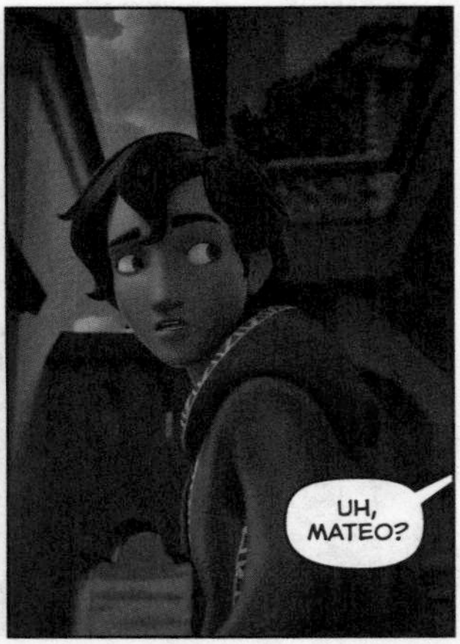
UH, MATEO?

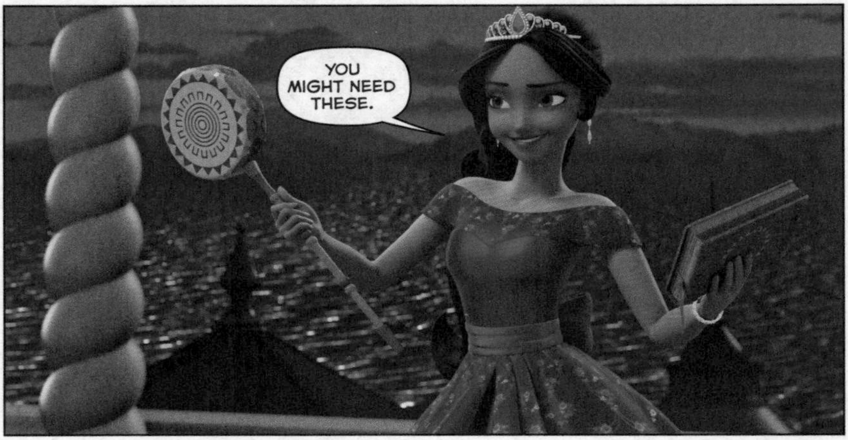
YOU MIGHT NEED THESE.

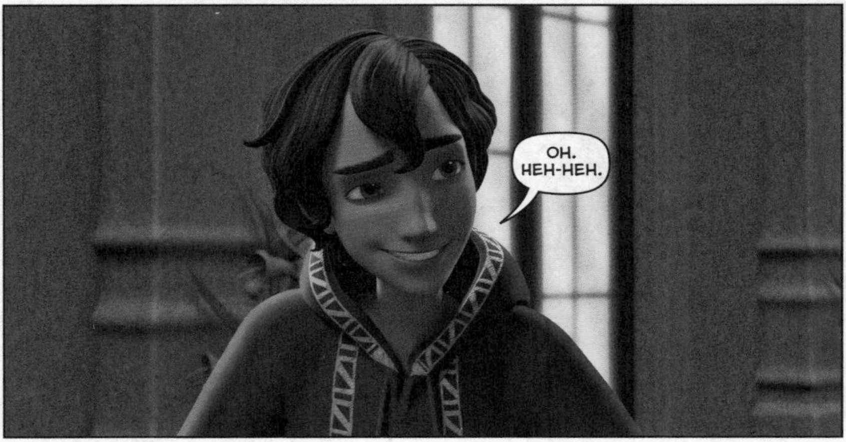
OH. HEH-HEH.

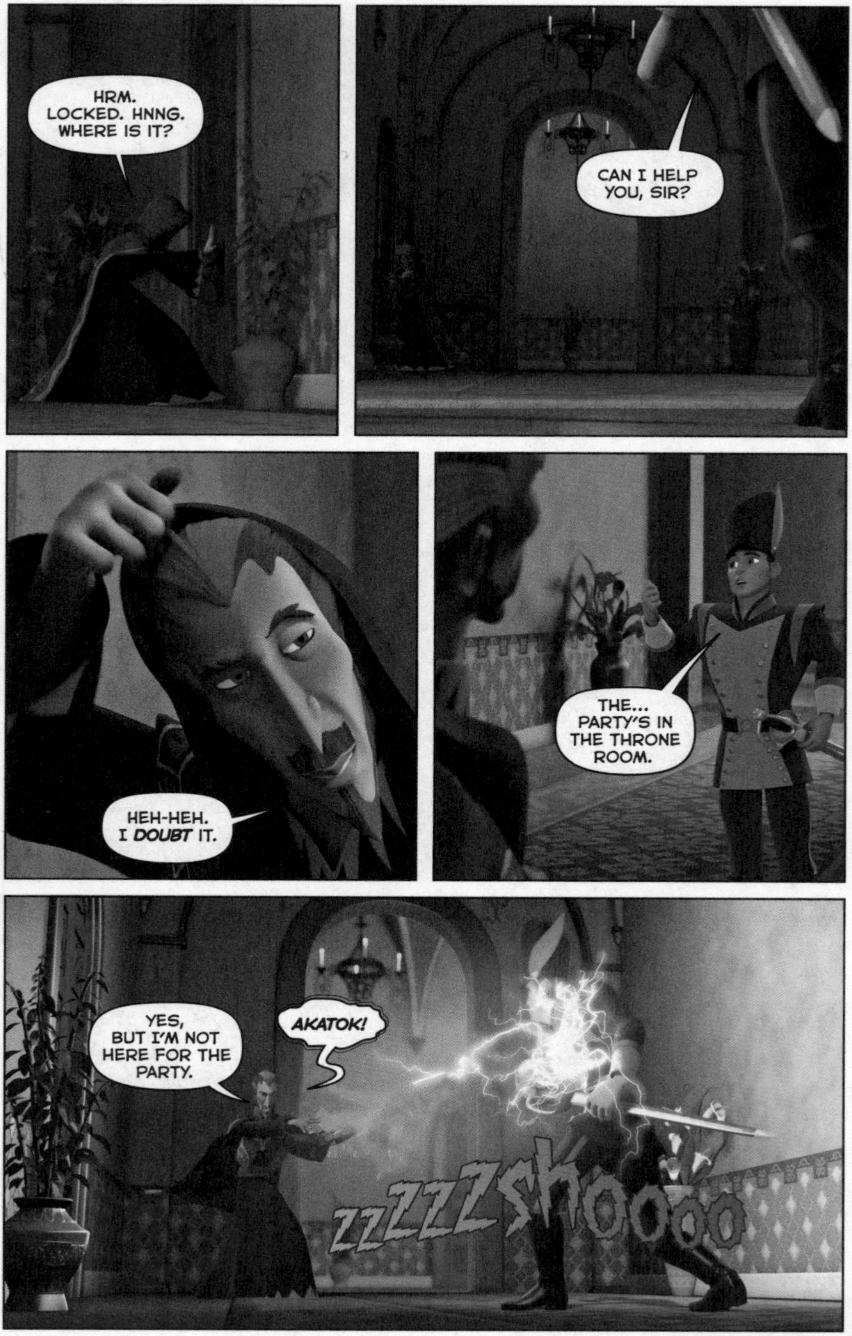
HRM. LOCKED. HNNG. WHERE IS IT?
CAN I HELP YOU, SIR?
HEH-HEH. I *DOUBT* IT.
THE... PARTY'S IN THE THRONE ROOM.
YES, BUT I'M NOT HERE FOR THE PARTY.
AKATOK!
ZZZZZSHOOOOO

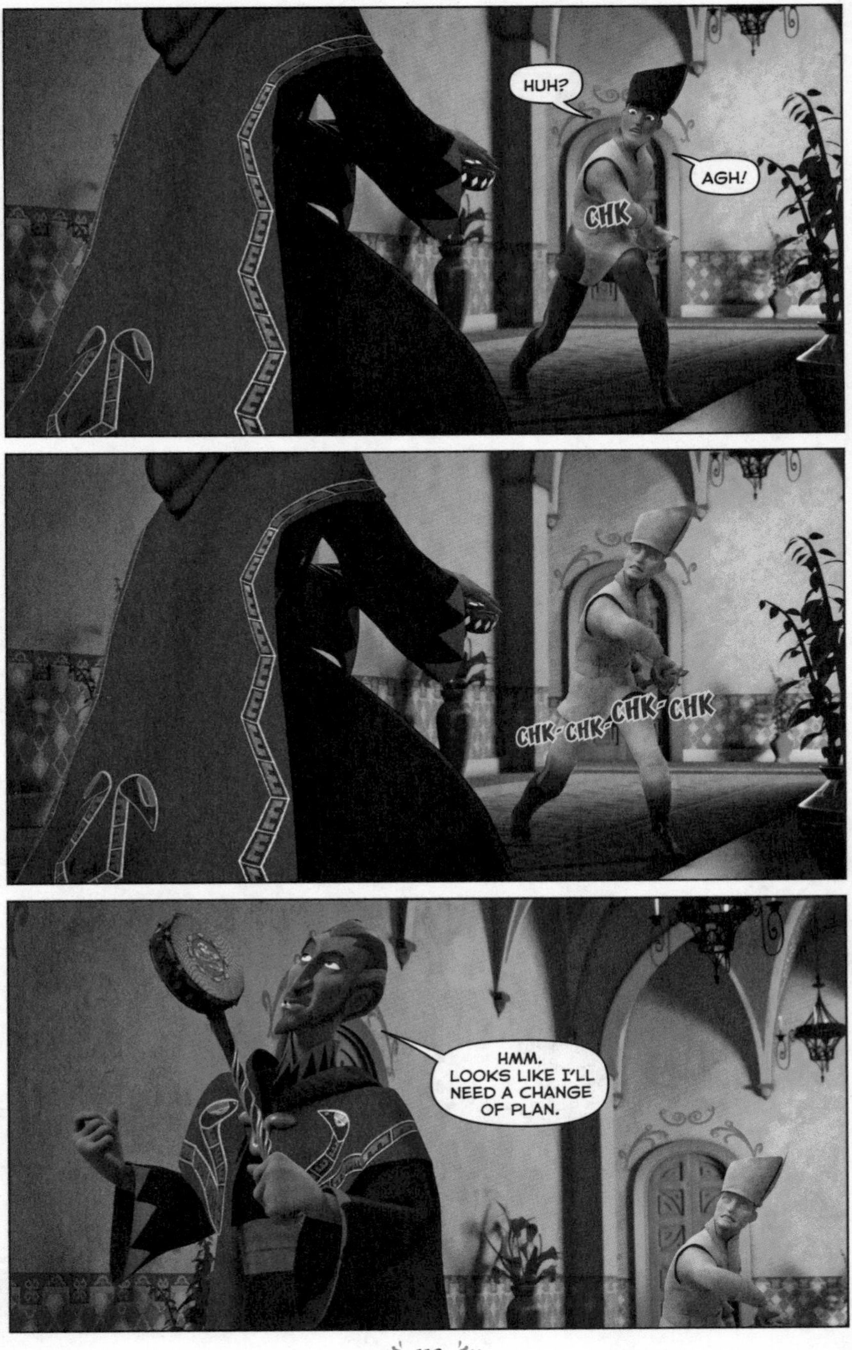
HUH?
AGH!
CHK
CHK-CHK-CHK-CHK
HMM. LOOKS LIKE I'LL NEED A CHANGE OF PLAN.

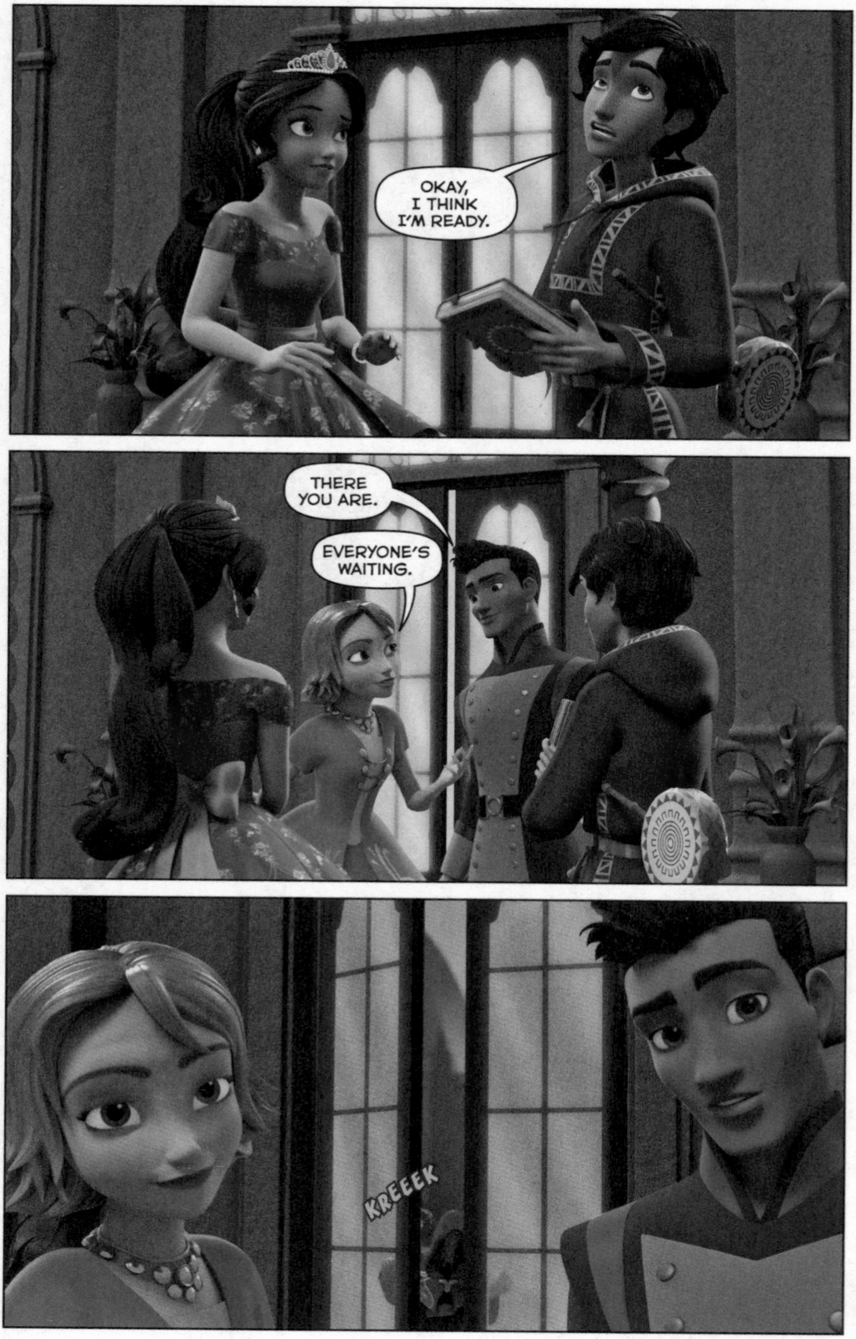
OKAY, I THINK I'M READY.
THERE YOU ARE.
EVERYONE'S WAITING.
KREEEK

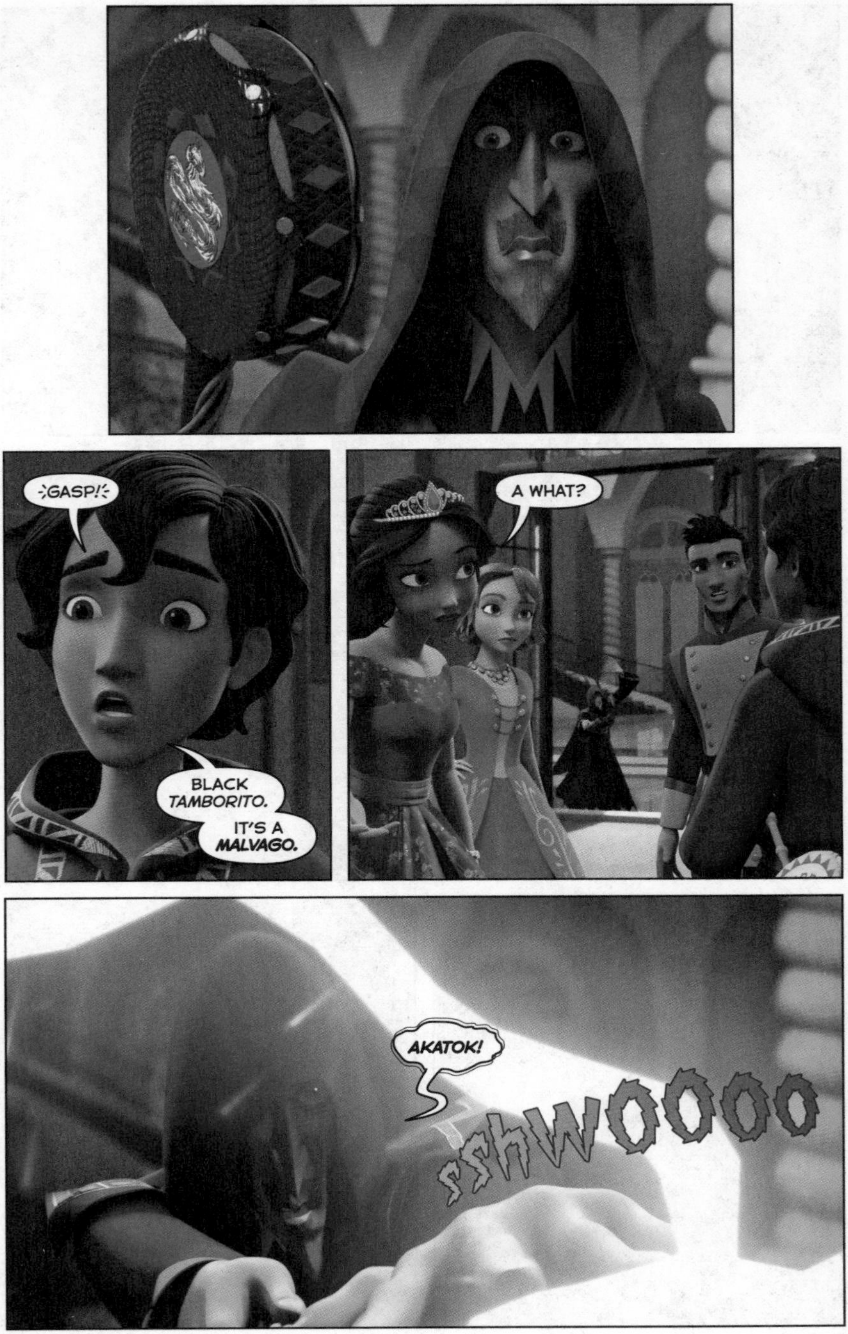

GASP!
BLACK TAMBORITO.
IT'S A *MALVAGO.*
A WHAT?
AKATOK!
SHWOOOO

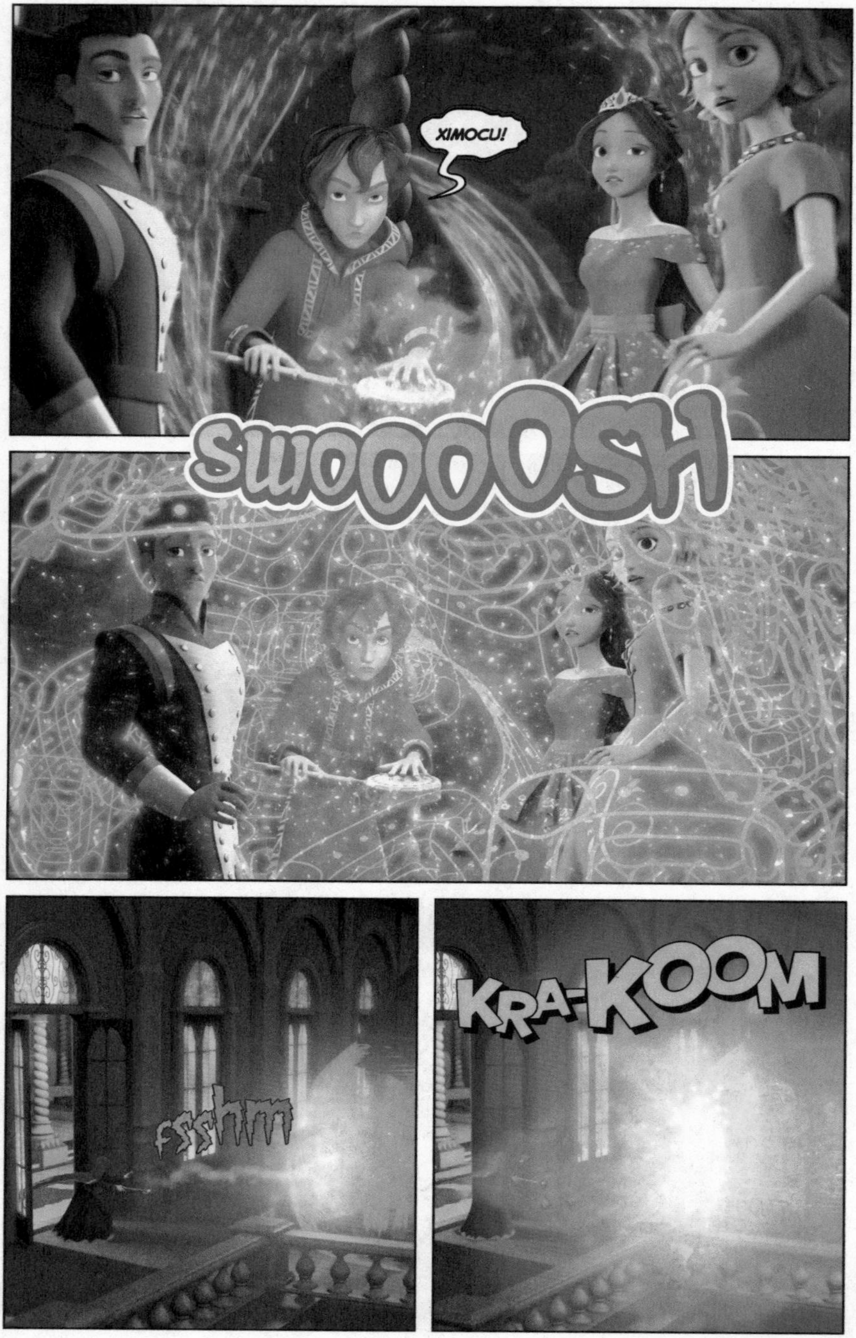
XIMOCU!
SWOOOOOSH
FSSHHH
KRA-KOOM

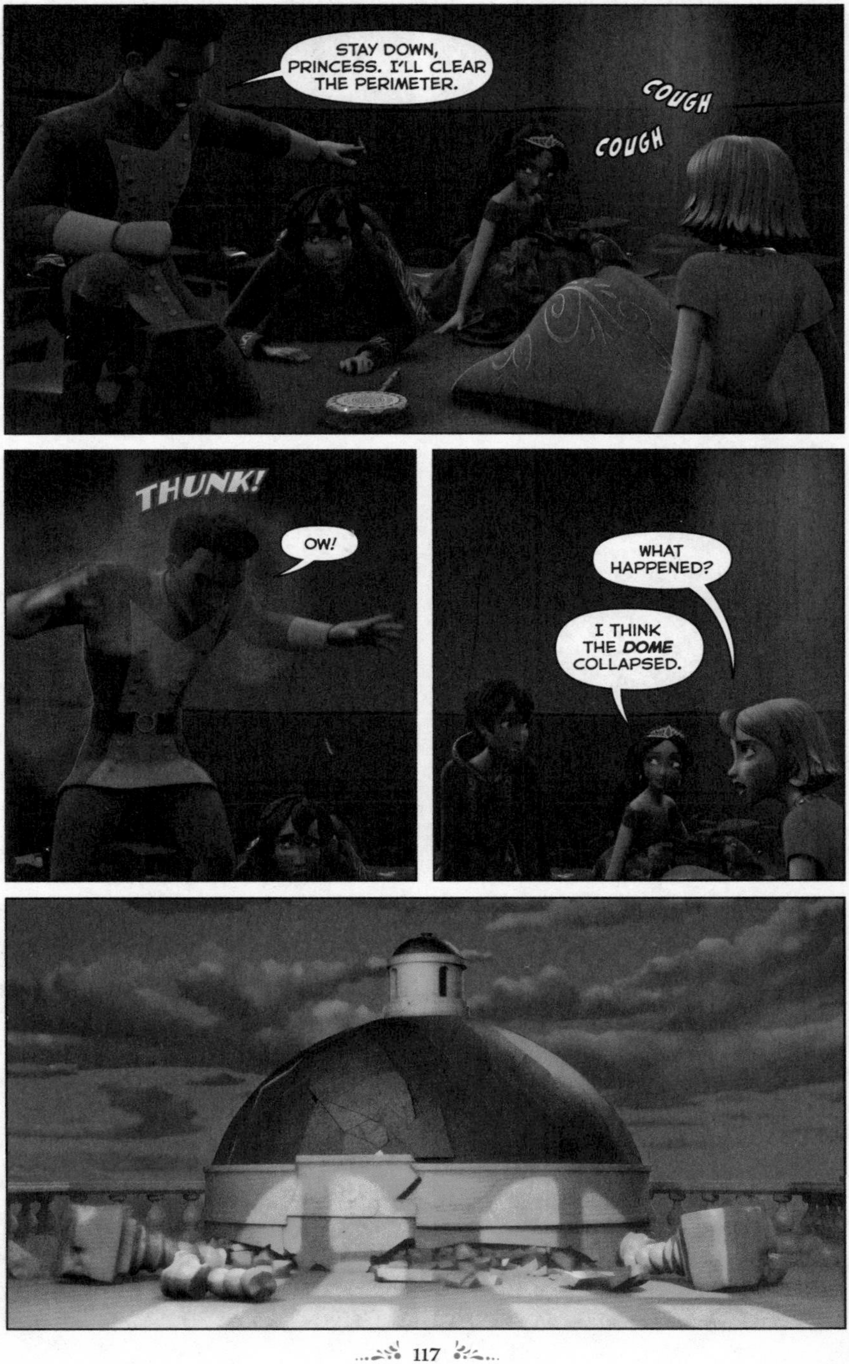
STAY DOWN, PRINCESS. I'LL CLEAR THE PERIMETER.
COUGH
COUGH
THUNK!
OW!
WHAT HAPPENED?
I THINK THE *DOME* COLLAPSED.

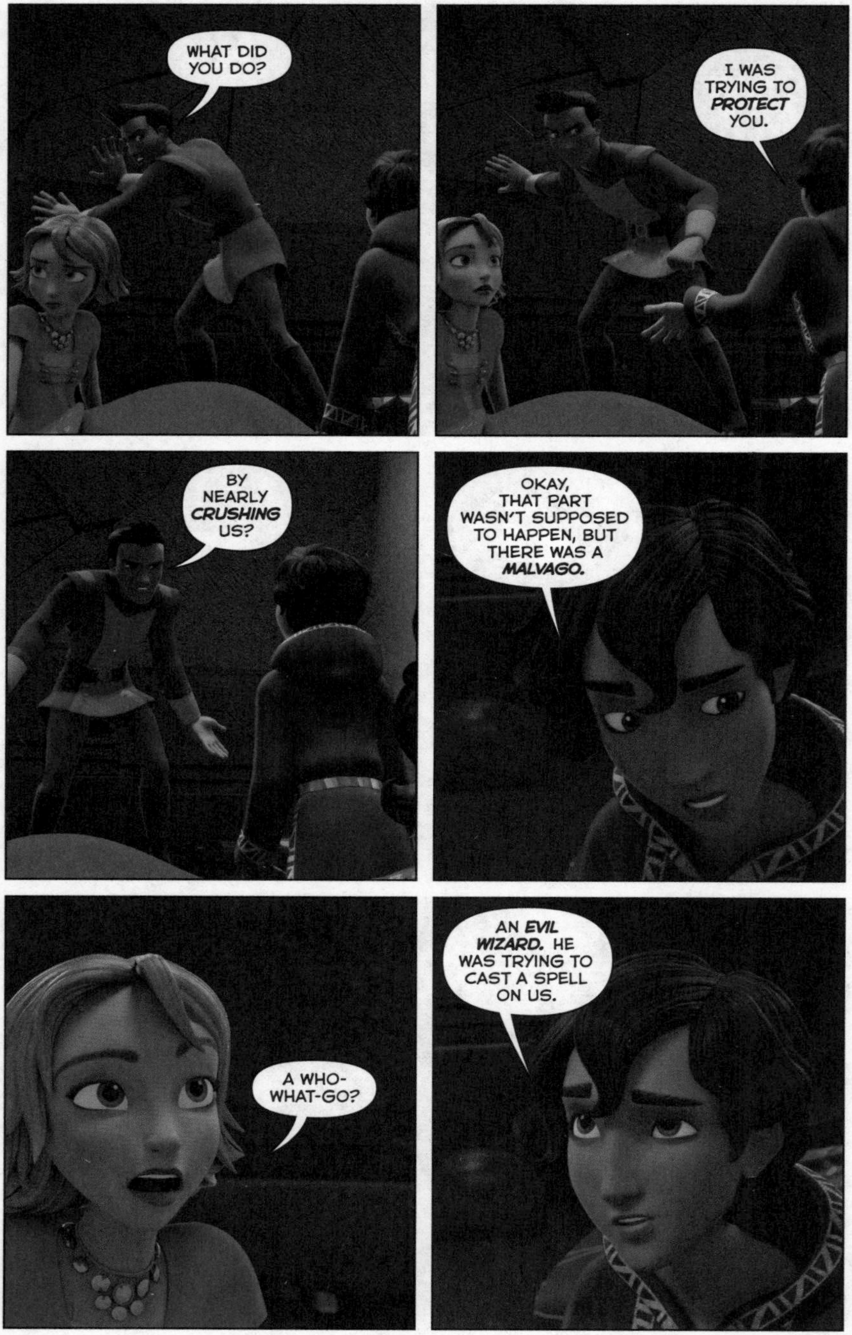
WHAT DID YOU DO?
I WAS TRYING TO *PROTECT* YOU.
BY NEARLY *CRUSHING* US?
OKAY, THAT PART WASN'T SUPPOSED TO HAPPEN, BUT THERE WAS A *MALVAGO.*
A WHO-WHAT-GO?
AN *EVIL WIZARD.* HE WAS TRYING TO CAST A SPELL ON US.

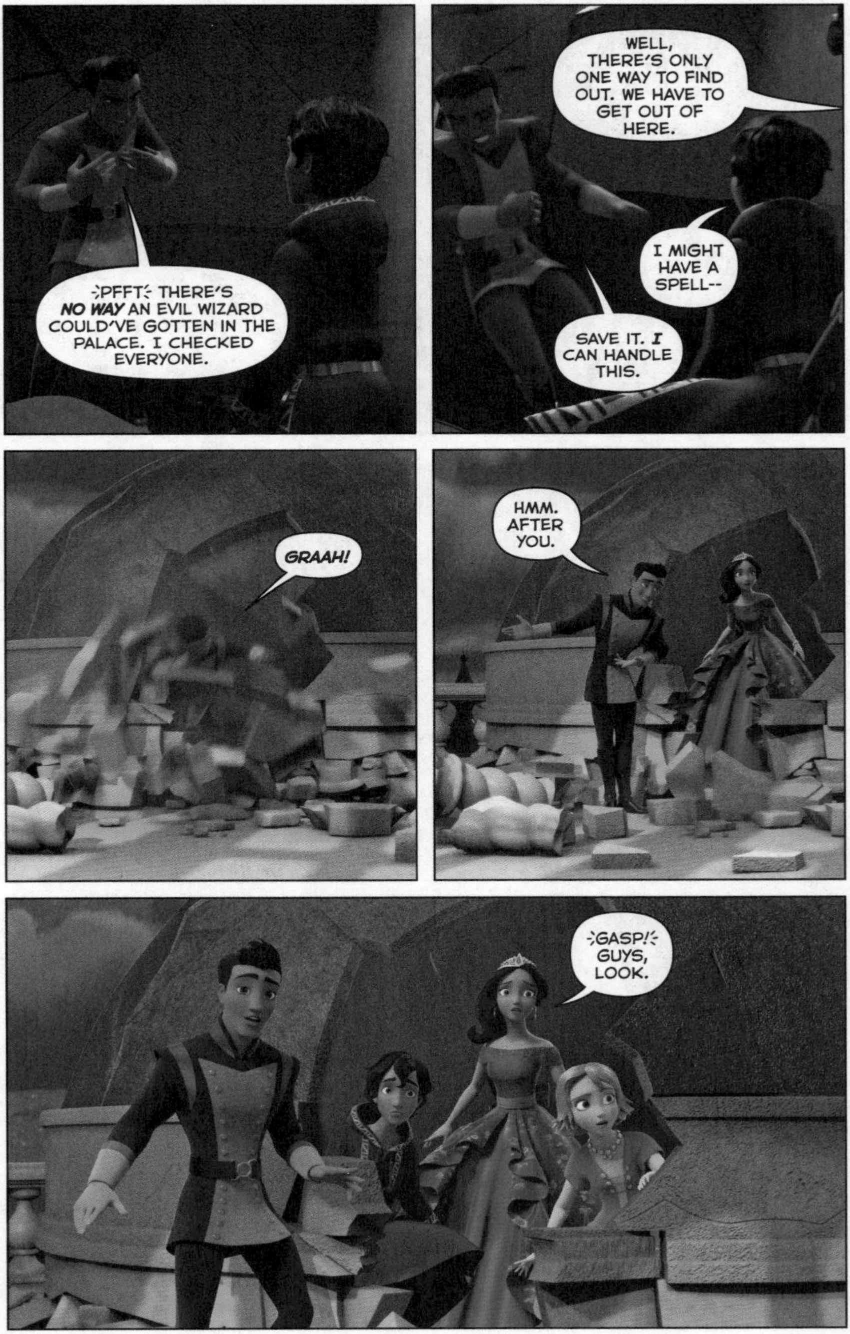

PFFT THERE'S **NO WAY** AN EVIL WIZARD COULD'VE GOTTEN IN THE PALACE. I CHECKED EVERYONE.
WELL, THERE'S ONLY ONE WAY TO FIND OUT. WE HAVE TO GET OUT OF HERE.
I MIGHT HAVE A SPELL--
SAVE IT. ***I*** CAN HANDLE THIS.
GRAAH!
HMM. AFTER YOU.
GASP! GUYS, LOOK.

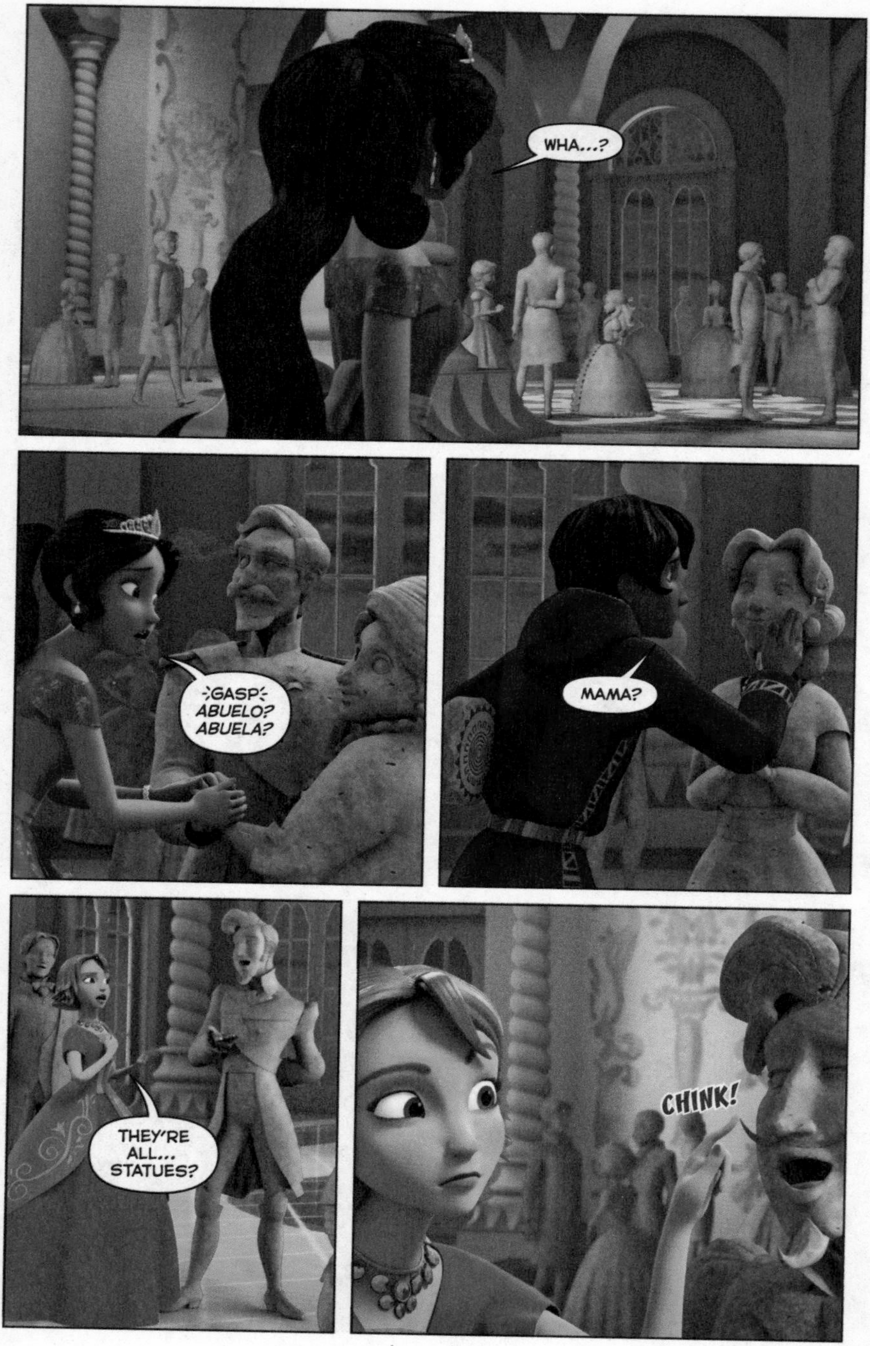
WHA...?
-GASP- ABUELO? ABUELA?
MAMA?
THEY'RE ALL... STATUES?
CHINK!

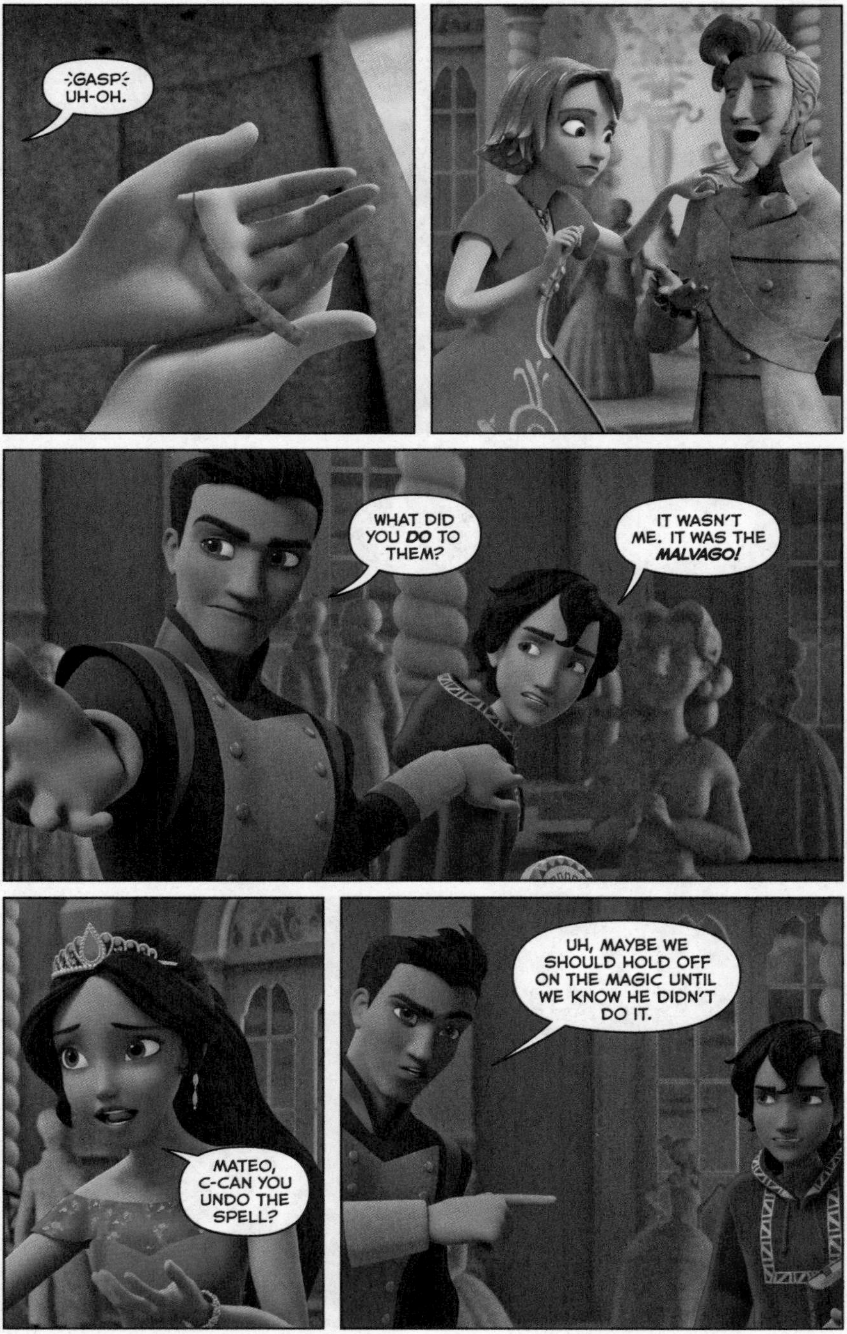
GASP
UH-OH.
WHAT DID YOU DO TO THEM?
IT WASN'T ME. IT WAS THE MALVAGO!
MATEO, C-CAN YOU UNDO THE SPELL?
UH, MAYBE WE SHOULD HOLD OFF ON THE MAGIC UNTIL WE KNOW HE DIDN'T DO IT.

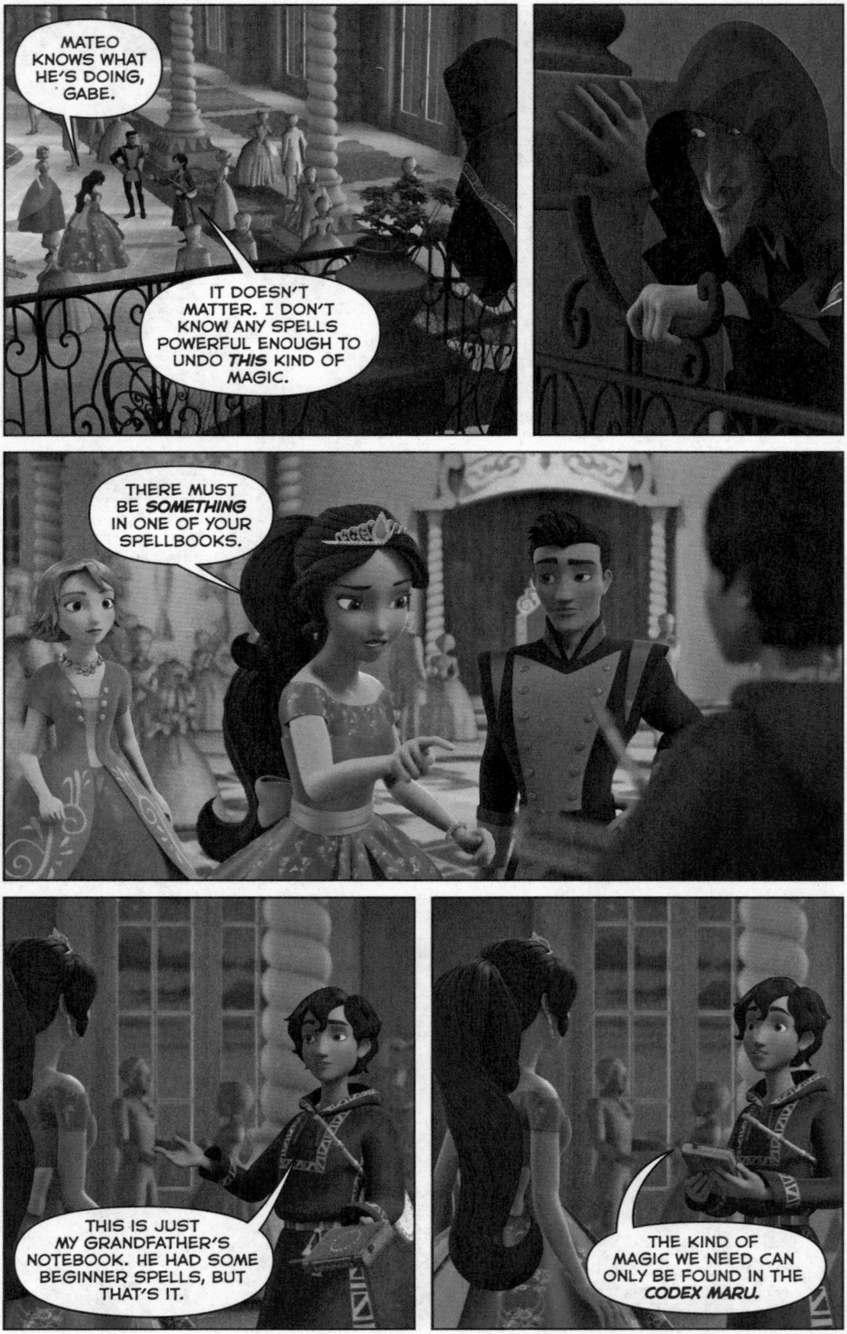
MATEO KNOWS WHAT HE'S DOING, GABE.
IT DOESN'T MATTER. I DON'T KNOW ANY SPELLS POWERFUL ENOUGH TO UNDO *THIS* KIND OF MAGIC.
THERE MUST BE *SOMETHING* IN ONE OF YOUR SPELLBOOKS.
THIS IS JUST MY GRANDFATHER'S NOTEBOOK. HE HAD SOME BEGINNER SPELLS, BUT THAT'S IT.
THE KIND OF MAGIC WE NEED CAN ONLY BE FOUND IN THE *CODEX MARU.*

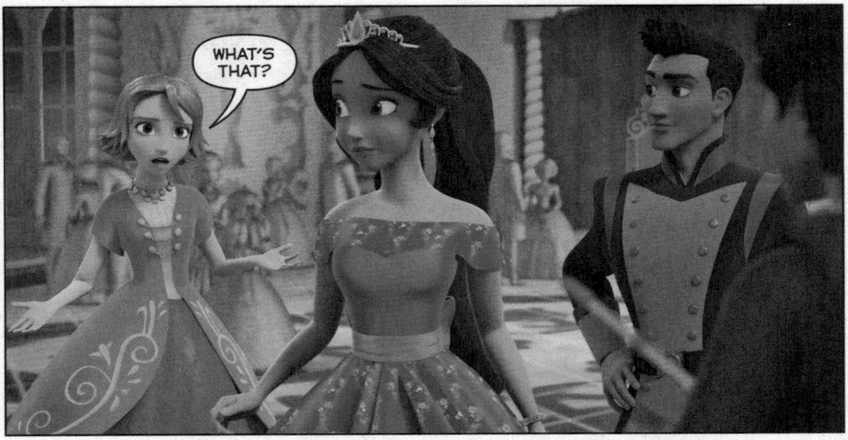
WHAT'S THAT?

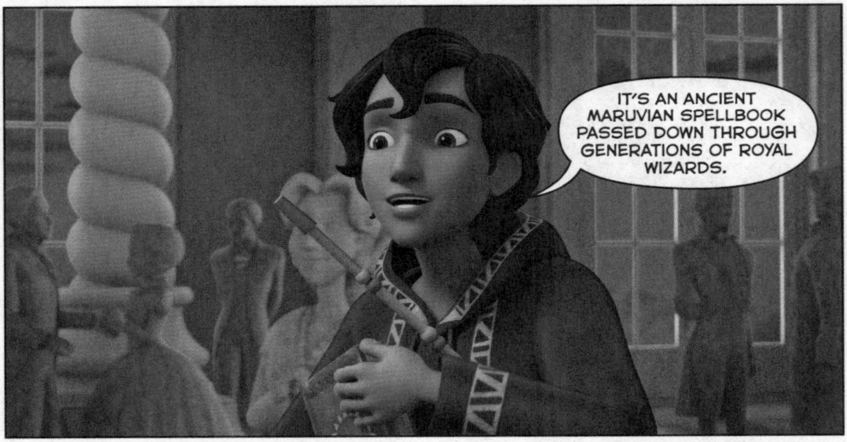
IT'S AN ANCIENT MARUVIAN SPELLBOOK PASSED DOWN THROUGH GENERATIONS OF ROYAL WIZARDS.

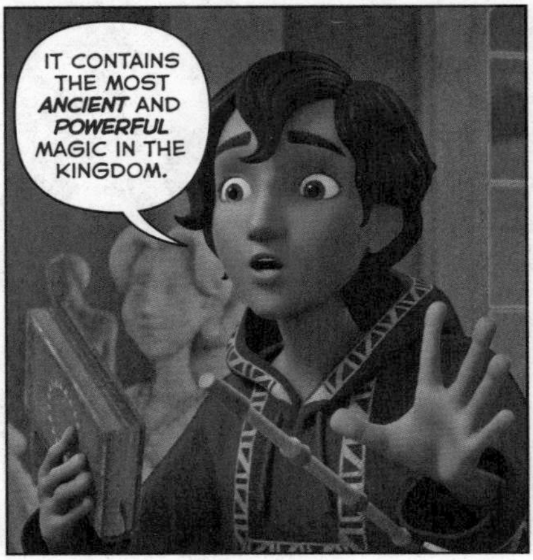
IT CONTAINS THE MOST *ANCIENT* AND *POWERFUL* MAGIC IN THE KINGDOM.

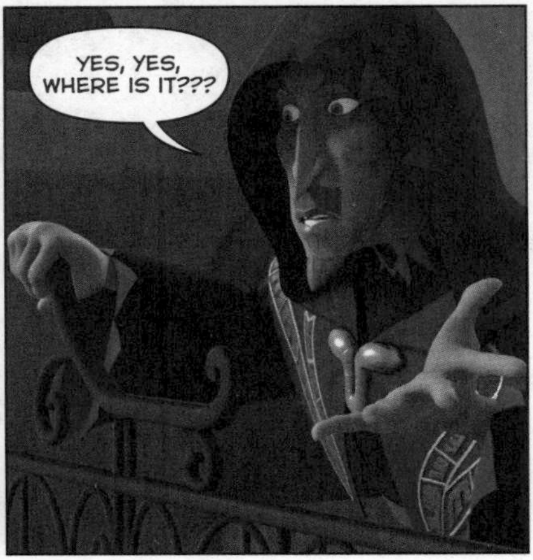
YES, YES, WHERE IS IT???

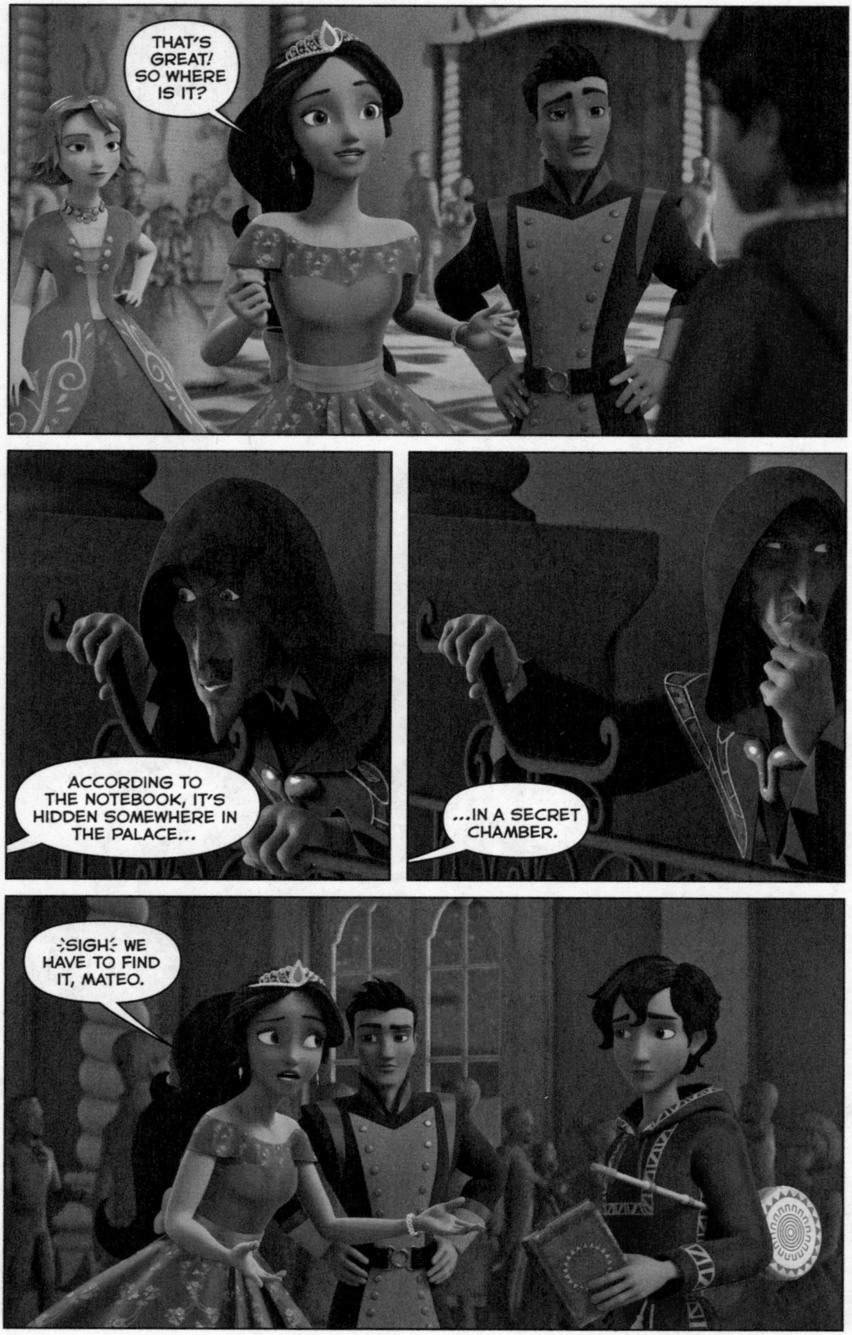
THAT'S GREAT! SO WHERE IS IT?
ACCORDING TO THE NOTEBOOK, IT'S HIDDEN SOMEWHERE IN THE PALACE...
...IN A SECRET CHAMBER.
SIGH WE HAVE TO FIND IT, MATEO.

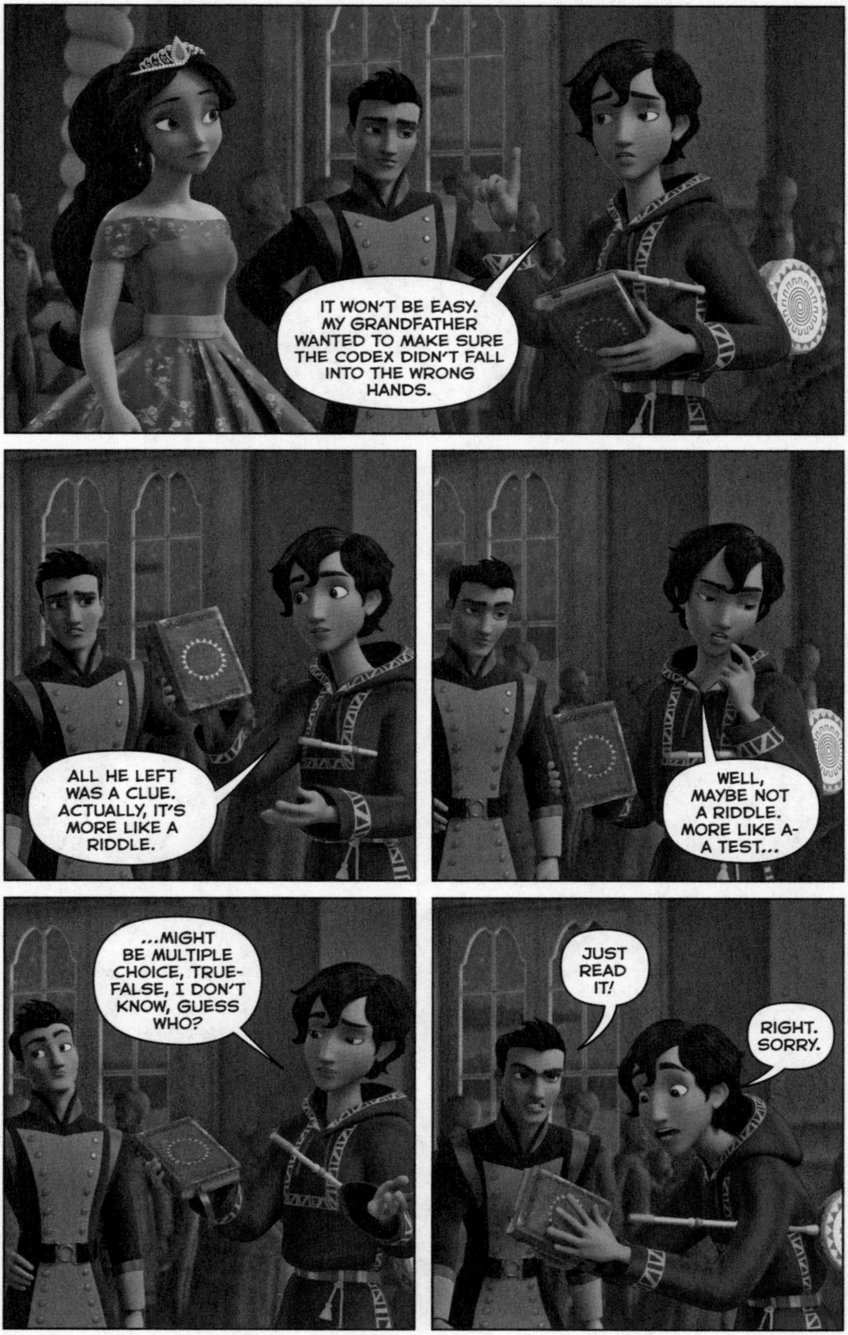
IT WON'T BE EASY. MY GRANDFATHER WANTED TO MAKE SURE THE CODEX DIDN'T FALL INTO THE WRONG HANDS.
ALL HE LEFT WAS A CLUE. ACTUALLY, IT'S MORE LIKE A RIDDLE.
WELL, MAYBE NOT A RIDDLE. MORE LIKE A- A TEST...
...MIGHT BE MULTIPLE CHOICE, TRUE-FALSE, I DON'T KNOW, GUESS WHO?
JUST READ IT!
RIGHT. SORRY.

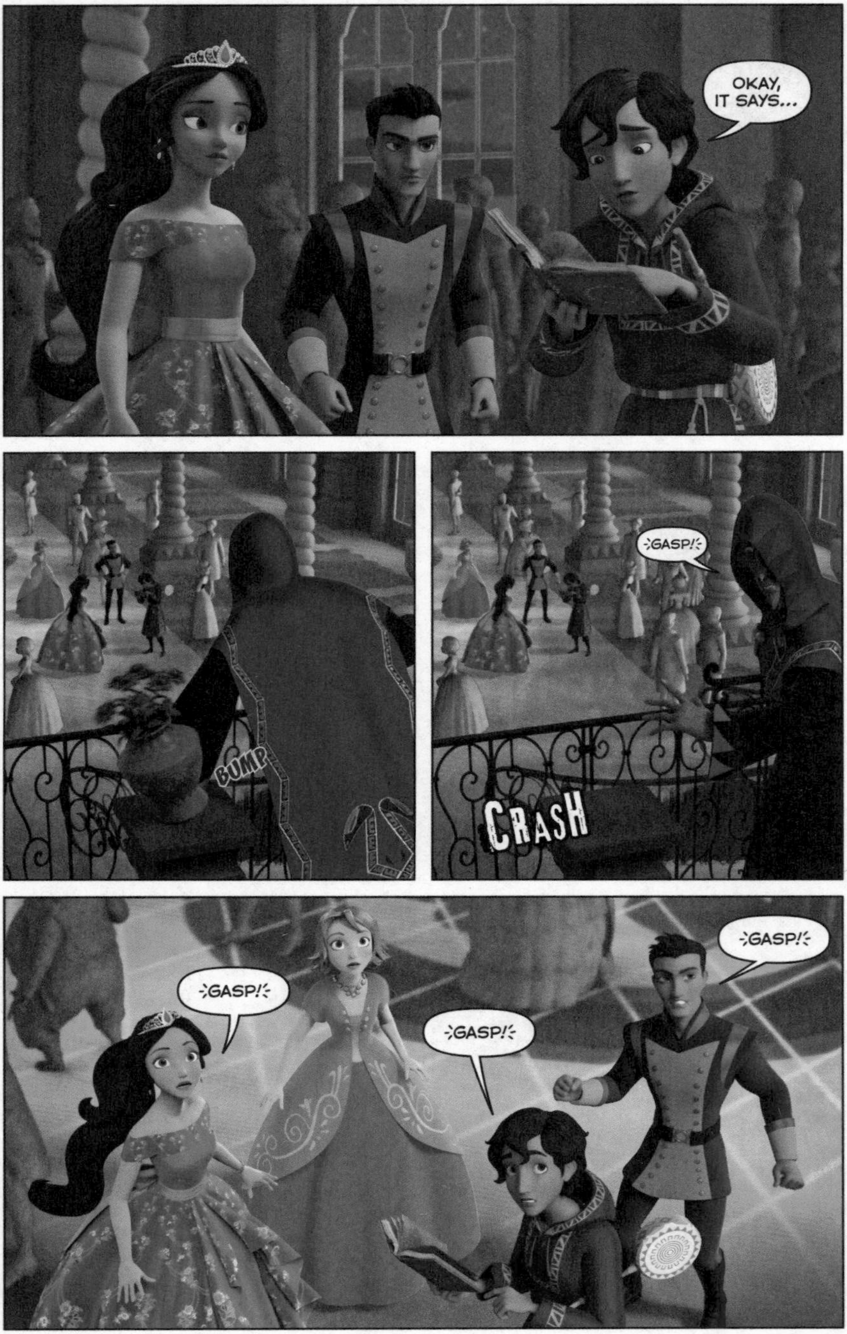
OKAY, IT SAYS...
BUMP
GASP!
CRASH
GASP!
GASP!
GASP!

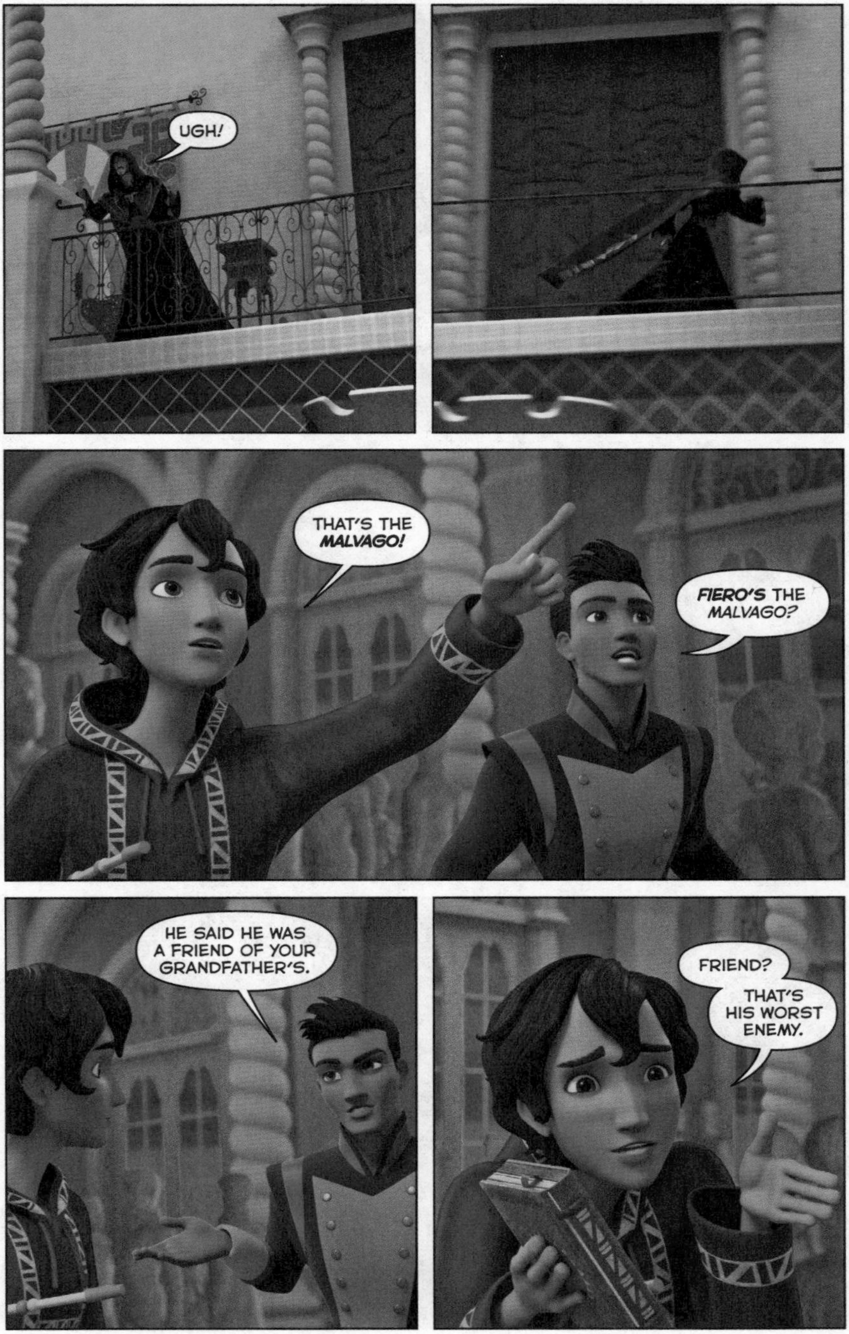
UGH!
THAT'S THE MALVAGO!
FIERO'S THE MALVAGO?
HE SAID HE WAS A FRIEND OF YOUR GRANDFATHER'S.
FRIEND?
THAT'S HIS WORST ENEMY.

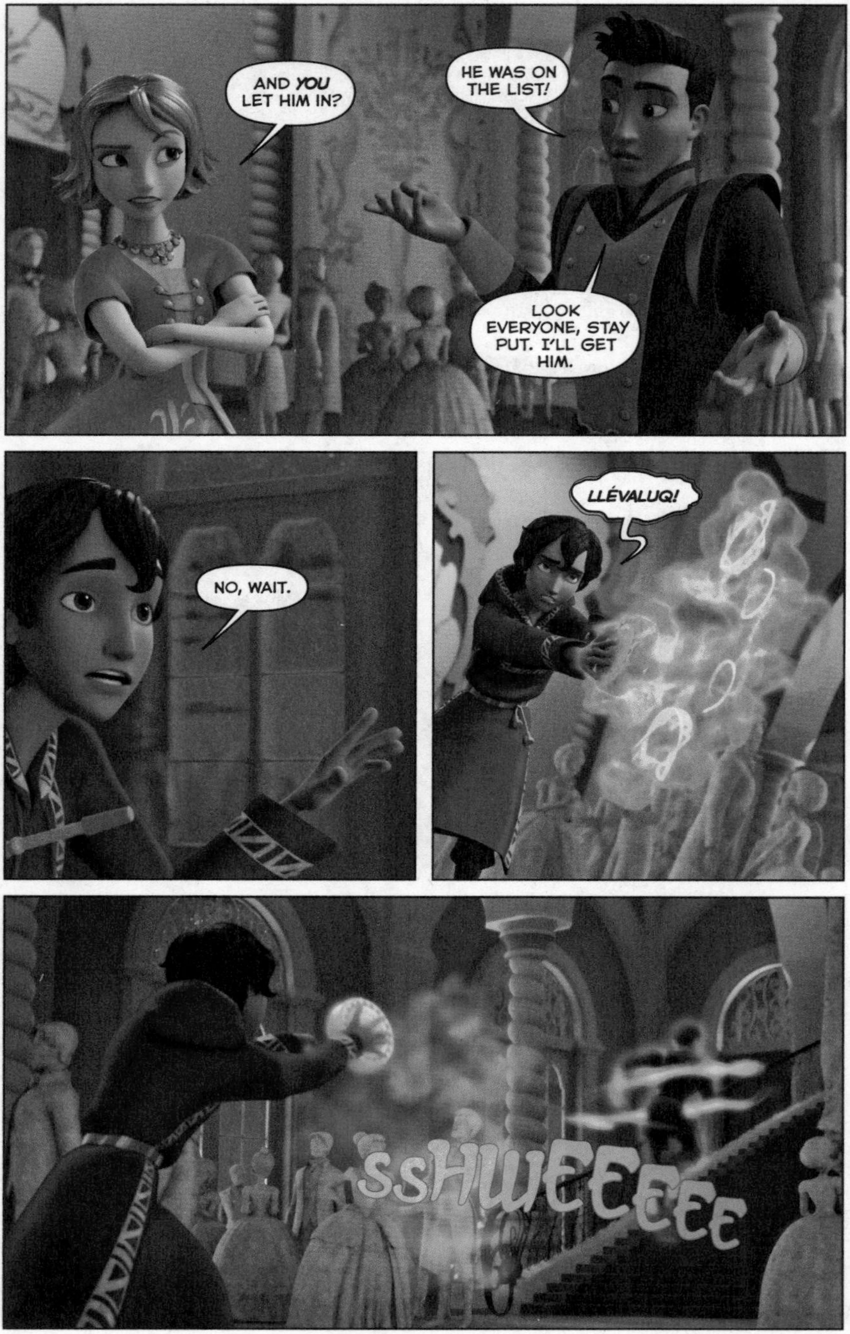
AND *YOU* LET HIM IN?
HE WAS ON THE LIST!
LOOK EVERYONE, STAY PUT. I'LL GET HIM.
NO, WAIT.
LLÉVALUQ!
SSHWEEEEEE

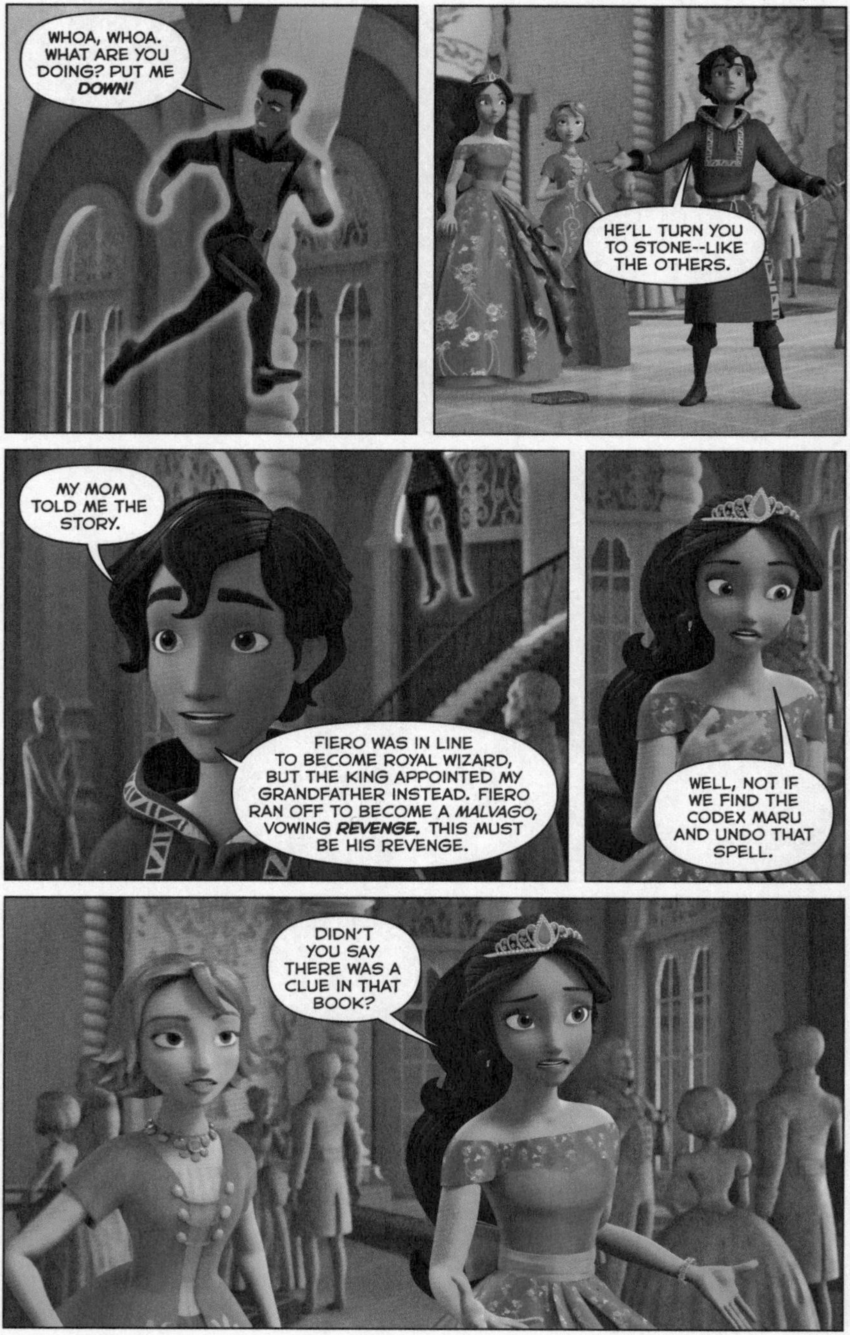
WHOA, WHOA. WHAT ARE YOU DOING? PUT ME *DOWN!*
HE'LL TURN YOU TO STONE--LIKE THE OTHERS.
MY MOM TOLD ME THE STORY.
FIERO WAS IN LINE TO BECOME ROYAL WIZARD, BUT THE KING APPOINTED MY GRANDFATHER INSTEAD. FIERO RAN OFF TO BECOME A *MALVAGO,* VOWING ***REVENGE.*** THIS MUST BE HIS REVENGE.
WELL, NOT IF WE FIND THE CODEX MARU AND UNDO THAT SPELL.
DIDN'T YOU SAY THERE WAS A CLUE IN THAT BOOK?

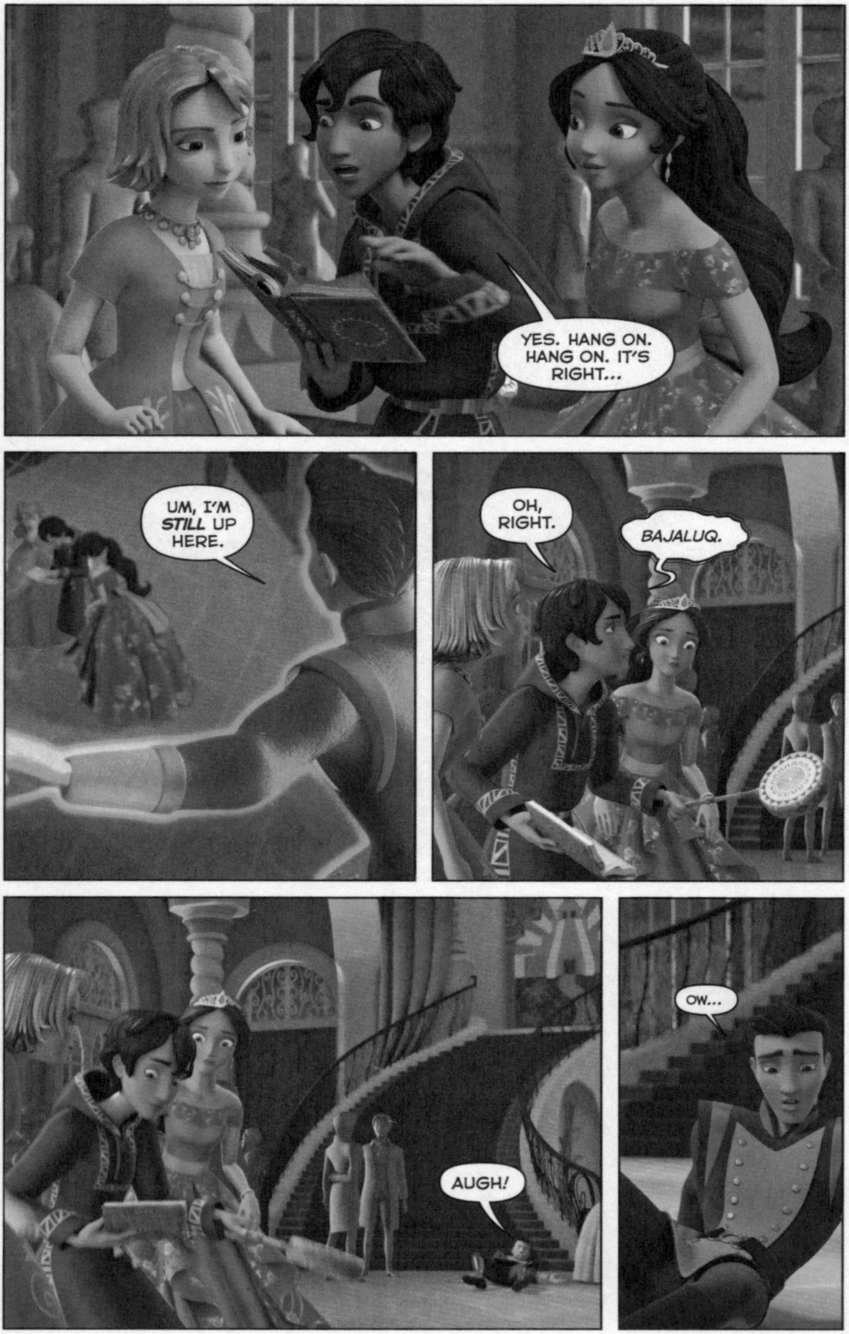
YES. HANG ON. HANG ON. IT'S RIGHT...
UM, I'M *STILL* UP HERE.
OH, RIGHT.
BAJALUQ.
AUGH!
OW...

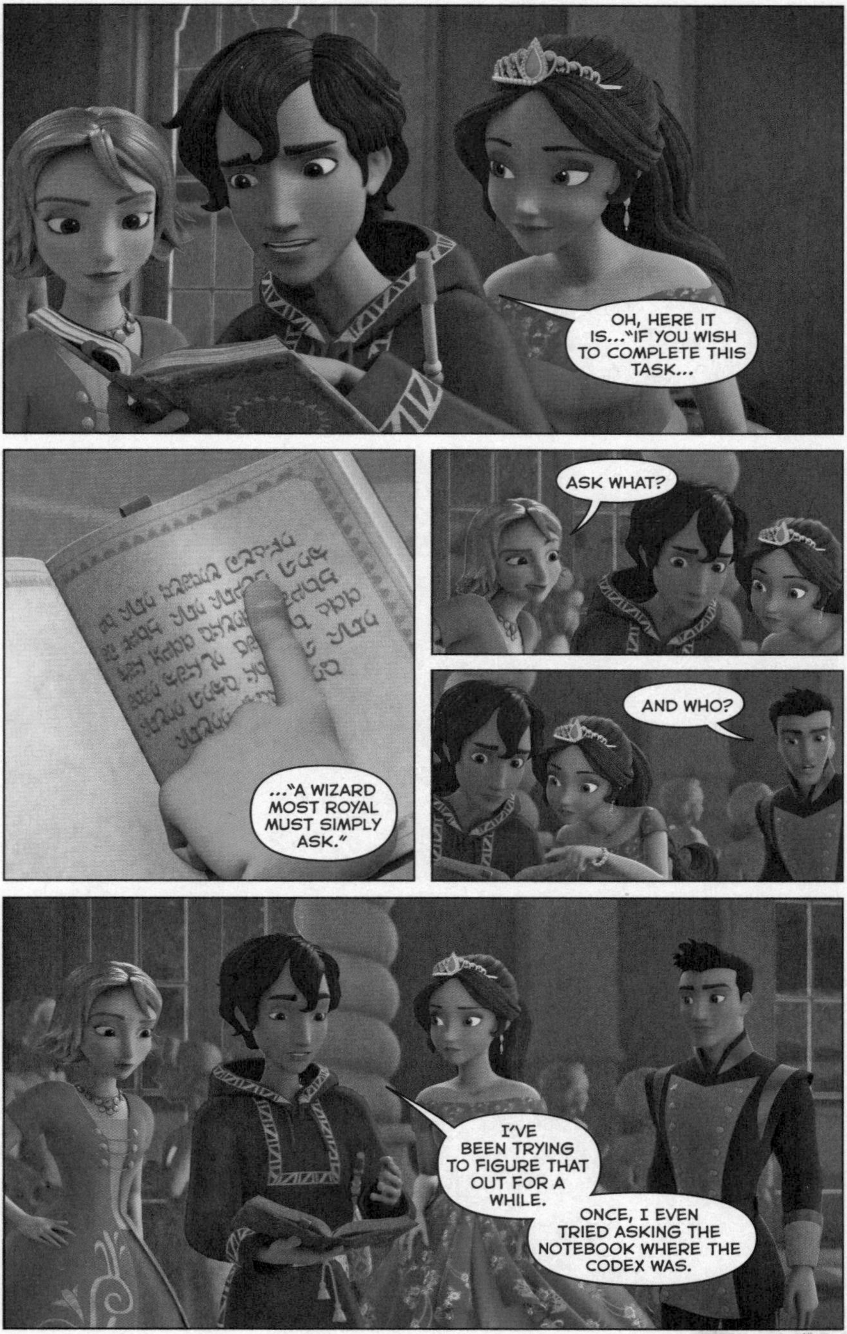
OH, HERE IT IS..."IF YOU WISH TO COMPLETE THIS TASK...
..."A WIZARD MOST ROYAL MUST SIMPLY ASK."
ASK WHAT?
AND WHO?
I'VE BEEN TRYING TO FIGURE THAT OUT FOR A WHILE.
ONCE, I EVEN TRIED ASKING THE NOTEBOOK WHERE THE CODEX WAS.

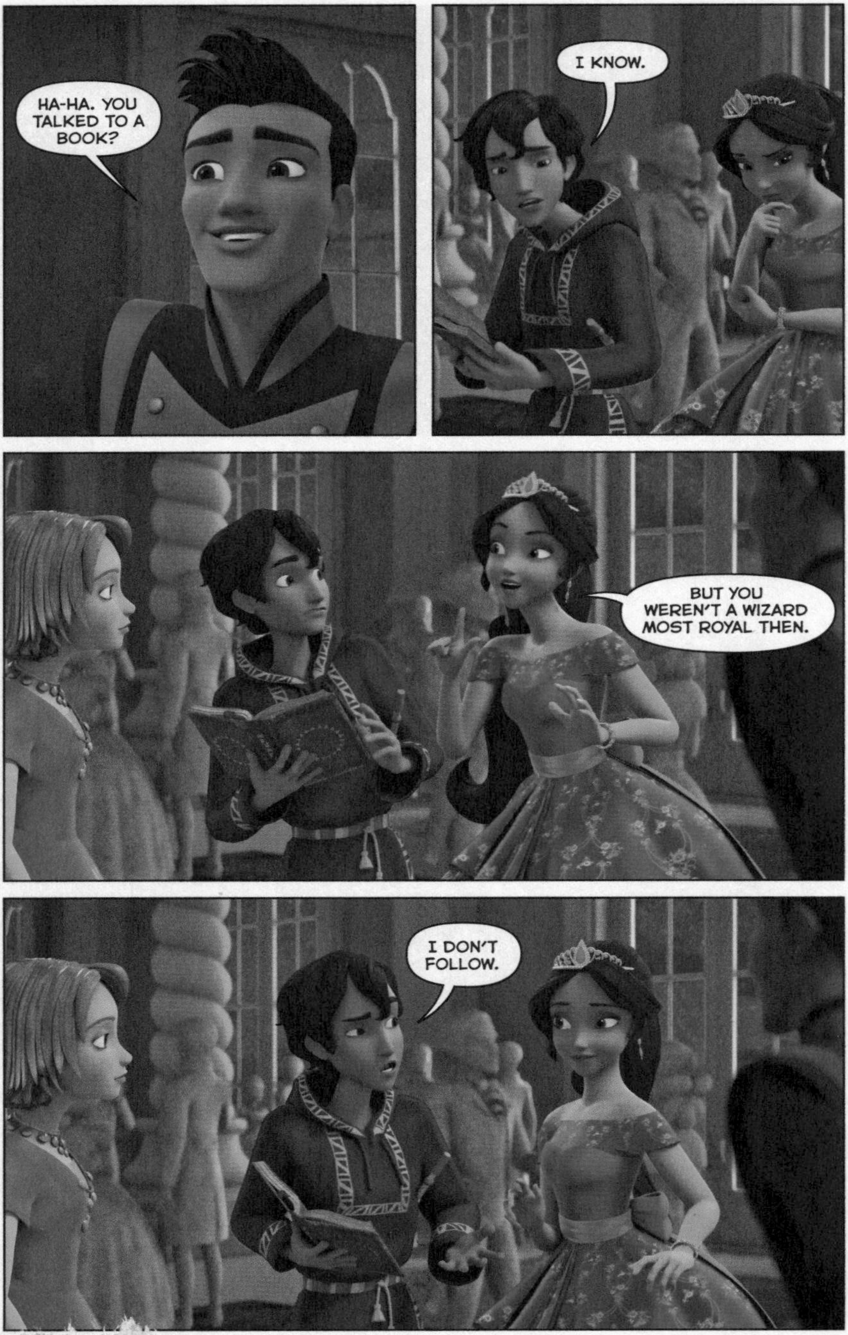
HA-HA. YOU TALKED TO A BOOK?
I KNOW.
BUT YOU WEREN'T A WIZARD MOST ROYAL THEN.
I DON'T FOLLOW.

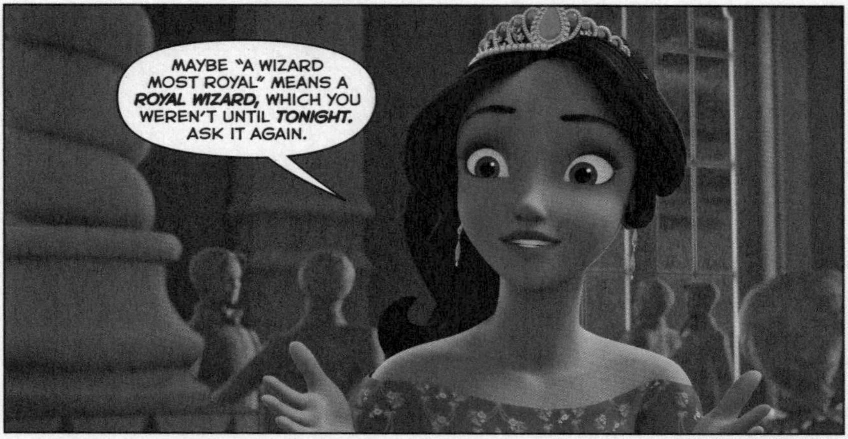
MAYBE "A WIZARD MOST ROYAL" MEANS A ***ROYAL WIZARD,*** WHICH YOU WEREN'T UNTIL ***TONIGHT.*** ASK IT AGAIN.

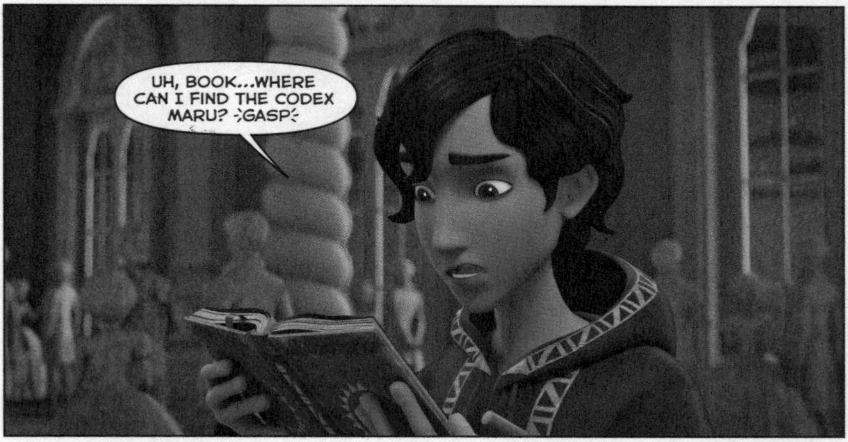
UH, BOOK...WHERE CAN I FIND THE CODEX MARU? -GASP-

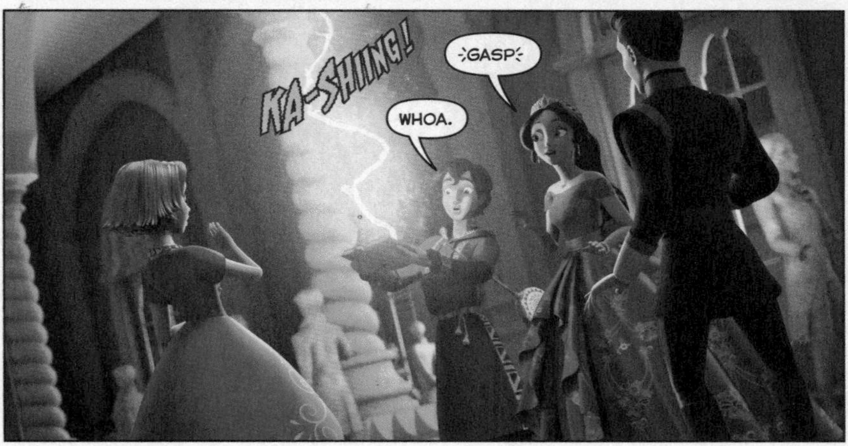
KA-SHIING!
-GASP-
WHOA.

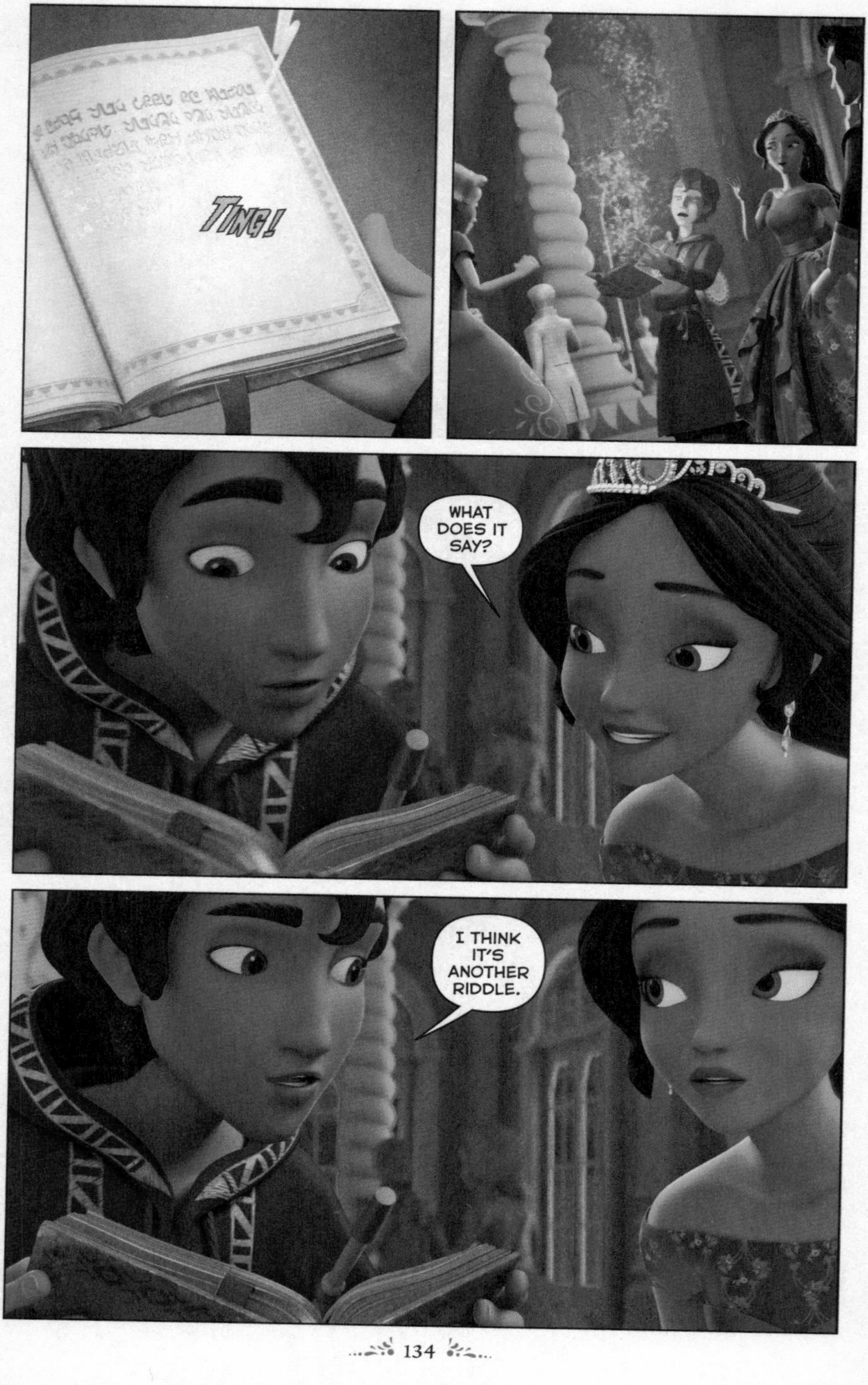
TING!
WHAT DOES IT SAY?
I THINK IT'S ANOTHER RIDDLE.

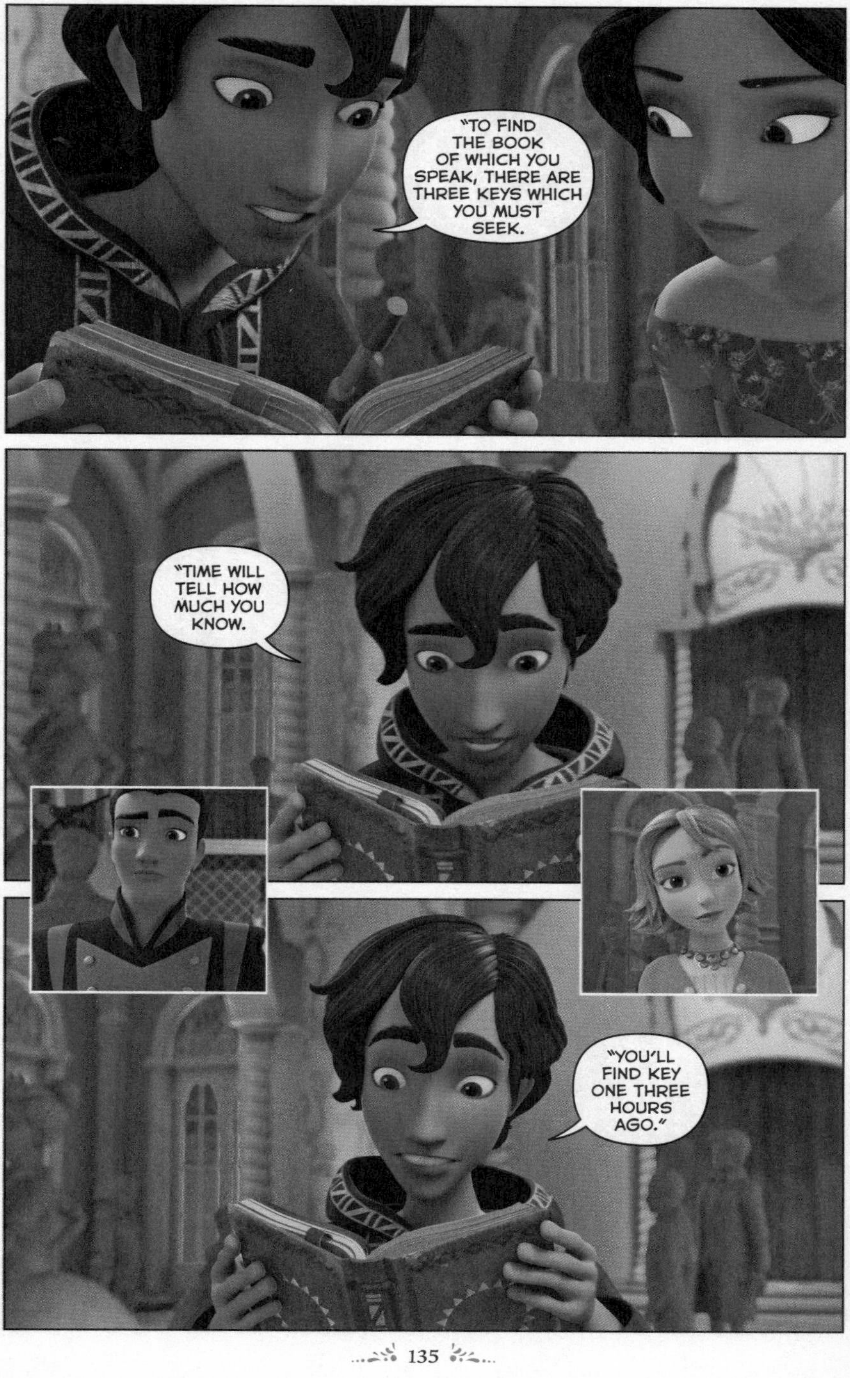
"TO FIND THE BOOK OF WHICH YOU SPEAK, THERE ARE THREE KEYS WHICH YOU MUST SEEK.
"TIME WILL TELL HOW MUCH YOU KNOW.
"YOU'LL FIND KEY ONE THREE HOURS AGO."

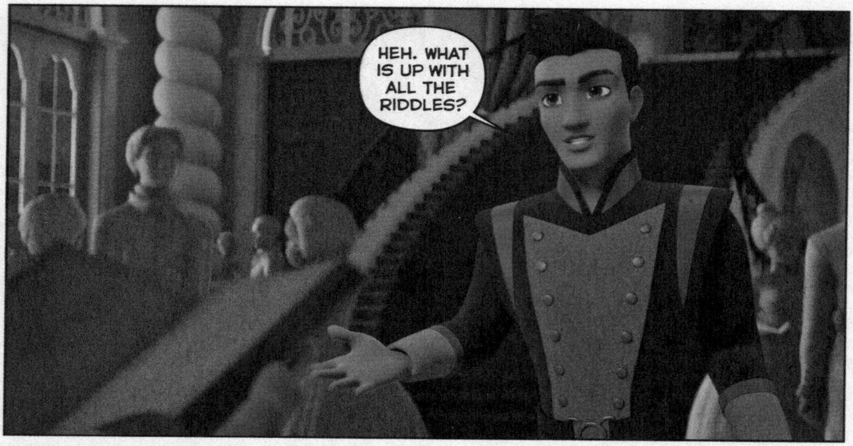
HEH. WHAT IS UP WITH ALL THE RIDDLES?

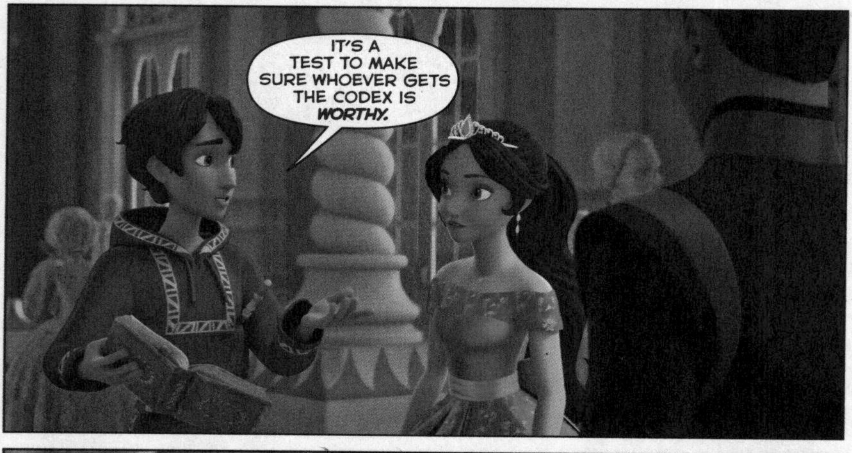
IT'S A TEST TO MAKE SURE WHOEVER GETS THE CODEX IS *WORTHY.*

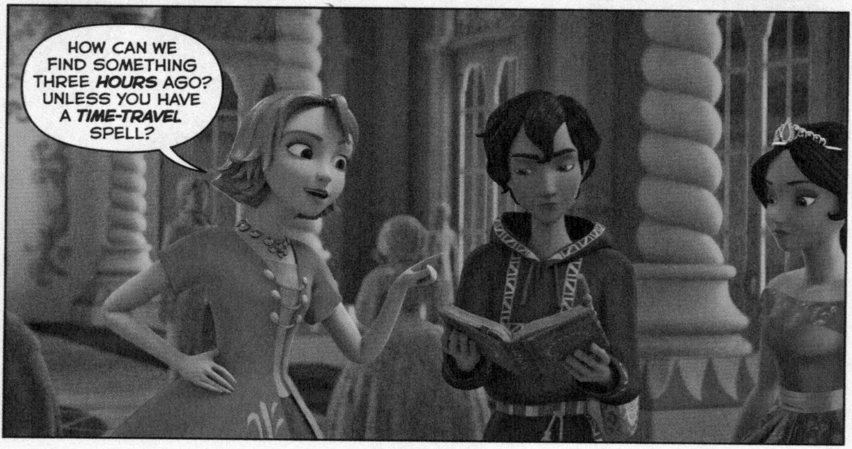
HOW CAN WE FIND SOMETHING THREE *HOURS* AGO? UNLESS YOU HAVE A *TIME-TRAVEL* SPELL?

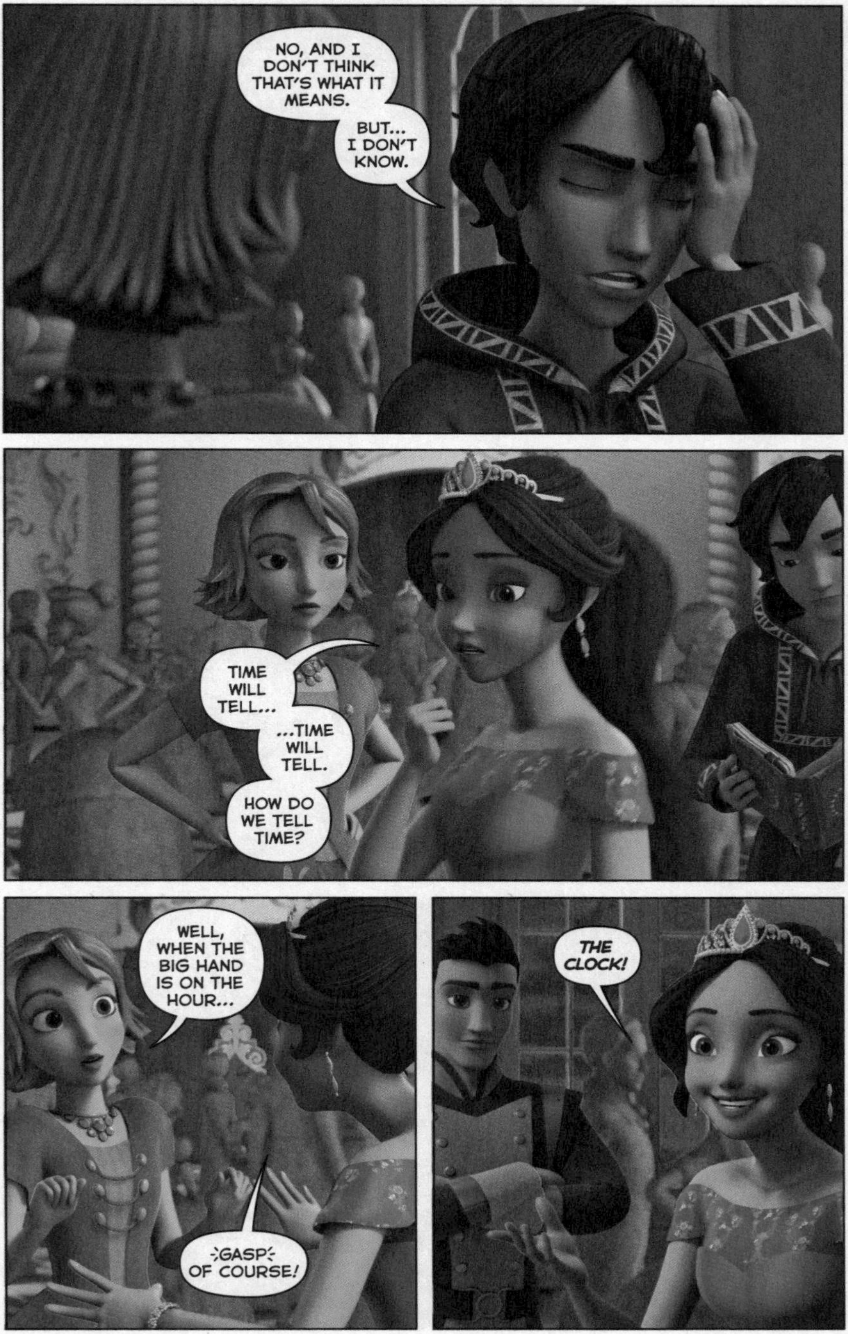
NO, AND I DON'T THINK THAT'S WHAT IT MEANS.
BUT... I DON'T KNOW.
TIME WILL TELL...
...TIME WILL TELL.
HOW DO WE TELL TIME?
WELL, WHEN THE BIG HAND IS ON THE HOUR...
GASP OF COURSE!
THE CLOCK!

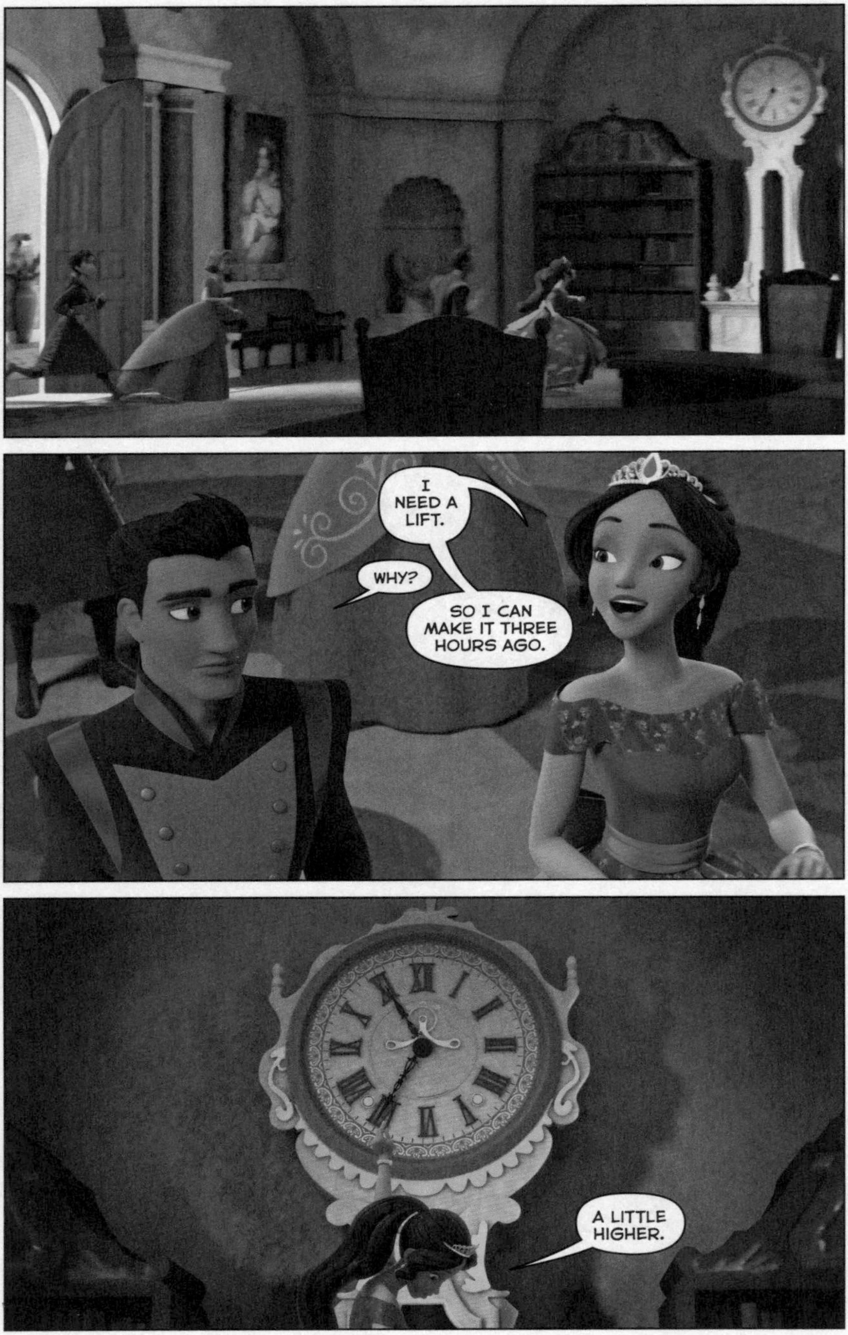
I NEED A LIFT.
WHY?
SO I CAN MAKE IT THREE HOURS AGO.
A LITTLE HIGHER.

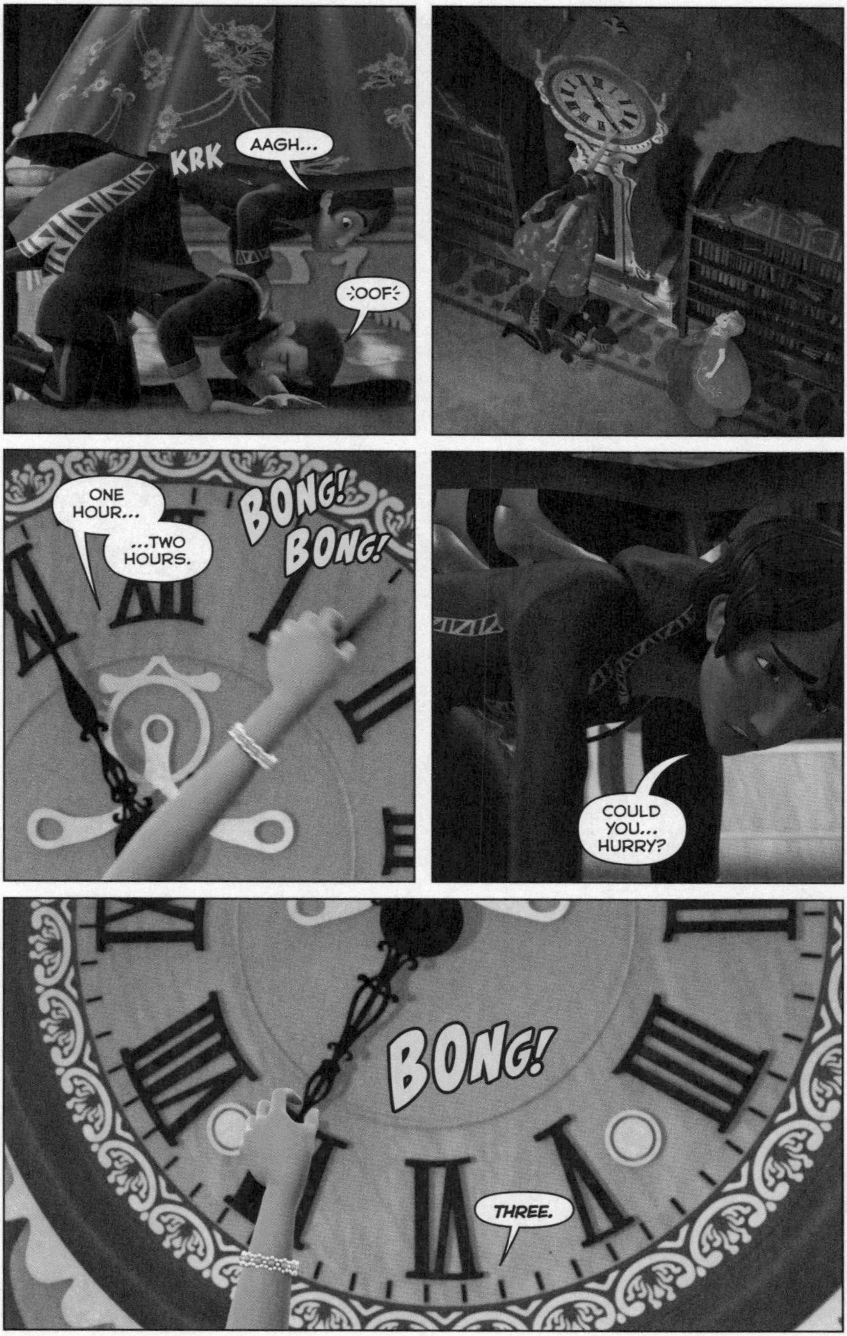
KRK
AAGH...
OOF
ONE HOUR...
...TWO HOURS.
BONG!
BONG!
COULD YOU... HURRY?
BONG!
THREE.

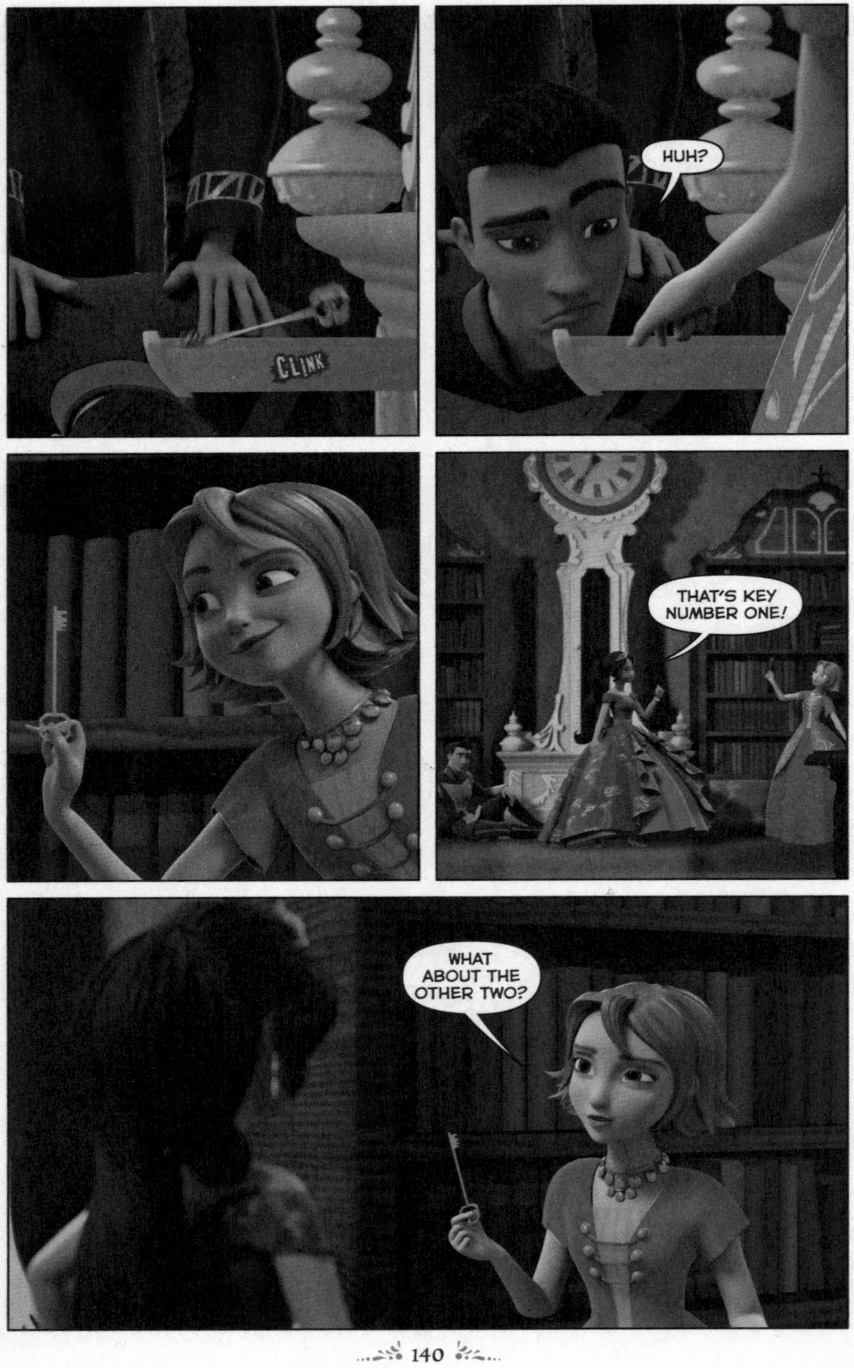
CLINK
HUH?
THAT'S KEY NUMBER ONE!
WHAT ABOUT THE OTHER TWO?

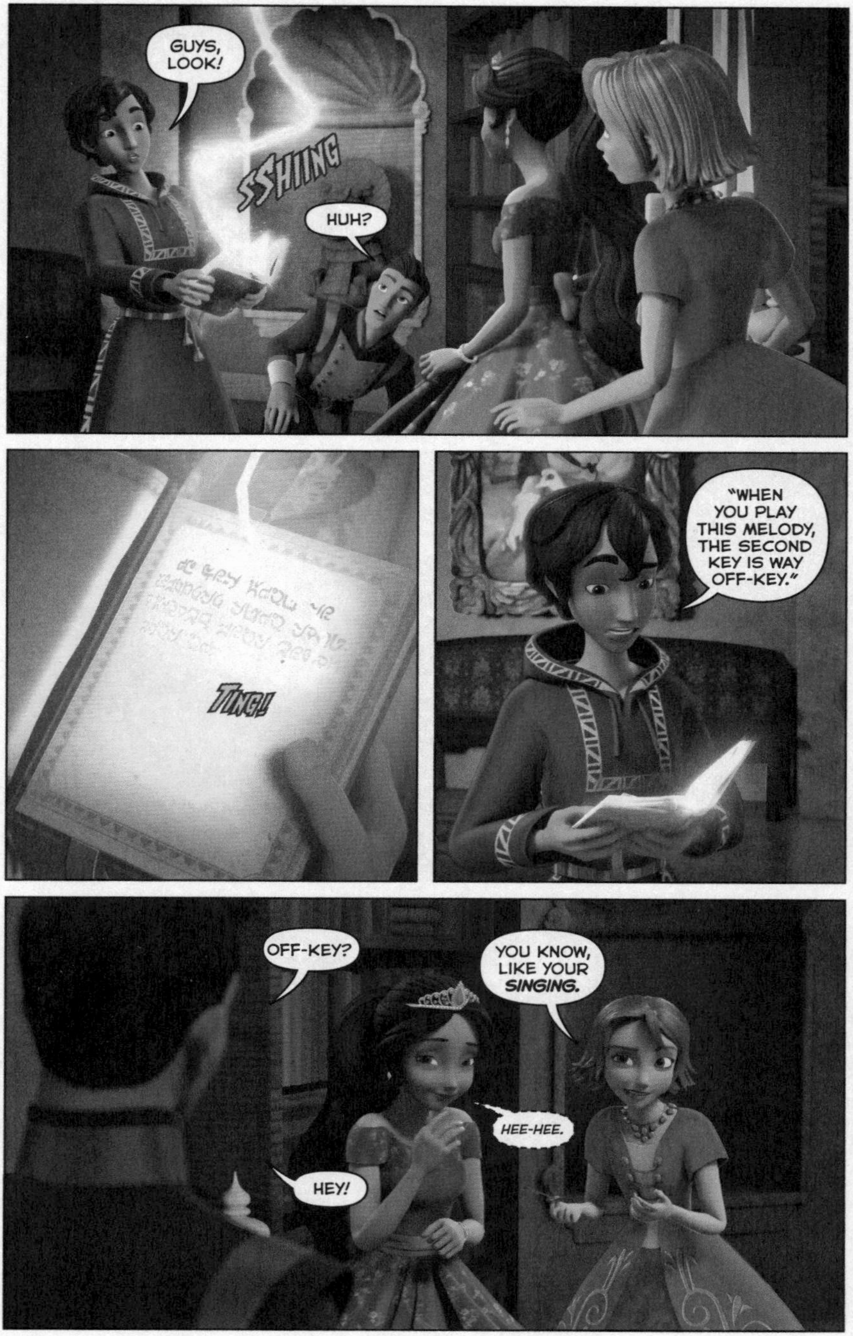
GUYS, LOOK!
SSHIING
HUH?
TING!
"WHEN YOU PLAY THIS MELODY, THE SECOND KEY IS WAY OFF-KEY."
OFF-KEY?
YOU KNOW, LIKE YOUR SINGING.
HEE-HEE.
HEY!

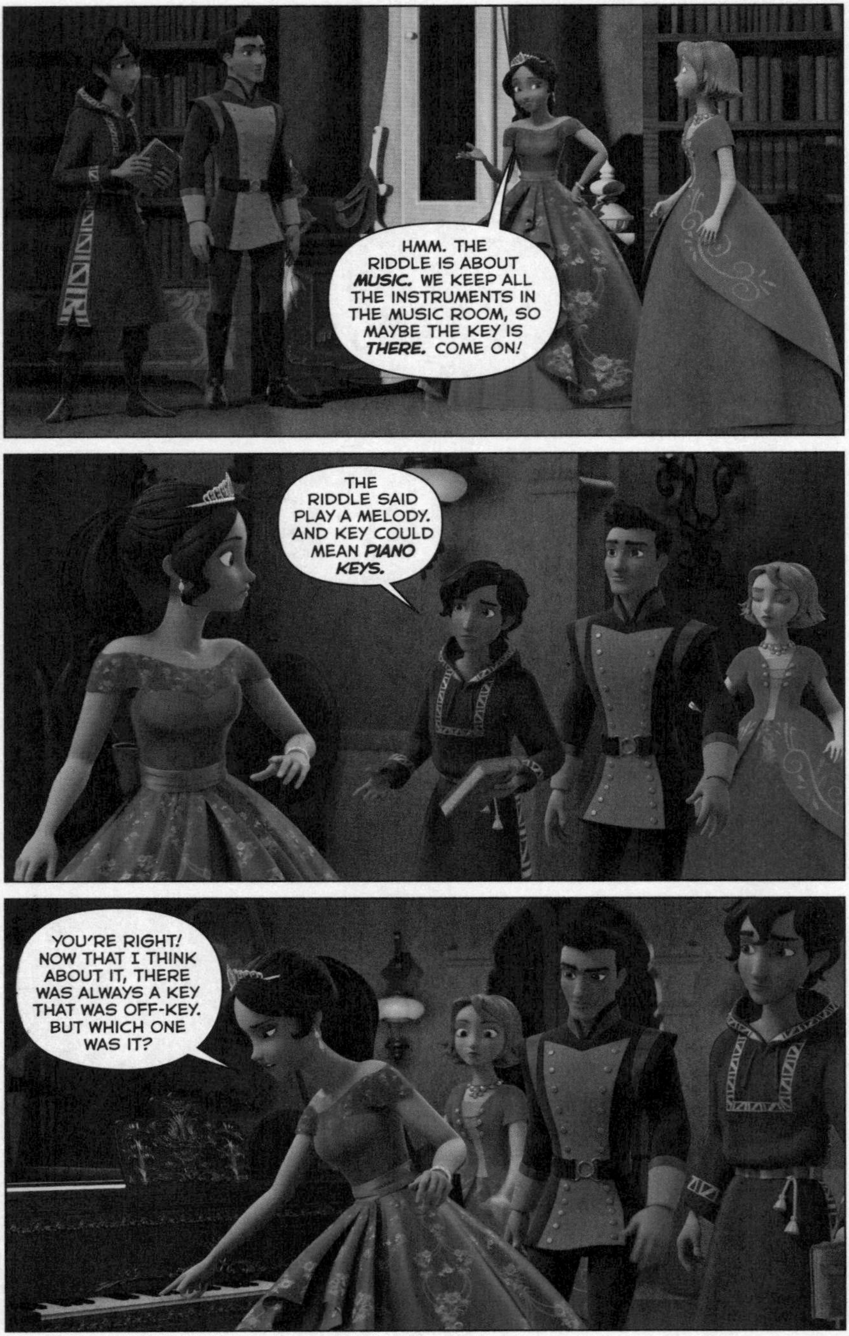
HMM. THE RIDDLE IS ABOUT *MUSIC.* WE KEEP ALL THE INSTRUMENTS IN THE MUSIC ROOM, SO MAYBE THE KEY IS *THERE.* COME ON!
THE RIDDLE SAID PLAY A MELODY. AND KEY COULD MEAN *PIANO KEYS.*
YOU'RE RIGHT! NOW THAT I THINK ABOUT IT, THERE WAS ALWAYS A KEY THAT WAS OFF-KEY. BUT WHICH ONE WAS IT?

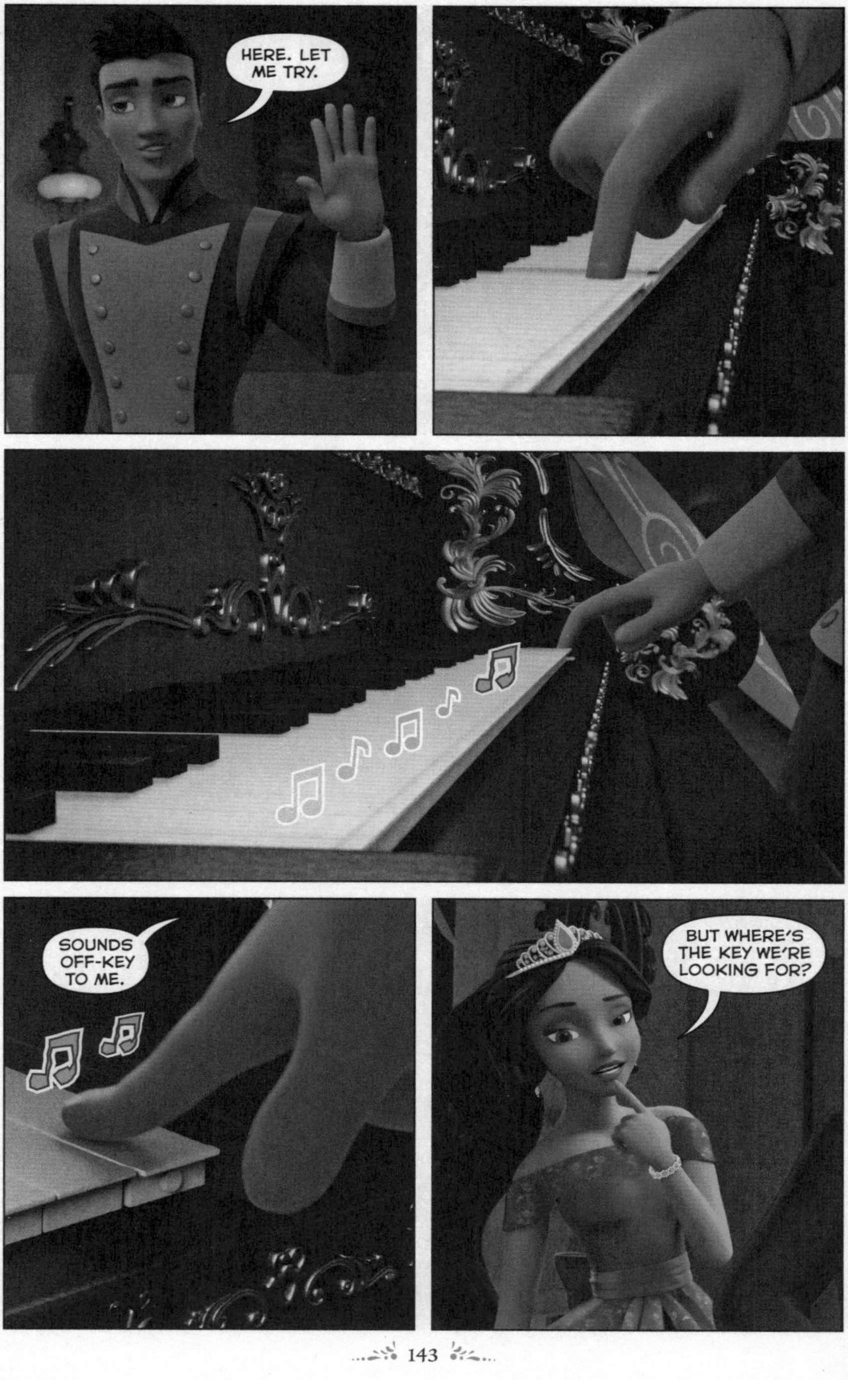
HERE. LET ME TRY.
SOUNDS OFF-KEY TO ME.
BUT WHERE'S THE KEY WE'RE LOOKING FOR?

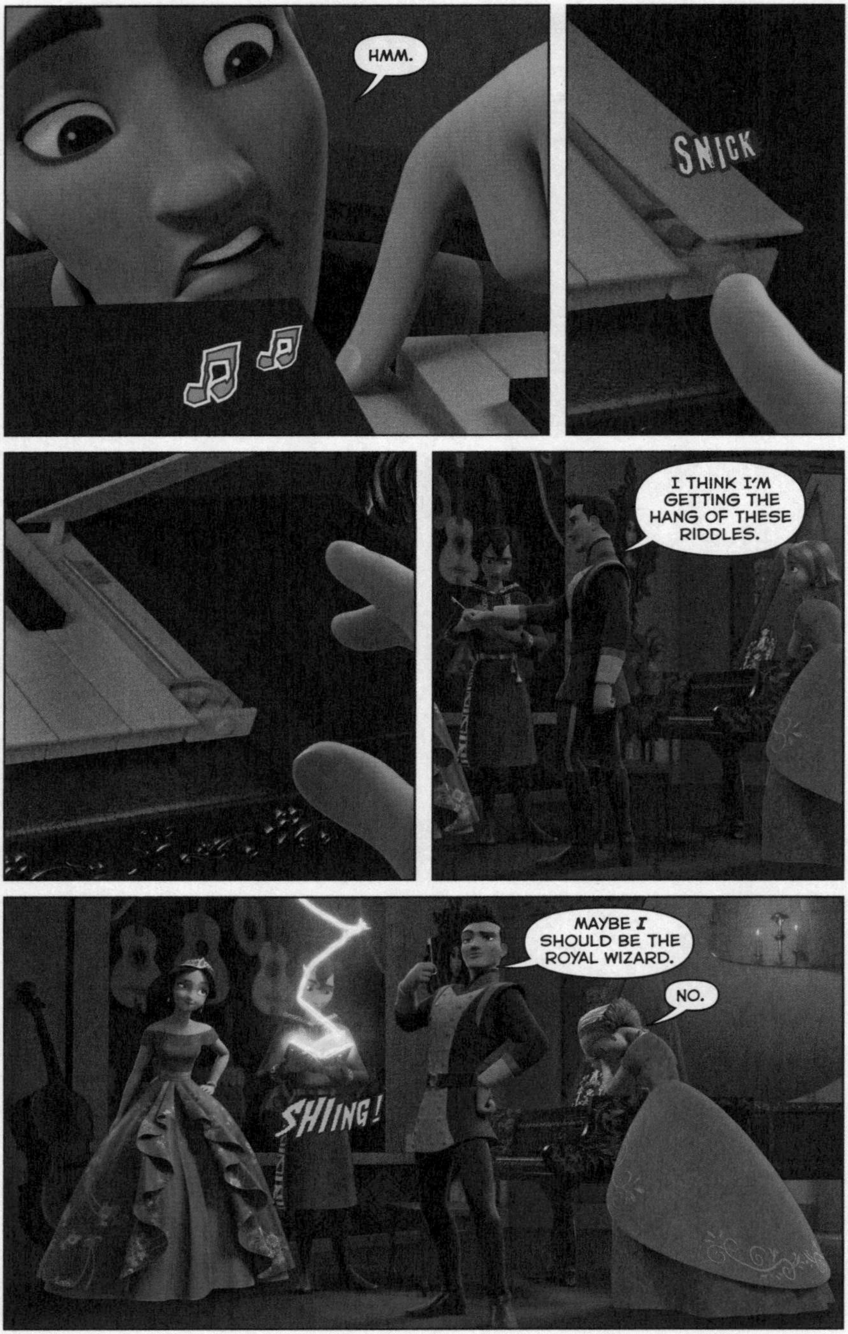
HMM.
SNICK
I THINK I'M GETTING THE HANG OF THESE RIDDLES.
MAYBE I SHOULD BE THE ROYAL WIZARD.
NO.
SHIING!

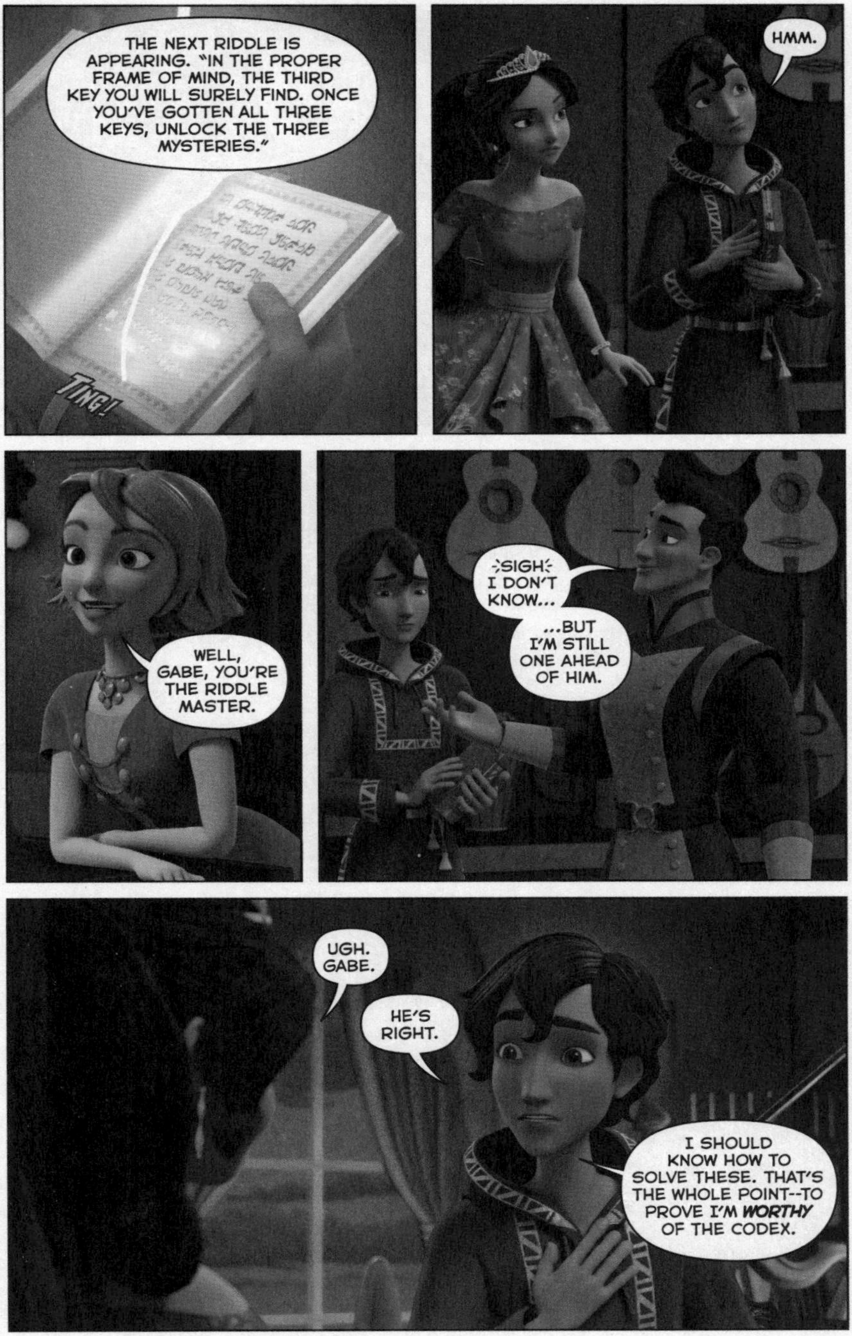
THE NEXT RIDDLE IS APPEARING. "IN THE PROPER FRAME OF MIND, THE THIRD KEY YOU WILL SURELY FIND. ONCE YOU'VE GOTTEN ALL THREE KEYS, UNLOCK THE THREE MYSTERIES."
TING!
HMM.
WELL, GABE, YOU'RE THE RIDDLE MASTER.
-SIGH- I DON'T KNOW...
...BUT I'M STILL ONE AHEAD OF HIM.
UGH. GABE.
HE'S RIGHT.
I SHOULD KNOW HOW TO SOLVE THESE. THAT'S THE WHOLE POINT--TO PROVE I'M *WORTHY* OF THE CODEX.

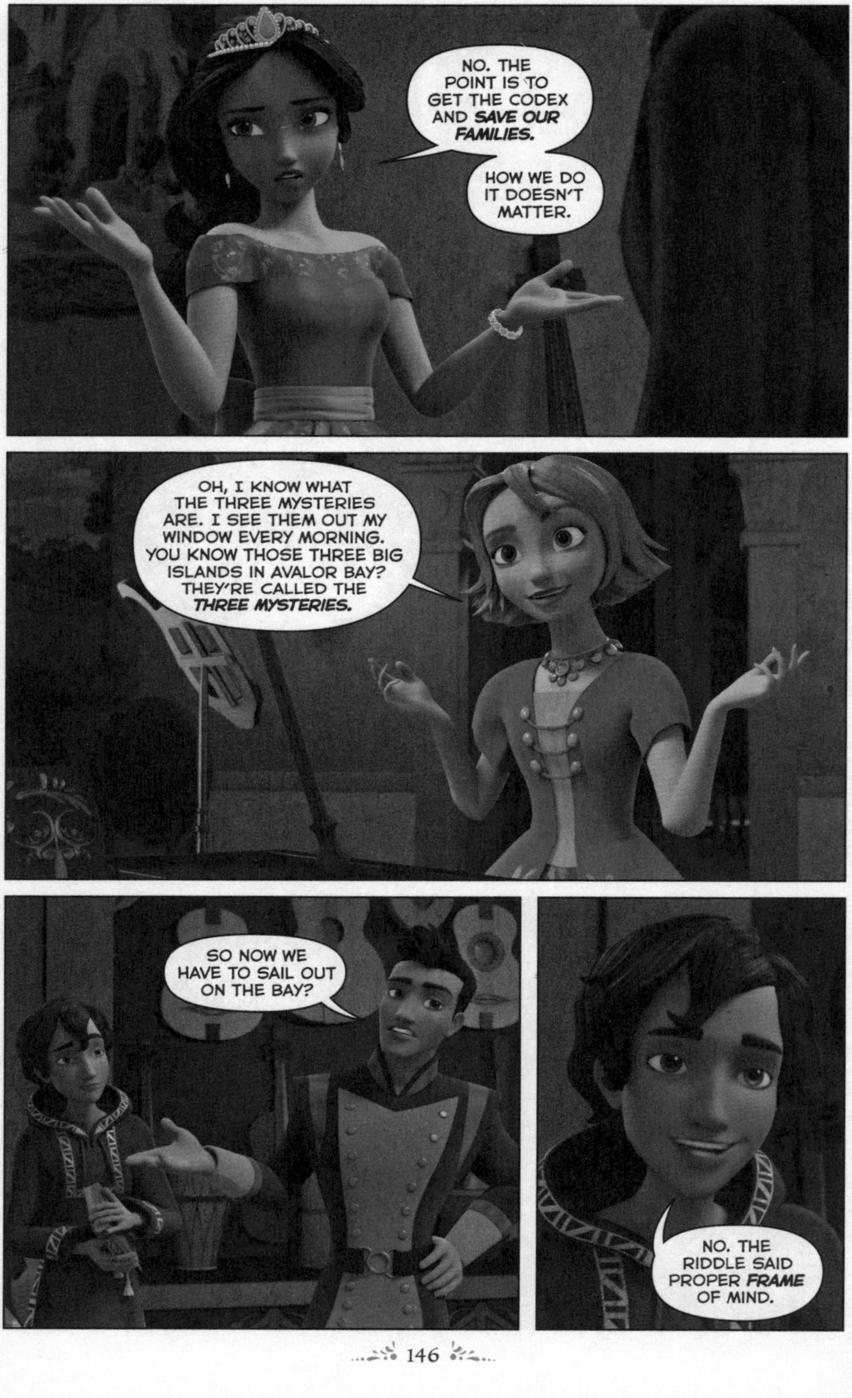
NO. THE POINT IS TO GET THE CODEX AND SAVE OUR FAMILIES.
HOW WE DO IT DOESN'T MATTER.
OH, I KNOW WHAT THE THREE MYSTERIES ARE. I SEE THEM OUT MY WINDOW EVERY MORNING. YOU KNOW THOSE THREE BIG ISLANDS IN AVALOR BAY? THEY'RE CALLED THE THREE MYSTERIES.
SO NOW WE HAVE TO SAIL OUT ON THE BAY?
NO. THE RIDDLE SAID PROPER FRAME OF MIND.

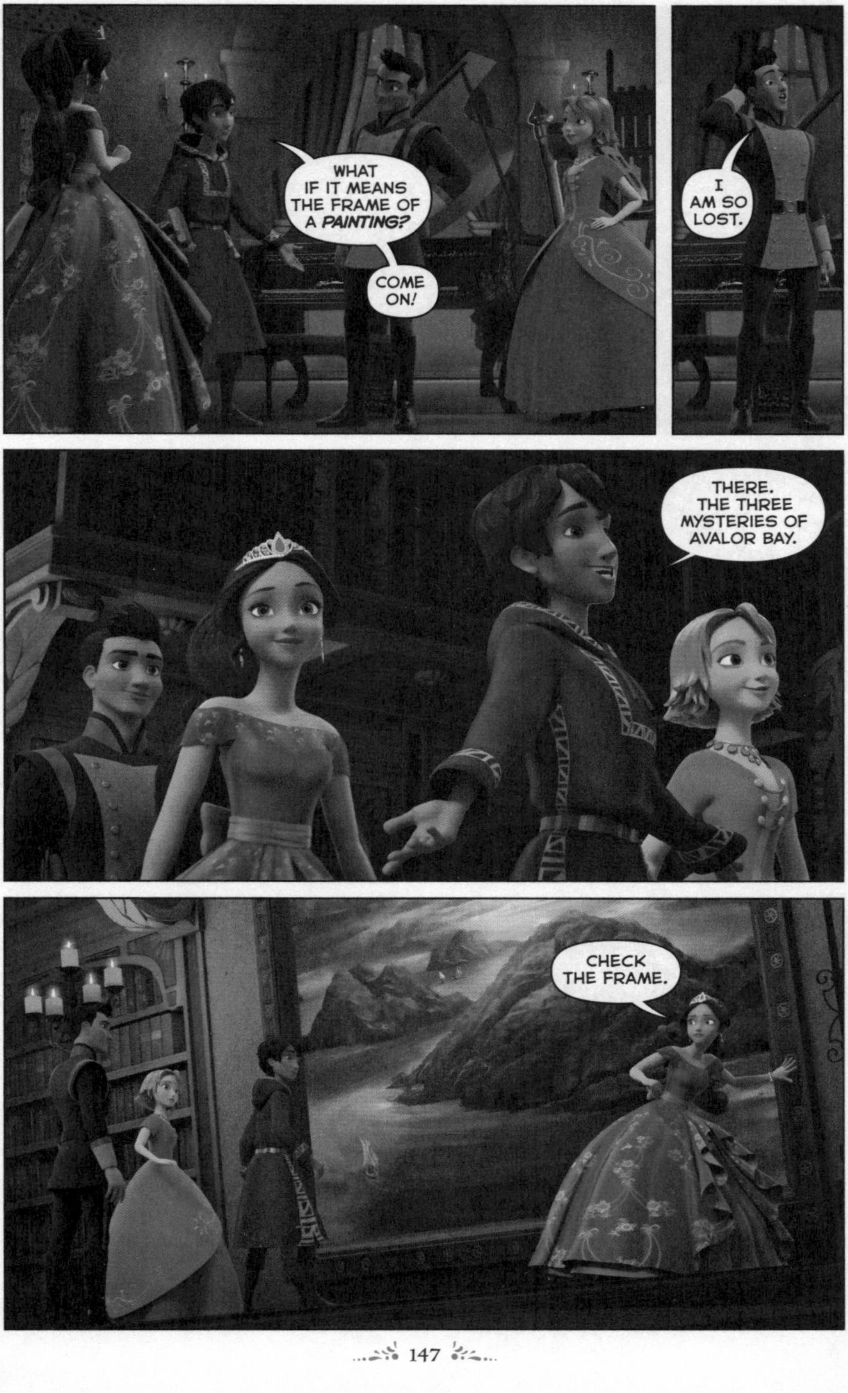

WHAT IF IT MEANS THE FRAME OF A *PAINTING?*
COME ON!
I AM SO LOST.
THERE. THE THREE MYSTERIES OF AVALOR BAY.
CHECK THE FRAME.

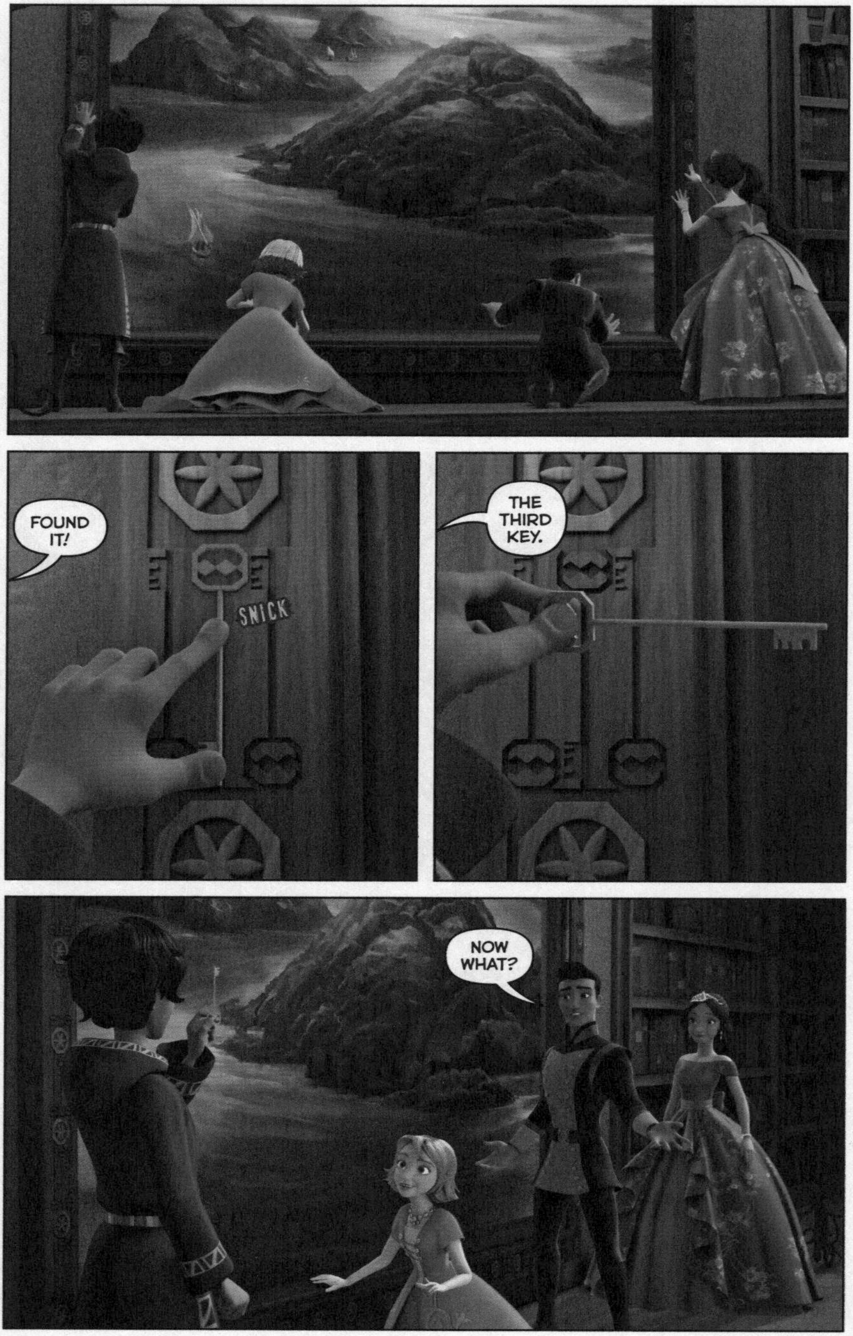
FOUND IT!
SNICK
THE THIRD KEY.
NOW WHAT?

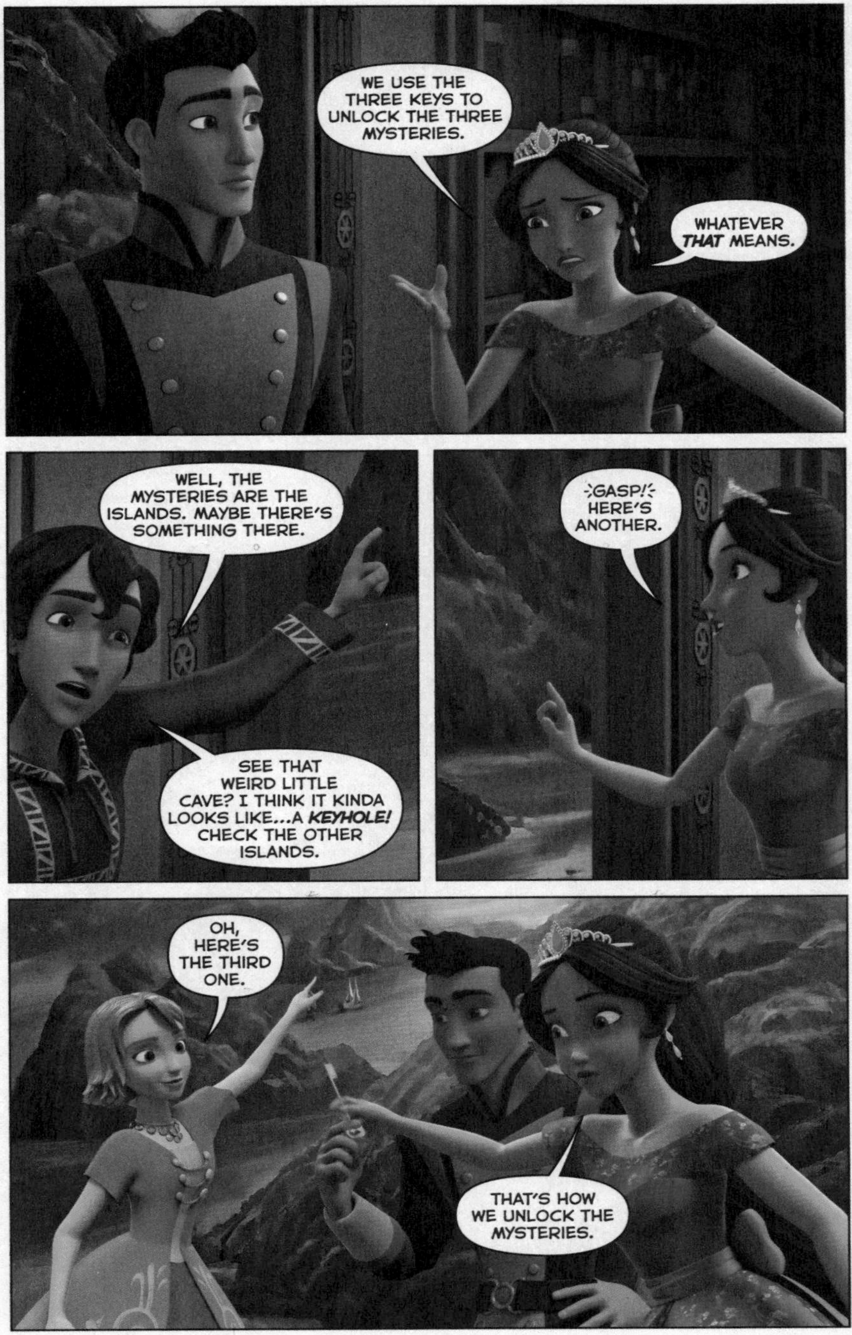
WE USE THE THREE KEYS TO UNLOCK THE THREE MYSTERIES.
WHATEVER *THAT* MEANS.
WELL, THE MYSTERIES ARE THE ISLANDS. MAYBE THERE'S SOMETHING THERE.
SEE THAT WEIRD LITTLE CAVE? I THINK IT KINDA LOOKS LIKE...A *KEYHOLE!* CHECK THE OTHER ISLANDS.
-GASP!- HERE'S ANOTHER.
OH, HERE'S THE THIRD ONE.
THAT'S HOW WE UNLOCK THE MYSTERIES.

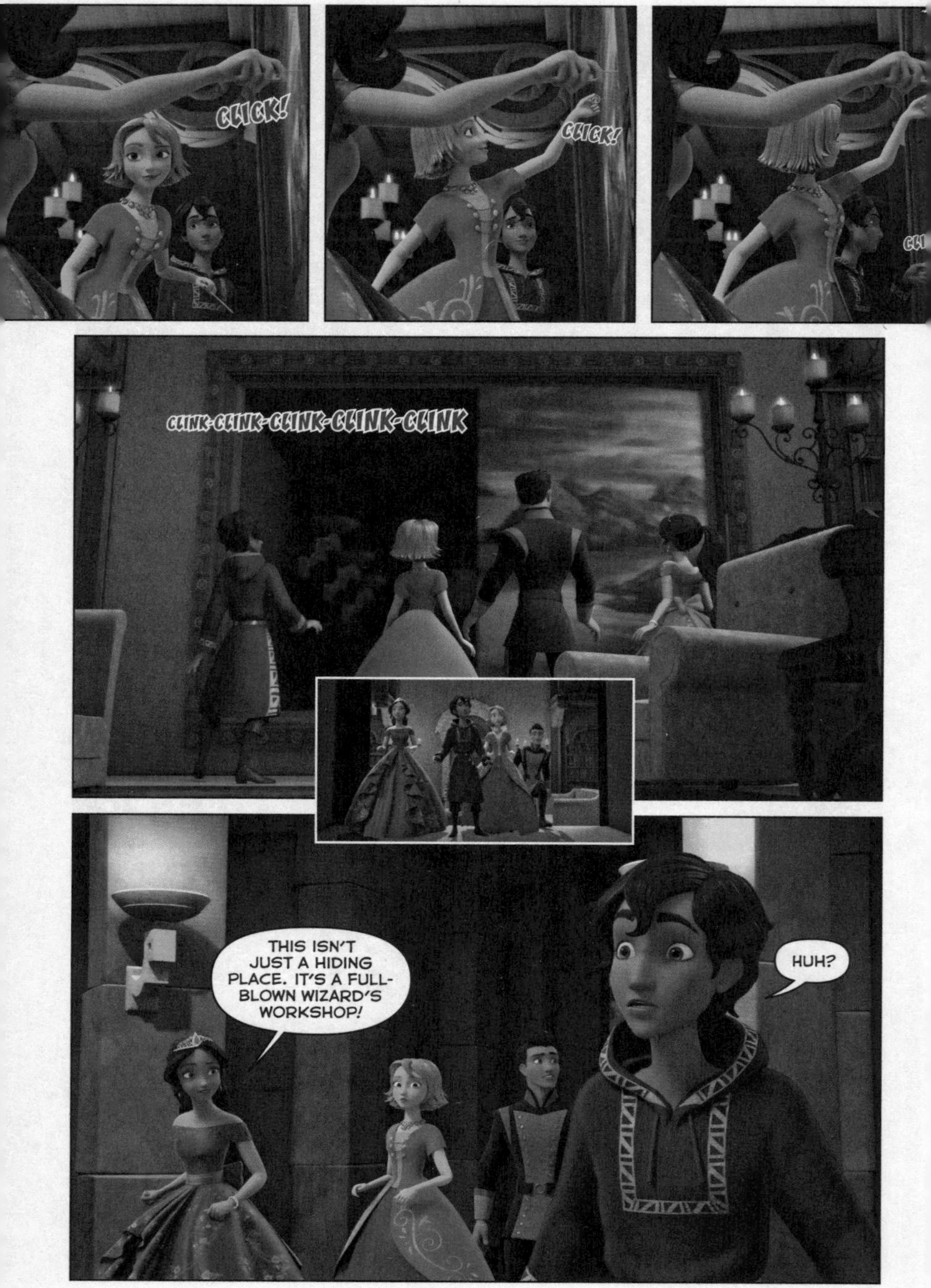
CLICK!
CLICK!
CLINK-CLINK-CLINK-CLINK-CLINK
THIS ISN'T JUST A HIDING PLACE. IT'S A FULL-BLOWN WIZARD'S WORKSHOP!
HUH?

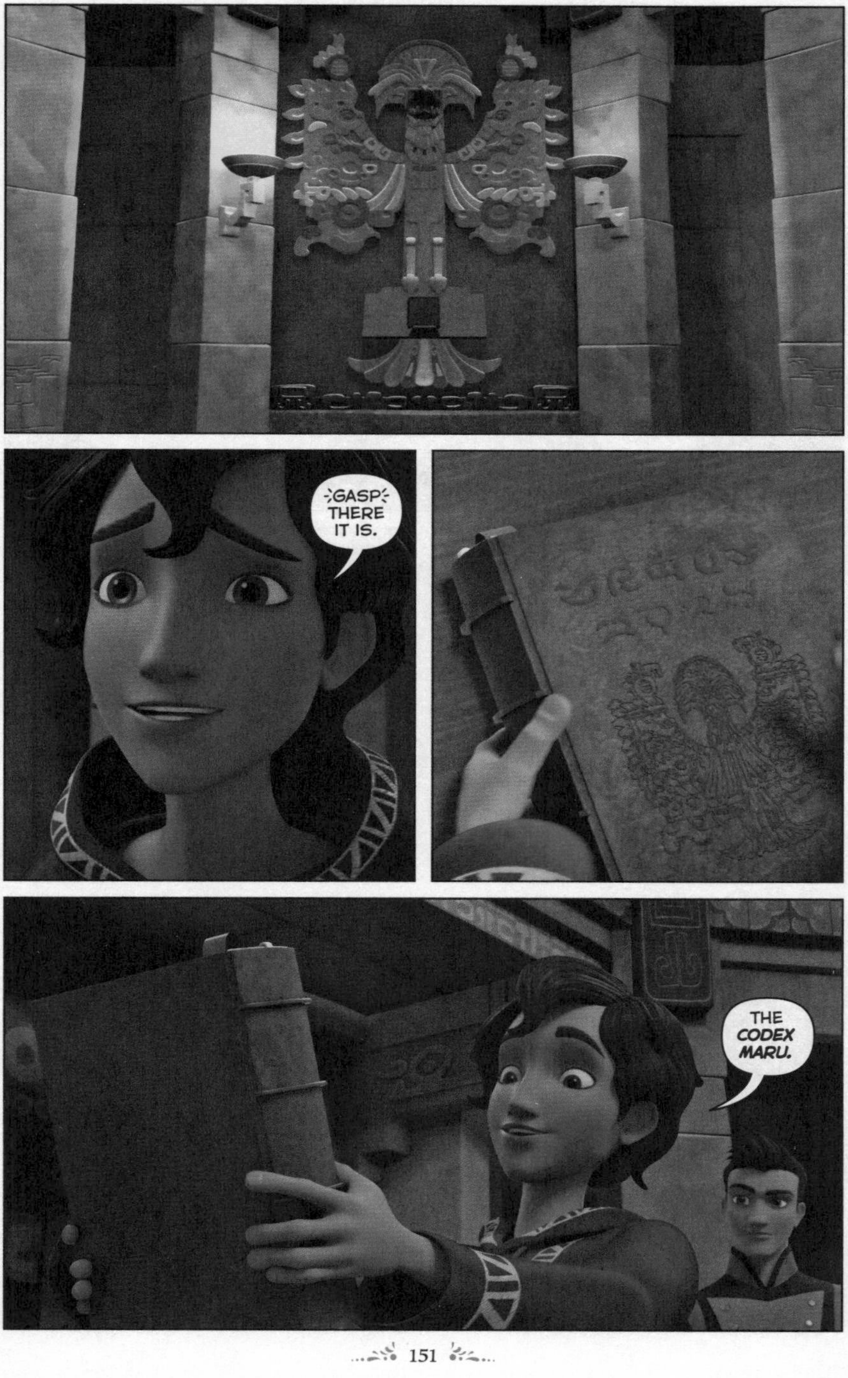
GASP
THERE IT IS.
THE CODEX MARU.

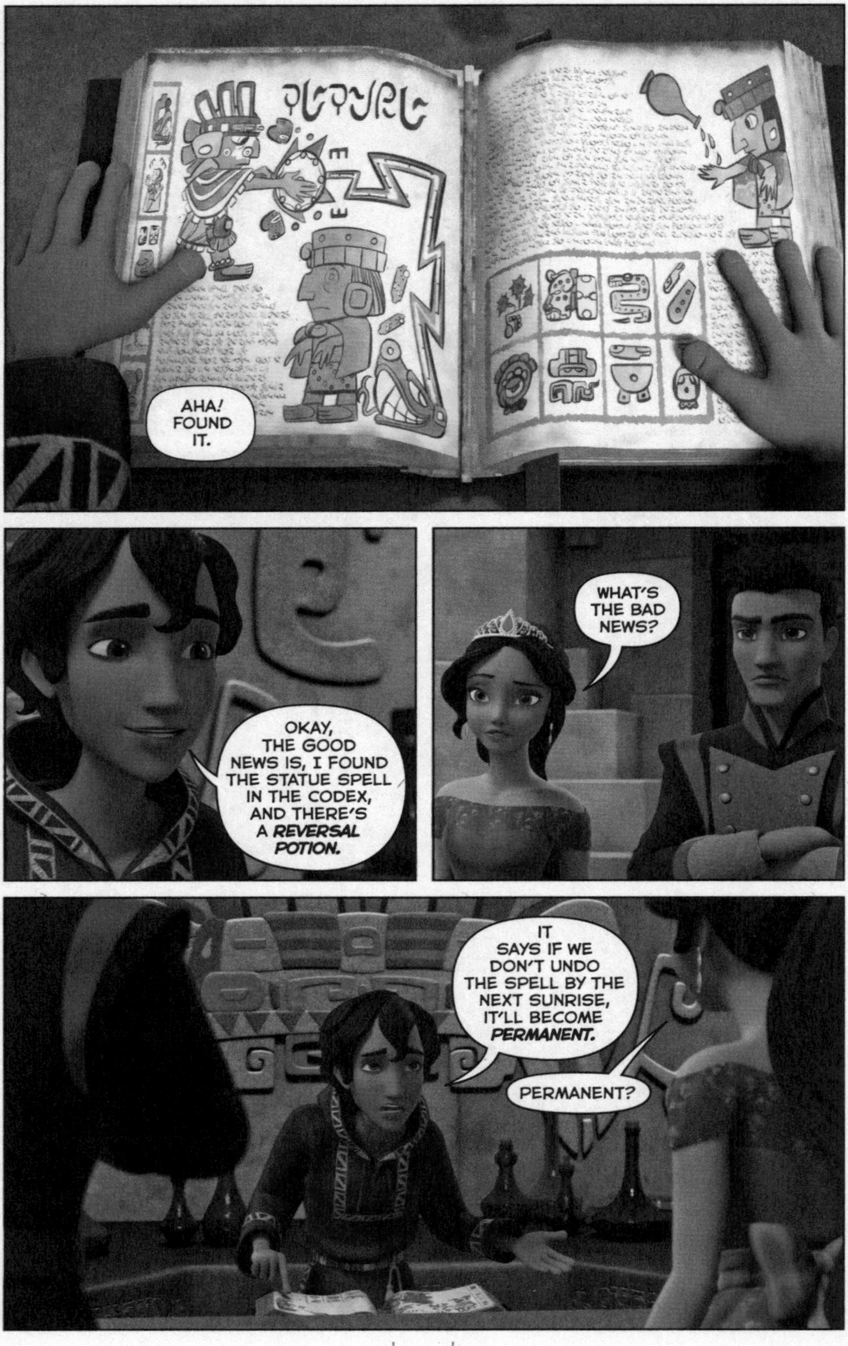
AHA! FOUND IT.
OKAY, THE GOOD NEWS IS, I FOUND THE STATUE SPELL IN THE CODEX, AND THERE'S A *REVERSAL POTION.*
WHAT'S THE BAD NEWS?
IT SAYS IF WE DON'T UNDO THE SPELL BY THE NEXT SUNRISE, IT'LL BECOME *PERMANENT.*
PERMANENT?

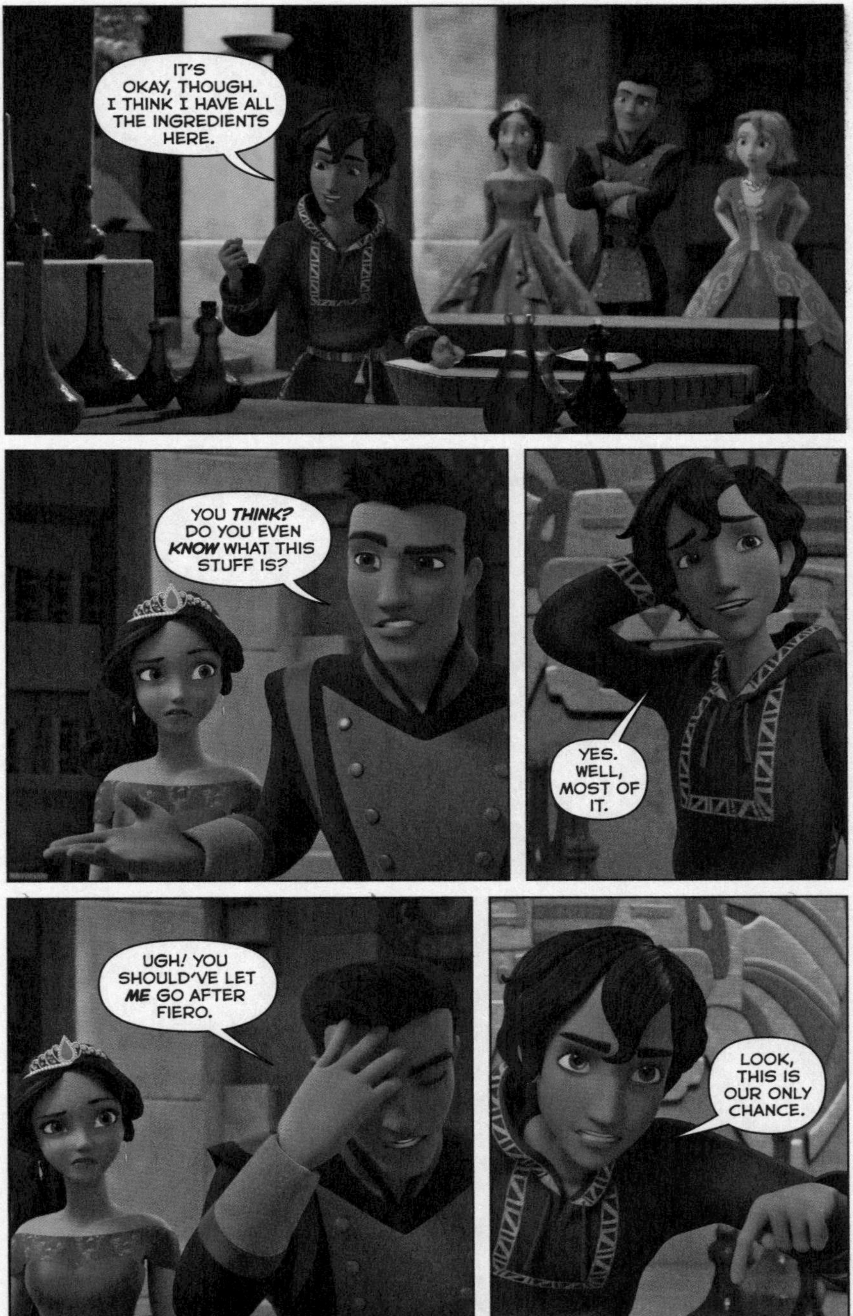
IT'S OKAY, THOUGH. I THINK I HAVE ALL THE INGREDIENTS HERE.
YOU *THINK?* DO YOU EVEN *KNOW* WHAT THIS STUFF IS?
YES. WELL, MOST OF IT.
UGH! YOU SHOULD'VE LET *ME* GO AFTER FIERO.
LOOK, THIS IS OUR ONLY CHANCE.

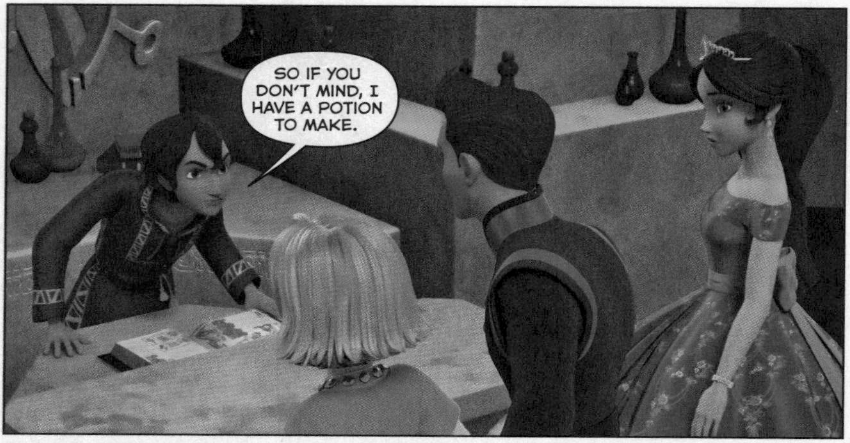
SO IF YOU DON'T MIND, I HAVE A POTION TO MAKE.

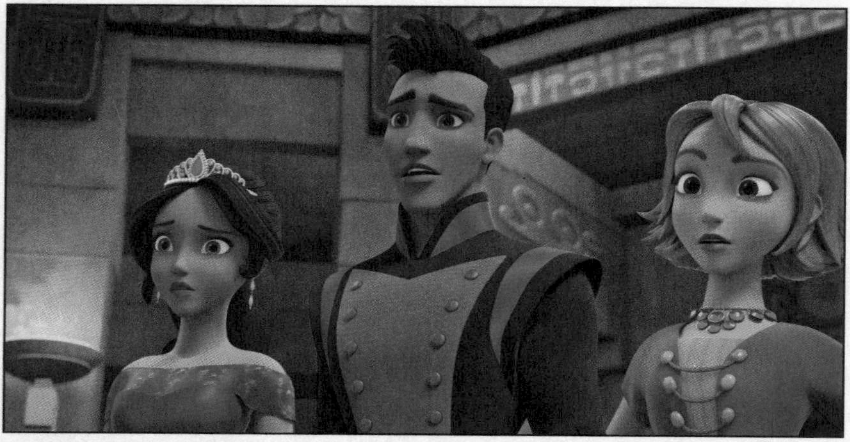

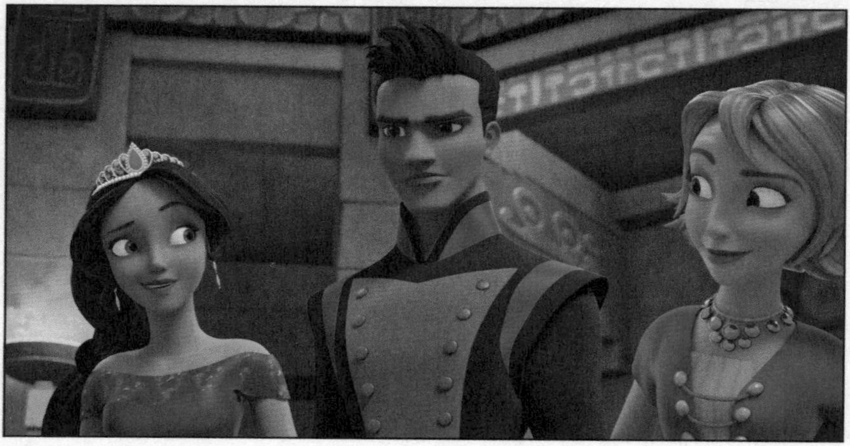

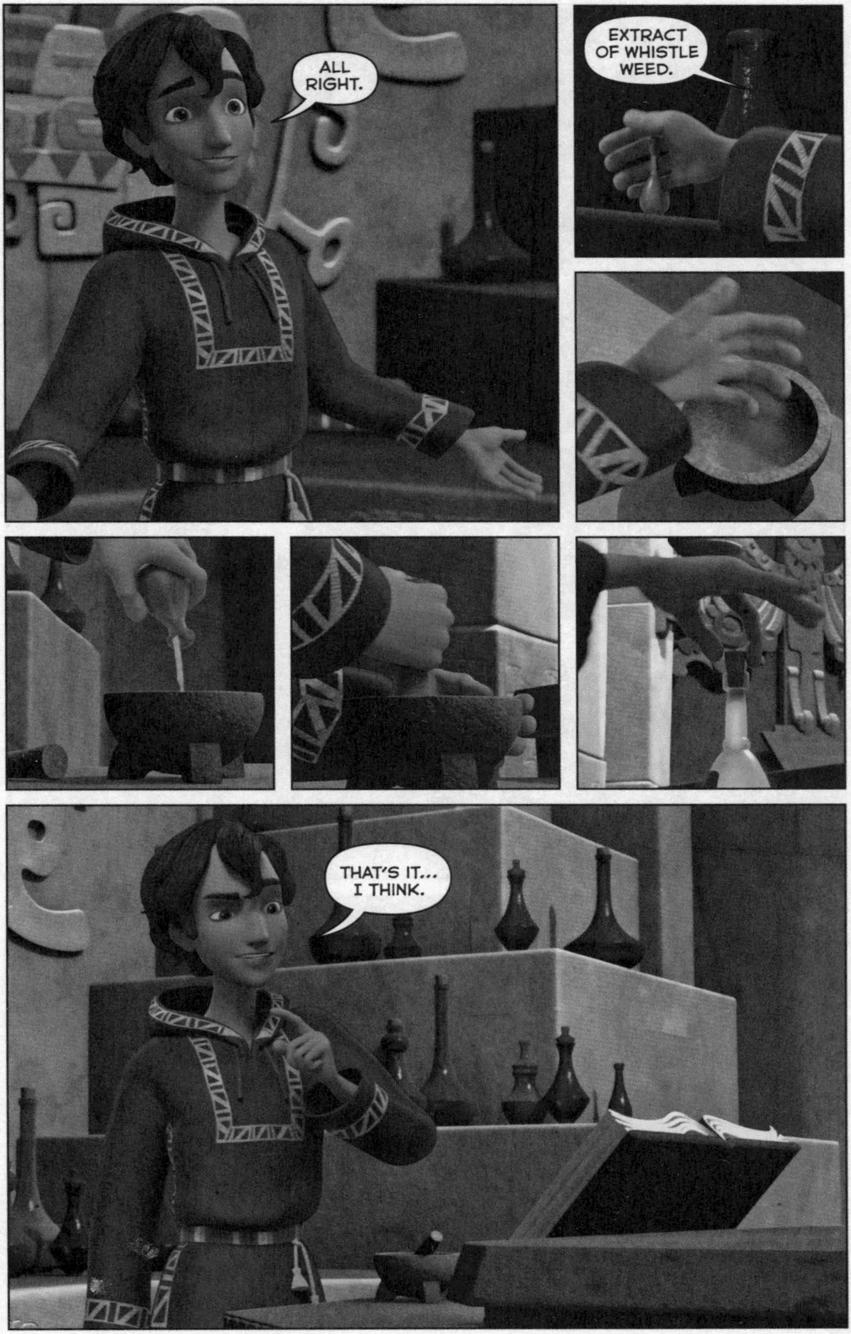
ALL RIGHT.
EXTRACT OF WHISTLE WEED.
THAT'S IT... I THINK.

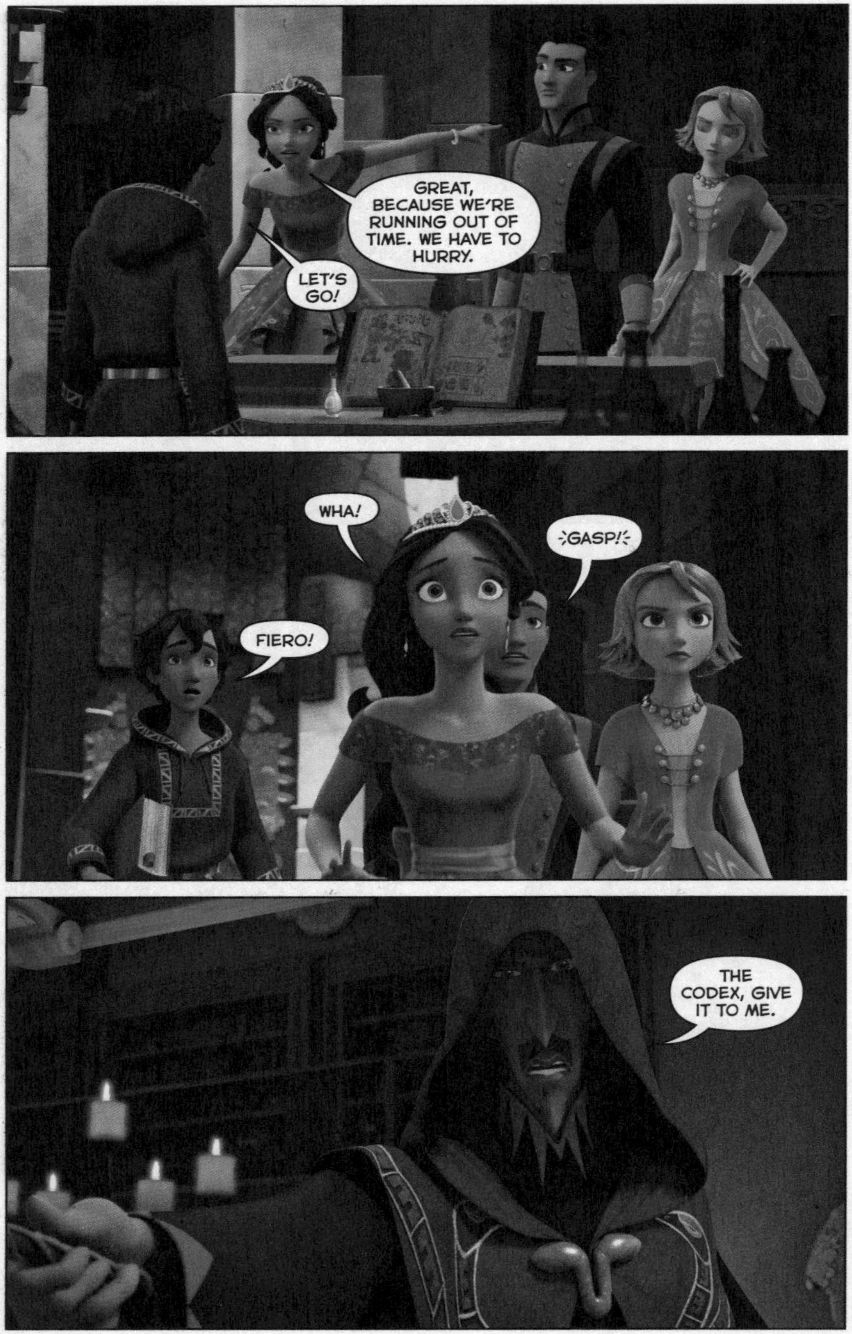
GREAT, BECAUSE WE'RE RUNNING OUT OF TIME. WE HAVE TO HURRY.
LET'S GO!
WHA!
-GASP!-
FIERO!
THE CODEX, GIVE IT TO ME.

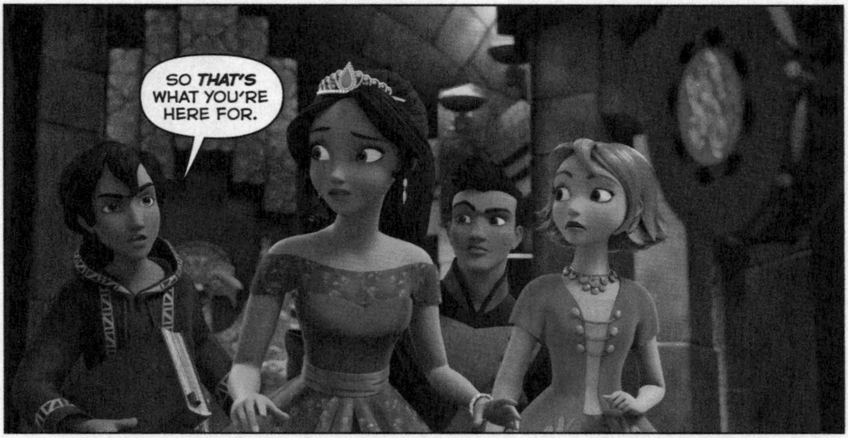
SO *THAT'S* WHAT YOU'RE HERE FOR.

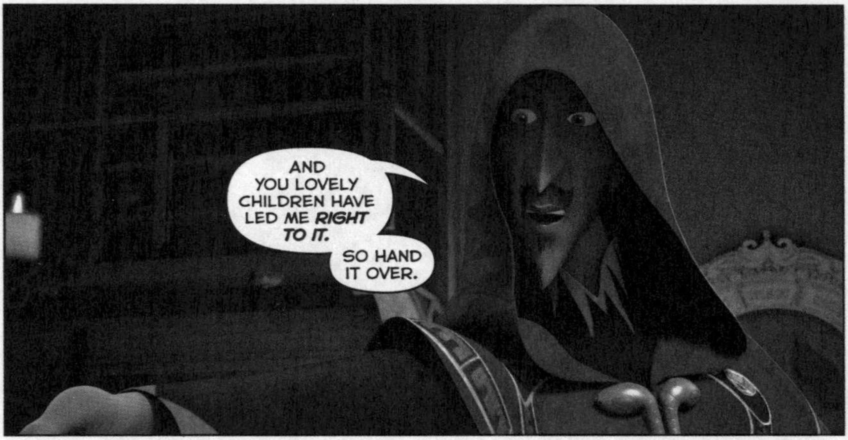
AND YOU LOVELY CHILDREN HAVE LED ME *RIGHT TO IT.*
SO HAND IT OVER.

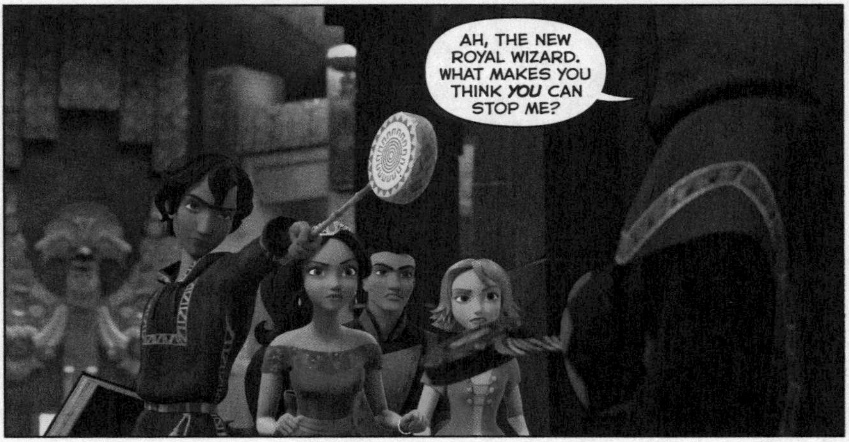
AH, THE NEW ROYAL WIZARD. WHAT MAKES YOU THINK *YOU* CAN STOP ME?

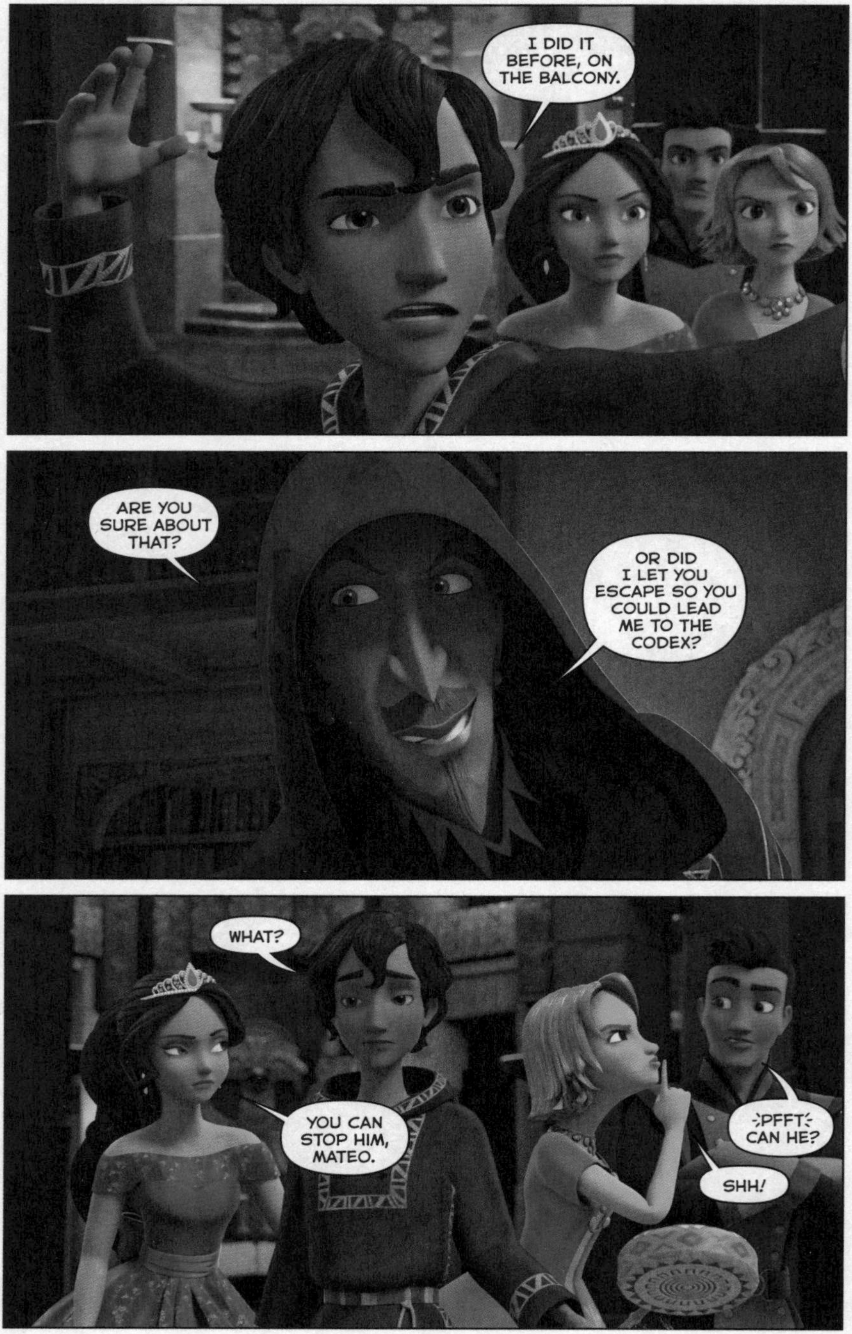
I DID IT BEFORE, ON THE BALCONY.
ARE YOU SURE ABOUT THAT?
OR DID I LET YOU ESCAPE SO YOU COULD LEAD ME TO THE CODEX?
WHAT?
YOU CAN STOP HIM, MATEO.
PFFT CAN HE?
SHH!

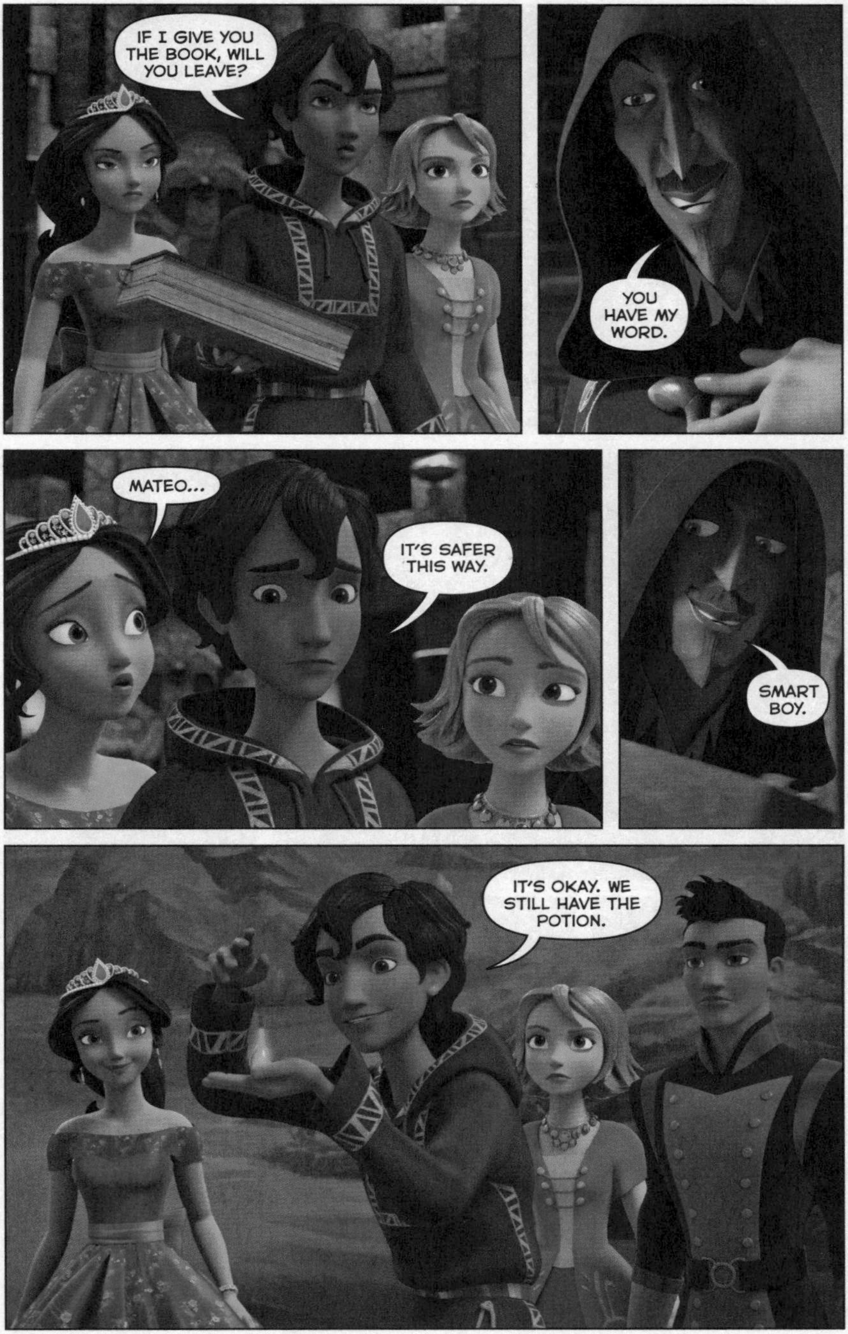
IF I GIVE YOU THE BOOK, WILL YOU LEAVE?
YOU HAVE MY WORD.
MATEO...
IT'S SAFER THIS WAY.
SMART BOY.
IT'S OKAY. WE STILL HAVE THE POTION.

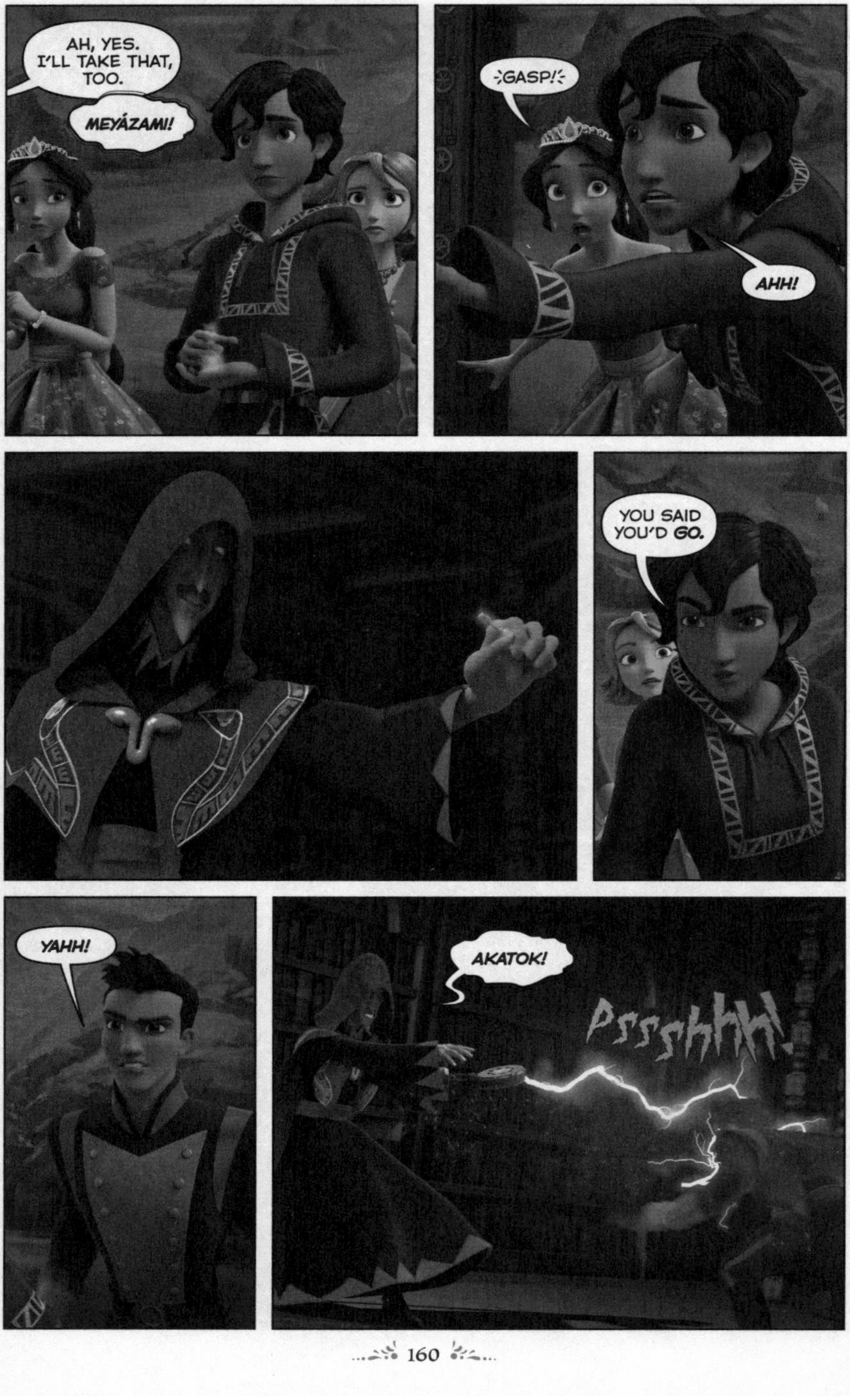
AH, YES. I'LL TAKE THAT, TOO.
MEYÁZAMI!
-GASP!-
AHH!
YOU SAID YOU'D GO.
YAHH!
AKATOK!
Psssshhh!

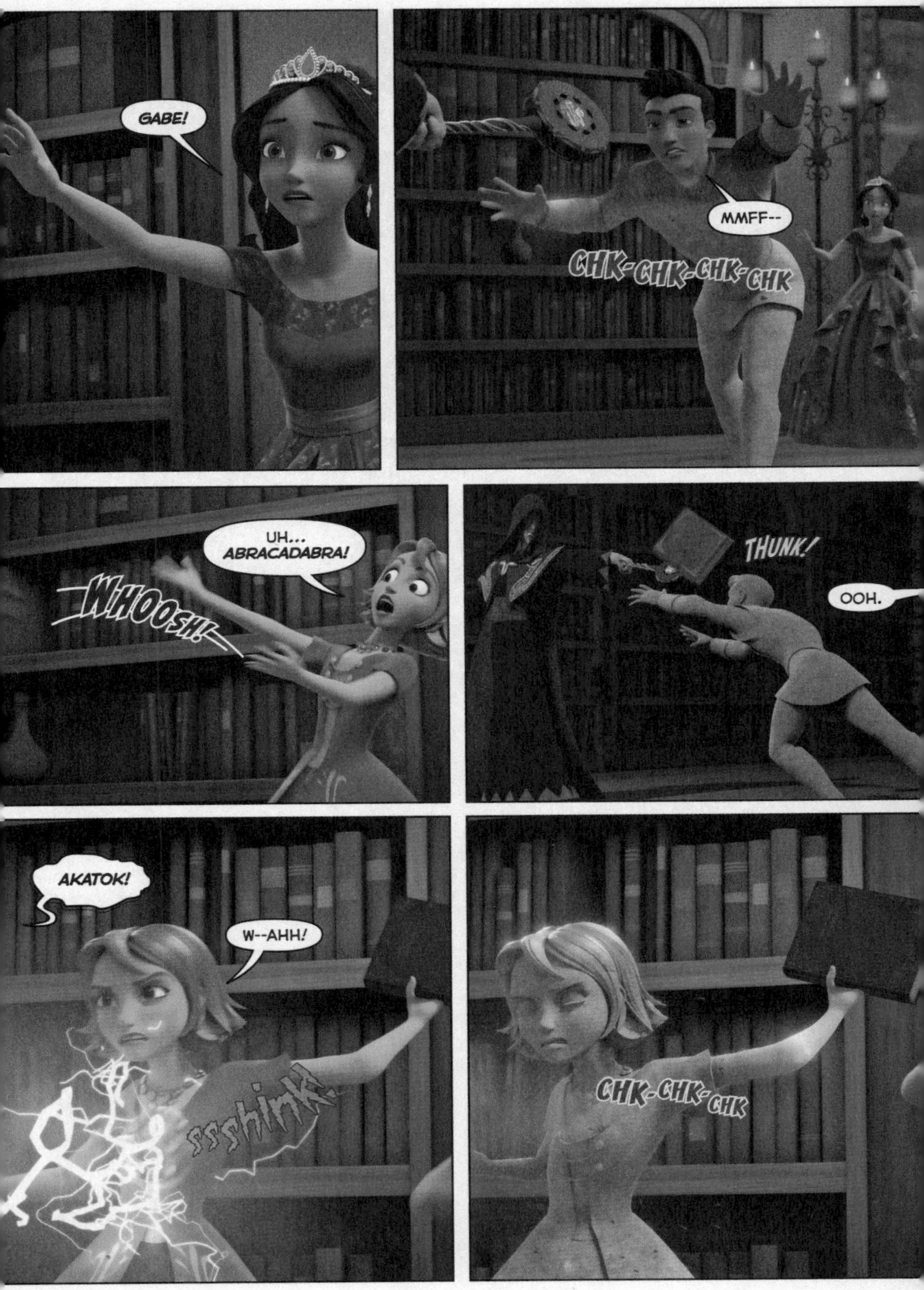
GABE!
MMFF--
CHK-CHK-CHK-CHK
UH... ABRACADABRA!
WHOOSH!
THUNK!
OOH.
AKATOK!
W--AHH!
SSSHINK!
CHK-CHK-CHK

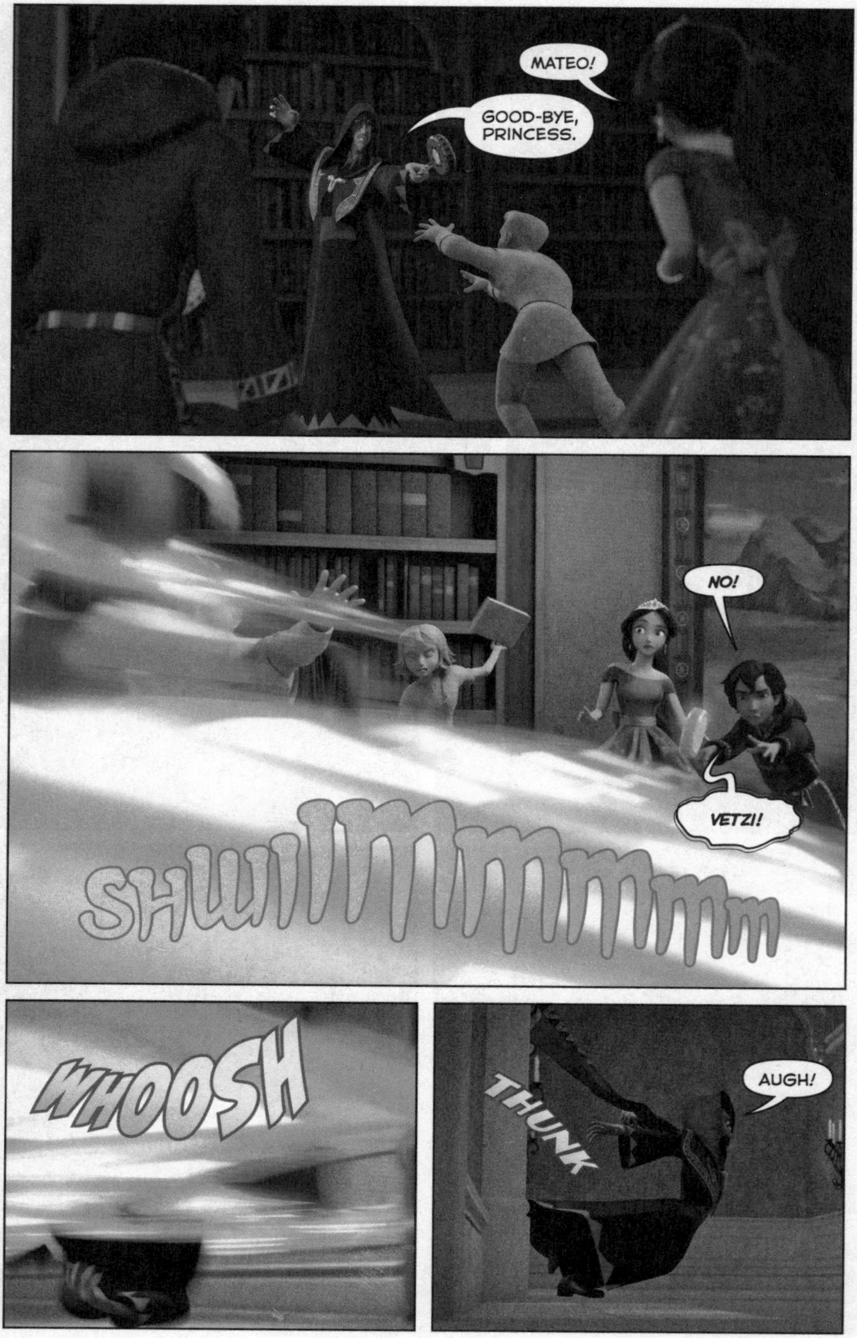
MATEO!
GOOD-BYE, PRINCESS.
NO!
VETZI!
SHWIIMMMMMM
WHOOSH
THUNK
AUGH!

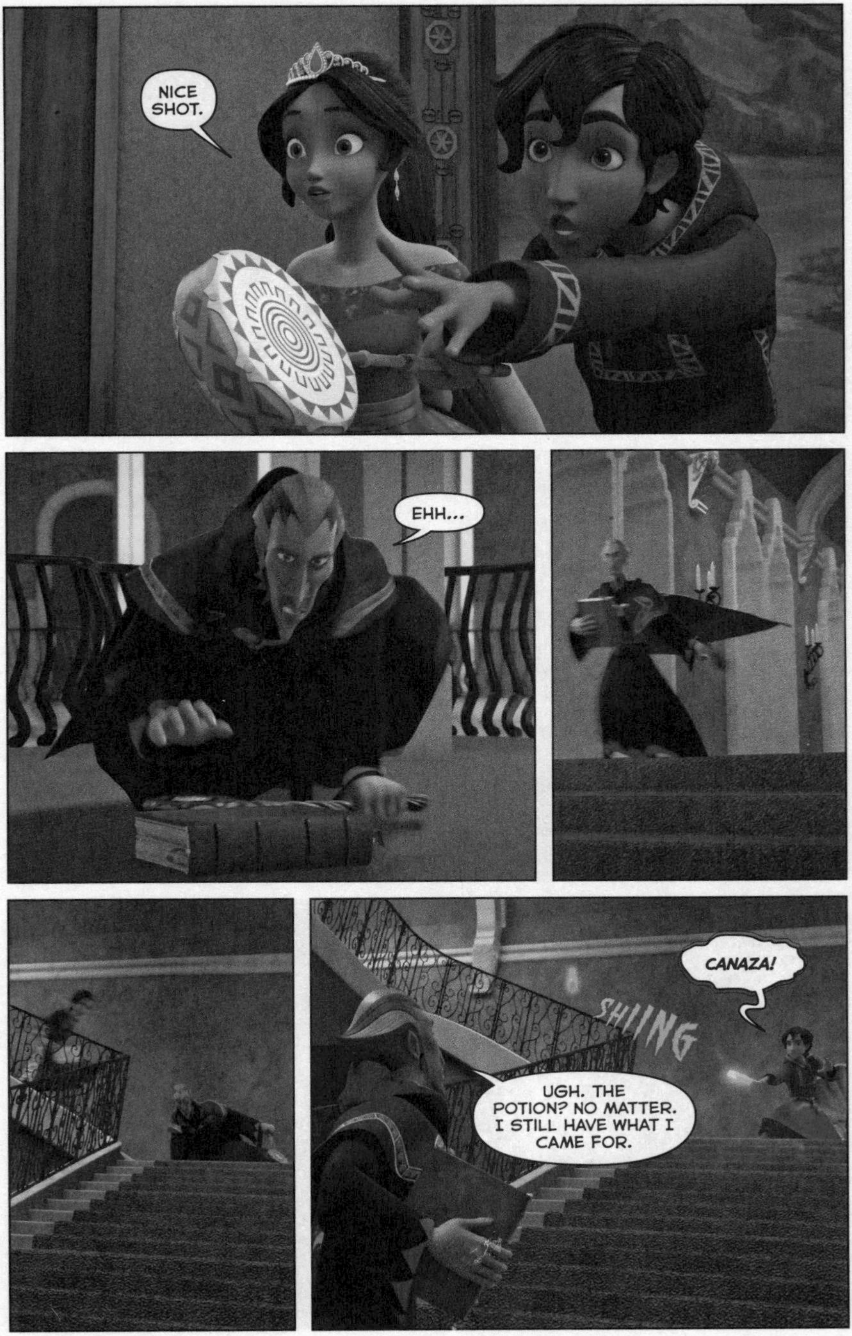
NICE SHOT.
EHH...
CANAZA!
SHIING
UGH. THE POTION? NO MATTER. I STILL HAVE WHAT I CAME FOR.

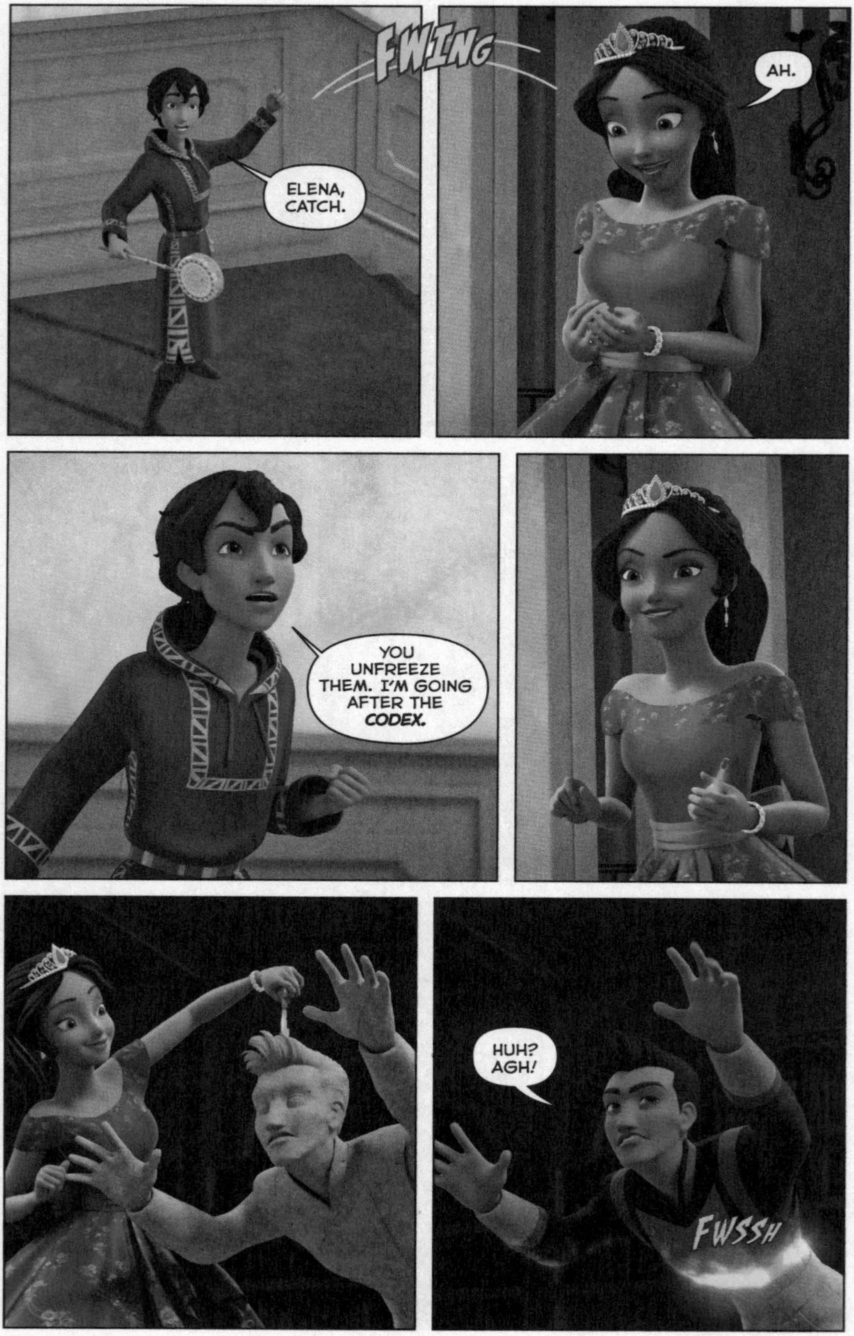
FWING
ELENA, CATCH.
AH.
YOU UNFREEZE THEM. I'M GOING AFTER THE *CODEX.*
HUH? AGH!
FWSSH

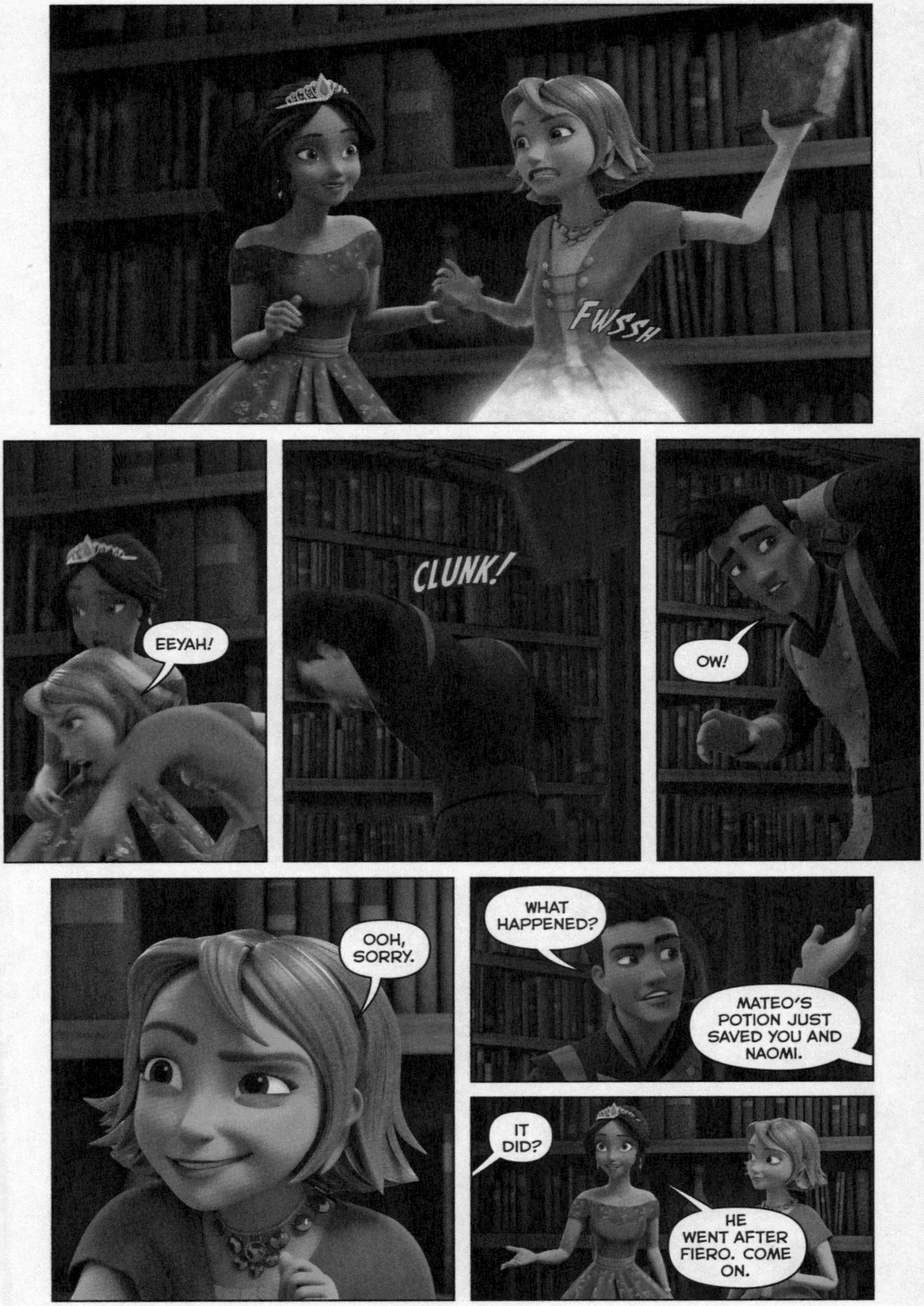
FWSSH
EEYAH!
CLUNK!
OW!
OOH, SORRY.
WHAT HAPPENED?
MATEO'S POTION JUST SAVED YOU AND NAOMI.
IT DID?
HE WENT AFTER FIERO. COME ON.

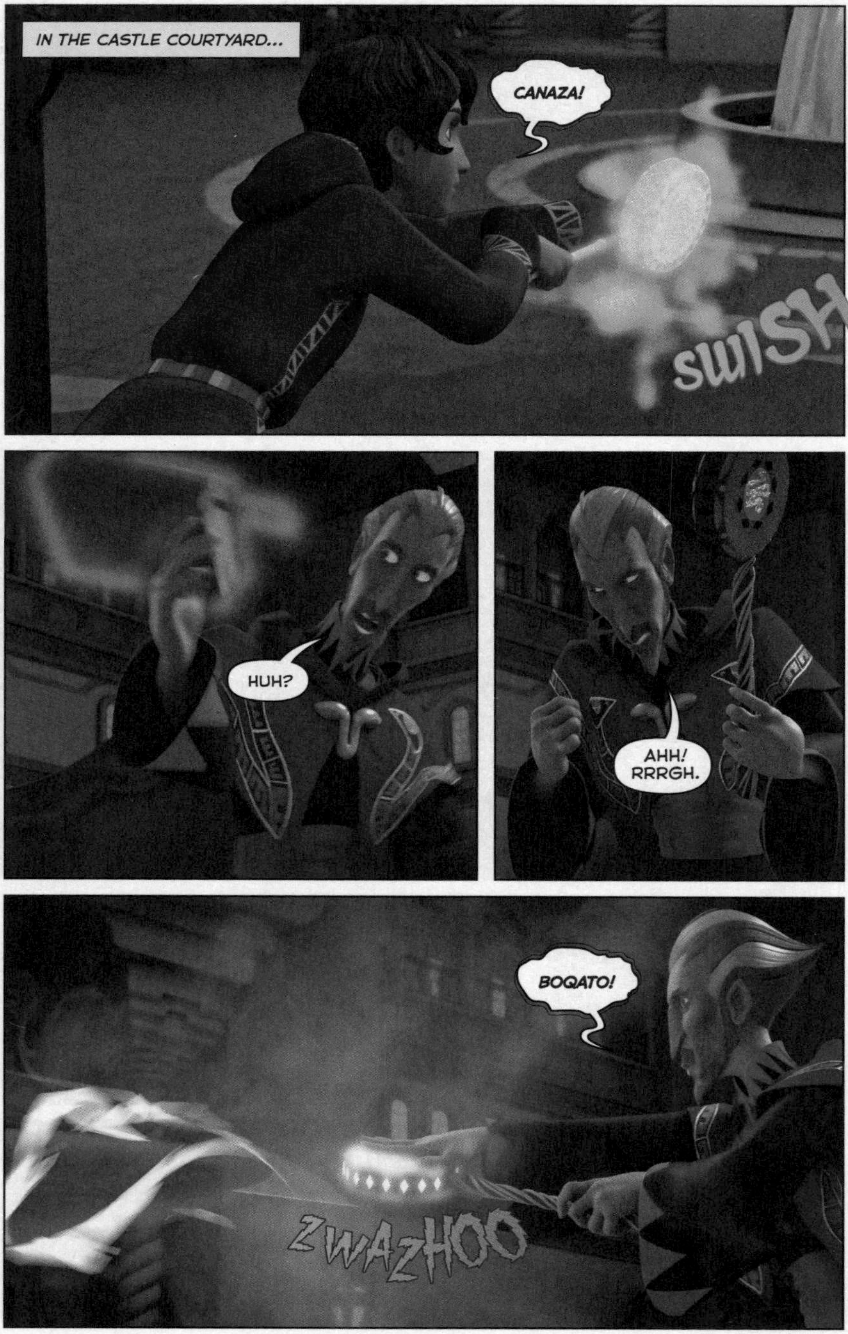
IN THE CASTLE COURTYARD...
CANAZA!
SWISH
HUH?
AHH! RRRGH.
BOQATO!
ZWAZHOO

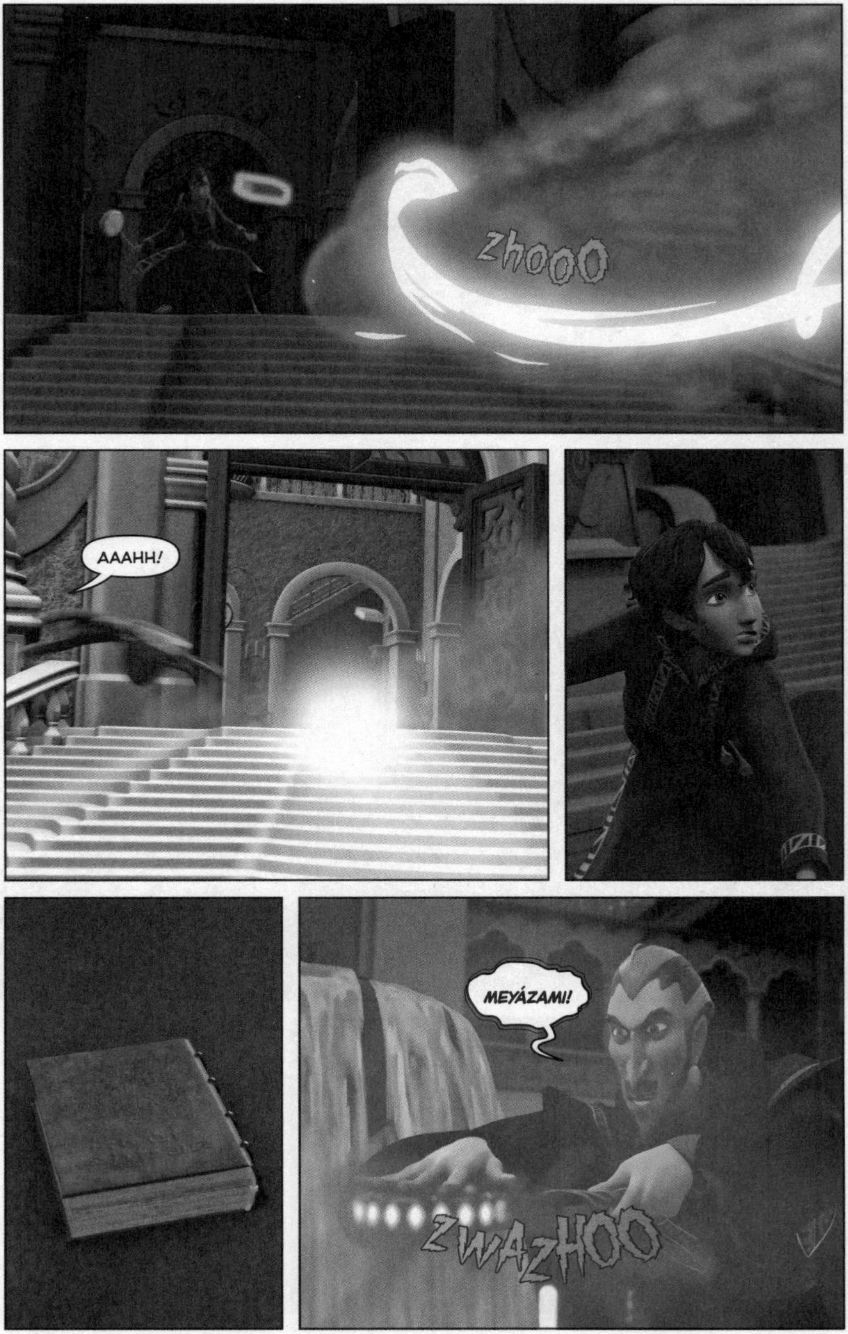
ZHOOO
AAAHH!
MEYÁZAMI!
ZWAZHOO

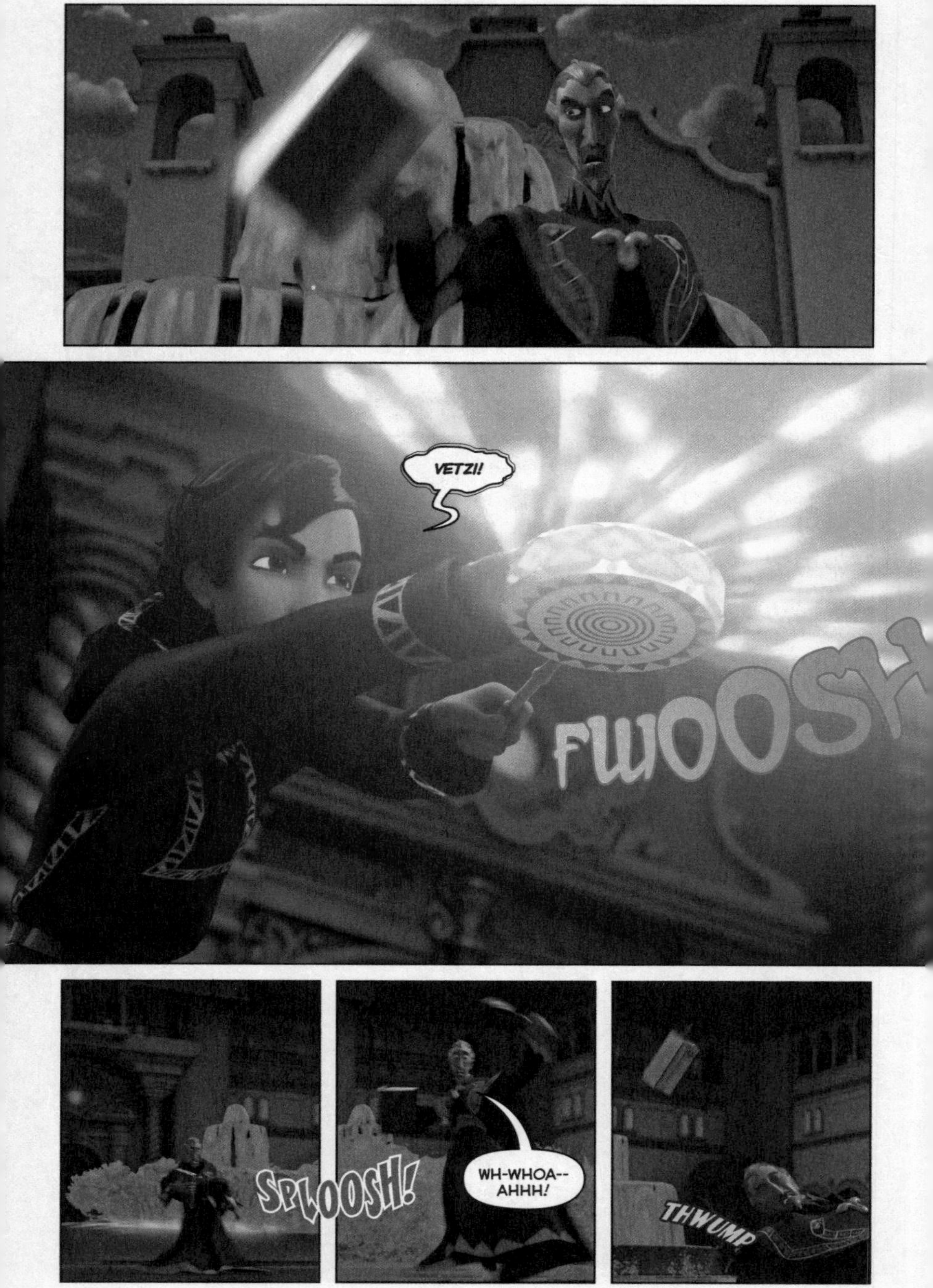
VETZI!
FWOOSH
SPLOOSH!
WH-WHOA--
AHHH!
THWUMP

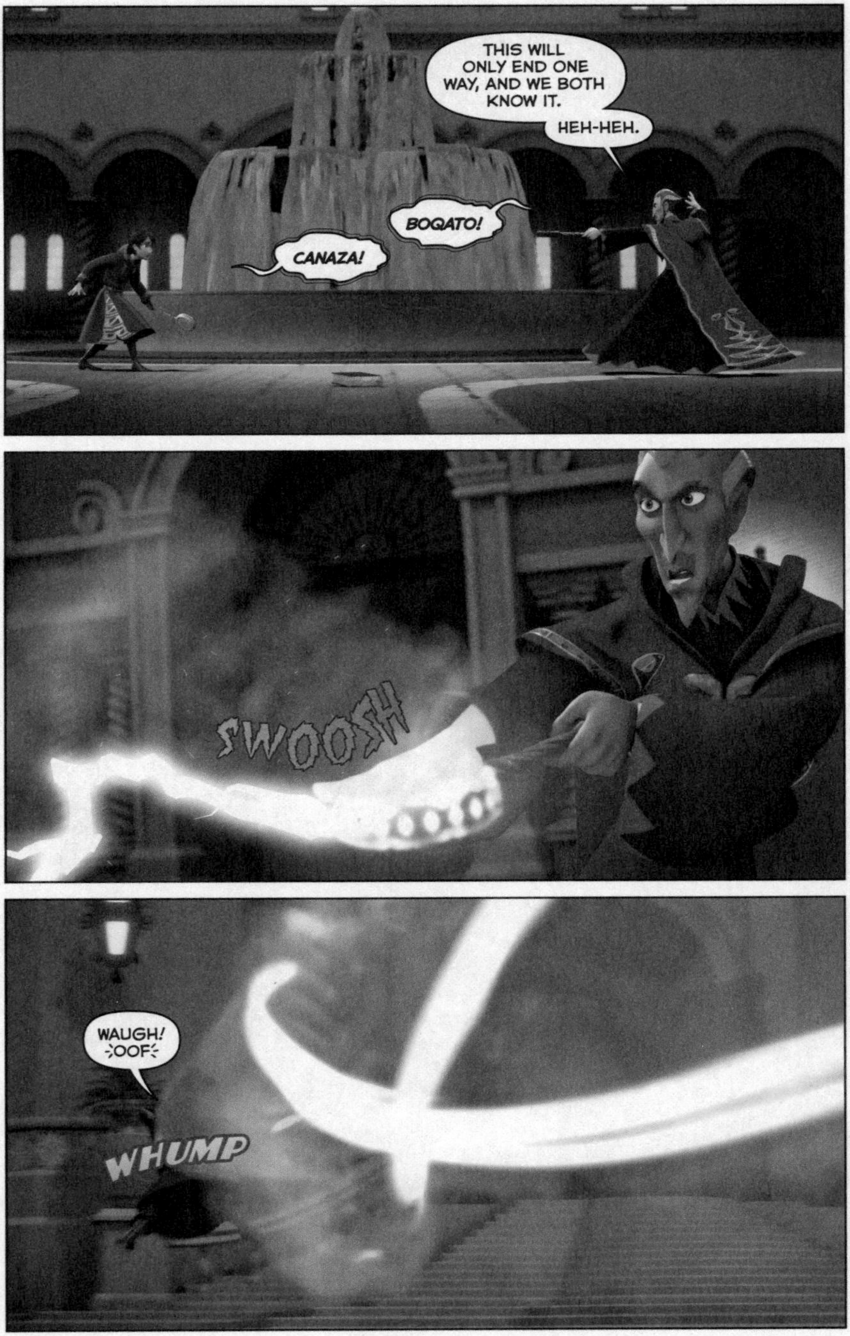
THIS WILL ONLY END ONE WAY, AND WE BOTH KNOW IT.
HEH-HEH.
BOQATO!
CANAZA!
SWOOSH
WAUGH! OOF!
WHUMP

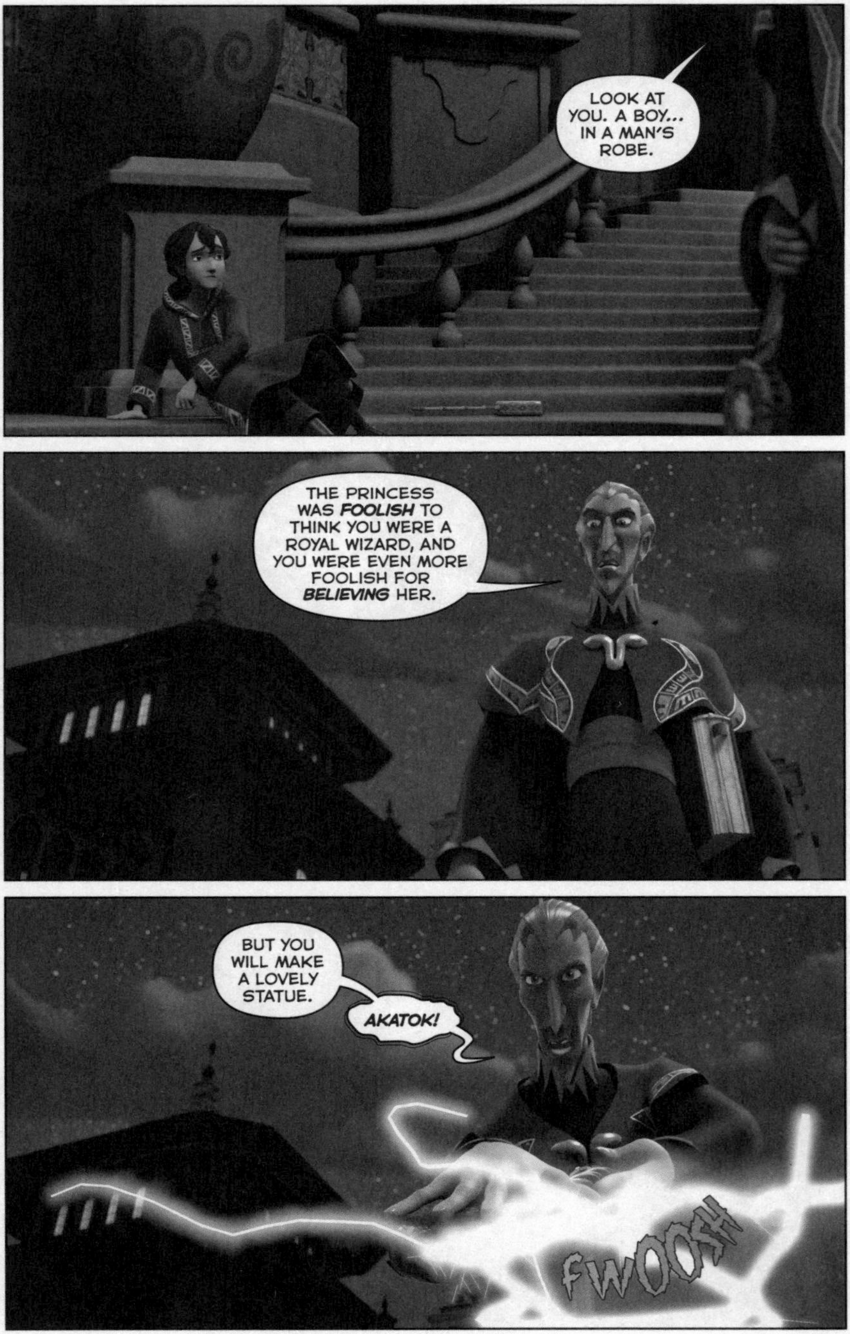
LOOK AT YOU. A BOY... IN A MAN'S ROBE.
THE PRINCESS WAS *FOOLISH* TO THINK YOU WERE A ROYAL WIZARD, AND YOU WERE EVEN MORE FOOLISH FOR *BELIEVING* HER.
BUT YOU WILL MAKE A LOVELY STATUE.
AKATOK!
FWOOSH

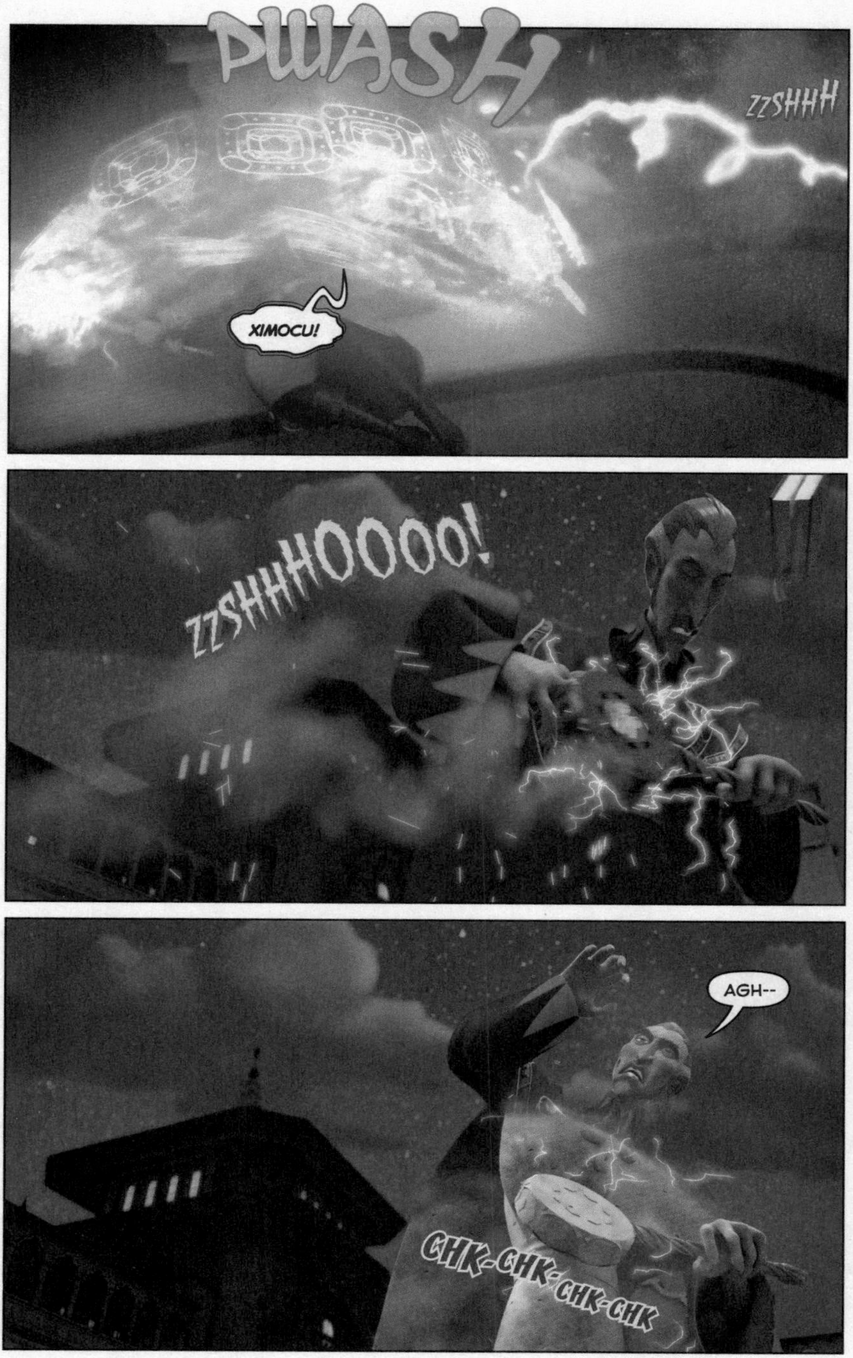
PWASH
ZZSHHH
XIMOCU!
ZZSHHHOOOO!
AGH--
CHK-CHK-CHK-CHK

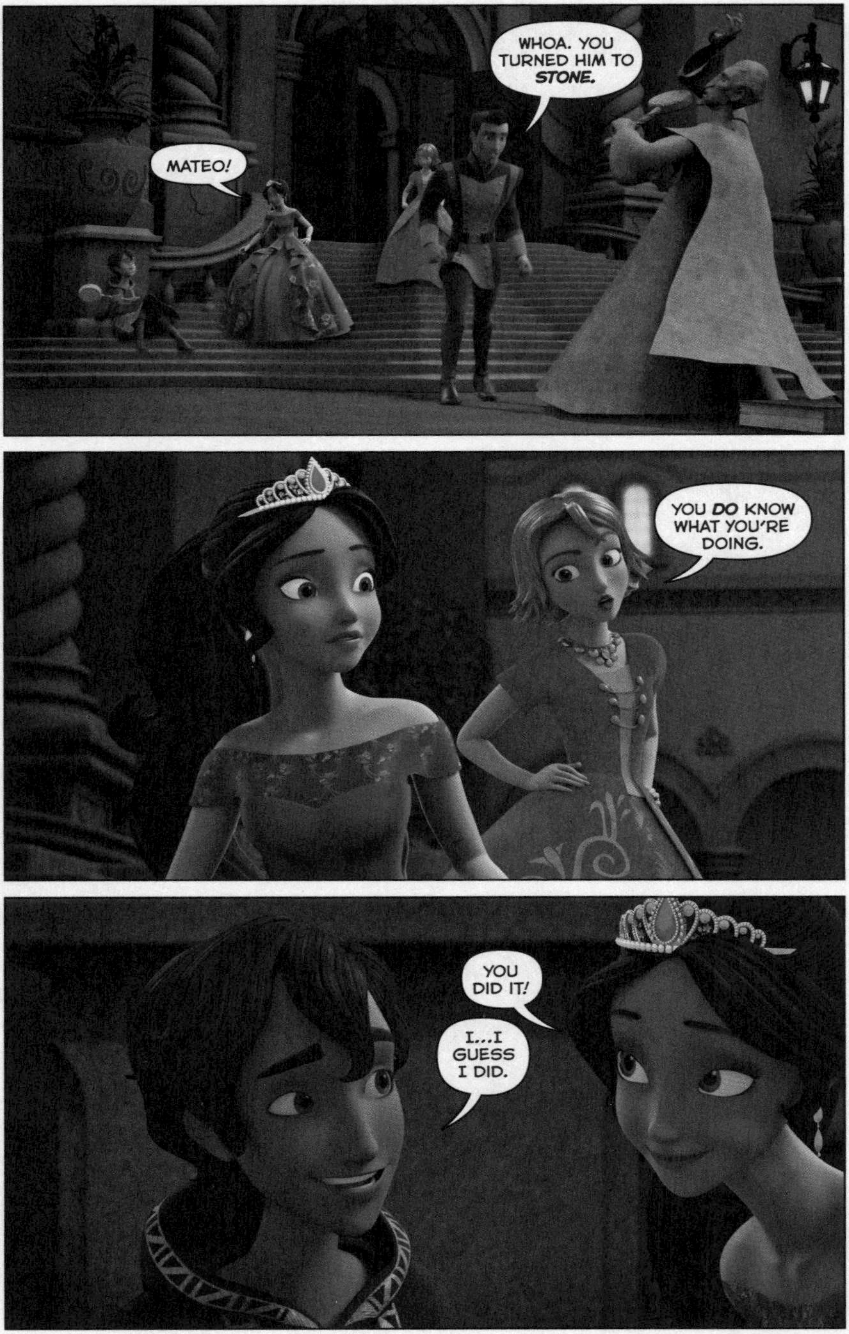
MATEO!
WHOA. YOU TURNED HIM TO *STONE.*
YOU *DO* KNOW WHAT YOU'RE DOING.
YOU DID IT!
I...I GUESS I DID.

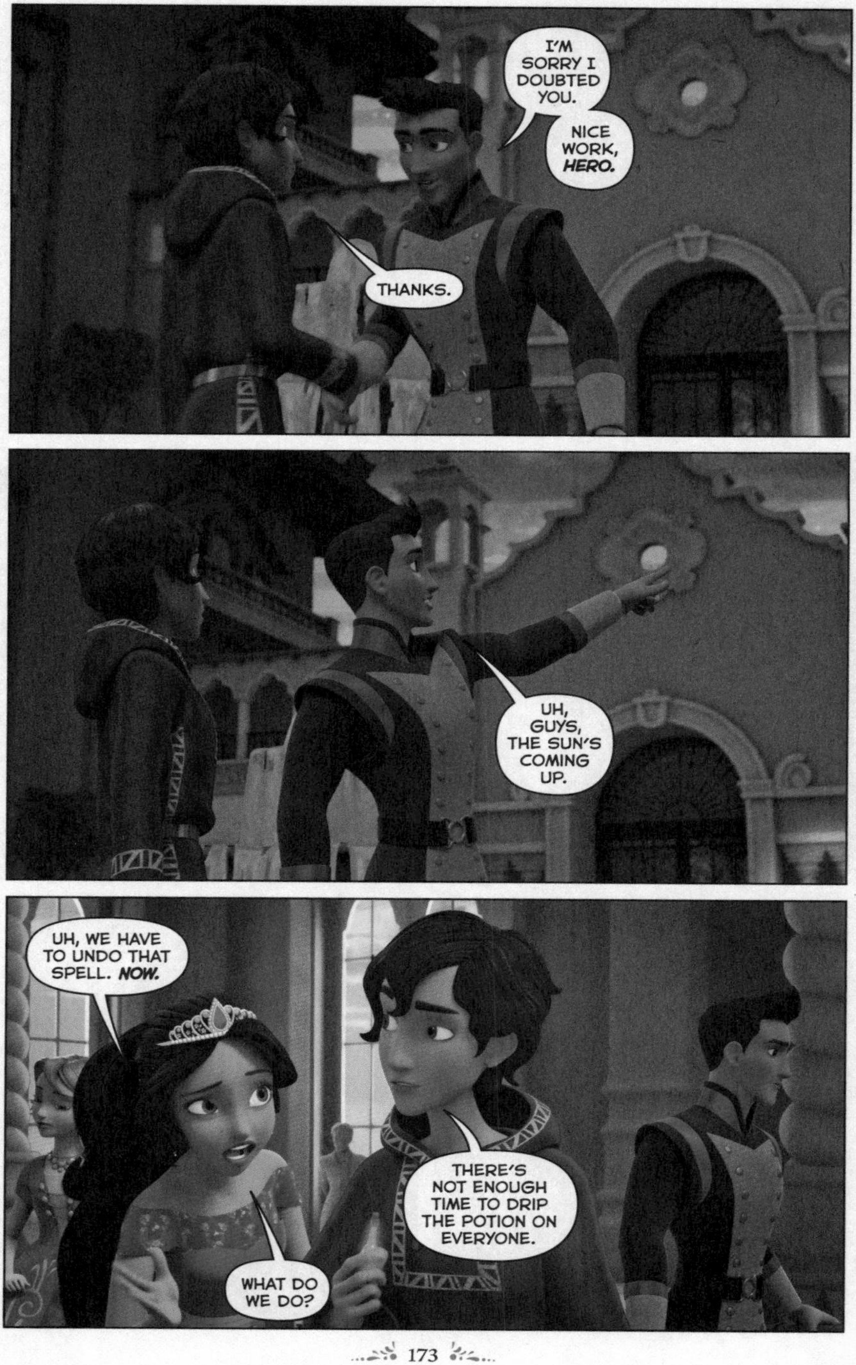
I'M SORRY I DOUBTED YOU.
NICE WORK, *HERO.*
THANKS.
UH, GUYS, THE SUN'S COMING UP.
UH, WE HAVE TO UNDO THAT SPELL. *NOW.*
THERE'S NOT ENOUGH TIME TO DRIP THE POTION ON EVERYONE.
WHAT DO WE DO?

GASP
GABE, HOW'S YOUR THROWING ARM?

LIKE A CANNON.

HIGH AS YOU CAN...RIGHT IN THE CENTER OF THE ROOM.

YOU GOT IT!

SOLAZA!

PWISSHHH

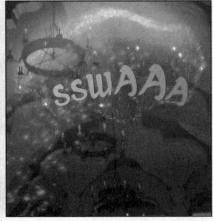

SSWAAA

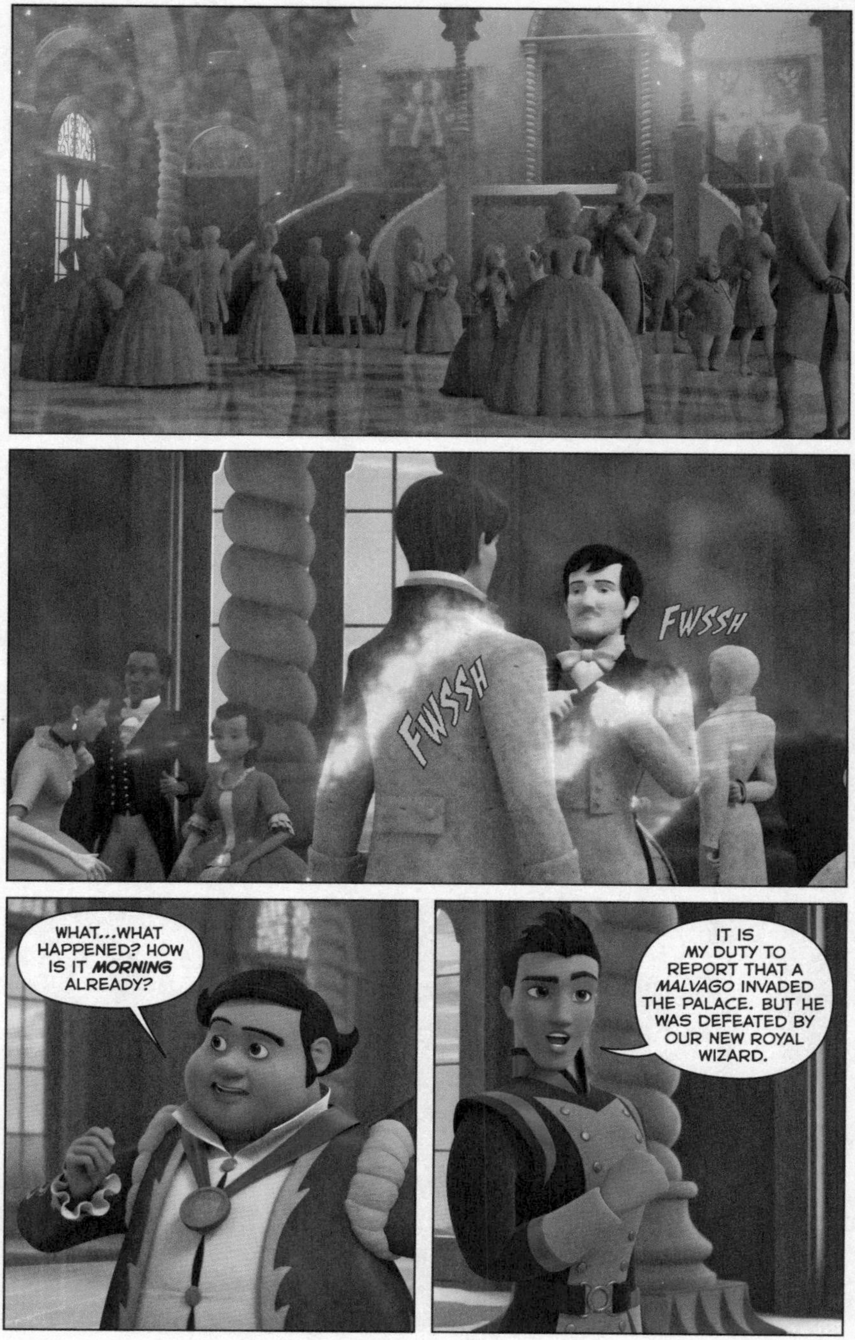
FWSSH
FWSSH
WHAT...WHAT HAPPENED? HOW IS IT *MORNING* ALREADY?
IT IS MY DUTY TO REPORT THAT A *MALVAGO* INVADED THE PALACE. BUT HE WAS DEFEATED BY OUR NEW ROYAL WIZARD.

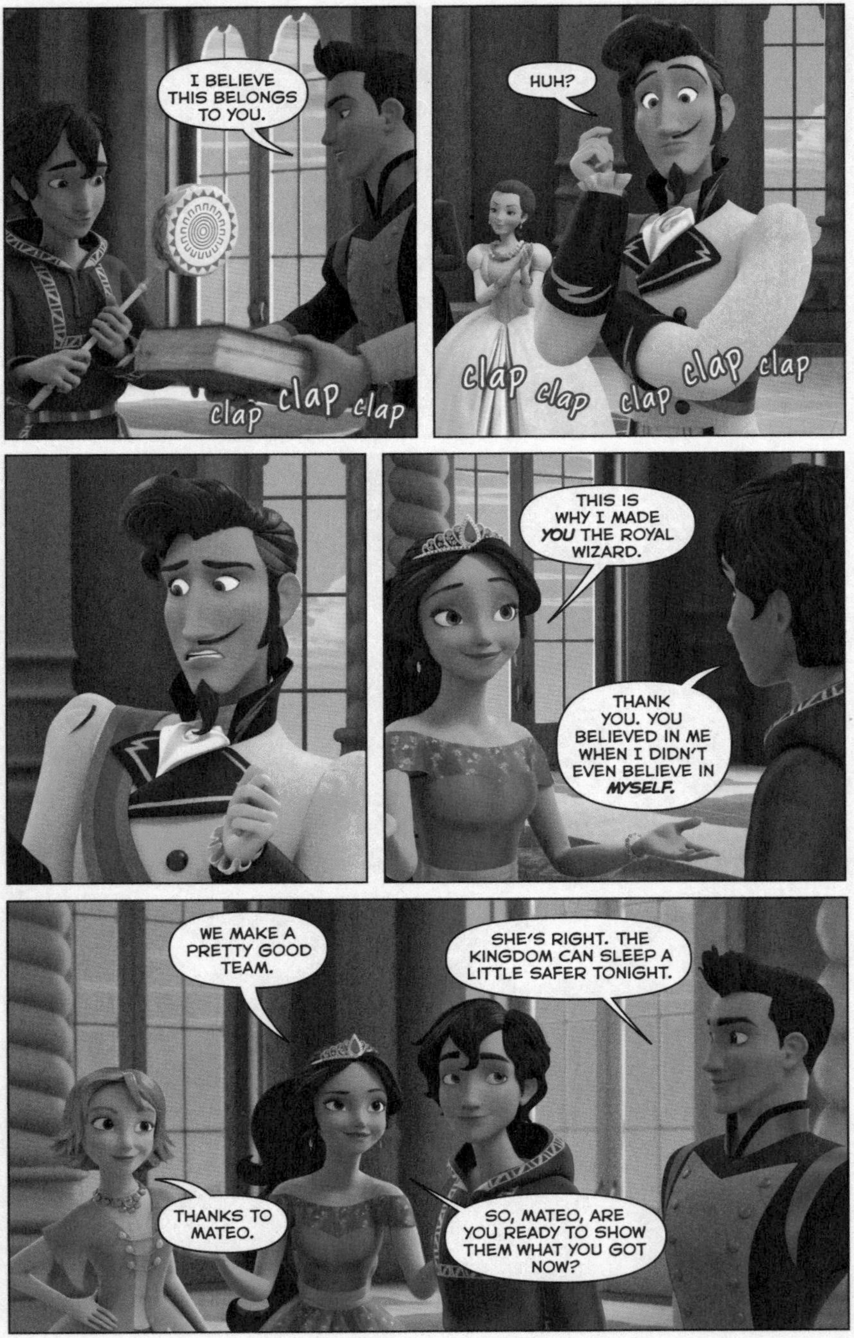
I BELIEVE THIS BELONGS TO YOU.
clap clap clap
HUH?
clap clap clap clap clap
THIS IS WHY I MADE *YOU* THE ROYAL WIZARD.
THANK YOU. YOU BELIEVED IN ME WHEN I DIDN'T EVEN BELIEVE IN ***MYSELF.***
WE MAKE A PRETTY GOOD TEAM.
SHE'S RIGHT. THE KINGDOM CAN SLEEP A LITTLE SAFER TONIGHT.
THANKS TO MATEO.
SO, MATEO, ARE YOU READY TO SHOW THEM WHAT YOU GOT NOW?

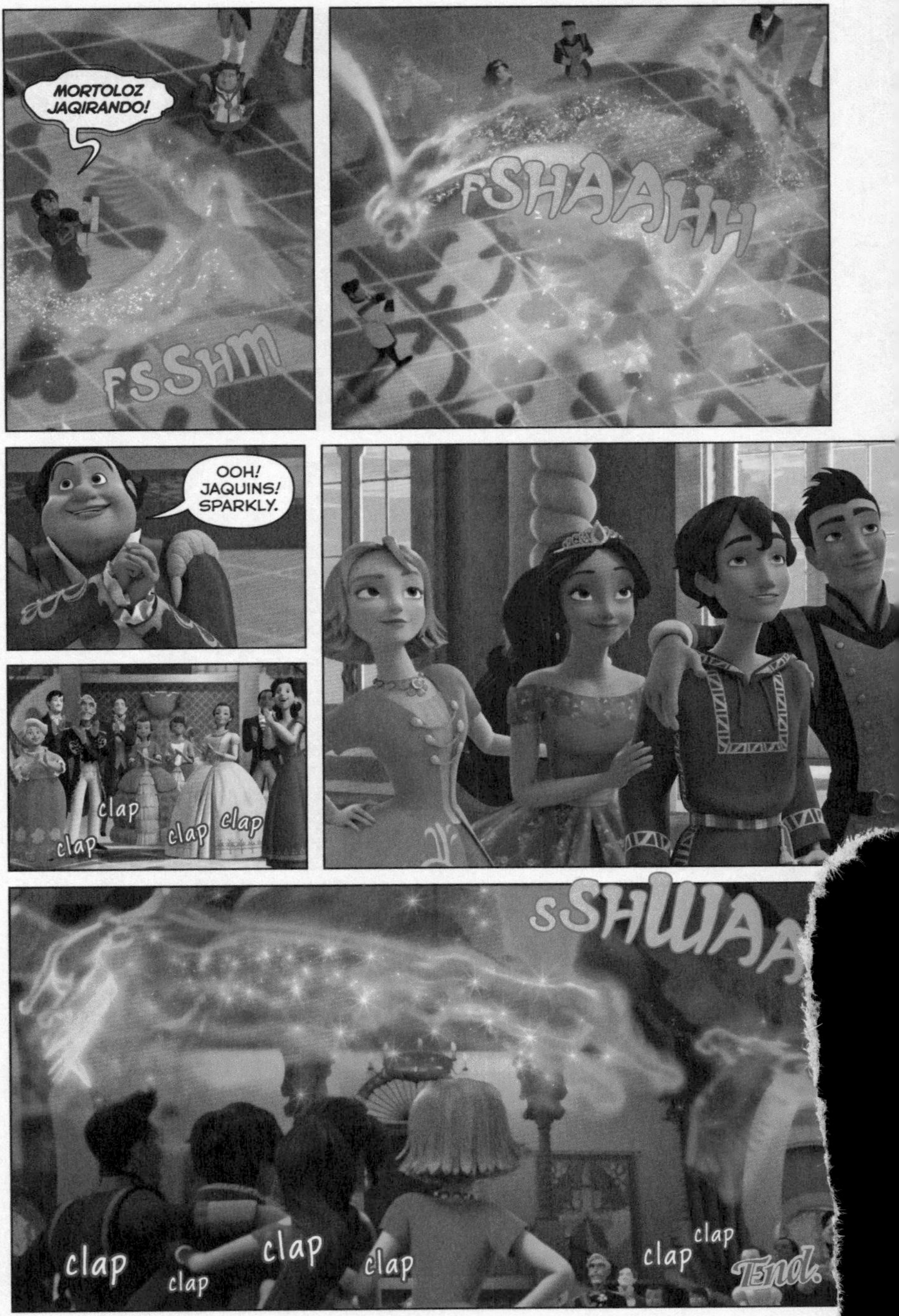
MORTOLOZ JAQIRANDO!
fSSHM
fSHAAHH
OOH! JAQUINS! SPARKLY.
clap
clap
clap
clap
sSHUAA
clap
clap
clap
clap
clap
clap
End.

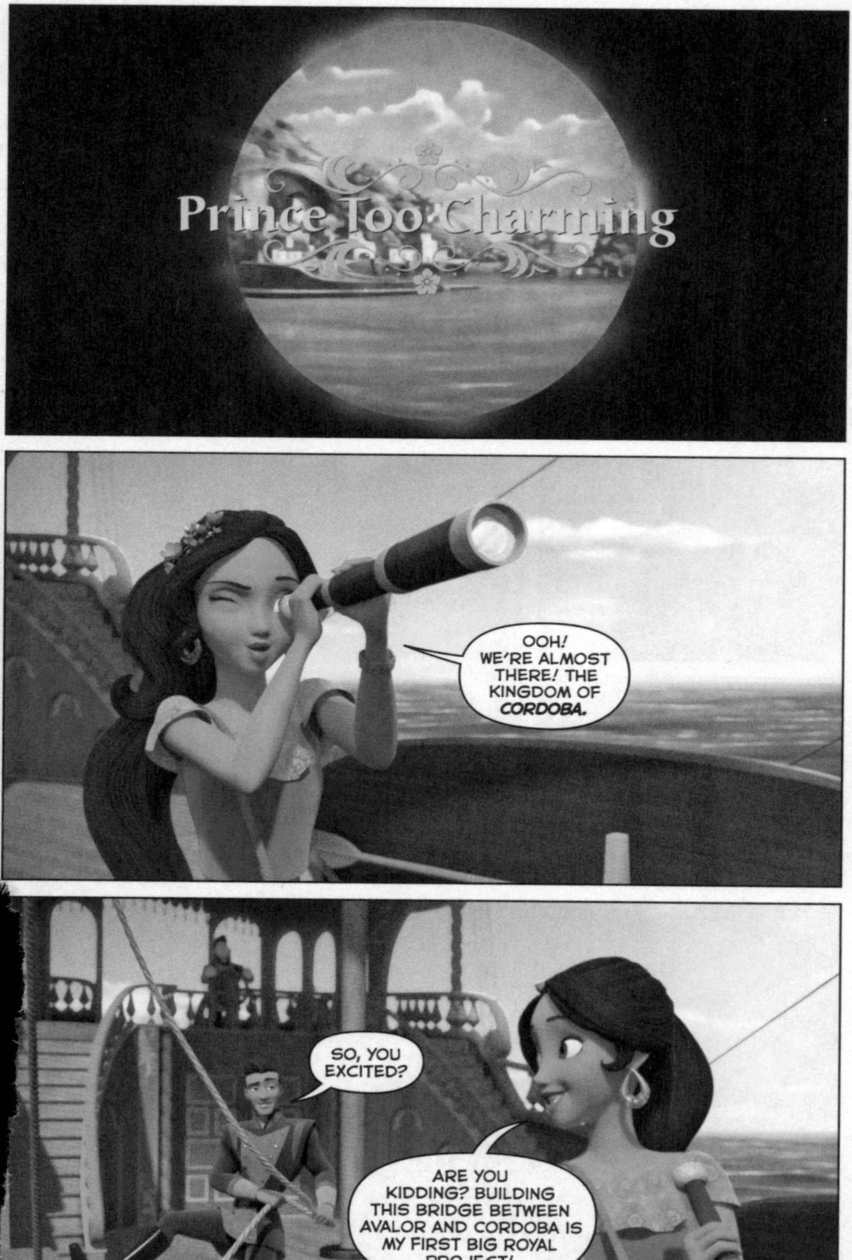
Prince Too Charming
OOH! WE'RE ALMOST THERE! THE KINGDOM OF CORDOBA.
SO, YOU EXCITED?
ARE YOU KIDDING? BUILDING THIS BRIDGE BETWEEN AVALOR AND CORDOBA IS MY FIRST BIG ROYAL PROJECT!

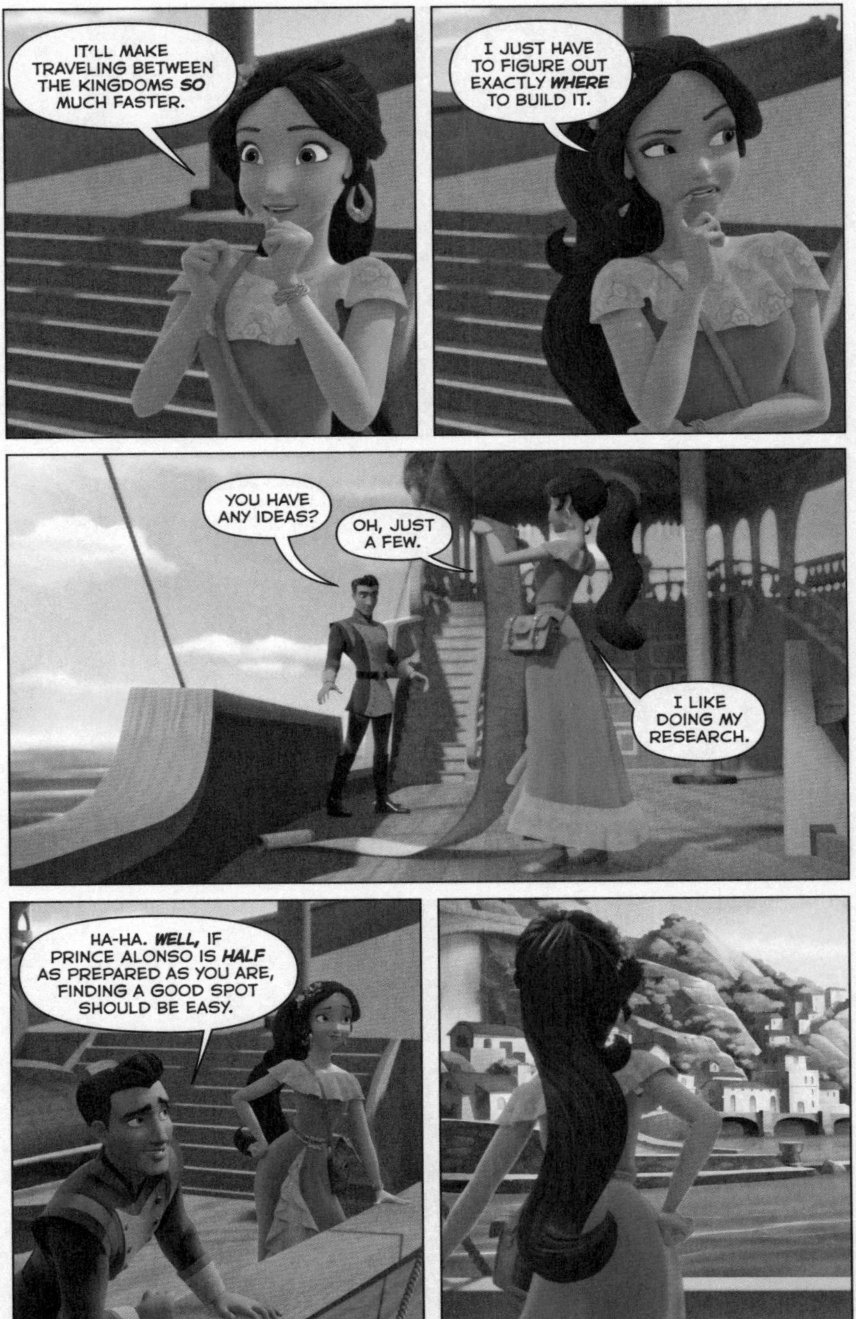
IT'LL MAKE TRAVELING BETWEEN THE KINGDOMS **SO** MUCH FASTER.
I JUST HAVE TO FIGURE OUT EXACTLY ***WHERE*** TO BUILD IT.
YOU HAVE ANY IDEAS?
OH, JUST A FEW.
I LIKE DOING MY RESEARCH.
HA-HA. ***WELL,*** IF PRINCE ALONSO IS ***HALF*** AS PREPARED AS YOU ARE, FINDING A GOOD SPOT SHOULD BE EASY.

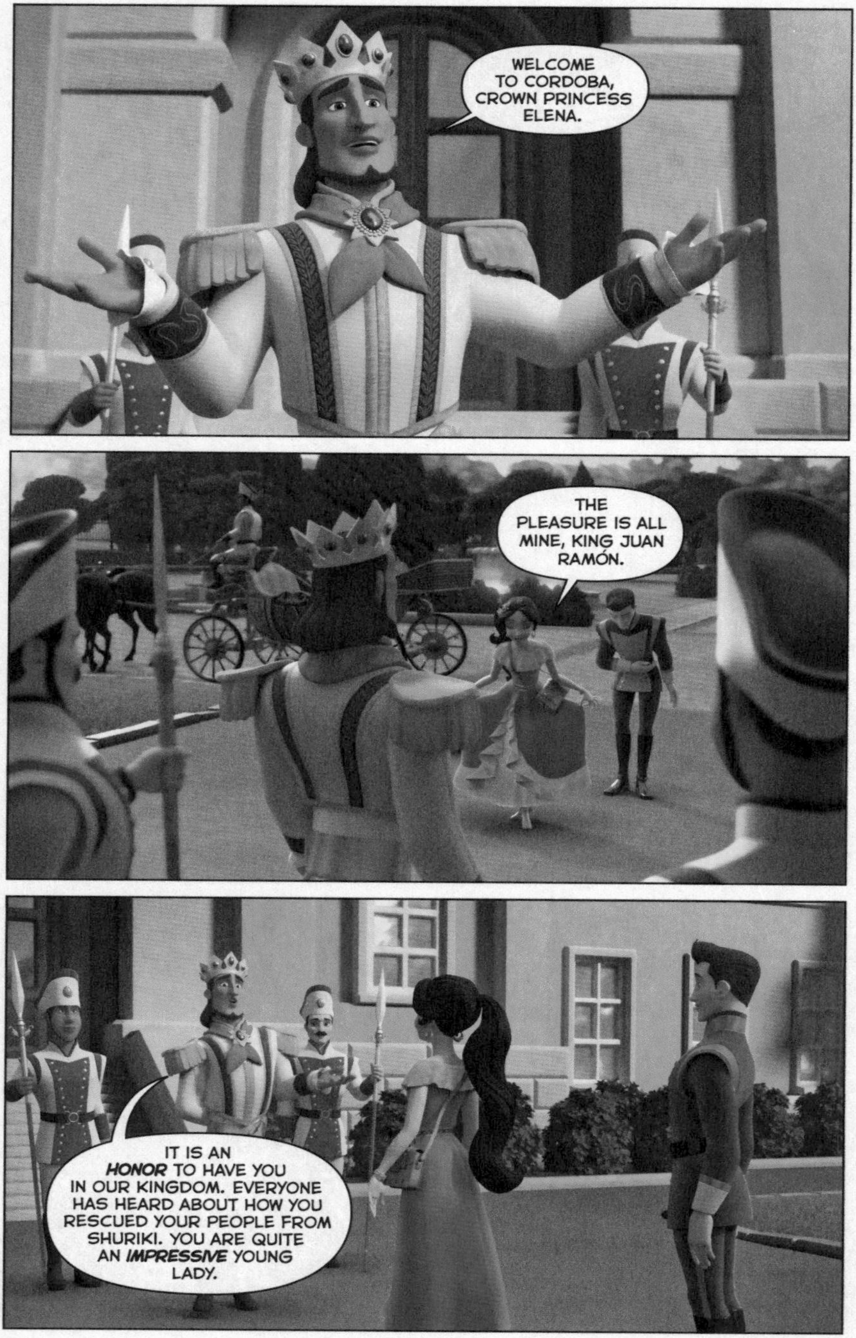
WELCOME TO CORDOBA, CROWN PRINCESS ELENA.
THE PLEASURE IS ALL MINE, KING JUAN RAMÓN.
IT IS AN *HONOR* TO HAVE YOU IN OUR KINGDOM. EVERYONE HAS HEARD ABOUT HOW YOU RESCUED YOUR PEOPLE FROM SHURIKI. YOU ARE QUITE AN *IMPRESSIVE* YOUNG LADY.

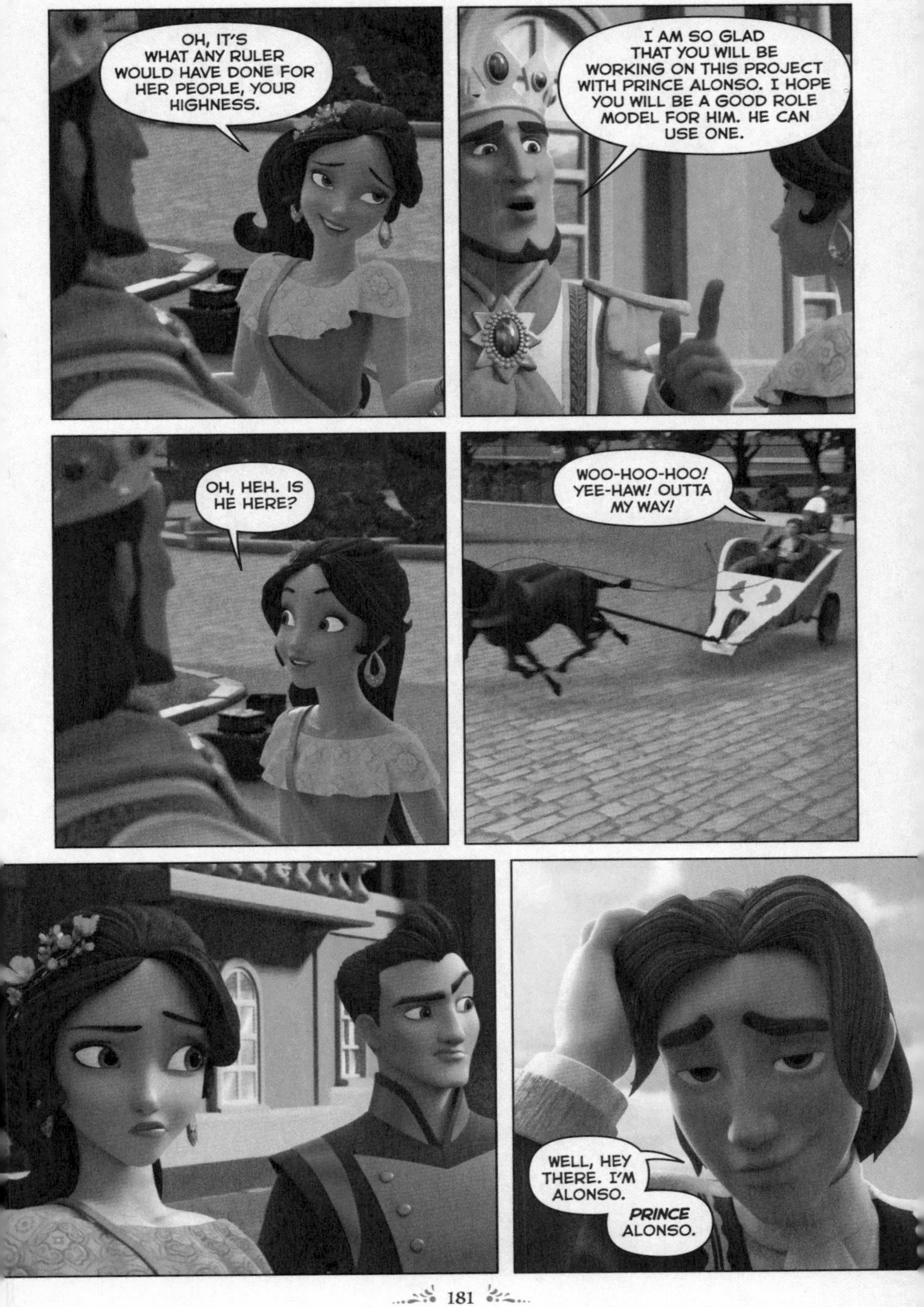
OH, IT'S WHAT ANY RULER WOULD HAVE DONE FOR HER PEOPLE, YOUR HIGHNESS.
I AM SO GLAD THAT YOU WILL BE WORKING ON THIS PROJECT WITH PRINCE ALONSO. I HOPE YOU WILL BE A GOOD ROLE MODEL FOR HIM. HE CAN USE ONE.
OH, HEH. IS HE HERE?
WOO-HOO-HOO! YEE-HAW! OUTTA MY WAY!
WELL, HEY THERE. I'M ALONSO.
PRINCE ALONSO.

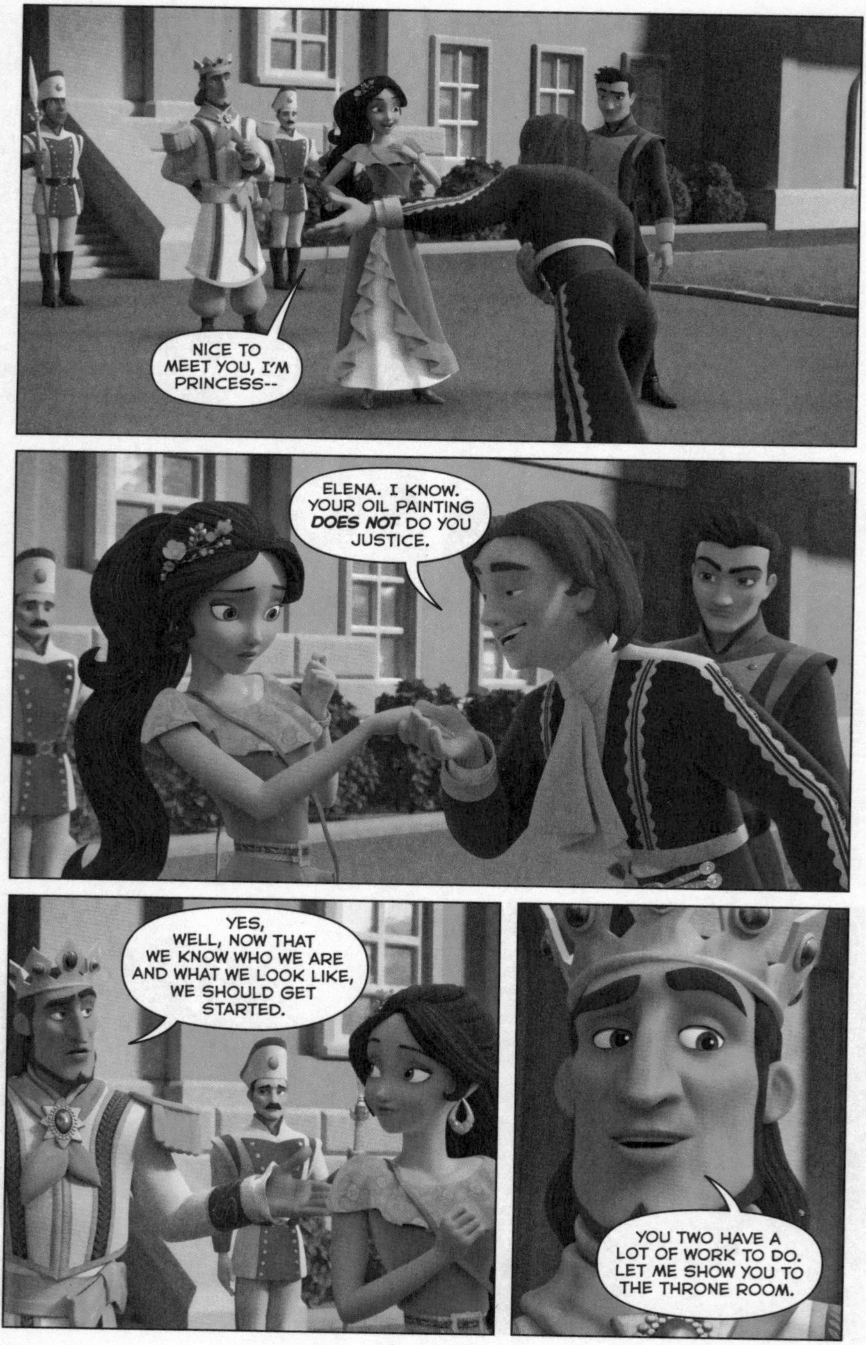
NICE TO MEET YOU, I'M PRINCESS--
ELENA. I KNOW. YOUR OIL PAINTING **DOES NOT** DO YOU JUSTICE.
YES, WELL, NOW THAT WE KNOW WHO WE ARE AND WHAT WE LOOK LIKE, WE SHOULD GET STARTED.
YOU TWO HAVE A LOT OF WORK TO DO. LET ME SHOW YOU TO THE THRONE ROOM.

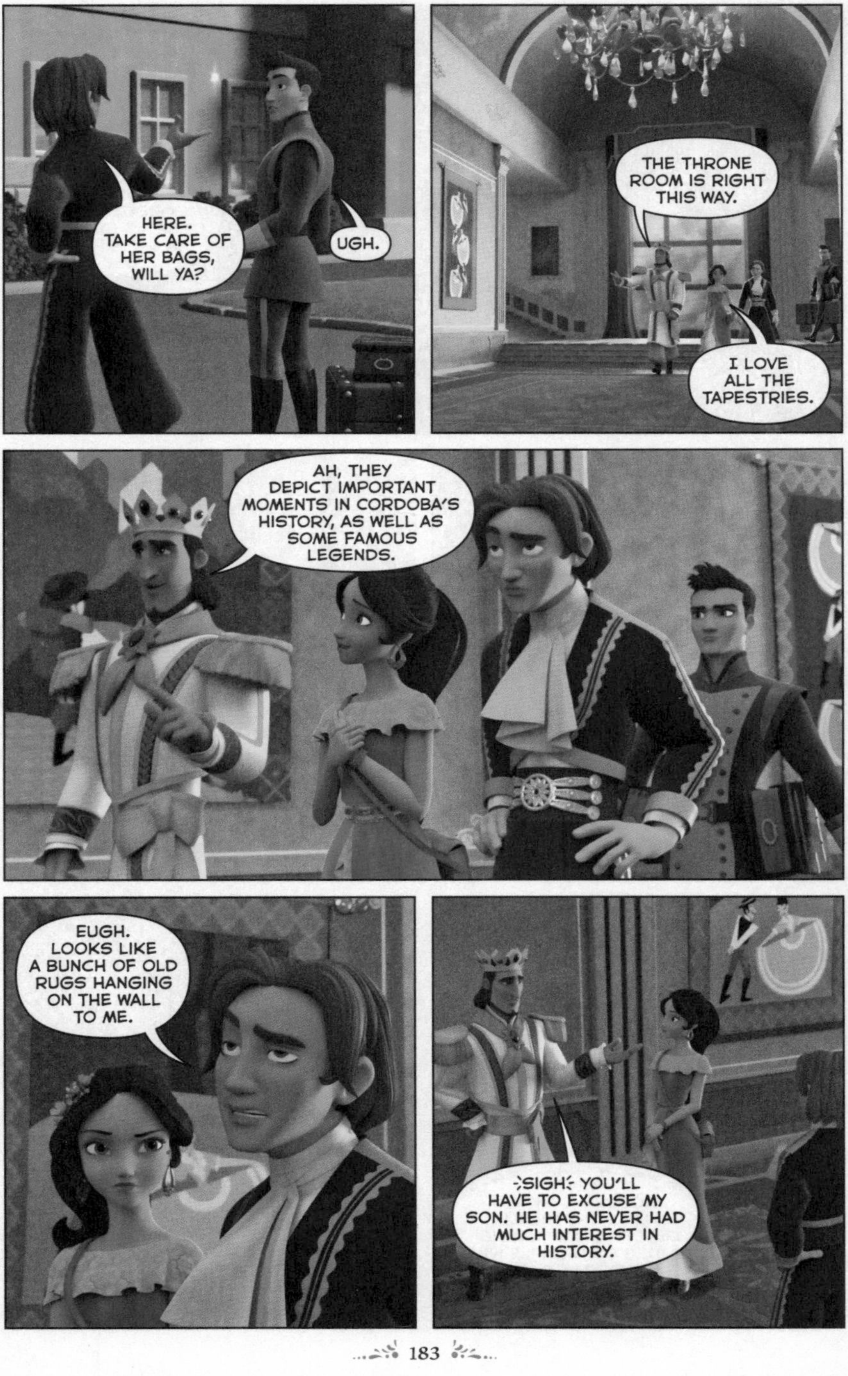
HERE. TAKE CARE OF HER BAGS, WILL YA?
UGH.
THE THRONE ROOM IS RIGHT THIS WAY.
I LOVE ALL THE TAPESTRIES.
AH, THEY DEPICT IMPORTANT MOMENTS IN CORDOBA'S HISTORY, AS WELL AS SOME FAMOUS LEGENDS.
EUGH. LOOKS LIKE A BUNCH OF OLD RUGS HANGING ON THE WALL TO ME.
SIGH YOU'LL HAVE TO EXCUSE MY SON. HE HAS NEVER HAD MUCH INTEREST IN HISTORY.

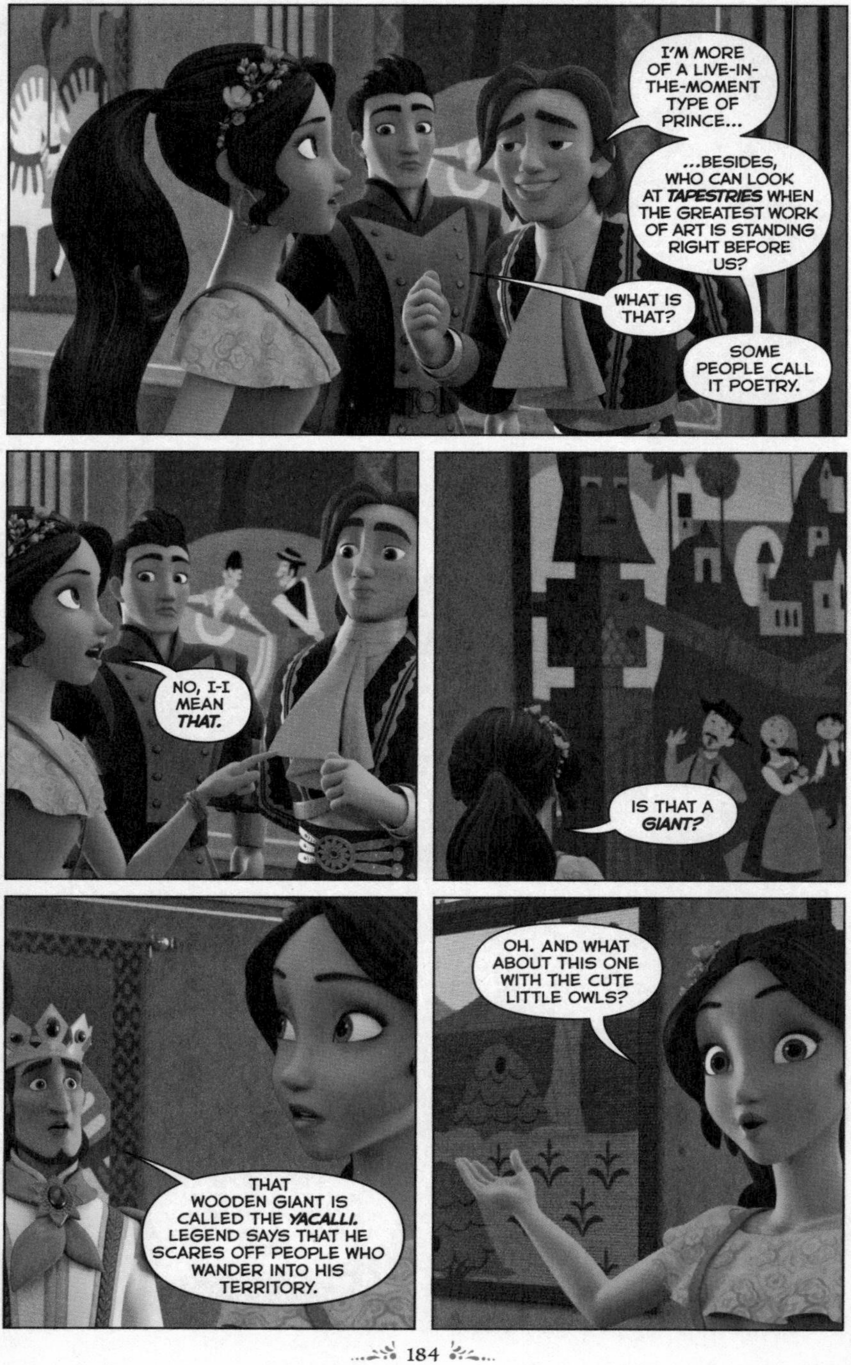
I'M MORE OF A LIVE-IN-THE-MOMENT TYPE OF PRINCE...
...BESIDES, WHO CAN LOOK AT TAPESTRIES WHEN THE GREATEST WORK OF ART IS STANDING RIGHT BEFORE US?
WHAT IS THAT?
SOME PEOPLE CALL IT POETRY.
NO, I-I MEAN THAT.
IS THAT A GIANT?
THAT WOODEN GIANT IS CALLED THE YACALLI. LEGEND SAYS THAT HE SCARES OFF PEOPLE WHO WANDER INTO HIS TERRITORY.
OH. AND WHAT ABOUT THIS ONE WITH THE CUTE LITTLE OWLS?

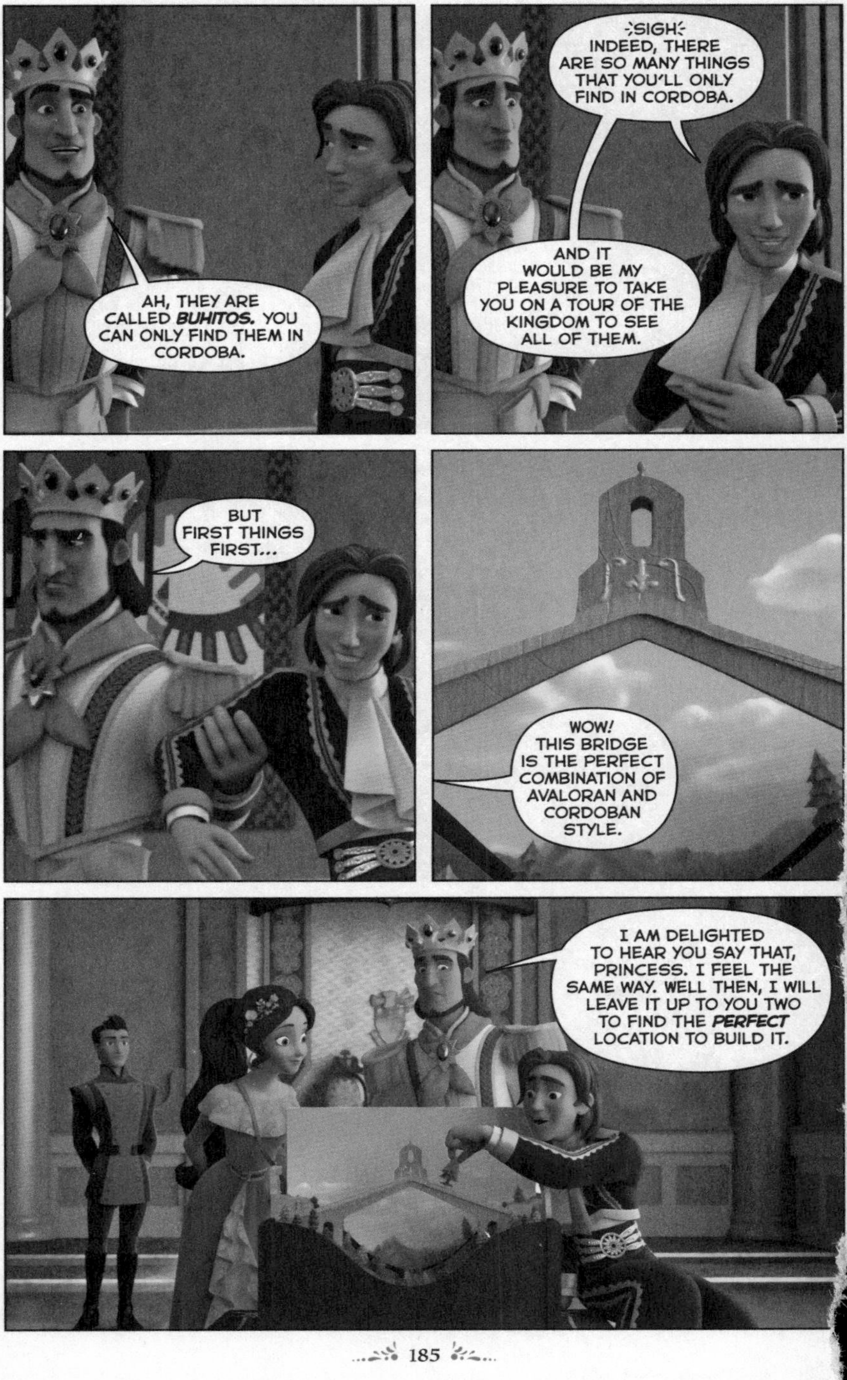
AH, THEY ARE CALLED *BUHITOS.* YOU CAN ONLY FIND THEM IN CORDOBA.
SIGH INDEED, THERE ARE SO MANY THINGS THAT YOU'LL ONLY FIND IN CORDOBA.
AND IT WOULD BE MY PLEASURE TO TAKE YOU ON A TOUR OF THE KINGDOM TO SEE ALL OF THEM.
BUT FIRST THINGS FIRST...
WOW! THIS BRIDGE IS THE PERFECT COMBINATION OF AVALORAN AND CORDOBAN STYLE.
I AM DELIGHTED TO HEAR YOU SAY THAT, PRINCESS. I FEEL THE SAME WAY. WELL THEN, I WILL LEAVE IT UP TO YOU TWO TO FIND THE *PERFECT* LOCATION TO BUILD IT.

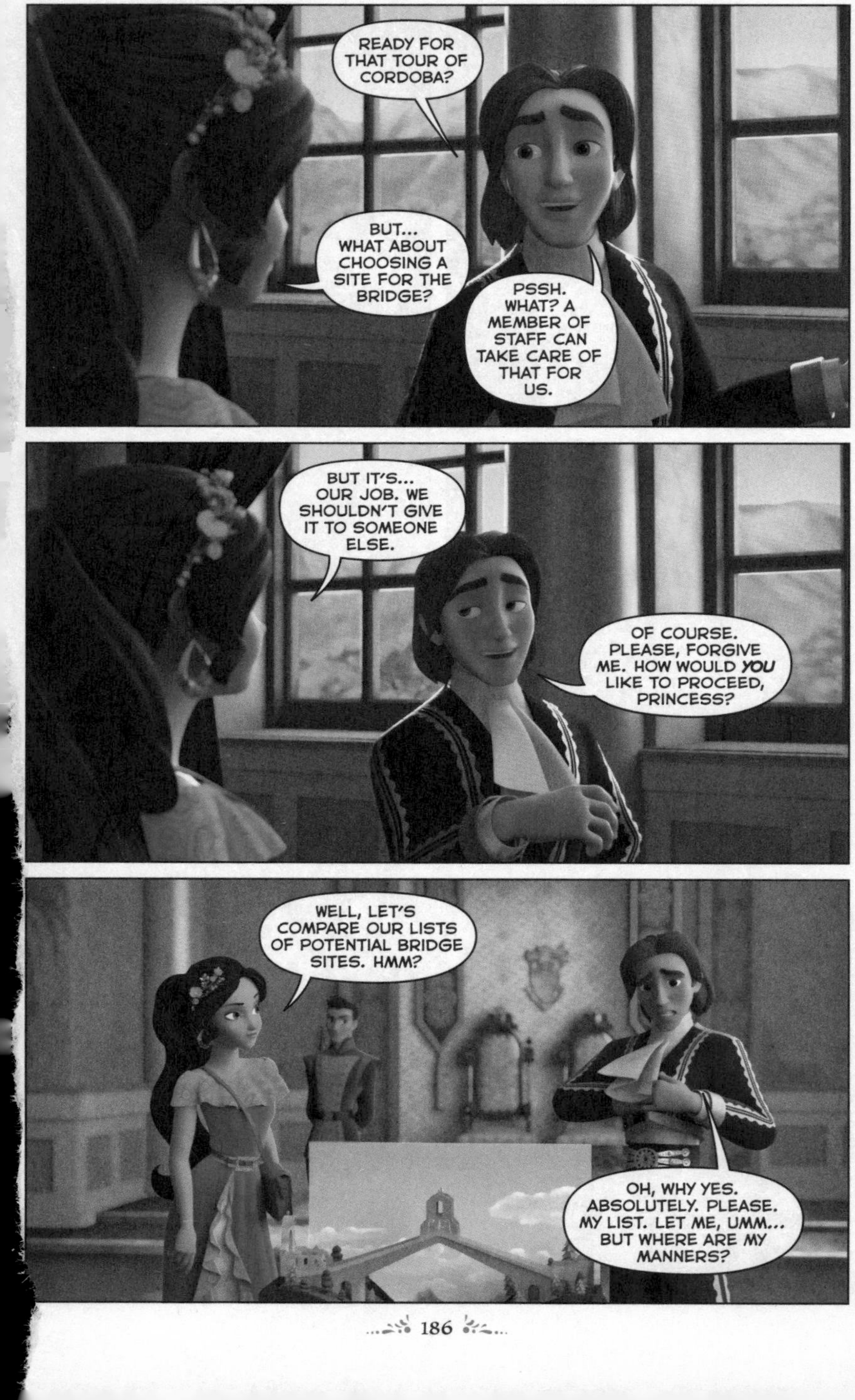
READY FOR THAT TOUR OF CORDOBA?
BUT... WHAT ABOUT CHOOSING A SITE FOR THE BRIDGE?
PSSH. WHAT? A MEMBER OF STAFF CAN TAKE CARE OF THAT FOR US.
BUT IT'S... OUR JOB. WE SHOULDN'T GIVE IT TO SOMEONE ELSE.
OF COURSE. PLEASE, FORGIVE ME. HOW WOULD *YOU* LIKE TO PROCEED, PRINCESS?
WELL, LET'S COMPARE OUR LISTS OF POTENTIAL BRIDGE SITES. HMM?
OH, WHY YES. ABSOLUTELY. PLEASE. MY LIST. LET ME, UMM... BUT WHERE ARE MY MANNERS?

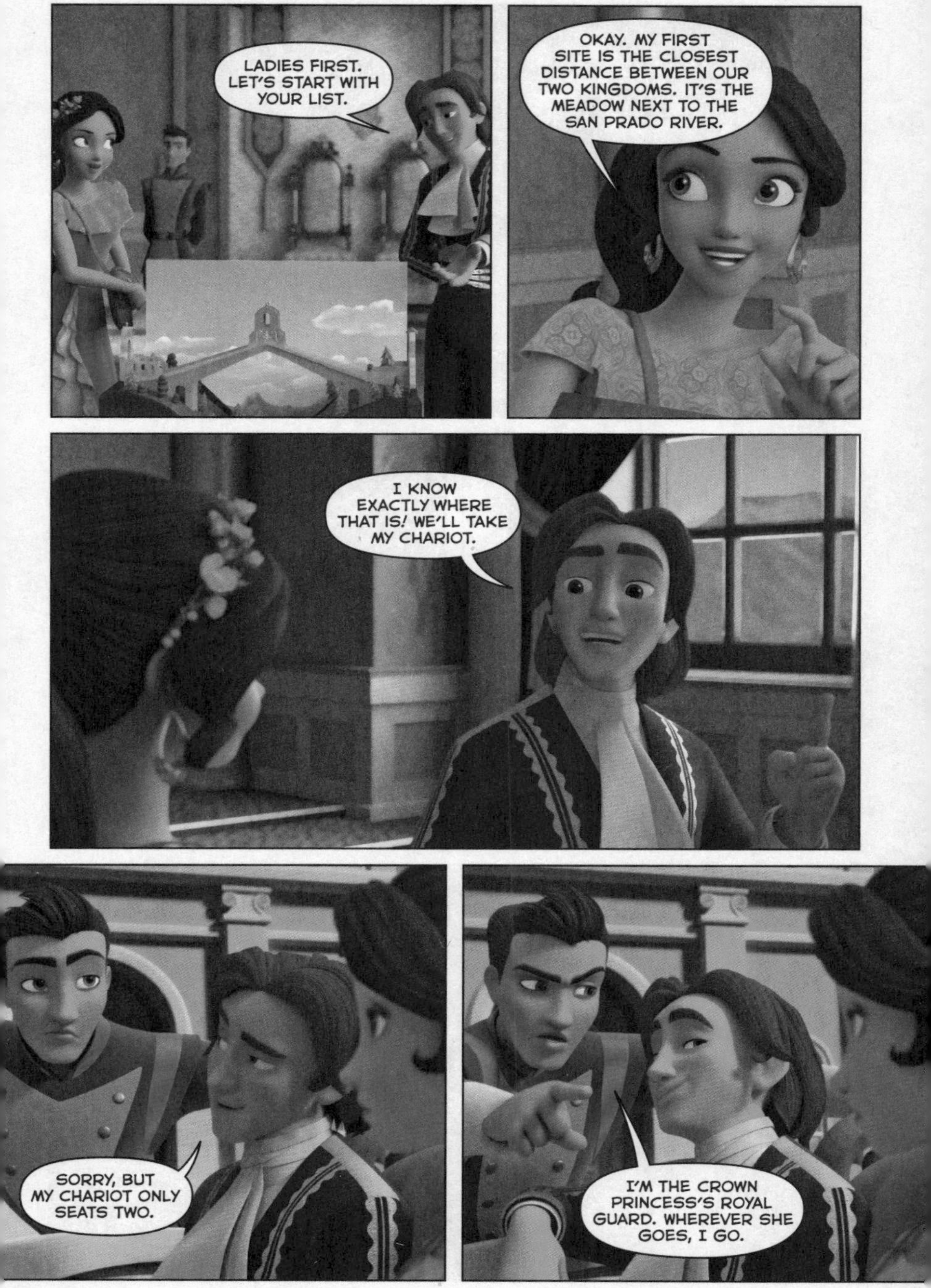
LADIES FIRST. LET'S START WITH YOUR LIST.
OKAY. MY FIRST SITE IS THE CLOSEST DISTANCE BETWEEN OUR TWO KINGDOMS. IT'S THE MEADOW NEXT TO THE SAN PRADO RIVER.
I KNOW EXACTLY WHERE THAT IS! WE'LL TAKE MY CHARIOT.
SORRY, BUT MY CHARIOT ONLY SEATS TWO.
I'M THE CROWN PRINCESS'S ROYAL GUARD. WHEREVER SHE GOES, I GO.

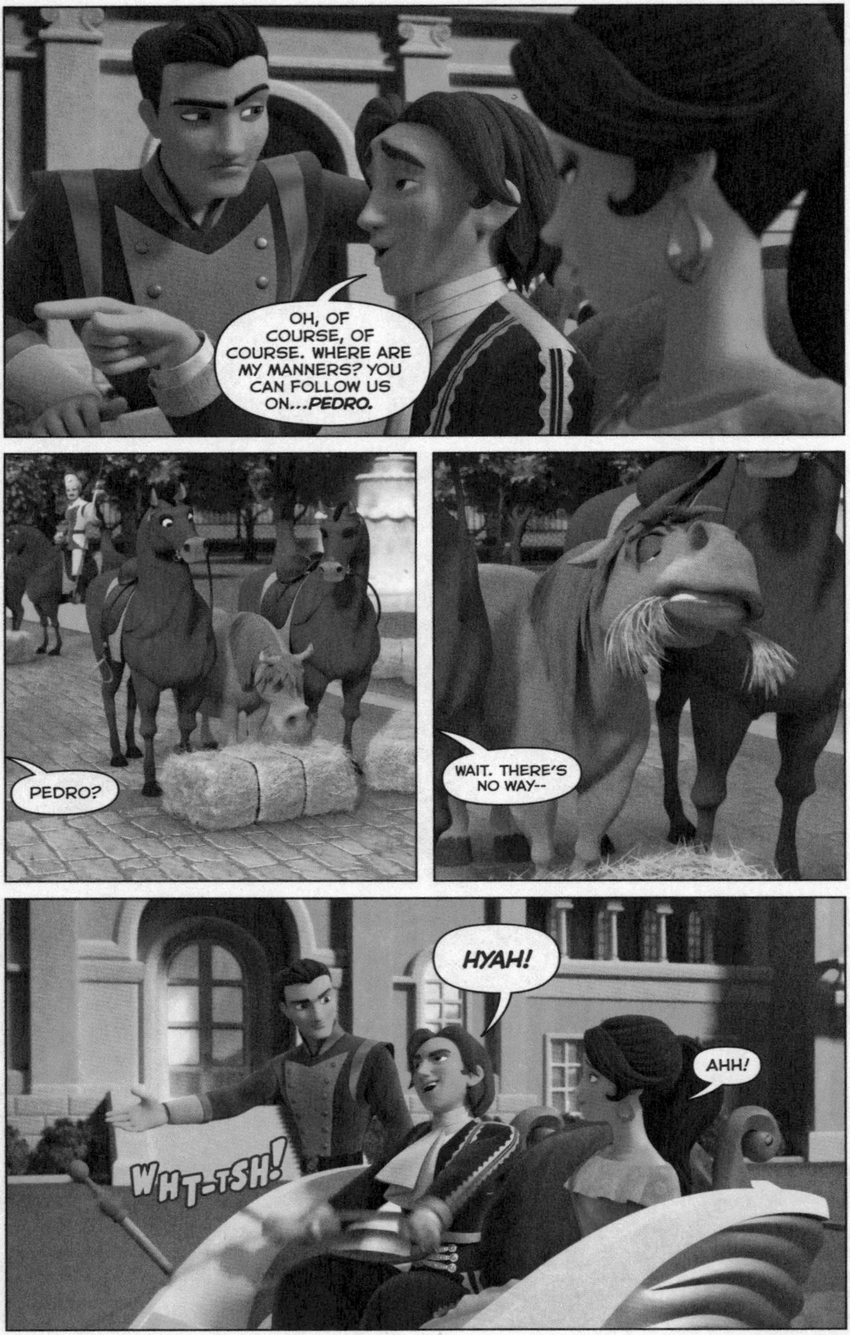

OH, OF COURSE, OF COURSE. WHERE ARE MY MANNERS? YOU CAN FOLLOW US ON...PEDRO.
PEDRO?
WAIT. THERE'S NO WAY--
HYAH!
AHH!
WHT-TSH!

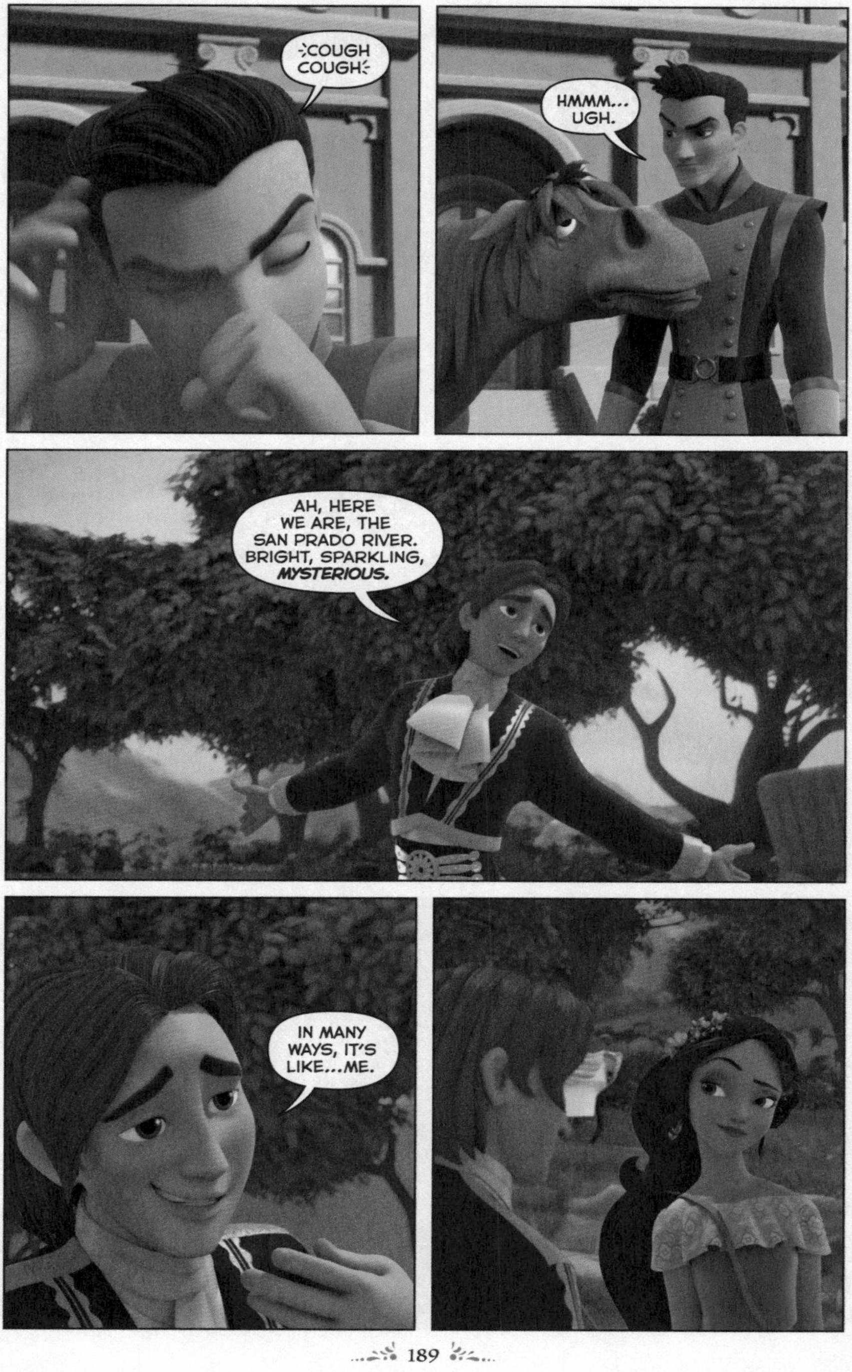

COUGH COUGH
HMMM... UGH.
AH, HERE WE ARE, THE SAN PRADO RIVER. BRIGHT, SPARKLING, ***MYSTERIOUS.***
IN MANY WAYS, IT'S LIKE...ME.

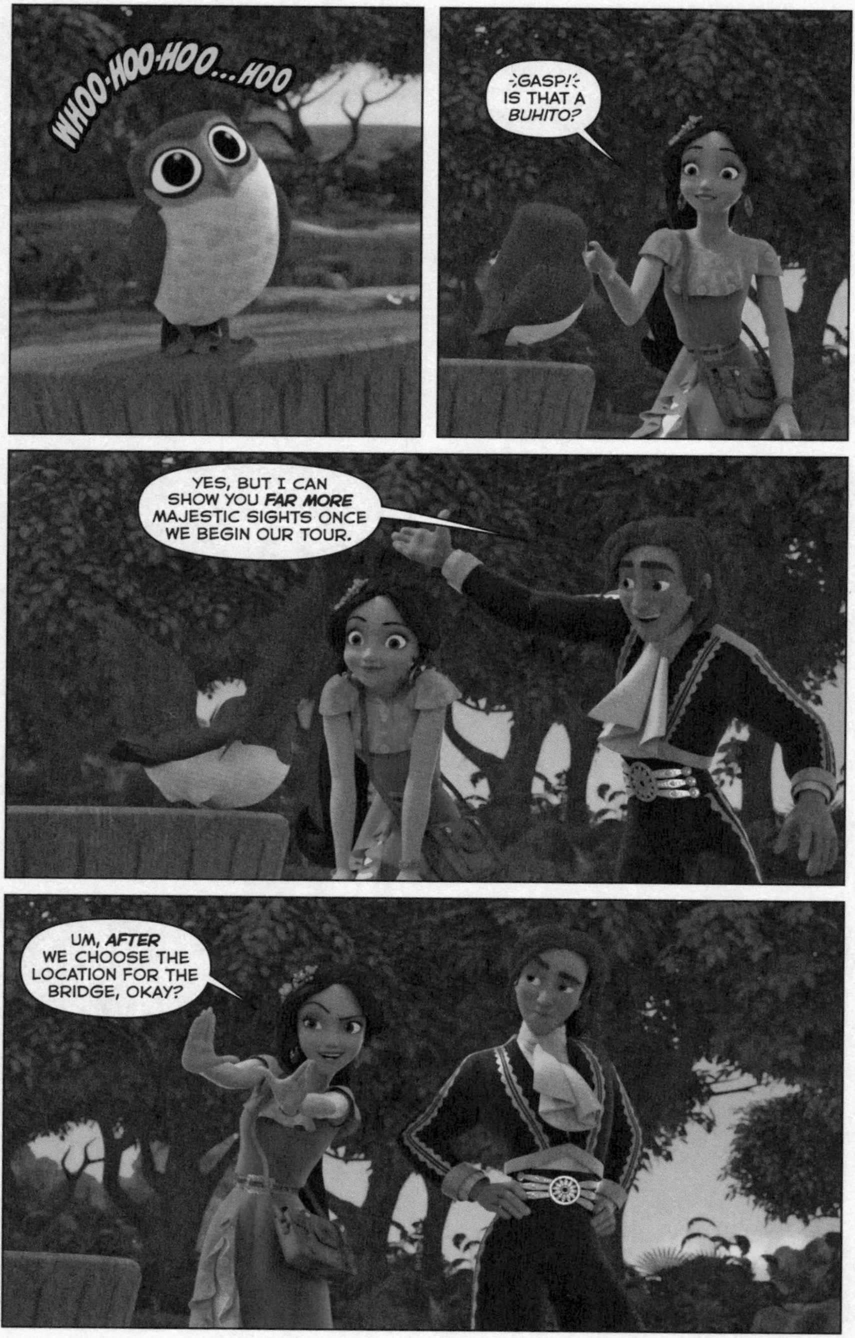
WHOO-HOO-HOO...HOO
¡GASP! IS THAT A *BUHITO?*
YES, BUT I CAN SHOW YOU ***FAR MORE*** MAJESTIC SIGHTS ONCE WE BEGIN OUR TOUR.
UM, ***AFTER*** WE CHOOSE THE LOCATION FOR THE BRIDGE, OKAY?

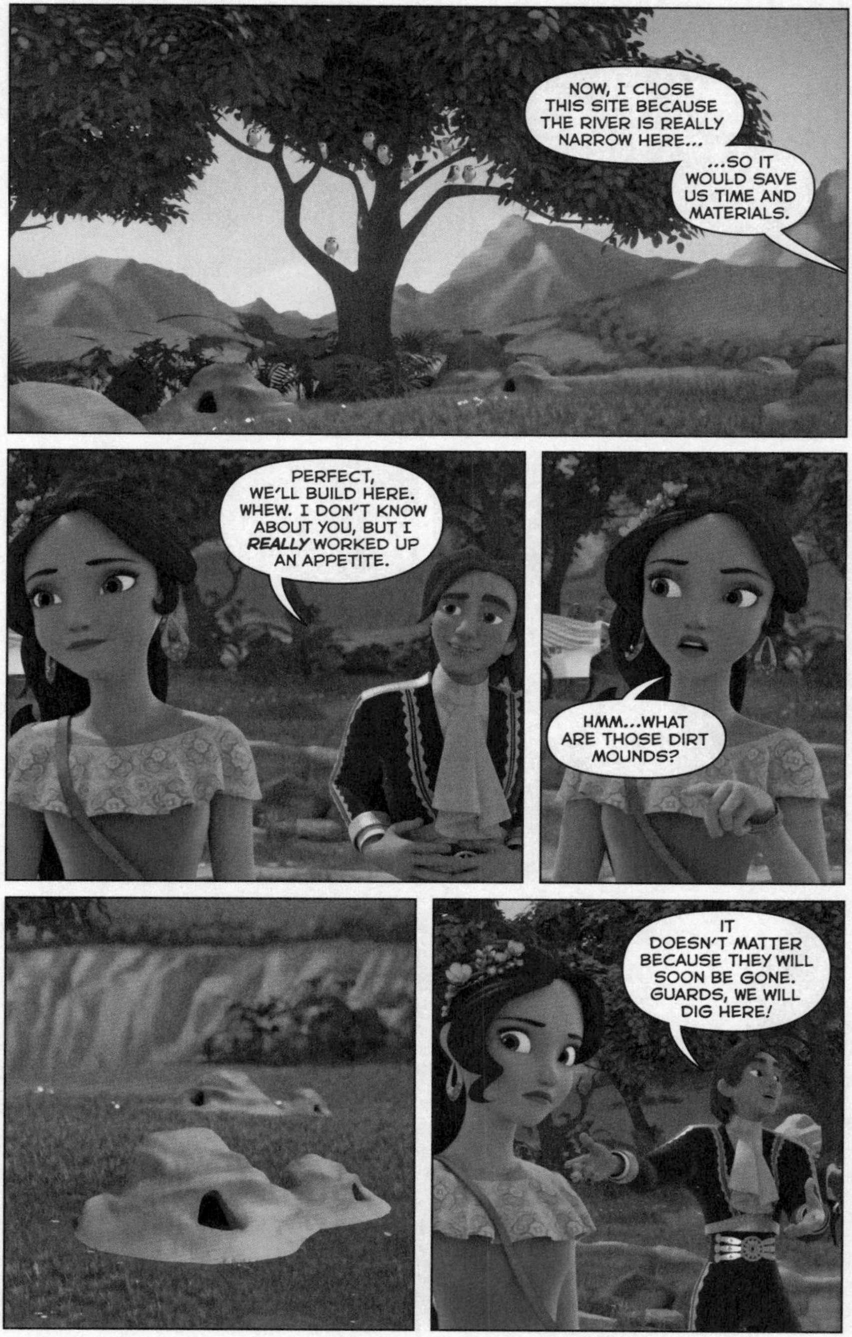
NOW, I CHOSE THIS SITE BECAUSE THE RIVER IS REALLY NARROW HERE...
...SO IT WOULD SAVE US TIME AND MATERIALS.
PERFECT, WE'LL BUILD HERE. WHEW. I DON'T KNOW ABOUT YOU, BUT I *REALLY* WORKED UP AN APPETITE.
HMM...WHAT ARE THOSE DIRT MOUNDS?
IT DOESN'T MATTER BECAUSE THEY WILL SOON BE GONE. GUARDS, WE WILL DIG HERE!

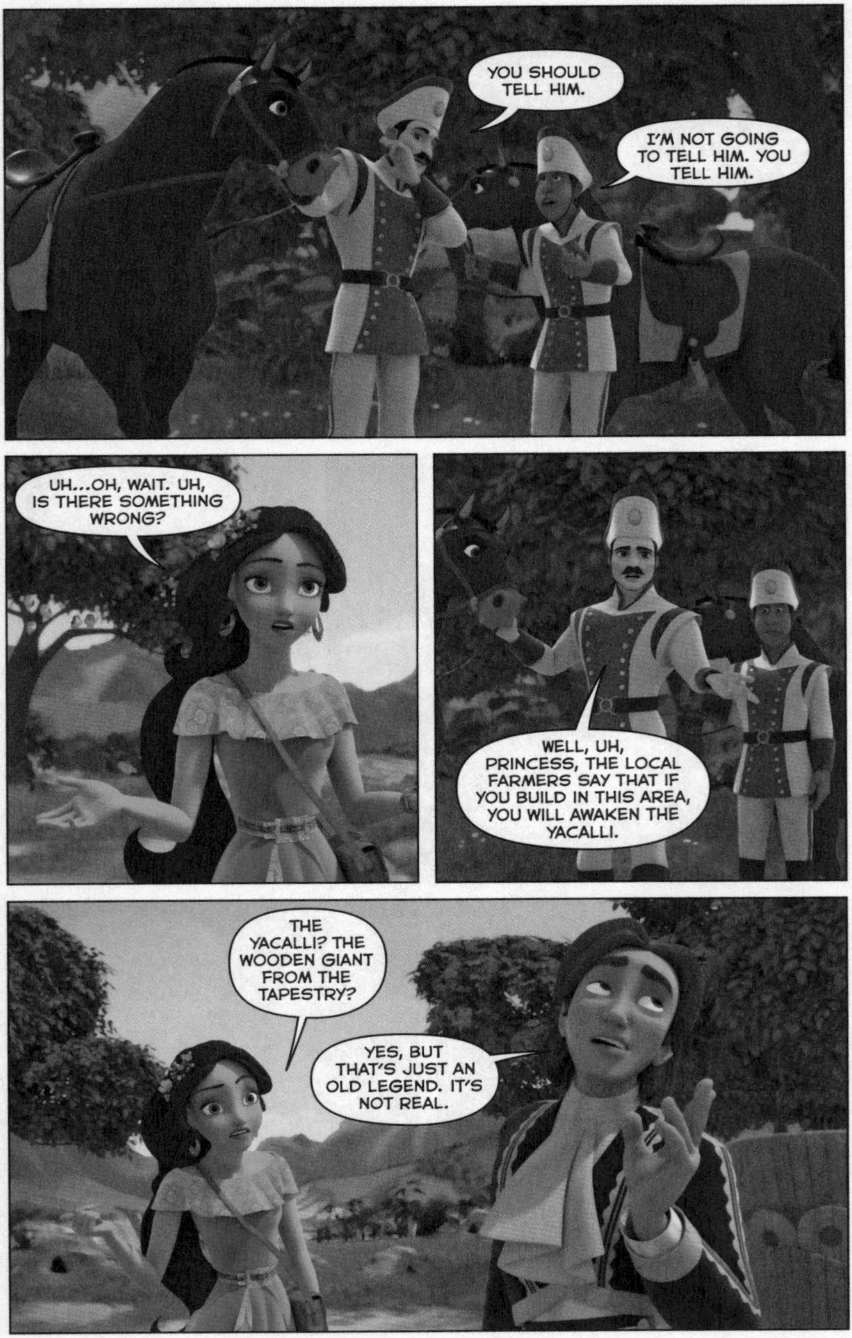
YOU SHOULD TELL HIM.
I'M NOT GOING TO TELL HIM. YOU TELL HIM.
UH...OH, WAIT. UH, IS THERE SOMETHING WRONG?
WELL, UH, PRINCESS, THE LOCAL FARMERS SAY THAT IF YOU BUILD IN THIS AREA, YOU WILL AWAKEN THE YACALLI.
THE YACALLI? THE WOODEN GIANT FROM THE TAPESTRY?
YES, BUT THAT'S JUST AN OLD LEGEND. IT'S NOT REAL.

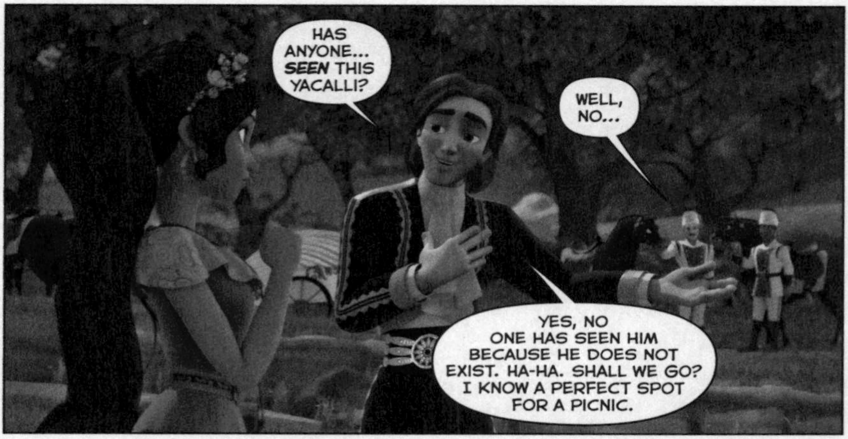
HAS ANYONE... SEEN THIS YACALLI?
WELL, NO...
YES, NO ONE HAS SEEN HIM BECAUSE HE DOES NOT EXIST. HA-HA. SHALL WE GO? I KNOW A PERFECT SPOT FOR A PICNIC.

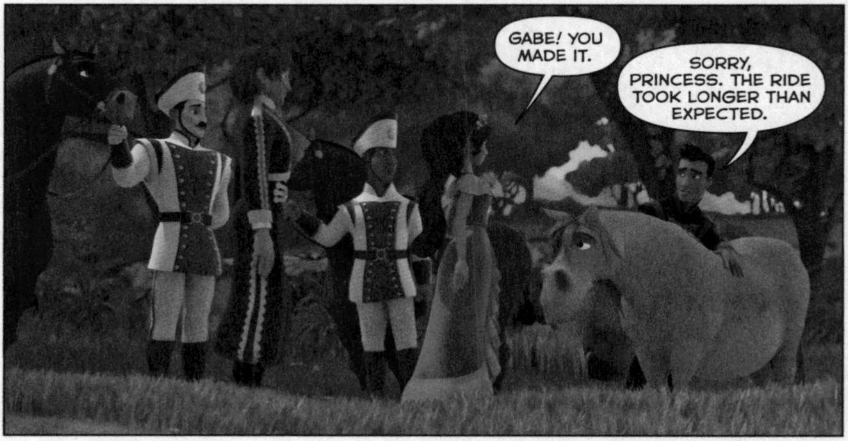
GABE! YOU MADE IT.
SORRY, PRINCESS. THE RIDE TOOK LONGER THAN EXPECTED.

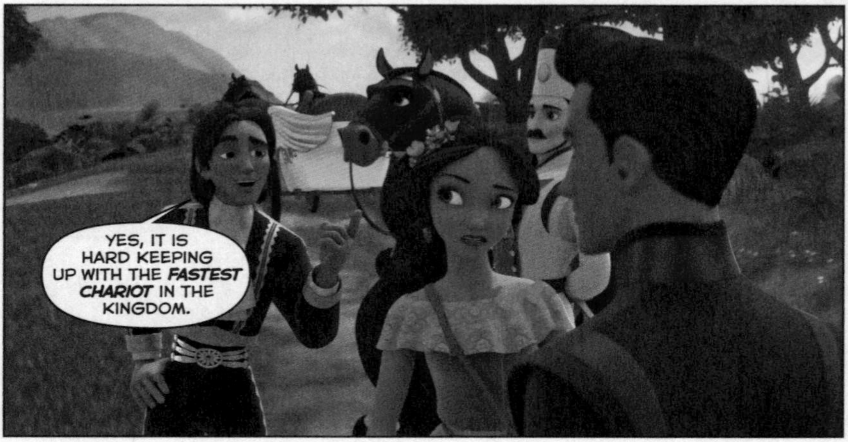
YES, IT IS HARD KEEPING UP WITH THE FASTEST CHARIOT IN THE KINGDOM.

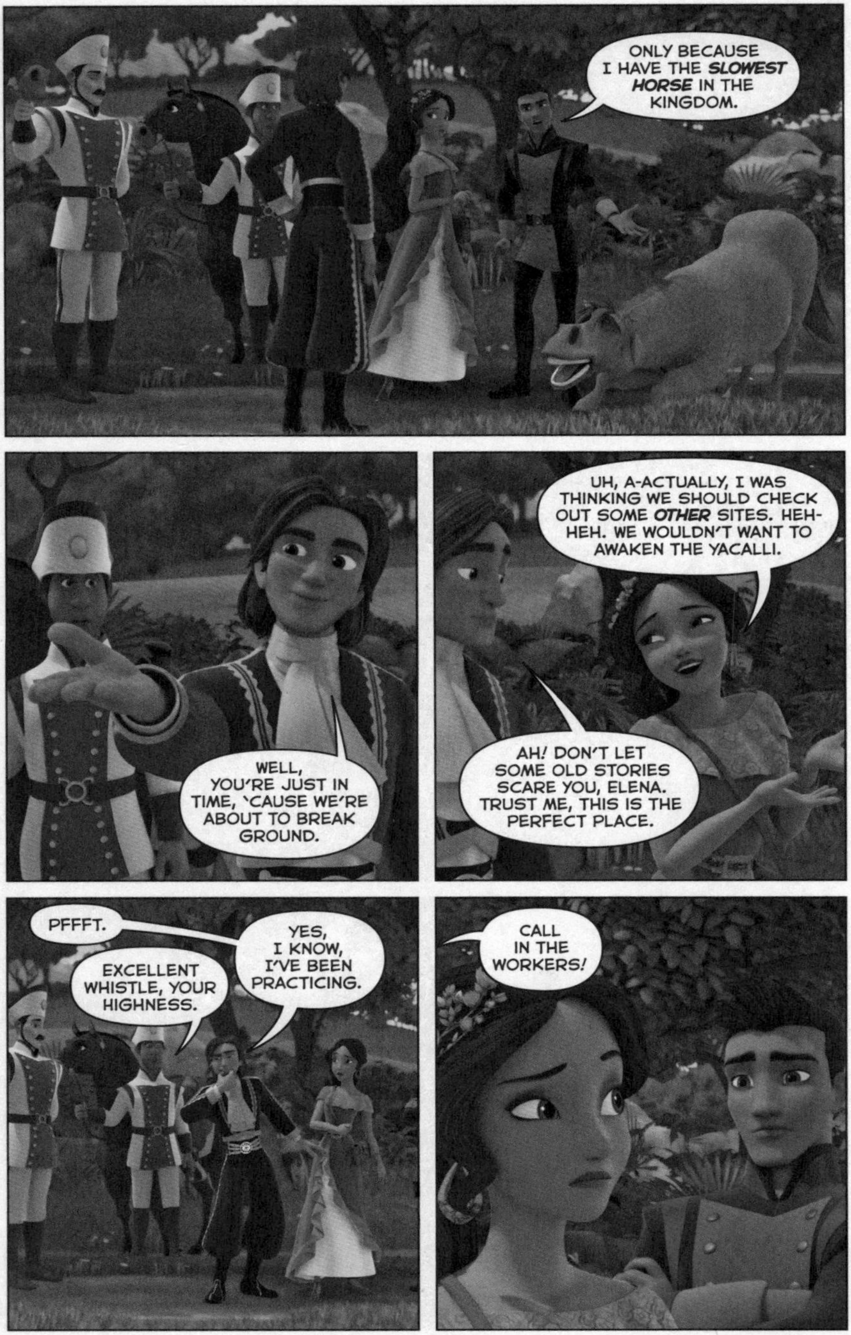
ONLY BECAUSE I HAVE THE *SLOWEST HORSE* IN THE KINGDOM.
WELL, YOU'RE JUST IN TIME, 'CAUSE WE'RE ABOUT TO BREAK GROUND.
UH, A-ACTUALLY, I WAS THINKING WE SHOULD CHECK OUT SOME *OTHER* SITES. HEH-HEH. WE WOULDN'T WANT TO AWAKEN THE YACALLI.
AH! DON'T LET SOME OLD STORIES SCARE YOU, ELENA. TRUST ME, THIS IS THE PERFECT PLACE.
PFFFT.
EXCELLENT WHISTLE, YOUR HIGHNESS.
YES, I KNOW, I'VE BEEN PRACTICING.
CALL IN THE WORKERS!

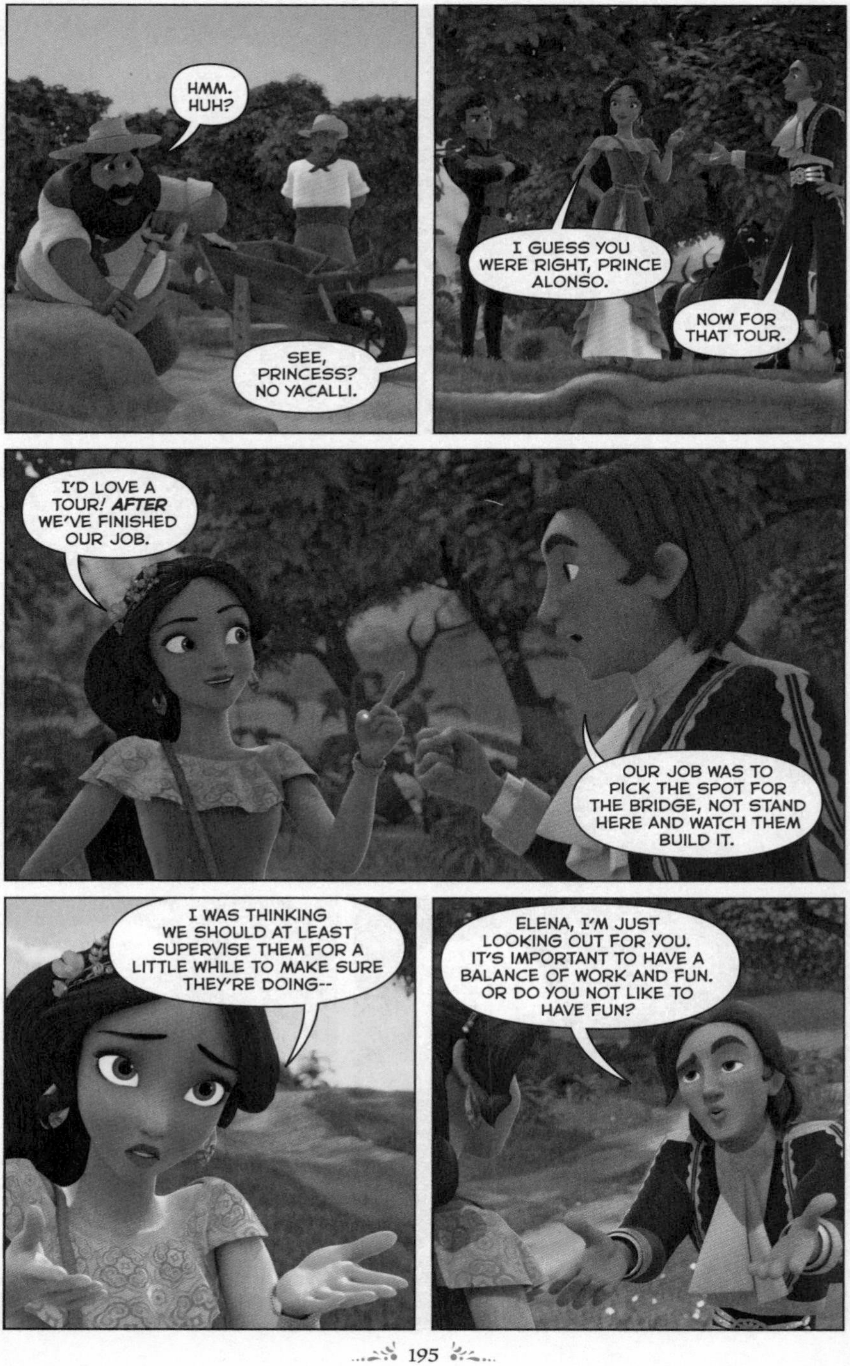
HMM. HUH?
SEE, PRINCESS? NO YACALLI.
I GUESS YOU WERE RIGHT, PRINCE ALONSO.
NOW FOR THAT TOUR.
I'D LOVE A TOUR! **AFTER** WE'VE FINISHED OUR JOB.
OUR JOB WAS TO PICK THE SPOT FOR THE BRIDGE, NOT STAND HERE AND WATCH THEM BUILD IT.
I WAS THINKING WE SHOULD AT LEAST SUPERVISE THEM FOR A LITTLE WHILE TO MAKE SURE THEY'RE DOING--
ELENA, I'M JUST LOOKING OUT FOR YOU. IT'S IMPORTANT TO HAVE A BALANCE OF WORK AND FUN. OR DO YOU NOT LIKE TO HAVE FUN?

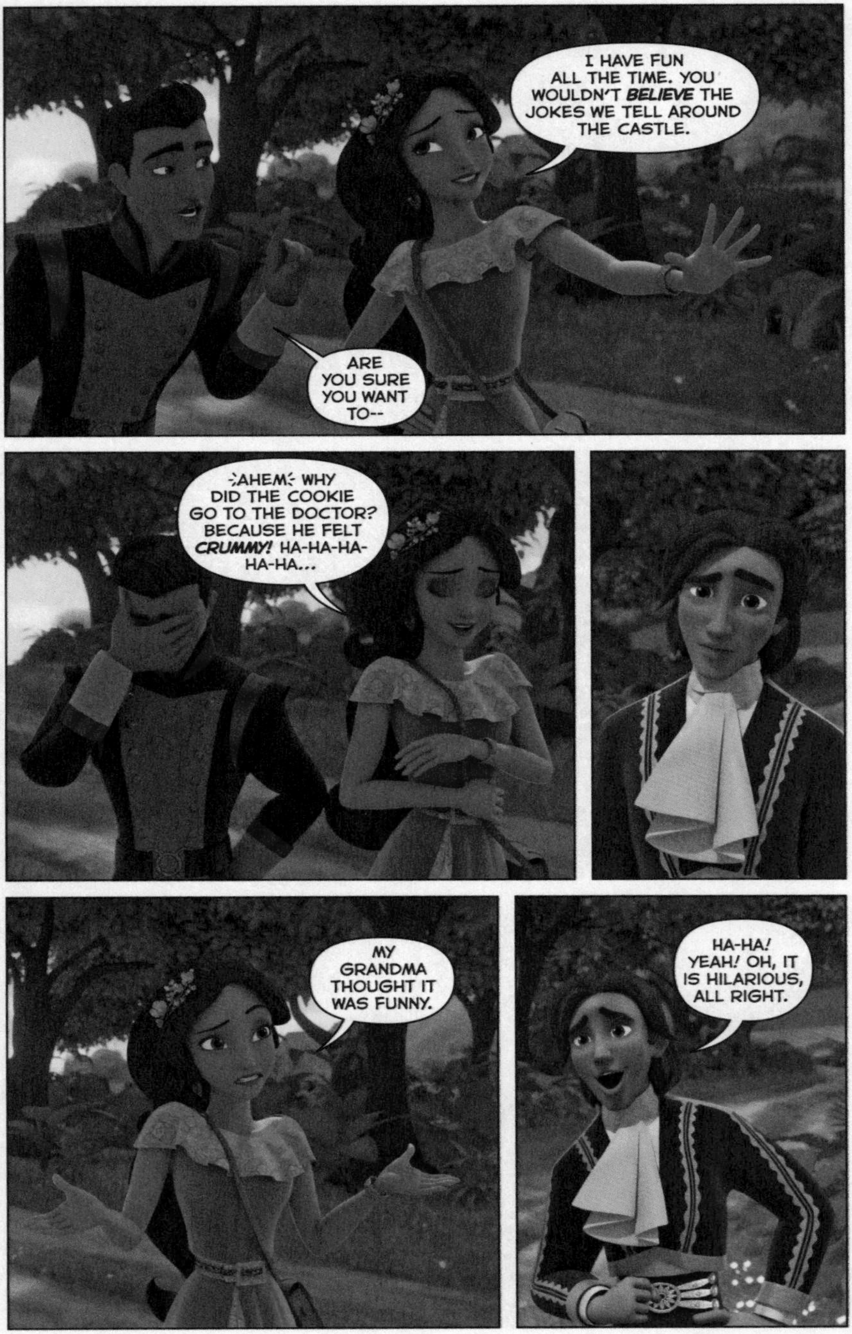
I HAVE FUN ALL THE TIME. YOU WOULDN'T *BELIEVE* THE JOKES WE TELL AROUND THE CASTLE.
ARE YOU SURE YOU WANT TO--
-AHEM- WHY DID THE COOKIE GO TO THE DOCTOR? BECAUSE HE FELT *CRUMMY!* HA-HA-HA-HA-HA...
MY GRANDMA THOUGHT IT WAS FUNNY.
HA-HA! YEAH! OH, IT IS HILARIOUS, ALL RIGHT.

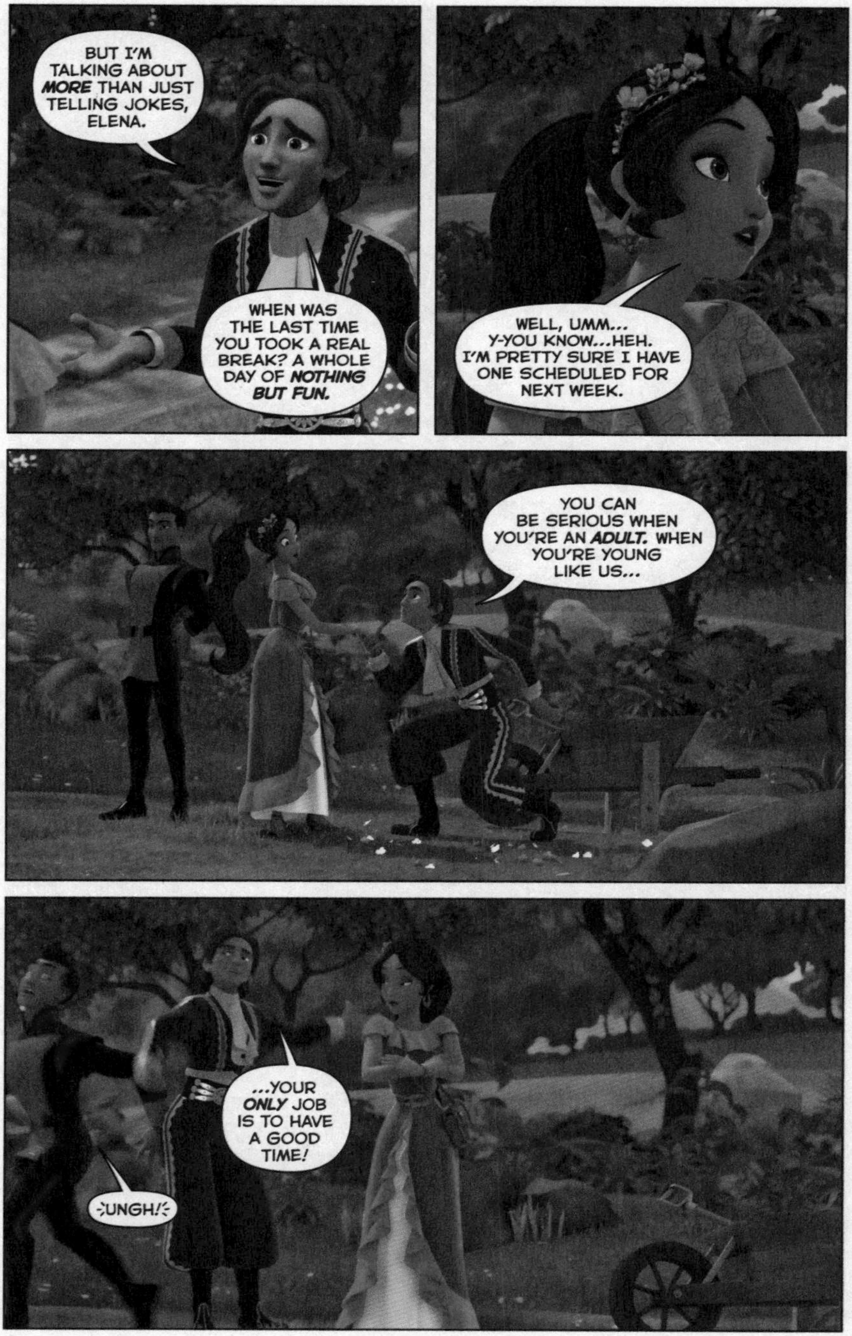
BUT I'M TALKING ABOUT **MORE** THAN JUST TELLING JOKES, ELENA.
WHEN WAS THE LAST TIME YOU TOOK A REAL BREAK? A WHOLE DAY OF **NOTHING BUT FUN.**
WELL, UMM... Y-YOU KNOW...HEH. I'M PRETTY SURE I HAVE ONE SCHEDULED FOR NEXT WEEK.
YOU CAN BE SERIOUS WHEN YOU'RE AN **ADULT.** WHEN YOU'RE YOUNG LIKE US...
...YOUR **ONLY** JOB IS TO HAVE A GOOD TIME!
UNGH!

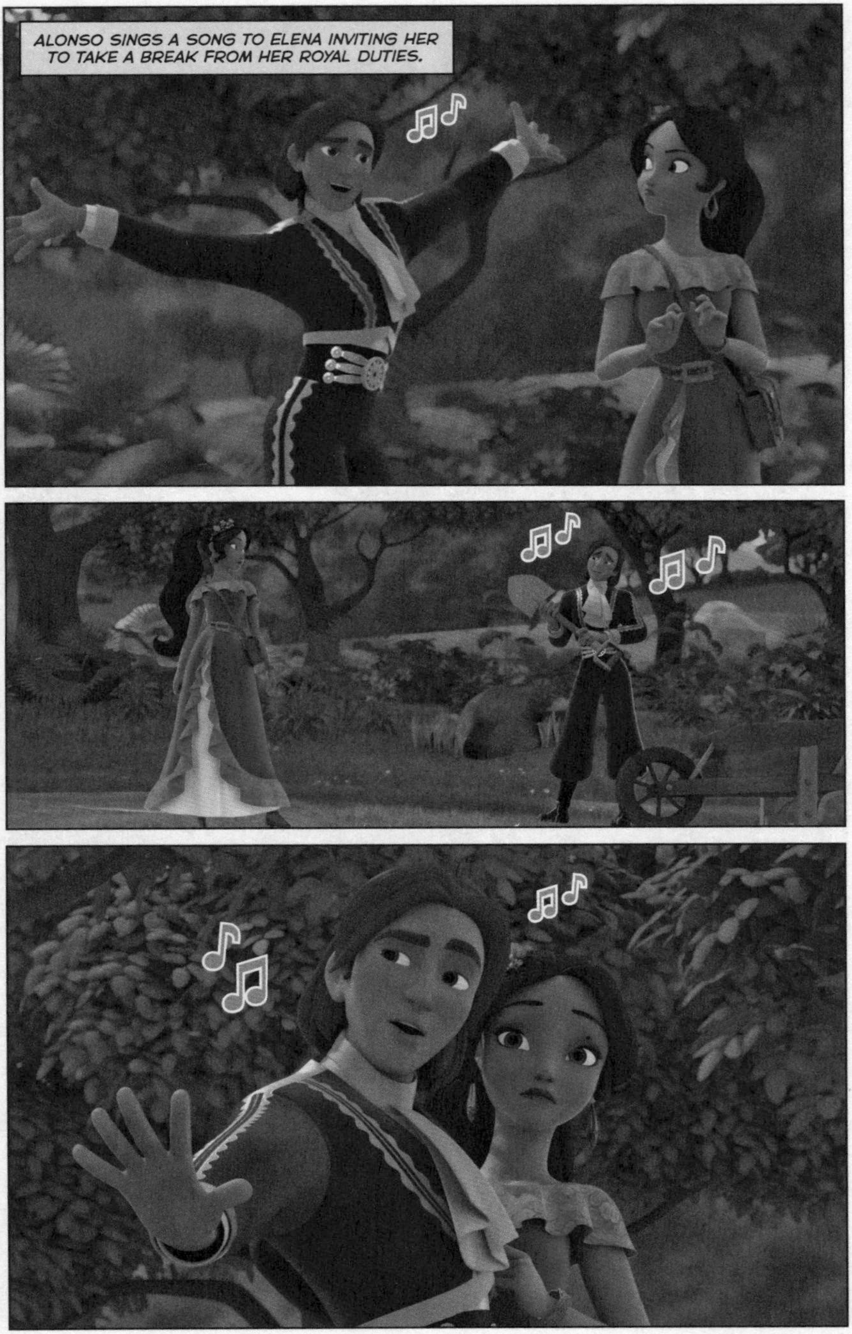
ALONSO SINGS A SONG TO ELENA INVITING HER TO TAKE A BREAK FROM HER ROYAL DUTIES.

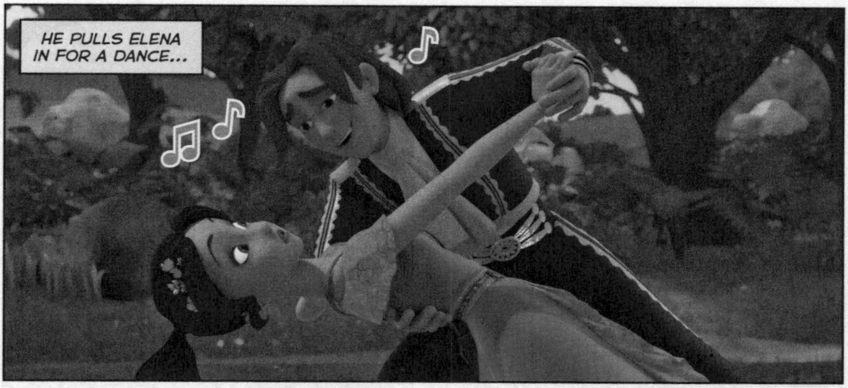
HE PULLS ELENA IN FOR A DANCE...

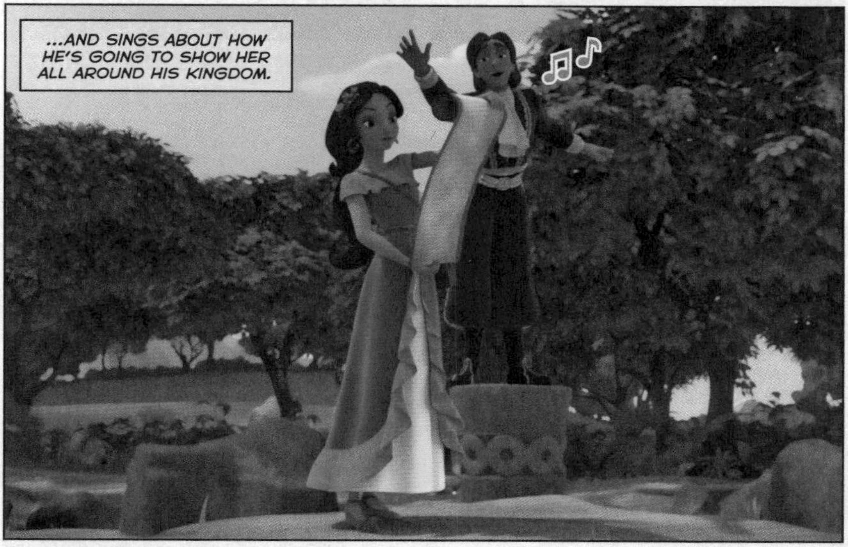
...AND SINGS ABOUT HOW HE'S GOING TO SHOW HER ALL AROUND HIS KINGDOM.

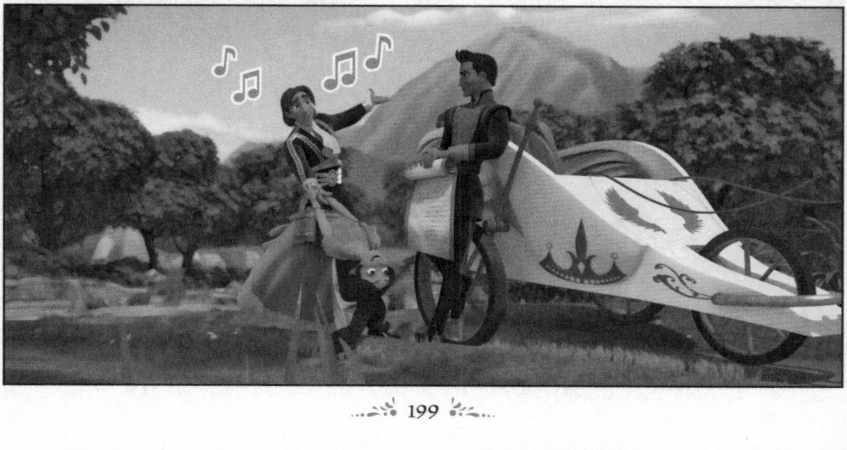

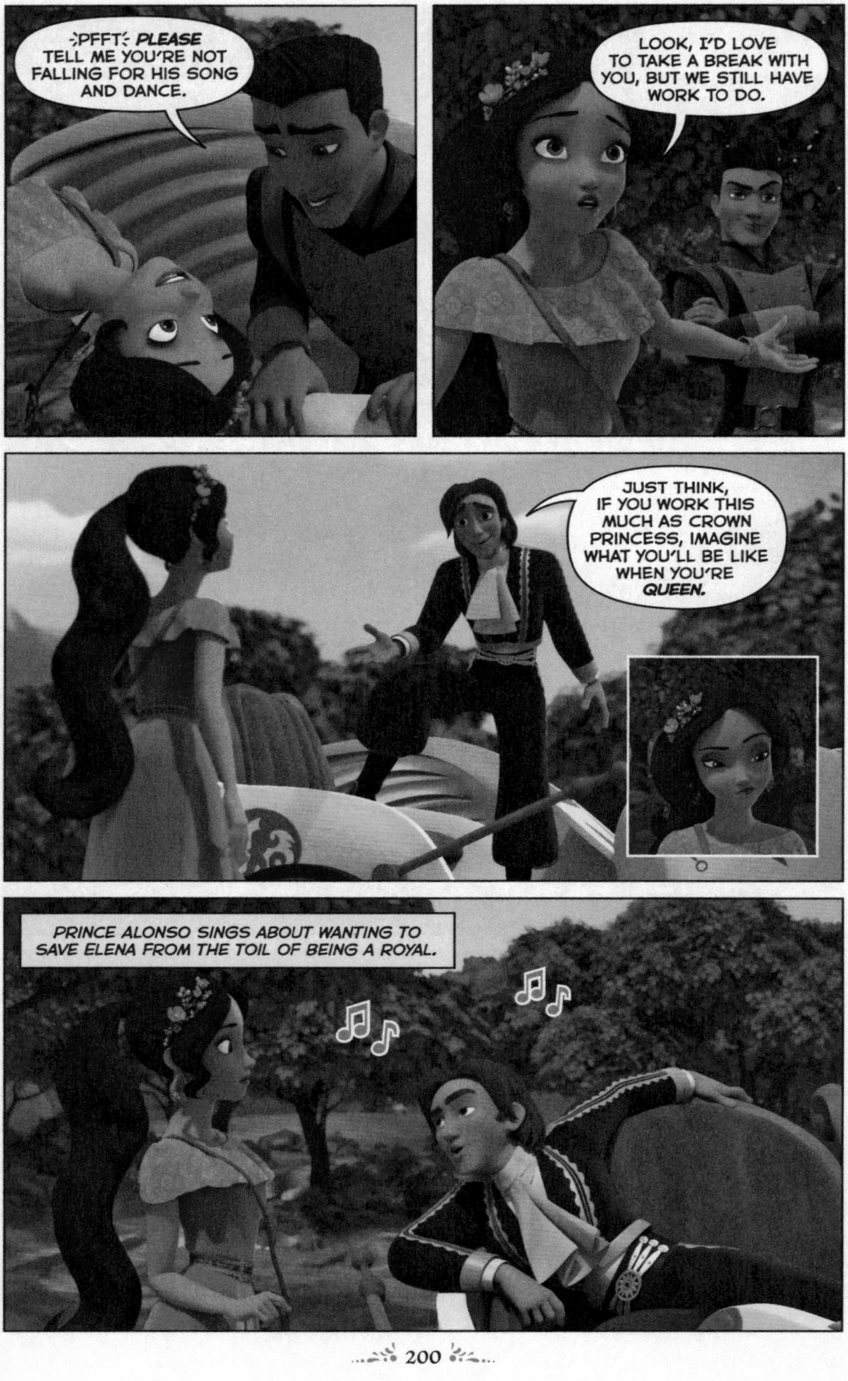

PFFT ***PLEASE*** TELL ME YOU'RE NOT FALLING FOR HIS SONG AND DANCE.
LOOK, I'D LOVE TO TAKE A BREAK WITH YOU, BUT WE STILL HAVE WORK TO DO.
JUST THINK, IF YOU WORK THIS MUCH AS CROWN PRINCESS, IMAGINE WHAT YOU'LL BE LIKE WHEN YOU'RE ***QUEEN.***
PRINCE ALONSO SINGS ABOUT WANTING TO SAVE ELENA FROM THE TOIL OF BEING A ROYAL.

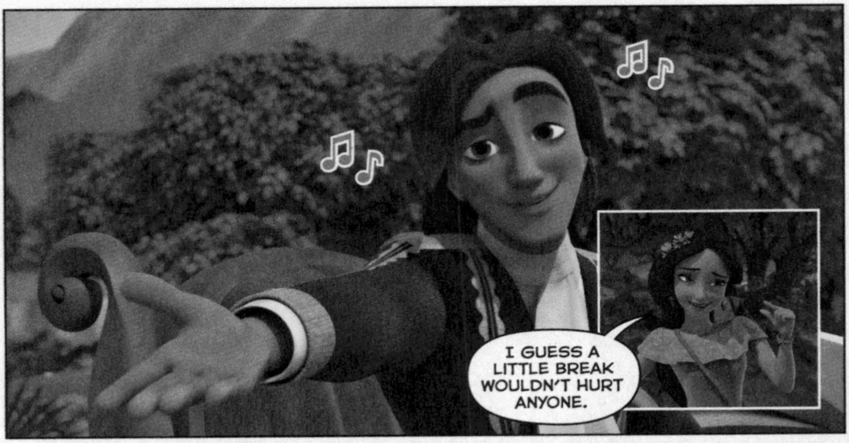
I GUESS A LITTLE BREAK WOULDN'T HURT ANYONE.

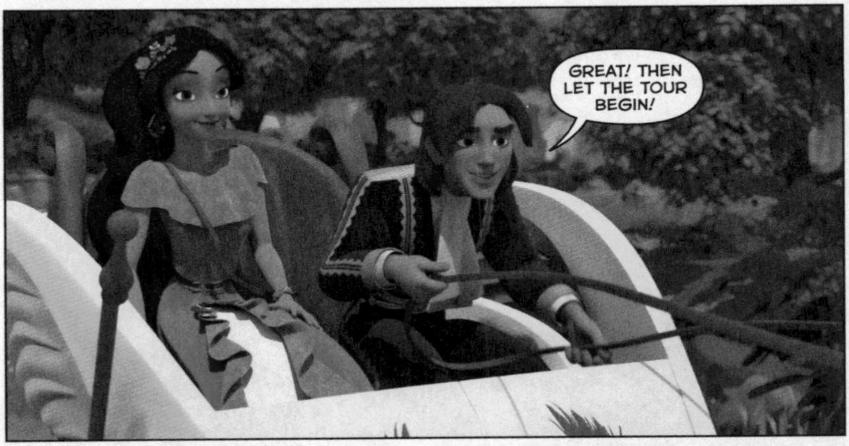
GREAT! THEN LET THE TOUR BEGIN!

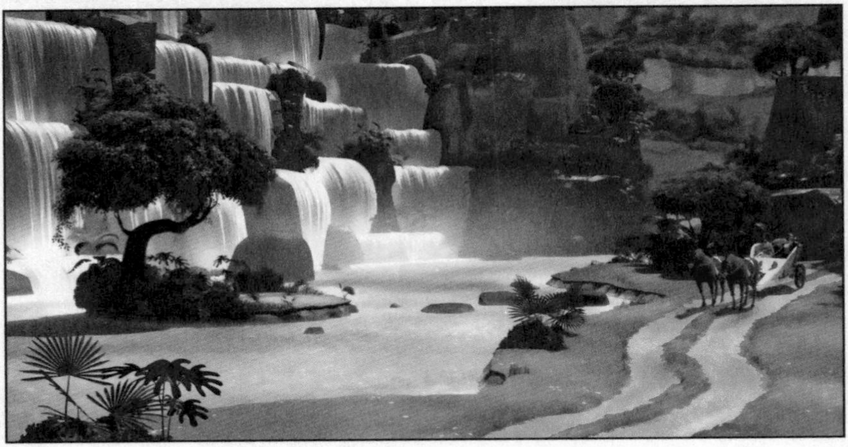

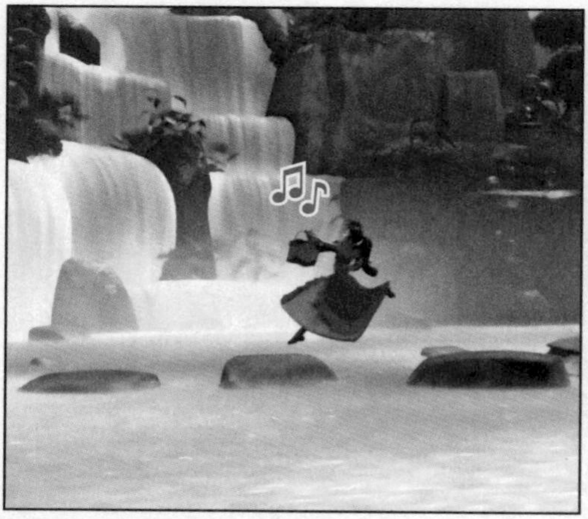

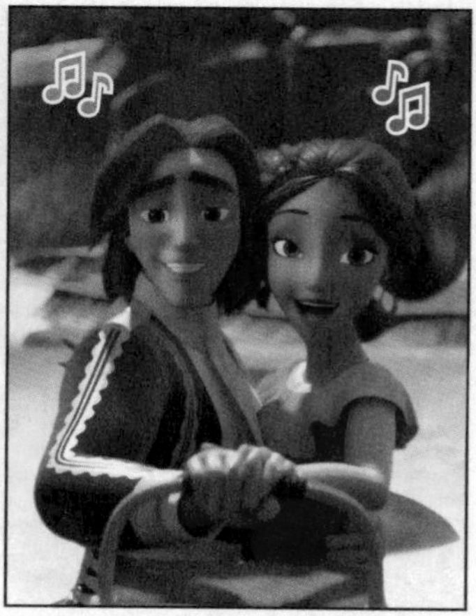

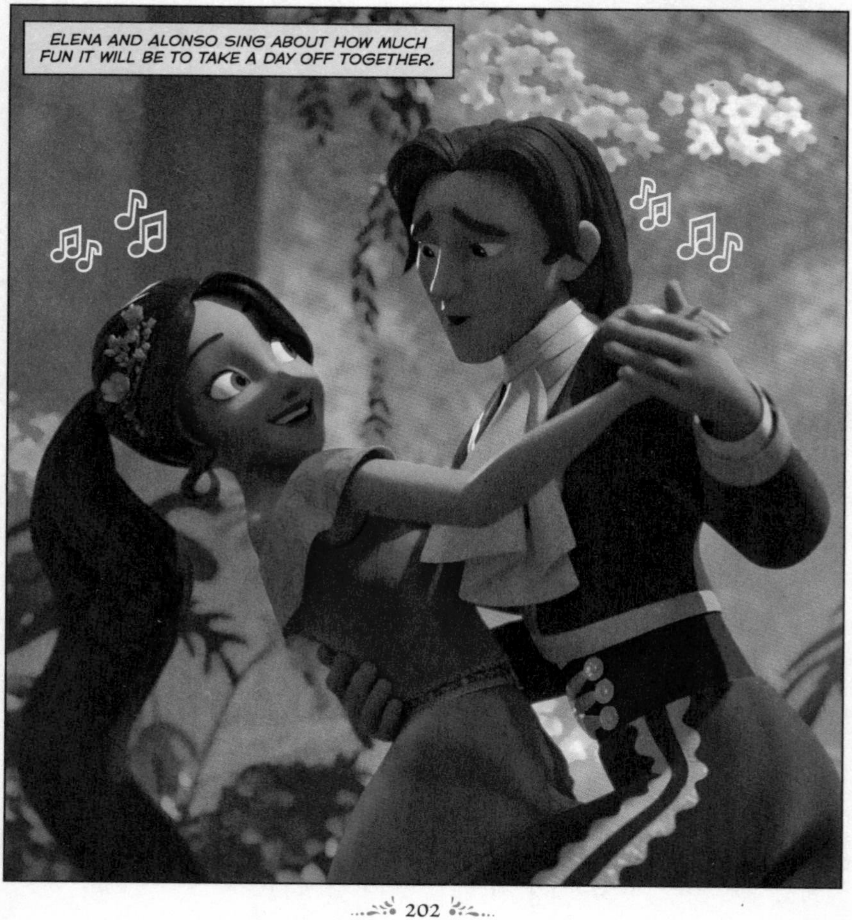
ELENA AND ALONSO SING ABOUT HOW MUCH FUN IT WILL BE TO TAKE A DAY OFF TOGETHER.

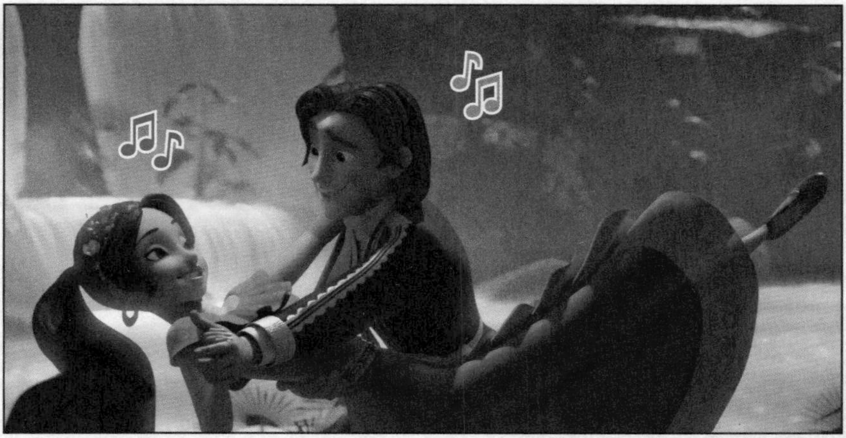

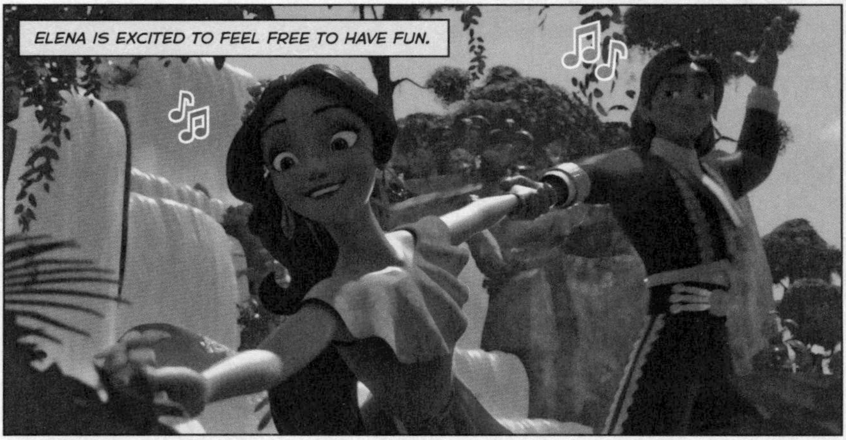
ELENA IS EXCITED TO FEEL FREE TO HAVE FUN.

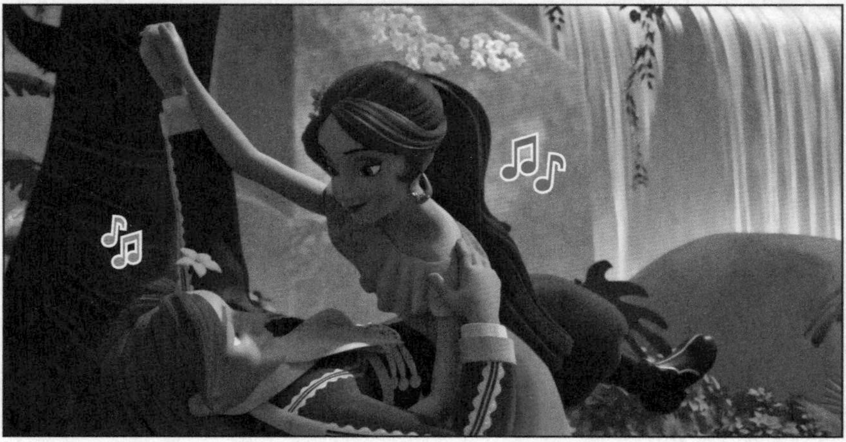

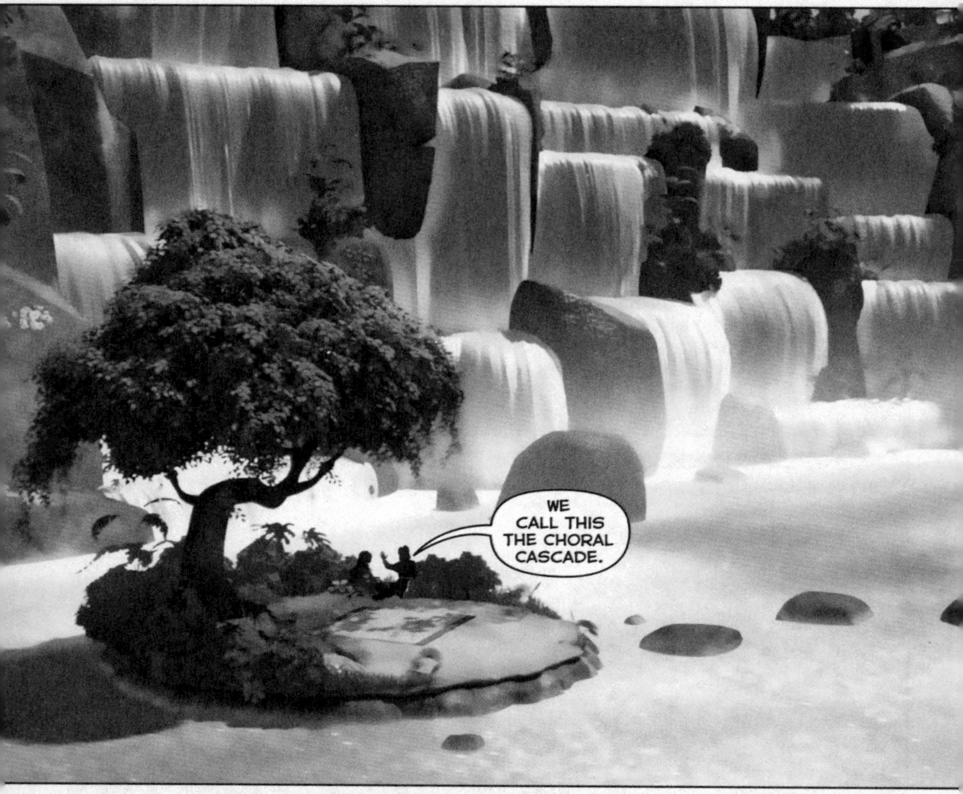
WE CALL THIS THE CHORAL CASCADE.

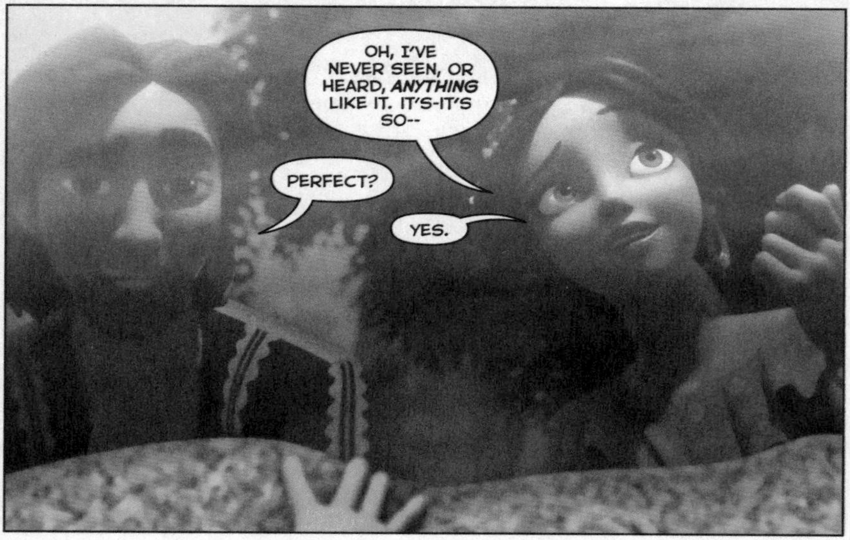
OH, I'VE NEVER SEEN, OR HEARD, *ANYTHING* LIKE IT. IT'S-IT'S SO--
PERFECT?
YES.

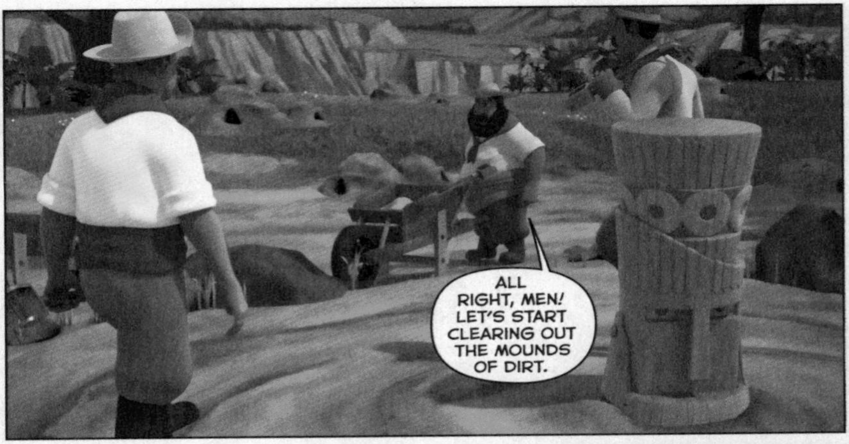
ALL RIGHT, MEN! LET'S START CLEARING OUT THE MOUNDS OF DIRT.

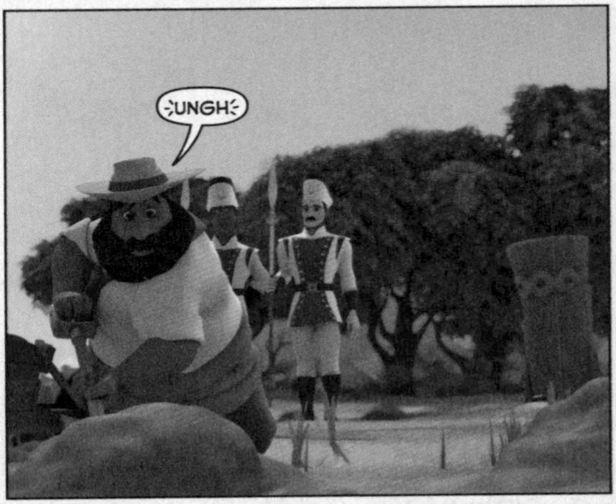
UNGH

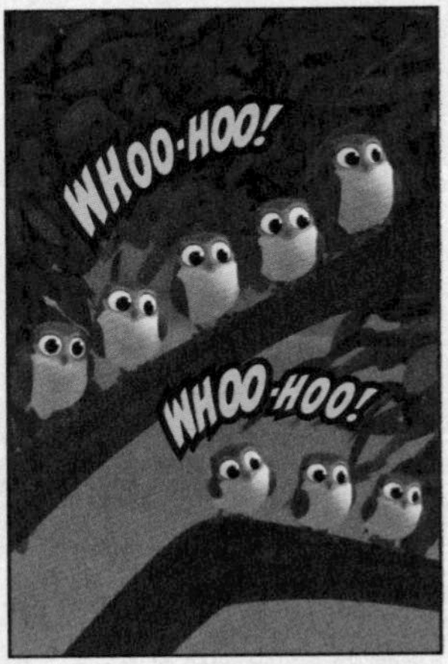
WHOO-HOO!
WHOO-HOO!

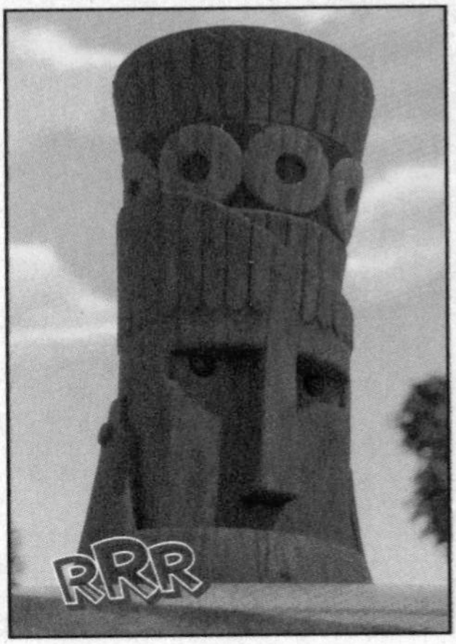
RRR

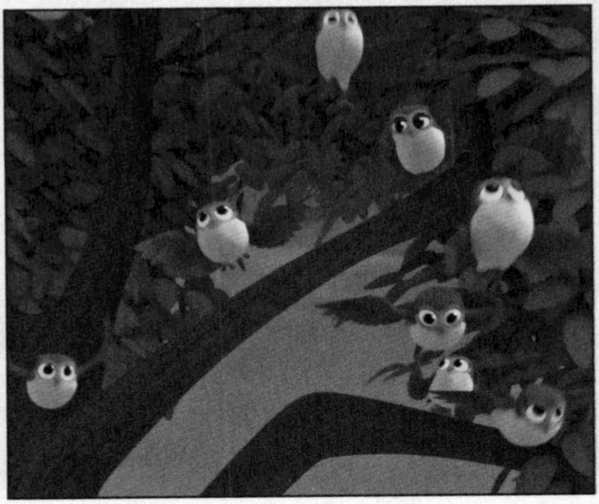

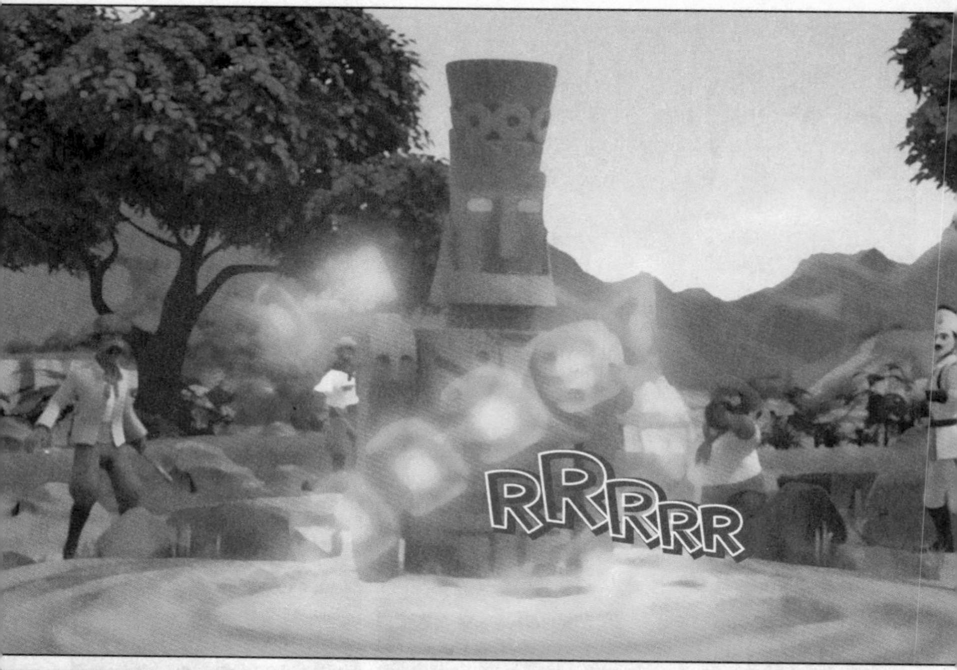
RRRRRR

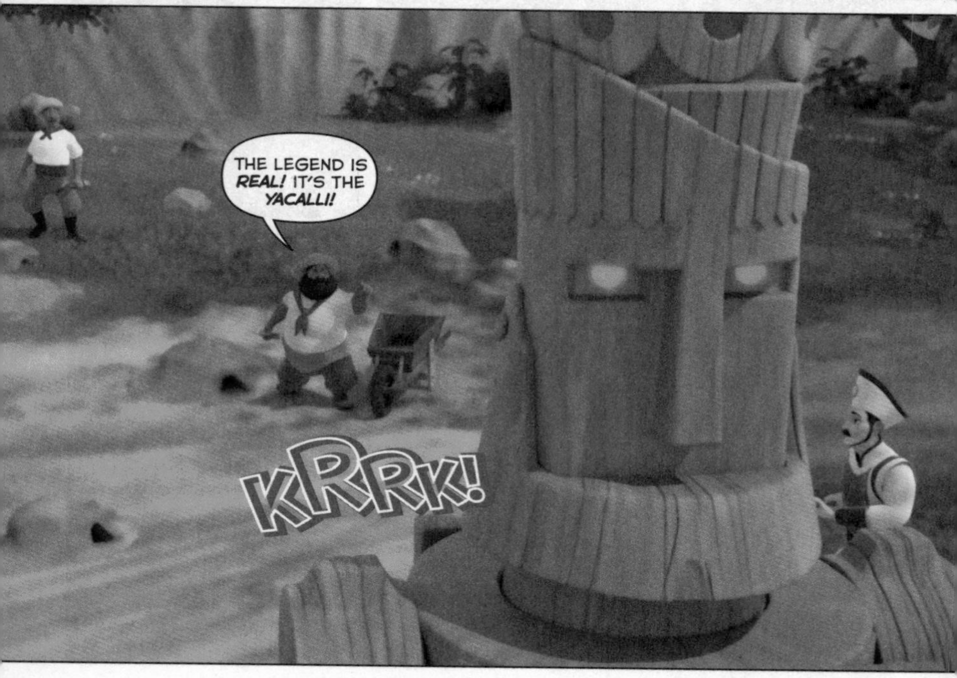
THE LEGEND IS *REAL!* IT'S THE *YACALLI!*
KRRK!

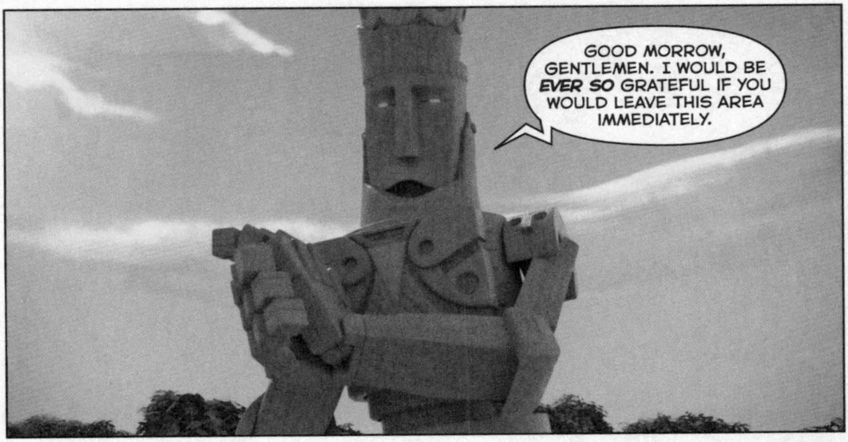
GOOD MORROW, GENTLEMEN. I WOULD BE EVER SO GRATEFUL IF YOU WOULD LEAVE THIS AREA IMMEDIATELY.

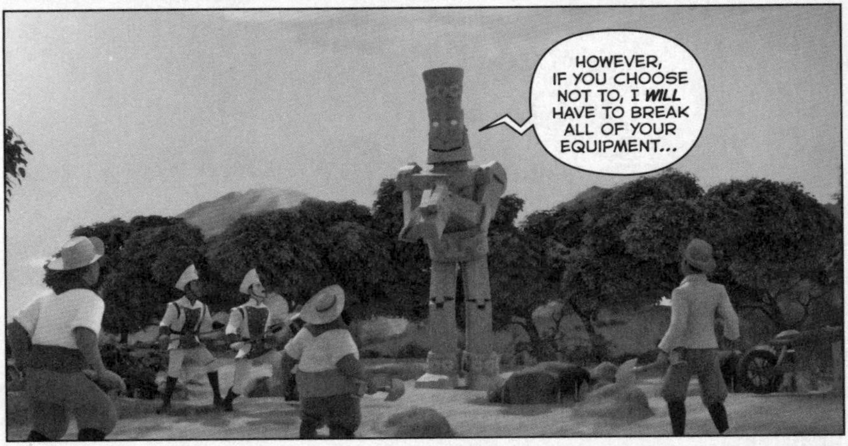
HOWEVER, IF YOU CHOOSE NOT TO, I WILL HAVE TO BREAK ALL OF YOUR EQUIPMENT...

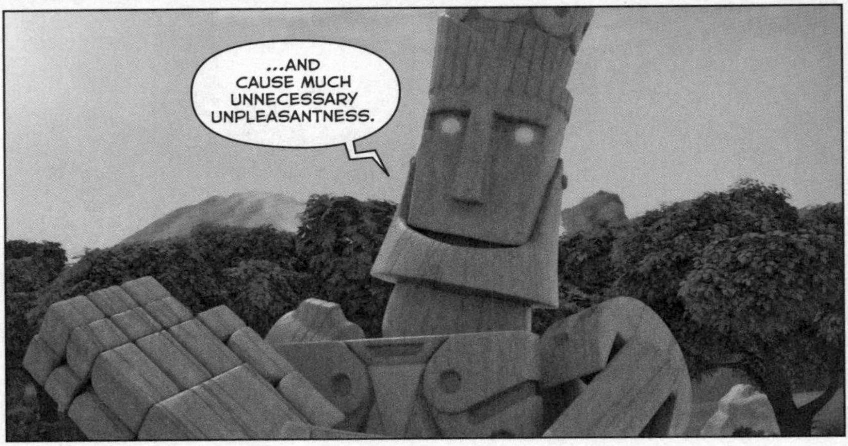
...AND CAUSE MUCH UNNECESSARY UNPLEASANTNESS.

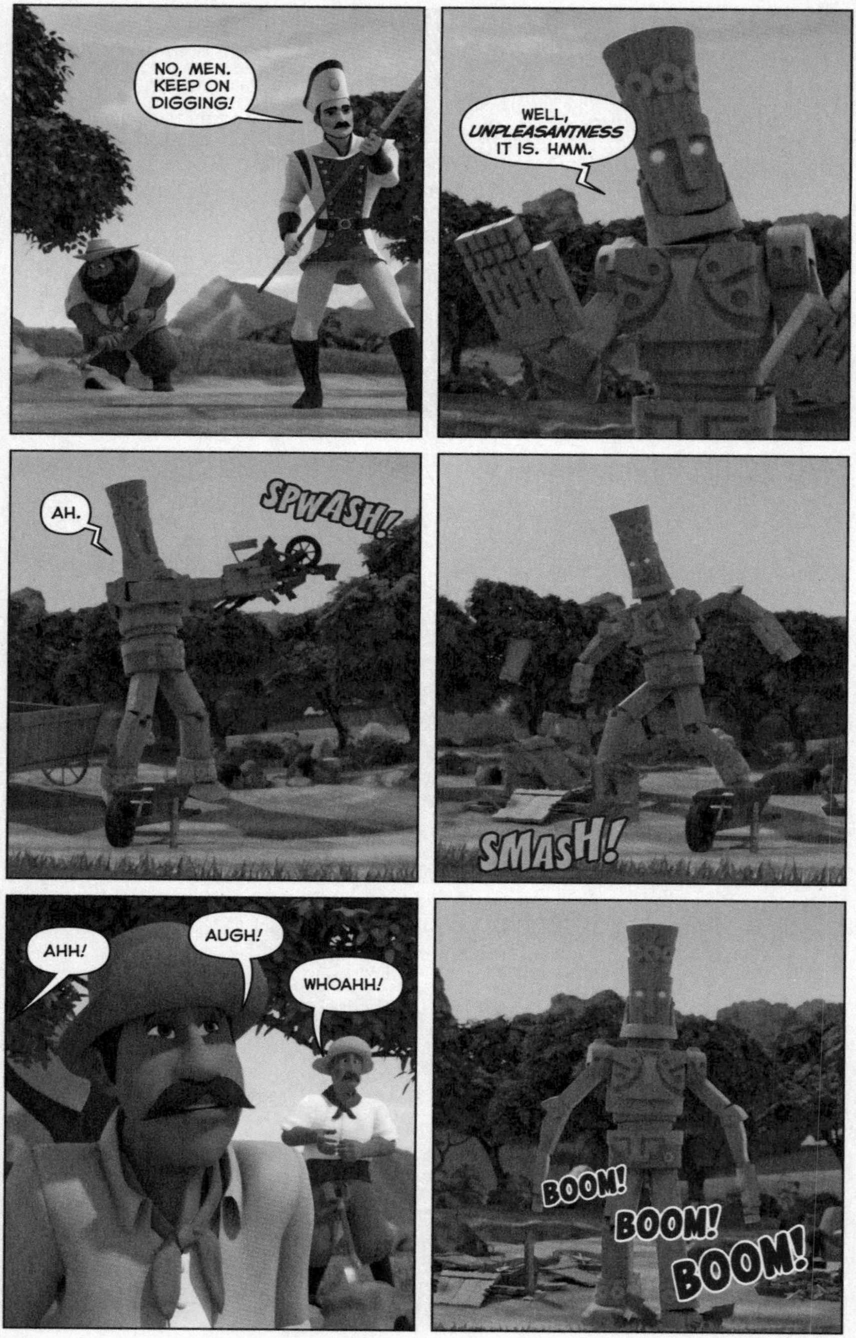
NO, MEN. KEEP ON DIGGING!
WELL, *UNPLEASANTNESS* IT IS. HMM.
AH.
SPWASH!
SMASH!
AHH!
AUGH!
WHOAHH!
BOOM!
BOOM!
BOOM!

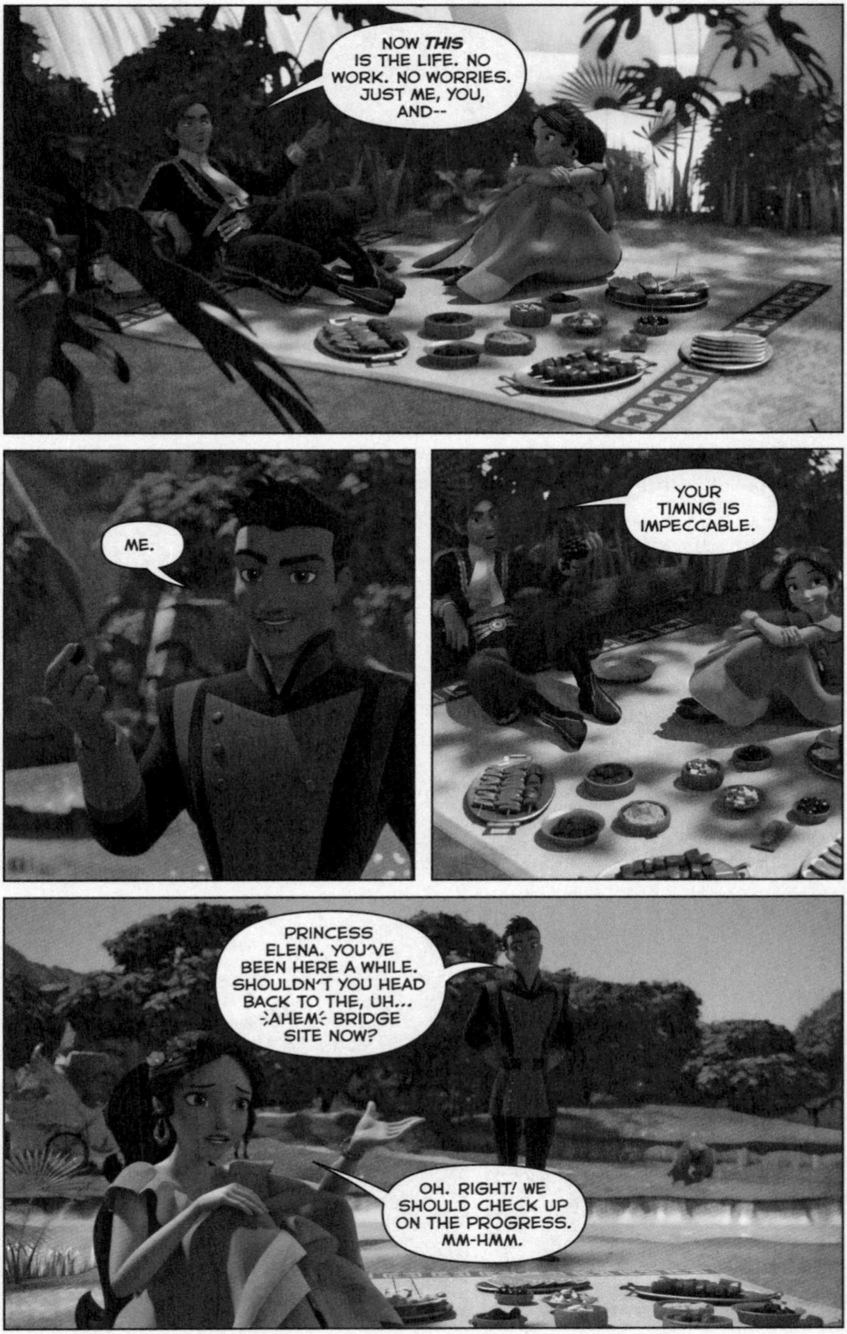
NOW *THIS* IS THE LIFE. NO WORK. NO WORRIES. JUST ME, YOU, AND--
ME.
YOUR TIMING IS IMPECCABLE.
PRINCESS ELENA. YOU'VE BEEN HERE A WHILE. SHOULDN'T YOU HEAD BACK TO THE, UH... AHEM BRIDGE SITE NOW?
OH. RIGHT! WE SHOULD CHECK UP ON THE PROGRESS. MM-HMM.

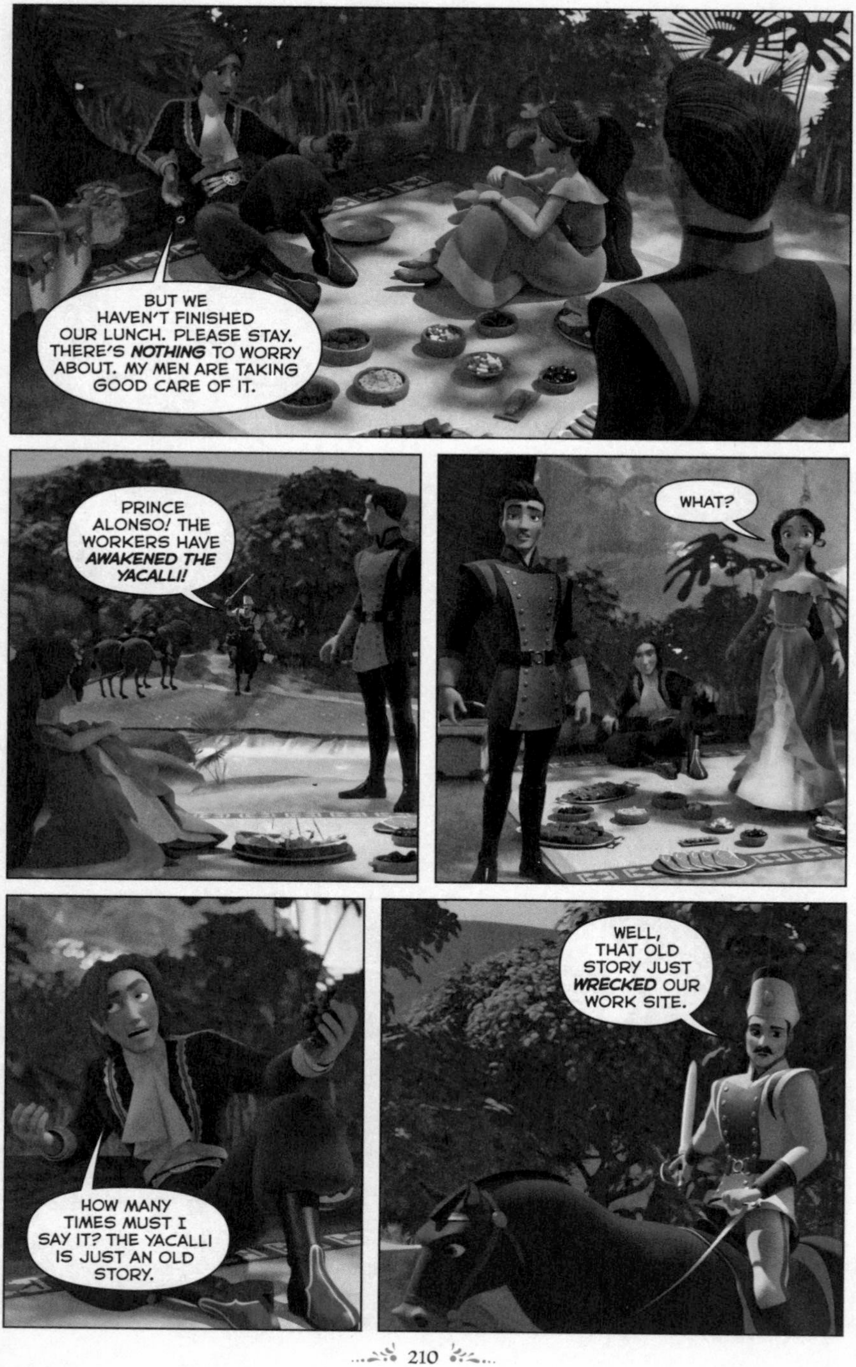
BUT WE HAVEN'T FINISHED OUR LUNCH. PLEASE STAY. THERE'S ***NOTHING*** TO WORRY ABOUT. MY MEN ARE TAKING GOOD CARE OF IT.
PRINCE ALONSO! THE WORKERS HAVE ***AWAKENED THE YACALLI!***
WHAT?
HOW MANY TIMES MUST I SAY IT? THE YACALLI IS JUST AN OLD STORY.
WELL, THAT OLD STORY JUST ***WRECKED*** OUR WORK SITE.

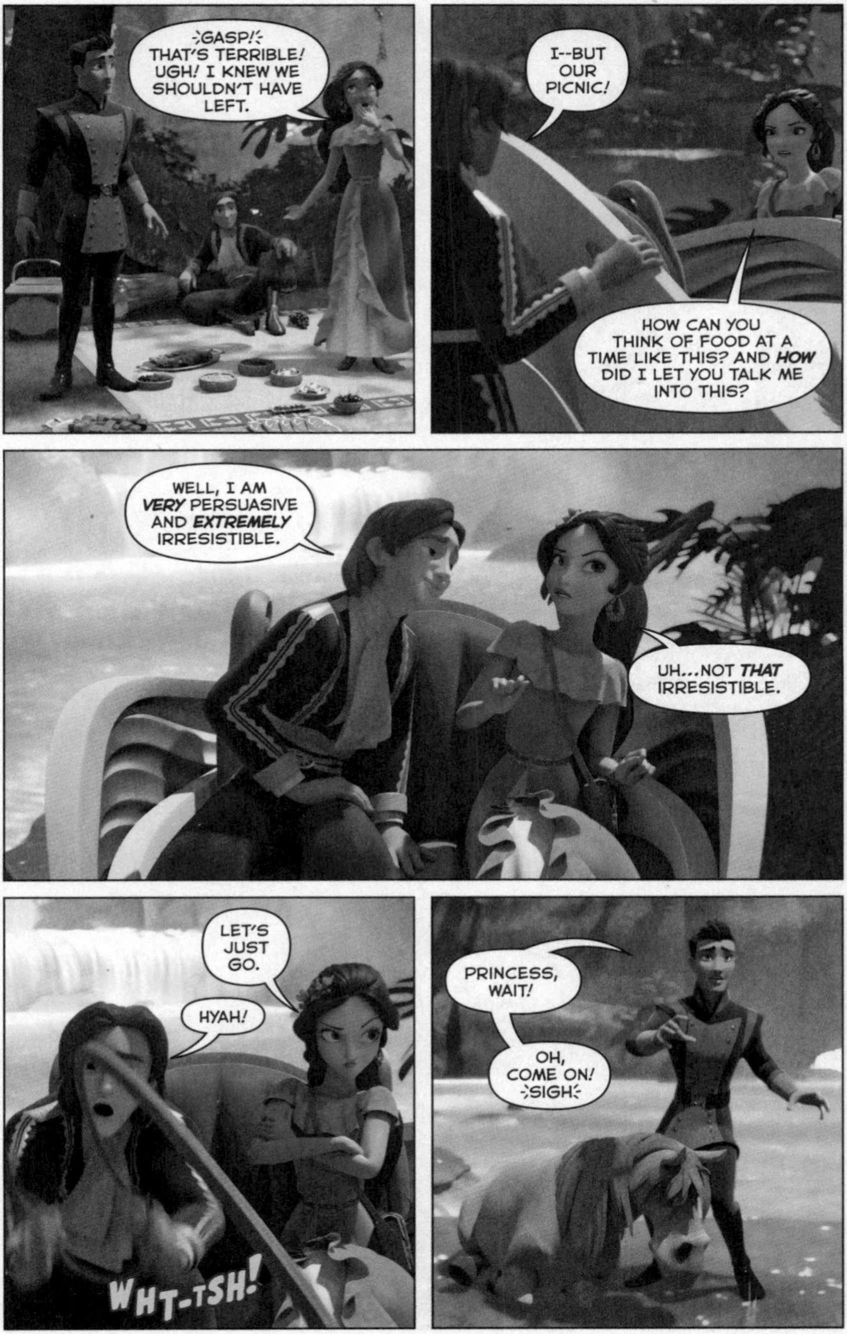

-GASP!- THAT'S TERRIBLE! UGH! I KNEW WE SHOULDN'T HAVE LEFT.
I--BUT OUR PICNIC!
HOW CAN YOU THINK OF FOOD AT A TIME LIKE THIS? AND *HOW* DID I LET YOU TALK ME INTO THIS?
WELL, I AM *VERY* PERSUASIVE AND *EXTREMELY* IRRESISTIBLE.
UH...NOT *THAT* IRRESISTIBLE.
LET'S JUST GO.
HYAH!
WHT-TSH!
PRINCESS, WAIT!
OH, COME ON! -SIGH-

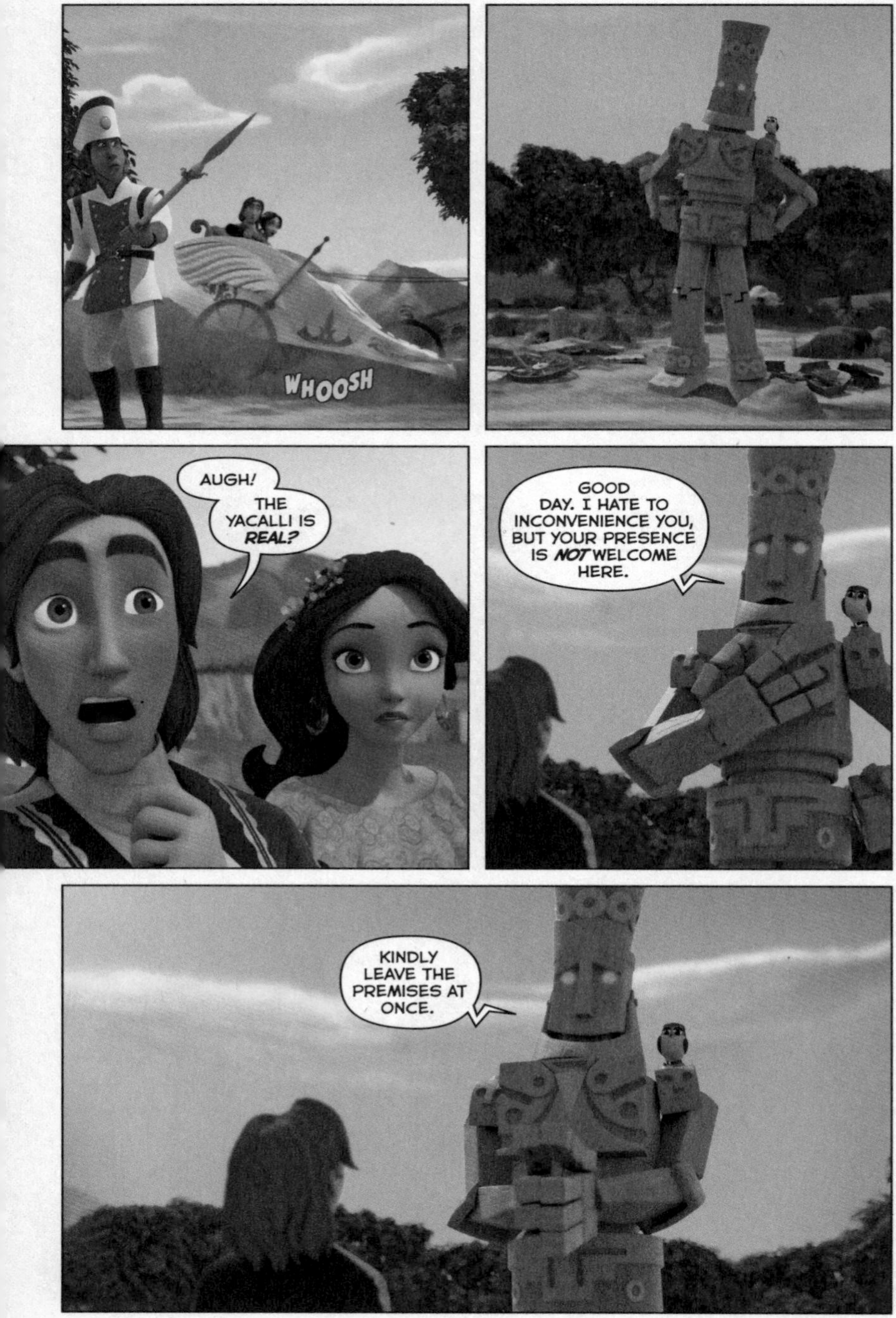
WHOOSH
AUGH!
THE YACALLI IS REAL?
GOOD DAY. I HATE TO INCONVENIENCE YOU, BUT YOUR PRESENCE IS NOT WELCOME HERE.
KINDLY LEAVE THE PREMISES AT ONCE.

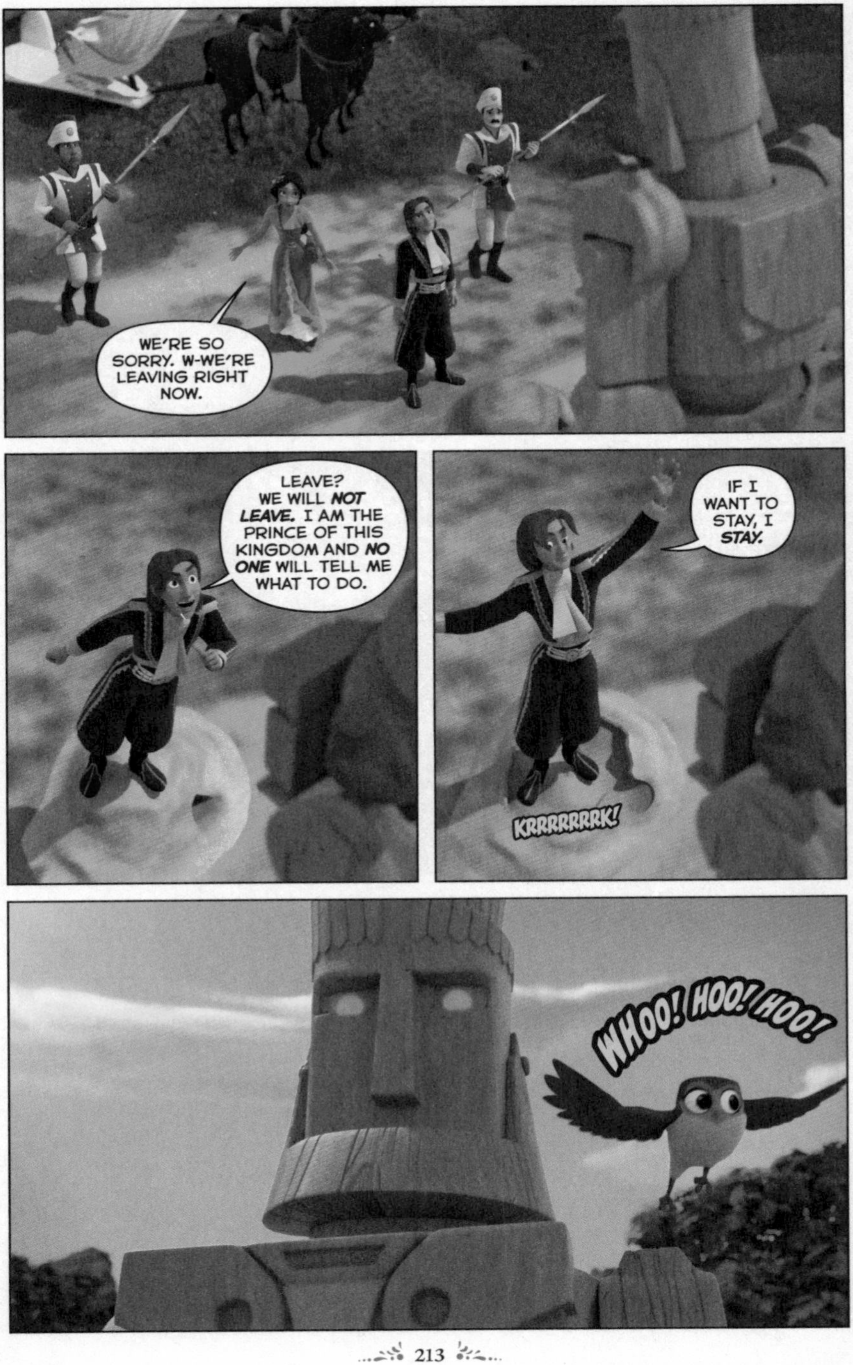
WE'RE SO SORRY. W-WE'RE LEAVING RIGHT NOW.
LEAVE? WE WILL ***NOT LEAVE.*** I AM THE PRINCE OF THIS KINGDOM AND ***NO ONE*** WILL TELL ME WHAT TO DO.
IF I WANT TO STAY, I ***STAY.***
KRRRRRRRK!
WHOO! HOO! HOO!

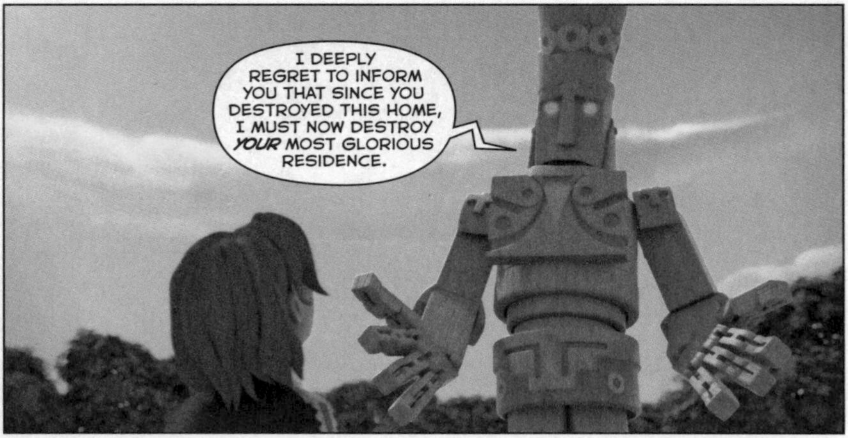
I DEEPLY REGRET TO INFORM YOU THAT SINCE YOU DESTROYED THIS HOME, I MUST NOW DESTROY *YOUR* MOST GLORIOUS RESIDENCE.

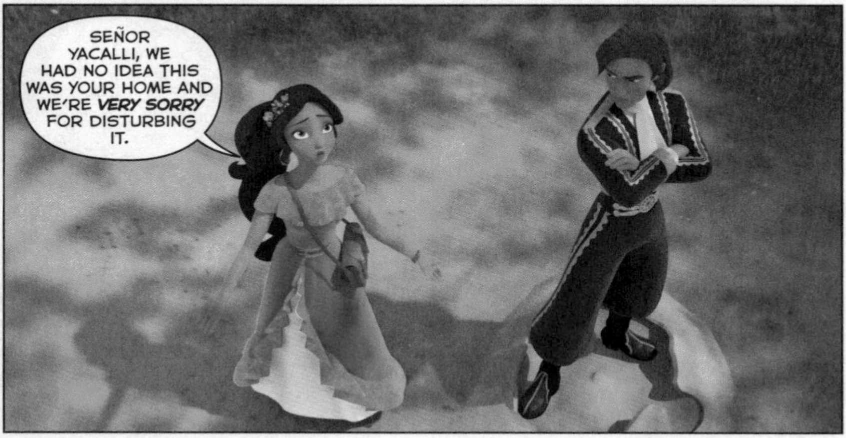
SEÑOR YACALLI, WE HAD NO IDEA THIS WAS YOUR HOME AND WE'RE *VERY SORRY* FOR DISTURBING IT.

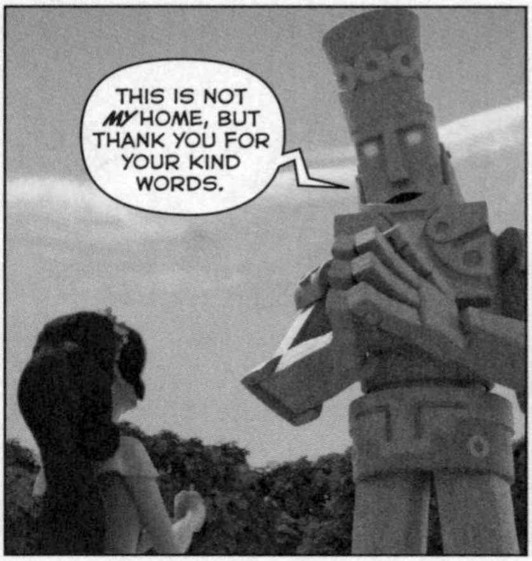
THIS IS NOT *MY* HOME, BUT THANK YOU FOR YOUR KIND WORDS.

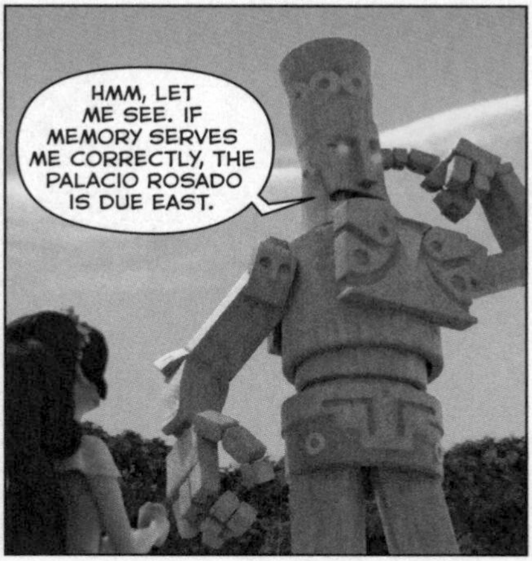
HMM, LET ME SEE. IF MEMORY SERVES ME CORRECTLY, THE PALACIO ROSADO IS DUE EAST.

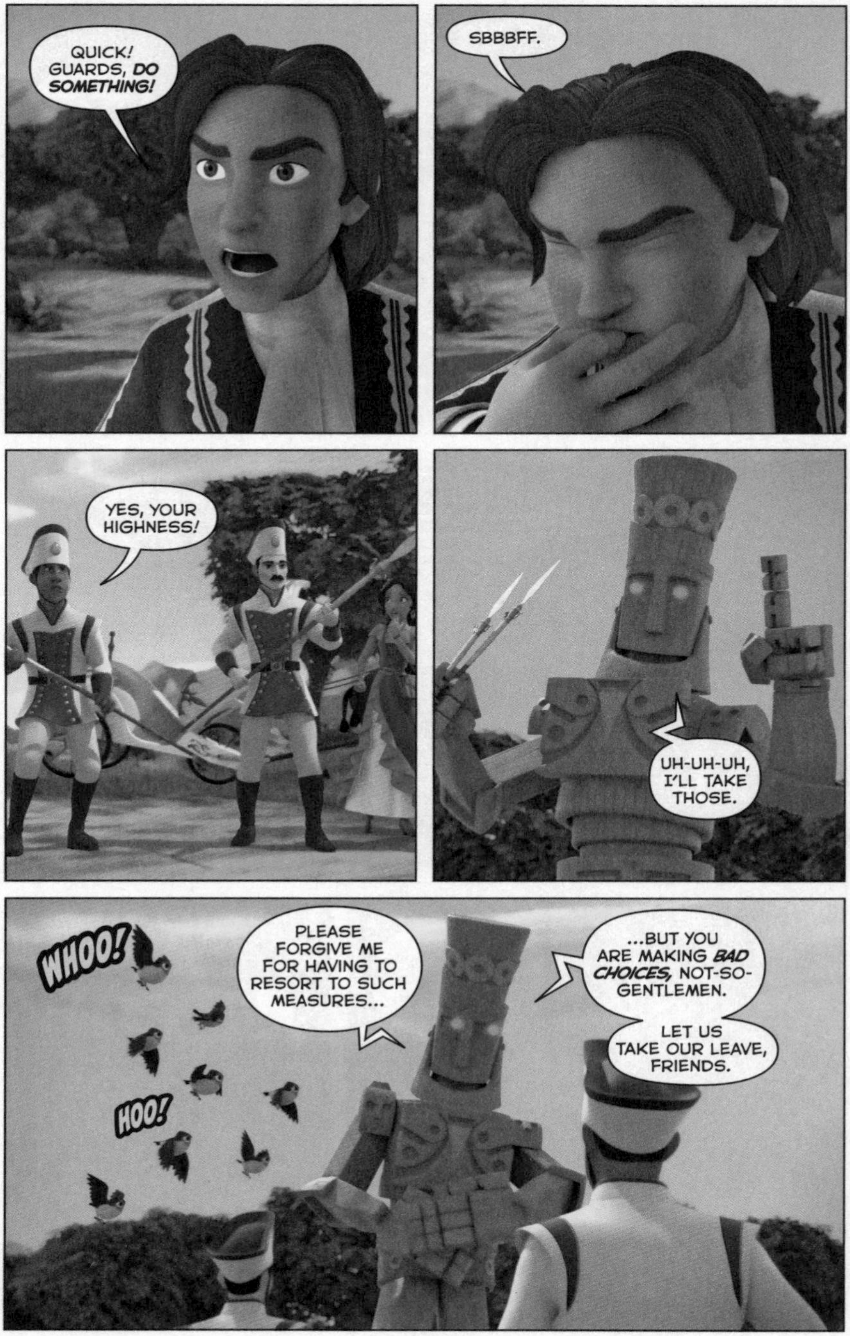
QUICK! GUARDS, DO SOMETHING!
SBBBFF.
YES, YOUR HIGHNESS!
UH-UH-UH, I'LL TAKE THOSE.
WHOO!
HOO!
PLEASE FORGIVE ME FOR HAVING TO RESORT TO SUCH MEASURES...
...BUT YOU ARE MAKING BAD CHOICES, NOT-SO-GENTLEMEN.
LET US TAKE OUR LEAVE, FRIENDS.

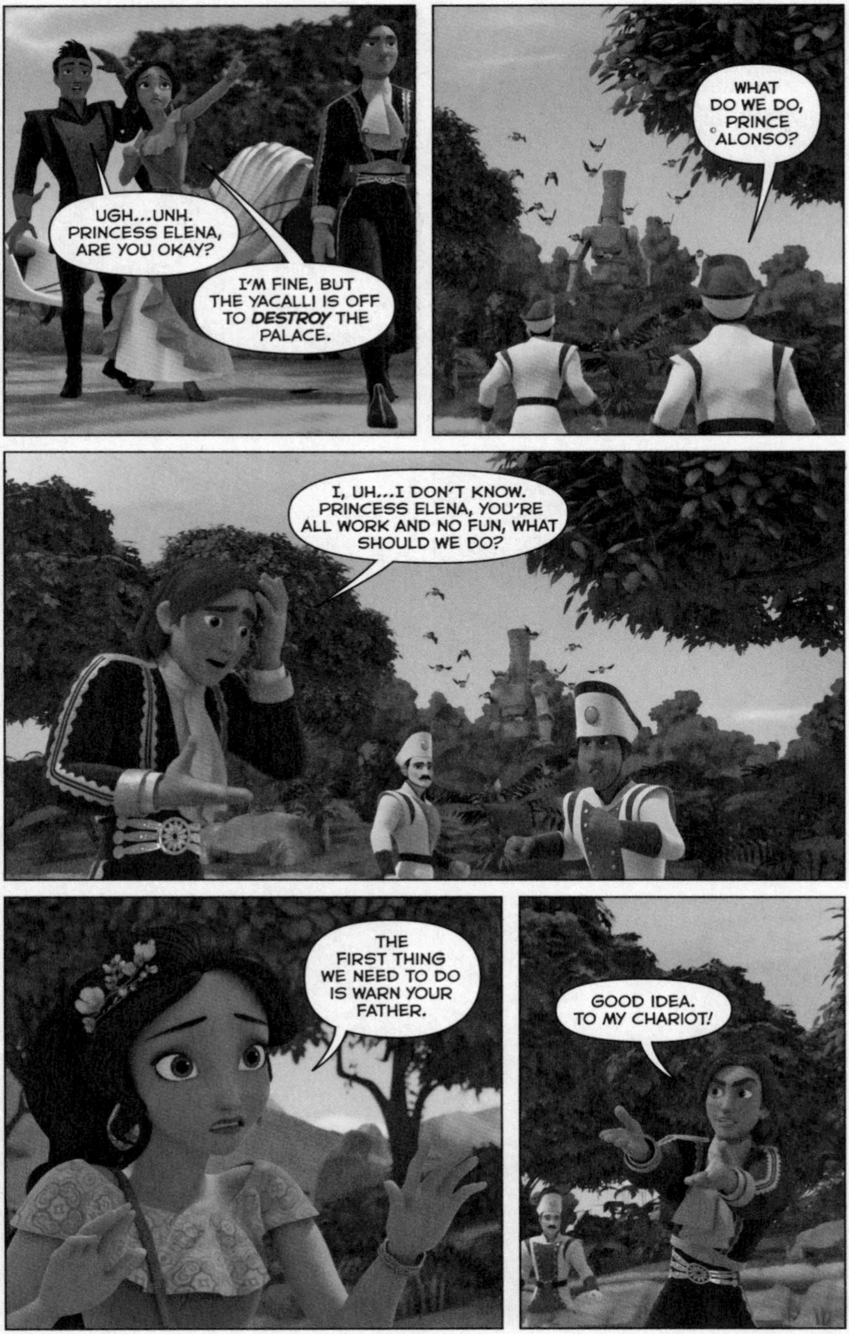
UGH...UNH. PRINCESS ELENA, ARE YOU OKAY?
I'M FINE, BUT THE YACALLI IS OFF TO *DESTROY* THE PALACE.
WHAT DO WE DO, PRINCE ALONSO?
I, UH...I DON'T KNOW. PRINCESS ELENA, YOU'RE ALL WORK AND NO FUN, WHAT SHOULD WE DO?
THE FIRST THING WE NEED TO DO IS WARN YOUR FATHER.
GOOD IDEA. TO MY CHARIOT!

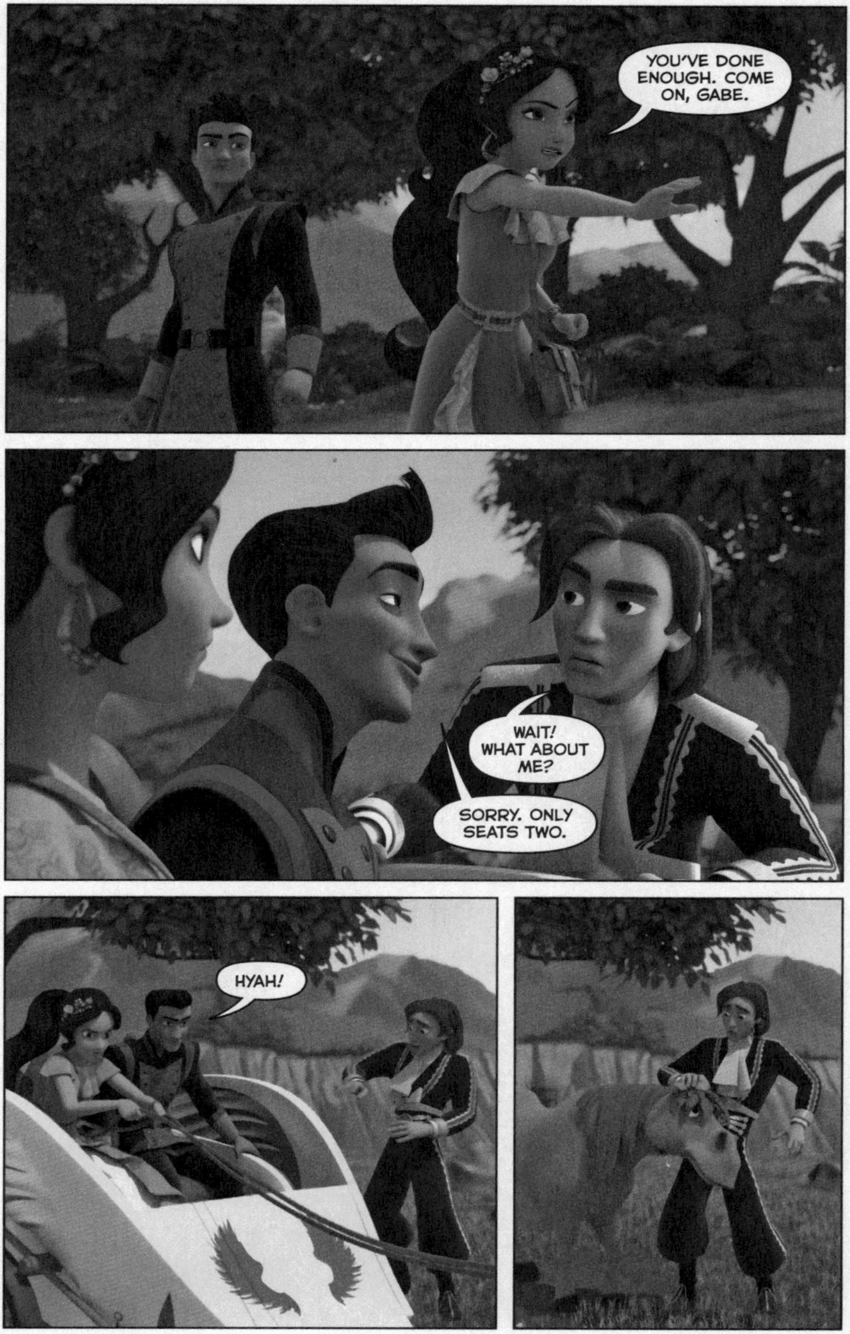
YOU'VE DONE ENOUGH. COME ON, GABE.
WAIT! WHAT ABOUT ME?
SORRY. ONLY SEATS TWO.
HYAH!

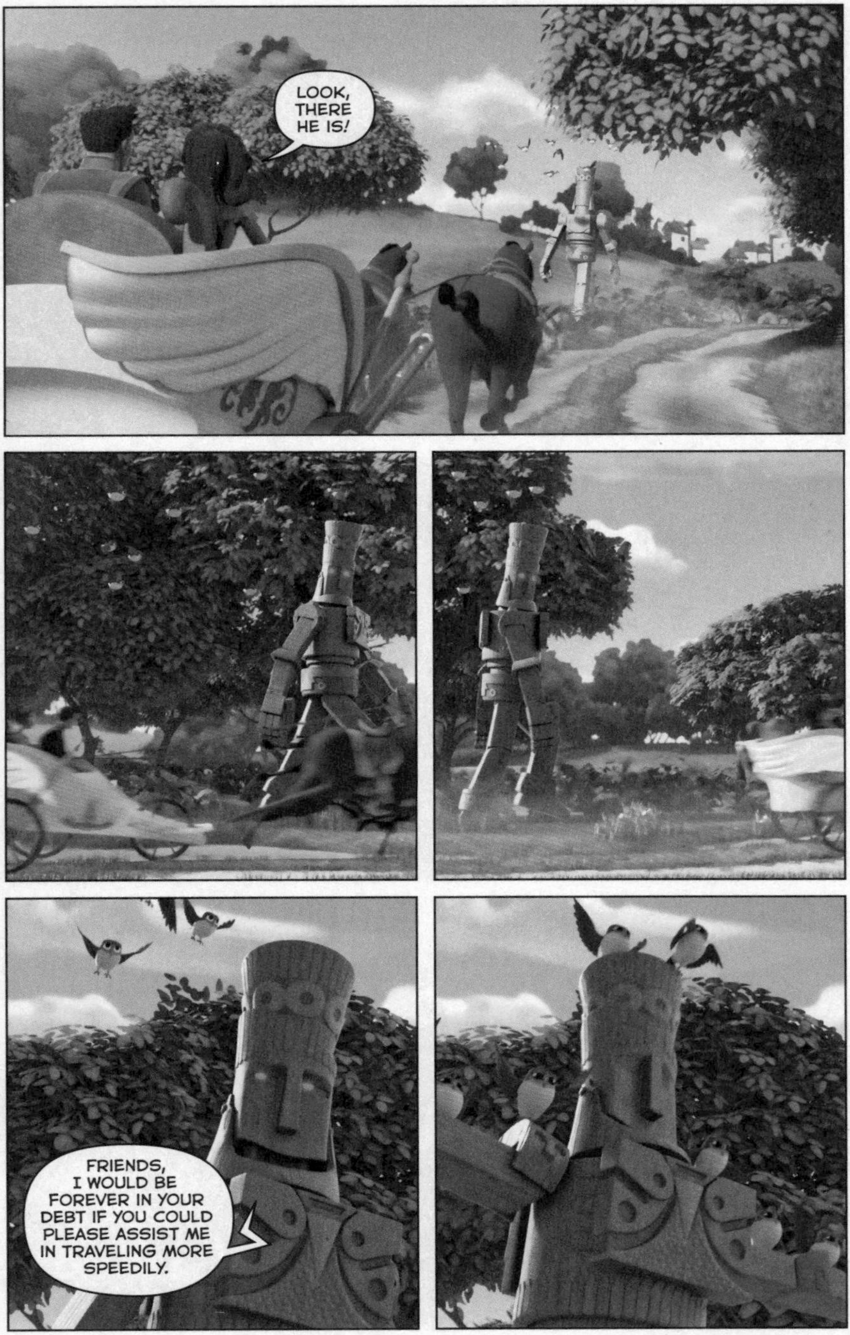
LOOK, THERE HE IS!
FRIENDS, I WOULD BE FOREVER IN YOUR DEBT IF YOU COULD PLEASE ASSIST ME IN TRAVELING MORE SPEEDILY.

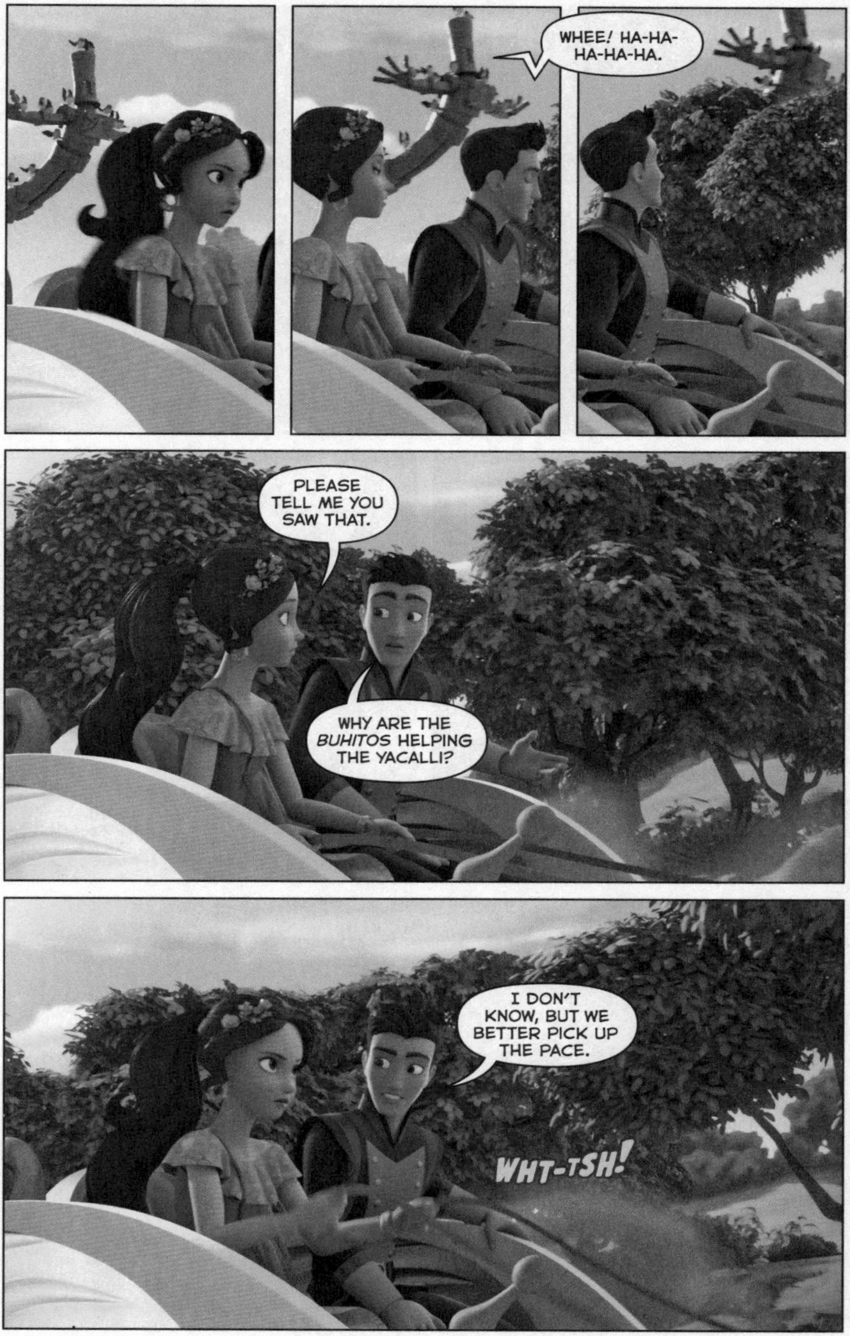
WHEE! HA-HA-HA-HA-HA.
PLEASE TELL ME YOU SAW THAT.
WHY ARE THE *BUHITOS* HELPING THE YACALLI?
I DON'T KNOW, BUT WE BETTER PICK UP THE PACE.
WHT-TSH!

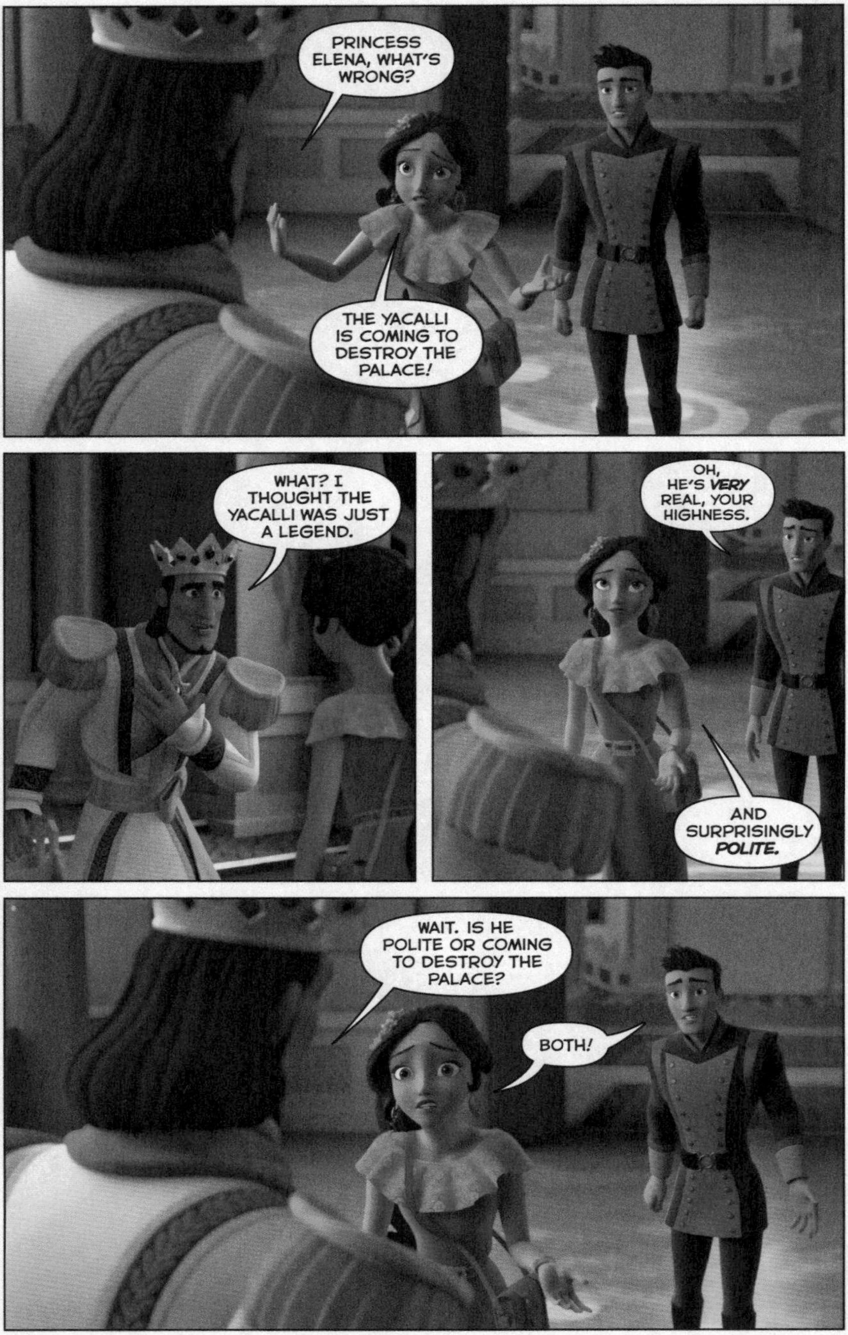
PRINCESS ELENA, WHAT'S WRONG?
THE YACALLI IS COMING TO DESTROY THE PALACE!
WHAT? I THOUGHT THE YACALLI WAS JUST A LEGEND.
OH, HE'S *VERY* REAL, YOUR HIGHNESS.
AND SURPRISINGLY ***POLITE.***
WAIT. IS HE POLITE OR COMING TO DESTROY THE PALACE?
BOTH!

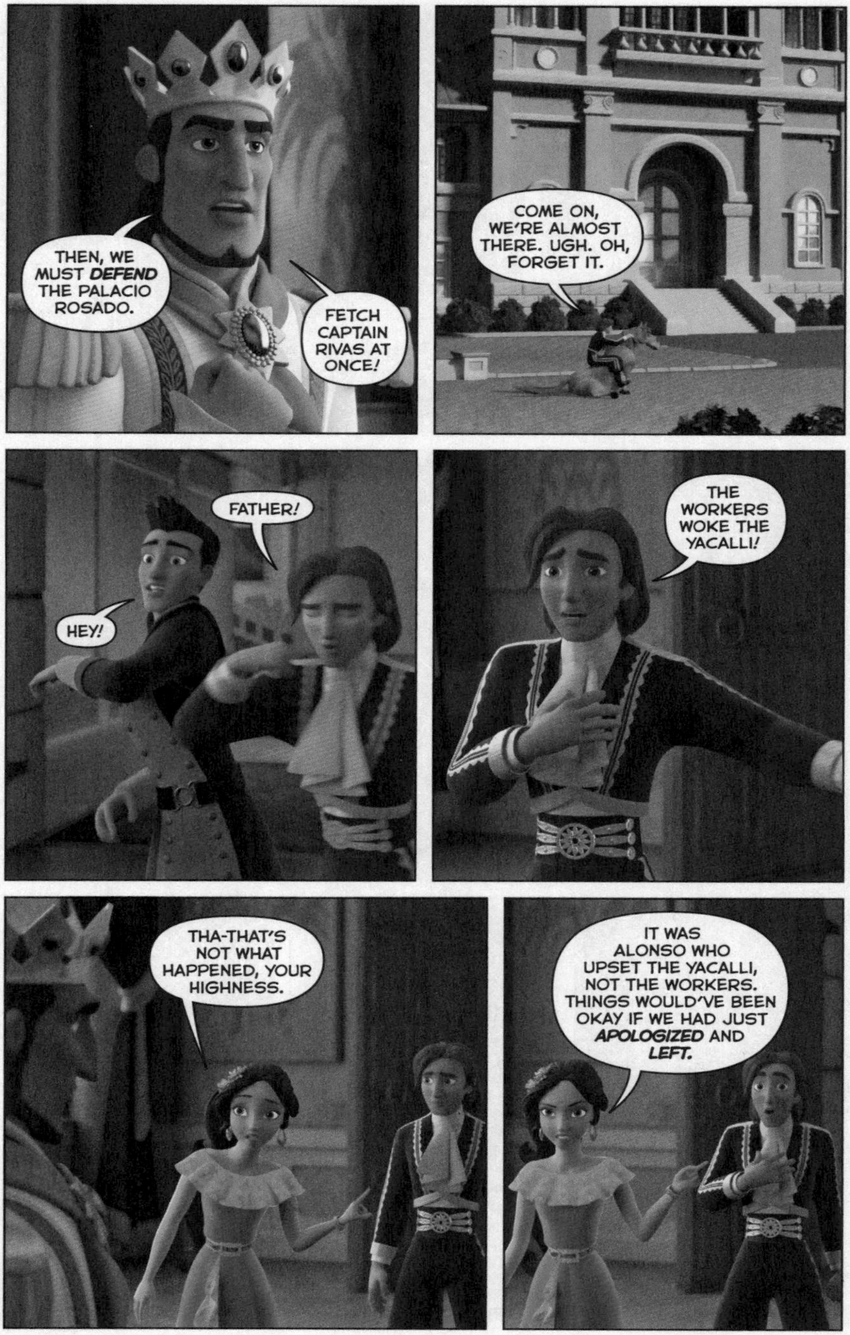
THEN, WE MUST DEFEND THE PALACIO ROSADO.
FETCH CAPTAIN RIVAS AT ONCE!
COME ON, WE'RE ALMOST THERE. UGH. OH, FORGET IT.
FATHER!
HEY!
THE WORKERS WOKE THE YACALLI!
THA-THAT'S NOT WHAT HAPPENED, YOUR HIGHNESS.
IT WAS ALONSO WHO UPSET THE YACALLI, NOT THE WORKERS. THINGS WOULD'VE BEEN OKAY IF WE HAD JUST APOLOGIZED AND LEFT.

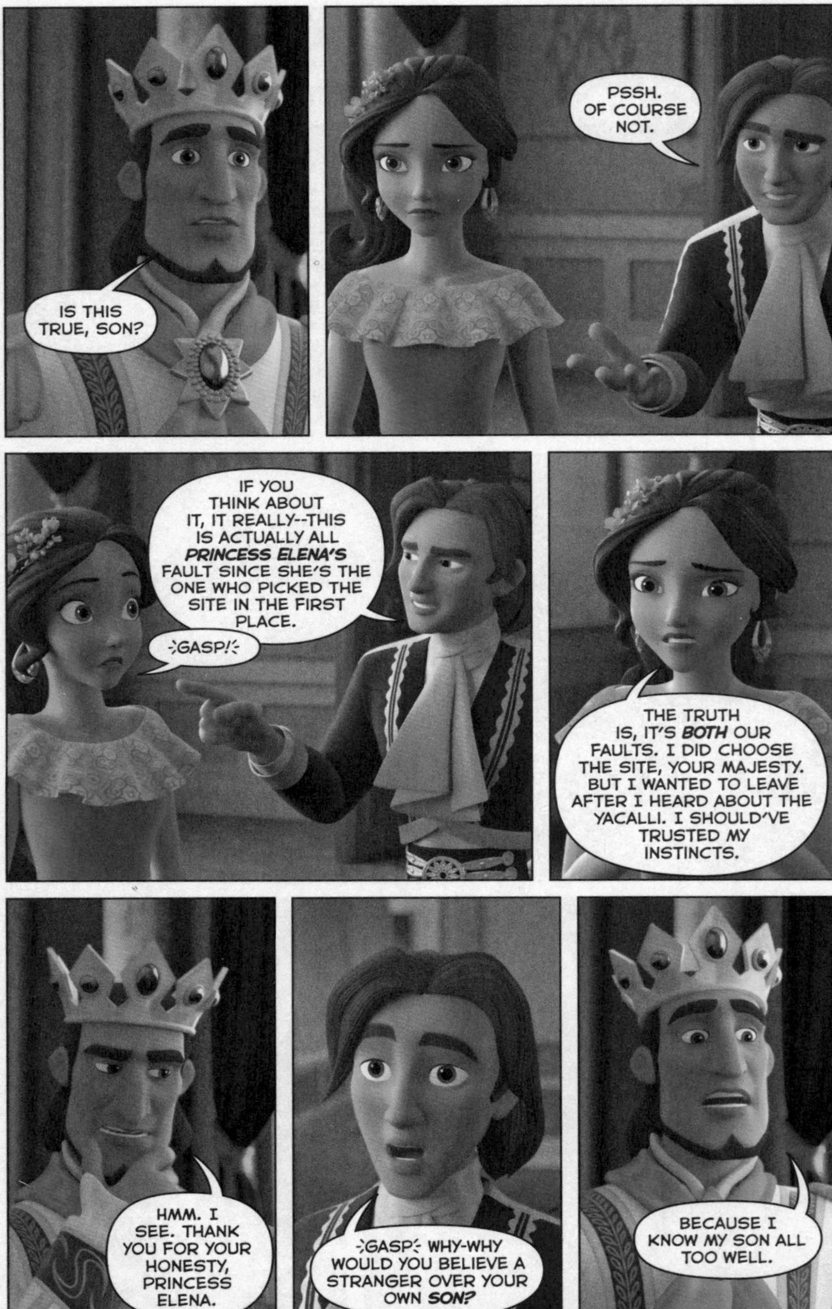
IS THIS TRUE, SON?
PSSH. OF COURSE NOT.
IF YOU THINK ABOUT IT, IT REALLY--THIS IS ACTUALLY ALL *PRINCESS ELENA'S* FAULT SINCE SHE'S THE ONE WHO PICKED THE SITE IN THE FIRST PLACE.
GASP!
THE TRUTH IS, IT'S *BOTH* OUR FAULTS. I DID CHOOSE THE SITE, YOUR MAJESTY. BUT I WANTED TO LEAVE AFTER I HEARD ABOUT THE YACALLI. I SHOULD'VE TRUSTED MY INSTINCTS.
HMM. I SEE. THANK YOU FOR YOUR HONESTY, PRINCESS ELENA.
GASP WHY-WHY WOULD YOU BELIEVE A STRANGER OVER YOUR OWN *SON?*
BECAUSE I KNOW MY SON ALL TOO WELL.

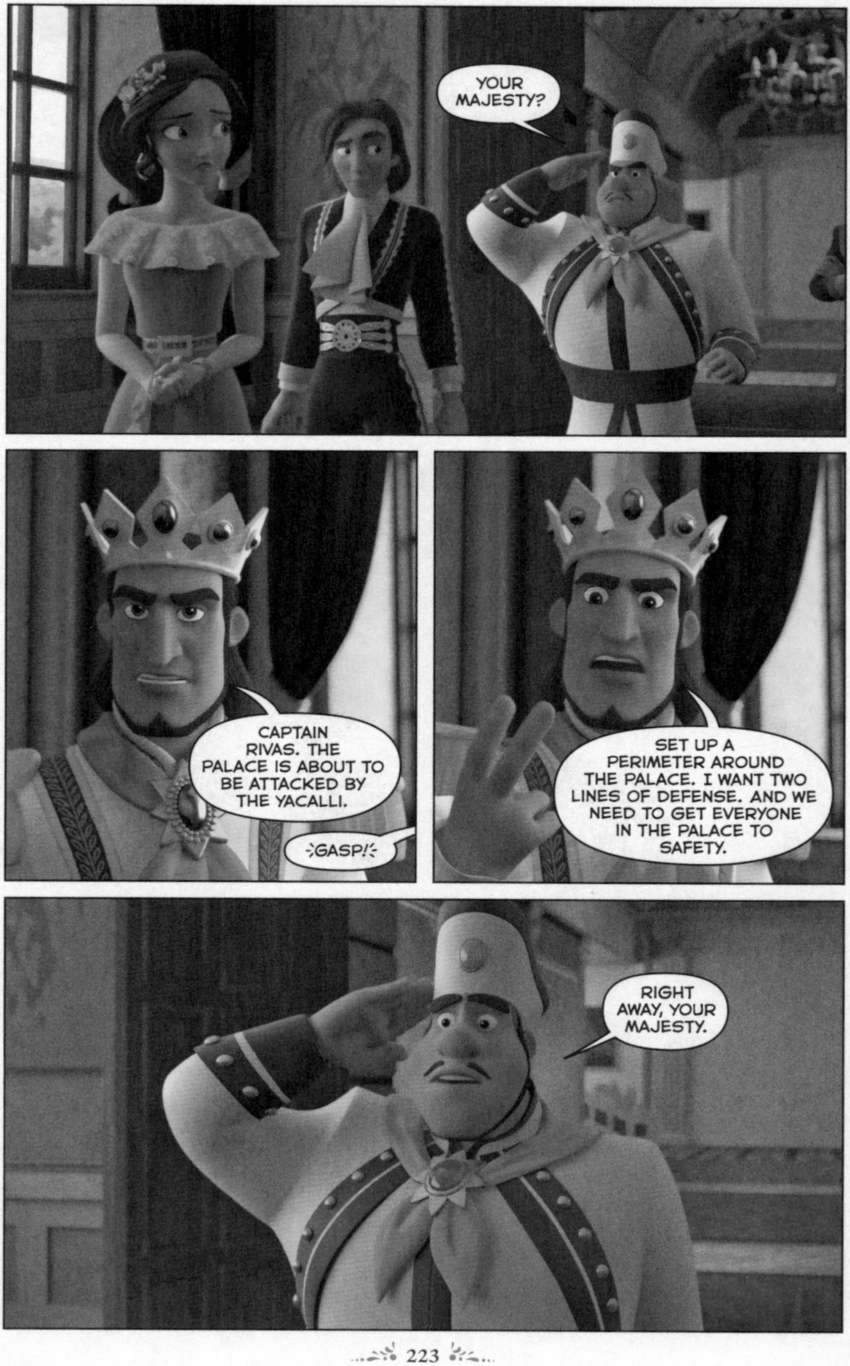
YOUR MAJESTY?
CAPTAIN RIVAS. THE PALACE IS ABOUT TO BE ATTACKED BY THE YACALLI.
GASP!
SET UP A PERIMETER AROUND THE PALACE. I WANT TWO LINES OF DEFENSE. AND WE NEED TO GET EVERYONE IN THE PALACE TO SAFETY.
RIGHT AWAY, YOUR MAJESTY.

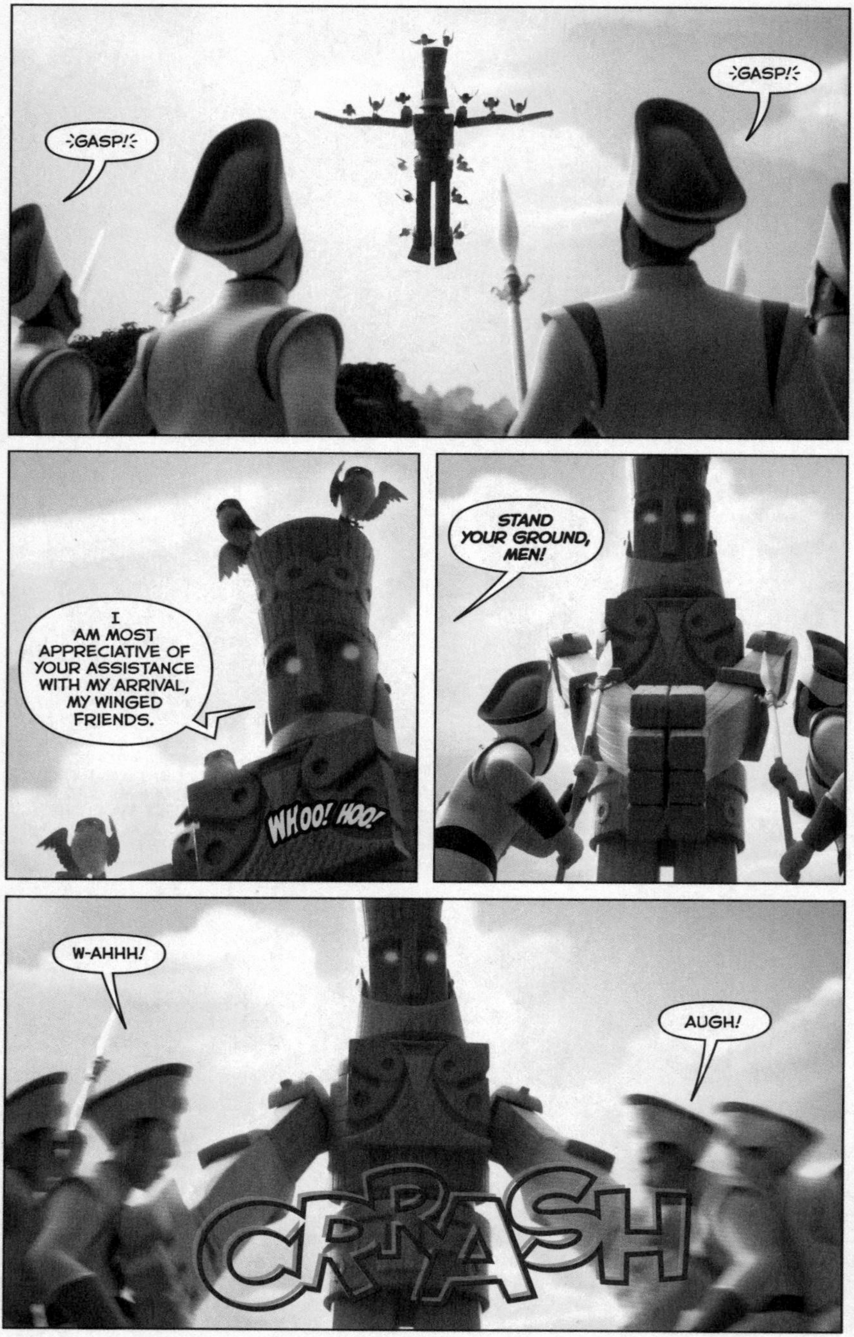
GASP!
GASP!
I AM MOST APPRECIATIVE OF YOUR ASSISTANCE WITH MY ARRIVAL, MY WINGED FRIENDS.
WHOO! HOO!
STAND YOUR GROUND, MEN!
W-AHHH!
AUGH!
CRASH

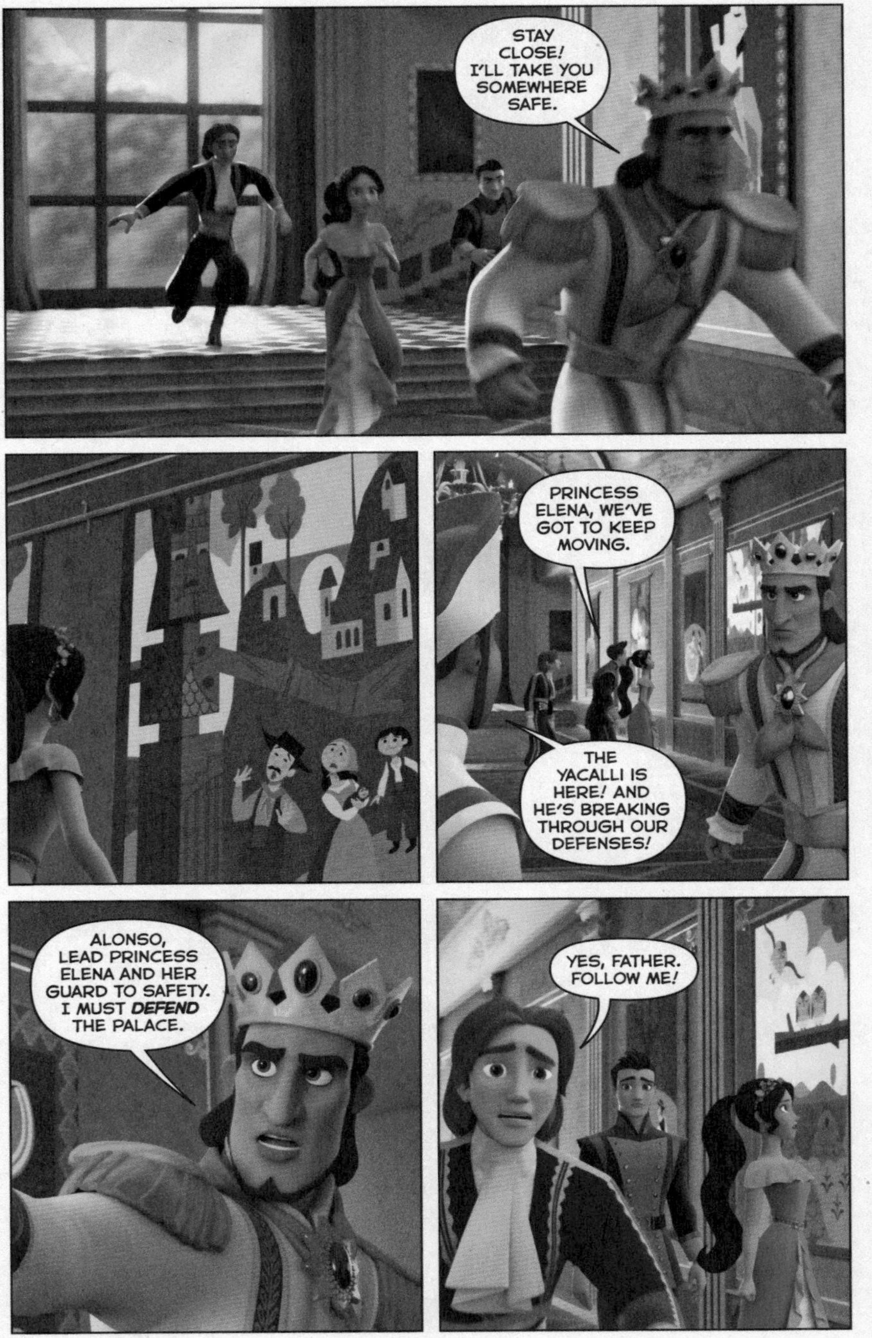
STAY CLOSE! I'LL TAKE YOU SOMEWHERE SAFE.
PRINCESS ELENA, WE'VE GOT TO KEEP MOVING.
THE YACALLI IS HERE! AND HE'S BREAKING THROUGH OUR DEFENSES!
ALONSO, LEAD PRINCESS ELENA AND HER GUARD TO SAFETY. I MUST *DEFEND* THE PALACE.
YES, FATHER. FOLLOW ME!

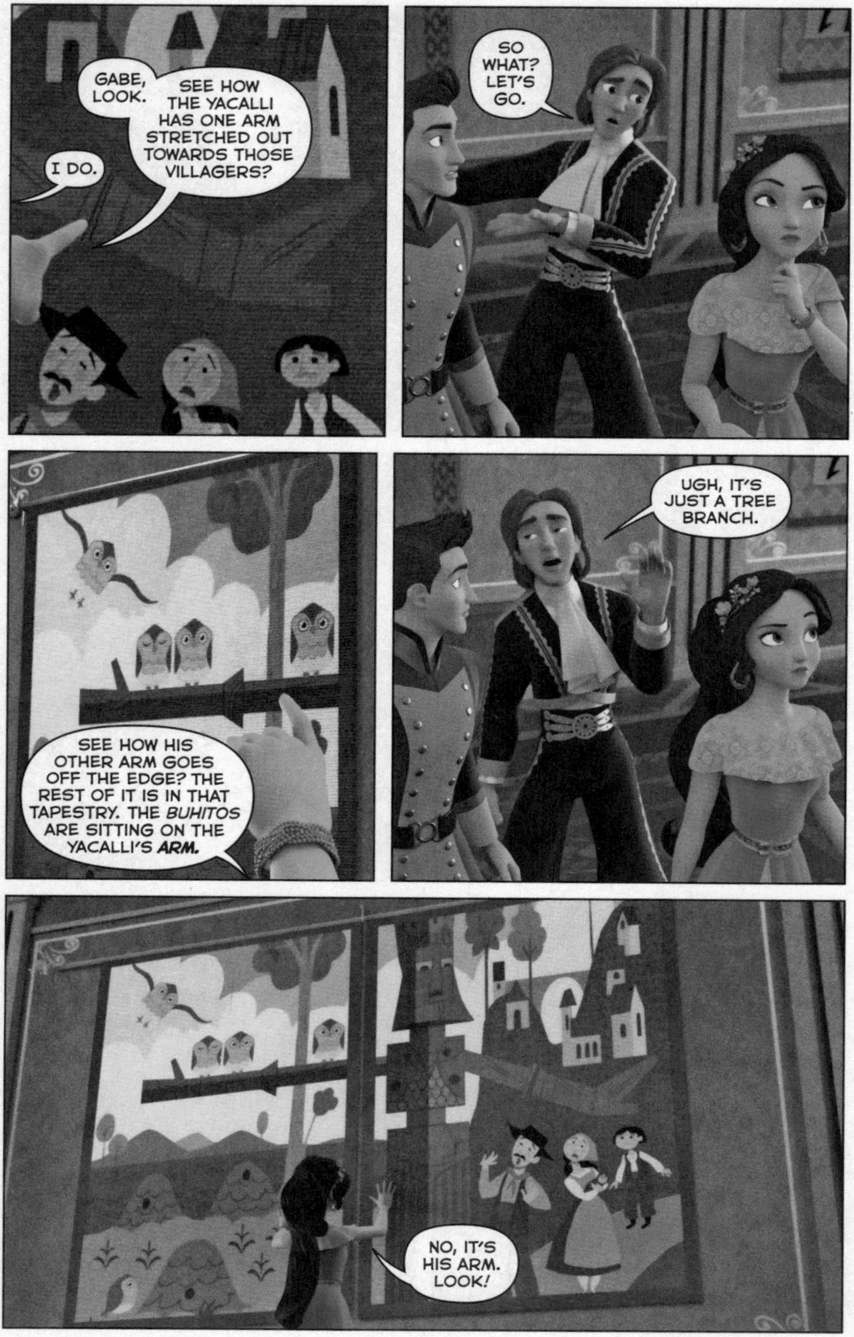
GABE, LOOK.
SEE HOW THE YACALLI HAS ONE ARM STRETCHED OUT TOWARDS THOSE VILLAGERS?
I DO.
SO WHAT? LET'S GO.
SEE HOW HIS OTHER ARM GOES OFF THE EDGE? THE REST OF IT IS IN THAT TAPESTRY. THE *BUHITOS* ARE SITTING ON THE YACALLI'S ***ARM.***
UGH, IT'S JUST A TREE BRANCH.
NO, IT'S HIS ARM. LOOK!

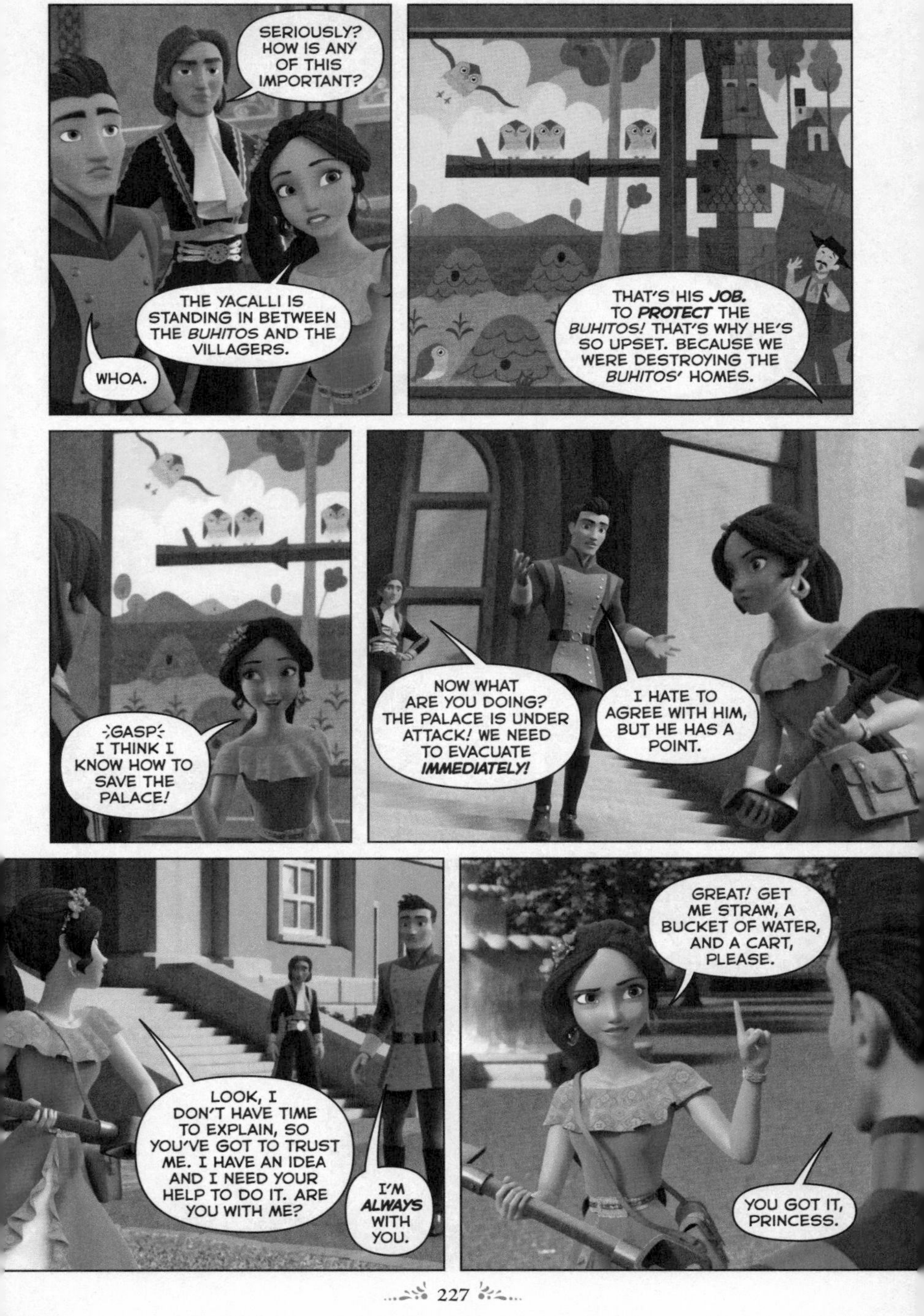
SERIOUSLY? HOW IS ANY OF THIS IMPORTANT?
THE YACALLI IS STANDING IN BETWEEN THE BUHITOS AND THE VILLAGERS.
WHOA.
THAT'S HIS JOB. TO PROTECT THE BUHITOS! THAT'S WHY HE'S SO UPSET. BECAUSE WE WERE DESTROYING THE BUHITOS' HOMES.
GASP I THINK I KNOW HOW TO SAVE THE PALACE!
NOW WHAT ARE YOU DOING? THE PALACE IS UNDER ATTACK! WE NEED TO EVACUATE IMMEDIATELY!
I HATE TO AGREE WITH HIM, BUT HE HAS A POINT.
LOOK, I DON'T HAVE TIME TO EXPLAIN, SO YOU'VE GOT TO TRUST ME. I HAVE AN IDEA AND I NEED YOUR HELP TO DO IT. ARE YOU WITH ME?
I'M ALWAYS WITH YOU.
GREAT! GET ME STRAW, A BUCKET OF WATER, AND A CART, PLEASE.
YOU GOT IT, PRINCESS.

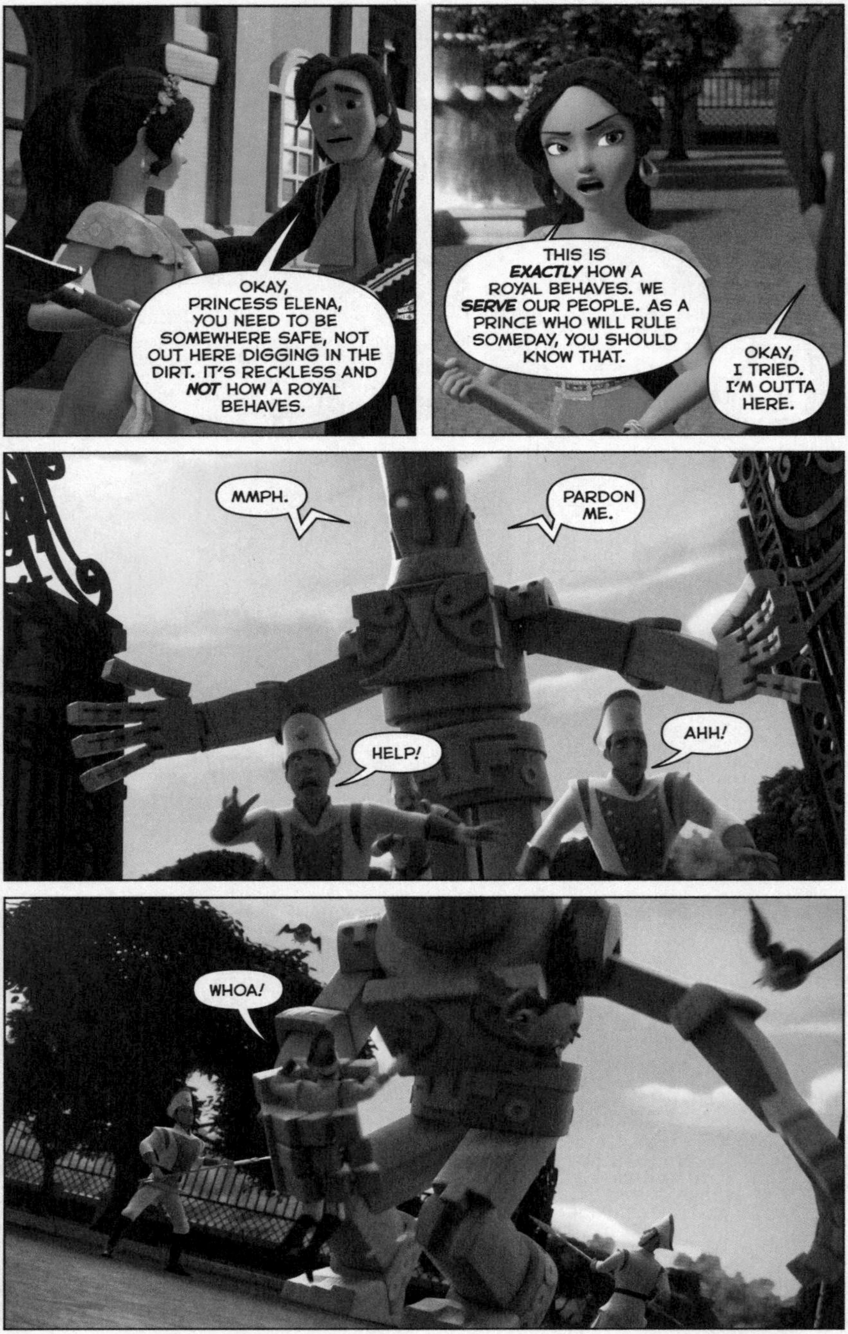

OKAY, PRINCESS ELENA, YOU NEED TO BE SOMEWHERE SAFE, NOT OUT HERE DIGGING IN THE DIRT. IT'S RECKLESS AND NOT HOW A ROYAL BEHAVES.
THIS IS EXACTLY HOW A ROYAL BEHAVES. WE SERVE OUR PEOPLE. AS A PRINCE WHO WILL RULE SOMEDAY, YOU SHOULD KNOW THAT.
OKAY, I TRIED. I'M OUTTA HERE.
MMPH.
PARDON ME.
HELP!
AHH!
WHOA!

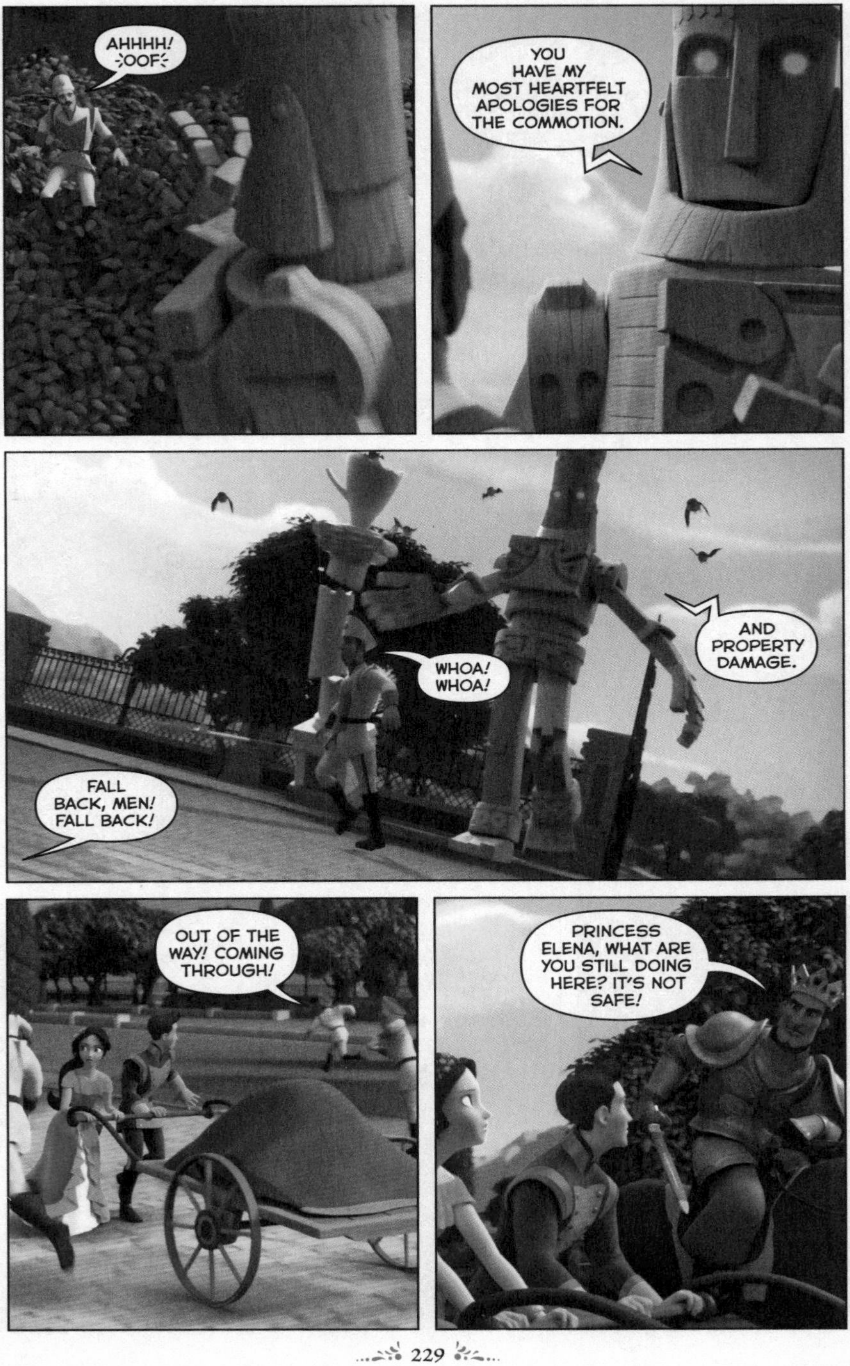
AHHHH! OOF!
YOU HAVE MY MOST HEARTFELT APOLOGIES FOR THE COMMOTION.
AND PROPERTY DAMAGE.
WHOA! WHOA!
FALL BACK, MEN! FALL BACK!
OUT OF THE WAY! COMING THROUGH!
PRINCESS ELENA, WHAT ARE YOU STILL DOING HERE? IT'S NOT SAFE!

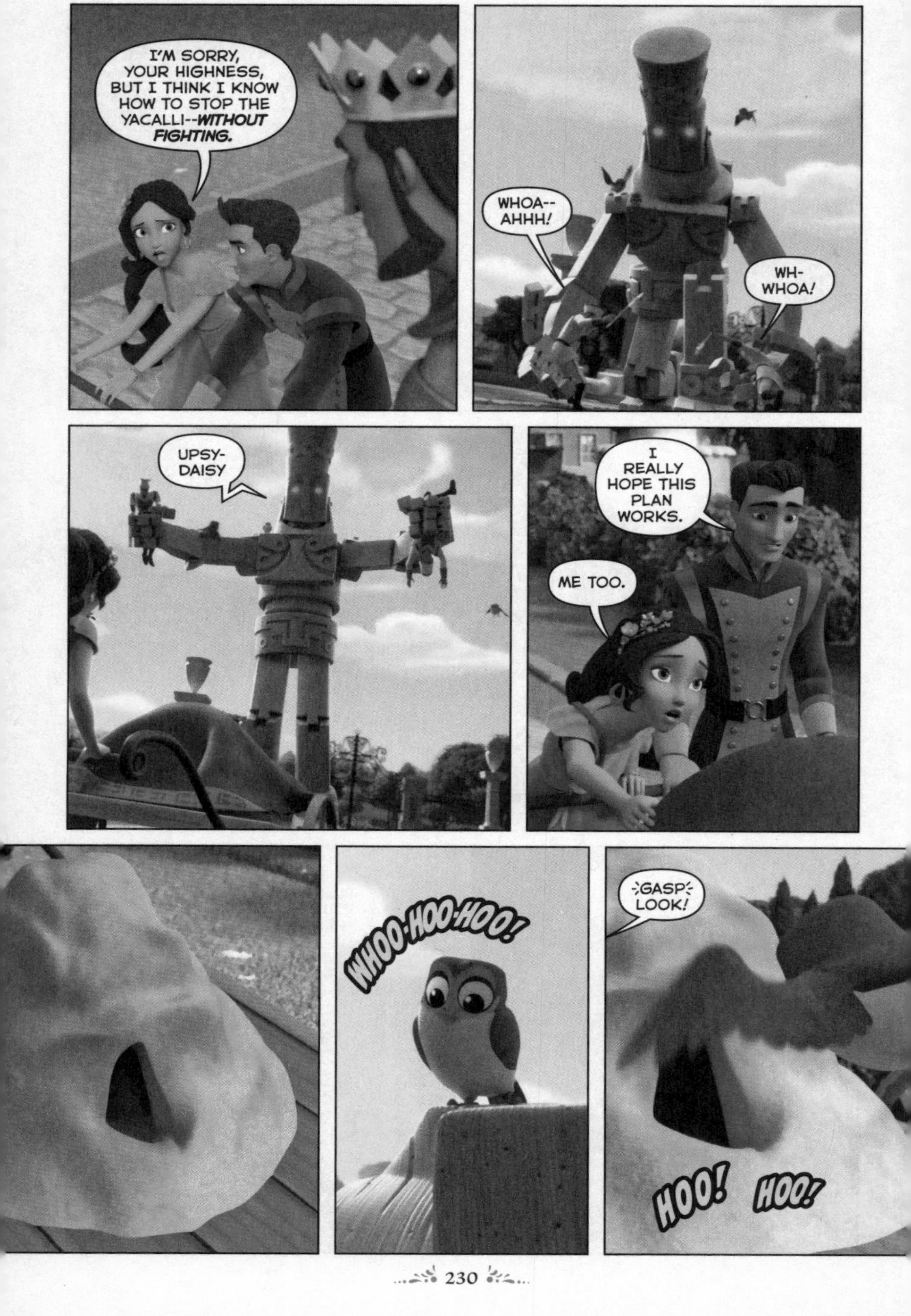
I'M SORRY, YOUR HIGHNESS, BUT I THINK I KNOW HOW TO STOP THE YACALLI--WITHOUT FIGHTING.
WHOA-- AHHH!
WH- WHOA!
UPSY- DAISY
I REALLY HOPE THIS PLAN WORKS.
ME TOO.
WHOO-HOO-HOO!
-GASP- LOOK!
HOO! HOO!

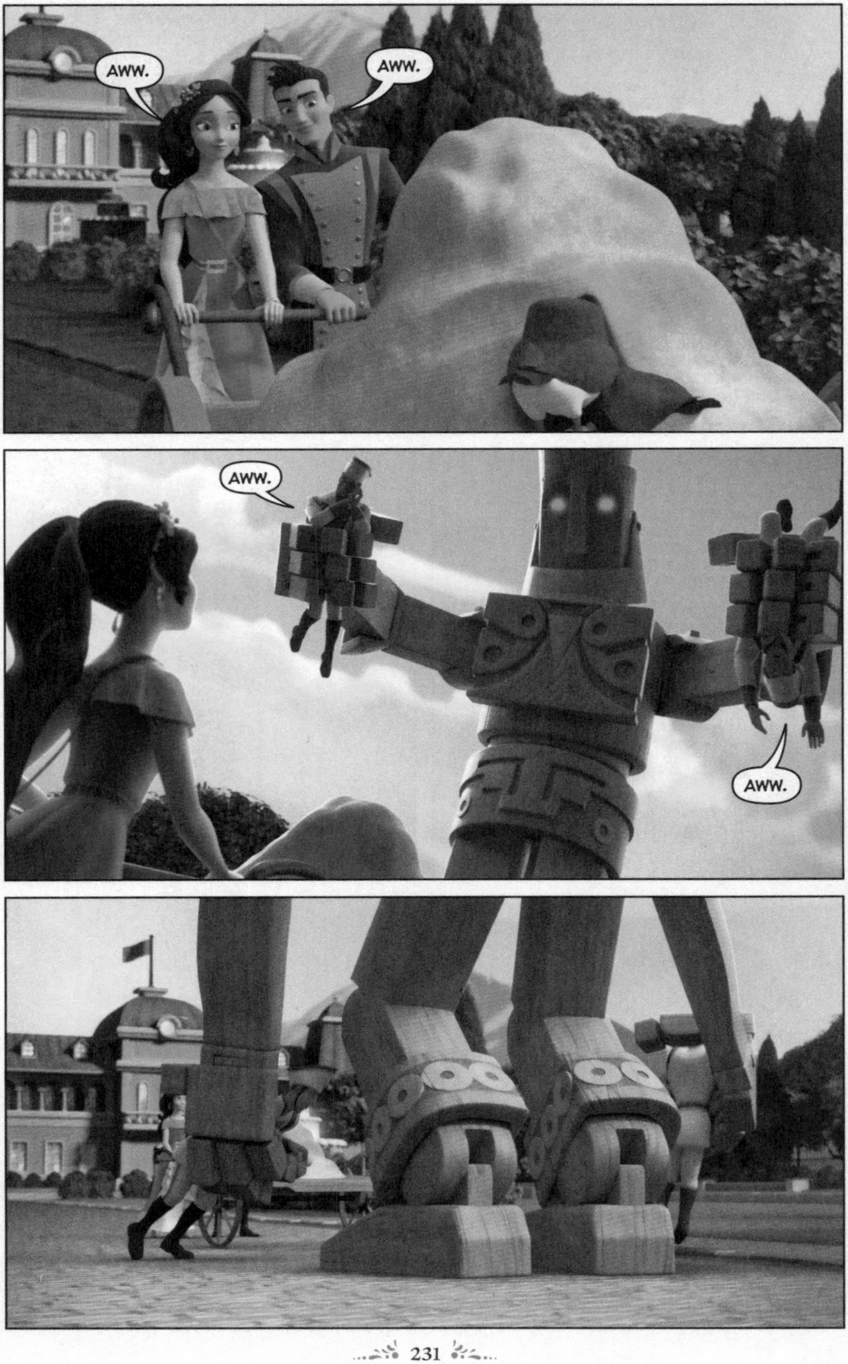
AWW.
AWW.
AWW.
AWW.

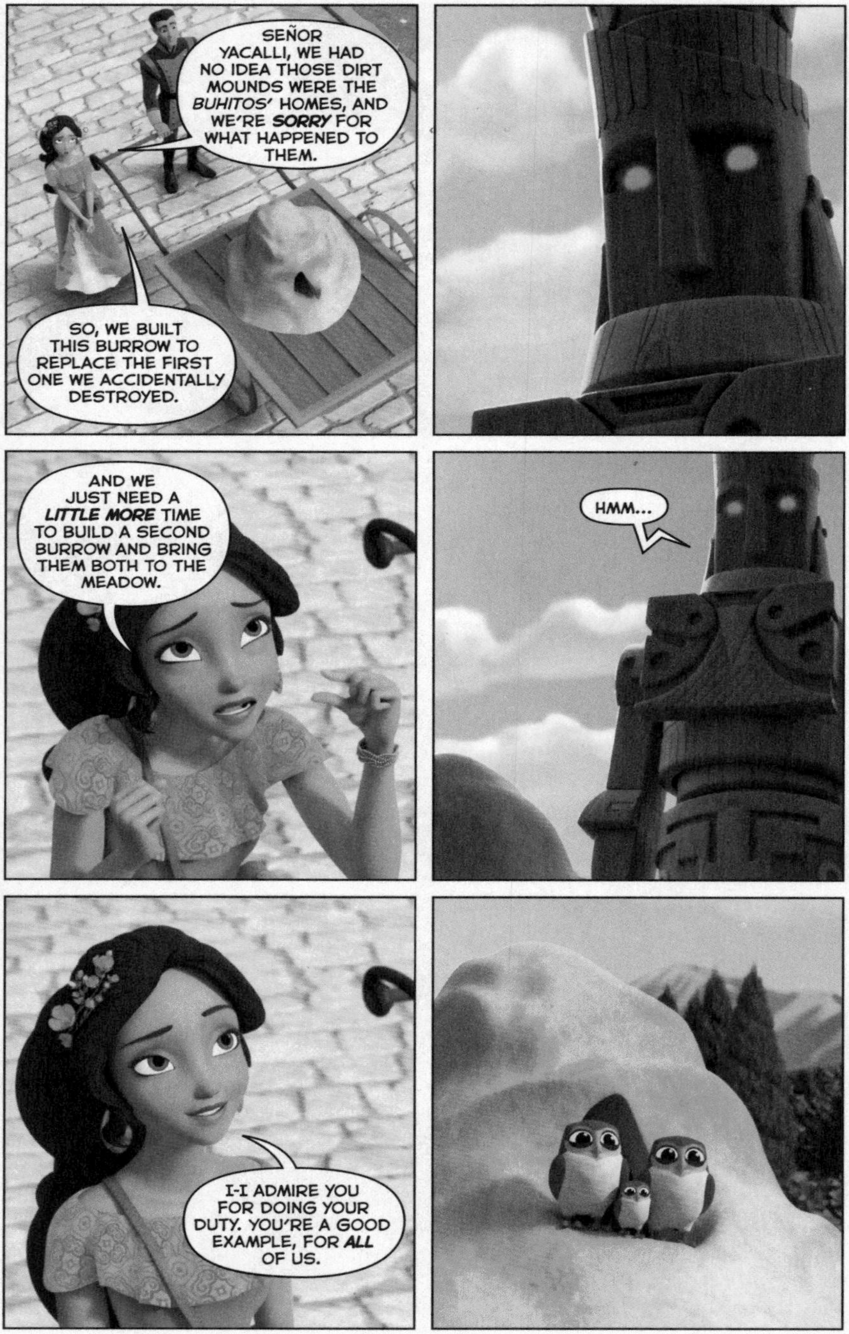

SEÑOR YACALLI, WE HAD NO IDEA THOSE DIRT MOUNDS WERE THE *BUHITOS'* HOMES, AND WE'RE ***SORRY*** FOR WHAT HAPPENED TO THEM.
SO, WE BUILT THIS BURROW TO REPLACE THE FIRST ONE WE ACCIDENTALLY DESTROYED.
AND WE JUST NEED A ***LITTLE MORE*** TIME TO BUILD A SECOND BURROW AND BRING THEM BOTH TO THE MEADOW.
HMM...
I-I ADMIRE YOU FOR DOING YOUR DUTY. YOU'RE A GOOD EXAMPLE, FOR ***ALL*** OF US.

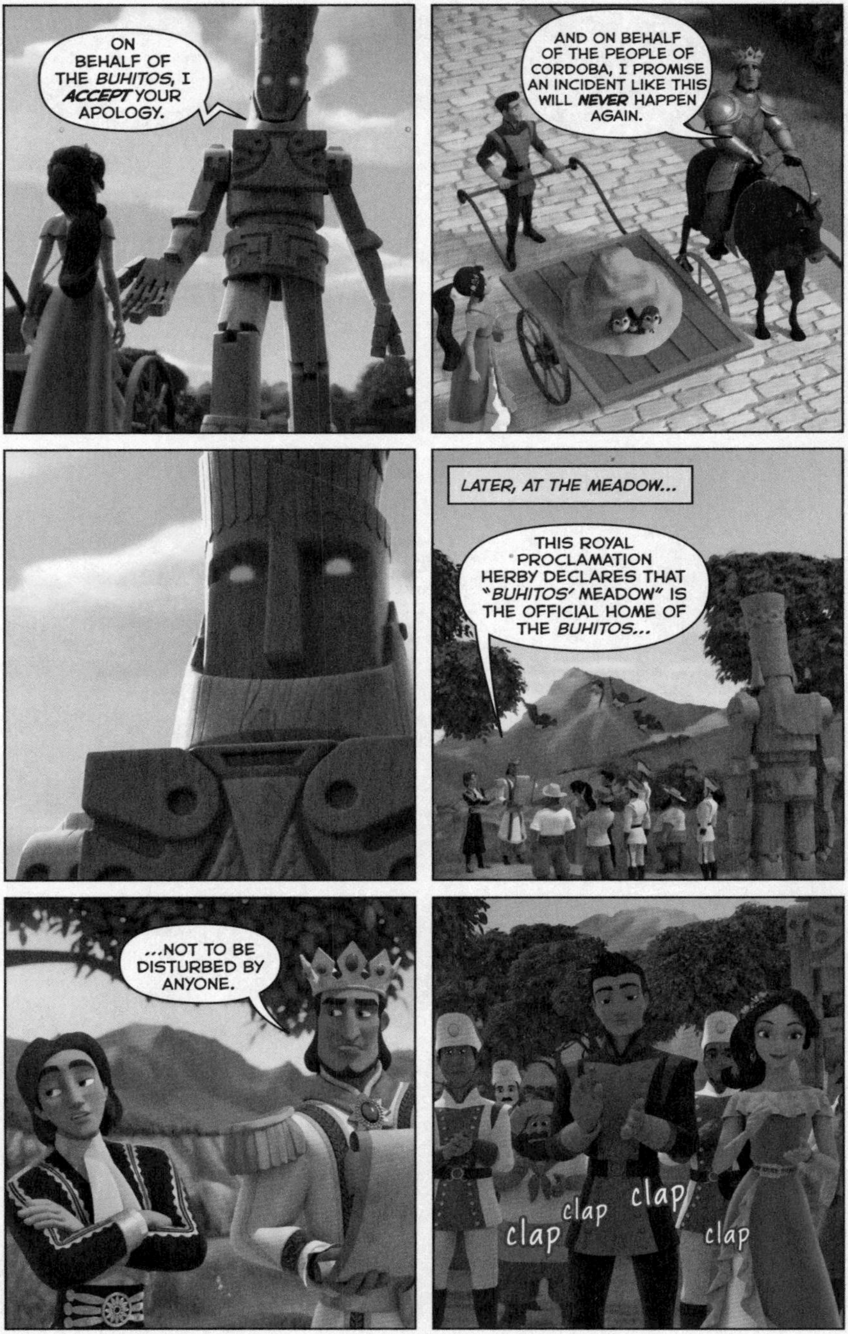
ON BEHALF OF THE *BUHITOS*, I ***ACCEPT*** YOUR APOLOGY.
AND ON BEHALF OF THE PEOPLE OF CORDOBA, I PROMISE AN INCIDENT LIKE THIS WILL ***NEVER*** HAPPEN AGAIN.
LATER, AT THE MEADOW...
THIS ROYAL PROCLAMATION HERBY DECLARES THAT "*BUHITOS'* MEADOW" IS THE OFFICIAL HOME OF THE *BUHITOS*...
...NOT TO BE DISTURBED BY ANYONE.
clap
clap
clap
clap

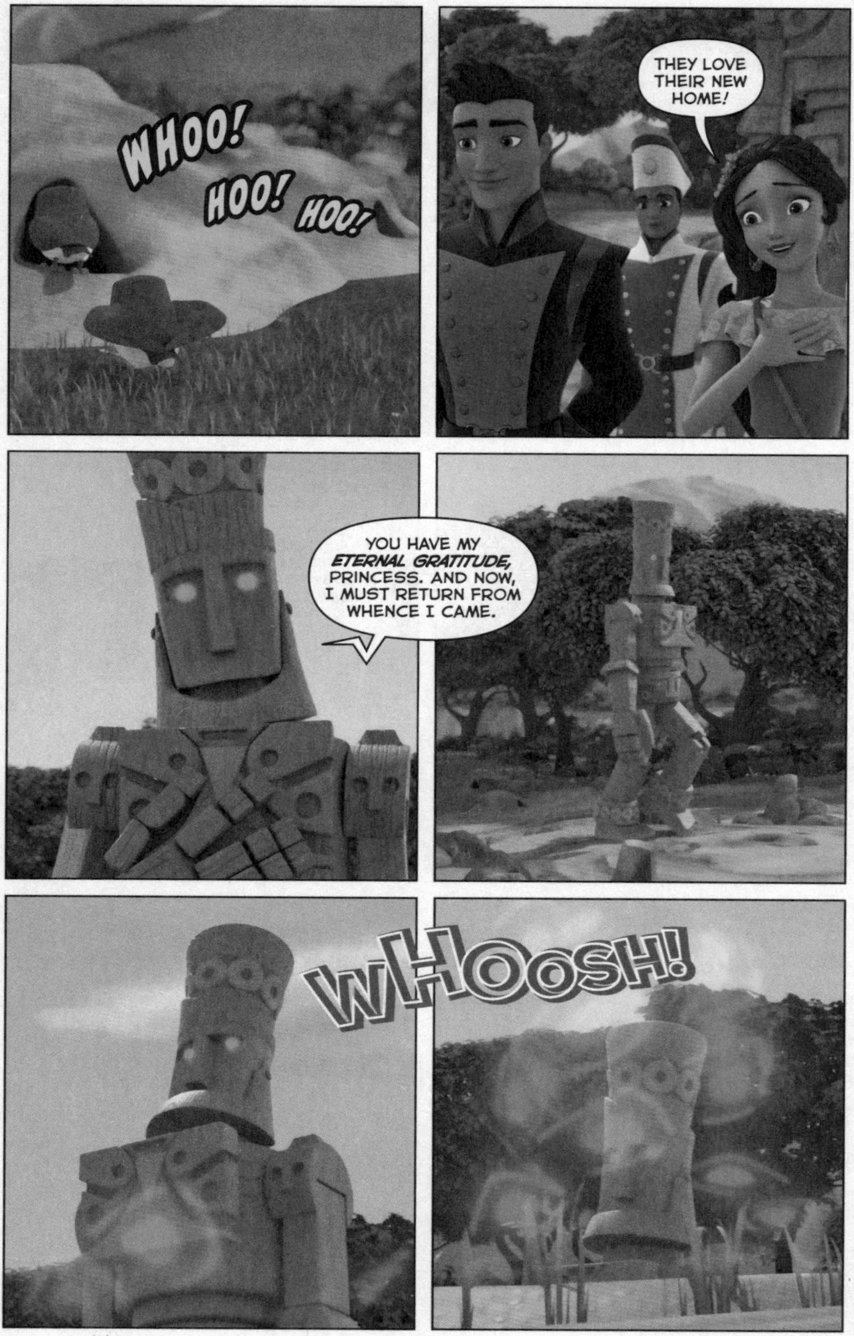
WHOO!
HOO!
HOO!
THEY LOVE THEIR NEW HOME!
YOU HAVE MY *ETERNAL GRATITUDE*, PRINCESS. AND NOW, I MUST RETURN FROM WHENCE I CAME.
WHOOSH!

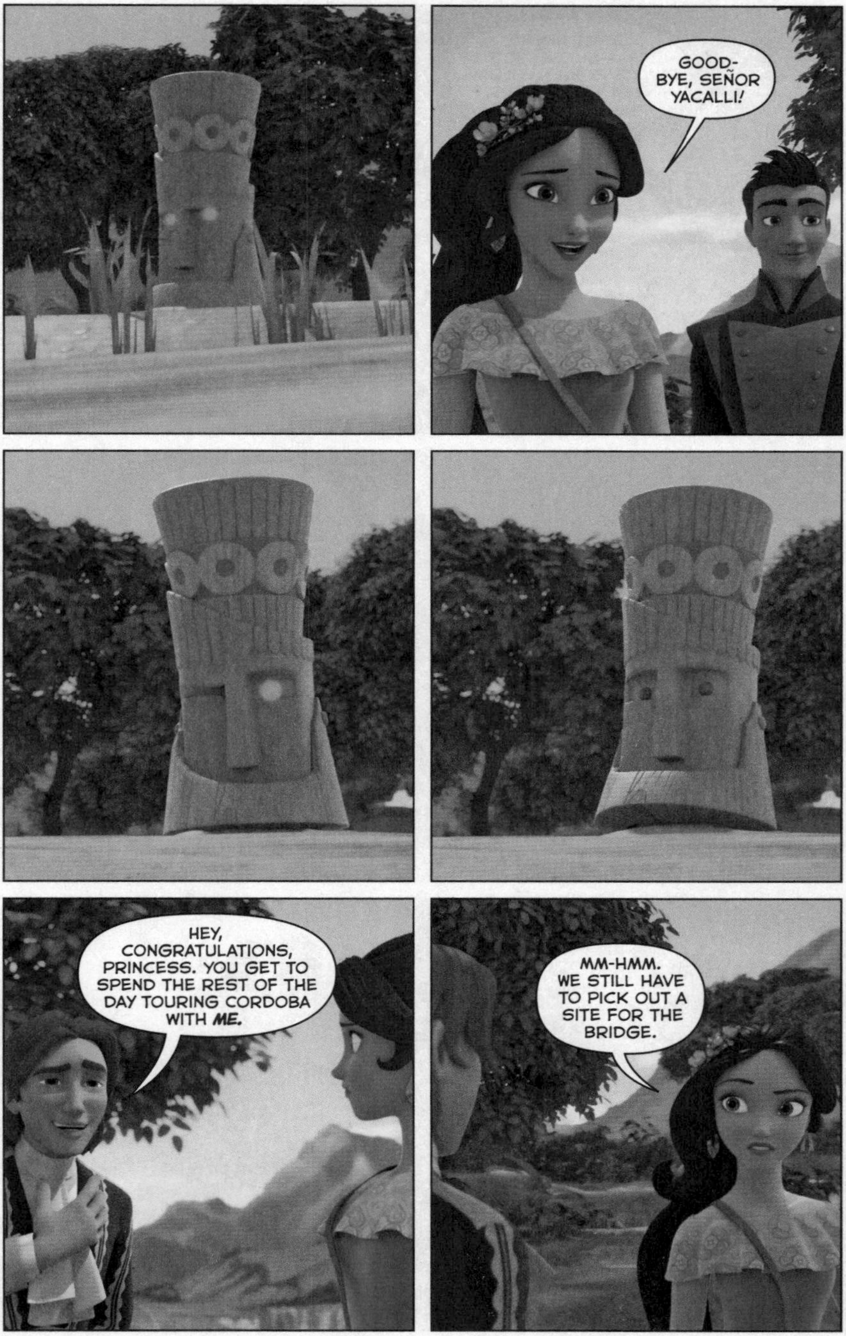
GOOD-BYE, SEÑOR YACALLI!
HEY, CONGRATULATIONS, PRINCESS. YOU GET TO SPEND THE REST OF THE DAY TOURING CORDOBA WITH *ME.*
MM-HMM. WE STILL HAVE TO PICK OUT A SITE FOR THE BRIDGE.

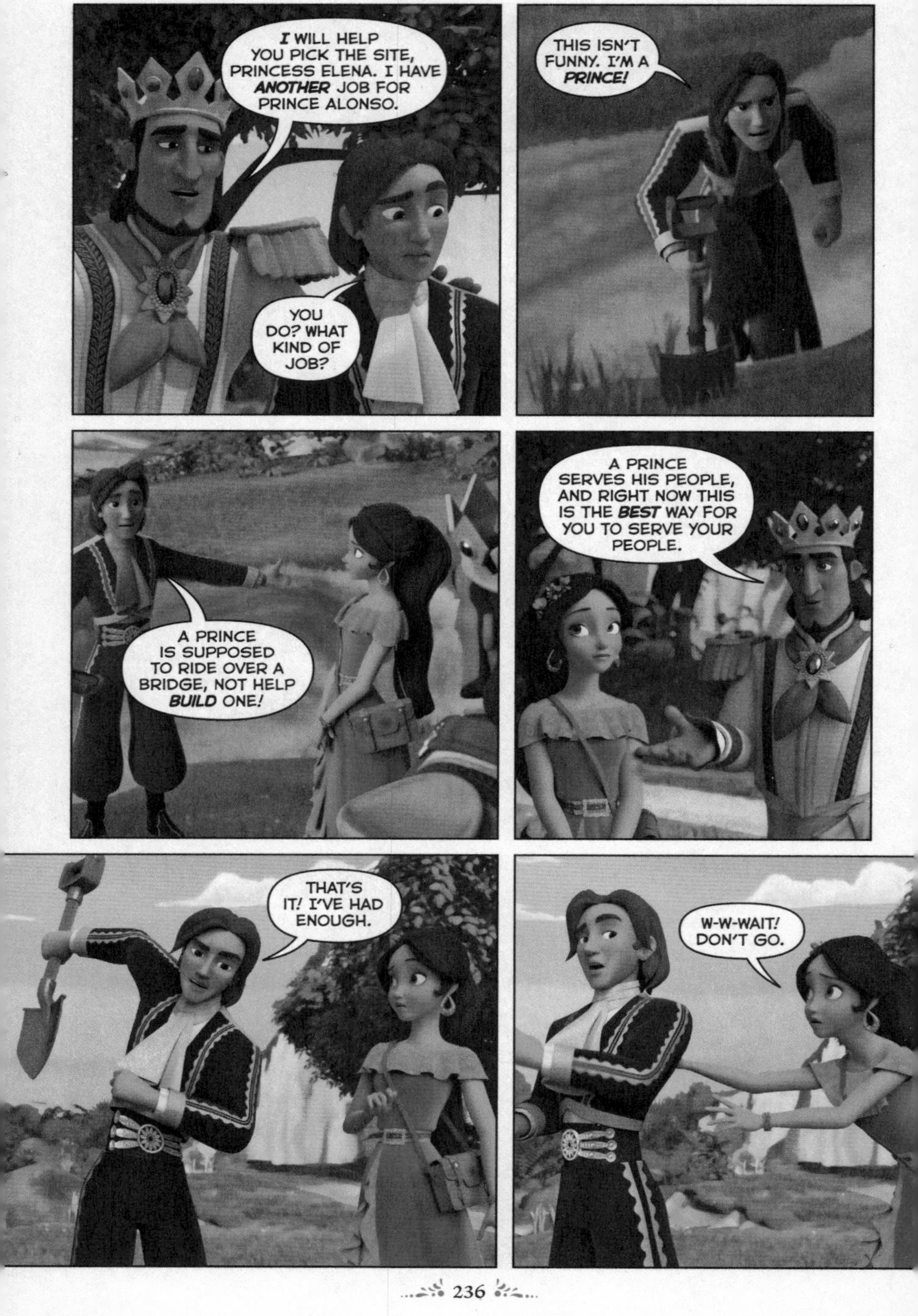
I WILL HELP YOU PICK THE SITE, PRINCESS ELENA. I HAVE ***ANOTHER*** JOB FOR PRINCE ALONSO.
YOU DO? WHAT KIND OF JOB?
THIS ISN'T FUNNY. I'M A ***PRINCE!***
A PRINCE IS SUPPOSED TO RIDE OVER A BRIDGE, NOT HELP ***BUILD*** ONE!
A PRINCE SERVES HIS PEOPLE, AND RIGHT NOW THIS IS THE ***BEST*** WAY FOR YOU TO SERVE YOUR PEOPLE.
THAT'S IT! I'VE HAD ENOUGH.
W-W-WAIT! DON'T GO.

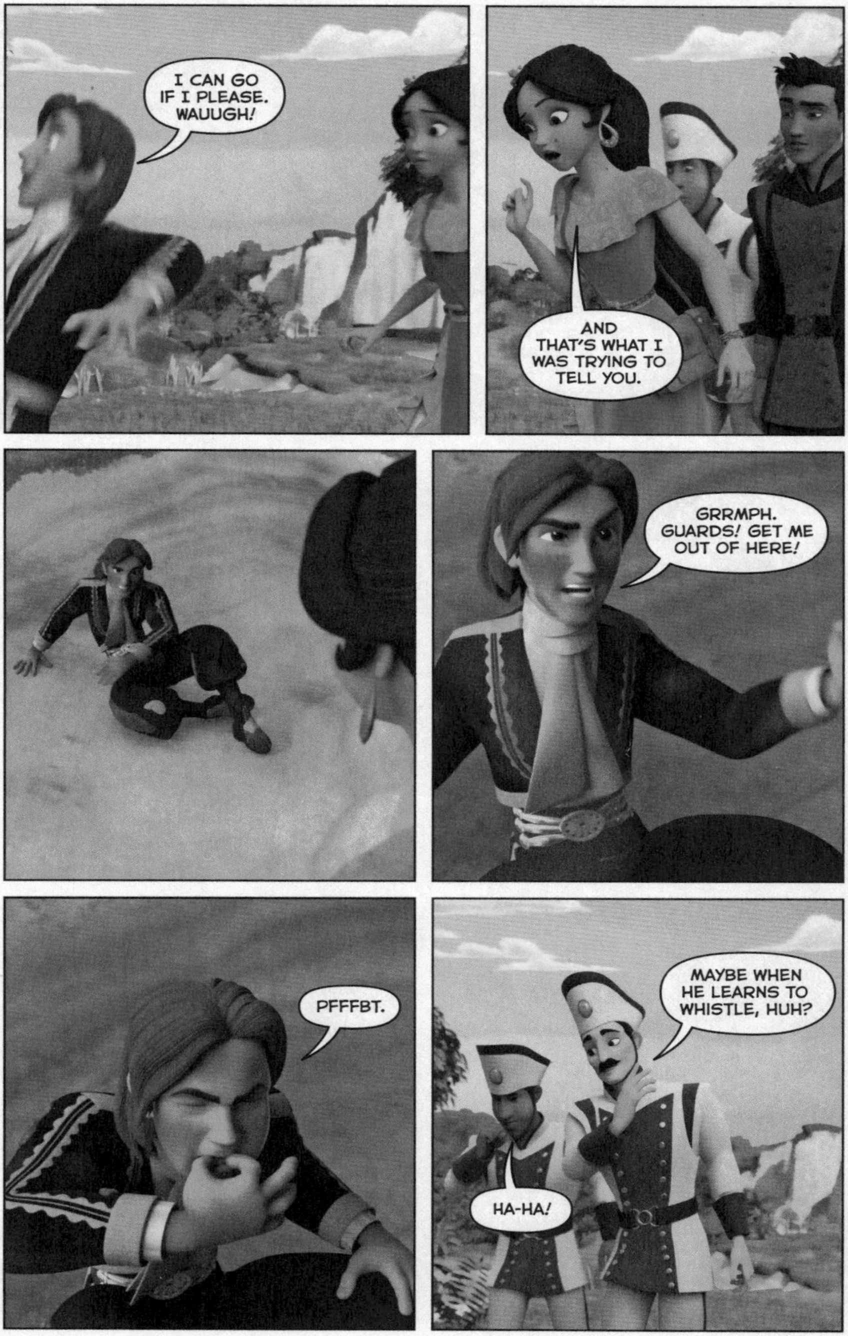
I CAN GO
IF I PLEASE.
WAUUGH!
AND
THAT'S WHAT I
WAS TRYING TO
TELL YOU.
GRRMPH.
GUARDS! GET ME
OUT OF HERE!
PFFFBT.
MAYBE WHEN
HE LEARNS TO
WHISTLE, HUH?
HA-HA!

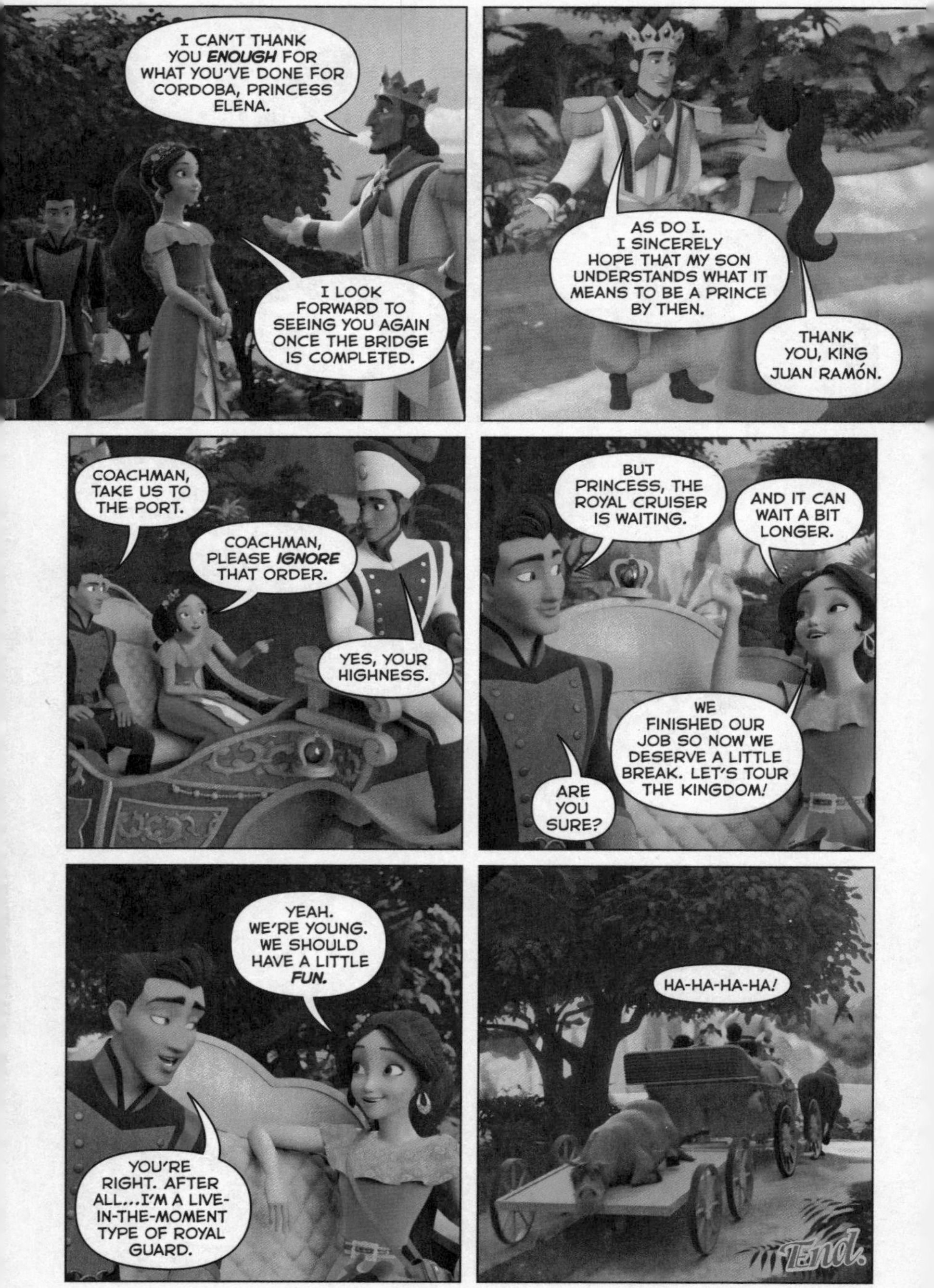
I CAN'T THANK YOU **ENOUGH** FOR WHAT YOU'VE DONE FOR CORDOBA, PRINCESS ELENA.
I LOOK FORWARD TO SEEING YOU AGAIN ONCE THE BRIDGE IS COMPLETED.
AS DO I. I SINCERELY HOPE THAT MY SON UNDERSTANDS WHAT IT MEANS TO BE A PRINCE BY THEN.
THANK YOU, KING JUAN RAMÓN.
COACHMAN, TAKE US TO THE PORT.
COACHMAN, PLEASE **IGNORE** THAT ORDER.
YES, YOUR HIGHNESS.
BUT PRINCESS, THE ROYAL CRUISER IS WAITING.
AND IT CAN WAIT A BIT LONGER.
WE FINISHED OUR JOB SO NOW WE DESERVE A LITTLE BREAK. LET'S TOUR THE KINGDOM!
ARE YOU SURE?
YEAH. WE'RE YOUNG. WE SHOULD HAVE A LITTLE **FUN.**
YOU'RE RIGHT. AFTER ALL...I'M A LIVE-IN-THE-MOMENT TYPE OF ROYAL GUARD.
HA-HA-HA-HA!
End.